Mystery Writers of America Grand Master
Winner of the Edgar® Award for Best Novel
Los Angeles Times Woman of the Year

"One of the most original and vital voices in all of American crime fiction."
—**Laura Lippman**

"No woman in twentieth-century American mystery writing is more important than Margaret Millar."
—**H.R.F. Keating**

"I long ago changed my writing name to Ross Macdonald for obvious reasons."
—**Kenneth Millar (Ross Macdonald), in a letter to the *Toronto Saturday Night* newspaper**

"Very Original."
—**Agatha Christie**

"Stunningly original."
—**Val McDermid**

"She has few peers, and no superior in the art of bamboozlement."
—**Julian Symons**

"Written with such complete realization of every character that the most bitter antagonist of mystery fiction may be forced to acknowledge it as a work of art."
—**Anthony Boucher reviewing *Beast in View* for the *New York Times***

"Margaret Millar can build up the sensation of fear so strongly that at the end it literally hits you like a battering ram."
—**BBC**

"Wonderfully ingenious."
—**The New Yorker**

"Brilliantly superlative . . . One of the most impressive additions to mystery literature—and the word "literature" is used in its fullest sense."
—**San Francisco Chronicle**

"In the whole of crime fiction's distinguished sisterhood, there is no one quite like Margaret Millar."
—**The Guardian**

"She writes minor classics."
—**Washington Post**

"Mrs. Millar doesn't attract fans she creates addicts."
—**Dilys Winn, namesake of the Dilys Award**

COLLECTED MILLAR

LEGENDARY NOVELS OF SUSPENSE

COLLECTED MILLAR

THE FIRST DETECTIVES
The Paul Prye Mysteries
The Invisible Worm (1941)
The Weak-Eyed Bat (1942)
The Devil Loves Me (1942)

Inspector Sands Mysteries
Wall of Eyes (1943)
The Iron Gates [Taste of Fears] (1945)

DAWN OF DOMESTIC SUSPENSE
Fire Will Freeze (1944)
Experiment in Springtime (1947)
The Cannibal Heart (1949)
Do Evil in Return (1950)
Rose's Last Summer (1952)

THE MASTER AT HER ZENITH
Vanish in an Instant (1952)
Wives and Lovers (1954)
Beast in View (1955)
An Air That Kills (1957)
The Listening Walls (1959)

LEGENDARY NOVELS OF SUSPENSE
A Stranger in My Grave (1960)
How Like an Angel (1962)
The Fiend (1964)
Beyond This Point Are Monsters (1970)

THE TOM ARAGON NOVELS
Ask for Me Tomorrow (1976)
The Murder of Miranda (1979)
Mermaid (1982)

FIRST THINGS, LAST THINGS
Banshee (1983)
Spider Webs (1986)
Collected Short Fiction (2016)
It's All in the Family (1948) (semi-autobiographical children's book)

MEMOIR
The Birds and the Beasts Were There (1968)

COLLECTED MILLAR

LEGENDARY NOVELS OF SUSPENSE

INCLUDING

A STRANGER IN MY GRAVE
HOW LIKE AN ANGEL
THE FIEND
BEYOND THIS POINT ARE MONSTERS

MARGARET
MILLAR

SYNDICATE BOOKS
NEW YORK

This volume published in 2016 by Syndicate Books

www.syndicatebooks.com

Distributed by
Soho Press, Inc.
853 Broadway
New York, NY 10003

Library of Congress Cataloging-in-Publication Data is available

ISBN: 978-1-68199-028-6
A Stranger in My Grave eISBN: 978-1-68199-015-6
How Like an Angel eISBN: 978-1-68199-016-3
The Fiend eISBN: 978-1-68199-017-0
Beyond This Point Are Monsters eISBN: 978-1-68199-018-7

Cover and interior design by Jeff Wong

Printed in the United States of America

10 9 8 7 6 5 4 3 2

The Graveyard

My beloved Daisy: It has been so many years since I have seen you . . .

THE TIMES OF terror began, not in the middle of the night when the quiet and the darkness made terror seem a natural thing, but on a bright and noisy morning during the first week of February. The acacia trees, in such full bloom that they looked leafless, were shaking the night fog off their blossoms like shaggy dogs shaking off rain, and the eucalyptus fluttered and played coquette with hundreds of tiny grey birds, no bigger than thumbs, whose name Daisy did not know.

She had tried to find out what species they belonged to by consulting the bird book Jim had given her when they'd first moved into the new house. But the little thumb-sized birds refused to stay still long enough to be identified, and Daisy dropped the subject. She didn't like birds anyway. The contrast between their blithe freedom in flight and their terrible vulnerability when grounded reminded her too strongly of herself.

Across the wooded canyon she could see parts of the new housing development. Less than a year ago, there had been nothing but scrub oak and castor beans pushing out through the stubborn adobe soil. Now the hills were sprouting with brick chimneys and television aerials, and the landscape was growing green with newly rooted ice plant and ivy. Noises floated across the canyon to Daisy's house, undiminished by distance on a windless day: the barking of dogs, the shrieks of children at play, snatches of music, the crying of a baby, the shout of an angry mother, the intermittent whirring of an electric saw.

Daisy enjoyed these morning sounds, sounds of life, of living. She sat at the breakfast table listening to them, a pretty dark-haired young woman wearing a bright blue robe that matched her eyes, and the faintest trace of a smile. The smile meant nothing. It was one of habit. She put it on in the morning along with her lipstick and removed it at night when she washed her face. Jim liked this smile of Daisy's. To him it indicated that she was a happy woman and that he, as her husband, deserved a major portion of the praise for making and keeping her that way. And so the smile, which intended no purpose, served one anyway: it convinced Jim that he was doing what at various times in the past he'd believed to be impossible—making Daisy happy.

He was reading the paper, some of it to himself, some of it aloud, when he came upon any item that he thought might interest her.

"There's a new storm front off the Oregon coast. Maybe it will get down this far. I hope to God it does. Did you know this has been the driest year since '48?"

"Mmm." It was not an answer or a comment, merely an encouragement for him to tell her more so she wouldn't have to talk. Usually she felt quite talkative at breakfast, recounting the day past, planning the day to come. But this morning she felt quiet, as if some part of her lay still asleep and dreaming.

"Only five and a half inches of rain since last July. That's eight months. It's amazing how all our trees have managed to survive, isn't it?"

"Mmm."

"Still, I suppose the bigger ones have their roots down to the creek bed by this time. The fire hazard's pretty bad, though. I hope you're careful with your cigarettes, Daisy. Our fire insurance wouldn't cover the replacement cost of the house. Are you?"

"What?"

"Careful with your cigarettes and matches?"

"Certainly. Very."

"Actually, it's your mother I'm concerned about." By looking over Daisy's left shoulder out through the picture window of the dinette, he could see the used-brick chimney of the mother-in-law cottage he'd built for Mrs. Fielding. It was some 200 yards away. Sometimes it seemed closer, sometimes he forgot about it entirely. "I know she's fussy about such things, but accidents can happen. Suppose she's sitting there smoking one night and has another stroke? I wonder if I ought to talk to her about it."

It was nine years ago, before Jim and Daisy had even met, that Mrs. Fielding had suffered a slight stroke, sold her dress shop in Denver, and retired to San Félice on the California coast. But Jim still worried about it, as if the stroke had just taken place yesterday and might recur tomorrow. He himself had always had a very active and healthy life, and the idea of illness appalled him. Since he had become successful as a land speculator, he'd met a great many doctors socially, but their presence made him uncomfortable. They were intruders, Cassandras, like morticians at a wedding or policemen at a child's party.

"I hope you won't mind, Daisy."

"What?"

"If I speak to your mother about it."

"Oh no."

He returned, satisfied, to his paper. The bacon and eggs Daisy had cooked for him because the day maid didn't arrive until nine o'clock lay untouched on his plate. Food meant little to Jim at breakfast time. It was the paper he devoured, paragraph by paragraph, eating up the facts and figures as if he could never get enough of them. He'd quit school at sixteen to join a construction crew.

"Now here's something interesting. Researchers have now proved that whales have a sonar system for avoiding collisions, something like bats."

"Mmm." Some part of her still slept and dreamed: she could think of nothing to say. So she sat gazing out the window, listening to Jim and the other morning sounds. Then, without warning, without apparent reason, the terror seized her.

The placid, steady beating of her heart turned into a fast, arrhythmic pounding. She began to breathe heavily and quickly, like a person engaged in some tremendous physical feat, and the blood swept up into her face as if driven before a wind. Her forehead and cheeks and the tips of her ears burned with sudden fever, and sweat poured into the palms of her hands from some secret well.

The sleeper had awakened.

"Jim."

"Yes?" He glanced at her over the top of the paper and thought how well Daisy was looking this morning, with a fine high color, like a young girl's. She seemed excited, as if she'd

4

just planned some new big project, and he wondered, indulgently, what it would be this time. The years were crammed with Daisy's projects, packed away and half forgotten, like old toys in a trunk, some of them broken, some barely used: ceramics, astrology, tuberous begonias, Spanish conversation, upholstering, Vedanta, mental hygiene, mosaics, Russian literature—all the toys Daisy had played with and discarded. "Do you want something, dear?"

"Some water."

"Sure thing." He brought a glass of water from the kitchen. "Here you are."

She reached for the glass, but she couldn't pick it up. The lower part of her body was frozen, the upper part burned with fever, and there seemed to be no connection between the two parts. She wanted the water to cool her parched mouth, but the hand on the glass would not respond, as if the lines of communication had been broken between desire and will.

"Daisy? What's the matter?"

"I feel—I think I'm—sick."

"Sick?" He looked surprised and hurt, like a boxer caught by a sudden low blow. "You don't look sick. I was thinking just a minute ago what a marvelous color you have this morning—oh God, Daisy, don't be sick."

"I can't help it."

"Here. Drink this. Let me carry you over to the davenport. Then I'll go and get your mother."

"No," she said sharply. "I don't want her to—"

"We have to do something. Perhaps I'd better call a doctor."

"No, don't. It will all be over by the time anyone could get here."

"How do you know?"

"It's happened before."

"When?"

"Last week. Twice."

"Why didn't you tell me?"

"I don't know." She had a reason, but she couldn't remember it. "I feel so—hot."

He pressed his right hand gently against her forehead. It was cold and moist. "I don't think you have a temperature," he said anxiously. "You sound all right. And you've still got that good healthy color."

He didn't recognize the color of terror.

Daisy leaned forward in her chair. The lines of communication between the two parts of her body, the frozen half and the feverish half, were gradually re-forming themselves. By an effort of will she was able to pick up the glass from the table and drink the water. The water tasted peculiar, and Jim's face, staring down at her, was out of focus, so that he looked not like Jim, but like some kind stranger who'd dropped in to help her.

Help.

How had this kind stranger gotten in? Had she called out to him as he was passing, had she cried, "Help!"?

"Daisy? Are you all right now?"

"Yes."

"Thank God. You had me scared for a minute there."

Scared.

"You should take regular daily exercise," Jim said. "It would be good for your nerves. I also think you haven't been getting enough sleep."

Sleep. Scared. Help. The words kept sweeping around and around in her mind like horses on a carousel. If there were only some way of stopping it or even slowing it down—*hey, operator; you at the controls, kind stranger, slow down, stop, stop, stop.*

"It might be a good idea to start taking vitamins every day."

"Stop," she said. "Stop."

Jim stopped, and so did the horses, but only for a second, long enough to jump right off the carousel and start galloping in the opposite direction, *sleep* and *scared* and *help* all running riderless together in a cloud of dust. She blinked.

"All right, dear. I was only trying to do the right thing." He smiled at her timidly, like a nervous parent at a fretful, ailing child who must, but can't, be pleased. "Listen, why don't you sit there quietly for a minute, and I'll go and make you some hot tea?"

"There's coffee in the percolator."

"Tea might be better for you when you're upset like this."

I'm not upset, stranger. I'm cold and calm.

Cold.

She began to shiver, as if the mere thinking of the word had conjured up a tangible thing, like a block of ice.

She could hear Jim bumbling around in the kitchen, opening drawers and cupboards, trying to find the tea bags and the kettle. The gold sunburst clock over the mantel said 8:30. In another half hour the maid, Stella, would be arriving, and shortly after that Daisy's mother would be coming over from her cottage, brisk and cheerful, as usual in the mornings, and inclined to be critical of anyone who wasn't, especially Daisy.

Half an hour to become brisk and cheerful. So little time, so much to do, so many things to figure out. *What happened to me? Why did it happen? I was just sitting here, doing nothing, thinking nothing, only listening to Jim and to the sounds from across the canyon, the children playing, the dogs barking, the saw whirring, the baby crying. I felt quite happy, in a sleepy kind of way. And then suddenly something woke me, and it began, the terror, the panic. What started it, which of those sounds?*

Perhaps it was the dog, she thought. One of the new families across the canyon had an Airedale that howled at passing planes. A howling dog, when she was a child, meant death. She was nearly thirty now, and she knew some dogs howled, particular breeds, and others didn't, and it had nothing to do with death.

Death. As soon as the word entered her mind, she knew that it was the real one; the others going around on the carousel had been merely substitutes for it.

"Jim."

"Be with you in a minute. I'm waiting for the kettle to boil."

"Don't bother making any tea."

"How about some milk, then? It'd be good for you. You're going to have to take better care of yourself."

No, it's too late for that, she thought. *All the milk and vitamins and exercise and fresh air and sleep in the world don't make an antidote for death.*

Jim came back, carrying a glass of milk. "Here you are. Drink up."

She shook her head.

"Come on, Daisy."

"No. No, it's too late."

"What do you mean it's too late? Too late for what?" He put the glass down on the table so hard that some of the milk splashed on the cloth. "What the hell are you talking about?"

"Don't swear at me."

"I have to swear at you. You're so damned exasperating."

"You'd better go to your office."

"And leave you here like this, in this condition?"

"I'm all right."

"Okay, okay, you're all right. But I'm sticking around anyway." He sat down, stubbornly, opposite her. "Now, what's this all about, Daisy?"

"I can't—tell you."

"Can't, or don't want to? Which?"

6

She covered her eyes with her hands. She was not aware that she was crying until she felt the tears drip down between her fingers.

"What's the matter, Daisy? Have you done something you don't want to tell me about—wrecked your car, overdrawn your bank account?"

"No."

"What, then?"

"I'm frightened."

"Frightened?" The word displeased him. He didn't like his loved ones to be frightened or sick; it seemed to cast a reflection on him and his ability to look after them properly. "Frightened of what?"

She didn't answer.

"You can't be frightened without having something to be frightened about. So what is it?"

"You'll laugh."

"Believe me, I never felt less like laughing in my life. Come on, try me."

She wiped her eyes with the sleeve of her robe. "I had a dream."

He didn't laugh, but he looked amused. "And you're crying because of a *dream?* Come, come, you're a big girl now, Daisy."

She was staring at him across the table, mute and melancholy, and he knew he had said the wrong thing, but he couldn't think of any right thing. How did you treat a wife, a grown woman, who cried because she had a dream?

"I'm sorry, Daisy. I didn't meant to—"

"No apology is necessary," she said stiffly. "You have a perfect right to be amused. Now we'll drop the subject if you don't mind."

"I do mind. I want to hear about it."

"No. I wouldn't like to send you into hysterics; it gets a lot funnier."

He looked at her soberly. "Does it?"

"Oh yes. It's quite a scream. There's nothing funnier than death, really, especially if you have an advanced sense of humor." She wiped her eyes again, though there were no fresh tears. The heat of anger had dried them at their source. "You'd better go to your office."

"What the hell are you so mad about?"

"Stop swearing at—"

"I'll stop swearing if you'll stop acting childish." He reached for her hand, smiling. "Bargain?"

"I guess so."

"Then tell me about the dream."

"There's not very much to tell." She lapsed into silence, her hand moving uneasily beneath his, like a little animal wanting to escape but too timid to make any bold attempt. "I dreamed I was dead."

"Well, there's nothing so terrible about that, is there? People often dream they're dead."

"Not like this. It wasn't a nightmare like the kind of dream you're talking about. There was no emotion connected with it at all. It was just a *fact.*"

"The fact must have been presented in some way. How?"

"I saw my tombstone." Although she'd denied that there was any emotion connected with the dream, she was beginning to breathe heavily again, and her voice was rising in pitch. "I was walking along the beach below the cemetery with Prince. Suddenly Prince took off up the side of the cliff. I could hear him howling, but he was out of sight, and when I whistled for him, he didn't come. I started up the path after him."

She hesitated again. Jim didn't prompt her. It sounded real enough, he thought, like something that actually happened, except that there was no path up that cliff and Prince never howled.

"I found Prince at the top. He was sitting beside a grey tombstone, his head thrown back, howling like a wolf. I called to him, but he paid no attention. I went over to the tombstone.

It was mine. It had my name on it. The letters were distinct, but weathered, as if it had been there for some time. It had."

"How do you know?"

"The dates were on it, too. DAISY FIELDING HARKER, it said. BORN NOVEMBER 13, 1930. DIED DECEMBER 2, 1955." She looked at him as if she expected him to laugh. When he didn't, she raised her chin in a half-challenging manner. "There. I told you it was funny, didn't I? I've been dead for four years."

"Have you?" He forced a smile, hoping it would camouflage his sudden feeling of panic, of helplessness. It was not the dream that disturbed him; it was the reality it suggested: someday Daisy would die, and there would be a genuine tombstone in that very cemetery with her name on it. *Oh God, Daisy, don't die.* "You look very much alive to me," he said, but the words, meant to be light and airy, came out like feathers turned to stone and dropped heavily on the table. He picked them up and tried again. "In fact, you look pretty as a picture, to coin a phrase."

Her quick changes of mood teased and bewildered him. He had never reached the point of being able to predict them, so he was completely unprepared for her sudden, explosive little laugh. "I went to the best embalmer."

Whether she was going up or coming down, he was always willing to share the ride. "You found him in the Yellow Pages, no doubt?"

"Of course. I find everything in the Yellow Pages."

Their initial meeting through the Yellow Pages of the telephone directory had become a standard joke between them. When Daisy and her mother had arrived in San Félice from Denver and were looking for a house to buy, they had consulted the phone book for a list of real-estate brokers. Jim had been chosen because Ada Fielding was interested in numerology at the time and the name James Harker contained the same number of letters as her own.

In that first week of taking Daisy and her mother around to look at various houses, he'd learned quite a lot about them. Daisy had put up a great pretense of being alert to all the details of construction, drainage, interest rates, taxes, but in the end she picked a house because it had a fireplace she fell in love with. The property was overpriced, the terms unsuitable, it had no termite clearance, and the roof leaked, but Daisy refused to consider any other house. "It has such a darling fireplace," she said, and that was that.

Jim, a practical, coolheaded man, found himself fascinated by what he believed to be proof of Daisy's impulsive and sentimental nature. Before the week was over, he was in love. He deliberately delayed putting the papers for the house through escrow, making excuses which Ada Fielding later admitted she'd seen through from the beginning. Daisy suspected nothing. Within two months they were married, and the house they moved into, all three of them, was not the one with the darling fireplace that Daisy had chosen, but Jim's own place on Laurel Street. It was Jim who insisted that Daisy's mother share the house. He had a vague idea, even then, that the very qualities he admired in Daisy might make her hard to handle at times and that Mrs. Fielding, who was as practical as Jim himself, might be of assistance. The arrangement had worked out adequately, if not perfectly. Later, Jim had built the canyon house they were now occupying, with separate quarters for his mother-in-law. Their life was quiet and well run. There was no place in it for unscheduled dreams.

"Daisy," he said softly, "don't worry about the dream."

"I can't help it. It must have some meaning, with everything so specific, my name, the dates—"

"Stop thinking about it."

"I will. It's just that I can't help wondering what happened on that day, December 2, 1955."

"Probably a great many things happened, as on any day of any year."

"To me, I mean," she said impatiently. "Something must have happened to *me* that day, something very important."

"Why?"

"Otherwise my unconscious mind wouldn't have picked that particular date to put on a tombstone."

"If your unconscious mind is as flighty and unpredictable as your conscious mind—"

"No, I'm serious about it, Jim."

"I know, and I wish you weren't. In fact, I wish you'd stop thinking about it."

"I said I would."

"Promise?"

"All right."

The promise was as frail as a bubble; it broke before his car was out of the driveway.

Daisy got up and began to pace the room, her step heavy, her shoulders stooped, as if she were carrying the weight of the tombstone on her back.

2

Perhaps, at this hour that is very late for me, I should not step back into your life . . .

Daisy DIDN'T WATCH the car leave, so she had no way of knowing that Jim had stopped off at Mrs. Fielding's cottage. The first suspicion occurred to her when her mother, who was constantly and acutely aware of time, appeared at the back door half an hour before she was due. She had Prince, the collie, with her on a leash. When the leash was removed, Prince bounced around the kitchen as if he'd just been released after a year or two in leg-irons.

Since Mrs. Fielding lived alone, it was considered good policy for her to keep Prince, a zealous and indefatigable barker, at her cottage every night for protection. Because of this talent for barking, he enjoyed the reputation of being an excellent watchdog. The fact was, Prince's talent was spread pretty thin; he barked with as much enthusiasm at acorns falling on the roof as he would have at intruders bursting in the door. Although Prince had never been put to a proper test so far, the general feeling was that he would come through when the appropriate time arrived, and protect his people and property with ferocious loyalty.

Daisy greeted the dog affectionately, because she wanted to and because he expected it. The two women saw each other too frequently to make any fuss over good-mornings.

"You're early," Daisy said.

"Am I?"

"You know you are."

"Ah well," Mrs. Fielding said lightly, "it's time I stopped living by the clock. And it was such a lovely morning, and I heard on the radio that there's a storm coming, and I didn't want to waste the sun while it lasted—"

"Mother, stop that."

"Stop what, for goodness' sake?"

"Jim came over to see you, didn't he?"

"For a moment, yes."

"What did he tell you?"

"Oh, nothing much, actually."

"That's no answer," Daisy said. "I wish the two of you would stop treating me like an idiot child."

"Well, Jim made some remark about your needing a tonic, perhaps, for your nerves. Oh, not that I think your nerves are bad or anything, but a tonic certainly wouldn't do any harm, would it?"

"I don't know."

"I'll phone that nice new doctor at the clinic and ask him to prescribe something loaded with vitamins and minerals and whatever. Or perhaps protein would be better."

"I don't want any protein, vitamins, minerals, or anything else."

"We're just a mite irritable this morning, aren't we?" Mrs. Fielding said with a cool little smile. "Mind if I have some coffee?"

"Go ahead."

"Would you like some?"

"No."

"No, *thanks*, if you don't mind. Private problems don't constitute an excuse for bad manners." She poured some coffee from the electric percolator. "I take it there are private problems?"

"Jim told you everything, I suppose?"

"He mentioned something about a silly little dream you had which upset you. Poor Jim was very upset himself. Perhaps you shouldn't worry him with trivial things. He's terribly wrapped up in you, Daisy."

"Wrapped up." The words didn't conjure up the picture they were intended to. All Daisy could see was a double mummy, two people long dead, wrapped together in a winding sheet. Death again. No matter which direction her mind turned, death was around the corner or the next bend in the road, like a shadow that always walked in front of her. "It wasn't," Daisy said, "a silly little dream. It was very real and very important."

"It may seem so to you now while you're still upset. Wait till you calm down and think about it objectively."

"It's quite difficult," Daisy said dryly, "to be objective about one's own death."

"But you're not dead. You're here and alive and well, and, I thought, happy . . . You *are* happy, aren't you?"

"I don't know."

Prince, with the sensitivity of his breed to a troubled atmosphere, was standing in the doorway with his tail between his legs, watching the two women.

They were similar in appearance and perhaps had had, at one time, some similarity of temperament. But the circumstances of Mrs. Fielding's life had forced her to discipline herself to a high degree of practicality. Mr. Fielding, a man of great charm, had proved a fainthearted and spasmodic breadwinner, and Daisy's mother had been the main support of the family for many years. Mrs. Fielding seldom referred to her ex-husband, unless she was very angry, and she never heard from him at all. Daisy did, every now and then, always from a different address in a different city, but with the same message: *Daisy baby, I wonder if you could spare a bit of cash. I'm a little low at the moment, just temporarily, I'm expecting something big any day now . . .* Daisy, without informing her mother, answered all the letters.

"Daisy, listen. The maid will be here in ten minutes." Mrs. Fielding never called Stella by name because she didn't approve of her. "Now's our chance to have a little private talk, the kind we always used to have."

Daisy was aware that the private little talk would eventually become a rather exhaustive survey of her own faults: she was too emotional, weak-willed, selfish, too much like her father, in fact. Daisy's weaknesses invariably turned out to be duplications of her father's.

"We've always been so close," Mrs. Fielding said, "because there were just the two of us together for so many years."

"You talk as if I never had a father."

"Of course you had a father. But . . ."

There was no need to go on. Daisy knew the rest of it: Father wasn't around much, and he wasn't much when he was around.

Silently Daisy turned and started to go into the next room. Prince saw her coming, but he didn't budge from the doorway, and when she stepped over him, he let out a little snarl to indicate his disapproval of her mood and the way things were going in general. She reprimanded him, without conviction. She'd had the dog throughout the eight years of her marriage, and she sometimes thought Prince was more conscious of her real emotions than Jim or her mother or even herself. He followed her now into the living room, and when she sat down, he sat down, too, putting one paw in her lap, his brown eyes staring gravely into her face, his mouth open, ready to speak if it could: *Come on, old girl, cheer up. The world's not so bad. I'm in it.*

Even when the maid arrived at the back door, usually an occasion for loud and boisterous conduct, Prince didn't move.

Stella was a city girl. She didn't like working in the country. Though Daisy had explained frequently and patiently that it took only ten minutes to drive from the house to the nearest supermarket, Stella was not convinced. She knew the country when she saw it, and this was it, and she didn't like it one bit. All that nature around, it made her nervous. Wasps and hummingbirds coming at you, snails sneaking about, bees swarming in the eucalyptus trees, fleas breeding in the dry soil, every once in a while taking a sizable nip out of Stella's ankles or wrists.

Stella and her current husband occupied a second-floor apartment in the lower end of town where all she had to cope with was the odd housefly. In the city, things were civilized, not a wasp or snail or bird in sight, just people: shoppers and shopkeepers by day, drunks and prostitutes at night. Sometimes they were arrested right below Stella's front window, and occasionally there was a knife fight, very quick and quiet, among the Mexican nationals relaxing after a day of picking lemons or avocados. Stella enjoyed these excitements. They made her feel both alive (all those things happening) and virtuous (but not to her. No prostitute or drunk, she; just a couple of bucks on a horse, in the back room of the Sea Esta Café every morning before she came to work).

While the Harkers were still living in town, Stella was content enough with her job. They were nice people to work for, as people to work for went, never snippy or mean-spirited. But she couldn't stand the country. The fresh air made her cough, and the quietness depressed her—no cars passing, or hardly ever, no radios turned on full blast, no people chattering.

Before entering the house, Stella stepped on three ants and squashed a snail. It was the least she could do on behalf of civilization. *Those ants sure knew they was stepped on,* she thought, and pushed her two hundred pounds through the kitchen door. Since neither Mrs. Harker nor the old lady was around, Stella began her day's labors by making a fresh pot of coffee and eating five slices of bread and jam. One nice thing about the Harkers, they bought only the best victuals and plenty of.

"She's eating," Mrs. Fielding said in the living room. "Already. She hardly ever does anything else."

"The last one was no prize either."

"This one's impossible. You should be firmer with her, Daisy, show her who's boss."

"I'm not sure I know who's boss," Daisy said, looking faintly puzzled.

"Of course you do. *You* are."

"I don't feel as if I am. Or want to be."

"Well, you are, whether you want to be or not, and it's up to you to exercise your authority and stop being willy-nilly about it. If you want her to do something or not to do something, say so. The woman's not a mind reader, you know. She expects to be told things, to be ordered around."

"I don't think that would work with Stella."

"At least try. This habit of yours—and it is a habit, not a personality defect as I used to believe—this habit of letting everything slide because you won't take the trouble, because you can't be bothered, it's just like your—"

"Father. Yes. I know. You can stop right there."

"I wish I could. I wish I'd never had to begin in the first place. But when I see quite unnecessary mismanagement, I feel I must do something about it."

"Why? Stella's not so bad. She muddles through, and that's about all you can expect of anyone."

"I don't agree," Mrs. Fielding said grimly. "In fact, we don't seem to be agreeing on anything this morning. I don't understand what the trouble is. *I* feel quite the same as usual—or did, until this absurd business of a dream came up."

"It's not absurd."

"Isn't it? Well, I won't argue." Mrs. Fielding leaned forward stiffly and put her empty cup on the coffee table. Jim had made the table himself, of teakwood and ivory-colored ceramic tile. "I don't know why you won't talk to me freely anymore, Daisy."

"I'm growing up, perhaps that's the reason."

"Growing up? Or just growing away?"

"They go together."

"Yes, I suppose they do, but—"

"Maybe you don't want me to grow up."

"What nonsense. Of course I do."

"Sometimes I think you're not even sorry I can't have a child, because if I had a child, it would show I was no longer one myself." Daisy paused, biting her lower lip. "No, no, I don't really mean that. I'm sorry, it just came out. I don't mean it."

Mrs. Fielding had turned pale, and her hands were clenched in her lap. "I won't accept your apology. It was a stupid and cruel remark. But at least I realize now what the trouble is. You've started thinking about it again, perhaps even hoping."

"No," Daisy said. "Not hoping."

"When are you going to accept the inevitable, Daisy? I thought you'd become adjusted by this time. You've known about it for five whole years."

"Yes."

"The specialist in Los Angeles made it very clear."

"Yes." Daisy didn't remember how long ago it was, or the month or the week. She only remembered the day itself, beginning the first thing in the morning when she was so ill. Then, afterward, the phone call to a friend of hers who worked at a local medical clinic: "Eleanor? It's Daisy Harker. You'll never guess, never. I'm so happy I could burst. I think I'm pregnant. I'm almost sure I am. Isn't it wonderful? I've been sick as a dog all morning and yet so happy, if you know what I mean. Listen, I know there are all sorts of obstetricians in town, but I want you to recommend the very best in the whole country, the very, very best specialist . . ."

She remembered the trip down to Los Angeles, with her mother driving. She'd felt so ecstatic and alive, seeing everything in a fresh new light, watching, noticing things, as if she were preparing herself to point out all the wonders of the world to her child. Later the specialist spoke quite bluntly: "I'm sorry, Mrs. Harker. I detect no signs of pregnancy . . ."

This was all Daisy could bear to hear. She'd broken down then, and cried and carried on so much that the doctor made the rest of his report to Mrs. Fielding, and she had told Daisy: there were to be no children ever.

Mrs. Fielding had talked nearly all the way home while Daisy watched the dreary landscape (where were the green hills?) and the slate-grey sea (had it ever been blue?) and the barren dunes (barren, barren, barren). It wasn't the end of the world, Mrs. Fielding had said, count blessings, look at silver linings. But Mrs. Fielding herself was so disturbed she couldn't go on driving. She was forced to stop at a little café by the sea, and the two women had sat for a long time facing each other across a greasy, crumb-covered table. Mrs. Fielding kept right on talking, raising her voice against the crash of waves on pilings and the clatter of dishes from the kitchen.

Now, five years later, she was still using some of the same words. "Count your blessings, Daisy. You're secure and comfortable, you're in good health, surely you have the world's nicest husband."

"Yes," Daisy said. "Yes." She thought of the tombstone in her dream, and the date of her death, December 2, 1955. Four years ago, not five. And the trip to see the specialist must have taken place in the spring, not in December, because the hills had been green. There was no connection between the day of the trip and what Daisy now capitalized in her mind as The Day.

"Also," Mrs. Fielding continued, "you should be hearing from one of the adoption agencies any day now—you've been on the list for some time. Perhaps you should have applied sooner than last year, but it's too late to worry about that now. Look on the bright side. One of these days you'll have a baby, and you'll love it just as much as you would your own, and so will Jim. You don't realize sometimes how lucky you are simply to have Jim. When I think of what some women have to put up with in their marriages . . ."

Meaning herself, Daisy thought.

". . . you are a lucky, lucky girl, Daisy."

"Yes."

"I think the main trouble with you is that you haven't enough to do. You've let so many of your activities slide lately. Why did you drop your course in Russian literature?"

"I couldn't keep the names straight."

"And the mosaic you were making . . ."

"I have no talent."

As if to demonstrate that there was at least some talent around the house, Stella burst into song while she washed the breakfast dishes.

Mrs. Fielding went over and closed the kitchen door, not too subtly. "It's time you started a new activity, one that will *absorb* you. Why don't you come with me to the Drama Club luncheon this noon? Someday you might even want to try out for one of our plays."

"I doubt that very—"

"There's absolutely nothing to acting. You just do what the director tells you. They're having a very interesting speaker at the luncheon. It would be a lot better for you to go out than to sit here brooding because you dreamed somebody killed you."

Daisy leaned forward suddenly in her chair, pushed the dog's paw off her lap, and got up. "What did you say?"

"Didn't you hear me?"

"Say it again."

"I see no reason to . . ." Mrs. Fielding paused, flushed with annoyance. "Well, all right. Anything to humor you. I simply stated that I thought it would be better for you to come with me to the luncheon than to sit here brooding because you had a bad dream."

"I don't think that's quite accurate."

"It's as close as I can remember."

"You said, 'because I dreamed somebody killed me.'" There was a brief silence. "Didn't you?"

"I may have." Mrs. Fielding's annoyance was turning into something deeper. "Why fuss about a little difference in words?"

Not a little difference, Daisy thought. *An enormous one.* "I died" had become "someone killed me."

She began to pace up and down the room again, followed by the reproachful eyes of the dog and the disapproving eyes of her mother. Twenty-two steps up, twenty-two steps down. After a while the dog started walking with her, heeling, as if they were out for a stroll together.

We were walking along the beach below the cemetery, Prince and I, and suddenly Prince disappeared up the cliff. I could hear him howling. I whistled for him, but he didn't come.

I went up the path after him. He was sitting beside a tombstone. It had my name on it:
Daisy Fielding Harker. Born November 13, 1930. Killed December 2, 1955 . . .

3

But I cannot help it. My blood runs in your veins . . .

At noon Jim called and asked her to meet him downtown for lunch. They ate soup and salad at a café on State Street. The place was crowded and noisy, and Daisy was grateful that Jim had chosen it. There was no need to force conversation. With so many others talking, silence between any two particular people seemed to go unnoticed. Jim even had the illusion that they'd enjoyed a lively lunch, and when they parted in front of the café, he said, "You're feeling better, aren't you?"

"Yes."

"No more skirmishes with your unconscious?"

"Oh no."

"Good girl." He pressed her shoulder affectionately. "See you for dinner."

She watched him until he turned the corner to the parking lot. Then she began walking slowly down the street in the opposite direction, with no special destination in mind, only a strong desire to stay away from the house as long as she could.

A rising wind prodded her, and on the tips of the purple mountains storm clouds were gathering like great plumes of black smoke. For the first time that day she thought of something unconnected with herself: *Rain. It's going to rain.*

As the wind pushed the storm clouds toward the city, everyone on the street was caught up in the excitement of the coming rain. They walked faster, talked louder. Strangers spoke to strangers: "How about that, look at those clouds . . ." "We're going to catch it this time . . ." "When I hung up the wash this morning, there wasn't a cloud in sight . . ." "Just in time for my cinerarias . . ."

"Rain," they said, and lifted their faces to the sky as if they were expecting not just rain but a shower of gold.

It had been a year without winter. The hot, sunny days, which usually ended in November, had stretched through Christmas and the New Year. It was now February, and the reservoirs were getting low, and large sections of the mountains had been closed to picnickers and campers because of the fire hazard. Cloud seeders were standing by, waiting for clouds, like actors ready with their roles waiting for a stage to appear.

The clouds came, their blacks and greys more beautiful than all the colors of the spectrum, and suddenly the sun vanished and the air turned cold.

I'll be caught in the rain, Daisy thought. *I should start for home.* But her feet kept right on going as if they had a mind of their own and would not be led by a timid girl afraid of getting a little wet.

Behind her, someone called her name: "Daisy Harker."

She stopped and turned, recognizing the voice immediately—Adam Burnett's. Burnett was a lawyer, an old friend of Jim's, who shared Jim's interest in cabinetmaking. Adam came over to the house quite frequently as a refugee from his family of eight, but Daisy didn't see much of him. The two men usually shut themselves up in Jim's hobby shop downstairs.

All morning Daisy had been thinking off and on of going to talk to Adam, and this sudden meeting confused her, as if she had conjured up his person out of her thoughts. She didn't even greet him. She said uncertainly, "How funny, running into you like this."

"Not so funny. My office is just two doors down the street, and the place where I eat lunch is directly across the road." He was a tall, heavily built man in his forties, with a brisk but pleasant professional manner. He noticed Daisy's confusion immediately but could think of no reason for it. "I'm pretty hard to miss in this neck of the woods."

"I'd—forgotten where your office was."

"Oh? For a moment when I first spotted you, I thought you might be on your way to see me."

"No. No." *I didn't, I couldn't possibly have, come this way deliberately. Why, I didn't even remember his office was near here, or I can't remember remembering.* "I wasn't on my way to anywhere. I was just walking. It's such a lovely day."

"It's cold." He glanced briefly at the sky. "And about to be wet."

"I like rain."

"At this point, don't we all."

"I meant, I like to *walk* in the rain."

His smile was friendly but a little puzzled. "That's fine. Go right ahead. The exercise will do you good, and the rain probably won't hurt you."

She didn't move. "The reason I thought it was funny running into you like this was because—well, I was thinking about you this morning."

"Oh?"

"I was even thinking of—of making an appointment to see you."

"Why?"

"Something has sort of happened."

"How can anything sort of happen? It happens or it doesn't."

"I don't quite know how to explain." The first drops of rain had begun to fall. She didn't notice them. "Do you consider me a neurotic woman?"

"This is hardly the time or place to discuss a subject like that," he said dryly. "*You* may like walking in the rain. Some of us don't."

"Adam, listen."

"You'd better come up to my office." He consulted his wristwatch. "I've got twenty-five minutes before I'm due at the courthouse."

"I don't want to."

"I think you want to."

"No, I feel like such a fool."

"So do I, standing around in the pouring rain. Come on, Daisy."

They took the elevator up to the third floor. Adam's receptionist and his secretary were both still out to lunch, and the suite was quiet and dark. Adam turned on the lamps in the reception room; then he went into his office, hung up his wet tweed jacket to dry on an old-fashioned brass clothes rack.

"Sit down, Daisy. You're looking great. How's Jim?"

"Fine."

"Has he been making any new furniture?"

"No. He's refinishing an old bird's-eye maple desk for the den."

"Where did he get hold of it?"

"The former owners of the house he bought left it behind as trash. I guess they didn't know what it was—it had so many layers of paint on it. Ten at least, Jim says."

She knew this was part of his technique, getting her started talking about safe, impersonal things first, and she half resented the fact that it was working. It was as if he'd applied a few drops of oil to the proper places and suddenly wheels began turning and she told him about the dream. The rain beat in torrents against the windows, but Daisy was walking on a sunny beach with her dog, Prince.

Adam leaned back in his chair and listened, his only outward reaction an occasional blink. Inwardly, he was surprised, not at the dream itself, but at the way she related it, coldly and without emotion, as if she were describing a simple factual chain of events, not a mere fantasy of her own mind.

She completed her account by telling him the dates on the tombstone. "November 13, 1930, and December 2, 1955. My birthday," she said, "and my death day."

The strange word annoyed him; he didn't understand why. "Is there such a word?"

"Yes."

He grunted and leaned forward, the chair squeaking under his weight. "I'm no psychiatrist. I don't interpret dreams."

"I'm not asking you to. No interpretation is necessary. It's all quite clear. On December 2, 1955, something happened to me that was so terrible it caused my death. I was psychically murdered."

Psychic murder, Adam thought. *Now I've heard everything. These damned silly idle women who sit around dreaming up trouble for themselves and everyone else . . .*

"Do you really believe that, Daisy?"

"Yes."

"All right. Suppose something catastrophic actually happened on that day. Why is it you don't remember what it was?"

"I'm trying to. That's the real reason I wanted to talk to you. I've got to remember. I've got to reconstruct the whole day."

"Well, I can't help you. And even if I could, I wouldn't. I see no point in people deliberately trying to recall an unpleasant occurrence."

"Unpleasant occurrence? That's a pretty mild expression for what happened."

"If you don't recall what happened," he said with a touch of irony, "how do you know it's a pretty mild expression?"

"*I know.*"

"You know. Just like that, eh?"

"Yes."

"I wish all knowledge was as easy to come by."

Her gaze was cool and steady. "You don't take me very seriously, do you, Adam? That's too bad, because I'm actually quite a serious person. Jim and my mother treat me like a child, and I frequently respond like one because it's easier that way—it doesn't upset their image of me. My self-image is quite different. I consider myself fairly bright. I graduated from college when I was twenty-one . . . Well, we won't go into that. It's evident I'm not convincing you of anything." She rose suddenly and started toward the door. "Thanks for listening, anyway."

"What's your hurry? Wait a minute."

"Why?"

"Nothing's been settled, for one thing. For another, I'll admit your, ah, situation intrigues me. This business of reconstructing a whole day four years ago . . ."

"Well?"

"It's going to be very difficult."

"I'm aware of that."

"Suppose you're able to do it, what then, Daisy?"

"I will at least know what happened."

"What use would such knowledge be to you? It certainly won't make you any happier, will it? Or any wiser?"

"No."

"Why not let it drop, then? Forget the whole business. You have nothing to gain and perhaps a great deal to lose—have you considered that angle of it?"

"No. Not until now."

"Give it some thought, will you?" He got up and opened the door for her. "One more thing, Daisy. The chances are that nothing whatever happened to you on that particular day. Dreams are never that logical." He knew the word *never* was too strong in this

16

connection, but he used it deliberately. She needed strong words to lean on or to test her own strength against.

"Well, I must be going," Daisy said. "I've taken up too much of your time. You'll send a bill, of course?"

"Of course not."

"I'd feel better about it if you did. I mean it."

"All right, then, I will."

"And thanks a lot for the advice, Adam."

"You know, a lot of my clients thank me for my advice and then go right home and do the exact opposite. Is that going to be the case with you, Daisy?"

"I don't think so," she said seriously. "I appreciate your letting me talk to you. I can't discuss things—problems, I mean—with Jim or Mother. They're too involved with me. They get upset when I step out of my role as the happy innocent."

"You should be able to talk freely to Jim. You have a good marriage."

"Any good marriage involves a certain amount of playacting."

His grunt indicated neither agreement nor disagreement: *I'll have to think about that before I decide. Playacting? Maybe.*

He walked her to the elevator, feeling pleased with himself for handling the situation well and with her for reacting so sensibly. He realized that although he'd known Daisy for a long time, he had never talked seriously to her before; he had been willing to accept her in her role of the happy innocent, the gay little girl, long after he'd discovered that she was not happy or innocent or gay.

The elevator arrived, and even though someone else was already buzzing for it, Adam held the door back with one hand. He had a sudden, uneasy feeling that he shouldn't let Daisy go, that nothing had been settled after all and the good solid advice he'd given her had blown away like smoke on a windy day.

"Daisy . . ."

"Someone's buzzing for the elevator."

"I just wanted to say that I wish you'd feel free to call me whenever you get upset."

"I'm not upset anymore."

"Sure?"

"Adam, someone wants the elevator. We can't just—"

"I'll take you down to the ground floor."

"That isn't nec—"

"I like the ride."

He stepped inside, the door closed, and the slow descent began. It wasn't slow enough, though. By the time Adam thought of anything more to say, they had reached the ground floor and Daisy was thanking him again, too politely and formally, as if she were thanking a host for a very dull party.

4

When I die, part of me will still be alive, in you, in your children, in your children's children . . .

IT WAS 2:30 when Daisy arrived home. Stella met her at the front door looking so flushed and lively that Daisy thought for a moment she'd got into Jim's liquor cabinet.

"Some man's been trying to get hold of you," Stella said. "He's called three times in the last hour, kept telling me how urgent it was and when was I expecting you back and the like." It wasn't often that any excitement occurred out here in the sticks, and Stella was determined to stretch it out. "The first two times he wouldn't give no name, but the last time I just up and asked him, who is this calling please, I said. I could tell he didn't want to give it, but he did, and I got it written down right here on a magazine with a number for you to call."

Across the top of a magazine Stella had printed, "Stan Foster 67134 urgent." Daisy had never heard of any Stan Foster, and she thought either the caller or Stella had made an error: Stella may have misunderstood the name, or Mr. Foster might be wanting to get in touch with a different Mrs. Harker.

"You're sure of the name?" Daisy said.

"He spelled it out for me twice: S-t-a-n—"

"Yes. Thanks. I'll call after I change my clothes."

"How did you get so soaking wet? Is it raining even in the city?"

"Yes," Daisy said. "It's raining even in the city."

She was in the bedroom taking off her clothes when the phone started ringing again. A minute later Stella knocked on the door.

"It's that Mr. Foster on the line again. I told him you was home, is that all right?"

"Yes. I'll take the call in here." Throwing a bathrobe around her shoulders, she sat down on the bed and picked up the phone. "This is Mrs. Harker."

"Hello, Daisy baby."

Even if she hadn't recognized the voice, she would have known who it was. No one ever called her Daisy baby except her father.

"Daisy baby? You there?"

"Yes, Daddy." In that first moment of hearing his voice again, she felt neither pleasure nor pain, only a kind of surprise and relief that he was still alive. She hadn't received a letter from him for nearly a year, though she'd written several times, and the last time she'd spoken to him was three years ago, when he called from Chicago to wish her a happy birthday. He'd been very drunk, and it wasn't her birthday. "How are you feeling, Daddy?"

"Fine. Oh, I've got a touch of this and a touch of that, but in the main, fine."

"Are you in town?"

"Yes. Got here last night."

"Why didn't you call me?"

"I called you. Didn't she tell you?"

"Who?"

"Your mother. I asked for you, but you were out. She recognized my voice and hung up, just like that, wham."

Daisy remembered entering the house after taking Prince for a walk and finding her mother seated beside the telephone looking grim and granite-eyed. "A wrong number," Mrs. Fielding had said. "Some drunk." And the contrast of the voice, as soft and bland as marshmallows coming out of that stone face, had reminded Daisy of something ugly which she couldn't fit into a time or place. "Very drunk," Mrs. Fielding had said. "He called me baby." Later Daisy had gone to bed thinking not of the drunk that had called her mother baby, but of a real adopted baby that might someday soon belong to her and Jim.

"Why didn't you phone me back, Daddy?"

"One call is all they allow you."

"They?"

He gave a sheepish little laugh that broke in the middle like an elastic stretched too far. "The fact is, I'm in a bit of a pickle. Nothing serious, but I need a couple of hundred dollars. I didn't want *you* to get involved, so I gave them a false name. I mean, you have a reputation to maintain in the community, so I figured there was no sense getting you mixed up in—Daisy, for God's sake, help me!"

"I always do, don't I?" she said quietly.

"You do. You're a good girl, Daisy, a good daddy-loving girl. I'll never forget how—"

"Where are you now?"

"Downtown."

"In a hotel?"

"No. I'm in somebody's office. His name's Pinata."

"Is he there, too?"

"Yes."

"Listening to all this?"

"He knows it all anyway," her father said with that sheepish little laugh again. "I had to tell him everything, who I was and who you were, or he wouldn't have sprung me. He's a bail bondsman."

"So you were in jail. What for?"

"Oh, gad, Daisy, do I have to go into it?"

"I'd like to hear about it, yes."

"Well, all right. I was on my way to see you, and suddenly I needed a drink, see? So I stopped in this bar downtown. Things were slack, and I asked the waitress to have a drink with me, just out of friendliness, you might say. Nita, her name was, a very fine-looking young woman who's had a hard life. To make a long story short, suddenly out of the blue her husband came in and started to get tough with her about not staying home to look after the kids. They exchanged a few words, and then he began pushing her around. Well, I couldn't just sit there and watch that kind of thing going on without doing anything about it."

"So you got into a fight?"

"That's about it."

"That *is* it, you mean."

"Yes. Someone called the cops, and the husband and I were hauled off to the pokey. Drunk and disorderly and disturbing the peace. Nothing serious. I gave the cops a false name, though, so no one would know I was your father in case the incident gets into the papers. I've already cast enough shame on you and your mother."

"Please," Daisy said, "don't try to make yourself out a hero because you gave a false name to protect Mother and me. In the first place, that's illegal when you have any sort of record, isn't it?"

"Is it?" He sounded very innocent. "Well, it's too late to worry about that now. Mr. Pinata isn't likely to tell on me. He's a gentleman."

Daisy could well imagine her father's definition of the word: a gentleman was somebody who'd just helped him out of a jam. Her own mental picture of Pinata showed him as a wizened, beady-eyed old man who smelled of jails and corruption.

"When I explained my situation to Mr. Pinata, he very kindly paid my fine. He's not in business for his health, though, so of course I have to stay here in his office until I can raise the money to pay him. Two hundred dollars the fine was. I pleaded guilty to get the trial over with in a hurry. No sense in having to come up here from L.A. just to—"

"You're living in L.A.?"

"Yes. We—I moved there last week. I thought it would be nice to be closer to you, Daisy baby. Besides, the climate in Dallas didn't agree with me."

It was the first she'd heard that he'd been living in Dallas. Topeka, Kansas, had been his last address. Dallas, Topeka, Chicago, Toronto, Detroit, St. Louis, Montreal—they were all just names to Daisy, but she knew that her father had lived in all of these places, had walked along their streets, searching for something that was always a few hundred miles farther on.

"Daisy? You can get the money, can't you? I gave Pinata my solemn promise."

"I can get it."

"When? The fact is, I'm in kind of a hurry. I have to get back to L.A. tonight—someone's expecting me—and as you know, I can't leave Pinata's office until I pay up."

"I'll come down right away." Daisy could see him waiting in the office, Pinata's prisoner, not a free man at all. He had merely changed jails and jailers the way he changed towns and people, never realizing he would always be in bondage. "Where is the office?"

She could hear him consulting Pinata: "Just where is this place anyway?" And then Pinata's voice, surprisingly young and pleasant for an old man who'd spent his life hanging around jails: "107 East Opal Street, between the 800 and 900 blocks of State Street."

Her father repeated the directions, and Daisy said, "Yes, I know where it is. I'll be down in half an hour."

"Ah, Daisy baby, you're a good girl, a good daddy-loving girl."

"Yes," Daisy said wearily. "Yes."

Fielding put down the telephone and turned to Pinata, who was sitting at his desk writing a letter to his son, Johnny. The boy, who was ten, lived in New Orleans with his mother, and Pinata saw him only for a month out of every year, but he wrote to him regularly each week.

Pinata said, without looking up, "Is she coming?"

"Certainly she's coming. Right away. I told you she would, didn't I?"

"What people like you tell me I don't always believe."

"I could take exception to that remark but I won't, because I'm feeling good."

"You should be. You've gone through a pint of my bourbon."

"I called you a gentleman, didn't I? Didn't you hear me tell Daisy you were a gentleman?"

"So?"

"No gentleman ever begrudges a drink to a fellow gentleman in distress. That's one of the rules of civilized society."

"It is, eh?" Pinata finished his letter: *Be a good boy, Johnny, and don't forget to write. I enclose five dollars so you can buy your mother and your little sister a nice valentine. Best love from your loving Dad.*

He put the letter in an envelope and sealed it. He always had a sick, lost feeling when he wrote to this boy who was his only known relative; it made him mad at the world, or whatever part of the world happened to be available at the moment. This time it was Fielding.

Pinata pounded an airmail stamp on the envelope and said, "You're a bum, Foster."

"Fielding, if you please."

"Foster, Fielding, Smith, you're still a bum."

"I've had a lot of hard luck."

"For every ounce of hard luck you've had, I bet you've passed a pound of it along to other people. Mrs. Harker, for instance."

"That's a lie. I've never harmed a hair on Daisy's head. Why, I've never even asked her for money unless it was absolutely necessary. And it's not as if she can't afford it. She made a very good marriage—trust Mrs. Fielding to see to that. So what if I put the bite on her now and then? When you come right down to it—"

"Don't bother coming right down to it," Pinata said. "You bore me."

Fielding's lower lip began to pout as if it had been stung by the word. He hadn't minded so much being called a bum since there was some truth in the statement, but he'd never considered himself a bore. "If I'd known that was your opinion of me," he said with dignity, "I'd never have drunk your liquor."

"The hell you wouldn't."

"It was a very cheap brand anyway. Ordinarily I wouldn't demean myself by touching such stuff, but under the stress of the moment . . ."

Pinata threw back his head and laughed, and Fielding, who hadn't intended to be amusing, watched him with an aggrieved expression. But the laughter was contagious, and pretty soon Fielding joined in. The two of them stood in the dingy little rain-loud office, laughing: a middle-aged man in a torn shirt with dried blood on his face, and a young man wearing

20

"I am."

"It will be much better for him, having a life of his own."

"When has he ever had anything else?"

"Don't be bitter about it," Jim said, forcing patience into his voice. Daisy's combination of loyalty and resentment toward her father irritated him. He himself didn't think much or care much about Fielding, not even to the extent of begrudging him the money he cost. He considered, in fact, that the money was well spent if it kept Fielding at a distance. Los Angeles was a hundred miles away, not much of a distance. He hoped, for Daisy's sake, that Fielding would take a dislike to the city, the smog, the traffic, or living conditions, and head back to the East Coast or the Middle West. Jim knew, better than Daisy, how difficult it was to handle old family knots when they no longer held anything together and were too frayed to be retied.

The last time he'd seen his father-in-law was five years ago, when he'd gone to Chicago on a business trip. The two men met at the Town House, and the evening started well, with Fielding going out of his way to be charming and Jim out of his to be charmed. But by ten o'clock Fielding was drunk and blubbering about how Daisy baby had never had a real father: "You take good care of my little girl, you hear? Poor little Daisy baby. You take good care of her, you goddamn stuffed shirt." Later, Fielding was poured into a taxicab by a couple of waiters, and Jim put three twenty-dollar bills in the pocket of his understuffed shirt.

Well, I've taken good care of her, Jim thought now, *within my limits anyway. I haven't made a move without first thinking of her welfare. And sometimes the decisions have been almost impossibly difficult, like the business about Juanita. She never mentions Juanita. The corner of her mind where the girl lies has been sealed off like a tomb.*

His pipe had gone out. He relit it, and its hoarse wheezing brought back the memory of Fielding's voice: "You take good care of my little girl . . . you goddamn stuffed shirt."

6

This letter may never reach you, Daisy. If it doesn't, I will know why . . .

Two days later, on Wednesday afternoon, Jim Harker arrived home for dinner an hour earlier than usual. Daisy's car was missing from the garage, and the mail was still in the postbox. It meant that Daisy had been away since noon, when the mail arrived. The house seemed lifeless without her, in spite of the noise of Stella vacuuming the downstairs and singing bits of sad songs in a loud, cheerful voice.

He sorted the mail on the dining-room table, and was surprised to come across a bill from Adam Burnett for services rendered Mrs. James Harker, February 9, $2.50.

The bill was surprising in several ways: that Daisy had been to see Adam without telling him about it, that the fee was so small, less than minimal for a lawyer's, and that the timing was unusual. It had been sent directly after Daisy's visit instead of being postponed until the end of the month like ordinary bills for professional services. He concluded, after some thought, that sending the bill was Adam's way of informing him about Daisy's visit without actually breaking any code of ethics involving the confidences of a client.

It wasn't quite five o'clock, so he called Adam at his office. "Mr. Burnett, please. Jim Harker speaking."

"Just one second, Mr. Harker. Mr. Burnett's on his way out, but I think I can catch him. Hold on."

After a minute Adam said, "Hello, Jim."

"I received your bill today."

"Oh yes." Adam sounded embarrassed. "I wasn't going to send you any, but Daisy insisted."

"I didn't know until now that she'd been to see you."

"Oh?"

"What did she have in mind?"

"Come now, Jim, that's for Daisy to tell you, not me."

"You addressed the bill to me, so I presume you wanted me to know she'd consulted you."

"Well, yes. I thought it would be preferable if you were cognizant . . ."

"No lawyer talk, please," Jim said in a sharp, tense voice. "Did she come to you about— about a divorce?"

"Good Lord, no. What gave you such a crazy idea?"

"That's the usual reason women consult lawyers, isn't it?"

"As a matter of fact, no. Women make wills, sign contracts, fill out tax forms—"

"Stop beating around the bush."

"All right," Adam said cautiously. "I met Daisy by accident on the street early Monday afternoon. She seemed bewildered and anxious to talk. So we talked. I'd like to think that I gave her some good advice and that she took it."

"Was it concerning a dream she had about a certain day four years ago?"

"Yes."

"And she didn't mention a divorce?"

"Why, no. Where did you get this worm in your wig about a divorce? There was absolutely nothing in Daisy's attitude to indicate she was contemplating such a move. Besides, she couldn't get one in California. She has no grounds."

"You're forgetting, Adam."

"That was a long time ago," Adam said quickly. "What's the matter with you and Daisy anyway? A more lugubrious pair—"

"Nothing was the matter until she had this damned dream on Sunday night. Things have been going smoothly. We've been married eight years, and I honestly think this last year has been the best. Daisy has finally adjusted to the fact that she can't have children— maybe not adjusted, but at least reconciled—and she's looking forward eagerly to the one we're going to adopt. At least she had been, until this dream business cropped up. She hasn't mentioned our prospective child for three days now. You've had eight children, and you know how much preparation and talking and planning goes on ahead of time. I'm confused by her sudden lack of interest. Perhaps she doesn't want a child after all. If she doesn't, if she's changed her mind, God knows it wouldn't be fair for us to adopt one."

"Nonsense. Of course she wants a child." Adam spoke firmly, although he had no real convictions on the subject. Daisy, like most other women, had always puzzled him and always would. It seemed reasonable to suppose that she would want children, but she might have some deep, unspoken revulsion against adopting one. "The dream has confused her, Jim. Be patient. Play along with her."

"That might do more harm than good."

"I don't think so. In fact, I'm convinced this deathday business of hers will come to a dead end."

"How so?"

"There's no place else for it to go. She's attempting the impossible."

"Why are you so certain it's impossible?"

"Because I've been trying the same thing," Adam said. "The idea intrigued me, picking a day at random out of the past and reconstructing it. If it had been simply a matter of recalling a business appointment, I would have consulted my desk diary. But this was purely personal. Anyway, on Monday night, after the kids were in bed, Fran and I tried it. To make sure our choice of date was absolute chance, we picked it, blindfolded, from a set of calendars in the almanac. Now, Fran not only has a memory like an elephant, she also keeps a pretty complete record of the kids: baby books, report cards, artwork, and so on. But we didn't get to first base. I predict Daisy will have a similar experience. It's the kind of thing that sounds easy but isn't.

After Daisy runs into a few blind alleys, she'll lose interest and give up. So let her run. Or better still, run with her."

"How?"

"Try remembering her day yourself, whatever day it was. I've forgotten."

"If you didn't get to first base, how do you expect me to?"

"I don't expect you to. Just play along. Step up to the plate and swing."

"I don't think Daisy would be fooled," Jim said dryly. "Perhaps it would be better if I distracted her attention, took her on a trip, something like that."

"A trip might be fine."

"I have to go up north this weekend anyway to look at a parcel of land in Marin County. I'll take Daisy along. She's always liked San Francisco."

He spoke to Daisy about it that night after dinner, describing the trip, lunch at Cambria Pines, a stopover at Carmel, dinner at Amelio's, a play at the Curran or the Alcazar, and afterwards a drink and floor show at the Hungry I. She looked at him as if he were proposing a trip to the moon in a rocket earned with Rice Krispies box tops.

Her refusal was sharp and direct, with no hint of her usual hesitance. "I can't go."

"Why not?"

"I have something important to attend to."

"Such as?"

"I'm doing—research."

"Research?" He repeated the word as if it tasted foreign to his tongue. "I tried to phone you this afternoon three or four times. You were out again. You've been out every afternoon this week."

"There have only been three afternoons in the week so far."

"Even so."

"Your meals are on time," Daisy said. "Your house is well kept."

Her slight but definite emphasis on the word *your* made it sound to Jim as though she were disclaiming any further share or interest in the house, as if she had, in some obscure sense, moved out. "It's *our* house, Daisy."

"Very well, our house. It's well kept, isn't it?"

"Of course."

"Then why should it bother you if I go out during the afternoon while you're at work?"

"It doesn't bother me. It concerns me. Not your going out, your attitude."

"What's the matter with my attitude?"

"A week ago you wouldn't have asked that, especially not in that particular tone, as if you were challenging me to knock a chip off your shoulder . . . Daisy, what's happening to us?"

"Nothing." She knew what was happening, though; what had, in fact, already happened. She had stepped out of her usual role, had changed lines and costumes, and now the director was agitated because he no longer knew what play he was directing. *Poor Jim,* she thought, and reached over and took his hand. "Nothing," she said again.

They were sitting side by side on the davenport. The house was very quiet. The rain had stopped temporarily, Stella had gone home after surviving another day in the country, and Mrs. Fielding was at a concert with a friend. Prince, the collie, was sleeping in front of the fireplace, where he always slept in bad weather. Even though there was no fire in the grate, he liked the remembered warmth of other fires.

"Be fair, Daisy," Jim said, pressing her hand. "I'm not one of these heavy husbands who wants his wife to have no interests outside himself. Haven't I always encouraged your activities?"

"Yes."

"Well, then? What have you been doing, Daisy?"

"Walking around."

"In all this rain?"

"Yes."

"Walking around where?"

"The old neighborhood on Laurel Street."

"But why?"

"That was where we were living when I"—*when I died*—"when it happened."

His mouth looked as though she'd reached up and pinched it. "Did you imagine that what happened was still there, like a piece of furniture we forgot to bring along?"

"In a sense it's still there."

"Well, in that case, why didn't you walk up to the door and inquire? Why didn't you ask the occupants if they'd mind if you searched the attic for a lost day?"

"There was no one at home."

"Oh, for God's sake, you mean you actually *tried* to get in?"

"I rang the doorbell. No one answered."

"Thank heaven for small mercies. What would you have said if someone had answered?"

"Just that I used to live there once and would like to see the house again."

"Rather than have you make such an exhibition of yourself," he said coldly, "I'll buy the house back for you. Then you can spend all your afternoons there, you can search every nook and cranny of the damn place, examine every piece of junk you find."

She had withdrawn her hand from his. For a while the contact had been like a bridge between them, but the bridge had washed away in the bitter flood of his irony. "I'm not looking for—junk. I don't intend making an exhibition of myself either. I went back because I thought that if I found myself in the same situation as before, I might remember something valuable."

"Valuable? The golden moment of your death, perhaps? Isn't that just a little morbid? When did you fall in love with the idea of dying?"

She got up and crossed the room as if trying to get beyond the range of his sarcasm. The movement warned him that he was going too far, and he changed his tone.

"Are you so bored with your life, Daisy? Do you consider the past four years a living death? Is that what your dream means?"

"No."

"I think so."

"It's not your dream."

The dog had awakened and was moving his eyes back and forth, from Daisy to Jim and back to Daisy, like a spectator at a tennis match.

"I don't want to quarrel," Daisy said. "It upsets the dog."

"It upsets the—oh, for Pete's sake. All right, all right, we won't quarrel. Can't have the dog getting upset. It's okay, though, if the rest of us are reduced to gibbering idiocy. We're just people, we don't deserve any better."

She was petting the dog's head in a soothing, reassuring way, her touch telling him that everything was fine, his eyes and ears were liars, not to be taken seriously.

I should play along with her, Jim thought. *That was Adam's advice. God knows, my own approach doesn't work.* "So you went back to Laurel Street," he said finally, "and walked around."

"Yes."

"Any results?"

"This quarrel with you," she said with bitterness. "That's all."

"You didn't remember anything?"

"Nothing that would pinpoint the actual day."

"I suppose you realize how unlikely it is that you'll ever succeed in pinpointing it?"

"Yes."

"But you intend to keep on trying?"

"Yes."

"Over my objections?"

"Yes, if you won't change your mind." She was quiet a moment, and her hand had paused on the dog's neck. "I remembered the winter. Perhaps that's a start. As soon as I saw the jasmine bushes on the south side of the house, I recalled that that was the year of the big frost when we lost all the jasmines. At least I thought we'd lost them, they looked so dead. But in the spring they all came to life again." *I didn't, though. The jasmines were tougher than I. There was no spring for me that year, no new leaves, no little buds.* "That's a start, isn't it, remembering the winter?"

"I guess so," he said heavily. "I guess that's a start."

"One day there was even snow on the mountain peaks. A lot of the high school kids ditched classes to go up and see it, and afterwards they drove down State Street with the snow piled high on their fenders. They looked very happy. It was the first time some of them had seen snow."

"Daisy."

"Snow in California never seems real to me somehow, not like back home in Denver, where it was a part of my life and often not a very pleasant part. I wanted to go up and see the snow that day, just like the high school kids, to make sure it was the real stuff, not something blown out of a machine from Hollywood . . .The year of the frost, you must remember it, Jim. I ordered a cord of wood for the fireplace, but I didn't realize what a lot of wood a cord was, and when it came, we didn't have any place to store it except outside in the rain."

She seemed anxious to go on talking, as if she felt she was on her way to convincing him of the importance of her project and the necessity for carrying on with it. Jim didn't try again to interrupt her. He felt with relief that Adam had been right: the whole thing was impossible. All Daisy had been able to remember so far was a little snow on the mountain peaks and some high school kids riding down State Street and a few dead jasmine bushes.

7

Your mother has vowed to keep us apart at any cost because she is ashamed of me . . .

THE NEXT MORNING, between the time Jim left and Stella arrived, Daisy phoned Pinata at his office. She didn't expect him to be there so early, but he answered the phone on the second ring, his voice alert and wary, as if early calls were the kind to watch out for.

"Yes."

"This is Daisy Harker, Mr. Pinata."

"Oh. Good morning, Mrs. Harker." He sounded suddenly a little too cordial. She didn't have to wait long to find out why. "If you want to cancel our agreement, that's fine with me. There'll be no charge. I'll mail you the retainer you gave me."

"Your extrasensory perception isn't working very well this morning," she said coldly. "I'm calling merely to suggest that I meet you at your office this afternoon instead of at the *Monitor-Press* building."

"Why?"

She told him the truth without embarrassment. "Because you're young and good-looking, and I wouldn't want people to get the wrong impression if they saw us together."

"I gather you haven't informed your family that you've hired me?"

"No."

"Why not?"

"I tried to, but I couldn't face another argument with Jim. He's right, according to his lights, and I'm right, according to mine. What's the point of arguing?"

"He's bound to find out," Pinata said. "Word gets around pretty fast in this town."

"I know, but by that time perhaps everything will be settled, you will have solved—"

"Mrs. Harker, I can't solve a thing pussyfooting around back alleys trying to avoid your family and friends. In fact, we're going to need their cooperation. This day you're fixated on, it wasn't just your day. It belonged to a lot of other people, too—650,000,000 Chinese, to name a few of them."

"I fail to see what 650,000,000 Chinese have to do with it."

"No. Well, forget it." His sigh was quite audible. *Intentionally audible*, she thought, annoyed. "I'll be in front of the *Monitor-Press* building at three o'clock, Mrs. Harker."

"Isn't it usually the employer who gives the orders?"

"Most employers know their business and are in a position to give orders. I don't think that applies to you in this particular instance, no insult intended. So, unless you've come up with some new ideas, I suggest we go about it my way. Have you any new ideas?"

"No."

"Then I'll see you this afternoon."

"Why there, at that specific place?"

"Because we're going to need some official help," Pinata said. "The *Monitor* knows a great deal more about what happened on December 2, 1955, than you or I do at the moment."

"They surely don't keep copies of newspapers from that far back."

"Not in the sense that they're offering them for sale, no. But every edition they've printed is available on microfilm. Let's hope something interesting will turn up."

They were both exactly on time, Pinata because punctuality was a habit with him, Daisy because the occasion was very important to her. All day, ever since her phone call to Pinata, she'd been impatient and excited, as if she half expected the *Monitor* to open its pages and reveal some vital truth to her. Perhaps a very special event had taken place in the world on December 2, 1955, and once the event was recalled to her, she would remember her reactions to it; it would become the peg on which she could hang the rest of the day, hat and coat and dress and sweater and, finally, the woman who fitted into them.

The carillon in the courthouse tower was ringing out the hour of three when Pinata approached the front door of the *Monitor* building. Daisy was already there, looking inconspicuous and a little dowdy in a loosely cut grey cotton suit. He wondered whether she had dressed that way deliberately to avoid calling attention to herself, or whether this was one of the latest styles. He'd lost touch with the latest styles since Monica had left him.

He said, "I hope I didn't keep you waiting."

"No. I just arrived."

"The library's on the third floor. We can take the elevator. Or would you rather walk?"

"I like to walk."

"Yes, I know."

She seemed a little surprised. "How could you know that?"

"I saw you yesterday afternoon."

"Where?"

"On Laurel Street. You were walking in the rain. I figured that anyone who walks in the rain must be very fond of walking."

"The walking was incidental. I had a purpose in visiting Laurel Street."

"I know. You used to live there. From the time of your marriage in June 1950 until October of last year, to be exact."

Her surprise this time was mixed with annoyance. "Have you been investigating me?"

"Just a few black and white statistics. Not in living color." He squinted up at the afternoon sun and rubbed his eyes. "I imagine the place on Laurel Street has many pleasant memories for you."

"Certainly."

"Then why try to destroy them?"

She regarded him with a kind of weary patience, as if he were a backward child who must be told the same thing over and over.

"I'm giving you," Pinata said, "another chance to change your mind."

"And I'm refusing it."

"All right. Let's go inside."

They went through the swinging doors and headed for the staircase, walking some distance apart like two strangers accidentally going in the same direction. The apartness was of Daisy's choosing, not Pinata's. It reminded him of what she'd said over the phone about not wanting people to see them together because he was young and good-looking. The compliment, if it was one, had embarrassed him. He didn't like any reference, good or bad, made to his physical appearance, because he felt such things were, or should be, irrelevant.

In his early years Pinata had been extremely conscious of the fact that he didn't know his own racial origin and couldn't identify with any particular racial group. Now, in his maturity, this lack of group identification had the effect of making him tolerant of every race. He was able to think of men as his brothers because some of them might very well be his brothers, for all he knew. The name Pinata, which enabled him to mix freely with the Spanish Americans and the Mexicans who made up a large part of the city, was not his. It had been given to him by the Mother Superior of the orphanage in Los Angeles where he'd been abandoned.

He still visited the orphanage occasionally. The Mother Superior was very old now, and her eyesight and hearing were failing, but her tongue was as lively as a girl's when Pinata came to see her. More than any of the other hundreds of her children, he was hers, because she'd found him, in the chapel on Christmas Eve, and because she'd named him, Jesus Pinata. As the Mother Superior grew older, her mind, no longer nimble or inquisitive, chose to follow certain well-worn roads. Her favorite road led back to a Christmas Eve thirty-two years ago.

"There you were, in front of the altar, a wee mite of a bundle barely five pounds, and squalling so hard I thought your little lungs would break. Sister Mary Martha came in then, looking as white as a sheet, as if she'd never seen a brand-new baby before. She picked you up in her arms and called you the Lord Jesus, and immediately you stopped crying, like any lost soul recognizing his name called out in the wilderness. So we called you Jesus.

"Of course, it's a very difficult name to live up to," she would add with a sigh. "Ah, how well I remember as you got older, all the fighting you had to do every time one of the other children laughed at your name. All those bruises and black eyes and chipped teeth, dear me, it became quite a problem. You hardly looked human half the time. Jesus is a lovely name, but I felt something had to be done. So I asked Father Stevens for his advice, and he came over and talked to you. He asked you what name you would like to have, and you said Stevens. A very fine choice, too. Father Stevens was a great man."

At this point she always stopped to blow her nose, explaining that she had a touch of sinusitis because of the smog. "You could have changed the Pinata part as well. After all, it was just a name we picked because the children were playing the piñata game that Christmas Eve. We took a vote on it. Sister Mary Martha was the only one who objected to the name. 'Suppose he is a Smith or a Brown or an Anderson,' she said. I reminded her that very few whites lived in our neighborhood, and since you were to be brought up among us, you would do better as a Pinata than as a Brown or Anderson. I was right, too. You've developed into a fine young man we're all proud of. If the good Father were only here to see you . . . Dear me, I think this smog gets worse each year. If it were the will of the Lord, I wouldn't complain, but I fear it's just sheer human perversity."

Perversity. The word reminded him of Daisy. She was racing up the steps ahead of him as if she were in training for a track meet. He caught up with her on the third floor. "What's your hurry? The place stays open until 5:30."

"I like to move fast."

"So do I, when someone's chasing me."

The library was at the end of a long, elaborately tiled corridor. It was rumored that no two tiles in the entire building were alike. So far no one had gone to the trouble of checking this, but the rumor was repeated to tourists, who relayed it via postcard and letter to their friends and relatives in the East and Middle West.

In the small room marked LIBRARY, a girl in horn-rimmed glasses was seated behind a desk pasting clippings into a scrapbook. She ignored Daisy and fixed her bright, inquisitive eyes on Pinata. "Is there anything I can do for you?"

Pinata said, "You're new around here, aren't you?"

"Yes. The other girl had to quit. Allergic to paste, broke out all over her hands and arms. A real mess."

"Sorry to hear it."

"She's trying to get workman's compensation, but I'm not sure it applies to allergies. Can I help you with anything?"

"I'd like to see the microfilm of one of your back copies."

"Year and month?"

"December '55."

"One roll of film covers half a month. Which half are you interested in, the first or last?"

"The first."

She unlocked one drawer of a metal filing cabinet and brought out a roll of microfilm, which she fitted into the projection machine. Then she turned on the light in the machine and showed Pinata the hand crank. "You just keep turning this until you come to the day you want. It starts at December the first and goes through to the fifteenth."

"Yes. Thanks."

"Pull up a chair if you want." The girl for the first time looked directly at Daisy. "Or two chairs."

Pinata arranged a chair for Daisy. He remained standing, with one hand on the crank. Although the girl in charge had returned to her desk and was presumably intent on her work, Pinata lowered his voice. "Can you see properly?"

"Not too well."

"Close your eyes for a minute while I turn to the right day, or you might get dizzy."

She closed her eyes until he said crisply, "Well, here's your day, Mrs. Harker."

Her eyes remained closed, as if the lids had become calcified and too stiff and heavy to move.

"Aren't you going to look at it?"

"Yes. Of course."

She opened her eyes and blinked a couple of times, refocusing. The headlines meant nothing to her: CIO AND AFL MERGED AFTER TWENTY-YEAR SPLIT. BODY OF UNIDENTIFIED MAN FOUND NEAR RAILROAD JUNGLE. FEDERAL SCHOOL AID PLAN BACKED. YOUTH CONFESSES DOZEN BURGLARIES. BAD WEATHER MAY CLOSE AIRPORT. SEVEN HUNDRED TO PARTICIPATE IN CHRISTMAS PARADE TONIGHT. CRASH INJURES PIANIST GIESEKING, KILLS WIFE. MORE SNOW PREDICTED FOR MOUNTAIN AREAS.

Snow on the mountains, she thought, *the kids driving down State Street, the dead jasmines.* "Could you read the fine print to me, please?"

"Which fine print?"

"About the snow on the mountains."

"All right. 'Early risers were given a rare treat this morning in the form of a blanket of snow on the mountains. Forest rangers at La Cumbre peak reported a depth of seven inches in some places, and more is predicted during the night. Some senior classes of both public and private schools were dismissed for the morning so that students could drive up and experience, many of them for the first time, real snow. Damage to citrus crops—'"

"I remember that," she said, "the students with the snow piled on the fenders of their cars."

"So do I."

"Very clearly?"

"Yes. They made quite a parade out of it."

"Why should both of us remember a little thing like that?"

"Because it was very unusual, I suppose," Pinata said.

"So unusual that it could only have happened once that year?"

"Perhaps. I can't be sure of it, though."

"Wait." She turned to him, flushed with excitement. "It must have happened only once. Don't you see? The students wouldn't have been dismissed from class a second time. They'd already been given their chance to see the snow. The school authorities surely wouldn't keep repeating the dismissal if it snowed a second or third or fourth time."

Her logic surprised and convinced him. "I agree. But why is it so important to you?"

"Because it's the first *real* thing I remember about the day, the only thing that separates it from a lot of other days. If I saw those students parading in their cars, it means I must have gone downtown, perhaps to have lunch with Jim. And yet I can't remember Jim being with me, or my mother either. I think—I'm almost sure—I was alone."

"When you saw the kids, where were you? Walking along the street?"

"No. I think I was inside some place, looking out through a window."

"A restaurant? A store? Where did you usually shop in those days?"

"For groceries at the Fairway, for clothes at Dewolfe's."

"Neither of those is on State Street. How about a restaurant? Do you have a favorite place to eat lunch?"

"The Copper Kettle. It's a cafeteria in the 1100 block."

"Let's assume for a minute," Pinata said, "that you were having lunch at the Copper Kettle, alone. Did you often go downtown and have lunch alone?"

"Sometimes, on the days I worked."

"You had a job?"

"I was a volunteer for a while at the Neighborhood Clinic. It's a family counseling service. I worked there every Wednesday and Friday afternoon."

"December 2 was a Friday. Did you go to work that afternoon?"

"I don't remember. I don't even know if I was still working at that time. I quit because I wasn't very good with chil—with people."

"You were going to say 'with children,' weren't you?"

"Does it matter?"

"It might."

She shook her head. "My job wasn't important anyway. I'm not a trained social worker. I acted mainly as a babysitter for the children of the mothers and fathers who came in for counseling, some of them voluntarily, some by order of the courts or the Probation Department."

"You didn't like the job?"

"Oh, but I did. I was crazy about it. I just wasn't competent enough. I couldn't handle the children. I felt too sorry for them. I was too—personal. Children, especially children of families who reach the point of going to the Clinic, need a firmer and more objective approach. The fact is," she added with a grim little smile, "if I hadn't quit, they'd probably have fired me."

"What gave you that idea?"

"Nothing specific. But I got the impression that I was more of a hindrance than a help around the place, so I simply failed to show up the next time."

"The next time after what?"

"After—after I got the impression that I was a hindrance."

"But something must have given you that impression at a definite time or you wouldn't have used the phrase 'the next time.'"

"I don't follow you."

He thought, *You follow me, Daisy baby. You just don't like the bumps in the road I'm taking. Well, it's not my road; it's yours. If there are potholes in it, don't blame me.*

"I don't follow you," she repeated.

"All right, let's skip it."

She looked relieved, as if he'd pointed out to her a nice, easy detour. "I don't see how a little detail like that could be important when I'm not even sure I was working at the Clinic at the time."

"We can make sure. They keep records, and I shouldn't have any trouble getting the information you want. Charles Alston, the director, is an old friend of mine. We've had a lot of clients in common—on their way up they land in his lap; on their way down they land in mine."

"Will you have to use my name?"

"Of course. How else—"

"Can't you think of any other way?"

"Look, Mrs. Harker. If you worked at the Clinic, you must know that their file room isn't open to the public. If I want information, I ask Mr. Alston, and he decides whether I get it or not. How am I going to find out if you were working on a certain Friday or not if I don't mention your name?"

"Well, I wish you didn't have to." She pleated a corner of her grey jacket, smoothed it out carefully, and began all over again. "Jim said I mustn't make an—an exhibition of myself. He's very conscious of public opinion. He's had to be," she added, raising her head in a sudden defensive gesture, "to get where he is."

"And where is that?"

"The end of the rainbow, I guess you'd call it. Years ago, when he had nothing at all, Jim made plans for himself: how he would live, the type of house he would build, how much money he'd make, yes, even the kind of wife he would choose—he had everything on the drawing board when he was still in his teens."

"And it's all worked out?"

"Most of it," she said. *One thing hasn't, and never will. Jim wanted two boys and two girls.*

"What, if I may ask, was on your drawing board, Mrs. Harker?"

"I'm not a planner." She fixed her eyes on the projector again. "Shall we continue with the newspaper?"

"All right."

He turned the crank, and the headlines of the next page rolled into view. Gunman John Kendrick, one of the FBI's most wanted men, was captured in Chicago. California had nine traffic deaths on Safe Driving Day. The Abbott murder trial was still going on in San Francisco. A woman celebrated her 110th birthday in Dublin. High tides were demolishing several houses at Redondo Beach. In Sacramento the future of the State Junior College was discussed by educators, and in Georgia 2,000 students rioted over the racial ban in the Bowl game.

"Any bells ringing?" Pinata said.

"No."

"Well, let's try the local news. The American Penwomen gave a Christmas party and the Trinity Guild a bazaar. The Bert Petersons celebrated their thirtieth anniversary. The harbor dredging contract was okayed. A Peeping Tom was apprehended on Colina Street. A four-year-old boy was bitten by a cocker spaniel and the dog ordered confined for fourteen days. A woman called Juanita Garcia, age twenty-three, was given probation on charges of neglecting her five children by locking them in her apartment while she visited several west-side taverns. The city council referred to the water commission a petition concerning—"

He stopped. Daisy had turned away from the projector with a noise that sounded like a sigh of boredom. She didn't look bored, though. She looked angry. Her jaw was set tight, and blotches of color appeared on her cheeks as if she'd been slapped, silently, invisibly, hard. Her reaction puzzled Pinata: did she have a grudge against the city council or the water commission? Was she afraid of biting dogs, Peeping Toms, thirtieth anniversaries?

He said, "Don't you want to go on with this, Mrs. Harker?"

The slight movement of her head was neither negative nor affirmative. "It seems hopeless. I mean, what difference does it make to me whether a woman called Juanita Garcia got probation or not? I don't know any Juanita Garcia." She spoke the words with unnecessary force, as if Pinata had accused her of having had a part in Mrs. Garcia's case. "How would I know a woman like that?"

"Through your work at the Clinic, perhaps. According to the newspaper account, one of the conditions of Mrs. Garcia's two-year probation was that she get some psychiatric help. Since she had five children and was expecting a sixth, and her husband was an Army private stationed in Germany, it seems unlikely she could afford a private psychiatrist. That leaves the Clinic."

"No doubt your reasoning is sound. But it has no connection with me. I have never met Mrs. Garcia, at the Clinic or anywhere else. As I told you before, my work there was concerned entirely with the children of patients, not the patients themselves."

"Then perhaps you knew Mrs. Garcia's children. She had five."

"Why do you keep harping like this on the name Garcia?"

"Because I got the impression it meant something to you."

"I've denied that, haven't I?"

"Several times, yes."

"Then why are you accusing me of lying to you?"

"Not to me, exactly," Pinata said. "But there's the possibility that you may be lying to yourself without realizing it. Think about it, Mrs. Harker. You overreacted to the name . . ."

"Perhaps I overreacted. Or perhaps you overinterpreted."

"That could be."

"It was. It is."

She got up and walked over to the window. The movement was so obviously one of protest and escape that Pinata felt as if she'd told him to shut up and leave her alone. He had no intention of doing either.

"It will be easy enough to check up on Mrs. Garcia," he said. "The police will have a file on her, as well as the Probation Department and probably Charles Alston at the Clinic."

She turned and gave him a weary look. "I wish I could convince you that I never in my life heard of the woman. But it's a free country; you can check everyone in the city directory if you like."

"I may have to. You've given me very little to go on. The only facts I have are that on December 2, 1955, there was snow on the mountains, and you ate lunch at a cafeteria downtown. How did you get downtown, by the way?"

"I must have driven. I had my own car."

"What kind?"

"An Oldsmobile convertible."

"Did you usually drive with the top up or down?"

"Down. But I can't see how all this is important."

"When we don't know what's important, anything can be. You can't tell what particular detail will jog your memory. For instance, that Friday was a cold day. Maybe you can remember putting the top up. Or you might have had trouble starting your car."

She looked honestly bewildered. "I *seem* to remember that I did. But that may be only because you suggested it. You say things in such a positive way. Like about the Garcia woman—you're so sure I know her or knew her." She sat down again and began repleating the corner of her jacket. "If I did know her, why have I forgotten? I'd have no reason to forget a friend or a casual acquaintance, and I'm not forceful enough to make enemies. Yet you seem so positive."

"Seeming and being are two different things," Pinata said with a faint smile. "No, I'm not positive, Mrs. Harker. I saw a straw and grasped it."

"But you're holding on?"

"Only until I find something more substantial to hold on to."

"I wish I could help. I'm trying. I'm really *trying*."

"Well, don't get tense about it. Perhaps we should stop for today. Have you had enough?"

"I guess so."

"You'd better go home. Back to Rainbow's End."

She stood up stiffly. "I regret telling you that about my husband. It seems to amuse you."

"On the contrary. It depresses me. I had a few plans on the drawing board myself." *Just one of them worked out,* Pinata thought. *His name is Johnny. And the only reason I'm trying to track down your precious day, Daisy baby, is because Johnny's having his teeth straightened, not because you got your head stuck in the pot of gold at the end of the rainbow.*

He turned the roll of microfilm back to the beginning and switched off the light in the projector.

The girl in the horn-rimmed spectacles came hurrying over, looking alarmed as if she expected him to wreck the machine or at least run off with the film. "Let me handle that," she said. "These things are quite valuable, you know. History being made right before our eyes, you might say. Did you find what you wanted?"

Pinata glanced at Daisy. "Did you?"

"Yes," Daisy said. "Yes, thank you very much."

Pinata opened the door for her, and she began walking slowly and silently down the corridor, her head bent as if she were studying the tiles on the floor.

"No two are alike," he said.

"Pardon?"

"The tiles. There are no two alike in the whole building."

"Oh."

"Someday when this current project of yours is finished and you need something new to amuse yourself with, you could come down here and check."

He said it to get a rise out of her, preferring her hostility to her sudden, unexpected withdrawal, but she gave no indication that she'd heard him or even that he was there at all. Whatever corridor she was walking along, it wasn't this one and it wasn't with him. As far as she was concerned, he had already gone back to his office or was still up in the library looking at microfilm. He felt canceled, erased.

When they reached the front of the building, the carillon in the courthouse tower across the street was chiming four o'clock. The sound brought her to attention.

"I must hurry," she said.

"Why?"

"The cemetery closes in an hour."

He looked at her irritably. "Are you going to take some flowers to yourself?"

"All week," she said, ignoring his question, "ever since Monday, I've been trying to gather up enough courage to go there. Then last night I had the same dream again, of the sea and the cliff and Prince and the tombstone with my name on it. I can't endure it any longer. I must satisfy myself that it's not there, it doesn't exist."

"How will you go about it, just wander around reading off names?"

"That won't be necessary. I'm quite familiar with the place. I've visited it often with Jim and my mother—Jim's parents are buried there, and one of my mother's cousins. I know exactly what to look for, and where, because in all my dreams the tombstone is the same, a rough-hewn unpolished grey cross, about five feet high, and it's always in the same place, by the edge of the cliff, underneath the Moreton Bay fig tree. There's only one tree of that kind in the area. It's a famous sailor's landmark."

Pinata didn't know what a Moreton Bay fig tree looked like, and he had never been a sailor or visited the cemetery, but he was willing to take her word. She seemed sure of her facts. He thought, *So she's familiar with the place, she's been there often. The dream didn't just come out of nowhere. The locale is real, perhaps even the tombstone is real.*

"You'd better let me come along," he said.

"Why? I'm not afraid anymore."

"Oh, let's just say I'm curious." He touched her sleeve very delicately, as if he were directing a highly trained but nervous mare who would go to pieces under too much pressure. "My car's over on Piedra Street."

8

Right from the beginning, she has been ashamed, not only of me but of herself, too . . .

THE IRON GATES looked as though they had been made for giants to swing on. Bougainvillea concealed the twelve-foot steel fence, its fluttery crimson flowers looking innocent of the curved spikes lurking beneath the leaves, sharper than any barbed wire. Between the street and the fence, rows of silver dollar trees shook their money like demented gamblers.

The grey stone gatehouse resembled a miniature prison, with its barred windows and padlocked iron door. Both the door and the lock were rusted, as if the gatekeeper had long since vanished into another part of the cemetery. Century plants, huge enough to be approaching the end of their designated time, lined both sides of the road to the chapel, alternating with orange and blue birds of paradise that looked ready to sing or to fly away.

In contrast to the gatehouse, the chapel was decorated with vividly colored Mexican tiles, and organ music was pouring out of its open doors, loud and lively. Only one person was visible, the organist. He seemed to be playing to and for himself; perhaps a funeral had just taken place, and he had stayed on to practice or to drown out a persistent choir of ghosts.

There was a threat of darkness in the air, and a threat of fog. Daisy buttoned her jacket to the throat and put on her white gloves. They were pretty gloves, of nylon net and linen, but they looked to her now like the kind that were passed out to pallbearers. She would have taken them off immediately and stuffed them back in her purse if she hadn't been afraid Pinata would observe the gesture and put his own interpretation on it. His interpretations were too quick and sure and, at least in one case, wrong. She thought, *I know no person called Juanita, only an old song we sang at home when I was a child. Nita, Juanita, ask thy soul if we should part . . .*

She began to hum it unconsciously, and Pinata, listening, recognized the tune and wondered why it disturbed him. There was something about the words. *Nita, Juanita, ask thy soul if we should part . . .* Nita, that was it. Nita was the name of the waitress in the Velada Café, the one Fielding had "rescued" from her husband. It could be, and probably was, a coincidence.

And even if it wasn't a coincidence, and Nita Donelli and Juanita Garcia were the same woman, it meant nothing more than that she had divorced Garcia and married Donelli. She was the kind of woman who would ordinarily seek employment in places like the Velada, and Fielding was the kind of man who frequented them. It seemed perfectly natural that their paths should cross. As for the fight with the woman's husband, that certainly hadn't been planned by Fielding. He'd told the police when he was arrested that she was a stranger to him, a lady in distress, and he'd gone to her assistance out of his respect for womanhood. It was the type of thing Fielding, at the euphoric level of the bottle, would say and do.

They had come to a fork in the road at the top of the mesa which formed the main part of the cemetery. Pinata stopped the car and looked over at Daisy. "Have you heard from your father?"

"No. We turn right here. We're going to the west end."

"The waitress your father got into a fight over was named Nita. Possibly Juanita."

"I know that. My father told me when he phoned about the bail money. He also told me she was a stranger to him, a good-looking young woman who'd led a hard life—those were his words. Don't you believe him?"

"Yes. Yes, I do."

"Well, then?"

Pinata shrugged. "Nothing. I just thought I'd mention it."

"What a fool he is." The contempt in her voice was softened by pity and sorrow. "What a fool. Will he *never* learn that you can't walk into a squalid little café and pick up waitresses without inviting disaster? He could have been seriously injured, even killed."

"He's pretty tough."

"Tough? My father?" She shook her head. "No, I wish he were. He's like a marshmallow."

"Speaking from my own experience, some marshmallows can be very tough. Depends on their age."

She changed the subject by pointing out of the window. "The fig tree is over there by the cliff. You can see the top of it from here. It's a very unusual specimen, the largest of its kind in this hemisphere, Jim says. He's taken dozens of pictures of it."

Pinata started the car, keeping down to the posted limit of ten miles an hour although he felt like speeding through the place and out again, and to hell with Daisy baby and her fig tree. The rolling lawns, the green and growing things, made too disquieting a contrast to the dead buried beneath them. A cemetery shouldn't be like a park, he thought, but like a desert: all tans and greys, rock and sand, and cacti which looked alive briefly only once a year, at the time of the resurrection.

Most of the visitors had gone for the day. A young woman dressed in black was arranging a bouquet of gladioli above a bronze nameplate, while her two children, T-shirted and blue-jeaned, played hide-and-seek among the crypts and tombstones. A hundred yards farther on, four workmen in overalls were starting to fill in a freshly dug grave. The green cloth, intended to simulate grass, had been pulled away from the excavated mound of earth, and the workmen were stabbing at it listlessly with their shovels. An old man with white hair sat on a nearby bench and looked down at the falling earth, stupefied by grief.

"I'm glad you came along," Daisy said suddenly. "I would have been frightened by myself or depressed."

"Why? You've been here before."

"It never affected me much. Whenever I came with Jim and my mother, it was more like taking part in a pageant, a ritual that meant nothing to me. How could it? I never even met Jim's parents or my mother's cousin. People can't seem dead to you unless they were once alive. It wasn't real, the flowers, the tears, the prayers."

"Whose tears?"

"Mother cries easily."

"Over a cousin so remote or so long dead that you hadn't even met her?"

Daisy leaned forward in the seat with a sigh of impatience or anxiety. "They were brought up together as children in Denver. Besides, the tears weren't really for her, I guess. They were for— oh, life in general. *Lacrimae rerum.*"

"Were you specifically invited to go on these excursions with your husband and mother?"

"Why? What's that got to do with anything?"

"I just wondered."

"I was invited. Jim thought it proper for me to go along, and Mother used me to lean on. It isn't often she does. I suppose I—I rather enjoyed the feeling of being strong enough for anyone else to lean on, especially my mother."

"Where are Jim's parents buried?"

"The west end."

"Anywhere near where we're headed?"

"No."

"You said your husband has taken many pictures of the fig tree?"

"Yes."

"Were you with him on some of those occasions?"

"Yes."

They were approaching the cliff, and the sound of breakers was like the roar of a great wind through a distant forest, rising and falling. As the roar increased, the fig tree came into full view: a huge green umbrella, twice as wide as it was tall. The glossy, leathery leaves showed cinnamon color on the undersides, as if they, too, like the lock and the iron door of the gatehouse, were rusting away in the sea air. The trunk and larger branches resembled grey marble shapes of subhuman figures entwined in static love. There were no graves directly under the tree because part of the vast root system grew above ground. The monuments began at the periphery—all shapes and sizes, angels, rectangles, crosses, columns, polished and unpolished, grey and white and black and pink—but only one of them exactly matched the description of the tombstone in Daisy's dream.

Pinata saw it as soon as he got out of the car: a rough-hewn grey stone cross about five feet high.

Daisy saw it, too. She said, with a look of terrible surprise, "It's there. It's—real."

He felt less surprise than she did. Everything in the dream was turning out to be real. He glanced toward the edge of the cliff as if he almost expected the dog Prince to come running up from the beach and start to howl.

Daisy had stepped out of the car and was leaning against the hood of the engine for support or warmth.

"I can't see any name on it at this distance," Pinata said. "Let's go over and examine it."

"I'm afraid."

"There's nothing to be afraid of, Mrs. Harker. What's obviously happened is that you've seen this particular stone in this particular location on one of your visits here. For some reason it impressed and interested you, you remembered it, and it cropped up in your dreams."

"Why should it have impressed me?"

"For one thing, it's a handsome and expensive piece of work. Or it might have reminded you of the old rugged cross in the hymn. But instead of standing here theorizing, why don't we go over and check the facts?"

"Facts?"

"Surely the important fact," Pinata said dryly, "is whose name is on it."

For a moment he thought she was going to turn and run for the exit gates. Instead, she straightened up, with a shake of her head, and stepped over the small lantana hedge onto the graveled path that wound around the periphery of the fig tree. She began walking toward the grey cross very quickly, as though she were putting her trust in momentum to keep her going if fear should try to stop her.

She had almost reached her destination when she stumbled and fell forward on her knees. He caught up with her and helped her to her feet. There were grass stains on the front of her skirt, and prickly little pellets of burr clover.

"It's not mine," she said in a whisper. "Thank God it's not mine."

A small rectangular area in the center of the cross had been cut and polished to hold the inscription:

CARLOS THEODORE CAMILLA
1907–1955

Pinata was sure from her reaction that the name meant nothing to her beyond the fact that it was not her own. She was looking relieved and a little embarrassed, like a child who's had the lights turned on and recognized the bogeyman for what it was, a discarded coat, a blowing curtain. Even with the lights on, there was one small bogeyman left that she apparently hadn't noticed yet—the year of Camilla's death. Perhaps from where she stood she couldn't discern the numbers; he suspected from her actions in the newspaper library that she was nearsighted and either didn't know it or didn't want to admit it.

He stepped directly in front of the tombstone to hide the inscription in case she came any closer. It made him feel uneasy, standing on this stranger's coffin, right where his face would be, or had been. Carlos Camilla. What kind of face had he once had? Dark, certainly. It was a Mexican name. Few Mexicans were buried in this cemetery, both because it was too expensive and because the ground was not consecrated by their church. Fewer still had such elaborate monuments.

"I feel guilty," Daisy said, "at being so glad that it's his and not mine. But I can't help it."

"No need to feel guilty."

"It must have happened just as you said it did. I saw the tombstone, and for some reason it stuck in my memory—perhaps it was the name on it. *Camilla*, it's a very pretty name. What does it mean, a camellia?"

"No, it means a stretcher, a little bed."

"Oh. It doesn't sound so pretty when you know what it means."

"That's true of a lot of things."

Fog had started to drift in from the sea. It moved in aimless wisps across the lawns and hung like tatters of chiffon among the leather leaves of the fig tree. Pinata wondered how quietly Camilla was resting, with the roots of the vast tree growing inexorably toward his little bed.

"They'll be closing the gates soon," he said. "We'd better leave."

"All right."

She turned toward the car. He waited for her to take a few steps before he moved away from the tombstone, feeling a little ashamed of himself for the deception. He didn't know it wasn't a deception until they were back inside the car and Daisy said suddenly, "Camilla died in 1955."

"So did a lot of other people."

"I'd like to find out the exact date, just out of curiosity. They must keep records of some kind on the premises—there's an office marked 'Superintendent' just behind the chapel, and a caretaker's cottage over on the east side."

"I was hoping you intended to drop this whole business."

"Why should I? Nothing's really changed, if you'll think about it."

He thought about it. Nothing had really changed, least of all Daisy baby's mind.

The superintendent's office was closed for the day, but there were lights burning in the caretaker's cottage. Through the living-room window Pinata could see a stout elderly man in suspenders watching a TV program: two cowboys were shooting freely at each other from behind two rocks. Both the cowboys and the rocks appeared exactly the same as the ones Pinata remembered from his boyhood.

He pressed the buzzer, and the old man got hurriedly to his feet and zigzagged across the living room as if he were dodging bullets. He turned off the TV set, with a furtive glance toward the window, and came running to open the door.

"I hardly never watch the stuff," he said, wheezing apology. "My son-in-law Harold don't approve, says it's bad for my heart, all them shootings."

"Are you the caretaker?"

"No, that's my son-in-law Harold. He's at the dentist, got himself an absence on the gum."

"Maybe you could give me some information?"

"Can't do no more than try. My name's Finchley. Come in and close the door. That fog clogs up my tubes, can't hardly breathe certain nights." He squinted out at the car. "Don't the lady care to come in out of the fog?"

"No."

"She must have good serviceable tubes." The old man closed the door. The small, neat living room was stifling hot and smelled of chocolate. "You looking for a particular gra—resting-place? Harold says never to say grave, customers don't like it, but all the time I keep forgetting. Now right here I got a map of the whole location, tells you who's buried where. That what you want?"

"Not exactly. I know where the man's buried, but I'd like some more information about the date and circumstances."

"Where's he buried?"

Pinata indicated the spot on the map while Finchley wheezed and grunted his disapproval. "That's a bad place, what with the spring tides eating away at the cliff and that big old tree getting bigger every day and 'tracting tourists that stomp on the grass. People buy there because of the view, but what's a view good for if you can't see it? Me, when I die, I want to lie safe and snug, not with no big old tree and them high tides coming after me hell-bent for leather . . . What's his name?"

"Carlos Camilla."

"I'd have to go to the file to look that up, and I ain't so sure I can find the key."

"You could try."

"I ain't so sure I oughta. It's near closing time, and I got to put supper on the stove. Absence or no absence, Harold likes to eat and eat good, same as me. All them dead people out there, they don't bother me none. When it comes quitting time, I close the door on them, never think of them again till next morning. They don't bother my sleep or my victuals none." But he belched suddenly, in a genteel way, as if he had, unawares, swallowed a few indigestible fibers of fear. "Anyhow, maybe Harold wouldn't like me messing with his file. That file's mighty important to him; it's exactly the same as the one the Super has in his office. You can tell from that how much the Super thinks of Harold."

Pinata was beginning to suspect that Finchley was stalling not because of his inability to find the key or any inhibitions about using it, but because he couldn't spell.

"You find the key," he said, "and I'll help you look up the name."

The old man looked relieved at having the burden of decision lifted from his shoulders. "Now that's fair enough, ain't it?"

"It won't take me a minute. Then you can turn on the TV again and catch the end of the program."

"I don't mind admitting I ain't sure which was the good guy and which was the bad guy. Now what's that name again?"

"Camilla."

"K-a—"

"C-a-m-i-l-l-a."

"You write it down, just like it shows on the cards, eh?"

Pinata wrote it down, and the old man took the paper and sped out of the room as if he'd been handed the baton in a relay race to the frontier where the bad guys were shooting it out with the good guys.

He returned in less than a minute, put the file drawer on the table, turned on the TV set, and retired from the world.

Pinata bent over the file. The card bearing the name Carlos Theodore Camilla bore little else: a technical description of his burial plot and the name of the funeral director, Roy Fondero. Next of kin, none. Address, none. Born April 3, 1907. Died December 2, 1955. *Sui mano.*

Coincidence, he thought. The date of Camilla's suicide must be just a crazy coincidence. After all, the chances were one in 365. Things a lot more coincidental than that happen every day.

But he didn't believe it, and he knew Daisy wouldn't either if he told her. The question was whether to tell her, and if he decided not to, the problem was how to lie successfully. She wasn't easily deceived. Her ears were quick to catch false notes, and her eyes were a good deal sharper than he'd thought.

A new and disturbing idea had begun to gnaw at a corner of his brain: suppose Daisy already knew how and when Camilla had died, suppose she had invented the whole business of the dreams as a means of getting him interested in Camilla without revealing her own connection with him. It seemed highly improbable, however. Her reaction to the name had been one of simple relief that it was not her own; she'd shown no signs of emotional involvement or confusion or guilt beyond the spoken artificial guilt over her gladness that the tombstone was Camilla's instead of hers. Besides, he could think of no valid reason why Daisy would choose such a devious way of accomplishing her purpose. *No*, he thought, *Daisy is a victim, not a manipulator of circumstances.* She didn't plan, couldn't possibly have planned the sequence of events that led to his meeting her in the first place: the arrest of her father, the bail, her visit to his office. If any planning had been done, it was on Fielding's part, but this was equally unlikely. Fielding seemed incapable of planning anything farther than the next minute and the next bottle.

All right, he thought irritably. *So nobody planned anything. Daisy had a dream, that's all. Daisy had a dream.*

He said, "Thanks very much, Mr. Finchley."

"Eh?"

"Thank you for letting me see the file."

"Oh my, look at him take that bullet right in the belly. I knew all along it was the bad guy in the black hat. You can always tell by the horse's eyes. A horse looks mean and shifty, and you can bet he's got a mean and shifty critter on his back. Well, he got his, yes sir, he got his." Finchley wrenched his eyes from the screen. "Program's changing, must be five o'clock. You better get a move on before Harold comes home and locks the gates. He won't be in so good a humor with that absence on his gum and all. Harold's fair," he added with a grunt, "but he ain't merciful. Not since his wife died. That's what women are put in this world for, mercy, ain't that right?"

"I guess so."

"Someday, you live long enough and you'll know so."

"Good night, Mr. Finchley."

"You get out of them gates before Harold comes."

Daisy had turned on the radio and the heater in the car, but she didn't look as though she were feeling any warmth or hearing any music. She said, "Please, let's hurry and get out of here."

"You could have come inside the house."

"I didn't want to interfere with your work. What did you find out?"

"Not much."

"Well, aren't you going to tell me?"

"I suppose I'll have to."

He told her, and she listened in silence while the car rolled noisily down the graveled hill past the chapel. It was dark. The organist was gone, leaving no echoes of music. The birds of paradise were voiceless. The money on the silver dollar trees was spent; the bougainvillea wept in the fog.

Harold, holding his swollen jaw, watched the car leave and closed the iron gates. The day was over; it was good to be home.

9

Even when she talked of love, her voice had bitterness in it, as if the relationship between us was the result of a physical defect she couldn't help, a weakness of the body which her mind despised . . .

THE LIGHTS OF the city were going on, in strings and clusters along the sea and highway, thinning out as they rose up the foothills until, at the very top, they looked like individual stars that had fallen on the mountains, still burning. Pinata knew that none of the lights belonged to him. His house was dark; there was no one in it, no Johnny, no Monica, not even Mrs. Dubrinski, who left at five o'clock to take care of her own family. He felt as excluded from life as Camilla in his grave under the great tree, as empty as Camilla's mind, as deaf as his ears to the sound of the sea, as blind as his eyes to the spindrift.

"What's a view good for," the old man had said, "if you can't see it?"

Well, the view's there, Pinata thought. *I'm looking at it, but I'm not part of it. None of those lights have been lit for me, and if anyone's waiting for me, it's some drunk in the city jail anxious to get out and buy another bottle.*

Beside him, Daisy was sitting mute and motionless, as if she were thinking of nothing at all or of so many things so quickly that they had crashed the sound barrier into silence. Glancing at her, he wanted suddenly to do something shocking, arresting, to force her to pay attention to him. But a second later the idea seemed so absurd that he went cold with anger at himself: *Christ, what's the matter with me? I must be losing my marbles. Johnny, I must think of Johnny. Or Camilla. That's safe, think of Camilla, the stranger in Daisy's grave.*

This stranger had died, and Daisy had dreamed the tombstone was her own—that much of it was explicable. The rest wasn't, unless Daisy had extrasensory perception, which seemed highly improbable, or a singular ability to deceive herself as well as other people. The latter was more likely, but he didn't believe it. As he became better acquainted with her, he was struck by her essential naïveté and innocence, as if she had somehow walked through life without touching anything or being touched, like a child wandering through a store where all the merchandise was out of reach and not for sale, and dummy clerks stood behind plate glass and sold nothing. Had Daisy baby been too well disciplined to protest, too docile to demand? And was she demanding now, through her dreams, for the plate glass to be removed and the dummy clerks put into action?

"The stranger," she said at last. "How did he die?"

"Suicide. His file card was marked *sui mano,* 'by his own hand.' I presume someone thought putting it in Latin would take the curse off it."

"So he killed himself. That makes it even worse."

"Why?"

"Perhaps I had some connection with his death. Perhaps I was responsible for it."

"That's pretty far-fetched," Pinata said quietly. "You've had a shock, Mrs. Harker. The best thing you can do now is to stop worrying and go home and have a rest." *Or take a pill, or a drink, or throw fits, or whatever else women like you do under the circumstances. Monica used to cry, but I don't think you will, Daisy baby. You'll brood, and God only knows what you'll hatch.* "Camilla was a stranger to you, wasn't he?"

"Yes."

"Then how is it possible that you were connected in any way with his death?"

"Possible? We're not dealing in 'possibles' anymore, Mr. Pinata. It isn't possible that I should have known the day he died. But it happened. It's a fact, not something whipped up by an over-imaginative or hysterical woman, which is probably how you've been regarding me up until now. My knowing the date of Camilla's death, that's changed things between us, hasn't it?"

"Yes." He would have liked to tell her that things between them had changed a great deal more than she thought, changed enough to send her running for cover back to Rainbow's End, Jim and Mamma. She would run, of course. But how soon and how fast? He glanced at his hands gripping the steering wheel. In the dim lights of the dashboard they looked very brown. *She would run very soon*, he thought, *and very fast. Even if she weren't married.* The fact dug painfully into his mind as though in her flight she wore the spiked shoes of a sprinter.

She was talking about Camilla again, the dead man who was more important to her than he ever would be, in all his youth and energy. Alive, present, eager, he was no match for the dead stranger lying under the fig tree at the edge of the cliff. Pinata thought, *I am, here beside her, in time and space, but Camilla is part of her dreams.* He was beginning to hate the name. *Damn you, Camilla, stretcher, little bed . . .*

"I have this very strong feeling," she said, "of involvement, even of guilt."

"Guilt feelings are often transferred to quite unrelated things or people. Yours may have nothing to do with Camilla."

"I think they have, though." She sounded perversely obstinate, as if she wanted to believe the worst about herself. "It's an odd coincidence that both the names are Mexican, first the girl's, Juanita Garcia, and now Camilla's. I hardly know, in fact I don't know, any Mexicans at all except casually through my work at the Clinic. It's not that I'm prejudiced like my mother; I simply never get to meet any."

"Your never getting to meet any means your prejudice or lack of it hasn't been tested. Perhaps your mother's has, and at least she's playing it straight by admitting it."

"And I'm not playing things straight?"

"I didn't say that."

"The implication was clear. Perhaps you think I found out the date of Camilla's death before this afternoon? Or that I knew the man himself?"

"Both have occurred to me."

"It's easier, of course, to distrust me than to believe the impossible. Camilla is a stranger to me," she repeated. "What motive would I have in lying to you?"

"I don't know." He had tried, and failed, to think of a reason why she should lie to him. He meant nothing to her; she was not interested in his approval or disapproval; she was not trying to influence, entice, convince, or impress him. He was no more to her than a wall you bounce balls off. Why bother lying to a wall?

"It's too bad," she said, "that you met my father before you met me. You were prepared to be suspicious of me before you even saw me, speaking of prejudice. My father and I aren't in the least alike, although Mother likes to tell me we are when she's angry. She even claims I look like him. Do I?"

"There's no physical resemblance."

"There's no resemblance in any other way either, not even in the good things. And there are a lot of good things about him, but I guess they didn't show up the day you met him."

"Some of them did. I never judge anyone by his parents, anyway. I can't afford to."

She turned and looked at him as if she expected him to elaborate on the subject. He said nothing more. The less she knew about him, the better. Walls weren't supposed to have family histories; walls were for protection, privacy, decoration, for hiding behind, jumping over, playing games. *Bounce some more balls at me, Daisy baby.*

"Camilla," she said. "You'll find out more about him, of course."

"Such as?"

"How he died, and why, and if he had any family or friends."

"And then what?"

"Then we'll know."

"Suppose it turns out to be the kind of knowledge that won't do anybody any good?"

"We've got to take that chance," she said. "We couldn't possibly stop now. It's unthinkable."

"I find it quite thinkable."

"You're bluffing, Mr. Pinata. You don't want to quit now any more than I do. You're much too curious."

She was half right. He didn't want to quit now, but a surplus of curiosity wasn't the reason.

"It's 5:15," she said. "If you drive faster, we can get back to the *Monitor* before they close the library. Since Camilla committed suicide, there's sure to be a report of it, as well as his obituary."

"Aren't you expected at home about this time?"

"Yes."

"Then I think you'd better go there and leave the Camilla business to me."

"Will you call me as soon as you find out anything?"

"Wouldn't that be a little foolish under the circumstances?" Pinata said. "You'd have some fancy explaining to do to your husband and your mother. Unless, of course, you've decided to come clean with them."

"I'll call you at your office tomorrow morning at the same time as this morning."

"Still playing secrets, eh?"

"I'm playing," she said distinctly, "exactly the way I've been taught to play. Your system of all cards face up on the table wouldn't work in my house, Mr. Pinata."

It didn't work in mine either, he thought. *Monica got herself a new partner.*

When he returned to the third floor of the *Monitor-Press* building, the girl in charge of the library was about to lock up for the day.

She jangled her keys at him unplayfully. "We're closing."

"You're ahead of yourself by four minutes."

"I can use four minutes."

"So can I. Let me see that microfilm again, will you?"

"This is just another example," she said bitterly, "of what it's like working on a newspaper. Everything's got to be done at the last minute. There's just one crisis after another."

She kept on grumbling as she took the microfilm out of the file and put it in the projection machine. But it was a mild kind of grumbling, not directed at Pinata or even the newspaper. It was a general indictment of life for not being planned and predictable. "I like things to be *orderly*," she said, switching on the light. "And they never are."

Camilla had made the front page of the December 3rd edition. The story was headlined SUICIDE LEAVES BIZARRE FAREWELL NOTE and accompanied by a sketch of the head of a gaunt-faced man with deep-set eyes and high cheekbones. Although age lines scarred the man's face, long dark hair curling over the tips of his ears gave him an incongruous look of innocence. According to the caption, the sketch had been made by *Monitor-Press* artist Gorham Smith, who'd been among the first at the scene. Smith's byline was also on the story:

The body of the suicide victim found yesterday near the railroad jungle by a police patrolman has been identified as that of Carlos Theodore Camilla, believed to be a transient.

No wallet or personal papers were found on the body, but further search of his clothing revealed an envelope containing a penciled note and the sum of $2,000 in large bills. Local authorities were surprised by the amount of money and by the nature of the note, which read as follows: "This ought to pay my way into heaven, you stinking rats. Carlos Theodore Camilla. Born, too soon, 1907. Died, too late, 1955."

The note was printed on Hotel Parker stationery, but the management of the hotel has no record of Camilla staying there. A check of other hotels and motor lodges in the area failed to uncover the suicide victim's place of residence. Police theorize that he was a transient who hitchhiked or rode the roads into the city after committing a holdup in some other part of the state. This would explain how Camilla, who appeared destitute and in an advanced stage of malnutrition, was carrying so much money. Inquiries have been sent to police headquarters and sheriffs' offices throughout the state in an effort to find the source of the $2,000. Burial services will be postponed until it is established that the money is not the proceeds of a robbery but belongs legally to the dead man. Meanwhile, Camilla's body is under the care of Roy Fondero, funeral director.

According to Sheriff-Coroner Robert Lerner, Camilla died of a self-inflicted knife wound late Thursday night or early Friday morning. The type of knife was identified by authorities as a *navaja*, often carried by Mexicans and Indians of the Southwest. The initials C.C. were carved on the handle. A dozen cigarette butts found at the scene of the tragedy indicate that Camilla spent considerable time debating whether to go through with the act or not. An empty wine bottle was also found nearby, but a blood test indicated that Camilla had not been drinking.

The residents of so-called Jungleland, the collection of shacks between the railway tracks and Highway 101, denied knowing anything about the dead man. Camilla's fingerprints are being sent to Washington to determine whether he had a criminal record or is registered with immigration authorities. An effort is being made to locate the dead man's place of residence, family, and friends. If no one claims the body and if the money is found to be legally his, Camilla will be buried in a local cemetery. The Coroner's inquest, scheduled for tomorrow morning, is expected to be brief.

It was brief. As reported in the December 5th edition, Camilla was found to have died of a knife wound, self-inflicted while in a state of despondency. Witnesses were few: the police patrolman who discovered him, a doctor who described the fatal wound, and a pathologist who stated that Camilla had been suffering from prolonged malnutrition and a number of serious physical disorders. The time of death was fixed at approximately 1:00 A.M. on December 2.

Probably, Pinata thought, *Daisy had read all this in the newspaper at the time it happened.* The pathos of the case must have struck her—a sick, starving man, fearful ("This ought to pay my way into heaven"), rebellious ("You stinking rats"), despairing ("Born too soon. Died too late"), had sent his final message to the world and committed his final act.

Pinata wondered whether the stinking rats referred to specific people, or whether the phrase, like the grumbling of the girl in charge of the library, was an indictment of life itself.

The girl was jangling her keys again. Pinata switched off the projector, thanked her, and left.

He drove back to his office, thinking of the money Camilla had left in the envelope. Obviously the police hadn't been able to prove it had come from a robbery, or Camilla wouldn't be lying now under his stone cross. The big question was why a destitute transient would want to spend $2,000 on his own funeral instead of on the food and clothing he needed. Cases of people dying of malnutrition with a fortune hidden in a mattress or under some floorboards were not common, but they happened every now and then. Had Camilla been one of these, a psychotic miser? It seemed improbable. The money in the envelope had been in large bills. The collection of misers was usually a hodgepodge of dimes, nickels, dollars, hoarded throughout the years. Furthermore, misers didn't travel. They stayed in one place, often in one room, to protect their hoard. Camilla had traveled, but from where and for what reason? Had he picked this town because it was a pretty place to die in? Or did he come here to see someone, find someone? If so, was it Daisy? But the only connection Daisy had with Camilla was in a dream, four years later.

His office was cold and dark, and although he turned on the gas heater and all the lights, the place still seemed cheerless and without warmth, as if Camilla's ghost was trapped inside the walls, emanating an eternal chill.

Camilla had come back, quietly, insidiously, through a dream. He had changed his mind—the sea was too noisy, the roots of the big tree too threatening, the little bed too dark and narrow—he was demanding reentry into the world, and he had chosen Daisy to help him. The destitute transient, whose body no one had claimed, was staking out a claim for himself in Daisy's mind.

I'm getting as screwy as she is, he thought. *I've got to keep this on a straightforward, factual basis. Daisy saw the report in the newspaper. It was painful to her, and she repressed it. For almost four years it was forgotten. Then some incident or emotion triggered her memory, and Camilla popped up in a dream, a pathetic creature whom she identified, for unknown reasons, with herself.*

That's all it amounted to. No mysticism was involved; it was merely a case of the complexities of memory.

"It's quite simple," he said aloud, and the sound of his own voice was comforting in the chilly room. It had been a long time since he'd actually listened to himself speak, and his voice seemed oddly pleasant and deep, like that of a wise old man. He wished he could think of some wise old remarks to match it, but none occurred to him. His mind seemed to have shrunk so that there was no room in it for anything except Daisy and the dead stranger of her dreams.

A drop of sweat slid down behind his left ear into his collar. He got up and opened the window and looked down at the busy street. Few whites ventured out on Opal Street after dark. This was his part of the city, his and Camilla's, and it had nothing to do with Daisy's part. Grease Alley, some of the cops called it, and when he was feeling calm and secure, he didn't blame them. Many of the knives used in brawls were greased. Maybe Camilla's had been, too.

"Welcome back to Grease Alley, Camilla," he said aloud, but his voice didn't sound like a wise old man's anymore. It was young and bitter and furious. It was the voice of the child in the orphanage, fighting for his name, Jesus.

"All those bruises and black eyes and chipped teeth," the Mother Superior had said. "You hardly looked human, half the time."

He closed the window and stared at his reflection in the dusty glass. There were no chipped teeth or bruises or black eyes visible, but he hardly looked human.

"Of course, it's a very difficult name to live up to . . ."

The City

10

But there was love, Daisy. You are proof there was love . . .

THROUGH ALL OF Fielding's travels only one object had remained with him constantly, a grimy, pockmarked, rawhide suitcase. It was so old now that the clasps no longer fastened, and it was held together by a dog's chain leash which he'd bought in a dime store in Kansas City. The few mementos of his life that Fielding had chosen to keep were packed inside this suitcase, and when he was feeling nostalgic or guilty or merely lonesome, he liked to bring them out and examine them, like a bankrupt shopkeeper taking stock of whatever he had left.

These mementos, although few in number, had such a strong content of emotion that the memories they evoked seemed to become more vivid with the passing of the years. The plastic cane from the circus at Madison Square Garden took him back to the big top so completely that he could recall every clown and juggler, every bulging-thighed aerialist and tired old elephant.

The suitcase contained, in addition to the cane:

A green derby from a St. Patrick's Day party in Newark. (Oh, what a beautiful binge that had been!)

Two pieces of petrified wood from Arizona.

A silver locket. (Poor Agnes.)

A ukulele, which Fielding couldn't play but liked to hold expertly in his hands while he hummed "Harvest Moon" or "Springtime in the Rockies."

A little box made of sweet grass and porcupine quills by an Indian in northern Ontario.

A beribboned cluster of small gilded pine cones that had been attached to a Christmas present from Daisy: a wristwatch, later hocked in Chicago.

Several newspaper clippings about exotic ports on the other side of the world.

A package of letters, most of them from Daisy; the money orders which had been enclosed were long since cashed.

A pen which didn't write, made of gold which wasn't real.

Two train schedules.

A splinter of wood—allegedly from the battleship *West Virginia* after it was bombed at Pearl Harbor—which he'd got from a sailor in Brooklyn in exchange for a bottle of muscatel.

There were also about a dozen pictures: Daisy holding her high school diploma; Daisy and Jim on their honeymoon; a framed photograph of two identical middle-aged matrons who ran a boardinghouse in Dallas and had inscribed across the picture "To Stan Fielding, hoping he won't forget 'the Heavenly Twins'"; an enlarged snapshot of a coal miner from Pennsylvania, who looked exactly like Abraham Lincoln and whose chief sorrow in life was that Lincoln was dead and no advantage could be taken of the resemblance. ("Think of it, Stan, all the fun we could have had, me being Abraham Lincoln, and you being my Secretary of State, and everybody bowing and scraping in front of us and buying us drinks. Oh, it just makes me sick thinking of all them free drinks we missed!")

Another picture, mounted on cardboard, showed Ada and Fielding himself and a ranch hand he'd worked with near Albuquerque, a handsome dark-eyed young man called Curly. On spring days, when dust storms obscured the range and made work impossible, the three of them used to play pinochle together. Ada had been a good sport in those early times, full of fun and life, ready for anything. Having a child had changed her. It was a year of drought. During the months of Ada's pregnancy more tears had come from her eyes than rain from the skies.

He brought the suitcase out now and began unpacking its contents on the big round table under the green-shaded ceiling light.

Muriel came in from the kitchen, the only other room in the apartment. She was a short, stout middle-aged woman with a hard mouth and eyes soft and round and pale green, like little mint patties with a licorice drop in the middle. She snorted at the sight of the open suitcase. "What do you want to go dragging out that old thing again for?"

"Memories, my dear. Memories."

"Well, I've got a few memories myself, but I don't go spreading them out in the middle of a table every couple of weeks." She leaned over his shoulder to get a closer look at the picture taken at the ranch. "You look like you were a real lively bunch."

"We were, thirty years ago."

"Oh go on, you haven't changed so much."

"Not as much as Curly anyway," he said grimly. "I looked him up last time I went through Albuquerque, and I hardly recognized him. He was an old man already, and his hands were so crippled by arthritis he couldn't even play pinochle anymore, let alone work cattle. We talked about old times for a while, and he said he'd drop in on me next time he came to Chicago. But we both knew he'd never make it."

"Well, don't *dwell* on it," Muriel said brusquely. "That's the trouble with your poking around in the past like this—you get to dwelling on things. You mark my words, Stan Fielding. That old suitcase of yours is your worst enemy in this world. And if you were smart, you'd take it right down to the pier and chuck it in the briny with a farewell and amen."

"I don't claim to be smart. I'm thirsty, though. Bring me out a beer like a good wife, will you? It's a hot day."

"You're not going to make it any cooler by lapping up beer," she said. But she went out to the kitchen anyway, because she liked his reference to her being a good wife. They'd only been married for a month, and while she wasn't passionately in love with him, he had many qualities she admired. He was kinder, in or out of his cups, than any man she'd ever known; he had a sense of humor and good manners and a fine head of hair and all his teeth. Above all, though, she appreciated his gift of gab. No matter what anyone said, really educated people with brains, Stan could always top them. Muriel was proud to be the wife of a man who had an answer for everything even though it might be, and often was, wrong. Being wrong, in a classy way, was to Muriel every bit as good as being right.

His easy manner of conversation had encouraged Muriel and emboldened her. From the taciturn and rather timid woman he'd met in Dallas she had developed into quite a loud and lively talker. She knew she had nothing to fear from him no matter what she said. He took all spoken words, including his own, with a grain of salt and a shrug. To written words his attitude was different. He believed absolutely everything he read, even flat contradictions, and when he received a letter, he treated it as if it were a message from a king, delivered via diplomatic pouch and much too special to be opened immediately. He always spent at least five minutes turning it over, examining it, holding it up to the light, before he finally slit the envelope.

When Muriel returned with his beer, she found him hunched over one of the letters, looking tense and anxious, as if this were the first time he'd read it instead of the fiftieth.

Most of the letters from Daisy he had read aloud to her, and she couldn't understand his excitement over such dull stuff: The weather was warm. Or cold. The roses were out. Or in. Went to the dentist, the park, the beach, the museum, the movies . . . Probably a nice girl, this Daisy of his, Muriel thought, but not very interesting.

"Stan."

"Eh?"

"Here's your beer."

"Thanks," he said, but he didn't reach for it immediately, as he usually did, and she knew this letter must be one of the bad ones he didn't read aloud or talk about.

"Stan, you won't get the blues, will you? I hate when you get the blues. It's lonesome for me. Bottoms up, eh?"

"In a minute."

"Hey, I know. Why don't you show me the picture of the guy that looked like Abraham Lincoln? He must have been a real card, that one. Tell me about him, Stan, about how you would have been Secretary of State, wearing a top hat and a cutaway—"

"You've heard it before."

"Tell me again. I'd like a good laugh. It's so hot in here I'd like a good laugh."

"So would I."

"What's stopping us, then? We've got a lot to laugh about."

"Sure. I know."

"Don't get the blues, Stan."

"Don't worry." He put the letter back in the envelope, wishing that he hadn't reread it. It had been written a long time ago, and there was nothing he could do now to change things. There was nothing he could have done then either. What bothered him was that he hadn't tried, hadn't phoned her, written to her, gone to see her.

"Come on, Stan. Bottoms up and mud in your eye, eh?"

"Sure." He drank the beer. It had a musky odor, as if it had been chilled and warmed too many times. He wondered if he had the same odor for the same reason. "You're a good woman, Muriel."

"Oh, can that now," she said with an embarrassed and pleased little laugh. "You're not so bad yourself."

"No? Don't bet on it."

"I think you're swell. I did right from that first night I saw you."

"Then you're dead wrong. Stone cold dead wrong."

"Oh, Stan, don't."

"There comes a time when every man must evaluate his own life."

"Why pick a time like this, a nice sunny Saturday morning when we could hop on a bus and go out to the zoo? Why don't we do that, eh, go out to the zoo?"

"No," he said heavily. "Let the monkeys come and look at me if they want a good laugh."

The fear in her eyes was turning into bitterness, and her mouth looked as though it had been tightened by a pair of pliers. "So you got the blues, you got them after all."

He didn't seem to hear. "I let her down. I always let her down. Even last Monday I walked out on her. I shouldn't have walked out on her like that without an apology or an explanation. I'm a coward, a bum. That's what Pinata called me, a bum."

"You told me that before. You told me all about it. Now why don't you forget it? If you ask me, he had his nerve. He may be a bigger bum than you are for all you know."

"So now you're calling me a bum, too."

"No, honest, I didn't mean it like the way it sounded. I only—"

"You should have meant it. It's true."

She reached down suddenly and pounded her fist on the table. "Why don't you keep that damned suitcase locked up the way it ought to be?"

He looked at her with a kind of sorrowful affection. "You really shouldn't scream like that, Muriel."

"And why not? I've got things to scream about, why shouldn't I scream?"

"Because it doesn't become a lady. 'The Devil hath not, in all his quiver's choice, an arrow for the heart like a sweet voice.' Remember that."

"You've got an answer for everything, haven't you, even if you got to pinch it from the Bible."

"Lord Byron, not the Bible."

"Stan, put the suitcase away, will you?" She picked up the chain leash from the floor and held it out to him. "Let's lock everything up and put the suitcase under the bed again and pretend you never opened it, how about that? I'll help you."

"No. I can do it myself."

"Do it, then. *Do* it."

"All right." He began replacing everything in the battered suitcase, the photographs and letters and clippings, the petrified wood and circus cane and box made of porcupine quills. "I'm fifty-three," he said abruptly.

"Well, I know. I must say you don't look it, though. You've got a fine head of hair. I bet there's many a man not forty yet who envies—"

"Fifty-three. And this is all I have to show for all those years. Not much, is it?"

"As much as most."

54

"No, Muriel, don't try to be kind. I've had too much kindness given to me in my life, too many allowances and excuses made for me. I don't deserve a good girl like Daisy. And then to think I walked out on her, didn't even stay to say hello or to see how she looked after all these years. She used to be such a pretty little girl with those big innocent blue eyes and a smile so shy and sweet—"

"I know," Muriel said shortly. "You told me. Now, have you got everything back in here? I'll close it up for you."

"Any decent father stays with his children even if he doesn't get along very well with his wife. Children, they're our only hope of immortality."

"Well, I'm fixed then. I've got two hopes of immortality chasing cows back in Texas."

"When my time comes, I won't completely die, because part of me will keep on living in Daisy." He wiped a little moisture from his eyes because it was so sad thinking of his own death, far sadder than thinking of anyone else's.

"If you're such a bum," Muriel said, "how come you want part of you to stay alive in Daisy?"

"Ah, you wouldn't understand, Muriel. You're not a man."

"Well, I'm glad you've noticed it. How about you notice it a little more often?"

Fielding winced. Muriel was a well-meaning woman, but her earthiness could be embarrassing, even destructive at times. When he was on a delicate train of thought, such as this one, it was a great shock to find himself suddenly derailed by the sound waves of Muriel's powerful voice.

To cushion the shock, he opened another bottle of beer while Muriel pushed the suitcase back under the bed.

"There," she said with satisfaction, and made a gesture of wiping her hands, like a doctor who has just stitched up an especially bad wound. "Out of sight, out of mind."

"Things are not that simple."

"They're not as complicated as you make out, Stan Fielding. If they were, we might as well all go jump in the ocean. Say, how about that? Why don't we go down to the beach and sit in the sand and watch the people? That always gives you a laugh, Stan, watching people."

"Not today. I don't feel like it."

"You just going to stay here and brood?"

"A little brooding may be exactly what I need. Maybe I haven't brooded enough in my lifetime. Whenever I became depressed, I simply packed up and moved on. I ran away, just as I ran away from Daisy. I shouldn't have done that, Muriel. I shouldn't have done it."

"Stop crying over spilled milk," she said harshly. "Every drunk I've ever known, that's their trouble. Bawling over things they done and then having to get tanked up to forget they done them and then going ahead and doing them all over again."

"Well," he said, blinking, "you're quite a psychologist, Muriel. That's an interesting theory."

"Nobody needs a fancy degree to figure it, just eyes and ears like I've got. And like you've got, too, if you'd use them." She came over to him, rather shyly, and put her hands on his shoulders. "Come on, Stan. Let's go to the beach and watch the people. How about trying to find that place where everybody's building up their muscles? We could take a bus."

"No, Muriel. I'm sorry. I have other things to do."

"Like what?"

"I'm going back to San Félice to see Daisy."

She didn't speak for a minute. She just backed away from him and sat down on the bed, looking bewildered. "What do you want to do that for, Stan?"

"I have my reasons."

"Why don't you take me along? I could see you didn't get into any trouble like you did last time over that waitress."

When he returned to Los Angeles on Monday night, he'd told her all about his encounter with Nita and Nita's husband in the bar. To diminish the importance of the incident, in his own mind and hers, he'd made quite a funny story of it, and they'd both had a good laugh. But Muriel's laughter hadn't been too genuine: suppose the girl's husband had been bigger and meaner? Suppose, and it often happened this way, that the girl Nita had suddenly decided to take her husband's side against Stan? Suppose no one had called the police? Suppose... "Stan," she said, "take me along to look out for you."

"No."

"Oh, I wouldn't ask you to introduce me to Daisy, if that's what you're thinking. I wouldn't dream of asking such a thing, her being so high class and everything. I could keep out of sight, Stan. I just want to be there to look out for you, see?"

"We haven't the money for bus fare."

"I could borrow some. The old lady in the apartment across the hall—I know she's got some hidden away. And she likes me, Stan; she says I look exactly like her younger sister that got put away last year. I don't think she'd mind lending me a little money on account of the resemblance, just enough for bus fare. How about it, Stan?"

"No. Stay away from the old lady. She's poison."

"All right, then, maybe we could hitchhike?"

He gathered from her hesitance and tone that she had never done any hitchhiking, and the thought of it scared her almost as much as the thought of his going to San Félice without her and getting into trouble. "No, Muriel, hitchhiking isn't for ladies."

She looked at him suspiciously. "You just don't want me along, that's it. You're afraid I might interfere if you decided to pick up some cheap waitress in a—"

"I didn't pick up anyone." Fielding's tone was all the sharper and more positive because he was lying. He'd gone deliberately into the café with the idea of finding the girl, but no one suspected this (except Muriel, who suspected everything), least of all the girl herself. Nothing had worked out as he planned, because the husband had walked in before he had a chance to ask her any questions or even to find out for sure if it was the right girl. "I was trying to protect a young woman who was being assaulted."

"How come you can protect everyone but yourself? The whole damn world you can protect, except Stan Fielding, who needs it worse than—"

"Now, Muriel, don't go on." He went over to the bed and sat down beside her. "Put your head on my shoulder, that's my girl. Now listen. I have a certain matter to take care of in San Félice. I won't be away long, no later than tomorrow night if things go well."

"What things? And why shouldn't they?"

"Daisy and Jim might be away for the weekend or something like that. In that case I won't be back until Monday night. But don't worry about me. In spite of your low opinion of my powers of self-protection, I can take care of myself."

"Sure you can. When you're sober."

"I intend to stay sober." No matter how many hundreds of times he had said this in his life, he still managed to put so much conviction into it that he believed himself. "This time, not one drink. Unless, of course, it would look conspicuous if I refused, and then I would take one—I repeat, one—and nurse it along."

She pressed her head hard against his shoulder as if she were trying to imprint on him by sheer force an image of herself which would go along with him on the trip, as her substitute, to protect him while he was protecting everyone else.

"Stan."

"Yes, my love."

"Don't get tanked up."

"I said I wouldn't, didn't I? No drinks, except maybe one to avoid looking conspicuous."

"Like for instance?"

"Suppose Daisy invites me to the house and opens a bottle of champagne to celebrate."

"Celebrate what?" With her head against his shoulder she couldn't see the sudden grimness of his face. "What's there to celebrate, Stan?"

"Nothing," he said. "Nothing."

"Then why should she open the bottle of champagne?"

"She won't."

"Then why did you say—"

"Please be quiet, Muriel."

"But—"

"There'll be no celebration, no champagne. I was just dreaming for a minute, see? People dream, even people like me, who should know better."

"There's no harm in a little dreaming now and then," Muriel said softly, stroking the back of his neck. "Say, you need a haircut, Stan. Could we spare the money for a haircut?"

"No."

"Well, wait right there while I go get my sewing scissors. Out on the ranch I always cut my kids' hair, there being nobody else to do it." She stood up, smoothing her dress down over her hips. "There was never any complaints either, once I got a little practiced."

"No, Muriel. Please—"

"It'll only take a minute. You want to look presentable, don't you, if you're going to that fancy house of hers? Remember that letter she wrote telling you her change of address? She described the whole house. It sounded just like a palace. You wouldn't want to go to a place like that needing a haircut, would you?"

"I don't care."

"You're always saying you don't care when you do." Muriel went out to the kitchen and returned with the sewing scissors. She said as she began trimming his hair, "You might meet up with your ex, think of that."

"Why should I?"

"There's nothing worse than meeting up with your ex when you're not looking your best. Hold your chin down a little."

"I don't intend to see my former wife."

"You might see her by accident on the street."

"Then I'd look the other way and cross the street."

She had been waiting and wanting to hear this. She exhaled suddenly and noisily, as if she'd been holding her breath until she was reassured. "You'd *really* look the other way?"

"Yes."

"Tell me about her, Stan. Is she pretty?"

"I'd prefer not to discuss it."

"You never ever talk about her—move your head a bit to the right—the way other men talk about their exes. What harm would it do if you told me a little about her, like is she pretty?"

"What good would it do?"

"Then at least I'd know. Chin down."

Chin down, he stared at his belt buckle. "And would you *like* to know she's pretty?"

"Well, no. I mean, it would be nicer if she wasn't."

"She's not," Fielding said. "Does that satisfy you?"

"No."

"All right, she's ugly as sin. Fat, pimply, cross-eyed, bow-legged, pigeon-toed—"

"Now you're kidding me, Stan."

"I'd be kidding you even more," he said soberly, "if I told you she looked pretty to me."

"She must have once, or you wouldn't have married her."

"I was seventeen. All the girls looked good in those days." It wasn't true. He couldn't even remember any of the other girls, only Ada, delicate and pink and fluffy like a cloud at sunset.

He had intended, in his youth and strength, to spend the rest of his life looking after her; instead, she had spent hers doing it for him. He didn't know, even now, at what point or for what reason their roles had been reversed.

"Some of them still look good to you." Muriel put down the sewing scissors. "You know what I bet? I bet that waitress of yours is nothing but a chippy."

"She's a married woman with six children."

"A husband and six kids don't make you an angel."

"Stop worrying, will you, Muriel? I'm not going up to San Félice to get involved with a waitress or my ex-wife. I'm going up solely to see Daisy."

"You had a chance to see her last Monday," Muriel said anxiously. "Why don't you just phone her long distance or write her a letter? Then you could go and see her some other time, when you're sure she's at home."

"I want to see her now, today."

"Why so all of a sudden?"

"I have reasons."

"Does it have something to do with Daisy's old letters you were reading?"

"Not a thing." He hadn't told her about the new letter, the one that had been sent special delivery to the warehouse where he worked and which was now hidden in his wallet, folded and refolded to the size of a postage stamp. This last letter wasn't like the others he kept in the suitcase. It contained no money, no news, no polite inquiries about his health or statements about her own: *Dear Father: I would be very much obliged if you'd let me know at once whether the name Carlos Theodore Camilla means anything to you. Please call collect, Robles 24663. Love, Daisy.* Fielding would have liked to pretend that the brief, brusque, almost unfriendly note had never reached him, but he realized he couldn't. He'd signed for it at the warehouse, and there would be a record of the signature at the post office. How had she got hold of the name and address of the warehouse? From Pinata, obviously, although Fielding couldn't remember telling Pinata about his job—he'd been feeling bad that day, fuzzy around the edges, not sure where one thing ended and another began. Or maybe Pinata had found out in some other way; he was a detective as well as a bail bondsman. A detective . . .

God Almighty, he thought suddenly. *Maybe she's hired him. But why? And what did it have to do with Camilla?*

"You look awful flushed, Stan, like maybe you've got a fever coming on."

"Stop making a pest of yourself, will you? I have to get ready."

While he washed and shaved in the bathroom they shared with the old lady across the hall, Muriel laid out fresh underwear for him and a clean shirt and the new blue-striped tie Pinata had lent him earlier in the week. He had told Muriel he bought the tie after seeing it in a store window, and she had believed him because it seemed too slight a thing to lie about. She hadn't known him long enough yet to realize that this secrecy about very trivial matters was as much a part of his nature as his devastating frankness about some of the important and serious ones. There had been no real need, for instance, for him to have recounted the details of the episode involving Nita and her husband and the jail and Pinata. Yet he had told her all about it, leaving out only the small detail of the tie he'd borrowed from Pinata.

When he returned from the bathroom and saw that this tie was the one she'd picked out for him to wear, he put it back in the bureau drawer.

"I like that one," Muriel protested. "It goes with your eyes."

"It's a little too gaudy. When you're hitchhiking, it pays to look as conservative as possible, like a gentleman whose Cadillac has just had a flat tire and he can't find a telephone."

"Like that, eh?"

"Yes."

"What are you going to use for a Cadillac?"

"My imagination, love. When I'm standing out there on the freeway, I'm going to imagine that Cadillac so hard that other people will see it."

"Why don't you start right now so's I can see it, too?"

"I *have* started." He went over to the window and pulled back the grimy pink net curtain. "There. What do you see?"

"Cars. About a million cars."

"One of them's my Cadillac." Letting the curtain drop into place, he drew himself up to his full height and adjusted an imaginary monocle to his eye. "I beg your pardon, madam, but I wonder if you would be so kind as to direct me to the nearest petrol parlor?"

She began to laugh, a girlish, giggly sound. "Oh Stan, honestly. You're a scream. You ought to be an actor."

"I hesitate to contradict you, madam, but I *am* an actor. Permit me to introduce myself. My name—ah, but I quite forgot I am traveling incognito. I must not identify myself for fear of the terrifying adulation of my millions of fanatic admirers."

"Gee, you could fool anybody, Stan. You talk just like a gentleman."

He stared down at her, suddenly sober. "Thanks."

"Why, I could see that Cadillac as plain as could be for a minute there. Red and black, with real leather upholstery and your initials on the door." She touched his arm. It had gone stiff as a board. "Stan?"

"Yeah."

"What the heck, we wouldn't know what to do with a Cadillac if we had one. We'd have to pay the license and insurance and gas and oil, and then we'd have to find a place to park it—well, it just wouldn't be worth the trouble, as far as I'm concerned, and I'm not just shooting the breeze either. I mean it."

"Sure. Sure you do, Muriel." He was touched by her loyalty, but at the same time it nagged at him; it reminded him that he didn't deserve it and that he would have to try harder to deserve it in the future. *The future,* he thought. When he was younger, the future always seemed to him like a bright and beribboned box full of gifts. Now it loomed in front of him, dark grey and impenetrable, like a leaden wall.

He picked out a tie from the bureau drawer, dark grey to match the wall.

"Stan? Take me with you?"

"No, Muriel. I'm sorry."

"Will you be back in time to go to your job Monday night?"

"I'll be back." He'd had the job, as night watchman for an electrical appliance warehouse on Figueroa Street, for only a week. The work was dull and lonely, but he made it more interesting for himself by imagining the place was going to be robbed any night now and visualizing how he would foil the robbers, with a flying tackle or a rabbit punch from behind, or a short, powerful left hook, or simply by outwitting them in a very clever way which he hadn't figured out yet. Having outthought, or outfought, the robbers, he would go on to receive his reward from the president of the appliance firm. The rewards varied from money or some shares in the company to a large bronze plaque inscribed with his name and a description of his deed of valor: "To Stanley Elliott Fielding, Who, Above and Beyond the Call of Duty, Did Resist the Onslaught of Seven Masked and Desperate Criminals . . ."

It was all fantasy, and he knew it. But it helped to pass the time and ease the tension he felt whenever he was alone.

Muriel helped him on with his jacket. "There. You look real nice, Stan. Nobody'd ever take you for a night watchman."

"Thank you."

"Where will you stay when you get there, Stan?"

"I haven't decided."

"I should know how to get in touch with you in case something comes up about your job. I suppose I could call Daisy's house if it was real important."

"No, don't," he said quickly. "I may not even be going to Daisy's house."

"But you said before you—"

"Listen. Remember the young man I told you about who paid my fine? Steve Pinata. His office is on East Opal Street. If anything urgent should come up, leave a message for me with Pinata."

She went with him to the door, clinging to his arm. "Remember what you promised, Stan, about laying off the liquor and behaving yourself in general."

"Of course."

"I wish I was going along."

"Next time."

He kissed her good-bye before he opened the door because of Miss Wittenburg, the old lady who lived across the hall. Miss Wittenburg kept the door of her apartment wide open all day and sat just inside it, with her spectacles on and a newspaper across her knee. Sometimes she read the paper in silence; at other times she became quite voluble, addressing her comments to her younger sister, who'd been gone for a year.

"There they are now, Rosemary," Miss Wittenburg said in her strong New England accent. "He appears to be groomed for the street. Good riddance, I say. I'm glad you agree. Did you notice the deplorable condition in which he left the bathroom again? All that wetness. Wet, wet, wet everywhere . . . I am surprised at you, Rosemary, making such a vulgar remark. Father would turn over in his grave to hear such a thing fall from your lips."

"Go inside and lock the door," Fielding said to Muriel. "And keep it locked."

"All right."

"And don't worry about me. I'll be home tomorrow night, or Monday at the latest."

"Whispering," said Miss Wittenburg, "is a mark of poor breeding."

"Stan, please take care of yourself, won't you?"

"I will. I promise."

"Do you love me?"

"You know I do, Muriel."

"Whispering," Miss Wittenburg repeated, "is not only a mark of poor breeding, but I have it on very good authority that it is going to be declared illegal in all states west of the Mississippi. The penalties, I understand, will be very severe."

Fielding raised his voice. "Good-bye, Rosemary. Good-bye, Miss Wittenburg."

"Pay no attention, Rosemary. What effrontery the man has, addressing you by your first name. Next thing he'll be trying to—oh, it makes me shudder even to think of it." She, too, raised her voice. "Good manners compel me to respond to your greeting, Mr. Whisper, but I do so with grave misgivings. Good-bye."

"Oh Lord," Fielding said, and began to laugh. Muriel laughed with him, while Miss Wittenburg described to Rosemary certain legislation which was about to go into effect in seventeen states prohibiting laughter, mockery, and fornication.

"Keep your door locked, Muriel."

"She's just a harmless old lady."

"There's no such thing as a harmless old lady."

"Wait. Stan, you forgot your toothbrush."

"I'll pick one up in San Félice. Good-bye, love."

"Good-bye, Stan. And good luck."

After he'd gone, Muriel locked herself in the apartment and, standing by the window, cried quietly and efficiently for five minutes. Then, red-eyed but calm, she dragged out from under the bed Fielding's battered rawhide suitcase.

11

Memories are crowding in on me so hard and fast that I can barely breathe . . .

THE NEIGHBORHOOD CLINIC was housed in an old adobe building off State Street near the middle of town. A great many of Pinata's clients had been in and out of its vast oak doors, and over the years Pinata had come to know the director, Charles Alston, quite well. Alston was neither a doctor nor a trained social worker. He was a retired insurance executive, a widower, who devoted most of his time and energy to the solution of other people's problems. To keep the clinic operating, he persuaded doctors and laymen to donate their services, fought city and county officials for funds, plagued the local newspaper for free publicity, addressed women's clubs and political rallies and church groups, and bearded the Lions in their den and the Rotarians and Knights of Columbus in theirs.

Whenever and wherever there was any group to be enlightened, Alston could be found doing the enlightening, shooting statistics at his audience with the speed of a machine gun. This rapid delivery was essential: it kept his listeners from examining the facts and figures too closely, an effect that Alston found highly desirable, since he frequently made up his own statistics. He had no qualms about doing this, believing that it was a legitimate part of his war on ignorance. "Did you know," he would cry out, pointing the finger of doom, "that one in seven of you good, unsuspecting, innocent people out there will spend some time in a mental institution?" If the audience appeared listless and unimpressionable, he changed this figure to one in five or even one in three. "Prevention is the answer. Prevention. We at the Clinic may not be able to solve everyone's problems. What we hope to do is to keep them small enough to be manageable."

At noon on Saturday, Alston put the CLOSED sign on the oak doors and locked up for the weekend. It had been a strenuous but successful week. The Democratic League and the Veterans of Foreign Wars had contributed toward the new children's wing, the Plasterers and Cement Finishers Local 341 had volunteered their services, and the *Monitor-Press* was planning a series of articles on the Clinic and offering a prize for the best essay entitled "An Ounce of Prevention."

Alston had just shoved the steel bolt into place when someone began pounding on the door. This frequently happened when the Clinic was closed for the night or the weekend. It was one of Alston's dreams that someday he might have enough personnel and money to keep it open at all times, like a hospital, or at least on Sundays. Sunday was a bad day for the frightened.

"We're closed," Alston shouted through the door. "If you're desperately in need of help, call Dr. Mercado, 5-3698. Have you got that?"

Pinata didn't say anything. He just waited, knowing that Alston would open the door because he couldn't turn anyone away.

"Dr. Mercado, 5-3698, if you need help. Oh, what the hell," Alston said, and pushed open the door. "If you need—oh, it's you, Steve."

"Hello, Charley. Sorry to bother you like this."

"Looking for one of your clients?"

"I'd like some information."

"I charge by the hour," Alston said. "Or shall I say that I accept donations for the new children's wing? A check will do, providing it's good. Come in."

Pinata followed him into his office, a small, high-ceilinged room painted a garish pink. The pink had been Alston's idea; it was a cheerful color for people who saw too many of the blues and grays and blacks of life.

"Sit down," Alston said. "How's business?"

"If I told you it was good, you'd put the bite on me."

"The bite's on you. This is after hours. I get time and a half."

In spite of the lightness of his tone, Pinata knew he was quite serious. "All right, that suits me. Say ten dollars?"

"Fifteen would look prettier on the books."

"On yours, sure, but not mine."

"Very well, I won't argue. I would, however, like to point out that one person in every five will—"

"I heard that last week at the Kiwanis."

Alston's face brightened. "That was a rousing good meeting, eh? I hate to scare the lads like that, but if fear is what makes them bring out their wallets, fear is what I have to provide."

"Today," Pinata said, "I'm just scared ten dollars' worth."

"Maybe I'll do better next time. Believe me, I'll try."

"I believe you."

"All right, so what's your problem?"

"Juanita Garcia."

"Good Lord," Alston said with a heavy sigh. "Is she back in town?"

"I have reason to think so."

"You know her, eh?"

"Not personally."

"Well, consider yourself lucky. We don't use the word *incorrigible* around here, but I never got closer to using it than when we were trying to cope with Juanita. Now, there's a case where an ounce of prevention might have been worth a few pounds of cure. If she'd been brought to us when she first showed signs of disturbance as a child—well, we might have done some good and we might not. With Juanita it's difficult to say. When we finally saw her, by order of the Juvenile Court, she was sixteen, already divorced from one man and about eight months pregnant by another. Because of her condition, we had to handle her with kid gloves. I think that's where she got the idea."

"What idea?"

Alston shook his head in a mixture of sorrow and grudging admiration. "She worked out a simple but absolutely stunning device for hog-tying the whole bunch of us: the courts, the Probation Department, our staff. Whenever she got in trouble, she outwitted us all with classic simplicity."

"How?"

"By becoming pregnant. A delinquent girl is one thing; an expectant mother is quite different." Alston stirred in his chair and sighed again. "To tell you the truth, none of us knows for sure if Juanita actually figured out this device in a conscious way. One of our psychologists believes that she used pregnancy as a means of making herself feel important. I'm not positive about that, though. The girl—woman, rather, she must be twenty-six or twenty-seven by this time—isn't stupid by any means. She did quite well on several of her tests, especially those that required use of imagination rather than knowledge of facts. She could study an ordinary little drawing and describe it with such vivid imagination that you'd think she was looking at something by Van Gogh. The term *psychopathic personality* is no longer in vogue, but it certainly would have applied to Juanita."

"What does she look like?"

"Fairly pretty in a flashing-eyed, toothy sort of way. About her figure I couldn't say. I never saw her between pregnancies. The tragic part of it," Alston added, "is that she didn't really care about the kids. When they were small babies, she liked to cuddle them and play with them as if they were dolls, but as soon as they grew up a little, she lost interest. Three or four years ago she was arrested on a child-neglect charge, but once again she was in the throes of reproduction and got off on probation. After the birth of that particular child—her sixth, I think it was—she broke probation and left town. Nobody tried very hard to find her, I'm afraid. I wouldn't be surprised if my own staff chipped in to pay her traveling expenses. Juanita herself was enough of a problem. But multiply her by six—oh Lord, I hate to think about it. So now she's back in town."

"I believe so."

"Doing what? Or need I ask?"

"Working as a waitress in a bar," Pinata said. "If it's the same girl."

"Is she married?"

"Yes."

"Are the kids with her?"

"Some of them are, anyway. She got into a fight with her husband a few days ago. He claimed she was neglecting them."

"If you don't even know the girl," Alston said, "where did you pick up all your information?"

"A friend of mine happened to be in the bar when the fight started."

"And this is how you became interested in the prolific Juanita, through a friend of yours who happened to witness a fight?"

"You might say that."

"I might say it but it wouldn't be the truth, is that it?" Alston peered over the top of his spectacles. "Is the girl in trouble again?"

"Not that I know of."

"Then why exactly are you here?"

Pinata hesitated. He didn't want to tell the whole story, even to Alston, who'd heard some whoppers in his day. "I'd like you to check your files and tell me if Juanita Garcia came here on a certain date."

"What date?"

"Friday, December 2, 1955."

"That's a funny request," Alston said. "Care to give me a reason for it?"

"No."

"I assume you have a good reason."

"I'm not sure how good it is. I have one, though. It concerns a—client of mine. I'd like to keep her name out of it, but I can't, since I need some information about her, too. Her name's Mrs. James Harker."

"Harker, Harker, let me think a min—Daisy Harker?"

"Yes."

"What's a woman like Daisy Harker doing getting mixed up with a bail bondsman?"

"It's a long, implausible story," Pinata said with a smile. "And since it's Saturday afternoon and I'm paying you time and a half, I'd rather go into it on some other occasion."

"What do you want to know about Mrs. Harker?"

"The same thing: if she was working at the Clinic on that particular day. Also when, and why, she stopped coming here."

"The why part I can't tell you, because I don't know. It mystified me at the time and still does. She made some excuse about her mother being ill and needing attention, but I happen to know Mrs. Fielding from my connection with the Women's Club. The old girl's as healthy as a horse. Quite an attractive woman, if she could remember to keep her velvet gloves on . . . No, it wasn't Mrs. Fielding's illness, I'm sure of that. As for the work itself, I believe Mrs. Harker enjoyed it."

"Was she good at it?" Pinata asked.

"Excellent. Sweet-natured, understanding, dependable. Oh, she had a tendency to get overexcited at times and lose her head a bit in an emergency, but nothing serious. And the kids all loved her. She had a way, as childless women sometimes have, of making the kids feel very important and special, not just something that happened from an accidental meeting of a sperm and ovum. A fine young woman, Mrs. Harker. We were sorry to lose her. Have you known her long?"

"No."

"Next time you see her, give her my kind regards, will you? And tell her we'd like to have her back whenever she can come."

"I'll do that."

"In fact, if I could find out the circumstances that made her quit, I might be able to change them."

"The circumstances are entirely Daisy's, not the Clinic's."

"Well, I just thought I'd check," Alston said. "We have occasional disagreements and disgruntlements among the members of our staff just like any other business. It's surprising we don't have more when you consider that psychology is not an exact science and there are consequently differences of opinion on diagnosis and procedure. Procedure especially," he added with a frown. "Just what does one *do* with a girl like Juanita, for instance? Sterilize her? Keep her locked up? Enforce psychiatric treatment? We did our best, but the reason it didn't work was that Juanita herself wouldn't admit there was anything the matter with her. Like most incorrigibles, she'd managed to convince herself (and tried, of course, to convince us) that women were all the same and that what made her different was the fact that she was honest and aboveboard about her activities. Honest and aboveboard, the favorite words of the self-deceiver. Take my advice, Steve. Whenever anyone insists too vigorously on his honesty, you run and check the till. And don't be too surprised if you find somebody's fingers in it."

"I don't believe in generalizations," Pinata said. "Especially that one."

"Why not?"

"Because it includes me. I make frequent claims to honesty. In fact, I'm making one now."

"Well, well. This puts me in the embarrassing position of either taking back the generalization or going to check the till. This is a serious decision. Let me meditate a moment." Alston leaned back in his chair and closed his eyes. "Very well. I take back the generalization. I'm afraid it's easy to become a bit cynical in this job. So many promises made and broken, so many hopes dashed—it leaves you with a tendency to believe in the psychology of opposites, that is, when a person comes in and tells me he is affable, honest, and simple, I tend to tag him as a complex and irritable cheat. This is an occupational hazard I must avoid. Thanks for pointing it out, Steve."

"I didn't point out anything," Pinata said, embarrassed. "I was merely defending myself."

"I insist upon thanking you."

"All right, all right, you're welcome. At time and a half I don't want to argue with you."

"Oh yes, time and a half. I must get on with the job. I address the Newcomers Club at two, a good, malleable group usually. I have considerable hopes for our treasury." He took a ring of keys from his desk drawer. "Please wait here. I can't ask you into the file room. Not that our records are top secret, but many people like to believe they are. Want something to read while I'm gone?"

"No thanks. I'll just think."

"Got a lot to think about?"

"Enough."

"Daisy Harker," Alston said casually, "is a very pretty and, I believe, an unhappy young woman. That's a bad combination."

"What's it got to do with me?"

"Not a thing, I hope."

"Save your hopes for the treasury," Pinata said. "My relationship with Mrs. Harker is strictly professional. She hired me to get some information about a certain day in her life."

"And Juanita was part of this day?"

"Possibly." Possibly Camilla was, too, though so far there was no indication of it. When Daisy called his office the previous morning, as scheduled, and learned the details of

Camilla's death, she was surprised, pained, curious—a perfectly normal reaction, which dispelled his last trace of doubt about her sincerity. She had, she said, asked both Jim and her mother if they'd ever known a man named Camilla, and she was waiting to hear from her father, to whom she'd sent a special delivery letter.

Alston was staring at him with a mixture of amusement and suspicion. "You're not very communicative today, Steve."

"I like to think of myself as the strong, silent type."

"You do, eh? Well, just watch out for that Lancelot syndrome you're carrying around. Rescuing ladies in distress can be dangerous, especially if the ladies happen to be married. Harker has the reputation of being a very good guy. And a smart one. Think it over, Steve. I'll be back in a few minutes."

Pinata thought it over. Lancelot syndrome, hell. *I'm not interested in saving Daisies in distress. Daisy, what a silly name for a grown woman. I'll bet that was Fielding's idea. Mrs. Fielding would have picked something a little more high-toned or exotic, Céleste, Stephanie, Gwendolyn.*

He got up and began pacing the room. Thinking about names depressed him because his own were only borrowed, from a parish priest and a child's Christmas game. During the past three years especially, since Monica had taken Johnny away, Pinata had wondered a great deal about his parents, trying, not too successfully, to follow the advice the Mother Superior had given him many times: "There's no room in this world for self-pity, Stevens. You're a strong man because you had no one to lean on, and that's a good thing sometimes, to live without leaning. Think of all the fixations you might have developed, and dear me, there are a lot of them around these days. The essential thing for a boy is to have a good man to pattern himself after. And you had that in Father Stevens . . . Your mother? What else could she have been but a young woman who found herself bearing too heavy a cross? You must not blame her for being unable to carry it. Perhaps she was just a schoolgirl . . ."

Or a Juanita, Pinata thought grimly. *But why should it matter now after more than thirty years? I could never trace her anyway; there wasn't a single clue. And even if I found her, what about him? It's possible she wouldn't even know which of the men in her life was my father. Or care.*

Alston returned, carrying several cards picked out of a file. "Well, you have something, Steve. I'm not sure what. December 2, '55, was the last day Mrs. Harker worked here. She was on duty from 1:00 to 5:30, in charge of the children's playroom. That's where the younger children are kept while their parents or relatives are being counseled. No actual therapy is done there, but it was part of Mrs. Harker's job to observe any behavior problems, such as excessive destructiveness or shyness, and report them in writing to the professional members of the staff. The way a three-year-old plays with a doll often gives us more of a clue to the cause of family trouble than several hours of talking on the part of the parents. So you can see Mrs. Harker's work was important. She took it seriously, too. I just checked one of her reports. It was full of details that some of our other volunteers would have failed to notice or at least to record."

"The report you checked, was it one from that particular day?"

"Yes."

"Did anything unusual or disturbing happen?"

"A lot of unusual and disturbing things happen here every day," Alston said cheerfully. "You can count on that."

"I meant, as far as Mrs. Harker was concerned. Did she have some trouble with any of the children, for instance?"

"Nothing on the record indicates it. Mrs. Harker might have had some trouble with a relative of one of the children or even a staff member, but such an incident wouldn't be included in her written report. And I very much doubt that one occurred. Mrs. Harker got along well with everybody. If I had to make a personal criticism of her, that would be it. She was overeager to please people; it led me to think that she didn't set a very high value on herself. These constant smilers usually don't."

"Constant smiler?" Pinata said. "Overeager to please? Could we possibly be talking about the same woman? Maybe there are two Daisy Harkers."

"Why? Has she changed?"

"She shows no signs of being eager to please, believe me."

"Now, that's highly interesting. I always knew she was putting up a front. It's probably a good sign that she's stopped. These little Daddy's-girl wiles can look pretty nonsensical in a grown woman. Perhaps she's maturing, and that's about all any of us can hope for. Maturity," he added, "is not a destination like Hong Kong, London, Paris, or heaven. It's a continuing process, rather like a road along which one travels. There's no Maturitytown, U.S.A. Say, I wonder if I could put that across to the Soroptimists at their banquet tonight . . . No, no, I don't think I'll try. It wouldn't be much of a fund-raiser. I'd better stick with my statistics. People, alas, are more impressed by statistics than they are by ideas."

"Especially yours?"

"Mine can be very impressive," Alston said with a grin. "But to get back to our subject, I'll admit I'm becoming curious about the connection between Juanita and Mrs. Harker."

"I'm not sure there is one."

"Then I guess this is just a coincidence." Alston tapped the cards he'd picked from the file. "Friday, December 2, was the last time Mrs. Harker appeared here. It was also the last time any of us heard from Juanita."

"Heard from?"

"She was scheduled to come in Friday morning to talk to Mrs. Huxley, one of our social workers. It wasn't to be a therapy session, merely a discussion of finances and what could be done with Juanita's children, who'd been released from Juvenile Hall into the custody of Juanita's mother, Mrs. Rosario. None of us considered this an ideal arrangement. Mrs. Rosario is a clean-living, respectable woman, but she's a bit of a nut on religion, and Mrs. Huxley was going to try to talk Juanita into allowing the children to be placed in foster homes for a time.

"At any rate Juanita called Mrs. Huxley early Friday morning and said she couldn't keep her appointment, because she wasn't feeling well. This was natural enough, since she was just a couple of jumps ahead of the obstetrician. Mrs. Huxley explained to her that the business about the children was urgent, and another appointment was made for late that afternoon. Juanita was quite docile about it, even amiable. That alone should have warned us. She didn't show up, of course. Thinking the baby might have arrived on the scene a bit prematurely, I called Mrs. Rosario next day. She was in a furious state. Juanita had left town, taking the children with her, and Mrs. Rosario blamed me."

"Why you?" Pinata asked.

"Because," Alston said, grimacing, "I have *mal ojo,* the evil eye."

"I hadn't noticed."

"In case you think belief in *mal ojo* has disappeared, let me hasten to correct you. Like many older members of her race, Mrs. Rosario is still living in the distant past, medically speaking: hospitals are places to die in, psychiatry is against the Church, illness is caused not by germs but by *mal ojo.* If you accused her of believing these things, she would probably deny it. Nevertheless, Juanita's first child was born in the kitchen of an elderly midwife, and when Juanita was sent to us for psychiatric help, Mrs. Rosario proved to be as big a stumbling block as the girl herself. Very few medical doctors, and not enough psychiatrists, have attempted to bridge this cultural gap. They tend to dismiss people like Mrs. Rosario as obstinate, backward, perverse, whereas she is simply reacting according to her cultural pattern. That pattern hasn't changed as much as we'd like to think it has. It will take more than time to change it. It will take effort, intent, training. But that's lecture number twenty-seven and not much of a fund-raiser either . . . I hope, by the way, that you're not taking any of my remarks about your race personally."

"Why should I?" Pinata said with a shrug. "I'm not even sure it is my race."

"But you think so?"

"Yes, I think so."

"You know, I've often wondered about that. You don't quite fit the—"

"Mrs. Rosario is a more interesting subject than I am."

"Very well. As I said, she was extremely angry when I called her. She'd gone to a special mass the previous night to pray for various lost souls, including, I hope, Juanita's. I've often wondered—haven't you?—how the parish priests handle people like Mrs. Rosario who believe with equal fervor in the Virgin Mary and the evil eye. Must be quite a problem. Anyway, on returning home, she discovered that Juanita had left, bag and baggage and five children. I'm not aware of any reason why Mrs. Rosario should have lied about it, but it did strike me at the time that it was a very convenient story. It saved her from having to answer questions from the police and the Probation Department. If she was at church when Juanita left, then obviously she couldn't be expected to know anything. She's a complex woman, Mrs. Rosario. She distrusts and disapproves of Juanita; she seems, in fact, to hate her; but she has a fierce maternal instinct."

"Well, there you have it." Alston leaned back in his chair and studied the pink ceiling. "The end of Juanita. Or what I fondly hoped was the end. After a year or so we closed her file. The last entry on it is in November 1956: Garcia, when he was released from the Army, brought suit for divorce, charging desertion. Which of the children belonged to him, I have no idea. Perhaps none. In any case he didn't ask for custody. Nor was any alimony or child support demanded of him, since Juanita didn't show up for the hearing. The chances are she knew about it, though. Most Mexican families here in the Southwest, in spite of dissension among themselves, have a way of retaining their tribal loyalties and ties when confronted with trouble from the whites. And the law is always 'white' to them. There's no doubt in my mind that Juanita remained in touch in some way with relatives who kept her posted on what was going on and when it was safe for her to come back here. I take it you're sure she *is* back?"

"Reasonably," Pinata said.

"Married again?"

"Yes, to an Italian called Donelli. I gather he's not a bad guy, but Juanita has given him a rough time, and he's carrying a chip on his shoulder."

"How do you know all that?"

"I saw him in court after he got into the fight in the bar. My client was involved in the fight. Donelli couldn't scrape up enough money to pay his fine, so he's still in jail. It could be that's exactly where Juanita wants him."

"What bar is she working at?"

"The Velada, on lower State."

Alston nodded. "That's where she's worked before, off and on. It's owned by a friend of her mother's, a Mrs. Brewster. Both Mrs. Brewster and the Velada are known to every health and welfare agency in the county, though the place has never actually been closed. It looks as if you're on the right track, Steve. If you find out the girl is really Juanita, let me know immediately, will you? I feel a certain responsibility towards her. If she's in trouble, I want to help her."

"How will I get in touch with you?"

"I'll be home about the middle of the afternoon. Call me there. Meanwhile, I'll keep hoping a mistake has been made and the real Juanita is happily and securely ensconced on an island in the middle of the Pacific."

Alston got up and closed and locked the window as an indication that as far as he was concerned, the interview was ended.

"Just one more minute," Pinata said.

"Hurry it up, will you? I don't want to keep the Newcomers Club waiting."

"If they knew how much you were going to touch them for, I don't think they'd mind waiting."

"Oh yes. Speaking of money . . ."

"Here." Pinata gave him a ten-dollar bill. "Have you ever heard of a man called Carlos Camilla?"

"Offhand, I'd say no. That's an unusual name. I think I'd remember if I'd ever heard it before. What about him?"

"He killed himself four years ago. Roy Fondero was in charge of the funeral."

"I know Fondero," Alston said. "He's an old friend of mine. A good man, level-headed and straight as die, no pun intended."

"Will you do me a favor?"

"I might."

"Call him up and tell him I'd like to ask some questions about the Camilla case."

"That's easy enough." Alston reached for the phone and dialed. "Mr. Fondero, please . . . When will he be back? This is Charles Alston speaking . . . Thanks. I'll call him back later this afternoon." He hung up. "Fondero's out on business. I'll try and set up an appointment for you. What time would you prefer?"

"As soon as possible."

"I'll see if I can arrange it for today, then."

"Thanks very much, Charley. Now, just one more question, and I'll leave. Did Mrs. Harker know Juanita?"

"Everyone at the Clinic did, by sight if not by name. But why ask me? Why not ask Mrs. Harker?" Alston leaned across the desk, his eyes narrowed. "Is there anything the matter with her?"

"I don't think so."

"I heard on the grapevine she and Harker are planning to adopt a child. Would this mysterious visit of yours have anything to do with that?"

"In a remote way," Pinata said. "I wish I could tell you more, Charley, but certain things are confidential. All I can do is assure you that the matter is, to everyone else but Mrs. Harker, quite trivial. There are no lives at stake, no money, no great issue."

He was wrong: all three were at stake. But he hadn't the imagination or the desire to see it.

12

I wish they were good memories, that like other men I could sit back in the security of my family and review the past kindly. But I cannot . . .

FIELDING'S FIRST HITCH got him as far as Ventura, and his second, with a jukebox repairman, landed him in San Félice at the corner of State Street and Highway 101. From there it was only a short walk up to the Velada Café, sandwiched between a pawnshop (WE BUY AND SELL ANYTHING) and a hotel for transients (ROOMS WITHOUT BATH, $2.00), modestly called the Ritz. Fielding registered at the hotel and was given a room on the second floor. He had stayed in a hundred rooms like it in his life, but he liked this one better than most, partly because he was feeling excited and partly because he could see through the dirty window the shimmer of sun on the ocean and some fishing boats lying at anchor beyond the wharf. They looked so tranquil and at ease that Fielding had a brief notion of going down and applying for a job as deckhand. Then he remembered that he'd even got seasick on the Staten Island ferry. And there was Muriel now, too. He was a married man with responsibilities; he couldn't go dashing off on a boat with Muriel expecting him home . . . *I should have gone to sea when I was younger,* he thought. *I might have been a captain by this time. Captain Fielding, it sounds very right and proper.*

"Heave to," Fielding said aloud, and as a substitute for going to sea, he rinsed his face in the washbasin. Then he combed his hair (the jukebox repairman had been driving a convertible with the top down) and went downstairs to the Velada Café.

There was no cocktail hour at the Velada. Anytime you had the money was the time for drinking, and business was often as brisk in midmorning as it was at night. Brisker, sometimes, since the smell of stale grease that permeated the place increased the agonies of a hangover and encouraged the customers to dull their senses as quickly as possible. The manager of the Ritz Hotel and the operator of the pawnshop frequently complained about this smell to the Department of Health, the police, the State Board of Equalization, but Mrs. Brewster, who owned the Velada, fought back tooth, nail, and tongue. She was a scrawny little miser of a woman who wore an oversize denim apron which she used for everything—wiping counters, swatting flies, mopping her face, handling hot pans, blowing her nose, shooing away newsboys who came in to sell papers, collecting her meager tips, drying her hands. This apron had become the expression of her whole personality. When she took it off at night before going home, she felt lost, as if some vital part of her had been amputated.

Fielding noticed the smell and the dirty apron, but they didn't bother him. He'd smelled worse and seen dirtier. He sat down at a booth near the front window. The waitress, Nita, wasn't in sight, and no one seemed interested in taking his order. A Mexican busboy, who looked about fifteen, was sweeping up cigarette butts from the floor. He worked very intently, as if he were new at the job or expected to find something more in the morning's debris than just cigarette butts.

"Where's the waitress?" Fielding said.

The boy raised his head. He had huge dark eyes, like prunes swelling in hot water. "Which one?"

"Nita."

"Fixing her face, I guess. She likes to fix her face."

"What's your name, son?"

"Chico."

"Tell the old lady behind the counter I want a ham on rye and a bottle of beer."

"I can't do that, sir. The girls get mad; they think I'm trying to con them out of their tips."

"How old are you, Chico?"

"Twenty-one."

"Come off it, kid."

The boy's face turned dark red. "I'm twenty-one," he said, and returned to his sweeping.

Five minutes passed. The other waitress, who was attending to the back booths, glanced casually in Fielding's direction a couple of times, but she didn't approach him, and neither did Mrs. Brewster, who was wiping off the grill with her apron.

Juanita finally appeared wearing fresh lipstick and powder. She had outlined her eyes so heavily with black pencil that she looked like a coal miner who'd been working in the pits for years. She acknowledged his presence with a little flick of her rump, like a mare twitching her tail out of recognition or interest.

She said, unsmiling, "So you're back again."

"Surprised?"

"Why should I be surprised? Nothing surprises me. What'll you have?"

"Ham on rye, bottle of Western beer."

She shouted the order at Mrs. Brewster, who gave no response at all, not even a flutter of her apron. Fielding wondered whether she'd recognized him as the man involved in the fight and was trying to freeze him out to avoid further trouble.

"The service in this place is lousy," he said.

"So's the food. Why come here?"

"Oh, I just wanted to see how everybody was doing after the fracas last Monday."

"I'm doing fine. Joe's still in the cooler. He got thirty days."

"I'm sorry to hear that."

Juanita put one hand on her hip in a half-pensive, half-aggressive manner. "Say, your being always sorry for people is going to get you in some real trouble one of these days. Like your being sorry for me, and pretty soon you're trading punches with Joe."

"I was a little drunk."

"Well, I just thought I'd warn you, you oughta let people feel sorry for themselves. Most of them are pretty damn good at it, me included. Wait a minute, I'll light a match under the old girl. She's having one of her spooky days."

"There's no hurry. Why don't you sit down for a while?"

"What for?" Juanita asked suspiciously.

"Rest your feet."

"So now you're feeling sorry for my *feet*? Say, you're a real spooky guy, you know that?"

"I've been told once or twice."

"Well, it's no skin off my elbows." She sat down, with considerably more squirming than was necessary. "Got a cigarette?"

"No."

"Well, I'll smoke my own, then. I figure there's no sense smoking my own if I can bum one."

"Smart girl."

"Me, smart? Nobody else thinks so. You should hear my old lady on the subject. She throws fits telling me how dumb I am. I don't have to stand it much longer, though. I'm just living with her for the time being while Joe's in the cooler, so I'll have someone to look after the kids. When Joe gets out, maybe we'll take off again. I've always hated this town; it's treated me rotten. But don't go feeling sorry for me. What they can dish out, I can take."

"They?" Fielding said. "Who are they?"

"Nobody. Just them. The town."

"Where have you been living?"

"L.A."

"Why'd you come back here?"

"Joe lost his job. It wasn't his fault or anything. The boss's nephew just got old enough to work, and Joe was thrown out on his can to make room for him. So I thought, why not come back here for a while? Maybe things are different, maybe the town's changed, I thought. Hell, *this* town *change*? I must of been crazy. The only thing'll change this place is the Russians, and me personally I couldn't care less if they started dropping bombs like confetti and everybody fell dead in their tracks." She lit a cigarette and blew the smoke across the table directly into his face, as if she were challenging him to disagree with her. "What do you think of that, eh?"

"I haven't thought about it yet."

"Joe has. Joe says when I talk like that, I oughta have my mouth washed out with soap. And I says, listen, Dago, you try it and you get a hand full of teeth." She smiled, not out of amusement, but as if she wanted to show she had the teeth to carry out the threat. "Joe's a real flag-waver. Hell, I bet while they were locking him in his cell, he was waving the flag. Some dagos are like that. Even with the cops sitting on their faces, they open their yaps and sing 'God Bless America.'"

Fielding started to laugh but immediately checked himself when he realized Juanita wasn't attempting to be funny; she was merely presenting her own personal picture of the world, a place where people sat on your face and you retaliated in the only logical way, which wasn't by singing "God Bless America."

Behind the counter Mrs. Brewster had come to life and was putting the finishing touches on the ham sandwich, a slice of pickle and five potato chips. Juanita went over to pick up the order, and Fielding could hear the two women talking.

"Since when am I paying you to sit with the customers?"

"He's a friend of mine."

"Since when, five minutes ago?"

"Being nice to customers," Juanita said smoothly, "is good for business. You'll make more money. You like money, don't you?"

Mrs. Brewster let out a sudden little giggle, as if she'd been tickled in some vulnerable place. Then she smothered the giggle with a corner of her apron, slammed the ham sandwich on a tray, and opened a bottle of beer.

Juanita returned with the order and sat down opposite Fielding again. The exchange of words with Mrs. Brewster had improved her spirits. "Didn't I tell you she was a real spook? But I can handle her. All I do is say 'money,' and she giggles like that every time. I always get along with spooks," she added with a touch of pride. "Maybe I ought to of been a nurse or a doctor. How's the sandwich?"

"It's not bad."

"You must be awful hungry. Me, I've got a cast-iron stomach, but you couldn't pay me to eat in this joint."

"It's lucky for you the old girl hasn't taken up lip-reading." Fielding finished half the sandwich, pushed the plate away, and reached for the beer. "So your mother looks after the children while you work, eh?"

"Sure."

"You look too young to have children."

"That's a laugh," she said, but she looked pleased. "I got six of them."

"Go on, you're pulling my leg."

"No, that's the honest-to-God fact. I got six."

"Why, you're hardly more than a child yourself."

"I started young," Juanita said with considerable truth. "I never liked school much, so I quit and got married."

"Six. Well, I'll be damned."

She was obviously enjoying his incredulity. She reached down and patted her stomach. "Of course I kept my figure. A lot of girls don't; they let themselves go. I never did."

"I'll say you didn't. Six. God, I can't believe it." He kept shaking his head as if he really couldn't believe it, although he'd known since Monday, the day of the fight, that she had six children. "How many boys?"

"The oldest and the youngest are boys; the middle ones are girls."

"I bet they're cute."

"They're okay." But a note of boredom was evident in her voice, as if the children themselves were not very interesting, only the fact that she'd had them was important. "I guess there's worse around."

"Have you any pictures of them?"

"What for?"

"A lot of people carry pictures of their family."

"Who would I show them to? Who'd want to look at pictures of my kids?"

"I would, for one."

"Why?"

The idea that a stranger might be legitimately interested in her children was incredible to her. Her eyes narrowed in suspicion, and he thought for a minute that he'd lost her confidence. But he said easily, "Say, what's got into you anyway? Your kids have two heads or something?"

"No, they haven't got two heads, Mr. Foster."

"How did you know my name?" This time his surprise was genuine, and she reacted to it as she'd reacted to his feigned disbelief that she'd had six children, with a look of mischievous pleasure. Apparently this was what Juanita liked best, to surprise people. "Where'd you find out who I was?"

"I can read. It was in the paper, about the fight. Joe never had his name in the paper before, so I clipped it out to save for him. Joe Donelli and Stan Foster, it said, was involved in a fight over a woman in a local café."

"Well," Fielding said, smiling. "Now you know my name, and I know yours. Juanita Garcia meet Stan Foster."

She half rose from the bench, then suddenly dropped back with a noisy expulsion of her breath. "Garcia? Why did you say Garcia? That's not my name."

"It used to be, didn't it?"

"It used to be a lot of different things. Now it's Donelli, nothing else, see? And it's Nita, not Juanita. Nita Donelli, that's my name, understand?"

Fielding nodded. "Of course."

"Where'd you get a hold of that Juanita business anyway?"

"I thought the two names were the same. There's this old song, see, about a girl called Nita, Juanita."

"There is, eh?"

"Yes, and I naturally assumed—"

"Hey, Chico." She motioned to the busboy, and he came over to the booth, pushing his broom ahead of him. "You ever hear tell of a song called 'Nita, Juanita'?"

"Nope."

Juanita turned back to Fielding, her full mouth pressed tight against her teeth, so that it seemed half its size. "Sing it for me. Let's hear how it sounds."

"Here? Now?"

"Sure, here now. Why not?"

"I don't remember all the words. Anyway, I can't sing. I have a voice like—"

"Try."

She was very quiet in her insistence. No one in the café was paying any attention to the scene except Mrs. Brewster, who was watching them with her bright, beady little eyes.

"Maybe there's no such song, eh?" Juanita said.

"Sure there is. It goes back a long way. You're too young to remember."

"So remind me."

Fielding was sweating from the heat, from the beer, and from something he didn't want to identify as fear. "Say, what's the matter with you anyway?"

"I like music, is all. Old songs. I like old songs."

Mrs. Brewster came out from behind the counter making little sweeps of her apron as if she were brushing away invisible cobwebs. Juanita saw her coming and turned her face stubbornly toward the wall.

"What's up?" Mrs. Brewster asked Fielding.

"Nothing, I just—that is, she just wanted me to sing a song."

"What's wrong with a bit of music?"

"It wouldn't be music. I can't sing."

"She's a little crazy," Mrs. Brewster said. "But I can handle her." She put a scrawny hand firmly on Juanita's right shoulder. "Snap out of it. You hear, girl?"

"Leave me alone," Juanita said.

"You don't snap out of it, I call your mother and tell her you're having trouble with your *cabeza* again. Also, I write to Joe. I tell him, Dear Joe, that wife of yours, you better come and get her locked up. Okay, you snap out of it now?"

"All I wanted was to hear a song."

"What song?"

"'Nita, Juanita.' He says it's a song. I never heard of it, I think he's lying. I think he's a spy from the police or the Probation Department."

"He's not lying."

"I think he is."

"I can spot a cop a mile away." Mrs. Brewster said. "Also, I know that song. I used to sing it when I was a girl. I had a pretty voice once, before I breathed in all this foul air. Now you believe me?"

"No."

"Okay, we sing it together for you, him and me. How about that, mister? We make a little music to cheer Nita up?"

Fielding cleared his throat. "I can't—"

"I begin. You follow."

"But—"

"Now. One, two, three, here we go:

'Soft o'er the fountain,
Lingering falls the southern moon;
Far o'er the mountain,
Breaks the day too soon.
In thy dark eyes' splendor
Where the warm light loves to dwell,
Weary looks yet tender,
Speak their fond farewell.'"

Juanita's face was still turned to the wall. Mrs. Brewster said, "You're not listening."

"I am so."

"Isn't it pretty, all that sadness? Now comes the chorus with your very own name in it."

Fielding joined, softly and a little off key, in the chorus:

"'Nita, Juanita,
Ask thy soul if we should part.
Nita, Juanita,
Lean thou on my heart.'"

During the chorus Juanita slowly turned her head to watch the two songsters, and her mouth began to move slightly, as if she were silently singing along with them. She looked like a child again in that moment, a little girl wanting desperately to be part of a song she never knew, a harmony she never heard.

When the chorus was over, Mrs. Brewster blew her nose on her apron, thinking of her pretty voice that had vanished in the foul air.

"I like the part with my name in it the best," Juanita said.

Mrs. Brewster patted her shoulder. "Naturally. That's the best part."

"'Lean thou on my heart.' Imagine anyone saying that to me. I'd drop dead."

"Things like that don't get said in real life. You feeling better now, girl?"

"I'm all right. I was all right before, too. I just wanted to hear the song to make sure he wasn't lying."

"She's a little crazy," Mrs. Brewster said to Fielding. "But she handles easy if you know how."

"I didn't really think you were lying," Juanita said when Mrs. Brewster had gone. "I have to check things, that's all. I always check things. It's funny the way spooks like her think everybody else is crazy."

Fielding nodded. "It *is* funny. I've noticed it myself."

"You didn't believe her for a minute, did you?"

"Not for a minute."

"I could tell you didn't. You have a very kind expression. I bet you like dogs."

"Dogs are fine."

His fear had gone now, leaving in his throat a little knot of pity which he couldn't swallow or cough up. It wasn't often that Fielding experienced pity for anyone but himself, and he didn't like the feeling. It seemed to immobilize him. He wanted to get up and run away and forget about this strange, sad girl, forget about the whole bunch of them—Daisy, Jim, Ada, Camilla. Camilla was dead. Jim and Daisy had their own lives, and Ada had hers . . . *What the hell am I doing here? It's dangerous. I may stir up a storm and get caught in the middle of it. I'd better go while the going's good.*

The girl was staring at him gravely. "What kind of dogs do you like best?"

"Sleeping ones."

"I had a fox terrier once, but it chewed up one of my old lady's crucifixes, and she made me take it to the pound."

"That's too bad."

"I get off work in fifteen minutes. Maybe we could take in a movie this afternoon."

It was the last thing in the world he wanted to do, but he didn't hesitate. "That would be very nice."

"I have to go home first and change clothes. I only live about three blocks away. You could wait here for me."

"Why don't I come along? It's a good day for a walk."

She looked suddenly tense again. "Who said I was going to walk?"

"I assumed—well, since you only live three blocks away . . ."

"I thought maybe you meant I wasn't the kind of girl that'd have a car."

"I didn't mean that at all."

"That's good, because it's not true. I've got a car. I just don't bring it to work. I don't like leaving it parked in the hot sun for all those niggers to lean against and scratch up the finish."

He wondered whether the car, and "all those niggers" who leaned against it, existed outside Juanita's mind. He hoped they were real and not symbols of the dark and ugly things that had happened to her, in or out of the hot sun.

"I take real good care of the finish."

"I'm sure you do."

"Here's your check. Eighty-five cents."

He gave her a dollar, and she went behind the counter to get his change.

"How you feeling now, girl?" Mrs. Brewster said softly.

"Fine."

"When you get off work, you go home to your mother, lie down, take a little rest. You do that, eh?"

"I'm going to the movies."

"With *him*?"

Both the women turned and looked at Fielding. He wasn't sure what was expected of him, so he smiled in a tentative way. Neither of them smiled back.

"He's all right," Juanita said. "He's old enough to be my father."

"Sure, *we* know that, but does *he*?"

"We're only going to the movies."

74

"He looks like a lush," Mrs. Brewster said, "all those broken veins on his nose and cheekbones, and see the way he shakes."

"He only had one beer."

"And suppose one of Joe's friends sees you with this man?"

"Joe doesn't know anybody in town."

Mrs. Brewster began fanning herself with her apron. "It's too hot to argue. Just you be careful, girl. Your mother and me, we're old friends; we don't want you to start running wild again. You're a respectable married woman with a husband and kids, remember that."

Juanita had heard it all a hundred times; she could have recited it forward and backward and in Spanish. She listened without interest, watching the clock on the wall, leaning her weight first on one foot, then another.

"You hear me, girl?"

"Yeah."

"Pay it some mind, then."

"Oh sure," Juanita said, and gave Fielding an amused little glance: *Listen to this spook, will you?* "Can I go now?"

"It's not two yet."

"Can't I go early just this once?"

"All right, just this once. But it's no way to conduct a business, I ought to have my head examined for soft spots."

Juanita went over to the booth where Fielding was sitting. "Here's your change."

"Keep it."

"Thanks. I can go now; the spook says it's okay. Shall I say 'money' and make her giggle again, just for fun?"

"No."

"Don't you want to hear it?"

"No."

For some reason she couldn't figure out, Juanita didn't want to hear it again either. She walked very quickly to the door without glancing back to see whether Mrs. Brewster was watching or Fielding was following.

Outside. This was what Juanita liked best, to be out and free, to be moving fast, going from one place to another, not being anywhere in particular or with anyone in particular, which was the same thing, because people were like places, like houses, they tied you down and made you live in them. She wanted to be a train, a huge, beautiful, shiny train, which never had to stop for fuel or to let people off or on. It just kept on going, blowing its big whistle, frightening everyone off the tracks.

These were the high points of her life, the times between places.

She was a train. *Awhoooeeeee* . . .

13

I am alone, surrounded by strangers in a strange place . . .

IT WAS 2:30 when Pinata reached the neighborhood of the Velada Café. Before he got out of the car, he took off his tie and sports coat, rolled up the sleeves of his shirt, and unbuttoned it at the neck. He planned on using the direct approach, asking for the girl and letting it be assumed he was one of her admirers.

But he hadn't figured on Mrs. Brewster's sharp, suspicious eyes. He was barely inside the door when she spotted him and said to Chico the busboy out of the corner of her mouth, "Cop. You in trouble?"

"No, Mrs. Brewster."

"Don't lie to me."

"I'm not lying. I'm—"

"If he asks your age, you're twenty-one, see?"

"He won't believe it. I know him. I mean, he knows me from the Y; he taught me handball."

"Okay, hide in the back room till he leaves."

Chico made a dash for the back room, riding his broom like a witch frightened by a bigger witch.

Pinata sat down at the counter. Mrs. Brewster approached him, holding her apron in front of her like a shield, and said very politely, "Can I get you something, sir?"

"What's your lunch special?"

"We're not serving lunch. It's after hours."

"How about a bowl of soup?"

"We're fresh out of soup."

"Coffee?"

"It's stale."

"I see."

"I could make you some fresh, but it'd take a long time. I move slow."

"Chico moves pretty fast," Pinata said. "Of course, he's young."

Mrs. Brewster's eyes glittered. "Not so young. Twenty-one."

"My guess would be sixteen."

"Twenty-one. He's got a birth certificate says twenty-one, all printed up proper."

"He must have his own printer."

"Chico looks young," Mrs. Brewster said stubbornly, "because his whiskers are slow to come through the skin."

Pinata was well aware by this time that his plans for a direct approach were useless, that it would be impossible to get information from a woman who'd refused to serve him lunch or coffee. He said, "Look, I'm not a policeman. It's not my concern if you're employing underage help. Chico just happens to be a friend of mine. I'd like to talk to him for a minute."

"What for?"

"To see how he's getting along."

"He's getting along good. He minds his own business, which is how everybody should do."

Pinata looked toward the rear of the café and saw Chico's eyes peering out at him through the little square of glass in one of the swinging doors. Pinata smiled, and the boy grinned back in a friendly way.

Seeing the grin, Mrs. Brewster hesitated, wiping her hands uneasily on her apron. "Chico's not in trouble?"

"No."

"And you met him at the Y, eh?"

"That's right."

Mrs. Brewster's snort indicated her low opinion of the Y, but she motioned to Chico with her apron, and he came sidling out of the door dragging his broom behind him. He was still wearing his grin, but it seemed in close-up to be less friendly than anxious.

"Hello, Chico."

"Hello, Mr. Pinata."

"I haven't seen you for a long time."

"No, well, I been busy, one thing and another like."

Three men in coveralls came in and sat at the far end of the counter. Mrs. Brewster went over to take their orders, giving Chico a little frown of warning as she passed.

"How's your schoolwork coming along?" Pinata said.

Chico stared up at an interesting spot on the ceiling. "Not so good."

"You're getting passing grades, I hope."

"That grade bit's all in the past. I quit school at Christmastime."

"Why?"

"I had to get a steady job to keep my car running. That after-school errand stuff wasn't enough. You can't take the chicks out in a machine that don't run good."

"That's a foolish reason for quitting school."

The boy shrugged. "You asked. I answered. Maybe in your day the chicks was different, maybe they liked to do things like walk in the park, see? Now when you ask a chick out, she wants to go to a drive-in movie like, and you can't go to a drive-in without you got a car."

"Unless you have a car."

"That's what I mean. Without you got a car, you don't rate, you're the most nothing."

In the past few years Pinata had heard this same story fifty times, often from brighter and more educable boys than Chico. Each time it depressed him a little further. He said, "You're pretty young to be working in a place like this, aren't you, Chico?"

"There ain't no harm in it," the boy said nervously. "Honest to God, Mr. Pinata. It's not like I go around lapping up what's left in the glasses. Croaky does that—he's the dishwasher. It's part of his salary like."

"What about the other people who work here? The waitresses, for example. How do they treat you?"

"Okay."

"The blonde standing beside the back booth, who's she?"

"Millie. The other one's called Sunny, short for sunshine on account of she never smiles. She says, what's to smile at." Chico was relieved to have the conversation switched from himself, and he intended to keep it that way if he could. "Millie's real cool. She used to teach dancing at one of them schools, you know, like cha cha cha, but it was too hard on her feet. They were flat to begin with and got flatter."

"I thought there was a new girl around, Nita somebody-or-other."

"Oh, her. She's a funny one. One minute you're her best friend—good morning, Chico, ain't it a beautiful morning, Chico—and the next minute she looks at me like I'm the thing from outer space. She's a snappy waitress, though. Real jet. Her and the old bird"—he indicated Mrs. Brewster with a slight movement of his head—"are pretty palsy because the old bird knows her mother. I hear them talking about it a lot."

"Isn't Nita working today?"

"She was. She took off an hour ago with a guy. There was some trouble about a song, ended up with Mrs. Brewster and the guy singing this real square song with her name in it, Juanita. Nobody was drunk; it wasn't that kind of singing."

"Could the man have been her husband?"

"Naw. He's in hock. This other guy, he's the one put him there."

God, Fielding's back in town. I wonder if Daisy knows.

"I spotted him soon as he came in," Chico added with pride. "I got a good memory for faces. Maybe I don't dig that math bit so good, but faces I never forget."

"How old a man was he?"

"Old enough to be my father. Maybe even old enough to be *your* father."

"That's pretty old," Pinata said wryly.

"Sure. I know. I was kinda surprised Nita'd want to go out with him."

"Out where?"

"To the movies. Nita and the old bird had an argument about it, not a real fight like, just quiet. You go home to your mother, the old bird says, but Nita wasn't having any of that stuff, so she and the guy take off. Nita don't like to be told a thing. Like the other day it's raining, see, and I says to her, look, it's raining. That's all, nothing personal. But she gets sore as hell, like I'd told her her lipstick was on crooked or something. Me, I think she's *zafada*, she needs a headshrinker."

Mrs. Brewster turned suddenly and called out in a sharp, penetrating voice, "Chico, sweep!"

"Sure. Yes, ma'am," Chico said. "I got to get back to work now, Mr. Pinata. See you at the Y, huh?"

"I hope so. I'd hate to think you've given up everything merely to support a car."

"That's the way it is these days, if you dig me."

"Yes, I guess I dig you, Chico."

"You can't change it, I can't change it, that's the way it is."

"Chico!" Mrs. Brewster screamed. "Sweep!"

Chico swept.

The public phone booth on the corner smelled as if it were used during the dark hours for more personal communication and needs than the telephone company had planned on. The walls were covered with telephone numbers, initials, names, messages: Winston tastes good. Winston, 93446. Sally M is cool. Don't be haf safe. Greetings from Jersey City. Life is rotten. You guys are all nutz. 24T, U4 me. Hello crule world goodby.

Pinata dialed Daisy's number and received a busy signal. Then he called Charles Alston at his house.

Alston himself answered. "Hello?"

"This is Steve Pinata, Charley."

"Any luck?"

"That depends on what you mean by luck. I went to the Velada. Juanita wasn't on duty, but there's no doubt she's the girl."

Alston's heavy sigh could be heard even above the street noises coming through the open door of the telephone booth. "I was afraid of this. Well, I have no alternative. I'll have to let the Probation Department know about her. I hate the idea, but the girl's got to be protected and so do the children. Do you think—that is, you agree, don't you, that I should notify the Probation Department?"

"That's up to you. You know the circumstances better than I do."

"They're closed for the weekend, of course, but I'll call them first thing Monday morning."

"And meanwhile?"

"Meanwhile we wait."

"Meanwhile you wait," Pinata said. "I don't. I'm going to try and find her."

"Why?"

"She happens to be out with an ex-client of mine. I'd like to see him again for various reasons."

"When you find her, go easy on her. For her sake," Alston added, "not yours. I assume you can take care of yourself. Where's she staying?"

"With her mother, I think. At least she's in contact with her, so I'll try there first. Where does Mrs. Rosario live?"

"When I knew her, she was living in a little house on Granada Street. It's very likely she's still there, since the house belongs to her. She bought it a long time ago. She used to be the housekeeper on the old Higginson ranch. When Mrs. Higginson died, she left Mrs. Rosario a few thousand dollars, as she did all her other employees. By the way, if Juanita is out with this ex-client of yours, why do you expect to find her at the house on Granada Street? Believe me, she isn't the type to bring the boys home to mother."

"I have a hunch she might have dropped in to change her clothes. She was working, in uniform, until two o'clock. She wouldn't be likely to keep a date while wearing a uniform."

"Definitely not. So?"

"I thought I'd try to get some information from Mrs. Rosario."

Alston's laugh was loud and brief. "You may or may not get it. It depends on whether you have a *mal ojo*. By the way, I set up your appointment with Roy Fondero for three o'clock."

"It's almost that now."

"Then you'd better get over there. He's driving down to L.A. for the game tonight. Oh yes, one more word of advice, Steve: in dealing with Mrs. Rosario, play up the clean-living, high-thinking angle. You never swear, drink, smoke, blaspheme, or fornicate. You go to Mass and confession and observe saints' days. You don't happen to have a brother or uncle who's a priest?"

"I might have."

"That would help," Alston said. "Incidentally, do you speak Spanish?"

"Some."

"Well, don't. Many Spanish Americans who've been here a long time, like Mrs. Rosario, resent people addressing them in Spanish, although they may use the language themselves with their friends and families."

A dozen Doric columns entwined with giant Burmese honeysuckle made the front of Fondero's place look like an old southern mansion. The impression was destroyed by the long black hearse parked by the side door. In the driveway behind the hearse stood a small bright red sports car. The incongruity of the two vehicles amused Pinata. *The death and the resurrection,* he thought. *Maybe that's how modern Americans imagine resurrection, as a bright red sports car whitewalling them along a Styrofoam road to a nylon-Orlon-Dacron nirvana.*

Pinata went in the side door and turned right.

Fondero was watering a planter full of maranta. He was a man of massive proportions, as if he'd been built to withstand the weight and pressure of other people's griefs.

"Sit down, Mr. Pinata. Charley Alston called me to say you want some information."

"That's right."

"What about?"

"You may recall Carlos Camilla?"

"Oh yes. Yes, indeed." Fondero finished watering the maranta and put the empty pitcher on the window ledge. "Camilla was my guest, shall we say, for over a month. As you know, the city has no official morgue, but Camilla's body had to be kept, pending investigation of the source of the money that was found on him. Nothing came of the investigation, so he was buried."

"Did anyone attend the funeral?"

"A hired priest and my wife."

"Your wife?"

Fondero sat down in a chair that looked too frail to bear him. "Betty refused to let Camilla be buried without mourners, so she acted as a substitute. It wasn't entirely acting, however. Camilla, perhaps because of the tragic circumstances of his death, perhaps because we had him around so long, had gotten under our skin. We kept hoping that someone would come along to claim him. No one did, but Betty still refused to believe that Camilla didn't have somebody in the world who cared about him. She insisted that the money found on Camilla be used for an imposing monument instead of an expensive coffin. She had the idea that someday a mourner might appear, and she wanted Camilla's grave to be conspicuous. As I recall, it is."

"It's conspicuous," Pinata said. *And a mourner did come along and find it, but the mourner was a stranger—Daisy.*

"You're a detective, Mr. Pinata?"

"I have a license that says so."

"Then perhaps you have some theory of how a man like Camilla got hold of $2,000."

"A holdup seems the most likely source."

"The police were never able to prove that," Fondero said, taking a gold cigarette case from his pocket. "Cigarette? No? Good for you. I wish I could give them up. Since this lung cancer business, some of the local wits have started calling cigarettes Fonderos. Well, it's publicity of a kind, I suppose."

"Where do you think Camilla got the money?"

"I'm inclined to believe he came by it honestly. Perhaps he saved it up, perhaps it was repayment of a loan. The latter theory is more logical. He was a dying man. He must have been aware of his condition, and knowing how little time he had left, he decided to collect money owing to him to pay for his funeral. That would explain his coming to town—the person who owed him money lived here. Or lives here."

"That sounds plausible," Pinata said, "except for one thing. According to the newspaper, the police made an appeal to the public for anyone who knew Camilla to come forward. No one did."

"No one came forward in person. But I had a peculiar telephone call after Camilla had been here a week or so. I told the police about it, and they thought, as I did at the time, it was the work of some religious crank."

The expression on Fondero's face as he leaned forward was an odd mixture of amusement and irritation. "If you want to hear from every crackpot and prankster in town, try going into this business. At Halloween it's the kids. At Christmas and Easter it's the religious nuts. In September it's college boys being initiated. Any month at all is good for a lewd suggestion from a sex deviate as to what goes on in my lab. I received the call about Camilla just before Christmas, which made it the right timing for one of the religious crackpots."

"Was it from a man or a woman?"

"A woman. Such calls usually are."

"What kind of voice did she have?"

"Medium in all respects, as I recall," Fondero said. "Medium- pitched, medium-aged, medium-cultured."

"Any trace of an accent?"

"No."

"Could it have been a young woman, say about thirty?"

"Maybe, but I don't think so."

"What did she want?"

"I can't remember her exact words after all this time. The gist of her conversation was that Camilla was a good Catholic and should be buried in consecrated ground. I told her about the difficulties involved in such an arrangement, since there was no evidence that Camilla had died in the Church. She claimed that Camilla had fulfilled all the requirements for burial in consecrated ground. Then she hung up. Except for the degree of self-control she displayed, it was an ordinary run-of-the-mill crank call. At least I thought so then."

"Camilla is buried in the Protestant cemetery," Pinata said.

"I talked it over with our parish priest. There was no alternative."

"Did the woman mention the money?"

"No."

"Or the manner of his death?"

"I got the impression," Fondero said cautiously, "from her insistence on Camilla being a *good* Catholic, that she didn't believe he had killed himself."

"Do you?"

"The experts called it suicide."

"I should think by this time you'd be something of an expert yourself along those lines."

"Experienced. Not expert."

"What's your private opinion?"

Outside the window Fondero's son had begun to whistle, loudly and off-key, "Take Me Out to the Ball Game."

"I work very closely with the police and the coroner's office," Fondero said. "It wouldn't be good business for me to have an opinion contrary to theirs."

"But you have one anyway?"

"Not for the record."

"All right, for me. Top secret."

Fondero went over to the window and then returned to his chair, facing Pinata. "Do you happen to recall the contents of the note he left?"

"Yes. 'This ought to pay my way into heaven, you stinking rats . . . Born, too soon, 1907. Died, too late, 1955.'"

"Now everybody seemed to take that as a suicide note. Perhaps that's what it was. But it could also be the message of a man who knew he was going to die, couldn't it?"

"I guess so," Pinata said. "The idea never occurred to me."

"Nor to me, until I made my own examination of the body. It was that of an old man—prematurely aged if we accept the date of his birth as given, and I see no reason why he should lie about it under the circumstances. Many degenerative processes had taken place: the liver was cirrhotic, there was considerable hardening of the arteries, and he was suffering from emphysema of the lungs and an advanced case of arthritis. It was this last thing that interested me the most. Camilla's hands were badly swollen and out of shape. I seriously doubt whether he could have grasped the knife firmly enough to have inflicted the wound himself. Maybe he could. Maybe he did. All I'm saying is, I doubt it."

"Did you express your doubts to the authorities?"

"I told Lieutenant Kirby. He wasn't in the least excited. He claimed that the suicide note was more valid evidence than the opinion of a layman. Although I don't hold a pathologist's degree, I hardly consider myself a layman after some twenty-five years in the business. Still, Kirby had a point: opinions don't constitute evidence. The police were satisfied with a suicide verdict, the coroner was satisfied, and if Camilla had any friends who weren't, they didn't bother complaining. You're a detective, what do you think?"

"I'd be inclined to agree with Kirby," Pinata said carefully, "on the basis of the facts. Camilla had good reason to kill himself. He wrote, if not a suicide note, at least a farewell note. He left money for his funeral expenses. The knife used had his own initials on it. In the face of all this, I can't put too much stock in your opinion that Camilla's hands were too crippled to have wielded the knife. But of course I've had no experience with arthritis."

"I have."

Fondero leaned forward, holding out his left hand as if it were some specimen from his lab. Pinata saw what he hadn't noticed before: that Fondero's knuckles were swollen to twice normal size, and the fingers were bent and stiffened into a claw.

"That," Fondero said, "used to be my pitching hand. Now I couldn't even field a bunt if the World Series depended on it. I sit in the stands as a spectator, and when Wally Moon belts one over the fence, I can't even applaud. All my lab work these days is done by my assistants. Believe me, if I wanted to kill myself, it would have to be with something other than a knife."

"Desperation often gives a man additional strength."

"It may give him strength, yes, but it can't loosen up fused joints or restore atrophied muscles. It's impossible."

Impossible. Pinata wondered how often the word had already come up in connection with Camilla. Too many times. Perhaps he'd been the kind of man destined for the impossible, born to botch up statistics and defy the laws of physics. The evidence of motive, weapon, suicide note, and funeral money was powerful enough, but fused joints couldn't be loosened overnight, nor atrophied muscles restored on impulse or by desire.

Fondero was still holding out his hand for exhibit like a freak at a sideshow. "Are you still inclined to believe Kirby, Mr. Pinata?"

"I don't know."

"I don't actually know, either. All I can say is that if Camilla grasped that knife with those hands of his, I wish he'd have stayed alive long enough to tell me how he did it. I could use some advice on the subject."

He hid his deformed hand in his pocket. The show was over; it had been an effective one.

"Kirby's a sharp man," Pinata said.

"That's right, he's a sharp man. He just doesn't happen to have arthritis."

"Wouldn't Camilla's condition have prevented him from writing the suicide note?"

"No. It was printed, not written. This is common among arthritics. It's a good deal easier to print legibly."

"From your examination of the body, what general information did you get about Camilla's manner of living?"

"I won't go into further medical details," Fondero said, "but the evidence indicates that he was a heavy drinker, a heavy smoker, and at some time in his life a heavy worker."

"Was there any clue about what kind of work?"

"One, although some orthopedists might not agree with me. He had a bone malformation known as *genu varum*, less politely called bowlegs. Now bowlegs can be caused by a number of things, but if I had to make a wild guess about Camilla's occupation, I'd say that, beginning early in his youth, he had a lot to do with horses. He may have worked on a ranch."

"Ranch," Pinata said, frowning. Someone had recently mentioned a ranch to him, but it wasn't until he got back to his car that he recalled the circumstances: Alston on the telephone had said that Mrs. Rosario, Juanita's mother, had been housekeeper on a ranch and had inherited enough money, when the owners died, to buy the house on Granada Street.

14

The hotel guests are looking at me queerly while I write this, as if they are wondering what a tramp like me is doing in their lobby where I don't belong, writing to a daughter who has never really belonged to me . . .

GRANADA WAS A street of small frame houses built so closely together that they seemed to be leaning on each other for moral and physical and economic support against the pressures from the white side of town. The pomegranate trees, for which the street was named, were fruitless now, but at Christmas time the gaudy orange balls of fruit hung from the branches looking quite unreasonable, as if they had not grown there at all but had been strung up to decorate the street for the holiday season.

Five-twelve hid its age and infirmities—and proclaimed its independence from its neighbors—with a fresh coat of bright pink paint that seemed to have been applied by a child or a nearsighted amateur. Blotches of paint stained the narrow sidewalk, the railing of the porch, the square yard of lawn; the calla lilies, the leaves of the holly bush and the pittosporum hedge, were pimpled with pink as if they'd broken out with some strange new plant disease. Pink footsteps, belonging to a child or a very small woman, led up the grey porch steps and disappeared in the coarse bristles of the coca mat outside the front door. These footsteps were the only evidence that a child or children might be living in the house. There were no toys or parts of toys on the porch or lawn, no discarded shoes or sweaters, no half-eaten oranges or jelly sandwiches. If Juanita and her six children had taken up residence here, someone was being careful to hide the fact, perhaps Juanita herself, perhaps Mrs. Rosario.

Pinata pressed the door buzzer and waited, trying to figure out why Juanita had suddenly decided to come back to town after an absence of more than three years. She must have known she'd be in trouble with the authorities for breaking probation when she disappeared in the first place. On the other hand, Juanita didn't behave on the logical level, so the reason for her return could be something quite trivial and capricious, or purely emotional: homesickness, a desire to see her mother again or to show off her latest husband and youngest child to her friends, perhaps a quarrel with a neighbor, wherever she'd been living, followed by a sudden violent desire to get away. It was difficult to guess her motives. She was like a puppet operated by dozens of strings; some of them had broken, and others had become so inextricably twisted that not one of them functioned as it was intended to. To remove these knots and tangles, and to splice the broken ends together, was the job of Alston and his staff. So far, they had failed. Juanita's soarings and somersaults, her leaps and landings were beyond the control of any puppeteer.

The door opened to reveal a short, thin middle-aged woman with black, expressionless eyes like ripe olives. She held her body so rigidly straight that she appeared to be wearing an iron brace on her back. Everything about her was stretched taut; her skin looked as if it had been starched, her hair was drawn back from her face in a tight and tidy little bun, and her mouth was compressed into a hard line. Pinata was surprised when it opened with such ease.

"What do you want?"

"Mrs. Rosario?"

"That is my name."

"I'm Steve Pinata. I'd like to talk to you for a minute, if I may."

"If it's about old Mr. Lopez next door, I have nothing more to say. I told the lady from the Department of Health yesterday, they had no right to take him away like that against his will. He's had that same cough all his life, and it's never done him a bit of harm. It's as natural to him as breathing. As for the rest of the neighborhood getting into that ray machine, free or not, I refused and so did the Gonzales and the Escobars. It's against nature, getting your lungs choked up with all those rays."

"I'm not connected with the Department of Health," Pinata said. "I'm looking for a man who may be calling himself Foster."

"Calling himself? What is this business, calling himself?"

"Your daughter knows him as Foster, let's put it that way."

Mrs. Rosario took a tuck in her mouth, like a sailor reefing a mainsail at the approach of a storm. "My daughter, Juanita, lives down south."

"But she's here now for a visit, isn't she?"

"Whose concern is it if she comes here for a visit? She has done no harm. I keep a sharp eye on her, she stays out of trouble. Who are you anyway to come asking questions about my Juanita?"

"My name is Stevens Pinata."

"So? What does that tell me? Nothing. It tells me nothing. I don't care about names, only people."

"I'm a private investigator, Mrs. Rosario. My job right now is to keep track of Foster."

The woman clapped one hand to her left breast as if something had suddenly broken under her dress, a heart or perhaps merely the strap of a slip. "He's a bad man, is that what you're saying? He's going to cause trouble for my Juanita?"

"I don't think he's a bad man. I can't guarantee there won't be trouble, though. He can be a little impulsive at times. Did he come here with your daughter, Mrs. Rosario?"

"Yes."

"And they went off together?"

"Yes. Half an hour ago."

A thin, red-cheeked girl about ten came out on the porch of the house next door and started rotating a hula hoop around her hips and chewing a wad of gum in matching rhythm. She appeared to be completely oblivious to what was taking place on the adjoining porch, but Mrs. Rosario said in a hurried whisper, "We can't talk out here. That Querida Lopez, she hears everything and tells more."

Still not looking in their direction, Querida announced to the world in a loud, bright voice, "I am going to the hospital. None of you can come and see me either, because I've got spots on my lungs. I don't care. I don't like any of you anyway. I'm going to the hospital like Grandpa and have lots of toys to play with and ice cream to eat, and I don't have to do any more dishes forever and ever. And don't any of you come and see me, because you can't, ha ha."

"Querida Lopez," Mrs. Rosario said sharply, "is this true?"

The only sign that the girl had heard was the increased speed of the hula hoop.

Mrs. Rosario's dark skin had taken on a yellowish tinge, and when she stepped back into her front room, it was as if Querida had pushed her in the stomach. "The girl lies sometimes. Perhaps it isn't true. If she is so sick as to go to a hospital, how could she be out playing like this? She coughs, yes, but all children cough. And you see for yourself what a fine, healthy color she has in her cheeks."

Pinata thought that the color might be caused by fever rather than health, but he didn't say so. He followed Mrs. Rosario into the house. Even after he closed the door behind him, he could hear Querida's rhythmic chanting: "Going to the hospital—I don't care. Can't come and see me—I don't care. Going in an ambulance . . ."

The rays of sun coming in through the lace curtains scarcely lightened the gloom of the small square parlor. All four walls were covered with religious ornaments and pictures, crucifixes and rosaries, Madonna's with and without child, heads of Christ, a little shrine presided over by the Holy Mother, haloed angels and blessed virgins. Many of these objects, which were intended to give hope and comfort to the living, had the effect of glorifying death while at the same time making it seem repulsive.

In this room, or another one just like it, Juanita had grown up, and this first glimpse of it did more to explain her to Pinata than all the words Alston had used. Here she had spent her childhood, surrounded by constant reminders that life was cruel and short, and the gates to heaven bristled with thorns, nails, and barbed wire. She must have looked a thousand times at the haloed mothers with their plump little babies, and unconsciously or deliberately, she had chosen this role for herself because it represented aliveness and creativity as well as sanctity.

Mrs. Rosario crossed herself in front of the little shrine and asked the Holy Mother for assurance that Querida Lopez, with her fine, healthy color, was lying. Then she tucked her thin body neatly into a chair, taking up as little space as possible because in this house there was hardly any room left for the living.

"Sit down," she said with a stiff nod. "I don't expect strangers to come into my house asking personal questions, but now you are here, it is only polite to ask you to sit down."

"Thanks."

The chairs all looked uncomfortable, as if they had been selected to discourage people from sitting. Pinata chose a small, wooden-backed, petit-point couch, which gave off a faint odor of cleaning fluid. From the couch he could look directly into what appeared to be Mrs. Rosario's bedroom. Here, too, the walls were crowded with religious paintings and ornaments, and on the night-stand beside the big carved double bed a candle was burning in front of the photograph of a smiling young man. Obviously, the young man had died, and the candle was burning for his soul. He wondered whether the young man had been Juanita's father and how many candles ago he had died.

Mrs. Rosario saw him staring at the photograph and immediately got up and crossed the room. "You must excuse me. It is not polite to display the sleeping quarters to strangers."

She pulled the bedroom door shut, and Pinata could see at once why she had left it open in the first place. The door looked as if it had been attacked by someone with a hammer. The wood was gouged and splintered, and one whole panel was missing. Through the jagged aperture, the young man continued to smile at Pinata. The flickering light of the candle made his face appear very lively; the eyes twinkled, the cheek muscles moved, the lips expanded and contracted, the black curls stirred in the wind behind the broken door.

"One of the children did it," Mrs. Rosario explained in a quiet voice. "I don't know which one. I was at the grocery store when it happened. I suspect Pedro, being the oldest. He's eleven, a boy, but the devil gets into him sometimes, and he plays rough."

Very rough, indeed, Pinata thought. *And playing isn't quite the word.*

"Pedro's down at the lumber mill now, seeing about a new door. For punishment, I made him take the other children with him. Then he's got to paint and hang the new door by himself. I'm a poor woman. I can't afford painters and carpenters with such prices they charge."

It was obvious to Pinata that she wasn't rich. But he could see no signs in the house of extreme poverty, and the religious items alone had cost quite a bit of money. Mrs. Rosario's former employer on the ranch must have been generous in his will, or else she earned extra money doing odd jobs.

He glanced at the door again. *Some of the hammer marks were at the very top; if an eleven-year-old boy did the damage, he must be a giant for his age. And what would be his motive for such an act? Revenge? Destruction for its own sake? Or maybe,* Pinata thought, *the boy had been trying to break down a door locked against him.*

It didn't occur to him that Mrs. Rosario was lying . . .

She'd seen them coming up Granada Street, Juanita in her green uniform and an older man. Mrs. Rosario didn't recognize the man, but the two of them were laughing and talking, and that was enough: they were up to no good.

She called the children in from the backyard. They were old enough now to notice things, to wonder, yes, and to talk, too. Pedro had the eyes and ears of a fox and a mouth like a hippopotamus. Even in church he talked out loud sometimes and had to be punished afterward with adhesive tape.

She gave them each an apple and took them all into the bedroom. If they were very good, she promised, if they sat quietly on the bed and said their beads to themselves, later they would all go over to Mrs. Brewster's to watch the television.

She had just locked the bedroom door when she heard Juanita's quick, light step on the porch and the sound of laughter. She took the key out of the lock and put her eye to the keyhole. Juanita was coming in the front door with the stranger, looking flushed and restless.

"Well, sit down," she said. "Take a look around. Some dump, eh?"

"It's different."

"I'll say it's different. Don't touch anything. She'll throw a fit."

"Where is your mother?"

Juanita raised her eyebrows, the corners of her mouth, and her shoulders in an elaborate combination of shrug and grimace. "How should I know? Maybe she dragged the kids over to church again."

"That's too bad."

"So what's too bad about it?"

"I was hoping to meet them." Fielding made his tone casual, as if he were expressing a polite desire instead of a deadly serious purpose. "I like children. I only had one of my own, a girl. She's about your age now."

"Yeah? How old do you think I am?"

"If you hadn't told me about the six children, I'd say about twenty."

"Sure," Juanita said. "I bet."

"I mean it. That goo you put on your eyes makes you look older, though. You should stop using it."

"It enhances them."

"They don't need enhancing."

"You can sure throw the bull around." But she began rubbing her eyelids with her two forefingers, as if she had more respect for his opinion than she cared to admit. "Is she pretty? Your kid, I mean."

"She was. I haven't seen her for a long time."

"How come you haven't seen her for a long time if you like children so much?"

It was a question with a hundred answers. He picked a couple at random. "I've been moving around. I've got itchy feet."

"So've I. Only I can't do much about it, saddled with six kids and an old lady that watches me like I got two heads." She flung herself almost violently on the couch, rolled over, and stared up at the ceiling. "Sometimes I wish a big wind would come along and blow this house away and me in it. I wouldn't care where I blew to. Even a foreign country would be okay."

From the bedroom came the sudden, sharp cry of a child, followed immediately by a noisy babble of voices, as if that first single cry had been the signal for a whole chorus to begin.

Juanita glanced toward the door, looking angry but not surprised. "So she's in there spying on me again. I should've guessed."

The noise from the bedroom had increased to a roar. Fielding could scarcely hear his own voice above it. "We'd better leave. I don't want to get mixed up in another brawl."

"I haven't changed my clothes."

"You look fine. Come on, let's go. I need a drink."

"You can wait."

"For Pete's sake, someone might call the police like last time. Two hundred bucks that cost me."

"I don't like being spied on."

She jumped off the couch and moved swiftly toward the bedroom, yanking a large crucifix off the wall as she passed.

"What are you doing in there?" She banged on the door with the crucifix. "Open this up, you hear me? Open it up!"

There was a sudden silence. Then one of the children began to wail, and another answered in a scared voice, "Grandma won't let us."

Finally Mrs. Rosario herself spoke. "The door will be opened when the gentleman leaves."

"It'll be opened *now*."

"When the gentleman leaves, not before. I will not allow the children to see their mother consorting with a strange man while her husband is away."

"Listen to me, you old spook!" Juanita screamed. "You know what I got here in my hand? I got Jesus Christ himself. And you know what I'm going to do with him? I'm going to pound him against this door—"

"You will not blaspheme in my house."

"—and pound him and pound him, until there's nothing left of him or it. Hear that, you witch? For once, Jesus is going to do me a good turn. He's going to break down this door."

"If there is any violence, I will take steps."

"He's on *my* side for a change, see? It's him and *me*, not you." She let out a brief, excited laugh. "Come on, Jesus baby, you're on my side."

She began striking the door with the crucifix, as rhythmically as a skilled carpenter driving nails. Fielding sat, his face frozen in a grimace of pain, listening to the sound of splintering wood and sobbing children. Suddenly the crucifix broke at the top, and the metal head flew through the air, narrowly missing Fielding's, and ricocheted off a table onto the floor.

The same blow that broke the crucifix had shattered one of the panels in the door, so that Mrs. Rosario could see what had happened. The door opened then, and the children scrambled out like cattle from a boxcar, confused and terrified.

With a cry of rage Mrs. Rosario darted across the room and picked up the head of Jesus.

"That'll teach you to spy on me," Juanita said triumphantly. "Next time it'll be more than Jesus; it'll be every lousy piece of junk in the house."

"Wicked girl. Blasphemer."

"I don't like being spied on. I don't like doors locked against me."

Three of the children had run directly out the front door. To the others, one hidden behind the couch and two clinging to Juanita's skirt, Mrs. Rosario said in a trembling voice, "Come. We must kneel together and ask forgiveness for your mother's sin."

"Pray for yourself, you old spook. You need it as bad as anybody."

"Come, children. To keep your mother's soul from the torments of eternal hell—"

"Leave my kids alone. If they don't want to pray, they don't have to."

"Marybeth, Paul, Rita . . ."

None of the children moved or uttered a sound. They seemed suspended in midair like aerialists aware of an imminent fall and not sure which side would be safer to fall on—God and Grandma's, or Juanita's. It was the youngest, Paul, who decided first. He pressed his dark, moist face against Juanita's thigh and began to wail again.

"Stop slobbering," Juanita said, and gave him a casual push in Fielding's direction.

Fielding found himself in the position of a spectator at a ball game who sees the ball suddenly coming off the field in his direction and has no choice but to catch it. He picked the child up and carried him into the bedroom to get him away from the screaming women.

"You'll go to hell, you wicked girl."

"That's okay by me. I got relatives there."

"Don't you dare speak his name. He is not in hell. The priest says by this time he is with the angels."

"Well, if he can get to be with the angels, so can I."

"'Hi diddle diddle,'" Fielding whispered in the boy's ear. "'The cat and the fiddle. The cow jumped over the moon. The little dog laughed to see such sport, and the dish ran away with the spoon.' Did you ever see a cow jump over the moon?"

The boy's black eyes looked grave, as if this were a very important question that deserved something better than a snap answer. "I saw a cow once."

"Jumping over the moon?"

"No, he was giving milk. Grandma took us to see a big ranch, and there was cows giving milk. Grandma says cows work hard to give milk, so I mustn't spill mine on the table."

"I had a job on a ranch once. And believe me, I worked harder than any old cows."

"Grandma's ranch?"

"No. This one was far away."

The noise from the next room stopped abruptly. Juanita had disappeared into another part of the house, and Mrs. Rosario was kneeling alone in front of the little shrine, the head of Jesus cradled in her left hand. She prayed silently, but from the vindictive look on her face Fielding thought she must be invoking punishment, not forgiveness.

"I want my daddy," the boy said.

"He'll be back one of these days. Now how about Miss Muffett, would you like to hear about her troubles? 'Little Miss Muffett sat on a tuffet, eating her curds and whey. Along came a spider and sat down beside her, and frightened Miss Muffett away.' Are you afraid of spiders?"

"No."

"Good boy. Spiders can be very useful."

Fielding's collar was damp with sweat, and every few seconds his heart gave a quick extra beat, as if it were being chased around inside his chest cavity. He often worried about having a heart attack, but when he was at home, he simply took a couple of drinks and forgot about it. Here he couldn't forget. It seemed, in fact, inevitable, a bang-up climax to the crazy afternoon of the broken crucifix and the shattered door, the grim praying woman and the terrified children, Juanita and Miss Muffett. *And now, ladies and gentlemen, for our grand finale of the day we give you Stanley Fielding and his death-defying coronary.*

"Miss Muffett," he said, listening to his heartbeat, "was a real little girl, did you know that?"

"As real as me?"

"That's right, just as real as you. She lived, oh, about two or three hundred years ago. Well, one day her father wrote a verse about her, and now children all over the world like to hear about little Miss Muffett."

"I don't." The boy shook his head, and his thick black curly hair tickled Fielding's throat.

"You don't, eh? What do you like to hear about? And not so loud; we mustn't disturb Grandma."

"Talk about the ranch."

"What ranch?"

"Where you worked."

"That was a long time ago." *Ladies and gentlemen, before our star performer does his death-defying act, he will entertain you with a few highlights from his life story.* "Well, I had a mare called Winnie. She was a cutting horse. A cutting horse has got to be fast and smart, and that's what she was. All I had to do was stay in the saddle, and Winnie could pick a cow from a herd as easy as you can pick an orange from a bowl of fruit."

"Grandma gave us an apple before you came. I hid mine. Want to know where?"

"I don't think you'd better confide in me. I'm not so good at keeping secrets."

"Do you tell?"

"Yeah. Sometimes I tell."

"I tell all the time. The apple is hid under the—"

"Shhh." Fielding patted his head. The boy, without speaking, had already told him what he'd come to find out. His black eyes and hair, his dark skin had spoken for him. One thing was clear now: a mistake had been made. But who had made it, and why? *My God, I need a drink. If I had a drink, I could think. I could think with a drink. Think . . .*

"What's your name?"

"Foster," Fielding said. He had used the name so often that it no longer seemed like lying. "Stan Foster."

"Do you know my daddy?"

"I'm not sure."

"Where is he?"

It was a good question, but an even better one was going around in Fielding's mind. Not where, but who. *Who's your daddy, kid?*

The boy was clinging to his neck so tightly that Fielding couldn't move his head even to look around the room. But he was suddenly aware of a peculiar odor which he'd been too excited to notice before. It took him a minute or two to identify it as burning wax.

Rising from the bed, he eased the child gently onto the floor. Then he turned and saw the picture of the curly-haired young man behind the flickering candle. His heart began to pound against his rib cage, and the noise of it seemed as loud as the noise Juanita had made banging on the door. Flashes of red struck his eyes, and his hands and legs felt numb and swollen to double size. *This is it*, he thought. *Ladies and gentlemen, this is it. Here I go . . .*

It was a trap.

He saw it now very clearly. The whole thing was a trap; it had been written, rehearsed, staged. Every line, even the little boy's, had been memorized. Every piece of business, including the shattering of the door, had been practiced over and over until it seemed real. And all of it had been leading up to this moment when he saw the picture.

He raised his swollen hand and wiped away the sweat that was dripping into his eyes, obscuring his vision.

They were in there now, in the other room, waiting to see what he would do, Mrs. Rosario pretending to pray, Juanita pretending to be getting ready to go out, the children pretending to be scared. They were in there listening, watching, waiting for him to give himself away, to make the wrong move. Even the little boy was a spy. Those innocent eyes looking up at him were not innocent at all, and the angelic mouth belonged to a demon.

"He is with the angels by this time," Mrs. Rosario had said. Fielding knew now whom she'd been talking about, and crazy laughter rose in his throat and stuck there until he began to choke. He loosened his tie to get more air but immediately tightened it again. He must not let the watchers see that the picture meant anything to him or that he was trying to find out about the little boy's father.

He was aware, in a vague way, that he wasn't thinking straight, but he couldn't clear his mind of the haze of suspicion that clouded it. In this haze, fact and fiction merged into paradox: a troubled girl became a master criminal, her mother a scheming witch, and the children were not children at all but adults whose bodies hadn't grown up.

"Hey, I'm ready," Juanita said.

Fielding whirled around so fast he lost his balance and had to steady himself by grabbing one of the bedposts.

"It's a brand-new dress. How do I look?"

He couldn't speak yet, but he managed to nod. The haze was beginning to lift, and he could see her quite clearly: a young woman, slim and pretty in a blue and white full-skirted dress, with a red sweater flung over her shoulders and red snakeskin shoes with heels like needles.

"Come on," she said. "Let's get out of this spookery."

He walked out of the bedroom, rubber-kneed, trembling with relief. There had been no plot, no trap. His mind had invented the whole business, molded it out of fear and guilt. Juanita, Mrs. Rosario, the children, they were all innocent. They didn't even know his real name or why he had come here. The picture beside the bed was one of those ugly coincidences that happen sometimes.

And yet . . .

I need a drink. My God, get me to a drink.

Mrs. Rosario crossed herself and turned from the little shrine. She still had made no acknowledgment of Fielding's presence, not even a casual glance in his direction. She looked over his shoulder, addressing Juanita. "Where are you going?"

"Out."

"You will buy me a new crucifix."

Juanita moistened a forefinger on her tongue and smoothed her eyebrows. "I will, eh? Fancy me being so bighearted."

"You are not bighearted," Mrs. Rosario said steadily. "But you're sensible enough to realize this is my house. If I lock the door against you, you'll be out on the street."

"You just tried the lock bit. See where it got you."

"If there's any more of that, I'll call the police. You'll be arrested, and the children will be taken to Juvenile Hall."

Juanita had turned quite pale, but she grinned and shrugged her shoulders so expressively that her sweater fell off onto the floor. When Fielding bent over to pick it up, she snatched it out of his hand. "So? The kids will be just as good off there as they are in this nuthouse with you crawling around on your knees half the time."

Mrs. Rosario for the first time looked directly at Fielding. "Where are you taking my daughter?"

"He's not taking me anyplace," Juanita said. "I'm taking him. I'm the one with the car."

"You leave that car in the garage. Joe says you're too wild to drive. You'll be killed. You can't afford to be killed with so many sins on your soul you haven't confessed."

"We had planned on going to a movie," Fielding said to Mrs. Rosario. "But if you don't approve—that is, I wouldn't want to be the cause of any family friction."

"Then you'd better leave. My daughter is a married woman. Married women don't go to movies with strangers, and gentlemen don't ask them to. I don't even know who you are."

"Stan Foster, ma'am."

"What does that tell me? Nothing."

"Leave him alone," Juanita said. "And keep your nose out of my business."

"This is my house; what goes on here is my business."

"Okay, take your damn house. Keep it. It's only a lousy little shack anyway."

"It's sheltered you and your children in times of trouble. You'd be out on the street if it wasn't for—"

"I *like* the street."

"Yes, sure, now that it's warm and sunny you like it. Wait till the night comes, wait till it's cold and maybe it starts to rain. You'll come crying."

"You'd love that, wouldn't you, me coming crying. All right, start praying for rain, see if I come crying." Juanita opened the front door and motioned to Fielding to go out ahead of her. "Just see if I come crying."

"Gypsy," Mrs. Rosario said in a soft, furious whisper. "You're no child of mine, gypsy. I found you in an open field. I took pity. There's none of my blood in you, gypsy."

Juanita slammed the door. The Madonnas on the wall shivered but continued to smile.

"I was born right here in St. Joseph's hospital," Juanita said. "It's on the records. You didn't believe that open field stuff, did you?"

"Let's go someplace and have a drink."

"Sure, but did you or didn't you?"

"What?"

"Believe that gypsy stuff."

"No." Fielding wanted to break into a run, to put as much distance as possible between himself and the weird house with the decapitated crucifix.

Juanita was tottering along beside him, crippled by her needle heels. "Hey, not so fast."

"I need a drink. My nerves are shot."

"She bugged you, eh?"

"Yeah."

"She didn't use to be so spooky when I lived at home before. Sure, she was religious, but it wasn't so bad until she started trying to get people into heaven. You saw the candle, didn't you?"

"I guess so."

"The car's just down here. I keep it in a separate garage so's the kids don't play around it and scratch the finish."

"We don't need a car," Fielding said. "I can't afford to be killed with all the sins on my soul, either."

"She's a crackpot."

"Yes. Only—"

"You heard that open field stuff, didn't you? That was all lies. It's on the records, how I was born in St. Joseph's hospital . . ."

Mrs. Rosario stood in front of the broken door as if she were trying to hide from Pinata the mortal wound of her house.

"Forgive me my curiosity," Pinata said. "But the young man in the picture, was he Juanita's father?"

"The name of Juanita's father has not been spoken in this house for twenty years. I would not waste good beeswax on his soul." She crossed her arms on her chest. "I must remind you that you were invited into my house to discuss Mr. Foster. No one else. Just Mr. Foster."

"All right. Where did he go when he left here with your daughter?"

"I don't know. They spoke of going to the movies. But Juanita hardly ever goes to the movies. She's afraid of being shut up in dark places."

"Well, what does she usually do when she gets off on a Saturday afternoon?"

"She shops or takes the children to the beach or maybe down to the wharf to fish. She likes being outdoors and talking and laughing with the fishermen that hang around the wharf. She can be a very happy girl sometimes." She studied her hands as if she were reading the past in their lines and finding it as inscrutable as the future. "Sometimes you never saw a happier girl."

"What does she do when she's miserable?"

"I don't follow her. I have the children to watch over."

"But you hear things?"

"Friends maybe tell me when they see her acting—acting, well, not so good."

"Does she do much drinking? I'm asking the question because Foster has a decided weakness in that direction. If Juanita shares it, it will give me some idea of where to start looking for them."

"She drinks sometimes."

"At the Velada?"

"No, never," Mrs. Rosario said sharply. "Never at the Velada. Mrs. Brewster wouldn't allow it, not even a glass of beer."

Strike the Velada, Pinata thought. That left some twenty-five or thirty places which could strictly be called taverns, and perhaps eighty or ninety restaurants in and around town which served liquor. A great many of these restaurants would be closed to Juanita because of her race, either obviously, with a quick brush-off at the door, or subtly, with small printed signs stating the proprietor's right to refuse service to anyone. The taverns, however, were mainly located in areas where discrimination would have meant bankruptcy. For this reason a tavern seemed the most logical place to look for Juanita. In spite of everything he'd been told about her aggressiveness, Pinata had a hunch that she was too timid to wander very far from the places where she felt welcome and at home.

"Mrs. Rosario," Pinata said, "Juanita left town nearly four years ago to live in Los Angeles. Why?"

"She got sick of being hounded by the police and the Probation Department and the people at the Clinic. Talk, talk, talk, that's all they did, tell her what was wrong with her, what to do, what to wear, how to manage the children."

"They were all trying to help her, weren't they?"

"It's a funny kind of help that hinders," she said scornfully. "The last time she was arrested, she wasn't doing any harm. It's hard, when you're young, always being followed by five children, never going anyplace alone. When she locked them in the apartment, it was for their own good, so they wouldn't run away or get in an accident. But the neighbors complained when they cried, and the police said what if there was a fire or an earthquake. So they arrested her and put the children in Juvenile Hall. Do you call this *helping*? I don't. If that's the only kind of help I can get, I'd rather fend for myself. Which is what she chose to do when she got out. She left right away, that same night. The children were in bed asleep, and I asked Mrs. Lopez to keep an eye on them while I went to church. When I came back, she was gone." She moved her head back and forth in remembered pain. "I didn't think she would leave so sudden, her with no husband, no friends, and another baby due in less than a month."

"Did she leave a message for you?"

"No."

"You didn't know where she was going?"

"No. I never heard from her or saw her again until two weeks ago. The Probation Department and someone from the Clinic came snooping around a few times. I told them just what I'm telling you now."

"I hear what you're telling me," Pinata said. "But is it the truth?"

Mrs. Rosario blinked, and the ripe-olive eyes disappeared for a fraction of a second under lids that looked withered from lack of tears. "Four years with no news of her, and suddenly comes a knock on the front door, and there she is, with six children and a husband and a car. She talked a blue streak telling me how happy she was, and didn't I think the baby was cute and the car beautiful and the husband handsome. But there was a look in her eye I didn't like, that restless look of hers. When she's like that, she hardly eats or sleeps, she just keeps on the go, day and night, one place to another, never getting tired."

One place to another, Pinata thought. *Twenty-five taverns, eighty restaurants, sixty thousand people. I'd better start moving.*

"This man she's with," Mrs. Rosario said, "this Mr. Foster, he is a drunk?"

"Yes."

"You find them and send Juanita home."

"I'll try."

"Tell her I'm sorry I called her a gypsy. I lost control of my tongue. She's no gypsy, my Juanita. I lost control—it's so easy sometimes. Afterwards I'm filled with such shame and sadness. You find her for me, will you? Tell her I'm sorry?"

"I'll do my best."

"Hurry up before this man gets her into trouble."

Pinata wasn't sure who was going to get whom into trouble, but he knew they made a bad combination, Juanita and Fielding. He wrote his name and the phone numbers of his office and residence on a slip of paper and gave it to Mrs. Rosario.

She held it at arm's length to read it. "Pinata," she said, nodding. "That's a good Catholic name."

"Yes."

"If my daughter went to church more often, she wouldn't suffer from this sickness."

"Perhaps not," Pinata said, knowing how useless it would be to argue the point. "I'd appreciate your letting me know right away if either Juanita or Fielding shows up here again."

"Fielding?"

"That's his real name."

"Fielding," she repeated quietly. Then she folded the piece of paper and tucked it into the pocket of her black dress. "I guess it doesn't matter what people call themselves. Fielding may not be his real name, either, maybe?"

"I'm sure it is."

"Well, it's no business of mine." She crossed the room and opened the front door. "You won't find Juanita, or Fielding, either. With a car, they could be anywhere by this time."

"I can try."

"Don't try for my sake."

"You asked me to find her and send her home."

"I'm tired," she said bitterly. "I'm *tired.* Let her stay lost."

"I have a job to do."

"Then do it. Good day to you, Mr. Pinata. If that is your name."

"It's the only one I have."

"I don't care anyway."

When he stepped across the threshold, she closed the door behind him so quickly that he felt he'd been forcibly ejected.

The porch of the Lopez house next door was empty, and Querida's purple hula hoop lay broken on the steps.

Mrs. Rosario waited until his car had turned the corner. Peering through the lace curtain, she felt faint and very cold, as if an iron hand had squeezed her heart and stopped its flow of blood. She touched the silver cross she wore at her throat, hoping it would warm and comfort her. But the metal was as cold as her skin. *Pinata. It sounded false. He hadn't even claimed that it was real, just that it was the only one he had.*

She went out into the kitchen and picked up the telephone directory. The name was listed. Stevens Pinata, and the phone numbers were the same ones he'd written on the slip of paper.

She stood leaning against the sink, paralyzed by indecision. She had orders not to call Mr. Burnett, the lawyer, at his office unless it was absolutely necessary, and never to call him at his home under any circumstances. But what right had he to give the orders? Maybe he'd even been the one who sent Pinata and Fielding to spy on her. Well, they had learned nothing, either of them. The picture had been taken thirty years ago and bore no resemblance to the way he'd looked when he died.

The minutes passed, ticking away like heartbeats. It had been a long, cruel day. So many of the days were long and cruel. Carlos was well out of it. He was with the angels by this time. No more candles would be necessary, the priest said. "He will certainly be in heaven by this time," the priest said. "You mustn't become a fanatic; it looks bad for the church. This has been going on long enough."

He was right, of course. Things had been going on long enough . . .

She picked up the phone.

15

Your mother kept her vow, Daisy. We are still apart, you and I. She has hidden her shame because she cannot bear it the way we weaker and humbler ones can and must and do . . .

ON SATURDAY AFTERNOON Ada Fielding had lunch at a downtown restaurant with a group of friends. After lunch she found herself being followed into the powder room by Mrs. Weldon, a member of the group whom she didn't know very well and didn't like at all. Mrs. Weldon's large, inquisitive eyes were always hidden by a veil, like windows by a net curtain, and her thin, sharp mouth moved constantly, even when she wasn't talking, as if she were chewing on some little regurgitated seeds from the past.

Adjusting her veil in front of the mirror above the washbasin, Mrs. Weldon said, "How's Daisy?"

"Daisy? Oh, fine, she couldn't be better, thanks."

"And Jim?"

She wasn't even aware that Mrs. Weldon knew the names of her daughter and son-in-law, but she concealed her surprise, as she had concealed a great many other things in her lifetime, under a slow, placid smile. "Jim is very well, too. He'd planned on going north this weekend to look at some land he's thinking of buying, but he decided to wait until it was cooler. Hasn't it been a fantastic year? All this heat and no rain to speak of."

But Mrs. Weldon did not intend to put up with weather-talk when she'd planned on people-talk. "A friend of mine saw Daisy the other day—Corinne, you've heard me mention Corinne, the lovely girl that lives next door to us—well, not a girl, really, she's almost forty, but she's kept her figure like a girl. Of course she was born skinny; that helps. Corinne saw Daisy just the other day and said she was looking quite peaked."

"Indeed? I certainly haven't noticed."

"Thursday, it was. Thursday afternoon, walking along Piedra Street with a young man. I knew it couldn't be Jim. Jim's so blond and fair-skinned, and this man was quite—well, dark."

"Daisy is acquainted with a great many men," Mrs. Fielding said casually. "Dark and fair."

"I meant dark in you-know-what sense."

"I'm afraid I don't understand."

"Of course you're not a native Californian . . ." Mrs. Weldon stopped and shook her head helplessly; these nonnative Californians could be very dense. "I meant, this man wasn't one of *us*."

Ada Fielding was well aware of her meaning, but it seemed advisable to feign innocence, to appear imperturbable; there was nothing a gossip enjoyed more than the signs of anxiety, a quickening of the breath, a sudden flush, a clenching of the hands. Mrs. Fielding's hands and breathing remained steady, and her flush was hidden by a layer of powder. Only she knew it was there, she could feel it in her cheeks and neck, and it annoyed her because there was nothing to get excited about. Daisy had been seen walking along a street with a dark young man. Very well, what of it? Daisy had all kinds of friends. Still, in a town like this, one had to be careful. There was a difference between being tolerant and being foolish, and Daisy, even with the best of intentions, could be quite foolish at times.

"No, I'm not a native Californian," she said blandly. "I was born in Colorado. Have you ever visited Colorado? The mountain scenery is perfectly magnificent."

But Mrs. Weldon was not interested in Colorado. "By a strange coincidence Corinne happened to recognize the man. She met him last year when she was in that little scrape with the police. All she had at the bridge party was one teensy cocktail, but when she ran through the red light—Corinne swears it was yellow—the police insisted she was drunk. She had a perfectly dreadful time. It was Saturday, the banks were closed, and her lawyer was out playing golf, and her parents were in Palm Springs for the weekend. And the poor girl is so delicate because she never eats anything. Anyway, along came this young man and bailed her out. Corinne can't recall his name, but she remembered his face because he was so good-looking—except of course he was—well, dark."

"That's a very interesting story about Corinne's scrape with the police," Mrs. Fielding said with a small, steely smile. "I must remember to pass it along."

For nearly a week Daisy had been trying to arrange to have the house to herself, and she had finally accomplished it. Her mother was downtown shopping, Stella had taken the weekend off after Daisy convinced her she wasn't feeling well, and Jim had gone out for a sail in Adam Burnett's new racing sloop. Both the invitation and its acceptance had been engineered by Daisy: Jim suffered from seasickness, and Adam, who wasn't accustomed to the new boat, would have preferred a more experienced crew, but neither man put up much of an argument.

From the kitchen window Daisy watched Jim's car until it disappeared around the first sharp turn of the road that wound down the canyon. Then she went down immediately to the lower part of the house. Here there was an extra bedroom and bath for guests; a lanai decorated in pale green and turquoise which, seen in a half-light, looked under water; Jim's hobby room; and, at the far end of the house off the lanai, Jim's den. The den was filled with various pieces of furniture Jim had made himself, some of it experimental and impractical, all of it modernistic in line. The largest object in the room looked incongruous beside the modern pieces: a huge, old-fashioned rolltop desk which Jim had bought at an auction so that he could study its design and work out an improved version. But the old desk had proved so useful and satisfactory that he'd never bothered trying to improve it.

The rolltop and the drawers were locked, though the key was in plain sight on the windowsill. Daisy thought how typical this was of Jim, to lock everything, as if he felt surrounded by thieves, then to leave the key available, as if he'd decided he had nothing worth stealing after all.

She unlocked the desk while the dog, Prince, stood in the doorway, his tail between his legs, his amber eyes indicating disapproval of this change in routine. He knew Daisy didn't belong down here in this room, and he sensed her nervousness.

The top part of the desk was very neat, with separate little drawers for stamps and for paper clips, compartments for pencils, current bills, unanswered letters, bankbooks, clippings from out-of-town newspapers advertising land for sale. In contrast to the top of the desk, the larger drawers were crammed with stuff—old letters and postcards, bank statements, half-empty packets of matches and cigarettes.

She began going through the drawers, taking everything out and laying each item on a half-finished free-form table which Jim was making for her mother's cottage. She had no real hope of finding anything, but she kept on searching, her hands moving clumsily as if they were weighted down by feelings of guilt and shame at what she was doing. Jim had always trusted her, and she had trusted him. Now, she thought, after eight years of marriage, she was going through his private papers like a common thief. And, as any common thief deserved, she was finding nothing. The postcards were impersonal, the letters innocent. Already, in her mind, apologies were forming: *Jim dear, I'm terribly sorry. I didn't mean any harm . . .*

At the back of the left bottom drawer she came across a pile of used checkbooks. They were not arranged in order of date. The one on the top was from a year ago and covered a period of four months.

Without expecting to find anything important, she began to turn the tiny pages listlessly, as if she were reading a dull book with lots of characters but no plot. She knew most of the characters: the pharmacist, Stella, the owners of the bookstore and dress shop and building supply company, the dentist, the veterinarian, the gardener, the paperboy. The largest amount, $250, had gone to Stella for wages. The stub with the next largest amount bore the name Ab and the amount $200. It was dated September 1.

She checked the next month's stubs, and here again she discovered an identical notation for October 1. When she came to the end of the book, she'd found four of them altogether, each for $200, paid to Ab at the beginning of the month.

Ab. She knew no one by that name, no Abner, Abbott, Abernathy, Abigail. The closest was Adam. Adam Burnett. A.B.

She was not actually surprised at first: it was natural enough for Adam to be receiving money from Jim. He was Jim's lawyer and did all his tax work. But the amount—$200 a month, $2,400 a year for a tax consultant—seemed excessive, and she was puzzled by the fact that Jim had not paid it through his office as a business expense. Was it possible that Jim was paying off a debt, that he had borrowed money from Adam and wanted to keep it secret from his business associates? That he was not as well off as he pretended to be in front of her and her mother?

How foolish of him not to tell me, she thought. *I could easily economize. Mother and I got along on a shoestring when we had to. And we usually had to.*

The dog, Prince, suddenly let out a bark and bounded noisily through the lanai and up the stairs. Although Daisy could hear nothing from the upper floor, she knew someone must have come into the house, and she began frantically cramming everything back into the drawers. She might have had a chance to finish if Prince hadn't decided that it was his duty to guide Mrs. Fielding down to the den and Daisy.

The two women stared at each other for a moment in the silence of mutual confusion. Then Daisy said awkwardly, "I thought you were going to spend the afternoon shopping."

"I changed my mind. It was too hot downtown."

"Oh."

"It's nice and cool down here, though."

"Yes."

"Just what do you think you're doing?"

It was, for Daisy, like a scene from her childhood, with her mother standing over her, strong and angry and, above all, right, and herself cringing and scared and, beneath all, wrong. But she was older now; she knew better than to sound scared or admit she was wrong. "I was looking for something I thought Jim might have put in his desk."

"Something so important that you couldn't wait until he comes home to ask him about it?"

"On the contrary, it's so trivial I wouldn't bother him about it. Jim has a lot on his mind."

"You should know. You put it there."

"Oh, Mother, for heaven's sake, don't. Don't start anything."

"Something has already been started," Ada Fielding said harshly. "You started it last Monday morning when you allowed yourself to get hysterical over some absurd little dream. That's how it all began, with a dream, and since then everything's been going to pieces. There have been times when I actually thought you were losing your mind—crying and carrying on, wandering around a cemetery alone looking for a tombstone you saw in a dream, cross-examining us all, even Stella, about a dead Mexican none of us ever heard of—it's sheer madness."

"If it's madness, it's mine, not yours. Don't worry about it."

"And now *this*, this sneaking around going through Jim's private papers, what does it mean? What are you looking for?"

"You know what I'm looking for. Jim must have told you. He tells you everything else."

"Only because you won't talk to him anymore."

Daisy stared at a section of the wall, wondering how many times during the past week Jim and her mother had discussed the situation. Perhaps they had a conference about her whenever she was absent, like two doctors in consultation over a very sick patient whose symptoms they didn't understand. *"She's looking for a lost day, Dr. Fielding." "That sounds pretty serious, Dr. Harker." "Oh, it is. First case I've ever had quite like it." "We may have to operate." "Good idea. Splendid. If the lost day is anywhere, it's inside her. We'll dig it out and dispose of it. Can't leave it in there festering."*

"You seem," Mrs. Fielding said, "to resent the fact that Jim confides in me."

"Not at all."

"Most young women are grateful for a decent relationship between in-laws. Jim and I have many differences of opinion, but we try to overlook them for your sake, because we both love you." Mrs. Fielding's eyes were moist, and the corners of her mouth turned down as if she was going to cry. She pressed her fingertips against her mouth to steady it. "You know that, don't you? That we both love you?"

"Yes." She knew they both loved her, each in a different way, neither of them completely. Jim loved her insofar as she fitted his conception of the ideal wife. Her mother loved her as a projection of herself, but the projected part must be without the flaws of the original. Oh yes, certainly, she was loved. Being loved was not the problem. The problem, when you were the focus of two such powerful people as Jim and her mother, was the loss of spontaneity, of being able to love.

She thought, suddenly and disturbingly, of Pinata, of the drive back to the city from the cemetery, how old and tormented his face had looked in the dashlights as if he thought no one was watching him and it was safe to show his sorrow.

She turned her head and saw her mother looking at her, and she knew she'd better stop thinking about Pinata. It was frightening the way her mother could read her mind sometimes. *But then I am her projection machine. She just sits back and watches the pictures, censoring, editing. She can't see Pinata, though. She doesn't even know about him. No one does.* Pinata was hers, locked up in a secret drawer inside herself.

She finished replacing the papers. Then she locked the desk and put the key back on the windowsill. Everything looked exactly the same as when she had come in. Jim need never know she'd searched the desk and found out about the monthly payments to Adam. Unless her mother told him.

"I suppose," Daisy said, "you'll tell him?"

"I consider it my duty."

"Do you have any duty to me?"

"If I thought you were acting in a logical and rational manner, I wouldn't dream of mentioning this episode to Jim. Yes, I have a duty to you, and that is to protect you from the consequences of your own irresponsibility."

"I'm irresponsible," Daisy repeated. "I'm illogical and irrational and irresponsible. Just like my father. Go on, say it. I'm just like my father."

"I don't have to say it. You did."

"In exactly what ways have I been irresponsible?"

"Several that I know of. One that I'd like to find out about."

"You could ask me."

"I'm going to."

Mrs. Fielding sat down, holding her back straight and her hands crossed on her lap. It was a posture Daisy had come to know well through the years. It indicated seriousness of purpose, great patience, maternal affection (this hurts me more than it does you), and anger with its bile so finely distilled that it was almost palatable. Wry whiskey.

"I had lunch with Mrs. Weldon today," Mrs. Fielding said. "Do you remember her?"

"Vaguely."

"She's an impossible woman, but she has a way of finding out odd bits of information. This time the information was about you. Perhaps you'll consider it trivial. I don't. It's an indication that you're not being as careful as you should be. You can't afford to get yourself talked about. Jim is becoming a prominent man in this town. And he's a devoted husband as well. There isn't a woman who knows him who doesn't envy you."

Daisy had heard it all before. The tone varied, the clichés varied, but the message was always the same: that she, Daisy, was a very lucky girl, who ought to be grateful every day of her life that Jim remained married to her even though she was sterile. Mrs. Fielding was too subtle to say any of this outright, but the implication was clearly made: Daisy had to be a super wife because she couldn't be a mother. The marriage was the important thing, not the individuals who contracted it. And the marriage was important, not for any religious or moral reasons, but because it meant, for Mrs. Fielding, the only real security she'd ever had. Daisy understood this and felt both sympathetic, because her mother had worked very hard to keep the family going, and resentful, because it seemed to Daisy that it wasn't her own life or marriage or husband; half, or more than half, belonged to her mother.

"Are you listening to me, Daisy?"

"Yes."

"On Piedra Street?"

"I may have been on Piedra Street. Why? What difference does it make?"

"Someone saw you," Mrs. Fielding said. "A next-door neighbor of Mrs. Weldon's, called Corinne. She claims you were walking with a good-looking dark young man who has some connection with jails or the Police Department. Were you, Daisy?"

She was tempted to lie about it, to keep Pinata safely and secretly locked inside her private drawer, but she was afraid that a lie would be more damaging than the truth. "Yes, I was there."

"Who was the man?"

"He's an investigator."

"Do you mean a *detective?*"

"Yes."

"Why on earth would you be walking around town with a detective?"

"Why not? It was a nice day, and I like walking."

There was a silence, then Mrs. Fielding's voice, as smooth and chilling as liquid air. "I warn you not to be flippant with me. How did you meet this man?"

"Through my—through a friend. I didn't know he was an investigator at the time. When I found out, I hired him."

"You hired him? What for?"

"To do a job. Now that's all I have to say on the subject."

She started toward the door, but her mother called her back with an urgent "Wait."

"I prefer not to discuss—"

"*You* prefer, do you? Well, *I* prefer to get this settled between the two of us before Jim finds out about it."

"There's nothing to settle," Daisy said, keeping her voice calm because she knew her mother was waiting for her to lose her temper. Her mother was always at her best when other people lost their tempers. "I hired Mr. Pinata to do some work for me, and he's doing it. Whether Jim finds out about it doesn't matter. He hires people at the office all the time. I don't make an issue of it, because it's none of my business."

"And you think it's none of Jim's business that you should go traipsing all over town with a Mexican?"

"Whether Mr. Pinata is a Mexican or not is beside the point. I hired him for his qualifications, not his racial background. I know nothing about him personally. He doesn't volunteer any information, and I don't ask for any."

"Tolerance is one thing. Foolishness is another." There was a curious rasp in Mrs. Fielding's voice, as if her fury, which had been denied admittance into words, had broken in through the back door of her larynx. "You know nothing about such people. They're cunning, treacherous. You're a babe in the woods. If you let him, he'll use you, cheat you—"

"Where did you learn so much about a man you've never even seen?"

"I don't have to see him. They're all alike. You must put a stop to this relationship before you find yourself in serious trouble."

"Relationship? For heaven's sake, you're talking as if he were my lover, not someone I happened to hire." She took a deep breath, fighting for control. "As for traipsing all over town, I didn't. Mr. Pinata escorted me to my car at the conclusion of our business appointment. Now does that satisfy you, *and* Mrs. Weldon, *and* Corinne?"

"No."

"I'm afraid it will have to. I have nothing further to say on the subject."

"Sit down," Mrs. Fielding said sharply. "Listen to me."

"I've already listened."

"Forget I'm your mother for a minute."

"All right." It was easy, she thought. The green watery light coming in through the doorway from the lanai made Mrs. Fielding's face look strange and opalescent, like something that lived in the depths of the sea.

"For your own sake," Mrs. Fielding said, "I want you to tell me what you hired this Pinata to do."

"I'm trying to reconstruct a certain day in my life. I needed someone—someone objective—to help me."

"And that's all? It has nothing to do with Jim?"

"No."

"What about this other man, the one whose name is on the tombstone?"

"I've found out nothing further about him," Daisy said.

"Are you trying to?"

"Of course."

"*Of course,*" Mrs. Fielding repeated shrilly. "What do you mean, *of course?* Are you still being foolish enough to believe that his tombstone is the same one you saw in your dream?"

"I know it's the same one. Mr. Pinata was with me at the cemetery. He recognized the tombstone before I did, from the description I'd given him from my dream."

There was a long silence, broken finally by Mrs. Fielding's painful whisper. "Oh, my God. What will I do? What's happening to you, Daisy?"

"Whatever is happening, it's to me, not to you."

"You're my only child. Your welfare and happiness are more important to me than my own. Your life is my life."

"Not anymore."

"Why have you changed like this?" Her eyes filled with tears of disappointment and anger and self-pity, all mixed up together and inseparable. "What's *happened* to us?"

"Please don't cry," Daisy said wearily. "Nothing's happened to us except that we're both getting a little older, and you want a little more of my life than I'm willing to give."

"God knows I only try to make things easier for you, to protect you. What's the use of my having gone through everything I did if I can't pass on to you the benefit of my experience? My own marriage was broken. Can you blame me for trying to keep yours from turning out the same way? Perhaps if I'd had someone to guide me, as I've guided you, I'd never have married Stan Fielding in the first place. I'd have waited for someone reliable and trustworthy, like Jim, instead of tying myself to a man who never told a straight story or did a straight thing from the day he was born."

She went on talking, pacing up and down the room as though it were the prison of the past. Daisy listened without hearing, while she tried to remember some of the lies her father had told her. But they hadn't been lies, really, only bits of dreams that hadn't come true. *Someday, Daisy baby, I'm going to take you and your mother to Paris to see the Eiffel Tower.* Or to Kenya on a safari, or London for the coronation, or Athens to see the Parthenon.

If they were lies, they belonged as much to life as to Fielding. No one believed them anyway.

"Daisy, are you paying attention to me?"

"Yes."

"Then you must stop all this nonsense, do you understand? We're not the kind of people who hire detectives. There's something squalid about the very word."

"I'm not sure what kind of people we are," Daisy said. "I know what we pretend to be."

"Pretense? Is that what you call putting up a good front to the world, pretense? Well, I don't. I call it simple common sense and self-respect." Mrs. Fielding pressed one hand to her throat as if she were choking on the torrent of words gushing up inside her. "What's your idea of how to get along in life—hiring a hall and shouting your secrets to the whole city?"

"I have no secrets."

"Haven't you? *Haven't you?* You fool. I despair of you." She fell into a chair like a stone falling into a pond. "Oh God. I despair." The words rose from the very bottom of the pond. "I'm so—tired."

Daisy looked at her with bitterness. "You have reason to be tired. It takes a lot of energy to lead two lives, yours and mine."

The only noise in the room was the nervous panting of the collie and the tea tree pawing at the windowpane as if it wanted to get in.

"You must leave me alone," Daisy said softly. "Do you hear me, Mother? It's very important, you must leave me alone."

"I would if I thought you were strong enough to do without me."

"Give me a chance to try."

"You've picked a bad time to declare your independence, Daisy. Worse than you realize."

"Any time would be a bad time as far as you're concerned, wouldn't it?"

"Listen to me, you little fool," Mrs. Fielding said. "Jim's been a wonderful husband to you. Your marriage is a good one. Now, for the sake of some silly whim, you're putting it in jeopardy."

"Are you trying to tell me that Jim would actually divorce me simply because I've hired a detective?"

"All I meant—"

"Or could it be that you're afraid the detective might find out something Jim doesn't want found out?"

"If you were younger," Mrs. Fielding said steadily, "I'd wash your mouth out with soap for that remark. Your husband is the most decent, the most moral man I've ever met. Someday, when you're mature enough to understand, I'll be able to tell you some things about Jim that will surprise you."

"One thing about him surprises me right now. And I discovered it without the help of any detective." Daisy glanced briefly at the rolltop desk. "He's been paying Adam Burnett $200 a month. I found the check stubs."

"So?"

"It seems peculiar, doesn't it?"

"Obviously it does to you."

"You sound as if you know something about it."

"I know everything about it," Mrs. Fielding said dryly. "Jim bought some acreage Adam owned up near Santa Inez Pass. He intended to build a mountain hideaway on it as a surprise anniversary present for you. I'm sorry I've been forced to tell. But it seemed wiser to spoil the surprise than to let your suspicions keep on growing. You must have a guilty conscience, Daisy, or you wouldn't be so quick to accuse others."

"I didn't accuse him. I was simply curious."

"Oh? Just what did you think Adam was being paid for?" Mrs. Fielding got up out of the chair as though her joints had stiffened during the hour. "This man Pinata is obviously a bad influence on you to have affected your thinking like this."

"He has nothing to do with—"

"I want you to call him immediately and tell him he is no longer in your employ. Now I'm going over to my cottage and get some rest. The doctor says I must avoid scenes like this. The next time I see you, I hope the cause of them will have been removed."

"You think firing Pinata will solve everything?"

"It will be a start. Someone has to start somewhere."

She walked to the door with brisk, determined steps, but there was a weary stoop to her shoulders that Daisy had never seen before. "I despair," her mother had said.

Why, it's true, Daisy thought. *She despairs. How extraordinary to despair on a bright, sunny afternoon with Pinata somewhere in the city.*

She looked across the room at the telephone. Its shiny black cord seemed like a lifeline to her. All she had to do was pick up the receiver and dial, and even if she couldn't reach him personally, he would get her message through his answering service: *Call me, meet me, I want to see you.*

The phone began to ring while the sound of her mother's step was still on the stairs. She crossed the room, forcing herself to walk slowly because she wanted to run.

"Hello?"

"Long distance for Mrs. Daisy Harker."

"This is Mrs. Harker."

"Go ahead, ma'am. Your party's on the line."

Daisy waited, still hoping, though she had no reason to hope, that it was Pinata, that this was his way of reaching her in the event Jim or her mother might be around when he called.

But the voice was a woman's, high-pitched and nervous. "I know I shouldn't be phoning you like this, Mrs. Harker, or maybe I should say Daisy, though it don't seem socially proper to call you Daisy when we never even been introduced yet—"

"Who is this calling, please?"

"Muriel. Your new—new stepmother." Muriel let out an anxious little giggle. "I guess this is kind of a shock to you, picking up the phone and hearing a perfect stranger say she's your stepmother."

"No. I knew my father had married again."

"Did he write and tell you?"

"No. I heard it the way I hear everything else about my father—not from him but from somebody else."

"I'm sorry," Muriel said in her quick, nervous voice. "I told him to write. I kept reminding him."

"It's certainly not your fault. You have my best wishes, by the way. I hope you'll both be very happy."

"Thank you."

"Where are you calling from?"

"I'm in Miss Wittenburg's apartment across the hall. Miss Wittenburg promised not to listen; she has her fingers in her ears."

To Daisy it was beginning to sound like an April Fools' joke: *I am your new stepmother—Miss Wittenburg has her fingers in her ears* . . . "Is my father there with you?"

"No. That's why I decided to phone you. I'm worried about him. I shouldn't have let him go off by himself the way he did. Hitchhiking can be dangerous even when you're young and strong and have no outstanding weaknesses. I guess," Muriel added cautiously, "being as you're his daughter, you know he drinks?"

"Yes. I know he drinks."

"He's been pretty good lately, with me to keep an eye on him. But today he wouldn't take me along. He said we didn't have the money for bus fare for both of us, so he was going to hitchhike up alone."

"Do you mean up here, to San Félice?"

"Yes. He wanted to see you. His conscience was bothering him on account of he walked out on you last time when he lost his nerve. Stan has a very strong conscience; it drives him to drink. It's like he always has a bad pain that has to be numbed."

"I haven't seen him or heard from him," Daisy said. "Are you sure he intended to come right here to the house?"

"Why, yes. Why, he even mentioned how maybe you'd all have some champagne to celebrate being together again."

Daisy thought how typical it was of her father: *to Paris to see the Eiffel Tower, to London for the coronation, to San Félice for a champagne celebration.* Her sorrow and anger met and merged in a relationship that weakened them both and conceived a monster child. This child, half formed, tongueless, without a name, lay heavy inside her, refusing to be born, refusing to die.

"Stan wouldn't like me phoning you like this," Muriel said, "but I just couldn't help it. Last time he was up there, he got involved with that waitress, Nita."

"Nita?"

"Nita Garcia. That's what he called her."

"The report in the paper said her name was Donelli."

"It said Stan's name was Foster. That don't make it true." Muriel's dry little laugh was like a cough of disapproval. "Sure, I'm suspicious—women are—but I can't help thinking he's going to see her again, maybe get in some more trouble. I was hoping— well, that maybe he'd be in touch with you by this time and you could set him straight about associating with the wrong people."

"He hasn't been in touch," Daisy said. "And I'm afraid I couldn't set him straight if he were."

"No. Well. Well, I'm sorry to have bothered you." She seemed ready to hang up.

Daisy said hurriedly, "Just a minute, Muriel. I wrote my father a special delivery letter on Thursday night asking him an important question. Was this the reason he suddenly decided to come and see me?"

"I don't know about any special delivery letter."

"I sent it to the warehouse."

"He didn't mention it to me. Maybe he never got it. He was reading some other letters from you, though, just before he decided to leave. He kept them in his old suitcase. You know that old suitcase of his that he lugs around full of junk?"

Daisy remembered the suitcase. It was the only thing he'd taken with him when he'd left the apartment in Denver on a winter afternoon: "Daisy baby, I'm going to take a little trip. Don't you stop loving your daddy." The trip had lasted fifteen years, and she hadn't stopped.

"He was reading a letter of yours," Muriel said, "when he suddenly got the blues."

"How do you know it was from me?"

"Right away he started talking about how he'd failed as a father. Besides," she added bluntly, "nobody else writes to him."

"Did he mention what was in the letter?"

"No."

"Did he put it back in the suitcase?"

"No. I looked right after he left, and it wasn't there, so I guess he took it with him." Muriel sounded both apologetic and defensive. "He doesn't keep the suitcase *locked*, just chained."

"How did you know what particular letter to look for?"

"It was in a pink envelope."

Daisy was on the point of saying she didn't use colored stationery when she remembered that a friend of hers had given her some for her birthday several years ago. "What was the address on the envelope?"

"Some hotel in Albuquerque."

"I see." The Albuquerque address and the pink stationery dated the letter positively as being written in December of 1955. Her father had moved from Illinois to New Mexico at the end of that year, but he had stayed barely a month. She recalled sending his Christmas presents and check to a hotel in Albuquerque and receiving a postcard from Topeka, Kansas, a couple of weeks later thanking her for the gifts and saying he didn't like New Mexico, it was too dusty. There'd been a doleful quality about the postcard, and the handwriting was shaky, as if he'd been ill or on a drinking spree or, more likely, both.

"Stan will be awful mad about me phoning you like this," Muriel said nervously. "Maybe you just sort of keep it a secret when you see him?"

"I may not see him. He may not be anywhere near San Félice."

"But he said—"

"Yes. He said." He'd said, too, that he was taking a little trip, and the trip had lasted fifteen years. Perhaps he'd started on another little trip, and Muriel, as naive as Daisy had been in her early teens, would walk up and down the city streets searching for him in crowds of strangers; she would catch a glimpse of him passing in a speeding car or walking into an elevator just before the door closed. Daisy had seen him a hundred times, but the car was too fast, the face in the crowd too far away, the elevator door too final.

"Well, I'm sorry to have bothered you," Muriel repeated.

"It was no bother. In fact, I'm very grateful for the information."

"Stan gave me another number to call in case of emergency, a Mr. Pinata. But I didn't want to call a stranger about—well, about Stan's certain weakness."

Daisy wondered how many strangers, the length and breadth of the country, knew about Stan's certain weakness and how many more were finding out right now. "Muriel?"

"Yes."

"Don't worry about anything. I'm going to get in touch with Mr. Pinata. If my father's in town, we'll find him and look after him."

"Thank you." There were tears in Muriel's voice. "Thank you ever so much. You're a good girl. Stan's always said you were a real good girl."

"Don't take everything my father says too seriously."

"He really meant it. And I do, too. I'm ever so grateful for all the things you've done for him. I don't mean just the money. Having somebody who really cares about him, that's what's important."

Oh yes, I care, Daisy thought bitterly when she'd hung up. *I still love Daddy after his little trip of fifteen years. And if he's in town, I'll find him. I'll get to the elevator door before it closes; the speeding car will be stopped by a red light, a policeman, a flat tire; the face in the crowd will be his.*

The wind had increased, and the air was filled with the rush of birds and flying leaves, and the scratching of the tea tree against the window sounded like the paws of a dozen animals.

Daisy sat with the phone in her hands, shivering, as if there were no glass between her and the cold wind. She could barely dial Pinata's number, and when she was told he wasn't in, she wanted to scream at the girl on the other end of the line and accuse her of bungling or fraud.

She took a deep breath to steady herself. "When do you expect him?"

"This is his answering service. He left word that he'd be in his office at seven. He'll check in for his calls before that, though. Is there any message?"

"Tell him to call . . ." She stopped, dubious about leaving her name, even more dubious about Pinata phoning the house when her mother or Jim might be present. "I'll meet him at his office at seven."

"What name shall I put on that?"

"Just say it's about a tombstone."

16

Shame—it is my daily bread. No wonder the flesh is falling off my bones . . .

JIM HAD BEEN waiting at the dock for nearly an hour when Adam Burnett finally showed up. He came running along the seawall, moving heavily but quietly in his sailing sneakers.

"Sorry I'm late. I was delayed."

"Obviously."

"Don't get sore. I couldn't help it." The lawyer sat down beside Jim on the seawall. "The sail's off, anyway. They've raised a smallcraft warning at the end of the wharf."

"Well, I suppose I might as well go home, then."

"No, you'd better wait a minute."

"What for?"

Although there was no one within hearing distance, Adam kept his voice low. "I had a phone call half an hour ago from Mrs. Rosario. Juanita's back in town. What's worse, so is Fielding."

"Fielding? Daisy's father?"

"What's worse still, the two of them are together."

"But they don't even know each other."

"Well, they're getting acquainted in a hurry, if Mrs. Rosario can be believed."

"It just doesn't make sense," Jim said in a bewildered voice. "Fielding had nothing to do with the—the arrangements."

"Mrs. Rosario somehow got the impression that you—or I—sent him to spy on her."

"I haven't seen Fielding for years."

"And I never have. I pointed these facts out to her, but she was pretty excited, almost incoherent toward the end. She insisted I swear on the soul of her dead brother that I had nothing to do with Fielding's going to her house." Adam squinted out at the whitecaps, multiplying under the wind. "Know anything about a dead brother?"

"No."

"His name was Carlos, apparently."

"I said I knew nothing about a dead brother, didn't I?"

"Well, don't get waspish. I was just asking."

"You asked twice," Jim said curtly. "That's once too often. My relationship with Mrs. Rosario has been brief and impersonal. You should be aware of that better than anyone."

"Impersonal isn't quite the word, surely?"

"As far as I'm concerned, it is. I wouldn't recognize her if I met her on the street."

A fishing boat was coming into port, her catch measurable by the squat of her stern and the number of gulls quarreling in her wake, trying to snatch pieces of fish from each other's beaks.

"What does she want?" Jim said. "More money?"

"Money wasn't mentioned. Apparently there'd been some violence when Fielding was at the house, though he didn't have anything to do with it as far as I was able to make out. Mrs. Rosario was upset and needed reassurance."

"You gave it to her, I hope?"

"Oh, certainly. I swore on the soul of her dead brother. Whom you don't know."

"Whom I don't know. As I have now stated three times. Why the persistence, Adam?"

"She kept raving about him, and I'm curious, that's all. How does a dead brother fit into the arrangements we made about Juanita?"

"The woman's obviously unstable."

"I agree. But I wonder how unstable."

Jim got up and stretched his arms. "Well, I'll leave you to your wonderings. I must get home. Daisy will think we've both drowned."

"I don't believe," Adam said carefully, "that Daisy is thinking about us at all."

"What's that supposed to mean?"

"Just before I left the house, I had a phone call from Ada Fielding. She asked me to tell you that Daisy had hired a detective a few days ago, a man named Pinata."

"Oh, for God's sake."

"Mrs. Fielding thinks you ought to do something about it."

"She does, eh?" Jim's face was grim and weary. "Such as what?"

"I gather she meant unhire him. After all, it's your money he's getting." Adam paused, watching the fishing boat as it tied up to the dock, wishing he were on it. "There's more if you want to hear it."

"I'm not sure I do."

"You'd better listen anyway. Daisy's meeting this man at his office tonight at seven o'clock. She promised Fielding's new wife that she and Pinata would go looking for Fielding."

"Fielding's new wife? How the hell did she come into it?"

"She was worried about Fielding getting into trouble and phoned Daisy from Los Angeles."

"What's it all about anyway?"

"I was hoping that you'd tell me."

Jim shook his head. "I can't. I have no idea how Fielding got involved in this thing, if he is involved. As for his wife, I didn't know of her existence until Daisy informed me this week. I'm at a complete loss, I tell you."

"You tell me, yes."

"Your tone suggests disbelief."

"Let's put it this way. It's better to lie to your wife than to your lawyer."

"I play it safe," Jim said, "by not lying to either."

"What about the girl?"

"I told Daisy all about that when it happened—names and everything—and she took it very calmly. She seems to have forgotten now, and that's not my fault. I told her."

"Why?"

"Why? Because it was the reasonable, the honorable, thing to do."

"It may have been honorable as all get-out," Adam said with a cryptic little smile. "But reasonable, no."

"She'd have found out sooner or later anyway."

"Your logic reminds me of the first time I took my brother-in-law sailing. It was a brisk day, we were going along at a nice clip with just the right angle of heel, but Tom was so afraid we'd tip that he jumped overboard and swam to shore. I know you don't enjoy sailing much, so you probably think Tom did the sensible thing. It wasn't, though. It was both silly and dangerous. He almost didn't make it to shore, and of course, the boat didn't tip."

"She'd have found out eventually," Jim repeated.

"How? The girl left town and remarried. She'd have nothing to gain by talking. As for the mother, all arrangements were made by me. You were never brought into it except as a name. I don't want to pry"—he leaned over to remove a pebble caught in the tread of his sneakers—"but I've often wondered why you didn't let me take the case into court, especially since you never intended to keep it secret from Daisy."

"I couldn't afford the scandal."

"But I'm sure we could have won it."

"The scandal would still be there. Besides, the child was—and is—mine. Would you ask me to perjure myself?"

"Of course not. But the girl's reputation alone would certainly have cast doubt on the legitimacy of her claim."

"In other words, I should have stayed on the boat until it tipped?"

"It didn't tip," Adam said.

"Well, this one would have."

"You didn't wait around to find out. You jumped overboard."

"Oh, stop it, Adam. It happened. It happened a long time ago. Why go into it all over again now?"

"Do you remember exactly how long ago it happened?"

"No. I try not to think about it."

"It was four years ago. To be precise, it was on December 2, 1955, that I made the first payment to Mrs. Rosario in my office. I looked it up before I left." He pulled the hood of his sea jacket over his head. "You'd better go home and have a talk with Daisy."

"Yes, I guess so."

"Well, I'll see you later. I want to stay down and make sure everything's tight and tidy on the sloop. I don't like the size of those swells. Sorry we missed our sail, by the way."

"I'm not. I didn't want to go anyway."

"As a matter of fact, I didn't want to ask you, either."

"So Daisy arranged it."

"Yes."

"Daisy's getting to be quite an arranger." Jim turned abruptly and walked toward the parking lot.

But he was not thinking of Daisy as he climbed into his car. He was thinking of the boat that hadn't tipped, and of the man who'd jumped overboard and almost hadn't made it to shore. A silly and dangerous thing, Adam had called it. Sometimes, though, silly and dangerous things were necessary. Sometimes people didn't jump; they were pushed.

She pretended, in case any of the fishermen or the dockhands were observing her, that she was standing against the wall of the harbormaster's office for shelter from the wind. She made a show of being cold—shivering, pulling up her coat collar, rubbing her hands together—until, as time passed, the show became real and the coldness penetrated every tissue of her body.

She watched the two of them talking on the seawall fifty yards away. They looked as though they might have been discussing the weather, but Daisy knew it couldn't have been the weather when Jim suddenly turned and walked away in a peculiarly abrupt manner, as if he and Adam had been quarreling. She waited until Jim got into his car. Then she started running toward Adam, who was going down the floating ramp to the mooring slips.

"Adam."

He turned and came back up the ramp to the guardrail, swaying with the movement of the waves. "Hello, Daisy. You missed Jim by a couple of minutes. He just left."

"That's too bad." There was nothing in her voice to indicate how long she had waited for Jim to leave.

"I may be able to catch him for you."

"Oh no, don't bother."

"He told me he was going home."

"I'll see him there, then," Daisy said. "You didn't stay out very long, did you?"

"We didn't get out at all. The storm warnings are up."

"That's a pity."

"Jim didn't seem to mind," Adam said dryly. "By the way, next time you arrange a sailing partner for me, make it someone who likes water, will you?"

"I'll try." Daisy leaned against the guardrail and looked down at the crabs scuttling around the rocks as if they were trying to find the biggest and safest one to weather out the storm. "Since you couldn't sail, what did you and Jim do?"

"We talked."

"About me?"

"Certainly. We always talk about you. I ask Jim how you are, and he tells me."

"Well, how am I? I'd like Jim's version of the state of my health, mental and otherwise."

Adam's smile was imperturbable. "Obviously, you're a little cranky today. That's my version, not Jim's."

"Did he tell you his plans for our anniversary?"

"We discussed a great many—"

"He's made some lovely plans, only I'm not supposed to know about them."

"Only you do."

"Oh yes. Word gets around. I must say you've kept the secret from me very well, considering the fact that you must have been the first to know."

"Keeping secrets," Adam said coolly, "is part of my job."

"How large is it going to be, my surprise, I mean?"

"Large enough but not too large."

"And the style?"

"The style will be stylish. Naturally."

"And you haven't the faintest notion what I am talking about, have you?"

He took her arm. "Come on, I'll buy you a cup of coffee at the Yacht Club."

"No."

"You don't have to snap at me. What's the matter with you today?"

"I'm glad you asked. I intended to tell you anyway. I found some check stubs this afternoon in Jim's desk. They indicate that he's been paying you $200 a month for some time."

"Well?"

"I asked my mother about it, and she claimed the money was for some acreage Jim was buying from you to build a mountain cabin on. I gather she was lying?"

"She may have been lying," Adam said with a shrug. "Or she may actually believe it's the truth."

"It isn't, of course."

"No."

"What was that money for, Adam?"

"To pay for the support of Jim's child by another woman." He deliberately looked away from her as he spoke because he didn't want to see the pain and shock in her face. "You were told about it at the time, Daisy. Don't you remember?"

"Jim's—child. How funny that sounds. So f-funny." She was clutching the guardrail as if she were afraid she was going to fling herself into the sea against her own will. "Was it—is it a boy or a girl?"

"I don't know."

"You don't *know?* Haven't you even asked him?"

"That wouldn't do much good. Jim doesn't know, either."

She turned to Adam, and her eyes looked blind, as if a film of ice had formed over the pupils. "You mean he hasn't even seen the child?"

"No. The woman left town before her delivery. Jim hasn't heard from her since."

"Surely she must have written him a letter when the baby was born."

"There was a mutual agreement between the two parties involved that no contact be made, and no correspondence entered into."

"But what a terrible thing, not to see your own child. It's inhuman. I can't believe that Jim would evade his responsibilities like—"

"Now wait a minute," Adam said crisply. "Jim evaded nothing. In fact, if he'd taken my advice, he wouldn't have admitted paternity at all. The woman had a flock of other children whose paternity was in question. She also had a husband, although he was allegedly out of the country at the time. If she had brought charges against him—and I doubt that she'd have had the nerve—she would have had a tough time proving anything. As things turned out, Jim quietly admitted paternity, and financial arrangements were made with Mrs. Rosario, the girl's mother, through me. That's all there was to it."

"All there was to it," she repeated. "You talk like a lawyer, Adam, in terms of cases and bringing charges, of proving or not proving. You don't talk about justice."

"In this case, I think justice was done."

"Do you call it justice that Jim, who so desperately wanted to father a child, should cut himself off from his own flesh and blood?"

"The arrangements were his."

"I can't believe that."

"Ask him."

"I can't believe that any man, let alone Jim, wouldn't want to see his own child at least once."

"Jim did the only sensible thing under the circumstances," Adam said. "And the circumstances weren't in the least what you seem to imagine in your sentimental way. No sentiment was involved. The girl thought nothing of Jim personally, nor he of her. The child was not the product of love. If it's still alive—and neither Juanita nor Mrs. Rosario would be in a hurry to inform us otherwise—it's half Mexican, its mother is mentally unstable—"

"Stop it. I don't want to hear anymore."

"I must present the facts bluntly to prevent you from sentimentalizing and perhaps doing something foolish which you might regret."

"Foolish?"

Adam pushed back the hood of his sea jacket, as if the day had suddenly turned warm. "I think you hired the detective to find that child."

"So you know about Pinata?"

"Yes."

"Does Jim know, too?"

"Yes."

"Well, I don't care," she said listlessly. "I don't really care. I guess it's time we laid our cards on the table. You're wrong, though, about my reason for hiring Pinata. Why should I hire someone to find a child I didn't even know existed?"

"You knew. You were told."

"I can't remember."

"You were told."

"Stop repeating it like that, as if forgetting were a cardinal sin. All right, I was told. I forgot. It's not the kind of thing a woman likes to remember about her husband."

"Some part of you remembered," Adam said. "Your dream shows that. The date on your tombstone was the day the first payment was made to Mrs. Rosario. It was also the day that Juanita left town, and, possibly, the day Jim confessed the affair to you. Was it?"

"I don't—I don't know."

"Try to think about it. Where were you that day?"

"Working. At the Clinic."

"What happened when you had finished working?"

"I went home, I guess."

"How?"

"I drove the car—no. No, I didn't." She was looking down at the water as if it were the deep dark well of memory. "Jim called for me. He was waiting in the car when I went out the back door. I started to cross the parking lot. Then I saw this young woman getting out of Jim's car. I'd seen her around the Clinic before. She was one of the regular patients, but I'd never paid much attention to her. I wouldn't have then either, if she hadn't been talking to Jim and if she hadn't been so terribly pregnant. Jim opened the door for me . . ."

"*Who was the girl?*" *Daisy said.*

"*Her name's Juanita Garcia.*"

"*I hope she has her hospital reservations all set.*"

"*Yes, so do I.*"

"*You look pale, Jim. Are you feeling sick?*"

He reached out and took her hand and held it so tightly that it began to feel numb. "*Listen to me, Daisy. I love you. You won't ever forget that, will you? I love you. Promise never to forget it. There's nothing in the world I wouldn't do to make you happy.*"

"*You don't very often talk like this, as if you were going to die or something.*"

"*The girl—the child—I've got to tell you—*"

"*I don't want to hear.*" *She turned and looked out of the car window, smiling the little smile she put on in the morning and washed off at night.* "*It gets dark so early, it's a pity we don't have daylight saving time all year.*"

"*Daisy, listen, nothing's going to happen. She won't cause any trouble. She's going away.*"

"*The paper says there'll be snow on the mountains again tomorrow.*"

"*Daisy, give me a chance to explain.*"

"*The mountains always look so much prettier with a little snow on them . . .*"

The Stranger

17

I have nothing to live for. Yet, as I move through the days, shackled to this dying body, I yearn to step free of it long enough to see you again, you and Ada, my beloved ones still . . .

THEY HAD ALREADY visited five taverns, and Fielding was getting tired of moving from place to place. But Juanita was all set to go again. She sat on the very edge of the stool as though she were waiting for some whistle to blow inside her as a signal to take off. *Aawouhee . . .*

"For Pete's sake, can't you settle down?" Fielding said. He was beginning to feel the drinks, not in his head, which was marvelously clear and sharp and full of wit and information, but in his legs, which were getting older and heavier and harder to drag in and out of doors. His legs wanted to sit down and rest while his head informed and amused Juanita or the bartender or the guy on the next stool. None of them was in his class, of course. He had to talk down to them, way down. But they listened; they could see he was a gentleman of the old school.

"What old school?" the bartender said, and his left eye closed in a quick, expert wink directed at Juanita.

"You miss the point, old chap," Fielding said. "No particular school is involved. It's a figure of speech."

"It is, eh?"

"Precisely. Speaking of old schools, Winston Churchill went to Harrow. You know what people who went to Harrow are called?"

"I guess they're called the same names as the rest of us."

"No, no, no. They are Harrovians."

"You don't say."

"It's God's truth."

"Your friend's getting crocked," the bartender told Juanita.

Juanita gave him a blank stare. "No, he's not. He always talks that way. Hey, Foster, are you getting crocked?"

"Absolutely not," Fielding said. "I'm feeling absolutely shape-ship. How are you feeling, my dear?"

"My feet hurt."

"Take off your shoes."

Juanita began tugging at her left shoe, using both hands. "They're genuine snakeskin. I paid $19 for them."

"Your tips must be good."

"No. I got a rich uncle."

She put the sharp-toed, needle-heeled shoes side by side on the counter in front of her. She had ordinary-sized feet, but out of their proper place the shoes looked enormous and misshapen, as if they belonged to some giant with a taste for pain.

Fielding's drink seemed extremely small in comparison with the shoes, and he pointed this out to the bartender, who told Juanita to put the shoes on again and quit messing around.

"I'm not messing around."

"When I come over to your joint for a drink, I don't undress and leave my clothes on the counter."

"Well, why don't you?" Juanita said. "I think it'd be a riot. I can just see Mrs. Brewster swelling up and turning blue."

"If you want to do a striptease, sit in the back booth so the police patrol can't see you. Saturday night they go past maybe ten times."

"I'm not scared of the cops."

"Yeah? You want to know what happened up in Frisco the other day? I read it in the paper. This girl wasn't doing nothing except walking around in her bare feet, and by God, the cops arrested her."

Juanita said she didn't believe it, but she picked up the shoes and her half-finished drink and headed for the back booth, trailed by Fielding.

"Hurry up and finish your drink," she said as she sat down. "I'm sick of this place."

"We just got here."

"I want to go where we can have some fun. Nobody's having any fun around here."

"I am. Can't you hear me laughing? Ho ho ho. Ha ha ha."

Juanita was sitting with both hands clenched around her glass as if she were trying to crush it. "I hate this town. I wish I'd never've come back. I wish I was a million miles away and never had to see my old lady again or anyone else. I'd like to go where everybody is a stranger and don't know anything about me."

"They'd find out soon enough."

"How?"

"You'd tell them," Fielding said. "Just the way I did. I've hit a hundred towns as a stranger, and inside of ten minutes I was talking to somebody about myself. Maybe I wasn't speaking the truth, and maybe I was using a false name, but I was talking, see? And talking is telling. So pretty soon you're no stranger any longer, so you head for the next town. Don't be a patsy, kid. You stick around here, close to that rich uncle of yours."

Juanita let out an unexpected little giggle. "I can't very well stick close to him. He's dead."

"He is, eh?"

"You sound like you don't believe I ever had a rich uncle."

"Did you ever see him?"

"When I was a kid, he came to visit us. He brought me a silver belt, real silver made by the Indians."

"Where did he live?"

"New Mexico. He had important cattle interests there. That's how he made all his money."

He didn't have any money, Fielding thought, *except a few bucks on Saturday, which were gone by Sunday because he couldn't help drawing to an inside straight.* "And he left this money of his to you?"

"To my mother, on account of she was his sister. Every month she gets a check from the lawyer, regular as clockwork, out of the—I guess you call it the trust fund."

"Did you ever see any of these checks?"

"I saw the money. My mother sent me some every month to help feed the kids. Two hundred dollars," she added proudly. "So in case you think I've *got* to work in a crummy dive like the Velada, you got another think coming. I do it for the kicks. It's more fun than sticking around the house watching a bunch of kids."

To Fielding, the story was getting crazier by the minute. He signaled the bartender to bring another round of drinks while he did some rapid calculation. An income of $200 a month would mean a trust fund of around $50,000. The last time he'd seen Camilla, the man had been unemployed and trying desperately to raise the money for some food and clothing. Yet Juanita didn't appear to be lying. Her pride in having a rich uncle with important cattle interests was as obviously genuine as her pride in the $19 snakeskin shoes. The whole thing was beginning to smell like a shakedown, but Fielding felt almost certain that if Juanita was part of it, she had no knowledge of her role. The girl was being used by someone more intelligent and cunning than she was. *But that's crazy,* he thought. *She's the one who gets the money; she's admitted it.*

"What was the name of the lawyer?" he said.

"What lawyer?"

"The one who sends the checks?"

"Why should I tell you?"

"Because we're friends, aren't we?"

"I don't know if we're friends or not," Juanita said with a shrug. "You ask a lot of questions."

"That's because I'm interested in you."

"A lot of people have been interested in me. It never got me nowhere. Anyhow, I don't know his name."

"Does he live in town?"

"Are you deaf or something? I told you I never saw the checks, and I don't know the lawyer. My old lady sent me the money every month from my uncle's trust fund."

"This uncle of yours, how did he die?"

"He was killed."

"What do you mean, killed?"

Juanita's mouth opened in a yawn a little too wide and loud to be genuine. "What do you want to talk about an old dead uncle for?"

"Old dead uncles intrigue me, if they happen to be rich."

"There's nothing in it for you."

"I know that. I'm just curious. How did he die?"

"He got in an automobile accident in New Mexico about four years ago." In an attempt to appear detached, Juanita stared at a patch of grimy pink roses on the wallpaper. But Fielding had the idea that this was a subject which interested and puzzled her and which she actually wanted to discuss in spite of her apparent reluctance. "He was killed right away, before the priest could give him the last rites. That's why my old lady's always praying and burning candles for him, so he'll get into heaven anyway. You saw the candle, didn't you?"

"Yes."

"It's funny her making such a fuss over a brother she never saw for years. It's like she did something wrong to him and is trying to make up for it."

"If she did something wrong to him, he surely wouldn't have left her his money."

"Maybe he didn't know about whatever she'd done." She reached out and began tracing the outlines of one of the pink roses on the wallpaper. Her sharp fingernail cut a path through the grease. "It's like he only got to be important by dying and leaving the money. She didn't even talk about him when he was alive."

He didn't talk about her, either, Fielding thought. Only once, right at the end: *"I'd like to see my sister Filomena before I go." "You can't do it, Curly." "I want her to pray for me; she's a good woman." "You're crazy to take a chance seeing anyone now. It's too dangerous." "No. I must say good-bye to her."* At the time he'd barely had a voice to say good-bye, let alone a cent to leave anyone.

"Did he make a will?" Fielding asked.

"I never saw it. She says he did."

"Don't you believe her?"

"I don't know."

"When did you first hear about it?"

"One day before Paul was born, she suddenly announced that Uncle Carl had died and left a will. If I did this and that, I would get $200 a month."

"And what was 'this and that'?"

"Mostly I was to leave town right away and have the baby born in L.A. It seemed kind of crazy him being interested in the baby when he never even sent the other kids anything at Christmastime. When I asked my old lady about it, she said Uncle Carl wanted the baby born in L.A. because that's where he was born. For sentimental reasons, like."

He was born in Arizona, Fielding thought. *He must have told me a dozen times. Flagstaff, Arizona. And nobody knows better than me that he didn't die in any automobile accident in New Mexico. He died right here, less than a mile from this very spot, with his own knife between his ribs.*

Only on one count was the girl's story correct: there had been no last rites for Camilla.

"I guess he must have been very sentimental," Juanita said. "So's my old lady sometimes. A funny thing, there I was in L.A. with everything going pretty good, and suddenly she gets this idea she wants to see me again, me and the kids. She wrote me a letter how she was getting old and she had a bad heart and she was lonely all by herself and she wanted me to come visit her for a while. Well, Joe had just lost his job, and it seemed like a good time to come. I must've been crazy. An hour after I stepped inside that door, she was screaming at me and I was screaming back. That's the way it is. She wants me around, and she wants me far away. How the hell can I be both? Well, this time I'm going to settle it for good. I'm never coming back once I get out of this town again."

"Just make sure you get out."

"Why?"

"Be careful."

"What's to be careful about?"

"Oh, things. People." He would have liked to tell her the truth at this point, or as much of it as he knew. But he didn't trust her not to talk. And if she talked in front of the wrong people, she would put herself in danger as well as him. Perhaps she was already in danger, but she certainly seemed unaware of it. She was still busy outlining the wallpaper roses with her fingernail, looking as rapt and dedicated as an artist or a child.

Fielding said, "Stop that for a minute, will you?"

"What?"

"Stop fooling around with the wallpaper."

"I'm making it prettier."

"Yeah, I know that, but I want you to listen to me. Are you listening?"

"Well, sure."

"I came to town to see Jim Harker." He leaned across the table and repeated the name carefully. "Jim Harker."

"So what?"

"You remember him, don't you?"

"I never heard of him before."

"Think."

Her two eyebrows leaped at each other into the middle of her forehead, like animals about to fight. They didn't quite meet. "I wish people would quit telling me to think. I think. Thinking's easy. It's *not* thinking that's hard. I think all the time, but I can't think about Jim Harker if I never even heard of Jim Harker. Think, hell."

The single monosyllable had destroyed her creative impulse as well as her good mood. She turned from the wall and began wiping the grime off her hands with a paper napkin. When she had finished, she crumpled the napkin into a ball and threw it on the floor with a sound of despair that she had ever tried to make things prettier in the world.

The bartender came around the end of the counter, frowning as if he intended to rebuke her for messing up his place. Instead, he said, "Mrs. Brewster just called, wanted to know if you were here."

Juanita's face immediately assumed the peculiarly bland expression that indicated she was interested. "What'd you say to her?"

"That I'd keep an eye out for you, and if you showed up, I'd tell you to call her back. So now I'm telling you."

"Thanks," Juanita said without moving.

"You gonna do it?"

"So she can go blabbing to my old lady? What do you think I am, like stupid?"

"You better call her," the bartender said stubbornly. "She's at the Velada."

"So she's at the Velada. And I'm here, at—what's the name of this dump?"

"El Paraiso."

"The Paradise. Hey, Foster, ain't that a laugh? You and me are strangers in paradise."

The bartender turned to Fielding. One of his eyelids was twitching in unexpressed irritation. "If you're a friend of hers, you better persuade her to talk to Mrs. Brewster. There've been a couple of men looking for her at the Velada. One of them was a private detective."

A *detective*, Fielding thought. *So Pinata was in this, too.*

He wasn't exactly surprised. He'd been half expecting it ever since Daisy's letter was delivered to him at the warehouse. There was no other way for her to have found out where he was working except through Pinata. Obviously, if Pinata was looking for Juanita, that was what Daisy had hired him to do. But how did Camilla come into it? As far as Fielding knew, the name hadn't been mentioned in Daisy's presence; she was unaware such a man had ever existed.

He realized suddenly that both Juanita and the bartender were staring at him as if they were waiting for an answer. He hadn't heard any question.

"Well," the bartender said.

"Well, what?"

"You know any private detective around town?"

"No."

"That's funny, because he was looking for you, too."

"Why me? I haven't done anything."

Juanita protested shrilly that she hadn't done anything, either, but neither of the men paid any attention.

Fielding was squinting up at the bartender as if he found it difficult to focus his eyes. "You said two men came to the Velada. Who was the other one?"

"Search me."

"A cop?"

"Mrs. Brewster would have mentioned it if he'd been a cop. All she told me, he was a big man with blond hair and he acted funny. Jumpy, like. You know anybody like that?"

"Sure, lots of them." *One in particular,* Fielding thought. *He warn't jumpy the last time I saw him, in Chicago, but now he has reason to be.* "Some of my best friends are jumpy."

"Yeah, I bet." The bartender glanced briefly at Juanita. "I gotta get back to work. Don't say I didn't warn you."

When he had gone, Juanita leaned across the table and said confidentially, "I think Mrs. Brewster was making it all up so I'll get scared and go home. I don't believe there's any detective looking for me, or any big blond man, either. Why would they want to see me for?"

"Maybe they have some questions."

"What about?"

He hesitated a minute. He wanted to help the girl because in a disturbing way she reminded him of Daisy. It was as if some perverse fate had singled them both out to be victims, Daisy and Juanita, who had never met and perhaps never would, although they had so much in common. He felt sorry for them. But Fielding's pity, like his love and even his hate, was a variable thing, subject to changes in the weather, melting in the summer, freezing in the winter, blowing away in a high wind. Only by a miracle did it survive at all.

Proof of its survival was in the single monosyllable he spoke now. "Paul."

"Paul who?"

"Your son."

"Why would they ask questions about him? He's too young to be in any trouble. He's not even four. All he can do is maybe break windows or steal a little."

"Don't be naive, girl."

"What's that mean?"

"Innocent."

Juanita's eyes widened in outrage. "I'm not innocent. I may be dumb, but I'm not innocent."

"All right, all right, skip it."

"I'm not going to skip it. I want to know how come two men are so interested in my kids all of a sudden."

"Not the others, just Paul."

"Why?"

"I think they're trying to find out who his father is."

"Well, of all the goddamn nerve," Juanita said. "What business is it of theirs?"

"I can't answer that."

"Not that it's any of your business, either, but it so happens I was *married* at the time. I had a *husband*."

"What was his name?"

"Pedro Garcia."

"And that's who Paul's father is?"

Juanita picked up one of the snakeskin shoes, and Fielding thought for a moment that she was going to hit him with it. Instead, she began pushing it on her left foot. "By God, I don't have to sit here and be insulted by no lousy imitation district attorney."

"I'm sorry, I have to ask these questions. I'm trying to help you, but I've got my own hide to save, too. What happened to Garcia?"

"I divorced him."

Fielding knew that at least this part of her story was a deliberate lie. After he'd left Pinata's office the previous Monday, he'd gone to City Hall to check the records. It was Garcia who'd brought the divorce suit; Juanita had not contested it or asked for alimony or child support, a curious omission if the child was actually Garcia's. It occurred to Fielding now, not for the first time, that perhaps Juanita herself didn't know who the boy's father was and didn't care much, either. He might have been someone she picked up in a bar or on the street, or a sailor from a ship visiting the harbor or an airman down from Vandenberg. Juanita's pregnancies were inclined to be casual. One thing was certain: the little boy Paul bore no resemblance to Jim Harker.

Juanita finished squeezing her feet into the shoes and tucked her purse under her arm. She seemed ready to leave, but she made no move to do so. "What do you mean, you got your own hide to save?"

"The detective's looking for me, too."

"That's funny when you come to think of it. Someone must've told him we were together."

"Mrs. Brewster maybe."

"No." Her tone was positive. "She wouldn't give a detective the time of day."

"No one else knows except her and your mother."

"By God, that's it. That's who told him, my old lady."

"But first someone else must have given him your address," Fielding said. "Maybe the busboy or one of the waitresses."

"They don't know my address. I never tell people like that nothing personal about myself."

"He found out from somewhere."

"All right, so he found out from somewhere. What do I care? I haven't committed any crime. Why should I run away?"

"It's possible," Fielding said carefully, "that you're a part of something you're not fully aware of."

"Like what?"

"I can't explain it to you." He couldn't explain it to himself, either, because there were gaps in his knowledge that must be filled in. Once they were filled in, his duty would be done and he could be on his away again. The important thing now was to get rid of the girl. She was too conspicuous, and he had to travel light and fast and, if he was unlucky, far.

Luck. Fielding believed in it as some men believed in God, country, or mother. To luck he credited his triumphs; on lack of it he blamed his misfortunes. Several times a day he rubbed the tiny rabbit's foot that dangled from his watch chain, always expecting miracles from the fragile inert scrap of bone and fur, but not complaining if a miracle failed to occur. It was this quality of fatalism that always baffled his second wife and enraged his first. He knew now, for example, that he was inviting disaster in the same way that he knew he was getting drunk. He accepted both as things over which he personally had no control. Whatever happened, how the dice rolled, the ball bounced, the cookie crumbled, would be a matter of luck or lack of it. His sense of responsibility was no greater than that of the severed paw he wore on his watch chain.

"Why can't you explain things to me?" Juanita said.

"Because I can't."

"All this hinting around like I was going to be killed or something—well, it don't scare me. Nobody'd want to kill me. Why, nobody even hates me except my old lady and sometimes Joe and maybe a few others."

"I didn't say you were going to be killed."

"It sounded like that."

"I just warned you to be careful."

"How the hell can I be careful if I don't know who of or what of?" She leaned across the table, studying him soberly and carefully. "You know what I think? I think you're a crackpot."

"That's your considered opinion, eh?"

"It sure is."

Fielding wasn't offended. He was, in fact, quite pleased because once again luck had taken charge of his affairs. By calling him a crackpot the girl had relieved him of any sense of responsibility toward her. It made what he intended to do to her easier, even inevitable: *She called me a crackpot, therefore it's all right to steal her car.*

The immediate problem was to get her away from the table for a few minutes and make sure she left her purse behind with the keys in it.

He said abruptly, "You'd better call Mrs. Brewster."

"Why?"

"For your own sake—leaving me out of it entirely—you should find out everything you can about the two men who are looking for you."

"I don't want to talk to her. She's always telling me what to do."

"Well, in case you change your mind . . . " He took a dime out of his pocket and laid it on the table in front of her.

Juanita stared at the coin with a child's petty avarice. "I don't know what to say to her."

"Let her do the talking."

"Maybe it's all lies about the two men. She wants me to get scared and go home."

"I don't think so. It strikes me she's a pretty good friend of yours."

It was the dime that clinched her decision. She slid it off the table with the casual ease of an experienced waitress. "Watch my purse, will you?"

"All right."

"I'll be back."

"Sure."

She teetered across the floor to the phone booth, which was jammed in a corner between the end of the bar and the door to the kitchen. Fielding waited, stroking his little rabbit's foot with affection as one might stroke a living pet. Once again it was a matter of luck whether Juanita could remember Mrs. Brewster's phone number or whether she would have to look it up in the directory. If she had to look it up, he would have thirty seconds or more to open the purse, search through all Juanita's junk to find the keys, and reach the front door. If she dialed the number directly, he'd be forced to grab the purse and run, taking a chance on getting past the bartender and the half-dozen customers he was serving. The sentimental side of Fielding's nature, always erratic after a few drinks and apt to disappear entirely after a few more, balked at the idea of stealing a woman's purse. The car was a different matter. He'd stolen quite a few cars in his lifetime; he had also put the bite on a great many women. But he had never actually stolen a purse from any of them. Besides, there were the risks involved: the thing was too large to put in his pocket or hide under his coat. There seemed only one other alternative—to dump its contents out of sight on the seat beside him, pick out the car keys, and replace the purse on the table. The whole operation would require no more than four or five seconds . . .

Juanita was dialing.

The purse lay within reach of his hand, a black plastic rectangle with a gold clasp and handle. The plastic was so shiny that Fielding could see in miniature the reflection of his own face. It looked curiously young and unlined and innocent, not the image that stared back at him in the mornings between flyspecks and dabs of toothpaste and other unidentified residues of life. This face in the plastic belonged to his youth, as the picture in Mrs. Rosario's bedroom belonged to Camilla's youth. *Camilla*, he thought, and the knife of pain that stabbed him between the ribs seemed as real as the *navaja* that had so senselessly killed his friend. *We were both young together, Curly and I. It's too late for him now, but there's still a chance for me.*

He wanted suddenly and desperately to take the purse, not for the money or for the car keys which were in it, but for that reflection of his own face, that innocence intact, that youth preserved in plastic and protected from the sins of time.

He glanced across at the phone booth. Juanita, scowling, was in the act of hanging up. He thought that his opportunity was lost, that she had reached the Velada and been told Mrs. Brewster had gone. Then he saw her pick up the directory chained to the wall, and he knew she must have received a busy signal and decided to recheck the phone number. Luck was giving him another chance.

His eyes returned to the purse, but this time his angle of vision was different and the image that stared back at him was like the images in a fun house. The forehead projected out to the right and the jaw to the left, and in between was a distorted nose and two malevolent slits of eyes. With a little cry of rage he grabbed the purse off the table and dumped its contents on the seat beside him. The car keys were on a small chain separate from Juanita's other keys. He slid them into his pocket, stood up, and walked toward the front door. He didn't hurry. The trick was to appear casual. It was the kind of thing he'd done a hundred times before, the friendly, final good-bye-see-you-later to the landlady or grocer or hotel clerk or liquor dealer whom he had no intention of paying or ever seeing again.

He smiled at the bartender as he passed. "Tell Juanita I'll be back in a few minutes, will you?"

"You didn't pay for the last round of drinks."

"Oh, didn't I? Terribly sorry." It was a delay he hadn't anticipated, but he kept the smile on his face as he fished around in his pocket for a dollar. The only sign of his anxiety was a brief, nervous glance in the direction of the phone booth. "Here you are."

"Thanks," the bartender said.

"Juanita's talking to Mrs. Brewster. I thought I'd take a little walk to clear my head."

"You do that."

"See you later."

As soon as Fielding was outside, he dropped the pretense of being casual. He hurried along the sidewalk, the cold brisk air slapping his face with a wintry hand.

At this point he had no clear or extensive plan of action. Impulsively and without thought of the consequences, he had rushed into the middle of something he only half understood.

Getting the car and going to Daisy's house—this was as far ahead as he could see. At Daisy's house he would almost inevitably run into Ada, and the idea excited him. At this stage he was quite ready to meet her. Sober, he couldn't have faced her; drunk, he would certainly pick a quarrel, perhaps a very violent one. But right now, somewhere in between, he felt able to deal with her, confront her without malice, expose her without cruelty. Right now he could teach her a few lessons in civilization, in manners: *My dear Ada, it grieves me to bring this to your attention but in the interests of justice, I must insist you reveal the truth about your part in this devious little scheme . . .*

It didn't even seem ironic to him that he should be planning remarks about truth and justice when, in fact, his whole life had been a marathon race, with truth a few jumps ahead of him and justice a few jumps behind. He had never caught up with the one, and the other had never caught up with him.

The car was at the end of the block, parked in front of a long frame building with a dimly lit sign announcing its function: *billar.* The sign, printed only in Spanish, made it clear that whites were not welcome. Although the place was jammed, the noise coming out of the open door was subdued, punctuated by the click of balls and score racks. A group of young Negroes and Mexicans were hanging around outside, one of them with a cue in his hand. He was using the cue like a drum major, raising it and lowering it in time to some rhythms he heard in his head or felt in his bones.

As Fielding approached, the boy pointed the cue at him and said, "Rat ta ta ta ta. Man, you're dead."

Sober, Fielding might have been a little intimidated by the group; drunk, he would certainly have made trouble. But in between, right now—"That's pretty funny, kid. You ought to be on TV"—and he brushed past the boy with a grin and made his way to the car.

There were two keys on the ring he'd taken from Juanita's purse—one for the luggage compartment, the other for the doors and ignition. He tried the wrong key on the door first. It was a bad start, made worse by the fact that the boys were watching him with sober interest, as if they knew perfectly well what he intended to do and were waiting to see how he did it and if he would get caught. Later—if there was a later—they would be able to give a good description of both him and the car. Or perhaps Juanita had already called the police, and they had a description on the radio right now. He had counted on her distrust of officials to prevent such a move, but Juanita was unpredictable.

Once inside her car, he had a moment of panic when he looked at the dashboard. He hadn't driven a car for a long time, and never one like this, with so many buttons and switches that he couldn't tell which was supposed to turn on the lights. Even without lights, though, he knew where to find the most important object in the car—the half-pint of whiskey he'd bought at one of the bars and later hidden on the floorboard under the seat. The bottle had hardly touched his lips before he began feeling the effects of its contents. First there was a fleeting moment of guilt, followed by the transition of guilt to blame, blame to revenge, revenge to power: *By God, I'm going to teach all of them a lesson.*

In an ordinary person these changes of emotion would take time to evolve. But Fielding was like a man who's been hypnotized so often that a snap of the fingers will put him under. A smell of the cork, a tilt of the bottle, and *By God, I'll teach those smug, hypocritical, patronizing bastards.*

One of the young Negro men had approached the car and was kicking the right rear tire absently, as if he had no motive other than that the tire was there to kick and he didn't have anything more important to do.

Fielding shouted through the closed window, "Get your black feet off that tire, coon boy!" He knew these were fighting words, but he knew, too, in that corner of his mind which still had access to the real world, that the insult had been muffled by the window glass and scrambled by the wind.

He pressed the starter button. The car gave a couple of forward lurches, then the engine died, and he saw that he hadn't released the emergency brake. He released it, started the engine again, and looked in the rearview mirror to make sure the road was clear of traffic behind him. There were no nearby cars, and he was on the point of pulling away from the curb when he saw two Juanitas running down the middle of the road, barefooted, their arms flailing like windmills in a gale, their skirts ballooning around their thighs.

The sight of these two furies coming at him made him panic. He pressed the accelerator right down to the floorboard. The engine flooded and died again, and he knew that he had no choice but to wait.

He turned down the window and looked back at the road, narrowing his eyes until the two Juanitas merged into one. He could hear her screaming twenty yards away. A scream in this part of town was interpreted not as a cry for help, but as a sign of impending trouble: the group of young Negroes and Mexicans had disappeared without a trace, and the doors below the sign *billar* had closed as if in response to an electronic ear alert to the decibels of danger. When and if the police arrived, nobody would know anything about a car thief and a screaming woman.

Fielding glanced at the clock on the dashboard. It was 6:30. There was still plenty of time. All he had to do was keep his head, and the girl would be handled easily enough. The fact that she was running toward the car indicated that she hadn't called the police. The important thing was to stay calm, play it cool . . .

But as he watched her approach, rage beat against his temples and exploded behind his eyes with flashes of colored lights. Between flashes Juanita's face appeared, streaked with black tears, red from cold and exertion.

"You—sonna bitch—stole my car."

"I was coming to pick you up. I told the bartender I'd be right back."

"Dirty—liar."

He reached across the seat and unlocked and opened the right front door. "Get in."

"I'm gonna—calla cops."

"Get in."

The repetition of the direct order and the opening of the door had the same effect on her as his putting the dime on the table in the café. The dime was there to be picked up; the door was there to be entered. She went around the front of the car, keeping her eyes fixed steadily on Fielding as if she suspected he might try to run her down.

She got in, still breathing hard from her sprint down the road. "You sonofabitch, what've you got to say?"

"Nothing you'd believe."

"I wouldn't believe nothing you said, you—"

"Take it easy." Fielding lit a cigarette. The flare of the match blended with the lights flashing behind his eyes, so that he wasn't quite sure which was real. "I'm going to make a bargain with you."

"*You* make a bargain with *me?* That's a laugh. You've got more guts than a sausage factory."

"I want to borrow your car for a couple of hours."

"Oh, you do, eh? And what do I get out of it?"

"Some information."

"Who says I want information from an old crackpot like you?"

"Watch your language, girl."

Although he didn't raise his voice, she seemed to sense the force of his anger, and when she spoke again, she sounded almost conciliatory. "What kind of information?"

"About your rich uncle."

"Why should I want to hear about him for? He's been dead and buried for four years. Besides, how would you know anything about him that my old lady didn't tell me already?"

"There's no similarity between what your old mother told you and what I'm going to tell you. If you cooperate. All you have to do is lend me your car for a couple of hours. I'll drive you home now and bring the car back to your house when I've finished my errand."

Juanita rubbed her cheeks with the back of her hand, looking surprised to find tears there, as if she'd already forgotten that she had wept and why. "I don't want to go home."

"You will."

"Why will I?"

"You're going to be curious to find out why your mother has been lying in her teeth all these years."

He started the car and pulled away from the curb. Juanita seemed too astonished to object. "Lying? My old lady? You must be crazy. Why, she's so pure she . . ." Juanita used an ancient and earthy figure of speech without embarrassment. "I don't believe you, Foster. I think you're making all this up so you can get the car."

"You don't have to believe me. Just ask her."

"Ask her what?"

"Where your rich uncle got his money."

"He had cattle interests."

"He was a cowhand."

"He owned—"

"He owned nothing but the shirt on his back," Fielding said, "and ten chances to one he'd stolen that." This was not true, but Fielding couldn't admit it, even to himself. He had to keep himself convinced that Camilla had been a liar, a thief, and a scoundrel.

Juanita said, "Then where did the money come from that he left to me in the trust fund?"

"That's what I'm trying to tell you—there is no trust fund."

"But I get $200 regular every month. Where does it come from?"

"You'd better ask your mother."

"You talk like she's a crook or something."

"Or something."

He turned left at the next corner. He wasn't familiar with the city, but in his years of wandering, he had taught himself to observe landmarks carefully so he could always find his way back to his hotel or rooming house. He did it now automatically, like a blind man counting the number of steps between places.

Juanita was sitting on the edge of the seat, tense and rigid, one hand clutching her plastic purse and the other the snakeskin shoes. "She's no crook."

"Ask her."

"I don't have to. Her and me, maybe we don't get along so buddy-buddy, but I swear she's no crook. Unless she was doing something for somebody else."

"Unless that, yes," Fielding said blandly.

"How come you pretend to know so much about my uncle and my old lady?"

"Camilla was a friend of mine once."

"But you never even saw my old lady till this afternoon." She paused to give this some thought. "Why, you never even saw *me* till that day you got in the fight with Joe."

"I'd heard about you."

"Where? How?"

He was tempted, momentarily, to tell her where and how, to show her the letter from Daisy he'd taken out of the old suitcase that morning. It was this letter, dated almost four years previously, that had sent him to the Velada in the first place, in the hope of finding, or getting some information about, a young woman called Juanita Garcia. That she happened to be there at the time was luck, but he still wasn't sure whether it was good luck or bad luck.

That her husband happened to drop in and started the quarrel was pure bad luck: it had put Fielding's timing off, it had temporarily dislodged his whole purpose in coming to town, and, what might turn out to be the worst misfortune yet, it had brought Pinata into the affair. Pinata, and then Camilla. One of the most terrible shocks in Fielding's life occurred at the moment he looked across Mrs. Rosario's bedroom and saw the picture of Camilla.

That's when I should have stopped, he thought. *I should have walked away right then.*

Even now he didn't know why he hadn't stopped; he was just aware that the gnawing restlessness inside him disappeared when he was playing a game of danger, whether it was a simple matter of cheating at cards or defrauding a landlady, or whether it involved, as it did now, his own life or death.

"I don't believe you ever heard of me before," Juanita said, and it was obvious from her tone that she wanted to believe it, that she was flattered by the notion of being recognized by strangers, like a movie star. "I mean, I'm not famous or anything, so how could you?"

"Well, I did."

"Tell me about it."

"Some other time."

The idea of showing her the letter and watching her reactions appealed to his sense of dramatic irony. But the references to herself were decidedly unflattering, and he was afraid to take a chance on making her angry again. Besides, the letter was, in its way, a very special one. Of all the times that Daisy had written to him, this was the only time she had ever expressed genuine and deep emotions.

Dear Daddy, I wish you were here tonight so you and I could talk about things the way we used to. Talking to Mother or Jim isn't the same. It always ends up not as a conversation, but as their telling me.

Christmas is nearly here. How I've always loved it, the gaiety and the singing and the wrapping of presents. But this year I feel nothing. There is no good cheer in this childless house. I use that word, childless, with bitter irony: I found out a week ago today that another woman is giving—or has already given—birth to a baby fathered by Jim. I can almost see you now as you read this, and hear you saying, Now Daisy baby, are you sure you've got the facts straight? Yes, I'm sure. Jim has admitted it. And here's the awful thing about it—whatever I'm suffering, Jim is suffering twice as much, and neither of us seems able to help the other. Poor Jim, how desperately he's wanted children, but he will never even see this one. The woman has left town, and arrangements for her support have been made through Adam Burnett, Jim's lawyer.

After this letter is written, I will do my utmost to forget what has happened and to go on being a good wife to Jim. It's over and done with. I can't change anything, so I must forgive and forget. The forgiving is easy; the other might be impossible, but I'll try. After tonight, I'll try. Tonight I feel like wallowing in this ugly thing like a pig in a mudhole.

I've seen the woman many times. (How the ironies pile up once they start! It's as if they're self-multiplying like amoebae.) She has been a patient at the Clinic for years, off and on. Perhaps this is where Jim first met her while he was waiting for me. I haven't asked him, and he hasn't told me. Anyway, her name is Juanita Garcia, and she's been working as a waitress at the Velada Café, which is owned by a friend of her mother. She is married and has five other children. Jim didn't tell me this, either; I looked up her file at the Clinic. Also from her file I found out something else, and if you aren't already choking on ironies, try swallowing this one: Mrs. Garcia was arrested last week on charges of child neglect. I hope to God Jim never finds this out; it would only increase his misery to think of the kind of life his own child will have.

I haven't told Mother, but I suspect Jim has. She's going around with that kind of desperate, determined cheerfulness she puts on in emergencies. Like last year when I found out I was sterile, she drove me crazy counting blessings and pointing out silver linings.

One question keeps going through my mind: why did Jim have to tell me the truth? His confession hasn't lessened his own suffering. It has, in fact, added mine to his. Why, if he never intended to see the woman again, and the child, didn't he keep them both a secret? But I mustn't dwell on such things. I have promised myself I will forget, and I will. I must. Pray for me, Daddy. And please answer this. Please.

Your loving daughter, Daisy

He hadn't answered it. At the time there were a dozen reasons why not, but as the years passed, he'd forgotten the reasons and only the fact remained: he hadn't answered this simplest of requests. Every time he opened the old suitcase, that word *please* flew up out of it and struck him in the face . . .

Well, he was answering it now, and at a much greater risk than if he'd done it in the first place. It was a stroke of incredibly bad luck that the sister Camilla had referred to before he died had turned out to be Mrs. Rosario. And yet Fielding realized now that if he'd been thinking logically, he should have made some connection between Camilla, on the one hand, and Juanita, on the other. Daisy's letter was dated December 9. In it she stated she'd first heard about Juanita's child a week before, which would make it December 2. This was also the day Camilla had died and Juanita had left town. A connection between the two events was inescapable. And the link must be Mrs. Rosario, who, behind her crucifixes, madonnas, and shrines, seemed as devious an operator as Fielding himself.

"Ask your mother," he said, "how she wangled that money."

Juanita was stubborn. "Maybe someone gave it to her."

"Why?"

"There's some people that *like* to give away money."

"They do, eh? Well, I hope I meet one before I die."

They had reached Granada Street. It was lined on both sides with cars parked for the night; garages were a luxury in this part of town.

Fielding remembered the house not by number, but by its bright pink paint. As he braked the car, he noticed a new blue and white Cadillac pulling away from the curb with an anxious shriek of rubber.

"I'll be back in two hours," he told Juanita.

"You better be."

"I give you my word."

"I don't want your word. I want my car."

"You'll have it. In two hours."

He had no idea whether he'd be back in two hours, two days, or ever. It would all be a matter of luck.

18

I came here to see you, but I lack the courage. That is why I am writing, to feel in touch with you for a little, to remind myself that my death will be only partial; you will be left, you will be the proof that I ever lived at all. I leave nothing else . . .

THE BLUE AND white Cadillac was just as conspicuous on Opal Street as it had been on Granada, but there was no one around to notice. At the first drop of rain the sidewalks had emptied. Jim turned off the windshield wipers and the lights and waited in the cold darkness. Although he didn't look either at his watch or the clock on the dashboard, he knew it was five minutes to seven. During this week of crisis he seemed to carry around inside him his own clock, and he could hear the seconds ticking off with ominous accuracy. Time had become a living, breathing thing, attached to him as inexorably as a remora to a shark's belly, never sleeping or relaxing its grip, so that even when he awoke in the middle of the night, it would communicate to him the exact hour and minute.

Across the street the lights were on in Pinata's office, and a man's shadow was moving back and forth past the window. An overpowering hatred surged up Jim's body like a bore tide up a river, roiling his reason, muddying his perceptions. The hatred was divided equally between Pinata and Fielding—Pinata because he had dredged up the business about Carlos Camilla, Fielding because he had, in his impulsive, irresponsible manner, caused the events of the past week. It was his seemingly innocent phone call on Sunday night that had triggered Daisy's dream. If it hadn't been for the dream, Camilla would still be dead, Juanita forgotten, Mrs. Rosario unknown.

He had questioned Ada Fielding thoroughly about the phone call from Fielding, trying to make her remember exactly what she'd said that evening that might have disturbed Daisy and started the train of thought that led to the dream. "What did you say to her, Ada?" "I told her it was a wrong number." "What else?" "I said it was some drunk. God knows that part of it was true enough." "There must be something more." "Well, I wanted to make it sound realistic, so I told her the drunk had called me baby . . ."

Baby. The mere word might have caused the dream and led to Daisy's recollection of the day she'd forced herself to forget, the day Jim had told her about Juanita's baby. So it was Fielding who had started it, that unpredictable man whose friendship could be more disastrous than his enmity. Questions without answers dangled in Jim's mind like kites without strings. What had brought Fielding to San Félice in the first place? What were his intentions? Where was he now? Was the girl still with him? Mrs. Rosario hadn't been able to answer any of these questions, but she'd answered another before it was asked: Fielding had seen the boy, Paul.

Jim watched the raindrops zigzagging across the windshield, and he thought of Daisy walking in the rain on Laurel Street trying to find her lost day as if it were something that was still there in the old house. Tears came into his eyes, of love, of pity, of helplessness. He could no longer keep her safe and protect her from knowledge about her father that would cause her pain for the rest of her life. Yet he knew he must keep on trying, right to the end. "*We can't let her find out now, Jim,*" Ada Fielding had said, and he had replied, "*It's inevitable.*" "*No, Jim, don't talk like that.*" "*You shouldn't have lied to her in the first place.*" "*I did it for her own good, Jim. If she'd had children, they might have been like him. It would have killed her.*" "*People don't die so easily.*"

He realized now how true this was. He'd died a little more each day, each hour, of the past week, and there was still a long way to go.

He blinked away his tears and rubbed his eyes with his knuckles as if he were punishing them for having seen too much, or too little, or too late. When he looked up again, Daisy was coming down the street, half running, her dark hair uncovered and her raincoat blowing open. She appeared excited and happy, like a child walking along the edge of a steep precipice, confident that there would be no landslide, no loose stones under her feet.

Carrying the landslide and the loose stones in his pockets, he got out of the car and crossed the road, head bowed against the wind.

"Daisy?"

She gave a little jump of fright, as if she were being accosted by a strange man. When she recognized him, she didn't say anything, but he could see the happiness and excitement drain out of her face. It was like watching someone bleed.

"Have you been following me, Jim?"

"No."

"You're here."

"Ada told me you had an appointment at—at his office." He didn't want to say the name Pinata. It would have made the shadow moving behind the window too real. "Please come home with me, Daisy."

"No."

"If I have to plead with you, I will."

"It won't do the slightest good."

"I must make the attempt anyway, for your sake."

She turned away with a skeptical little smile that was hardly more than a twist of the mouth. "How quick people are to do things for *my* sake, never their own."

"Married people have a mutual welfare that can't be divided like a pair of towels marked His and Hers."

"Then stop talking about *my* sake. If you mean for the sake of our marriage, say so. Though of course it doesn't sound quite so noble, does it?"

"Please don't be ironic," he said heavily. "The issue is too important."

"What is the issue?"

"You don't realize the kind of catastrophe you're bringing down on yourself."

"But *you* realize?"

"Yes."

"Then tell me."

He was silent.

"Tell me, Jim."

"I can't."

"You see your own wife headed for a catastrophe, as you put it, and you can't even tell her what it is?"

"No."

"Does it have anything to do with the man in my grave?"

"Don't talk like that," he said harshly. "You have no grave. You're alive, healthy—"

"You aren't answering my question about Camilla."

"I can't. Too many people are involved."

She raised her eyebrows, half in surprise, half in irony. "It sounds as if there's been some giant plot going on behind my back."

"It's been my duty to protect you. It still is." He put his hand on her arm. "Come with me now, Daisy. We'll forget this past week, pretend it never happened."

She stood silent in the noisy rain. It would have been easy, at that moment, to yield to the pressure of his hand, follow him across the street, letting him guide her back to safety. They would take up where they left off; it would be Monday morning again, with Jim reading aloud to her from the *Chronicle.* The days would pass quietly, and if they promised no excitement, they promised no catastrophe, either. It was the nights she feared, the return of the dream. She would climb back up the cliff from the sea and find the stranger under the stone cross, under the seamark tree.

"Come home with me now, Daisy, before it's too late."

"It's already too late."

He watched her disappear through the front door of the building. Then he crossed the road and got into his car, without looking up at the shadow behind the lighted window.

The noise of the rain beating on the tile roof was so loud that Pinata didn't hear her step in the corridor or her knocking at the door of his office. It was after seven o'clock. He'd been chasing around after Juanita and Fielding for three hours until he'd reached the point where all the bars, and the people in them, looked alike. He was feeling tired and irritable, and when he looked up and saw Daisy standing in the doorway, he said brusquely, "You're late."

He expected, in fact wanted, her to snap back at him and give him an excuse to express his anger.

She merely looked at him coolly. "Yes. I met Jim outside."

"Jim?"

"My husband." She sat down, brushing her wet hair back from her forehead with the back of her hand. "He wanted me to go home with him."

"Why didn't you?"

"Because I found out some things this afternoon that indicate we've been on the right track."

"What are they?"

"It won't be easy or pleasant for me to tell you, especially about the girl. But of course you have to know, so you can plan what to do next." She blinked several times, but Pinata couldn't tell whether it was because the overhead lights were bothering her eyes or whether she was on the point of weeping. "There's some connection between the girl and Camilla. I'm pretty sure Jim knows what it is, although he wouldn't admit it."

"Did you ask him?"

"Yes."

"Did he indicate that he was acquainted with Camilla?"

"No, but I think he was."

She told him then, in a detached voice, about the events of the afternoon: her discovery of the check stubs in Jim's desk, the call from Muriel about Fielding, her talk with Adam Burnett at the dock, and finally her meeting Jim. He listened carefully, his only comments being the tapping of his heels as he paced the floor.

He said, when she'd finished, "What was in the letter in the pink envelope that Muriel mentioned to you?"

"From the date I know it could have been only one thing—the news about Juanita and the child."

"And that's what motivated his trip up here?"

"Yes."

"Why four years after the fact?"

"Perhaps it wasn't possible for him to do anything about it at the time," she said defensively. "I know he wanted to."

"Do anything such as what?"

"Give me moral support, or sympathy, or let me talk it out with him. I think the fact that he didn't come when I needed him has been bothering him all these years. Then when he finally settled nearby, in Los Angeles, he decided to satisfy his conscience. Or his curiosity. I don't know which. It's hard to explain my father's actions, especially when he's been drinking."

It's even harder to explain your husband's, Pinata thought. He stopped pacing and leaned against the front of the desk, his hands in his pockets. "What do you make of your husband's insistence that he is 'protecting' you, Mrs. Harker?"

"He appears to be sincere."

"I don't doubt it. But why does he think you need protection?"

"To avoid a catastrophe, he said."

"That's a pretty strong word. I wonder if he meant it literally."

"I'm sure he did."

"Did he indicate who, or what, would be the cause of this catastrophe?"

"Me," Daisy said. "I'm bringing it down on my own head."

"How?"

"By persisting in this investigation."

"Suppose you don't persist?"

"If I go home like a good little girl and don't ask too many questions or overhear too much, presumably I will avoid catastrophe and live happily ever after. Well, I'm not a good little girl anymore, and I no longer trust my husband or my mother to decide what's best for me."

She had spoken very rapidly, as if she were afraid she might change her mind before the words were all out. He realized the pressure she was under to go home and resume her ordinary life, and while he admired her courage, he doubted the validity of the reasons behind it. *Go back, Daisy baby, to Rainbow's End and the pot of gold and the handsome prince. The real world is a rough place for thirty-year-old little girls in search of catastrophe.*

"I know what you're thinking," she said with a frown. "It's written all over your face."

He could feel the blood rising up his neck into his ears and cheeks. "So you read faces, Mrs. Harker?"

"When they're as obvious as yours."

"Don't be too sure. I might be a man of many masks."

"Well, they're made of cellophane."

"We're wasting time," he said brusquely. "We'd better go over to Mrs. Rosario's house and clear up a few—"

"Why do you get so terribly embarrassed when I bring up anything in the least personal?"

He stared at her in silence for a moment. Then he said, with cold deliberation, "Lay off, Daisy baby."

He had meant to shock her, but she seemed merely curious. "Why did you call me that?"

"It was just another way of saying, don't go looking for two catastrophes."

"I don't understand what you mean."

"No? Well,"—he picked up his raincoat from the back of the swivel chair—"are you coming along?"

"Not until you explain to me what you meant."

"Try reading my face again."

"I can't. You just look mad."

"Why, you're a regular face-reading genius, Mrs. Harker. I *am* mad."

"What about?"

"Let's just say I'm a sorehead."

"That's not an adequate answer."

"Okay, put it this way: I have dreams, too. But I don't dream about dead people, just live ones. And sometimes they do some pretty lively things, and sometimes you're one of them. To be any more explicit I would have to go beyond the bounds of propriety, and neither of us wants that, do we?"

She turned away, her jaws clenched.

"Do we?" he repeated.

"No."

"Well, that's that. To hell with dreams." He went to the door and opened it, looking back at her impatiently when she made no move to get up. "Aren't you coming?"

"I don't know."

"I'm sorry if I've frightened you."

"I'm—not frightened." But she hunched in her raincoat as if she had shrunk during the storm, the real one on the other side of the window or the more turbulent one inside herself. "I'm not frightened," she said again. "I just don't know what's ahead for me."

"Nobody does."

"I used to. Now I can't see where I'm going."

"Then you'd better turn back." There was finality in his voice. It was as if they had met, had come together, and had parted, all in the space of a minute, and he knew the minute was gone and would not return. "I'll take you home now, Daisy."

"No."

"Yes. The role of good little girl is better suited to you than this. Just don't listen too hard and don't see too much. You'll be all right."

She was crying, holding the sleeve of his raincoat against her face. He looked away and focused his eyes on an unidentifiable stain on the south wall. The stain had been there when he moved in; it would be there when he moved out. Three coats of paint had failed to obscure it, and it had become for Pinata a symbol of persistence.

"You'll be all right," he repeated. "Going home again might be easier than you think. This past week has been like—well, like a little trip from reality, for both of us. Now the trip's over. It's time to get off the boat, or the plane, or whatever we were on."

"No."

He turned his eyes from the wall to look at her, but her face was still hidden behind his coat sleeve. "Daisy, for God's sake, don't you realize it's impossible? You don't belong in this part of town, on this street, in this office."

"Neither do you."

"The difference is, I'm here. And I'm stuck here. Do you understand what that means?"

"No."

"I have nothing to offer you but a name that isn't my own, an income that ranges from meager to mediocre, and a house with a leaky roof. That's not much."

"If it happens to be what I want, then it's enough, isn't it?"

She spoke with a stubborn dignity that he found both touching and exasperating.

"Daisy, for God's sake, listen to me. Do you realize that I don't even know who my parents were or what race I belong to?"

"I don't care."

"Your mother will."

"My mother has always cared about a lot of the wrong things."

"Maybe they're not wrong."

"Why are you trying so hard to get rid of me, Steve?"

She had never before called him Steve, and the sound of it coming from her made him feel for the first time that the name was finally and truly his own, not something borrowed from a parish priest and tacked on by a Mother Superior. Even if he never saw Daisy again, he would always be grateful to her for this moment of strong, sure identity.

Daisy was wiping her eyes with a handkerchief. The lids were faintly pink, but unswollen, and he wondered whether a really powerful emotion could have caused such dainty and restrained weeping. Perhaps it had been no more than the weeping of a child denied a toy or an ice cream cone.

He said carefully, "We'd better not discuss this anymore tonight, Daisy. I'll take you back to your car."

"I want to come with you."

"You're making this tough for me. I can't force you to go home, and I can't leave you alone in this part of town even with the door locked."

"Why do you keep referring to this part of town as if it were a corner of hell?"

"It is."

"I'm coming with you," she said again.

"To Mrs. Rosario's house?"

"If that's where you're going, yes."

"Juanita might be there. And the child."

A spasm of pain twisted her mouth, but she said, "It may be a necessary part of my growing up, to meet them both."

Memories—how she cried before you were born, day in, day out, until I wished
there were a way of using all those tears to irrigate the dry, dusty rangeland . . .

SHE HAD TAKEN the children to the Brewsters' house and left them without explanation,
and Mr. Brewster, who was crippled and liked to have company while he watched television,
had demanded none. On her return trip she avoided the lighted streets, using shortcuts
across backyards and driveways, hunched under her umbrella like a gnome on night business. She was not afraid, either of the dark or its contents. She knew most of the people in
the neighborhood stood in awe of her because of the candles she burned and the number
of times she went to church.

The thin walls of poverty hold few secrets. Even before she reached the porch, she could
hear Juanita slamming around inside the house as if she were looking for something. Mrs.
Rosario shook the water off her umbrella and removed her dripping coat, thinking, *Maybe*
she's got it in her head that I am spying on her again, and she is looking for me all over the
house, even in places I couldn't possibly be if I were a midget. I must hurry . . .

But she couldn't hurry. Weariness dragged at her legs and arms, and ever since the scene
with Juanita in the afternoon, there'd been a sickness in her stomach that didn't get worse
but wouldn't go away. When she'd fed the children their supper, she had eaten nothing, just
sipped a little lemon and anise tea.

She let herself quietly into the house and went to the bedroom to hang up her coat. With
Pedro's help she had taken the broken door off its hinges and carried it out to the backyard,
where it would lie, with other damaged pieces of her life, to warp in the rain and bleach in the
sun. Next week she and Pedro would go to the junkyard and hunt for another door until they
found one almost the right size. They would fix it up with sandpaper and a little paint . . .

"Next week," she said aloud, as if making a promise of improvement to someone who'd
accused her of being slovenly. But the thought of the long trip to the junkyard, the grating
of sandpaper, the smell of paint, increased her nausea. "Or the week after, when I am feeling stronger."

Even without the door, the bedroom was her sanctuary, the only place where she could
be alone with her grief and guilt. The candle in front of Camilla's picture had burned low.
She put a fresh one in its place and lit it, addressing the dead man in the language they had
used as children.

"I am sorry, Carlos, little brother. I yearned to see justice done, out in the open, but I had
my Juanita to think of. Just that very week you came here, she had been arrested again, and
I knew wherever she went in this town from then on, she'd be watched; they'd never let her
alone—the police, the Probation Department, and the Clinic. I had to get her away where
she could start over and live in peace. I am a woman, a mother. No one else would look
after my Juanita, who was cursed at birth by the evil eye of the *curandera* masquerading
as a nurse at the hospital. Not a penny did I touch for myself, Carlos."

Every night she explained to Carlos what had happened, and every night his static smile
seemed to indicate disbelief, and she was forced to go on, to convince him she had meant
no wrong.

"I know you did not kill yourself, little brother. When you came to see me that night, I
heard you telephoning the woman, telling her to meet you. I heard you ask for money, and
I knew this was a bad thing, asking money from rich people; better to beg from the poor. I
was afraid for you, Carlos. You acted so queer, and you would tell me nothing, only to be
quiet and to pray for your soul.

"When the time came that you were to meet her, I went down to the jungle by the railroad
tracks. I lost my way. I couldn't find you at first. But then I saw a car, a big new car, and I

knew it must be hers. A moment later she came out from the bushes and began running towards the car, very fast, as if she was trying to escape. When I reached the bushes, you were lying there dead with a knife in you, and I knew she had put it there. I knelt over you and begged you to be alive again, Carlos, but you would not hear me. I went home and lit a candle for you. It is still burning, God rest your soul."

She remembered kneeling in the dark in front of the little shrine, praying for guidance. She couldn't confide in Juanita or Mrs. Brewster, because neither of them could be trusted with a secret, and she couldn't call in the police, who were Juanita's enemies and hence her own. They might even suspect she was lying about the woman in the green car in order to protect Juanita.

She'd prayed, and as she prayed, one thought grew in her mind and expanded until it pushed aside all others: Juanita and her unborn child must be taken care of, and there was no one else to do it but herself. She'd called the woman on the telephone, knowing only her name and the shape of her shadow and the color of her car . . .

"It is a bad and dangerous thing, Carlos, asking money from the rich, and I was afraid for my life knowing what she'd done to you. But she was more afraid because she had more to lose than I. I did not tell her my name or where I lived, only what I had come across in the bushes and her running away to the car. I said I wanted no trouble, I was a poor woman, but I would never seek money for myself, only for my daughter, Juanita, with her unborn child that had no father. She asked me whether I'd told anyone else about you, Carlos, and I said no, with truth. Then she said if I gave her my telephone number, she would call me back; there was someone she had to consult. When she called back a little later, she told me she wanted to take care of my daughter and her child. She didn't even mention you, Carlos, or argue about the money, or accuse me of blackmail. Just 'I would like to take care of your daughter and her child.' She gave me the address of an office I was to go to the next day at 12:30. When I went in, I thought at first it was a trap for me—she wasn't there, only a tall blond man, and then later the lawyer. No one talked about you, no one spoke your name, Carlos. It was as if you had never lived . . . "

She turned away from the picture with a groan as another spasm of nausea seized her stomach. The lemon and anise tea had failed to ease her, although it was made from a recipe handed down by her grandmother and had never failed in the past. Clutching her stomach with both hands, she hurried out to the kitchen, with the idea of trying some of the medicine the school doctor had sent home to cure Rita's boils. The medicine had not been opened; Mrs. Rosario was treating the boils herself with a poultice of ivy leaves and salt pork.

She was so intent on her errand, and her pain, that she didn't notice Juanita standing at the stove until she spoke. "Well, are you all through talking to yourself?"

"I was not—"

"I got ears. I heard you mumbling and moaning in there like a crazy woman."

Mrs. Rosario sat down, hunched over the kitchen table. In spite of the pain crawling around inside her like a live thing with cruel legs, merciless arms, she knew she must talk to Juanita now. Mr. Harker had warned her; he'd been very angry that she had permitted Juanita to come back to town.

The room felt hot and airless. Juanita had turned the oven up high to cook herself some supper, and she hadn't opened the window as she was supposed to. Mrs. Rosario dragged herself over to the window and opened it, gasping in the cold fresh air.

"Where are my kids?" Juanita said. "What have you done with them?"

"They're at the Brewsters'."

"Why aren't they home in bed?"

"Because I didn't want them to overhear what I am going to say to you." Mrs. Rosario returned to her place at the table, forcing herself to sit erect because she knew the disastrous effects which a show of weakness on her part sometimes had on her daughter. "The man who was with you—where is he?"

"He had some business to look after, but he'll be back."

"Here?"

"Why not here?"

"You mustn't let him in. He's a bad man. He lies. Even about his name, which is not Foster but Fielding."

Juanita masked her annoyance with a shrug. "I don't care. What difference does it—"

"Did you tell him anything?"

"Sure. I told him my feet hurt, and he said take off your shoes. So I took—"

"There is no time for insolence." The strain of holding herself erect had weakened Mrs. Rosario's voice to a whisper, but even her whisper had a sting in it.

Juanita felt the sting and resented it. She was afraid of this old woman who could invoke saints and devils against her, and her fear was compounded by her knowledge that she had talked too much and too loosely to Fielding. "I never told him a thing, so help me God."

"Did he ask you any questions about your Uncle Carlos?"

"No."

"Or about Paul?"

"No."

"Juanita, listen to me—I must have the truth this time."

"I swear by Mary."

"What do you swear?"

Juanita's face was expressionless. "Whatever you want me to."

"Juanita, are you frightened of me? Are you afraid to tell the truth? I smell drink on your breath. Maybe the drink has made you forget what you said, eh?"

"I never said a word."

"Nothing about Paul or Carlos?"

"I swear by Mary."

Mrs. Rosario's lips moved silently as she bowed her head and crossed herself. The familiar gesture loosened angry memories in Juanita's mind, and they came crashing down like an avalanche of gravel, covering her fear with dust and noise.

"Do you call me a liar, you old witch?" she shouted.

"Shhhh. You must keep your voice down. Someone might—"

"I don't care. I got nothing to hide. That's more than you can say."

"Please. We must have a quiet talk, we—"

"For all your moaning and groaning to God Almighty, you're no better than the rest of us, are you?"

"No. I am no better than the rest of you."

Juanita's loud, harsh laughter filled the little room. "Well, that's the first thing you ever admitted in your whole damn life."

"You must be quiet a minute and listen to me," Mrs. Rosario said. "Sit down here beside me."

"I can listen standing up."

"Mr. Harker was here half an hour ago."

Juanita had a vague memory of Fielding mentioning the name to her. It had meant nothing to her then and meant nothing now. "What's that got to do with me?"

"Mr. Harker is Paul's father."

"Are you crazy? I never even heard of a guy called Harker."

"You are hearing now. He is Paul's father."

"By God, what are you trying to do? Prove I'm so spooky I can't even remember my own kid's father? You want me to get locked up so's you can keep the money from the trust fund for yourself?"

"There never was a trust fund," Mrs. Rosario said quietly. "Carlos was a poor man."

"Why did you lie to me?"

"It was necessary. If you told anyone about Mr. Harker, the money would stop."

"How could I tell anyone about Harker when I don't even know him?" Juanita pounded the table with her fist, and the salt-shaker gave a little jump, fell over on its side, and began spilling, as if it had been shot.

Hurriedly Mrs. Rosario picked up a pinch of the salt and put it under her tongue to ward off the bad luck that plagued a house where there was waste. "Please, there must be no violence."

"Then answer me."

"Mr. Harker has been supporting Paul because he is Paul's father."

"He's not."

"You are to say so, whether you remember or not."

"I won't. It's not true."

Mrs. Rosario's voice was rising in pitch as if it were competing with Juanita's. "You are to do as I tell you, without arguing."

"You think I can't even remember Paul's father? He was in the Air Force, he went to Korea. I wrote to him. We were going to get married when he got out."

"No, no! You must listen to me. Mr. Harker—"

"I never even heard of a guy called Harker. Never in my life, do you hear me?"

"Shhhh!" Mrs. Rosario's face had turned grey, and her eyes, darkened by fear, were fixed on the back door. "There's someone out on the porch," she said in an urgent whisper. "Quick, lock the door, close the window."

"I got nothing to hide. Why should I?"

"Oh God, will you never listen to your mother? Will you never know how much I've endured for you, how much I've loved you?"

She reached out to touch Juanita's hand with her own, but Juanita stepped back with a sound of contempt and disbelief, and went to the door.

She opened it. A man was standing on the threshold, and behind him, at the bottom of the porch steps, a woman, faceless in the shadows.

The man, a stranger to Juanita, was politely apologetic. "I knocked on the front door, and when I didn't get any answer, I came around to the back."

"Well?"

"My name is Steve Pinata. If you don't mind, I'd like to—"

"I don't know you."

"Your mother does."

"He's a detective," Mrs. Rosario said dully. "Tell him nothing."

"I've brought Mrs. Harker with me, Mrs. Rosario. She wants to talk to you about something that's of great importance to her. May we come inside?"

"Go away. I can't talk to anyone. I'm sick."

Pinata knew from her color and her labored breathing that she was telling the truth. "You'd better let me call a doctor, Mrs. Rosario."

"No. Just leave me alone. My daughter and I were having . . . a little argument. It is no business of yours."

"From what I overheard, it's Mrs. Harker's business."

"Let her talk to her husband about it. Not me. I can say nothing."

"Then I'm afraid I'll have to ask Juanita."

"No, no! Juanita is innocent. She knows nothing."

Using the table as support, Mrs. Rosario tried to push herself to her feet, but she fell back into the chair with a sigh of exhaustion. Pinata crossed the room and took her by the arm. "Let me help you."

"No."

"You'd better lie down quietly while I call a doctor."

"No. A priest—Father Salvadore . . ."

"All right, a priest. Mrs. Harker and I will help you to your bedroom, and I'll send for Father Salvadore." He motioned to Daisy to come into the house, and she started up the porch steps.

Up to this point Juanita had been standing, blank-faced, beside the open door, as if what was happening was of no concern or interest to her. It was only when Daisy reached the periphery of light that Juanita let out a gasp of recognition.

She began screaming at her mother in Spanish. "It's the woman I used to see at the Clinic. She's come to take me away. Don't let her. I promise to be good. I promise to buy you a new crucifix, and go to Mass and confession, and never break things anymore. Don't let her take me away!"

"Be quiet," Pinata said. "Mrs. Harker's had no connection with the Clinic for years. Now listen to me. Your mother's very ill. She belongs in a hospital. I want you to help Mrs. Harker look after her while I call an ambulance."

At the word *ambulance* Mrs. Rosario tried once more to get to her feet. This time she fell across the table. The tabled tilted, and she slid slowly and gracefully to the floor. Almost immediately her face began to darken. Bending over her, Pinata felt for a pulse that wasn't there.

Juanita was staring down at her mother, her fists clasped against her cheeks in an infantile gesture of fright. "She looks so funny."

Daisy put her hand on Juanita's shoulder. "We'd better go into the other room."

"But why does she look so black, like a nigger?"

"Mr. Pinata has called an ambulance. There's nothing else we can do."

"She isn't dead? She can't be dead?"

"I don't know. We—"

"Oh, God, if she'd dead, they'll blame me."

"No, they won't," Daisy said. "People die. There's no use blaming anyone."

"They'll say it's my fault because I was bad to her. I broke her crucifix and the door."

"No one will blame you," Daisy said. "Come with me."

It was only by concentrating on helping Juanita that Daisy was able to keep herself under control. She led Juanita into the front room and closed the door. Here, among the shrines and madonnas and thorn-crowned Christs, death seemed more real than it had in the presence of the dead woman herself. It was as if the room had been waiting for someone to die in it.

The two women sat side by side on the couch in awkward silence, like guests waiting for a tardy hostess to introduce them to each other.

"I don't know what it was all about," Juanita said finally in a high, desperate voice. "I just don't *know*. She asked me to lie, and I wouldn't. I never met any Mr. Harker."

"He's my husband."

"All right, then. Ask him. He'll tell you himself."

"He's already told me."

"When?"

"Four years ago," Daisy said. "Before your son was born."

"What did he say?"

"That he was the boy's father."

"Why, he's crazy." Juanita's fists were clenched so tight that the broad, flat thumbs almost covered the knuckles. "Why, the whole bunch of you are *crazy*. I don't even know any Mr. Harker!"

"I saw you getting out of his car at the parking lot outside the Clinic just before your baby was born."

"Maybe he just gave me a ride. A lot of people give me rides when I'm pregnant. I can't remember them all. Maybe he was one of them. Or maybe it wasn't even me you saw."

"It was you."

"All right, maybe I'm the one that's crazy. Is that what you're getting at? They oughta maybe come and take me away and lock me up someplace."

"That isn't going to happen," Daisy said.

"Maybe it'd be better if it did. I can't make sense of things like they are now. Like the business about my Uncle Carlos and the money—he said my mother had been lying about Uncle Carlos."

"Who said?"

"Foster. Or Fielding. He said Uncle Carlos was an old friend of his and he knew a lot about him and what my mother told me was all lies."

"Your uncle's name is—was Camilla?"

"Yes."

"And you think my fa—Mr. Fielding was telling you the truth?"

"I guess so. Why shouldn't he?"

"Where is he now, this Mr. Fielding?"

"He had an important errand, he said. He asked to borrow my car for a couple hours. We made like a bargain. I gave him the car; he gave me the dope on my uncle."

Daisy had no reason to doubt the statement: it sounded exactly like the kind of bargain her father would make. As for the important errand, there was only one logical place it could have taken him—to her own home. Fielding, Juanita, Mrs. Rosario, Jim, her mother, Camilla, they were all beginning to merge and adhere into a multiple-headed monster that was crawling inexorably toward her.

Outside the house the ambulance had come to a stop with one last suffocated wail of its siren.

Juanita began to moan, bent double, so that her forehead pressed against her knees. "They're going to take her away."

"They have to."

"She's scared of hospitals; hospitals are where you die."

"She won't be scared of this one, Juanita."

After a time the noises from the kitchen ceased. A door opened and banged shut again, and a minute later the ambulance pulled away from the curb. Its siren was mute. The time for hurrying had passed.

Pinata came in from the kitchen and looked across the room at the moaning girl. "I called Mrs. Brewster, Juanita. She's coming over to get you right away."

"I'm not going with her."

"Mrs. Harker and I can't leave you here alone."

"I got to stay here and wait, in case they send my mother home. There won't be anybody to look after her if I—"

"She's not coming home."

The strange blankness had come over Juanita's face again, as concealing as the sheet that was used to cover her mother's. Without a sound, she rose to her feet and walked into the bedroom. The candle in front of Camilla's picture was still burning. She leaned down and blew it out. Then she flung herself across the bed, rolled over on her back, and stared up at the ceiling. "It's just wax. It's just ordinary beeswax."

Daisy stood at the foot of the bed. "We'll stay with you until Mrs. Brewster gets here."

"I don't care."

"Juanita, if there's anything I can do, if there's any way I can help you—"

"I don't want no help."

"I'm putting my card with my telephone number on it here on the bureau."

"Leave me alone. Go away."

"All right. We're leaving."

Their departure was marked by the same words as their arrival had been: *Go away.* Between the two, a woman had died and a monster had come to life.

20

Dust and tears, these are what I remember most about the day of your birth, your mother's weeping, and the dust sifting in through locked windows and bolted doors and the closed draft of the chimney . . .

THE DRAPES WERE drawn across all the windows as if there was no one at home, or the people who were at home didn't want to advertise the fact. A car, unfamiliar to Daisy, was parked beside the garage. Pinata opened the door and examined the registration card while Daisy stood waiting under a eucalyptus tree that towered a hundred feet above the house. The pungent odor of the tree's wet bark, half bitter, half sweet, stung her nostrils.

"It's Juanita's car," he said. "Your father must be here."

"Yes. I thought he would be."

"You look pale. Are you feeling all right?"

"I guess so."

"I love you, Daisy."

"Love." The sound of the word was like the scent of eucalyptus, half bitter, half sweet. "Why are you telling me that now?"

"I wanted you to know, so that no matter what happens tonight in connection with your father or mother or Jim—"

"An hour ago you were trying to get rid of me," she said painfully. "Have you changed your mind?"

"Yes."

"Why?"

"I saw a woman die." He couldn't explain to her the shock he'd had of complete realization that this was the only life he was given to live. There would be no second chance, no certificate of merit to be awarded for waiting, no diploma for patience.

She seemed to understand what he meant, without explanation. "I love you, too, Steve."

"Then everything will work out all right. Won't it?"

"I guess so."

"We don't have time for guessing, Daisy."

"Everything will work out," she said, and when he kissed her, she almost believed herself.

She clung to his arm as they walked toward the house where the dream had begun and where it was now to end. The front door was unlocked. When she opened it and went into the foyer, there was no sound from the adjoining living room, but the silence was curiously alive; the walls seemed to be still echoing with noises of anger.

Her mother's sharp voice sliced the silence. "Daisy? Is that you?"

"Yes."

"Is there anyone with you?"

"Yes."

"We are having a *private* family discussion in here. You must ask our guest to excuse you. Immediately."

"I won't do that."

"Your—your father is here."

"Yes," Daisy said. "Yes, I know."

She went into the living room, and Pinata followed her.

A small woman who looked like Daisy was huddled in a chair by the picture window, a handkerchief pressed tightly against her mouth as if to stem a bloody flow of words. Harker sat by himself on the chesterfield, an unlit pipe clenched between his teeth. His glance at Daisy was brief and reproachful.

Standing on the raised hearth, surveying the room like a man who'd just bought the place, was Fielding. Pinata realized immediately that Fielding was drunk on more than liquor, as if he'd been waiting for years for this moment of seeing his former wife cringing in fear before him. Perhaps this was his real motive for coming to San Félice, not any desire to help Daisy, but a thirst for revenge against Ada. Revenge was heady stuff; Fielding looked delirious, half mad.

Daisy was crossing the room toward him, slowly, as if she wasn't quite sure whether this strange man was her father or not. "Daddy?"

"Yes, Daisy baby." He seemed pleased, but he didn't step off the raised hearth to go and meet her. "You're as pretty as ever."

"Are you all right, Daddy?"

"Certainly. Certainly I am. Never better." He bent to touch her forehead lightly with his lips, then straightened up again quickly, as though he was afraid a usurper might steal his position of power. "So you've brought Mr. Pinata with you. That's unfortunate, Daisy baby. This is entirely a private family affair, Pinata wouldn't be interested."

"I was hired," Pinata said, "to make an investigation. Until it's concluded, or until I'm dismissed, I'm under Mrs. Harker's orders." He glanced at Daisy. "Do you want me to leave?"

She shook her head. "No."

"You might regret it, Daisy baby," Fielding said. "But then regrets are a part of life, aren't they, Ada? Maybe the main part, eh? Some regrets, of course, are slower in coming than others, and harder to take. Isn't that right, Ada?"

Mrs. Fielding spoke through the handkerchief she held to her mouth. "You're drunk."

"In wine is truth, old girl."

"Coming from you, truth is a dirty word."

"I know dirtier ones. Love, that's the dirtiest of all, isn't it, Ada? Tell us about it. Give us the lowdown."

"You're a—an evil man."

"Don't antagonize him, Ada," Jim said quietly. "There's nothing to be gained."

"Jim's right. Don't antagonize me, Ada, and maybe I'll go away like a good lad without telling any tales. Would you like that? Sure you would. Only it's too late. Some of your little tricks are catching up with you. My going away can't stop them."

"If there were any tricks, they were necessary." Her head had begun to shake, as if the neck muscles that held it up had suddenly gone flabby. "I was forced to lie to Daisy. I couldn't permit her to have children who would inherit certain—certain characteristics of her father."

"Tell Daisy about these characteristics. Name them."

"I—please, Stan. Don't."

"She's got a right to know about her old man, hasn't she? You made a decision that affected her life. Now justify it." Fielding's mouth cracked open in a mirthless smile. "Tell her about all the little monsters she might have brought into the world if it hadn't been for her wise, benevolent mother."

Daisy was standing with her back against the door, her eyes fixed, not on her father or mother, but on Jim. "Jim? What are they talking about, Jim?"

"You'll have to ask your mother."

"She was lying to me that day in the doctor's office? It's not true I can't have children?"

"No, it's not true."

"Why did she do it? Why did you let her?"

"I had to."

"You *had* to. Is that the only explanation you can offer me?" She crossed the room toward him, the rain dripping soundlessly from her coat onto the soft rug. "What about the girl, Juanita?"

"I only met her once in my life," he said. "I picked her up on the street and drove her three or four blocks to the Clinic. Deliberately. I knew who she was. I kept her talking in the car until you came out because I wanted you to see us together."

"Why?"

"I intended to claim her child."

"You must have had a reason."

"No man would take a drastic step like that without having reasons."

"I can think of one," she said in a brittle voice. "You wanted to make sure I kept on believing that our lack of children was my fault and not yours. You're admitting now that it has been your fault, right from the beginning."

"Yes."

"And the reason you and my mother lied to me and that you claimed Juanita's child was to make sure I'd never suspect you were the sterile one in our marriage."

He didn't try to deny it, although he knew it was only a small portion of the truth. "That was a factor, yes. I didn't originate the lie; your mother did. I went along with it when I found out— when it became necessary."

"Why did it become necessary?"

"I had to protect your mother."

Mrs. Fielding sprang out of her chair like a runner at the sound of the starter's gun. But there was nowhere to run; the course had no beginning and no ending. "Stop it, Jim. Let me tell her, please."

"You?" Daisy turned to face her mother. "I wouldn't believe you if you told me it was Saturday night and raining outside."

"It *is* Saturday night and it *is* raining outside. You'd be a fool not to believe the facts just because they came from me."

"Tell me some facts, then."

"There's a stranger present." Mrs. Fielding glanced at Pinata, then at Fielding. "Two strangers. Must I talk in front of them? Can't we wait until—"

"I've done enough waiting. Mr. Pinata can be trusted to be discreet, and my father wouldn't do anything to harm me."

Fielding nodded and smiled at her—"You bet I wouldn't, Daisy baby"—but there was a derisive, cynical quality about the smile that worried Pinata because he couldn't understand it. He wished the alcohol, and whatever other intoxicant was at work in Fielding's system, would wear off and leave him less sure of himself. One sign of its wearing off was already apparent, the fine tremor of Fielding's hands, which he attempted to cover up by hiding them in his pockets.

Mrs. Fielding had begun to talk again, her eyes on Daisy. "No matter what you think now, Daisy, Jim has done everything possible for your happiness. Remember that. The first lie was mine. I've already told you why it was necessary—your children would be marked by a stigma that must not be passed on. I can't talk about it in front of a stranger. Later, you and I will discuss it alone." She took a long breath, wincing as if it hurt her lungs, or heart, to probe so deep. "Four years ago, without warning, I received a telephone call from a man I hadn't seen for a very long time and never expected to see again. His name was Carlos Camilla, and Stan and I had known him as Curly when we were first married in New Mexico. He was a close friend to us both. You've always accused me of race prejudice, Daisy. But in those days Camilla was our friend; we went through bad times together and helped each other.

"He didn't mince words when he called. He said he had only a short time to live and needed money for his funeral. He reminded me of—of old times, and I—well, I agreed to meet him and give him some money."

"Two thousand dollars?" Pinata said.

"Yes."

"That's a lot to pay for memories of old times, Mrs. Fielding."

"I felt an obligation to help him," she said. "He sounded so terribly ill and broken, I knew he must be telling the truth about his approaching death. I asked him if I could send him the money instead of meeting him, but he said there wasn't time, and he had no address for me to send it to."

"Where did you get the money?"

"From Jim. I knew he had a lot of cash in the safe at his office. I explained the situation to him, and he thought it would be advisable to pay what Camilla asked."

"Advisable?" It seemed, to Pinata, a curious word to use under the circumstances.

"Jim is a very generous man."

"Obviously there were reasons for his generosity?"

"Yes."

"What were they?"

"I must refuse to answer."

"All right," Pinata said. "You went to meet Camilla. Where?"

"At the end of Greenwald Street, near the signalman's shack. It was very late and dark. I couldn't see anyone, and I thought I had misunderstood his instructions. I was about to leave when I heard him call my name, and a shadow stepped out from behind a bush. 'Come here and look at me,' he said. He lit a match and held it in front of his face. I'd known him when he was young and lively and handsome; the man in the matchlight was a living corpse, emaciated, misshapen. I couldn't speak. There were so many things to say, but I couldn't speak. I gave him the money, and he said, 'God bless you, Ada, and God bless me, Carlos.'"

The funereal words seemed, to Pinata, to contain a curious echo of another ceremony: *I, Ada, take thee, Carlos . . .*

"I thought I heard someone coming," Mrs. Fielding went on. "I panicked and ran back to my car and drove off. When I returned to the house, the phone was ringing. It was a woman."

"Mrs. Rosario?"

"Yes, although she didn't tell me her name then. She said she had found Carlos dead and that I had killed him. She wouldn't listen to my denials, my protests. She just kept talking about her daughter, Juanita, who needed taking care of because she was going to give birth to a fatherless child. She seemed obsessed with this single idea of money for her daughter and the baby. I said I would call her back, that I had to consult someone. She gave me her phone number. Then I went to Jim's room and woke him up."

She paused, looking at Daisy half in sorrow, half in reproach. "You'll never know how many times Jim has taken a burden off my shoulders, Daisy. I told him the situation. We both agreed that it was impossible for me to be dragged through a police investigation. Too many suspicious things would come out: that I knew Camilla, that I'd given him two thousand dollars. I couldn't face it. I realized I had to keep Mrs. Rosario quiet. The problem was how to pay her so that even if someone found out about the payments, the real reason for them would remain secret. The only possible way was to concoct a false reason and make it known to someone in a key position, like Adam Burnett."

"And the false reason," Pinata said, "was support for Juanita's child?"

"Yes. It was Mrs. Rosario who inadvertently suggested it by insisting that she wanted no money for herself, only for Juanita. So we decided that was how it would be done. Jim was to claim the child and pay for its support. It seemed, in a way, like a stroke of fate that the lie should fit in so perfectly with the lie I was forced to tell Daisy in the first place. It was all arranged in Adam Burnett's office the next day, by Adam and Jim and Mrs. Rosario. Adam was never told the truth. He even wanted to fight Juanita's 'claim' in court, but Jim managed to convince him that he must keep quiet. The next step was convincing Daisy.

That was easy enough. Jim found out through Mrs. Rosario that Juanita was to go to the Clinic late that afternoon. He picked her up in his car and kept her talking in the parking lot until Daisy came out and saw them together. Then he made his false confession to her.

"Cruel? Yes, it was a cruel thing to do, Daisy. But not as cruel as others, perhaps—and not as cruel as some of the real tricks life plays on us. The next days were terrible ones. Although the coroner's inquest ruled Camilla's death was a suicide, the police were still investigating the source of the money found on him and still trying to establish who Camilla was. But time passed and nothing happened. Camilla was buried, still unknown."

Pinata said, "Did you ever visit his grave, Mrs. Fielding?"

"I passed it several times when we went to leave flowers for Jim's parents."

"Did you leave flowers for Camilla, too?"

"No, I couldn't. Daisy was always with me."

"Why?"

"Because I—I wanted her along."

"Was there any display of emotion on these occasions?"

"I cried sometimes."

"Wasn't Daisy curious about the reason for your tears?"

"I told her that I had a cousin buried there, of whom I'd been very fond."

"What was this cousin's name?"

"I. . ."

Fielding's sudden fit of coughing sounded like stifled laughter. When he had finished, he wiped his eyes with his coat sleeve. "Ada has a very sentimental nature. She weeps at the drop of a dead cousin. The only difficulty in this instance is that neither of her parents had any siblings. So where did the cousin come from, Ada?"

She looked at him, her mouth moving in a soundless curse.

Pinata said, "There was no cousin, Mrs. Fielding?"

"I—no."

"The tears were for Camilla?"

"Yes."

"Why?"

"He died alone and was buried alone. I felt guilty."

"Guilt as strong as that," Pinata said, "makes me wonder whether Mrs. Rosario's accusation against you might not have some basis in fact."

"I had nothing whatever to do with Camilla's death. He killed himself, with his own knife. That was the coroner's verdict."

"This afternoon I talked to Mr. Fondero, the mortician in charge of Camilla's body. It's his opinion that Camilla's hands were too severely crippled by arthritis to have used that knife with the necessary force."

"When I left him," Mrs. Fielding said steadily, "he was still alive."

"But when Mrs. Rosario arrived—and let's assume that her coming was the noise you heard which frightened you away—he was dead. Suppose Fondero's opinion about Camilla's incapacity to handle the knife is correct. As far as we know, only two people were with Camilla that night, you and Mrs. Rosario. Do you think Mrs. Rosario killed her brother?"

"It's more reasonable than to think I did."

"What would her motive have been?"

"Perhaps a deliberate scheme to get money for the girl. I don't know. Why don't you ask her, not me?"

"I can't ask her," Pinata said. "Mrs. Rosario died tonight of a heart attack."

"Oh God." She dropped back into the chair, her hands pressing against her chest. "Death. It's beginning to surround me. All this death, and nothing to take the curse off it, no new life coming to take its place. This is my punishment, no new life." She gazed at Fielding with dull eyes. "Revenge is what you wanted, isn't it, Stan? Well, you have it. You might as well leave now. Go back to whatever hole you crawled out of."

Fielding's smile wobbled at the corners, but it stayed with him. "You won't be living so fancy yourself from now on, will you, Ada? Maybe you'll be glad to find a hole to crawl into. Your passport to the land of gracious living expires when Daisy leaves."

"Daisy won't leave."

"No? Ask her."

The two women looked at each other in silence. Then Daisy said, with a brief glance at her husband, "I think Jim already knows I won't be staying. I think he's known for the past few days. Haven't you, Jim?"

"Yes."

"Are you going to ask me to stay?"

"No."

"Well, *I* am," Mrs. Fielding said harshly. "You can't walk out now. I've worked so hard to keep this marriage secure—"

Fielding laughed. "People should work on their *own* marriages, my dear. Take yours, for instance. This man Fielding you married, he wasn't a bad guy. Oh, he was no world-beater. He could never have afforded a split-level deal like this. But he adored you, he thought you were the most wonderful, virtuous, truthful—"

"Stop it. I won't listen."

"Most truthful—"

"Leave her alone, Fielding," Jim said quietly. "You've drawn blood. Be satisfied."

"Maybe I've developed a taste for it and want more."

"Any more will be Daisy's. Think about it."

"Think about Daisy's blood? All right, I'll do that." Fielding put on a mock-serious expression like an actor playing a doctor on a television commercial. "In this blood of hers there are certain genes which will be transmitted to her children and make monsters out of them. Like her father. Right?"

"The word monster doesn't apply, as you well know."

"Ada thinks it does. In fact, she's not quite sane on the subject. But then perhaps guilt makes us all a little crazy eventually."

Pinata said, "You know a lot about guilt, Fielding."

"I'm an expert."

"That makes you a little crazy, too, eh?"

Fielding grinned like an old dog. "You have to be a little crazy to take the risks I took in coming here."

"Risks? Did you expect Mrs. Fielding or Mr. Harker to attack you?"

"You figure it out."

"I'm trying." Pinata crossed the room and stood beside Mrs. Fielding's chair. "When Camilla telephoned you that night from Mrs. Rosario's house, you said the call was a complete surprise to you?"

"Yes. I hadn't seen him or heard from him for many years."

"Then how did he find out that you were living in San Félice and that you were in a position where you could help him financially? A man in Camilla's physical state wouldn't start out across the country in the vague hope of locating a woman he hadn't seen in years and finding her prosperous enough to assist him. He must have had two facts before he decided to come here—your address and your financial situation. Who told him?"

"I don't know. Unless . . ." She stopped, turning her head slowly toward Fielding. "It was—it was you, Stan?"

After a moment's hesitation, Fielding shrugged and said, "Sure. I told him."

"Why? To make trouble for me?"

"I figured you could afford a little trouble. Things had gone pretty smooth for you. I didn't actually plan anything, though. Not at first. It happened accidentally. I hit Albuquerque the end of that November. I decided to look Camilla up, thinking there was an off-chance he had struck it rich and wouldn't mind passing some of it around. It was a bum guess, believe me. When I found him, he was on the last skid. His wife had died, and he was living, or half living, in a mud shack with a couple of Indians."

His mouth stretched back from his teeth with no more expression or purpose than a piece of elastic. "Oh yes, it was quite a reunion, Ada. I'm sorry you missed it. It might have taught you a simple lesson, the difference between poorness and destitution. Poorness is having no money. Destitution is a real, a positive thing. It lives with you every minute. It eats at your stomach during the night, it drags at your arms and legs when you move, it bites your hands and ears on cold mornings, it pinches your throat when you swallow, it squeezes the moisture out of you, drop by drop by drop. Camilla sat there on his iron cot, dying in front of my eyes. And you think, while I stood and watched him, that I was worried about making trouble for *you*? What an egotist you are, Ada. Why, you didn't even exist as a person anymore, for Camilla or for me. You were a possible source of money, and we both needed it desperately—Camilla to die with, and I to live with. So I said to him, why not put the bite on Ada? She's got Daisy fixed up with a rich man, I told him; they wouldn't miss a couple of thousand dollars."

Mrs. Fielding's face had stiffened with pain and shock. "And he agreed to—to put the bite on me?"

"You or anyone else. It hardly matters to a dying man. He knew he wasn't going to make it in this life, and he'd gotten obsessed with the idea of the next one, having a fine funeral and going to heaven. I guess the idea of getting money from you appealed to him, particularly because he had a sister living here in San Félice. He thought he'd kill two birds: get the money and see Mrs. Rosario again. He had an idea that Mrs. Rosario had influence with the Church that would do him some good when he kicked off."

"Then you were aware," Pinata said, "when you arrived here, that Camilla was Juanita's uncle?"

"No, no," said Fielding. "Camilla had never called his sister anything but her first name, Filomena. It was a complete surprise to me seeing his picture when I took Juanita home this afternoon. But that's when I began to be sure some dirty work was going on. Too many coincidences add up to a plan. Whose plan I didn't know. But I did know my former wife, and plans are her specialty."

"They've had to be," Mrs. Fielding said. "I've had to look ahead if no one else would."

"This time you looked so far ahead you didn't see the road in front of you. You were worried about your grandchildren; you should have worried about your child."

"Let's get back to Camilla," Pinata said to Fielding. "Obviously you expected a share of whatever money he could pry out of your former wife?"

"Of course. It was my idea."

"You were pretty sure she'd pay up?"

"Yes."

"Why?"

"Oh, auld lang syne, and that sort of thing. As I said, Ada has a very sentimental nature."

"And as I said, two thousand dollars is a heap of auld lang syne."

Fielding shrugged. "We were all good friends once. Around the ranch they called us the three musketeers."

"Oh?" It was difficult for Pinata to believe that Mrs. Fielding, with her strong racial prejudices, should ever have been one of a trio that included a Mexican ranch hand. But if Fielding's statement was untrue, Ada Fielding would certainly deny it, and she made no attempt to do so.

All right, so she's changed, Pinata thought. *Maybe the years she spent with Fielding embittered her to the point where she's prejudiced against anything that was a part of their life together. I can't blame her much.*

"The idea, then," he said, "was for Camilla to come to San Félice, get the money, and return to Albuquerque with your share of it?"

Fielding's hesitation was slight, but noticeable. "Sure."

"And you trusted him?"

"I had to."

"Oh, not necessarily. You could, for example, have accompanied him here. That would have been the logical thing to do under the circumstances, wouldn't it?"

"I don't care."

It seemed to Pinata a strangely inept answer for a glib man like Fielding. "As it turned out, you didn't receive your share of the money because he killed himself?"

"I didn't get my share," Fielding said, "because there wasn't anything to share."

"What do you mean?"

"Camilla didn't get the money. She didn't give it to him."

Mrs. Fielding looked stunned for a moment. "That's not true. I handed him two thousand dollars."

"You're lying, Ada. You promised him that much but you didn't come across with it."

"I swear I gave him the money. He put it in an envelope, then he hid the envelope under his shirt."

"I don't believe—"

"You'll have to believe it, Fielding," Pinata said. "That's where it was found, in an envelope inside his shirt."

"It was *on* him? It was there *on* him, all the time?"

"Certainly."

"Why, that dirty bastard . . ." He began to curse, and each word that damned Camilla damned himself, too, but he couldn't stop. It was as if he'd been saving up words for years, like money to be spent all at once, on one vast special project, his old friend, old enemy, Camilla. The violent emotion behind the flow of words surprised Pinata. Although he knew now that Fielding was responsible for Camilla's death, he still didn't understand why. Money alone couldn't be the reason: Fielding had never cared enough about money even to pursue it with much energy, let alone kill for it. Perhaps, then, he had acted out of anger at being cheated by Camilla. But this theory was less likely than the other. In the first place, he hadn't found out until now that he'd been cheated; in the second, he wasn't a stand-up-and-fight type of man. If he was angry, he would walk away, as he'd walked away from every other difficult situation in his life.

A spasm of coughing had seized Fielding. Pinata poured half a glass of whiskey from the decanter on the coffee table and took it over to him. Ten seconds after Fielding had gulped the drink, his coughing stopped. He wiped his mouth with the back of his hand, in a symbolic gesture of pushing back into it words that should never have escaped.

"No temperance lecture?" he said hoarsely. "Thanks, preacher man."

"You were with Camilla that night, Fielding?"

"Hell, you don't think I'd have trusted him to come all this way alone? Chances were he wouldn't have made it back to Albuquerque even if he wanted to. He was a dying man."

"Tell us what happened."

"I can't remember it all. I was drinking. I bought a bottle of wine because it was a cold night. Curly didn't touch any of it; he wanted to see his sister, and she didn't approve of drinking. When he came back from his sister's house, he told me he'd called Ada and she was going to bring the money right away. I waited behind the signalman's shack. I couldn't see anything; it was too dark. But I heard Ada's car arrive and leave again a few minutes later. I went over to Camilla. He said Ada had changed her mind and there was no money to share after all. I accused him of lying. He took the knife out of his pocket and switched the blade open. He threatened to kill me if I didn't go away. I tried to get the knife away from him, and suddenly he fell over and—well, he was dead. It happened so fast. Just like that, he was dead."

Pinata didn't believe the entire story, but he was pretty sure a jury could be convinced that Fielding had acted in self-defense. A strong possibility existed that the case wouldn't even reach a courtroom. Beyond Fielding's own word there was no evidence against him, and he wasn't likely to talk so freely in front of the police. Besides, the district attorney might be averse to reopening, without strong evidence, a case closed four years previously.

"I heard someone coming," Fielding went on. "I got scared and started running down the tracks. Next thing I knew I was on a freight car heading south. I kept going. I just kept going. When I got back to Albuquerque, I told the two Indians Camilla had been living with that he had died in L.A., in case they might get the idea of reporting him missing. They believed me. They didn't give a damn anyway. Camilla was no loss to them, or to the world. He was just a lousy no-good Mexican." His eyes shifted back to Mrs. Fielding. He was smiling again, like a man enjoying a joke he couldn't share, because it was too special or too involved. "Isn't that right, Ada?"

She shook her head listlessly. "I don't know."

"Oh, come on now, Ada. Tell the people. You knew Camilla better than I did. You used to say he had the feelings of a poet. But you've learned better than that since, haven't you? Tell them what a mean, worthless hunk of—"

"Stop it, Stan. Don't."

"Then say it."

"All right. What difference does it make?" she said wearily. "He was a—a worthless man."

"A lazy, stupid *cholo*, in spite of all your efforts to educate him. Isn't that correct?"

"I—yes."

"Repeat it, then."

"Camilla was a—a lazy, stupid *cholo*."

"Let's drink to that." Fielding stepped down off the hearth and started across the room toward the decanter. "How about it, Pinata? You're a *cholo* too, aren't you? Have a drink to another *cholo*, one who didn't play it so smart."

Pinata felt the blood rising up into his neck and face. *Cholo, cholo, grease your bolo . . .* The old familiar word was as stinging an insult now as it had been in his childhood . . . *Take a trip to the northern polo . . .* But the anger Pinata felt was instinctive and general, not directed against Fielding. He realized that the man, for all his blustering arrogance, was suffering, perhaps for the first time, a moral pain as intense as the mortal pain Mrs. Rosario had suffered; and the exact cause of the pain Pinata didn't understand any more than, as a layman, he understood the technical cause of Mrs. Rosario's. He said, "You'd better lay off the liquor, Fielding."

"Oh, preacher man, are you going to go into that routine again? Pour me a drink, Daisy baby, like a good girl."

There were tears in Daisy's eyes and in her voice when she spoke. "All right."

"You've always been a good Daddy-loving girl, haven't you, Daisy baby?"

"Yes."

"Then hurry up about it. I'm thirsty."

"All right."

She poured him half a glass of whiskey and turned her head away while he drank it, as if she couldn't bear to witness his need and his compulsion. She said to Pinata, "What's going to happen to my father? What will they do to him?"

"My guess is, not a thing." Pinata sounded more confident than the circumstances warranted.

"First they'll have to find me, Daisy baby," Fielding said. "It won't be easy. I've disappeared before. I can do it again. You might even say I've developed a real knack for it. This Eagle Scout here,"—he pointed a thumb contemptuously at Pinata—"he can blast off to the police till he runs out of steam . It won't do any good. There's no case against me, just the one I'm carrying around inside. And that—well, I'm used to it." He put his hand briefly and gently on Daisy's hair. "I can take it. Don't worry about me, Daisy baby. I'll be here and there and around. Someday I'll write to you."

"Don't go away like this, so quickly, so—"

"Come on now, you're too big a girl to cry."

"Don't. Don't go," she said.

But she knew he would and that her search must begin again. She would see his face in crowds of strangers; she would catch a glimpse of him passing in a speeding car or walking into an elevator just before the door closed.

She tried to hold on to his arm. He said quickly, "Good-bye, Daisy," and started across the room.

"Daddy . . ."

"Don't call me Daddy anymore. That's over. That's gone."

"Wait a minute, Fielding," Pinata said. "Off the record, what did Camilla say or do to you that made you furious enough to knife him?"

Fielding didn't reply. He just turned and looked at his former wife with a terrible hatred. Then he walked out of the house. The slam of the door behind him was as final as the closing of a crypt.

"Why?" Daisy said. "*Why?*" The melancholy little whisper seemed to echo around the room in search of an answer. "Why did it have to happen, Mother?"

Mrs. Fielding sat, mute and rigid, a snow statue awaiting the first ominous rays of the sun.

"You've got to answer me, Mother."

"Yes. Yes, of course."

"Now."

"All right."

With a sigh of reluctance Mrs. Fielding stood up. She was holding in her hand something she'd taken unobtrusively from her pocket. It was an envelope, yellowed by age and wrinkled as if it had been dragged in and out of dozens of pockets and drawers and corners and handbags. "This came for you a long time ago, Daisy. I never thought I'd have to give it to you. It's a letter from—from your father."

"Why did you keep it from me?"

"Your father makes that quite clear."

"Then you've read it?"

"Read it?" Mrs. Fielding repeated wearily. "A hundred times, two hundred—I lost count."

Daisy took the envelope. Her name and the old address on Laurel Street were printed in a shaky and unfamiliar hand. The postmark said, "San Félice, December 1, 1955."

As Pinata watched her unfold the letter, the malevolent chant from his childhood kept running through his head: *Cholo, cholo, grease your bolo.* He hoped that his own children would never have to hear it and remember. His children and Daisy's.

21

My beloved Daisy:

It has been so many years since I have seen you. Perhaps, at this hour that is very late for me, I should not step back into your life. But I cannot help it. My blood runs in your veins. When I die, part of me will still be alive, in you, in your children, in your children's children. It is a thought that takes some of the ugliness out of these cruel years, some of the sting out of the tricks of time.

This letter may never reach you, Daisy. If it doesn't, I will know why. Your mother has vowed to keep us apart at any cost because she is ashamed of me. Right from the beginning she has been ashamed, not only of me but of herself, too. Even when she talked of love, her voice had a bitterness in it, as if the relationship between us was the result of a physical defect she couldn't help, a weakness of the body which her mind despised. But there was love, Daisy. You are proof there was love.

Memories are crowding in on me so hard and fast that I can barely breathe. I wish they were good memories, that like other men I could sit back in the security of my family and review the past kindly. But I cannot. I am alone, surrounded by strangers in a strange place. The hotel guests are looking at me queerly while I write this, as if they are wondering what a tramp like me is doing in their lobby where I don't belong, writing to a daughter who has never really belonged to me. Your mother kept her vow, Daisy. We are still apart, you and I. She has hidden her shame because she cannot bear it the way we weaker and humbler ones can and must and do.

Shame—it is my daily bread. No wonder the flesh is falling off my bones. I have nothing to live for. Yet, as I move through the days, shackled to this dying body, I yearn to step free of it long enough to see you again, you and Ada, my beloved ones still. I came here to see you, but I lack the courage. That is why I am writing, to feel in touch with you for a little, to remind myself that my death will be only partial; you will be left, you will be the proof that I ever lived at all. I leave nothing else.

Memories—how she cried before you were born, day in, day out, until I wished there were a way of using all those tears to irrigate the dry, dusty rangeland. Dust and tears, these are what I remember most about the day of your birth, your mother's weeping, and the dust sifting in through locked windows and bolted doors and the closed draft of the chimney. And at the very last moment before you were born, she said to me when we were alone, "What if the baby is like you. Oh God, help us, my baby and me." Her baby, not mine.

Right from the first she kept you away from me. To protect you. I had germs, she said; I was dirty from working with cattle. I washed and washed, my shoulders ached pumping water from the drying wells, but I was always dirty. She had to safeguard her baby, she said. Her baby, never mine.

I couldn't protest, I couldn't even speak of it out loud to anyone, but I must tell you now before I die. I must claim you, though I swore to her I never would, as my daughter. I die in the hope and trust that your mother will bring you to visit my grave. May God bless you, Daisy, and your children, and your children's children.

Your loving father, Carlos Camilla

HOW LIKE AN ANGEL

This book is dedicated, with love, to
Betty Masterson Norton

What a piece of work is a man!
. . . in action, how like an angel! in
apprehension, how like a god! . . . And yet,
to me, what is this quintessence of dust?
man delights not me;
no, nor woman neither . . .
HAMLET

1

ALL NIGHT AND most of the day they had been driving, through mountains, and desert, and now mountains again. The old car was beginning to act skittish, the driver was getting irritable, and Quinn, to escape both, had gone to sleep in the back seat. He was awakened by the sudden shriek of brakes and Newhouser's voice, hoarse from exhaustion and the heat and the knowledge that once more he'd made a fool of himself at the tables.

"This is it, Quinn. The end of the line."

Quinn stirred and turned his head, expecting to find himself on one of the tree-lined streets of San Felice, with the ocean glittering in the distance like a jewel not to be touched or sold. Even before he opened his eyes he knew something was wrong. No city street was so quiet, no sea air so dry.

"Hey, Quinn. You awake?"

"Yes."

"Well, flake off, will you? I'm in a hurry."

Quinn looked out of the window. The scenery hadn't changed since he'd gone to sleep. There were mountains and more mountains and still more, all covered with the same scrub oak and chaparral, manzanita and wild holly, and a few pines growing meagerly from the parched earth.

"This is nowhere," he said. "You told me you were going to San Felice."

"I said *near* San Felice."

"How far is near?"

"Forty-five miles."

"For the love of—"

147

"You must be from the East," Newhouser said. "In California forty-five miles is near."

"You might have told me that before I got in the car."

"I did. You weren't listening. You seemed pretty anxious to get out of Reno. So now you're out. Be grateful."

"Oh, I am," Quinn said dryly. "You've satisfied my curiosity. I've always wondered where nowhere was."

"Before you start beefing, listen. My turn-off to the ranch is half a mile down the road. I'm a day late getting back to work, my wife's a hothead, I lost seven hundred in Reno and I haven't slept for two days. Now, you want to be glad you got a ride this far or you want to put up a squawk?"

"You might have dropped me off at a truck stop where food was available."

"You said you had no money."

"I was figuring on a small loan, say five bucks."

"If I had five bucks I'd still be in Reno. You know that. You got the disease same as I have."

Quinn didn't deny it. "Okay, forget about money. I have another idea. Maybe that wife of yours isn't such a hothead after all. Maybe she wouldn't object to a temporary guest—all right, all right, it was just a suggestion. Do you have a better one?"

"Naturally, or I wouldn't have stopped here. See that dirt road down the line?"

When Quinn got out of the car he saw a narrow lane that meandered off into a grove of young eucalyptus trees. "It doesn't look like much of a road."

"It's not supposed to. The people who live at the end of it don't like to advertise the fact. Let's just say they're peculiar."

"Let's just ask how peculiar?"

"Oh, they're harmless, don't worry about that. And they're always good for a handout to the poor." Newhouser pushed his ten-gallon hat back, revealing a strip of pure white forehead that looked painted across the top of his brown leathery face. "Listen, Quinn, I hate like the devil to leave you here but I have no choice and I know you'll make out all right. You're young and healthy."

"Also hungry and thirsty."

"You can pick up something to eat and drink at the Tower and then hitch another ride right into San Felice."

"The Tower," Quinn repeated. "Is that what's at the end of the quote road unquote?"

"Yes."

"Is it a ranch?"

"They do some ranching," Newhouser said cautiously. "It's a—well, sort of a self-contained little community. So I've heard. I've never seen it personally."

"Why not?"

"They don't encourage visitors."

"Then how come you're so sure I'll get a big welcome?"

"You're a poor sinner."

"You mean it's a religious outfit?"

Newhouser moved his head but Quinn wasn't sure whether he was indicating affirmation or denial. "I tell you, I never saw the place, I just heard things about it. Some rich old dame who was afraid she was going to die built a five-story tower. Maybe she thought she'd have a shorter hitch to heaven when her time came, a head start, like. Well, I've got to be on my way now, Quinn."

"Wait," Quinn said urgently. "Be reasonable. I'm on my way to San Felice to collect three hundred bucks a friend of mine owes me. I promise to give you fifty if you'll drive me to—"

"I can't."

"That's more than a buck a mile."

"Sorry."

Quinn stood on the side of the road and watched Newhouser's car disappear around a curve. When the sound of its engine died out, there was absolute silence. Not a bird chirped, not a branch swished in the wind. It was an experience Quinn had never had before and he wondered for a minute if he'd suddenly gone deaf from hunger and lack of sleep and the heat of the sun.

He had never much liked the sound of his own voice but it seemed very good to him then, he wanted to hear more, to spread it out and fill the silence.

"My name is Joe Quinn. Joseph Rudyard Quinn, but I don't tell anyone about the Rudyard. Yesterday I was in Reno. I had a job, a car, clothes, a girlfriend. Today I'm in the middle of nowhere with nothing and nobody."

He'd been in jams before but they'd always involved people, friends to confide in, strangers to persuade. He prided himself on being a glib talker. Now it no longer mattered, there wasn't anyone around to listen. He could talk himself to death in that wilderness without causing a leaf to stir or an insect to scurry out of range.

He took out a handkerchief and dabbed at the sweat that was trickling down behind his ears. Although he'd often visited the city of San Felice, he knew nothing about this bleak mountainous back country, seared by the sun in summer, eroded by the winter rains. It was summer now. In the river beds dust lay, and the bones of small animals which had come to find water.

The silence, more than the heat and desolation, bothered Quinn. It seemed unnatural not even to hear a bird call, and he wondered whether all the birds had died in the long drought or whether they'd moved on to be nearer a water supply, to the ranch where Newhouser worked, or perhaps to the Tower. He glanced across the road at the narrow lane that seemed to end suddenly in the grove of eucalyptus.

"Hell, a little religion's not going to kill me," he said, and crossed the road, squinting against the sun.

Beyond the eucalyptus trees the path started to climb, and signs of life became evident as he followed it. He passed a small herd of cows grazing, some sheep enclosed in a pen made of logs, a couple of goats tethered in the shade of a wild holly tree, an irrigation ditch with a little sluggish water at the bottom. All the animals looked well-fed and well-tended.

The ascent became steeper as he walked, and the trees denser and taller, pines and live oaks, madrones and cotoneaster. He had almost reached the top of a knoll when he came across the first building. It was so skillfully constructed that he was only fifteen or twenty yards away before he realized it was there, a long low structure made of logs and native stone. It bore no resemblance to a tower and he thought Newhouser might have made a mistake about the place, had been taken in by local rumors and exaggerations.

There was no one in sight, and no smoke coming out of the wide stone chimney. Crude half-log shutters were fastened over the windows on the outside as if the builder's idea had been to keep people in rather than to protect the place against intruders. With the huge sugar pines filtering the sunlight, the air seemed to Quinn suddenly cool and damp. Pine needles and orange-colored flakes of madrone bark muffled the sound of his footsteps as he approached.

Through a chink between the half-logs Brother Tongue of Prophets saw the stranger coming and began making small animal noises of distress.

"Now what are you making a fuss about?" Sister Blessing said briskly. "Here, let me see for myself." She took his place at the chink. "It's only a man. Don't get excited. His car probably broke down; Brother Crown of Thorns will help him fix it, and that will end the incident. Unless—"

It was part of Sister Blessing's nature to look for silver linings, find them, point them out to other people, and then ruin the whole effect by adding *unless*.

"—unless he's from the school board or one of the newspapers. In which case I shall deal firmly with him and send him on his way, wrapped in his original ignorance. It seems a bit early, though, for the school board to start harassing us about the fall term."

Brother Tongue nodded agreement and nervously stroked the neck of the parakeet perched on his forefinger.

"So he's probably a newspaperman. Unless he's another plain ordinary tramp. In which case I shall treat him with dispassionate kindness. There certainly isn't anything to get excited about, we've had tramps before, as you well know. Stop making those noises. You can talk if you want to, if you have to. Suppose the building caught on fire, you could yell 'fire,' couldn't you?"

Brother Tongue shook his head.

"Nonsense, I know better. Fire. Say it. Go on. Fire."

Brother Tongue stared mutely down at the floor. If the place caught on fire he wouldn't give the alarm, he wouldn't say a word. He'd just stand and watch it burn, making sure first that the parakeet was safe.

Quinn knocked on the unpainted wooden door. "Hello. Is anyone here? I've lost my way, I'm hungry and thirsty."

The door opened slowly, with a squawk of unoiled hinges, and a woman stepped out on the threshold. She was about fifty, tall and strong-looking, with a round face and very shiny red cheeks. She was barefooted. The long loose robe she wore reminded Quinn of the muu-muus he'd seen on the women in Hawaii except that the muu-muus were bright with color and the woman's robe was made of coarse grey wool without ornament of any kind.

"Welcome, stranger," she said, and though the words were kind, her tone was wary.

"I'm sorry to bother you, madam."

"Sister, if you please. Sister Blessing of the Salvation. So you're hungry and thirsty and you've lost your way, is that it?"

"More or less. It's a long story."

"Such stories usually are," she said dryly. "Come inside. We never turn away the poor, being poor ourselves."

"Thank you."

"Just mind your manners, that's all we ask. How long since you've eaten?"

"I don't recall exactly."

"So you've been on a bender, eh?"

"Not the kind you mean. But I guess you'd have to call it a bender. It bent me."

She glanced sharply at the tweed jacket Quinn was carrying over his arm. "I know a fine piece of wool when I see it, since we weave all our own cloth. Where'd you get this?"

"I bought it."

She seemed a little disappointed as if she had hoped he would say he had stolen it. "You don't look or act like a beggar to me."

"I haven't been one very long. I don't have the knack of it yet."

"Don't get sarcastic with me. I have to check up on our visitors, in self-protection. Every now and then some prying reporter comes along, or a member of the law bent on mischief."

"I'm bent only on food and water."

"Come in, then."

Quinn followed her inside. It was a single room with a stone floor that looked as if it had just been scrubbed. The biggest skylight Quinn had ever seen provided the place with light.

Sister Blessing saw him staring up at it and said, "If light is to come from heaven, according to the Master, let it come directly, not slanting in through windows."

A wooden table with benches along each side ran almost the entire length of the building. It was set with tin plates, stainless steel spoons, knives and forks, and several kerosene lamps, already cleaned and fueled for the night. At the far end of the room there was an old-fashioned icebox, a woodstove with a pile of neatly cut logs beside it, and a bird cage obviously made by an amateur. In front of the stove a man, middle-aged, thin and pale-faced, sat in a rocking chair with a bird on his shoulder. He wore the same kind of robe as Sister Blessing and he, too, was barefooted. His head was shaved and his scalp showed little nicks and scratches as if whoever had wielded the razor had bad eyes and a dull blade.

Sister Blessing closed the door. Her suspicions of Quinn seemed to be allayed for the time being and her manner now was more that of a hostess. "This is our communal eating room. And that is Brother Tongue of Prophets. The others are all at prayer in the Tower, but I'm the nurse; I must stay with Brother Tongue. He's been sickly, I keep him by the stove at night. How are you feeling now, Brother Tongue?"

The Brother nodded and smiled, while the little bird pecked gently at his ear.

"A most unfortunate choice of names," Sister Blessing added to Quinn in a whisper. "He seldom speaks. But then, perhaps prophets are better off not speaking too much. You may sit down, Mr.—?"

"Quinn."

"Quinn. Rhymes with sin. It could be a bad omen."

Quinn started to point out that it also rhymed with grin, spin, fin, but Sister Blessing replied brusquely that sin was by far the most obvious.

"I gather sin is what brought a young, able-bodied man like you to such a low estate?"

Quinn remembered what Newhouser had said about the people at the Tower, that they were especially hospitable to poor sinners. "I'm afraid so."

"Drinking?"

"Of course."

"Gambling?"

"Frequently."

"Womanizing?"

"On occasion."

"I thought so," Sister Blessing said with gloomy satisfaction. "Well, I'll make you a cheese sandwich."

"Thank you."

"With ham. There are rumors in town we don't eat meat. What nonsense. We work hard. We need meat to keep going. A ham and cheese sandwich for you, too, Brother Tongue? A drop of goat's milk?"

The Brother shook his head.

"Well, I can't force you to eat. But I can at least see that you get some fresh air. It's cool enough now to sit outside for a while. Put your little bird back in his cage and Mr. Quinn will help you with your chair."

Sister Blessing gave orders as if there was no doubt in her mind that they would be carried out promptly and properly. Quinn took the rocking chair outside while Brother Tongue returned the parakeet to its cage and Sister Blessing started to prepare some sandwiches. In spite of her strange clothes and surroundings she gave the impression of an ordinary housewife working in her own kitchen, pleased to be of service. Quinn didn't even try to guess what combination of circumstances had brought her to a place like the Tower.

She sat down on the bench opposite him and watched him eat. "Who told you about us, Mr. Quinn?"

"A man I hitched a ride with, he's a hand on a ranch near here."

"That sounds plausible."

"It should. It's true."

"Where do you come from?"

"First or last?" Quinn said.

"Either, perhaps both."

"I was born in Detroit and the last place I lived was Reno."

"A wicked place, Reno."

"At the moment I'm inclined to agree with you."

Sister Blessing gave a little grunt of disapproval. "I assume that you were, as they say in the vernacular, taken to the cleaners?"

"Thoroughly."

"Did you have a job in Reno?"

"I was a security officer at one of the clubs. Or a casino cop, however you want to put it. I still have a detective's license in Nevada but it probably won't be renewed."

"You were fired from your job?"

"Let's just say I was warned not to mix business with pleasure and I didn't get the message in time." Quinn started on the second sandwich. The bread was homemade and quite stale, but the cheese and ham were good and the butter sweet.

"How old are you, Mr. Quinn?"

"Thirty-five, thirty-six. Thirty-six, I guess."

"Most men your age are at home with their wives and families, not skittering about the mountainside looking for a handout . . . So you're thirty-six. Now what? Are you going to start your life all over again, on a higher plane?"

Quinn stared at her across the table. "Look, Sister, I appreciate the food and hospitality, but I may as well make it clear that I'm not a candidate for conversion."

"Dear me, I wasn't thinking of that at all, Mr. Quinn. We don't go out seeking converts. No, they come to us. When they weary of the world they come to us."

"Then what happens?"

"We prepare them for their ascension of the Tower. There are five levels. The bottom one, where we all begin, is the earth level. The second is the level of the trees, the third mountains, the fourth sky, and fifth is the Tower of Heaven where the Master lives. I've never gotten beyond the third level myself. In fact"—she leaned confidentially toward Quinn, frowning— "I have some difficulty staying there, even."

"Now why is that?"

"It's because of the spiritual vibrations. I don't feel them properly. Or when I do feel them it turns out there's a jet plane overhead, or something's exploded, and the vibrations aren't spiritual at all. Once a tree fell, and I thought I was having the best vibrations ever. I was bitterly disappointed."

Quinn attempted to look sympathetic. "That's too bad."

"Oh, you don't really think so."

"But I do."

"No. I can tell. Skeptics always get a certain twist to their mouths."

"I have a piece of ham caught in my front tooth."

Before she covered her mouth with her hand, a little giggle escaped. She seemed flustered by the sound of it, as if it were a frivolous memento of the past she thought she'd left behind.

She got up and walked over to the icebox. "Shall I pour you some goat's milk? It's very nourishing."

"No, thank you. A cup of coffee would be—"

"We never use stimulants."

"Maybe you should try. Your vibrations might improve."

"I must ask you to be more respectful, Mr. Quinn."

"Sorry. The good food has made me a little light-headed."

"Oh, it wasn't that good."

"I insist it was."

"Well, I admit the cheese isn't so bad. Brother Behold the Vision makes it from a secret recipe."

"Please congratulate him for me." Quinn rose, stretched, and concealed a yawn. "Now I'd better be on my way."

"Where?"

"San Felice."

"It's almost fifty miles. How will you get there?"

"Walk back to the road and hitch another ride."

"You won't find many cars. Most people going to San Felice prefer to take the long way around, by the main highway. And once the sun goes down, cars aren't so likely to stop for a hitchhiker, especially in the mountains. Also, the nights are very cold."

Quinn studied her for a minute. "What's on your mind, Sister?"

"Why, nothing. I mean, I'm concerned with your welfare. Alone in the mountains on a cold night, with no shelter, and wild animals roaming about—"

"What are you leading up to?"

"Well, it occurred to me," she said carefully, "that we might find a simpler solution. Tomorrow morning Brother Crown of Thorns will probably be driving the truck to San Felice. Something's gone wrong with our tractor and Brother Crown has to buy some new parts. I'm sure he wouldn't mind if you rode along with him."

"You're very kind."

"Nonsense," she said with a frown, "it's pure selfishness on my part. I don't want to lie awake worrying about a tenderfoot wandering loose around the mountains . . . We have a storage shed you can sleep in. There's a cot in it and a couple of blankets."

"Are you always this hospitable to strangers, Sister?"

"No, we're not," she said sharply. "We get thieves, vandals, drunkards. We handle them as they deserve."

"How is it I get the royal treatment?"

"Oh, it's not very royal, as you will find out when you try sleeping on that cot. But it's the best we can offer."

From somewhere nearby a gong began to ring.

"Prayers are over," Sister Blessing said. For a few seconds she stood absolutely still, her right hand touching her forehead. "There. Well, we'd better get out of the kitchen now. Sister Contrition will be coming to start the fire for supper and it makes her nervous to have a stranger around."

"What about the others?"

"Each Brother and Sister has a special task until sundown."

"What I meant was, how do the others feel about having a stranger around?"

"You will be treated with courtesy, Mr. Quinn, to the extent that you display it yourself. Poor Sister Contrition has many problems, it might be wise to avoid her. It's the schools. She has three children and the authorities keep insisting she send them to school. And what would they learn in school, I ask you, that the Master can't teach them here if it's fit to learn?"

"It's a subject I'm not prepared to take sides on, Sister."

"You know, for a minute when I first saw you, I thought you might be one of the school authorities."

"I'm flattered."

"You needn't be," Sister Blessing said brusquely. "They're an officious, thick-headed lot. And the trouble they've caused poor Sister Contrition you wouldn't believe. It's no wonder she has as much difficulty with spiritual vibrations as I have."

Quinn followed her outside. Brother Tongue of Prophets was dozing in his rocking chair under a madrone tree, little patches of sunlight glistening on his shaved head.

A short broad-shouldered woman came around the side of the building followed by a boy about eight, a girl a year or so older, and a young woman of sixteen or seventeen. They wore identical grey wool robes except that those of the two younger children reached just below the knees.

They went silently into the communal eating room, with only the young woman giving Quinn a brief questioning glance. Quinn returned the glance. The girl was pretty, with brilliant brown eyes and black wavy hair, but her skin was blotched with pimples.

"Sister Karma," Sister Blessing said. "The poor girl has acne, no amount of prayer seems to help. Come along, and I'll show you where you're to sleep. You won't be comfortable but then neither are we. Indulge the flesh, weaken the spirit. That's what you've always done, no doubt?"

"No doubt at all."

"Doesn't it worry you? Aren't you afraid of what's coming?"

Quinn was more afraid of what might not be coming, money and a job. But all he said was, "I try not to worry about it."

"You *must* worry, Mr. Quinn."

"Very well, Sister, I will begin now."

"You're joking again, aren't you? You're a very peculiar young man." She looked down at her grey robe and at her bare feet, wide and flat and calloused. "I suppose I must seem peculiar to you, too. Be that as it may. I would rather seem peculiar in this world than in the next." She added, "Amen," as if to close the subject.

From the outside, the storage room appeared to be a small replica of the other building. But inside, it was divided into compartments, each of them padlocked. One of the compartments had a small window and was furnished with a narrow iron cot with a thin grey mattress and a couple of blankets partially eaten by moths. Quinn felt the mattress with both hands. It was soft but without resilience.

"Hair," Sister Blessing said. "The Brothers' hair. It was an experiment on the part of Sister Glory of the Ascension, she's very thrifty. Unfortunately, it attracts fleas. Are you susceptible to fleas?"

"I'm susceptible to a lot of things, fleas are probably included."

"Then I'll have Brother Light of the Infinite dose the mattress with sheep dip. First, you'd better test your susceptibility, though."

"How do I do that?"

"Sit down and stay still for a few minutes."

Quinn sat down on the cot and waited.

"Are you being bitten?" Sister Blessing said, after a time.

"I don't think so."

"Well, do you feel anything?"

"Not even a vibration."

"Perhaps we won't bother with the sheep dip, then. You might not like the smell, and poor Brother Light of the Infinite has enough to do."

"As a matter of curiosity," Quinn said, "how many people live here at the Tower?"

"Twenty-seven, right now. At one time there were nearly eighty, but some have strayed, some have died, some have lost faith. Now and then a new convert comes to us, perhaps just casually appears on the doorstep as you did . . . Has it occurred to you that the Lord might have guided your footsteps here?"

"No."

"Think about it."

"I don't have to. I *know* how I got here. This man, Newhouser, picked me up in Reno, said he was going to San Felice. That's what I understood anyway, but it turned out he meant —oh well, it doesn't matter."

"It matters to me," Sister Blessing said.

"How?"

"It's a very odd thing that you should turn out to have a detective's license. I can't believe it's a coincidence. I have a feeling in my bones that it was the will of Lord."

"Your vibrations must be improving, Sister."

"Yes, I think so," she said earnestly. "I think they are."

"Now if you don't mind telling me what my being a detective has to do with—"

"I haven't time right now. I must go and inform the Master that you're here. He doesn't like surprises, especially at mealtimes. He has a weak stomach."

"Let me go with you," Quinn said, getting up from the cot.

"Oh no, I couldn't. Strangers aren't allowed in the Tower."

"Well, would any of the Brothers and Sisters object if I wandered around a little?"

"Some will, some won't. Although all of us here are dedicated to a common cause, we have as many personality differences as you find in other places."

"In brief, I'm to stay here. Is that it?"

"You look tired, a little rest will do you good." Sister Blessing went out and closed the door firmly behind her.

Quinn lay down on the cot, rubbing his chin. He needed a shave, a shower, a drink. Or a drink, a shower, a shave. He dozed off trying to make up his mind about the exact order and dreamed he was back in his hotel room in Reno. He'd won ten thousand dollars and he didn't notice until he spread it out on the bed to count that the bills were all fives and all bore a picture of Sister Blessing instead of Lincoln.

It was still daylight when he awoke, sweating and confused. It took him a minute to remember where he was, the little room looked like a prison.

Someone pounded on the door and Quinn sat up. "Who is it?"

"Brother Light of the Infinite. I've come about the mattress."

"Mattress?"

The door opened and Brother Light of the Infinite entered the room, carrying a gallon tin can. He was a big man with a face crisscrossed with lines like an old paper bag. His robe was dirty and smelled, not unpleasantly, of livestock.

Quinn said, "This is very kind of you, Brother."

"Ain't kindness. Orders. Me with a hundred things to do and that woman can think of a hundred more. Go fix the mattress, she says. Can't let the stranger get all bit up, says she, so here I am wasting my time on fleas. You all bit up?"

"I don't think so."

Brother Light put the can of sheep dip on the floor. "Take off your shirt and look at your belly. They like bellies, the skin's softer, easier to get their *teeth* into."

"While I'm undressing, is there any chance of a shower around here?"

"There's water in the washroom, can't call it a shower exactly . . . Why, you ain't even bit. Must have a hide like an elephant. No use wasting this stuff on you." He picked the can up again and started toward the door.

"Wait a minute," Quinn said. "Where's the washroom?"

"Off to the left a piece."

"I don't suppose you have a razor?"

Brother Light fingered his shaved scalp which bore numerous nicks and scratches like Brother Tongue's. "We got razors, you think I was *born* this way? Only today's not shaving day."

"It is for me."

"You take it up with Brother of the Steady Heart, he's the barber. Don't come bothering me, with all the things I got to do, cows to be milked, goats to be watered, chickens to be fed."

"Sorry to have put you to any trouble."

As he left, Brother Light banged the can of sheep dip against the door frame to indicate his low opinion of apologies.

Quinn, too, went outside, carrying his shirt and tie. He guessed, from the position of the sun, that it was between six and seven o'clock and that he'd slept for a couple of hours.

From the chimney of the communal dining room smoke billowed and the smell of it mingled with the smell of meat cooking and pine needles. The air was crisp and cool.

It seemed to Quinn very healthful air and he wondered whether it had cured the rich old lady who'd built the Tower or whether she had died here, a step closer to heaven. As for the Tower itself, he still hadn't seen it and the only indication he'd had that it actually existed had been the gong sounding the termination of prayers. He would have liked to wander around the place and find the Tower for himself but Brother Light's attitude made him doubt the wisdom of this. The others might be even less friendly.

In the washroom he pumped water into a pail by hand. It was cold and murky, and the grey gritty bar of homemade soap resisted Quinn's attempt to work up a lather. He looked around for a razor. Even if he had found one it wouldn't have done much good, since the washroom contained no mirror. Perhaps the sect had a religious taboo against mirrors. That would account for the necessity of having Brother of the Steady Heart act as barber.

While he was washing and dressing, he considered Sister Blessing's remarks about the Lord guiding his footsteps to the Tower. *She's got bats in the belfry,* he thought. *Which is fine with me unless one of them flies out and bites me.*

When he went back outside, the sun was setting and the mountains had turned from dark green to violet. Two Brothers passed him on their way to the washroom, bowed their heads briefly and silently, and went on. Quinn heard the clinking of metal dishes and the sounds of voices coming from the dining room and he started toward it. He was halfway there when he heard Sister Blessing calling his name.

She came hurrying toward him, her robe flapping in the wind, *like a bat's wings,* he thought, without amusement.

She was carrying a couple of candles and a package of wooden matches. "Mr. Quinn? Yoohoo, Mr. Quinn."

"Hello, Sister. I was just going to look for you."

She was flushed and out of breath. "I've made a terrible mistake. I forgot this was the Day of Renunciation; I was so busy getting Brother Tongue settled back in his own quarters in the Tower. He's well enough now not to need the heat of the stove at night."

"Take a minute to catch your breath, Sister."

"Yes, I must. I'm so flustered, the Master's stomach is bothering him again."

"And?"

"This being the Day of Renunciation, we can't eat with a stranger among us because of—dear me, I've forgotten the reason, but anyhow it's a rule."

"I'm not very hungry anyway," Quinn lied politely.

"Oh, you'll be *fed,* have no doubt of that. It's just that you'll have to wait until the others are through. It will take an hour, perhaps longer, depending on poor Brother Behold the Vision's teeth. They don't fit very well and he gets behind the others. It taxes Brother Light's patience since he works in the fields all day and has a manly appetite. You don't mind waiting?"

"Not at all."

"I've brought you candles and matches. And look what else." From the folds of her robe she produced a dog-eared book. "Something to *read,*" she said with an air of triumph. "We're not allowed books except about the Faith but this is from one year when Sister Karma had to go to school. It's about dinosaurs. Do you think that will interest you?"

"Oh yes. Highly."

"I've read it myself dozens of times. I'm practically an expert on dinosaurs by this time. Promise you won't tell anyone I gave it to you?"

"I promise."

"I'll let you know when the others have finished eating."

"Thank you, Sister."

Quinn could tell from the way she handled the book that it was something very precious to her and that it was a sacrifice on her part to lend it to him. He was touched by her gesture but also a little suspicious of it: *Why me? Why do I get the special treatment? What does she want from me?*

Back in the storage shed he lit the two candles, sat down on the cot and tried to make some plans for the future. First he would hitch a ride in the truck with Brother Crown as far as San Felice. Then he would drop in on Tom Jurgensen and collect his three-hundred dollars. After that—

After that no plans were necessary. He knew all too well what would happen. If he scraped together enough money he'd go back to Reno. If he couldn't make Reno, Las Vegas. If he couldn't get to Las Vegas, one of the poker parlors outside Los Angeles. A job, money; a game, no money. Every time he ran around the circle, the grooves got deeper. He knew he'd have to break out of it some time. Maybe this was it.

All right, he told himself, he'd get a job in San Felice where the only gambling was bingo at the country club once a week. He'd save some money, mail a check for his back rent to the hotel in Reno and have the clerk send on his clothes and the rest of the things he'd left as security. He might even, if everything turned out well, ask Doris to join him . . . No, Doris was part of the circle. Like most of the other people who worked at the clubs, she spent her off-hours at the tables. Some of them had their whole lives under one roof; they slept, ate, worked and played there, with as much single-minded dedication as the Brothers and Sisters of the Tower.

Doris. It was only twenty-four hours since he'd said goodbye to her. She'd offered to lend him money but for reasons he wasn't sure of, either then or now; he'd refused. Maybe he turned it down because he knew money had strings attached, no matter how carefully they were camouflaged. He looked down at the book Sister Blessing had given to him and he wondered what strings were attached to it.

"Mr. Quinn?"

He got up and opened the door. "Come in, Sister. Did you have a good Renunciation Day dinner?"

Sister Blessing glanced at him suspiciously. "Good enough, considering the troubled state of Sister Contrition's mind."

"Just what is one supposed to renounce? Not food, I gather."

"None of your business. Come along now and no smart talking. The dining room's empty and I have your lamb stew heated up and a nice cup of cocoa."

"I thought you didn't believe in stimulants."

"Cocoa is not a *true* stimulant. We had a meeting of the Council about that last year, and it was decided by a large majority that cocoa, because it contained other important nourishment, is quite permissible. Only Sister Glory of the Ascension voted no because she's so stin—thrifty. I told you about the hair in the mattress?"

"Yes," said Quinn, who preferred to forget it.

"You'd better hide the book. Not that anyone would spy on you, but why take a chance?"

"Why, indeed." He covered the book with a blanket.

"Have you read it?"

"Some."

"Don't you think it's very interesting?"

Quinn thought the strings attached to it might be more interesting but he didn't say so.

They went outside. An almost full moon hung low in the redwood trees. Stars studded the sky, hundreds more than Quinn had even seen, and even while he stood and watched, still more appeared.

"Haven't you ever seen a *sky* before?" Sister Blessing said with a touch of impatience.

"Not this one."

"It's the same as always."

"It looks different to me."

Sister Blessing peered anxiously up into his face. "Do you suppose you're having a religious experience?"

"I am admiring the universe," Quinn said. "If you want to put a tag on it, go ahead."

"You don't understand, Mr. Quinn. I prefer that you *not* have a religious experience right at the moment."

"Why?"

"It would be very inconvenient. I have something I want you to do for me and a conversion at this time would interfere."

"You can stop worrying, Sister. Now, about this something you want me to do—"

"I'll tell you later, when you've eaten."

The dining room was empty, and Brother Tongue's rocking chair was gone and so was the bird cage. One place was set at the end of the table nearest the stove.

Quinn sat down and Sister Blessing filled a tin plate with lamb stew and another with thick slices of bread. As she had in the afternoon, she watched Quinn eat with a kind of maternal interest.

"Your color's not very good," she said, after a time. "But you have a hearty appetite and you seem healthy enough. What I mean is, if you were frail, I naturally couldn't ask you to do me any favors."

"Contrary to appearances, I am extremely frail. I have a bad liver, weak chest, poor circulation—"

"Nonsense."

"All right, what's the favor?"

"I want you to find somebody for me. Not find him in person, exactly, but find out what happened to him. You understand?"

"Not yet."

"Before I go on, I'd like to make one thing clear: I can pay you, I have money. Nobody around here knows about it because we all renounce our worldly possessions when we come to the Tower. Our money, our very clothes on our backs, everything goes into the common fund."

"But you kept something of your own in case of emergency?"

"Nothing of the kind," she said sharply. "My son in Chicago sends me a twenty-dollar bill every Christmas with the understanding that I hold on to it for myself and not give it to the Master. My son doesn't approve of all this." She gestured vaguely around the room. "He doesn't understand the satisfactions of a life of service to the Lord and His True Believers. He thinks I went a little crazy when my husband died, and maybe I did. But I've found my real place in the world now, I will never leave. How can I? I am needed. Brother Tongue with his pleurisy attacks, the Master's weak stomach, Mother Pureza's heart—she is the Master's wife and very old."

Sister Blessing got up and stood in front of the stove, rubbing her hands together as if she'd felt the sudden chill of death in the air.

"I'm getting old myself," she said. "Some of the days are hard to face. My soul is at peace but my body rebels. It longs for some softness, some warmth, some sweetness. Mornings when I get out of bed my spirit feels a touch of heaven, but my feet—oh, the coldness of them, and the aches in my legs. Once in a Sears catalogue I saw a picture of a pair of slippers. I often think of them, though I shouldn't. They were pink and furry and soft and warm, they were the most beautiful slippers I ever did see, but of course an indulgence of the flesh."

"A very small one, surely?"

"They're the ones you have to watch out for. They grow, grow like weeds. You get warm slippers and pretty soon you're wanting other things."

"Such as?"

"A hot bath in a real bathtub, with two towels. There, you see?" she said, turning to Quinn. "It's happening already. *Two* towels I asked for, when one would be plenty. It proves my point about human nature—nothing is ever enough. If I had a hot bath, I would want another, and then one a week or even one every day. And if everyone at the Tower did the same we'd all be lolling around in hot baths while the cattle starved and the garden went to weeds. No, Mr. Quinn, if you offered me a hot bath right this minute I'd have to refuse it."

Quinn wanted to point out that he wasn't in the habit of offering hot baths to strange women but he was afraid of hurting the Sister's feelings. She was as earnest and intense about the subject as if she were arguing with the devil himself.

After a time she said, "Have you heard of a place called Chicote? It's a small city in the Central Valley, a hundred miles or so from here."

"I know where it is, Sister."

"I would like you to go there and find a man named Patrick O'Gorman."

"An old friend of yours? A relative?"

She didn't seem to hear the question. "I have a hundred and twenty dollars."

"That's a lot of fuzzy pink slippers, Sister."

Again she made no response. "It may be quite a simple job, I don't know."

"Suppose I find O'Gorman, what then? Do I give him a message? Wish him a happy Fourth of July?"

"You do nothing at all, except come back here and tell me about it, me and only me."

"What if he's no longer living in Chicote?"

"Find out where he went. But please don't try to contact him, no purpose would be served and mischief could be done. Will you accept the job?"

"I'm in no position to pick and choose at the moment, Sister. I must remind you, though, that you're taking quite a risk sending me away from here with a hundred and twenty dollars. I might not come back."

"You might not," she said calmly. "In which case I will have learned another lesson. But then again you might come back, so I have nothing to lose but money I can't spend anyway and can't give to the Master because of my promise to my son."

"You have a trick of making everything seem very reasonable on first examination."

"And on second?"

"I wonder why you're interested in O'Gorman."

"Wonder a little. It won't do you any harm. I will tell you only that what I've asked you to do is highly important to me."

"All right. Where's the money?"

"In a good safe place," Sister Blessing said blandly, "until tomorrow morning."

"Meaning you don't trust me? Or you don't trust the Brothers and Sisters?"

"Meaning I'm no fool, Mr. Quinn. You'll get the money when you're sitting in that truck beside Brother Crown of Thorns at dawn tomorrow."

"Dawn?"

"Early to bed and early to rise puts color in the cheeks and sparkle in the eyes."

"That isn't how I heard it."

"The Master has made certain changes in the proverbs to make them suitable for our children to learn."

"I'm curious about the Master," Quinn said. "I'd like to meet him."

"He's indisposed tonight. Perhaps when you come to visit us again—"

"You seem pretty sure I'll be coming back, Sister. Maybe you don't know about gamblers."

"I knew about gamblers," Sister Blessing said, "long before you saw your first ace of spades."

2

QUINN WAS AWAKENED, while it was still dark, by someone shaking him vigorously by the shoulder. He opened his eyes.

A short fat man, carrying a lantern, was peering down at him through thick-lensed spectacles. "My goodness gracious, I was beginning to think you were dead. You must get up now, immediately."

"Why? What's the matter?"

"Nothing's the matter. It's time to arise and greet the new day. I am Brother of the Steady Heart. Sister Blessing told me to give you a shave and some breakfast before the others get up."

"What time is it?"

"We have no clocks at the Tower. I'll be waiting for you in the washroom."

Quinn soon found out how some of the Brothers had acquired the scars on their chins and scalps. The razor was dull, the light from the lantern feeble, and Brother of the Steady Heart near-sighted.

"My, you are a jumpy one," Brother Heart said with amiable interest. "I guess you suffer from bad nerves, eh?"

"At times."

"While I'm at it I could give your hair a bit of a trim."

"No thanks. The shave's plenty. I wouldn't want to impose."

"Sister Blessing said I was to make you look as much like a gentleman as possible. She's taken quite a fancy to you, seems to me. It kind of rouses my curiosity."

"It kind of rouses mine, too, Brother."

Brother Heart looked as though he wanted to pursue the subject but didn't dare pry into Sister Blessing's affairs or state of mind. "Well, I'll go now and make breakfast. I have the fire lit, won't take a minute to boil some eggs for the two of us."

"Why will there just be two of us?"

Brother Heart's pudgy face turned pink. "It will be more peaceful without Sister Contrition around, she's the regular cook. Oh, but that woman's a devil in the morning. Sour, there's nothing worse than a woman gone sour."

By the time Quinn finished dressing and went over to the dining room, Brother of the Steady Heart had breakfast waiting on the table, boiled eggs and bread and jam. He continued the conversation as if it hadn't been interrupted: "In my day, the ladies didn't own such sharp tongues. They were quiet-spoken and fragile, and had small, delicate feet. Have you noticed what big feet the women have around here?"

"Not particularly."

"Alas, they have. Very large, flat feet."

For all his barbershop chattiness, Brother Heart seemed nervous. He barely touched his food and he kept glancing over his shoulder as if he expected someone to sneak up on him.

Quinn said, "Why the big hurry to get rid of me before the others are up?"

"Well, now. Well, I wouldn't exactly put it that way."

"I would."

"It has nothing to do with you personally, Mr. Quinn. It's just, well, you might call it a precautionary measure."

"I might, if I knew what you were talking about."

Brother Heart hesitated for a moment, biting his underlip as though it itched to talk. "I suppose there's no harm in telling you. It concerns Sister Contrition's oldest child, Karma. Last time the truck was going to the city the girl hid in the back, under some burlap sacks. Brother Crown of Thorns drove halfway to San Felice before he discovered her. The burlap made her sneeze. Karma went to school for a while; it filled her head with bad ideas. She wants to leave here and find work in the city."

"And that's not possible?"

"Oh no, no. The child would be lost in the city. Here at least she is poor among poor."

The sun was beginning to rise and a faint rosy glow filled the skylight. From the invisible Tower came the sound of the gong, and almost immediately Sister Blessing hurried in the door. "The truck is ready, Mr. Quinn. You mustn't keep Brother Crown of Thorns waiting. Here, let me have your coat and I'll give it a good brushing."

Quinn had already brushed it but he gave it to her anyway. She took it outside and made a few swipes at it with her hand.

"Come along, Mr. Quinn. Brother Crown has a long day ahead of him."

He put his coat back on and followed her down the path to the dirt road. She said nothing about either the money or O'Gorman. Quinn had an uneasy feeling that she'd forgotten what happened the previous night and that she was a little crazier than he'd thought at first.

An old Chevrolet truck, lights on and engine chugging, was parked in the middle of the road. Behind the wheel, wearing a straw hat over his shaved head, sat a man younger than the Brothers Quinn had met so far. Quinn guessed his age to be about forty. Brother Crown of Thorns acknowledged Sister Blessing's introduction with a brief smile that revealed a front tooth missing.

"At San Felice, Brother Crown will let you off wherever you wish, Mr. Quinn."

"Thanks," Quinn said, getting into the truck. "But about O'Gor—"

Sister Blessing looked blank. "Have a good trip. And drive carefully, Brother Crown. And don't forget, if there are temptations in the city, turn your back. If people stare, lower your eyes. If they make remarks, be deaf."

"Amen, Sister."

"As for you, Mr. Quinn, the most I can ask is that you behave with discretion."

"Sister, listen—about the money—"

"*Au revoir*, Mr. Quinn."

The truck started rolling down the road. Quinn turned to look back at Sister Blessing but she had already disappeared among the trees.

He thought, *Maybe the whole thing never happened and I'm crazier than the bunch of them put together. Which is quite a bit crazy.*

He said, shouting over the noise of the engine, "A fine woman, Sister Blessing."

"What's that? Can't hear you."

"Sister Blessing is a fine woman but she's getting old. Maybe she forgets things now and then?"

"I wish she would."

"Perhaps just little things, occasionally?"

"Not her," Brother Crown of Thorns said, shaking his head in reluctant admiration. "Memory like an elephant. Turn down your window, will you? God's air is fresh."

It was also cold, but Quinn turned the window down and his collar up and put his hands in his pockets. His fingers touched the cool smoothness of money.

He looked back in the direction of the Tower and said silently, "*Au revoir*, Sister. I think."

Because of the twisting roads and the age and temperament of the truck's engine, it took more than two hours to reach San Felice, a narrow strip of land wedged between the mountains and the sea. It was an old, rich, and very conservative city which held itself aloof from the rest of Southern California. Its streets were filled with spry elderly ladies and tanned elderly men and athletic young people who looked as if they'd been born on tennis courts and beaches and golf courses. Seeing the city again Quinn realized that Doris, with her platinum hair and heavy make-up, would feel conspicuous in it, and feeling that way she would make it a point to look even more conspicuous and end up beaten. No, Doris would never fit in. She was a night person and San Felice was a city of day people. For them dawn was the beginning of a day, not the tail-end of a night, and Sister Blessing and Brother Crown, for all their strange attire, would look more at home among them than Doris. *Or me,* Quinn thought, and he felt his plans and resolutions dissolving inside himself. *I don't belong here. I'm too old for tennis and skin-diving, and too young for checkers and canasta.*

His fingers curled around the money in his pocket. A hundred and twenty dollars plus the three hundred Tom Jurgensen owed him made four hundred and twenty. If he went back to Reno and played carefully, if his luck was good—

"Where do you want to get off at?" Brother Crown said. "I'm going to Sears myself."

"Sears will be fine."

"You got a friend in town?"

"I had one. Maybe I've still got him."

Brother Crown pulled into the parking lot behind Sears and braked the truck to a noisy stop. "Here you are, safe and sound, like I promised Sister Blessing. You and the Sister ever meet before?"

"No."

"She don't always make such a how-de-do over strangers."

"Maybe I remind her of somebody."

"You don't remind me of nobody." Brother Crown climbed down from the truck and started shuffling across the parking lot toward the back door of Sears.

"Thanks for the ride, Brother," Quinn called out after him.

"Amen."

It was nine o'clock, eighteen hours since Sister Blessing had welcomed him to the Tower as a stranger and treated him like a friend. He touched the money in his pocket again. He could feel its strings pulling at him and he wished he hadn't taken it. He thought of running after Brother Crown and giving it to him to return to Sister Blessing. Then he remembered that the possession of private money was not allowed at the Tower and handing it over now to Brother Crown would get Sister Blessing into trouble, perhaps of a very serious kind.

He turned and began walking quickly toward State Street.

Tom Jurgensen sold boats and marine insurance down at the foot of the breakwater. He had a tiny office whose windows were plastered with For Sale signs and pictures of yawls and sloops and ketches and cutters and schooners, most of them under sail.

When Quinn entered, Jurgensen was smoking a cigar and talking into the telephone which perched affectionately on his shoulder the way Brother Tongue's little bird had perched on his. "Sails by Rattsey, so what. The thing's a tub. I'm not bidding."

He put the phone down and leaned over the desk to shake Quinn's hand. "Well, Joe Quinn himself in person. How's the old boy?"

"Older. Also broke."

"I was hoping you wouldn't say that, Joe. Business has been lousy. This isn't a rich man's town anymore. The penny-pinching middle class has moved in and they don't care about teakwood or mahogany, all they want—" Jurgensen broke off with a sigh. "You're absolutely flat?"

"Except for a little money that belongs to someone else."

"Since when did you ever let that worry you, Joe? I'm being funny, of course, ha ha."

"Ha ha, sure you are," Quinn said. "I've got your I.O.U. for three hundred dollars. I want the money now."

"I don't have it. This is damned embarrassing, old boy, but I just don't have it. If you'd settle for a boat, I've got a nice little sea mew, 300-pound keel, Watts sails, gaff rig—"

"Just what I need to get around Venice. Only I'm not going to Venice."

"Keep your shirt on, it was just a suggestion. I suppose you already have a car?"

"Bad supposing, Tom."

"Well, there's this crate—this dandy little' 54 Ford Victoria my wife's been driving. She'll put up a terrible squawk if I take it away from her but what can I do? It's worth at least three hundred. Two-tone blue and cream, white-walls, heater, radio."

"I could do better than that on a' 54 Ford in Reno."

"You're not in Reno like you're not in Venice," Jurgensen said. "It's the best I can do for you right now. Either take the car in full payment or use it until I can scrape up your money. It will suit me better if you just borrow it. That way Helen will be a little easier to handle."

"It's a deal. Where's the car?"

"Parked in the garage behind my house, 631 Gaviota Road. It hasn't been used for a week—Helen's visiting her mother in Denver—so you might have a little trouble starting it. Here are the keys. You going to be in town for a while, Joe?"

"In and out, I expect."

"Call me in a couple of weeks. I may have your money then. And take care of the crate or Helen will accuse me of losing it in a poker game. She may anyway, but—" Jurgensen spread his hands and shrugged. "You're looking pretty good, Joe."

"Early to bed and early to rise puts color in the cheeks and sparkle in the eyes. Like they say."

"Like who says?"

"The Brothers and Sisters of the Tower of Heaven."

Jurgensen raised his eyebrows. "You taken up religion or something?"

"Something," Quinn said. "Thanks for the car and I'll see you later."

Quinn had no trouble starting the car. He drove to a gas station, filled up the tank, added a quart of oil and parted with the first of Sister Blessing's twenty-dollar bills.

He asked the attendant the best way to get to Chicote.

"If it was me now, I'd follow 101 to Ventura, then cut over to 99. It's longer that way but you don't get stuck on 150, which hasn't half a mile of straightaway from one end to the other. You save trading stamps, sir?"

"I guess I could start."

As soon as he turned inland, at Ventura, he began to regret not waiting until night to make the trip. The bare hills, alternating with lemon and walnut groves, shimmered in the relentless sun, and the air was so dry that the cigarettes he'd bought in San Felice snapped in two in his fingers. He tried to cool off by thinking of San Felice, the breeze from the ocean and the harbor dotted with sails, but the contrast only made him more uncomfortable and he stopped thinking entirely for a while, surrendering himself to the heat.

He reached Chicote at noon. Since his last visit the small city had changed, grown bigger but not up and certainly not better. Fringed by oil wells and inhabited by the people who lived off them, it lay flat and brown and hard like something a cook had forgotten to take out of the oven. Underprivileged trees grew stunted along streets dividing new housing tracts from old slums. Small children played in the dust and weeds of vacant lots, looking just as contented as the children playing in the clean white sand of the San Felice beaches. It was in the teenagers that Quinn saw the uneasiness caused by a too quick and easy prosperity. They cruised aimlessly up and down the streets in brand new convertibles and ranch wagons. They stopped only at drive-in movies and drive-in malt shops and restaurants, keeping to their cars the way soldiers in enemy territory kept to their tanks.

Quinn bought what he needed at a drugstore and checked in at a motel near the center of town. Then he ate lunch in an air-conditioned café that was so cold he had to turn up the collar of his tweed jacket while he ate.

When he had finished he went to the phone booth at the rear of the café. Patrick O'Gorman was listed in the directory as living at 702 Olive Street.

So that's all there is to it, Quinn thought with a mixture of pleasure and disappointment. O'Gorman's still in Chicote and I've made a quick hundred and twenty dollars. I'll drive

163

back to the Tower in the morning, give Sister Blessing the information, and then head for Reno.

It seemed very simple, and yet the simplicity of it worried Quinn. If this was all there was to it, why had Sister Blessing played it so close to the chest? Why hadn't she just asked Brother Crown to call O'Gorman from San Felice or look up his address in the out-of-town phone books stocked both by the public library and the main telephone office? Quinn couldn't believe that she hadn't thought of both these possibilities. She was, in her own words and by Quinn's own observation, no fool. Yet she had paid a hundred and twenty dollars for information she could have got from a two-dollar phone call.

He put a dime in the slot and dialed O'Gorman's number.

A girl answered, breathlessly, as if she had raced somebody else to the phone. "This is the O'Gorman residence."

"Is Mr. O'Gorman there, please?"

"Richard's not a mister," the girl said with a giggle. "He's only twelve."

"I meant your father."

"My fath—? Just a minute."

There was a scurry at the other end of the line, then a woman's voice, stilted and self-conscious: "To whom did you wish to speak?"

"Mr. Patrick O'Gorman."

"I'm sorry, he's not—not here."

"When do you expect him back?"

"I don't expect him back at all."

"Perhaps you could tell me where I can reach him?"

"Mr. O'Gorman died five years ago," the woman said and hung up.

3

OLIVE STREET WAS in a section of town that was beginning to show its age but still trying to preserve appearances. Seven-o-two was flanked by patches of well-kept lawn. In the middle of one a white oleander bloomed, and in the middle of the other stood an orange tree bearing both fruit and blossoms at the same time. A boy's bicycle leaned carelessly against the tree as if its owner had suddenly found something more interesting to do. The windows of the small stucco house were closed and the blinds drawn. Someone had recently hosed off the sidewalk and the porch. Little puddles steamed in the sun and disappeared even as Quinn watched.

The front door had an old-fashioned lion's-head knocker made of brass, newly polished. Reflected in it Quinn could see a tiny crooked reflection of himself. In a way it matched his own self-image.

The woman who answered the door was, like the house, small and neat and no longer young. Although her features were pretty and her figure still good, her face lacked any spark of interest or animation. It was as if, at some time during her life, she had stepped outside and had never been able to find her way back in.

Quinn said, "Mrs. O'Gorman?"

"Yes. But I'm not buying anything."

She's not selling either, Quinn thought. "I'm Joe Quinn. I used to know your husband."

She didn't exactly unbend but she seemed faintly interested. "That was you on the telephone?"

"Yes. It was kind of a shock to me, suddenly hearing that he was dead. I came by to offer my condolences and apologize if my call upset you in any way."

"Thank you. I'm sorry I hung up so abruptly. I wasn't sure whether it was a joke or not, or a piece of malice, having someone ask for Patrick after all these years. Everyone in Chicote knows that Patrick's gone."

Gone. Quinn registered the word and her hesitation before saying it.

"Where did you know my husband, Mr. Quinn?"

There was no safe reply to this but Quinn picked one he considered fairly safe. "Pat and I were in the service together."

"Oh. Well, come inside. I was just making some lemonade to have ready for the children when they get home."

The front room was small and seemed smaller because of the wallpaper and carpeting. Mrs. O'Gorman's taste—or perhaps O'Gorman's—ran to roses, large red ones in the carpet, pink and white ones in the wallpaper. An air-conditioner, fitted into the side window, was whirring noisily but without much effect. The room was still hot.

"Please sit down, Mr. Quinn."

"Thank you."

"Now tell me about my husband."

"I was hoping you'd tell me."

"But that isn't how it's done, is it?" Mrs. O'Gorman said. "When a man comes to offer condolences to the widow of his old war buddy, reminiscences are usually called for, aren't they? So please start reminiscing. You have my undivided attention."

Quinn sat in an uneasy silence.

"Perhaps you're the shy kind, Mr. Quinn, who needs a little help getting started. How about, 'I'll never forget the time that—'? Or you might prefer a more dramatic approach. For instance, the Germans were coming over the hill in swarms and you lay trapped inside your wrecked tank, injured, with only your good buddy Pat O'Gorman to look after you. You like that?"

Quinn shook his head. "Sorry, I never saw any Germans. Koreans, yes."

"All right, switch locales. The scene changes to Korea. There's not much sense in wasting that hill and the wrecked tank—"

"What's on your mind, Mrs. O'Gorman?"

"What's on yours?" she said with a small steely smile. "My husband was not in the service, and he never allowed anyone to call him Pat. So suppose you start all over, taking somewhat less liberty with the truth."

"There isn't any truth in this case, or very little. I never met your husband. I didn't know he was dead. In fact, all I knew was his name and the fact that he lived here in Chicote at one time."

"Then why are you here?"

"That's a good question," Quinn said. "I wish I could think of an equally good answer. The truth just isn't plausible."

"The listener is supposed to be the judge of plausibility. I'm listening."

Quinn did some fast thinking. He had already disobeyed Sister Blessing's orders not to try and contact O'Gorman. To bring her name into it now would serve no purpose. And ten chances to one Mrs. O'Gorman wouldn't believe a word of it anyway, since the Brothers and Sisters of the Tower of Heaven didn't make for a very convincing story. There was one possible way out: if O'Gorman's death had taken place under peculiar circumstances (and Quinn remembered the way Mrs. O'Gorman had hesitated over the word "gone") she might want to talk about it. And if she did the talking, he wouldn't have to.

He said, "The fact is, I'm a detective, Mrs. O'Gorman."

Her reaction was quicker and more intense than he had anticipated. "So they're going to start in all over again, are they? I get a year or two of peace, I reach the point where I can walk down the street without people staring at me, feeling sorry for me, whispering about me. Now things will be right back where they were in the first place, newspaper headlines, silly men asking silly questions. My husband died by accident, can't they get that through their thick skulls? He was *not* murdered, he did *not* commit suicide, he did *not* run away to begin a new life with a new identity. He was a devout and devoted man and I will not have his memory tarnished any further. As for you, I suggest you stick to tagging parked cars and picking up kids with expired bicycle licenses. There's a bicycle in the front yard you can start with; it hasn't had a license for two years. Now get out of here and don't come back."

Mrs. O'Gorman wasn't a woman either to argue with or to try and charm. She was intelligent, forceful and embittered, and the combination was too much for Quinn. He left quickly and quietly.

Driving back to Main Street, he attempted to convince himself that his job was done except for the final step of reporting to Sister Blessing. O'Gorman had died by accident, his wife claimed. But what kind of accident? If the police had once suspected voluntary disappearance, it meant the body had never been found.

"My work is over," he said aloud. "The whys and wheres and hows of O'Gorman's death are none of my business. After five years the trail's cold anyway. On to Reno."

Thinking of Reno didn't help erase O'Gorman from his mind. Part of Quinn's job at the club, often a large part, was to be on the alert for men and women wanted by the police in other states and countries. Photographs, descriptions and Wanted circulars arrived daily and were posted for the security officers to study. A great many arrests were made quietly and quickly without interfering with a single spin of the roulette wheels. Quinn had once been told that more people wanted by the police were picked up in Reno and Las Vegas than in any other places in the country. The two cities were magnets for bank robbers and embezzlers, conmen and gangsters, any crook with a bank roll and a double-or-nothing urge.

Quinn parked his car in front of a cigar store and went in to buy a newspaper. The rack contained a variety, three from Los Angeles, two from San Francisco, a San Felice *Daily Press*, a *Wall Street Journal*, and a local weekly, *The Chicote Beacon*. Quinn bought a *Beacon* and turned to the editorial page. The paper was published on Eighth Avenue, and the publisher and editor was a man named John Harrison Ronda.

Ronda's office was a cubicle surrounded by six-foot walls, the bottom-half wood paneling, the top-half plate glass. Standing, Ronda could see his whole staff, seated at his desk he could blot them all out. It was a convenient arrangement.

He was a tall, pleasant-faced, unhurried man in his fifties, with a deep resonant voice. "What can I do for you, Quinn?"

"I've just been talking to Patrick O'Gorman's wife. Or shall we say, widow?"

"Widow."

"Were you in Chicote when O'Gorman died?"

"Yes. Matter of fact I'd just used my last dime to buy this paper. It was in the red at the time and might still be there if the O'Gorman business hadn't occurred. I had two big breaks within a month. First O'Gorman, and then three or four weeks later one of the local bank tellers, a nice little lady—why are some of the worst embezzlers such nice little ladies?—was caught with her fingers in the till. All ten of them. The *Beacon's* circulation doubled within a year. Yes, I owe a lot to O'Gorman and I don't mind admitting it. He was the ill wind that blew the wolf away from my door. So you're a friend of his widow's, are you?"

"No," Quinn said cautiously. "Not exactly."

"You're sure?"

"I'm sure. She's surer."

Ronda seemed disappointed. "I've always kept hoping Martha O'Gorman would suddenly come up with a secret boyfriend. It would be a great thing if she married again, some nice man her own age."

"Sorry, I don't fit the picture. I'm older than I look and I have a vile temper."

"All right, all right, I get the message. What I said still goes, though. Martha should remarry, stop living in the past. Every year O'Gorman seems to become more perfect in her eyes. I admit he was a good guy—a devoted husband, a loving father —but dead good guys are about the same as dead bad ones where the survivors are concerned. In fact, Martha would be better off now if she found out O'Gorman had been a first-class villain."

"Perhaps that's still possible."

"Not on your life," Ronda said, shaking his head vigorously. "He was a gentle, timid man, the exact opposite of the fighting Irishman you hear about and maybe meet, though I never have myself. One of the things that drove the police crazy when they were on the murder kick was the fact that they couldn't find a single soul in Chicote who had a bad word to say about O'Gorman. No grudges, no peeves, no quarrels. If O'Gorman was done in—and there's no doubt of it, in my mind—it must have been by a stranger, probably a hitchhiker he picked up."

"Timid men don't usually go in for picking up hitchhikers."

"Well, he did. It was one of the few things he disagreed with Martha about. She thought it was a dangerous practice but that didn't stop him. Sympathy for the underdog was what motivated him. I guess he felt like an underdog himself."

"Why?"

"Oh, he was never much of a success, financially or any other way. Martha had the guts and force in the family, which is a good thing because in the following years she really needed them. The insurance company held off settling O'Gorman's policy for almost a year because his body wasn't found. Meanwhile Martha and the two children were penniless. She went back to work as a lab technician in the local hospital. She's still there."

"You seem to know her well."

"My wife's one of her close friends, they attended the same high school in Bakersfield. For a time there, when I had to print a lot of stuff about O'Gorman, things were cool between Martha and me. But she came to understanding that I was only doing my job. What's your interest in the case, Quinn?"

Quinn said something vague about his work in Reno involving missing persons. Ronda seemed satisfied. Or, if he wasn't, he pretended to be. He was a man who obviously enjoyed talking and welcomed an occasion for it.

"So he was murdered by a hitchhiker," Quinn said. "Under what circumstances?"

"I can't remember every detail after such a time lapse but I can give you a general picture if you like."

"I would."

"It was the middle of February, nearly five and a half years ago. It had been a winter of big rains—most of the news I printed was rainfall statistics and stories on whose basement was flooded and whose backyard had been washed out. That year the Rattlesnake River, about three miles east of town, was running high. Now, and every summer, it's nothing but a dry ravine, so it's kind of hard to imagine what a torrent it was then. To make a long story short, O'Gorman's car crashed through the guardrail of the bridge and into the river. It was found a couple of days later when the flood subsided. A piece of cloth snagged on the door hinge had bloodstains on it, barely visible to the naked eye but quite clearly identified in the police lab. The blood was O'Gorman's type and the cloth was a piece of the shirt he'd been wearing when he left the house that night after dinner."

"And the body?"

"A few miles farther on, the Rattlesnake River joins the Torcido, which is fed by mountain snow and lives up to its name. Torcido means angry, twisted, resentful, and that about describes it, especially that year. O'Gorman wasn't a big man. He could easily have been carried down the Rattlesnake River into the Torcido and never found again. That's what the police believed then and still believe. There's another possibility, that he was murdered in the car after a struggle which tore his shirt, and then buried some place. I myself go along with the river theory. O'Gorman picked up a hitchhiker— don't forget it was a stormy night and a soft-hearted man like O'Gorman wouldn't pass up anyone on the road—and the hitchhiker tried to rob him and O'Gorman put up a fight. I myself believe the man must have been a stranger in these parts and didn't realize the river was only temporary. He may have thought the car would never be found."

"And then what happened to the stranger?" Quinn said.

Ronda lit a cigarette and scowled at the burning match. "Well, there's the weak point of the story, of course. He disappeared as completely as O'Gorman. For a while there the sheriff was picking up damn near everyone who wasn't actually born in Chicote, but nothing was proved. I'm an amateur student of crime in a way, and it seems to me a crime of impulse like this one, even though it's often bungled by lack of planning, may remain unsolved because of the very lack of planning."

"Who decided that it was a crime of impulse?"

"The sheriff, the coroner, the coroner's jury. Why? Don't you agree?"

"All I know is what you've told me," Quinn said. "And that hitchhiking stranger seems a little vague."

"I admit that."

"If he had a bloody struggle with O'Gorman, we'll have to assume the stranger got some blood on his own clothes. Were there any shacks or cottages in the vicinity where he could have broken in to change his clothes, steal some food and so on?"

"A few. But they weren't broken into, the sheriff's men checked every one of them."

"So we're left with a very wet stranger, probably with blood on him."

"The rain could have washed it away."

"It's not that easy," Quinn said. "Put yourself in the stranger's place. What would you have done?"

"Walked into town, bought some dry clothes."

"It was night, the stores were closed."

"Then I'd have checked into a motel, I guess."

"You'd be pretty conspicuous, the clerk would certainly remember and probably report you."

"Well, dammit, he must have done something," Ronda said. "Maybe he got a ride with somebody else. All I know is, he disappeared."

"Or she. Or they."

"All right, she, it, him or her, they disappeared."

"If they ever existed."

Ronda leaned across the desk. "What are you getting at?"

"Suppose the person in the car wasn't a stranger. Let's say it was a friend, a close friend, even a relative."

"I told you before, the sheriff couldn't find a single person who'd say a word against O'Gorman."

"The kind of person I'm thinking of wouldn't be likely to come forward and admit he had a grudge if he'd just murdered O'Gorman. Or she."

"You keep repeating *or she*. Why?"

"Why not? We're only dealing in possibilities anyway."

"I think you mean Martha O'Gorman."

"Wives," Quinn said dryly, "have been known to harbor grudges against husbands."

"Not Martha. Besides, she was at home that night, with the children."

"Who were in bed, sleeping?"

"Naturally they were in bed, sleeping," Ronda said irritably. "It was about 10:30. What do you think they were doing, playing poker and having a few beers? Richard was only seven then, and Sally five."

"How old was O'Gorman at the time?"

"Around your age, say forty."

Quinn didn't correct him. He felt forty, it seemed only fair that he should look it. "What about O'Gorman's description?"

"Blue eyes, fair skin, black curly hair. Medium build, about five foot nine or ten. There was nothing particularly arresting about his appearance but he was nice-looking."

"Have you a picture of him?"

"Five or six blown-up snapshots. Martha let me have them while she was still hoping O'Gorman would be found alive, maybe suffering from amnesia. Her hopes died hard but once they died, that was it. She's utterly convinced O'Gorman's car hit the bridge accidentally and O'Gorman was swept away by the river."

"And the piece of shirt with the bloodstains?"

"She thinks he was cut by the impact of the car against the guardrail. The windshield was broken and two of the windows, so it's possible. There's one argument against it, though: O'Gorman had the reputation of being a very cautious driver."

"What about suicide?"

"Again, it's possible," Ronda said, "and again there are elements that refute it. First, he was a healthy man, with no real financial worries or emotional problems, none that came to light anyway. Second, he was a strict Catholic, as Martha is. And I mean the kind that practices religion and believes every last word and comma of it. Third, he was in love with his wife and crazy about his children."

"A lot of what you've just told me doesn't come under the heading of fact. Think about it, Ronda."

"You think about it," Ronda said, grimacing. "After five years of veering this way and veering that way, maybe I need a fresh approach. Go on."

"All right. Let's say a fact is what can be proved. Fact one, he was healthy. Fact two, he was a practicing Catholic for whom suicide would constitute a deadly sin. The other things you mentioned are not facts but inferences. He may have had financial and emotional problems he didn't talk about. He may not have been as crazy about his wife and children as he pretended to be."

"Then he put up quite a front. And, frankly, I don't believe O'Gorman had the brains to put up any kind of front. I'd never say anything like this to Martha, but to me O'Gorman seemed almost dull-witted, in fact, stupid."

"What did he do, for a living?"

"He was a payroll clerk for one of the oil companies. I'm pretty sure Martha helped him at night with his job though she'd die before admitting it. Martha's loyalties are strong, even to her own mistakes."

"Of which O'Gorman was one?"

"I think he'd have been a mistake for any really intelligent woman to marry. O'Gorman just didn't have it. The two of them were more like mother and son than husband and wife, though Martha was actually a few years younger. I suppose the truth is that the pickings in Chicote, for a woman as bright as Martha, weren't very good and she did the best she could. O'Gorman was, as I said, nice-looking with a lot of curly black hair and so on. When holes in the head are hidden by big blue eyes, even a woman like Martha can be susceptible. Fortunately, the kids take after her, they're both sharp as tacks."

"Mrs. O'Gorman," Quinn said, "appears to have quite an aversion to the police."

"It's justified. She went through a very rough experience, and this isn't a very civilized town. The sheriff's an eager beaver who couldn't build a dam if his life depended on it. His attitude throughout the whole affair seemed to be that Martha should have kept O'Gorman from going out in the rain that night, then nothing would have happened."

"Just why did he go out?"

"According to Martha, he thought he'd made an error in one of the books that day and wanted to return to the field office to check."

"Did anyone take the trouble to examine the books?"

"Oh yes. O'Gorman was right. A mistake had been made. The bookkeeper found it easily, a simple error in addition."

"What do you think that proves?"

"Proves?" Ronda repeated, frowning. "That O'Gorman was dull-witted but conscientious, just as I said he was."

"It could prove something else, though."

"Such as?"

"That O'Gorman made that mistake deliberately."

"Why would he do a thing like that?"

"So he'd have a legitimate excuse to go back to the field office that night. Did he often do work in the evenings?"

"I told you, I think Martha often helped him but she'd never admit it," Ronda said. "Anyway, you're out in left field as far as the facts are concerned. O'Gorman didn't have the brains or the character for intrigue of any kind. Granted, a man can put on an act of being stupider than he is. But he can't give a perfect performance twenty-four hours a day, 365 days a year, the way O'Gorman did. No, Quinn. There could only be one reason why he went back to the office that night, during the worst rainstorm of the year—he was scared stiff of being caught in an error and losing his job."

"You seem sure."

"Positive. You can sit there and dream up intrigues, secret meetings, conspiracies and whatever. I can't. I knew O'Gorman. He couldn't think his way out of a wet paper bag."

"As you pointed out yourself, however, he had Mrs. O'Gorman to assist him in his work. Maybe she helped him in other things, too."

"Look, Quinn," Ronda said, slapping the desk with the flat of his hand. "We're talking about two very nice people."

"As nice as the little lady you mentioned who was caught with her fingers in the till? I'm not trying to give you a bad time, Ronda, I'm just puzzling a few possibilities."

"The possibilities in this case are almost endless. Ask the sheriff, if you don't believe me. Practically every crime in the book, except arson and infanticide, was suggested and investigated. Maybe you'd be interested in seeing my file on the case?"

"Very much," Quinn said.

"I kept a personal file, in addition to what we printed in the *Beacon*, because of Martha being an old friend. Also because —well, frankly, I've always had the feeling that the case would be reopened some day, that maybe some burglar in Kansas City, or some guy up on another murder charge in New Orleans or Seattle, would confess to killing O'Gorman and settle everything once and for all."

"Didn't you ever think, or hope, that O'Gorman himself might turn up?"

"I hoped. I didn't think, though. When O'Gorman left the house that night he had two one-dollar bills in his wallet, his car, and the clothes on his back, and that's all. Martha handled the money for the family, she knew to a cent how much O'Gorman was carrying."

"No clothes were missing from his closet?"

"None," Ronda said.

"Did he have a bank account?"

"A joint one with Martha. He could easily have cashed a check that afternoon without Martha finding out about it until later, but he didn't. He also didn't borrow any money."

"Did he have anything valuable he might have taken along to pawn?"

"He owned a wrist watch worth about a hundred dollars, a present from Martha. It was found in his bureau drawer." Ronda lit another cigarette, leaned back in the swivel chair and studied the ceiling. "Aside from all the physical evidence which would rule out a voluntary disappearance, there is the emotional evidence: O'Gorman had become, over the years, completely dependent on Martha; he couldn't have lasted a week without her, he was like a little boy."

"Little boys his age can become a nuisance," Quinn said dryly. "Maybe the police were wrong to rule out infanticide."

"If that's a joke, it's a bad one."

"Most of mine are."

"I'll get that file for you," Ronda said, rising. "I don't know why I'm doing all this, except I guess I'd like to see the case closed once and for all so Martha could start seriously considering remarriage. She'd make a fine wife. You probably haven't seen her at her best."

"No, and I doubt that I will."

"She's lively, full of fun—"

"The pitch doesn't fit the product," Quinn said, "and I'm not in the market."

"You're very suspicious."

"By nature, training, experience and observation, yes."

Ronda went out and Quinn sat back in the chair, frowning. Through the glass paneling he could see the tops of three heads, Ronda's bushy grey one, a man's crew cut, and a woman's elaborate bee-hive-style coiffure, the color of persimmons.

The shirt, he thought. *That's it, it's the shirt that bothers me, the piece of cloth snagged on the hinge of the car door. On the stormiest night of the year why wasn't O'Gorman wearing a jacket or a raincoat?*

Ronda came back, carrying two cardboard boxes labeled simply Patrick O'Gorman. The boxes contained newspaper clippings, photographs, snapshots, copies of telegrams and letters to and from various police officials. Though most of them originated in California, Nevada and Arizona, others came from remote parts of the country and Mexico and Canada. The material was arranged in chronological order, but to go through it all would require considerable time and patience.

Quinn said, "May I borrow the file overnight?"

"What do you intend to do with it?"

"Take it to my motel and examine it. There are one or two points I'd like to go into more fully—the condition of the car, for instance. Was there a heater in it and was it switched on?"

"What's that got to do with anything?"

"If the accident happened the way Mrs. O'Gorman believes it did, O'Gorman was driving around on the stormiest night of the year in his shirt sleeves."

Ronda looked puzzled for a minute. "I don't think anything was ever brought up concerning a heater in the car."

"It should have been."

"All right, take the stuff with you for tonight. Maybe you'll come across some other little thing the rest of us missed."

He sounded as if he felt the project was hopeless, and by eight o'clock that night Quinn was beginning to share the feeling. The facts in the case were meager, and the possibilities seemed endless.

Including infanticide, Quinn thought. *Maybe Martha O'Gorman was getting pretty tired of her little boy, Patrick.*

One item that especially interested Quinn was from a transcript of Martha O'Gorman's testimony before the coroner's jury: "It was about 8:30. The children were in bed sleeping and I was reading the newspaper. Patrick acted restless and worried, he couldn't seem to settle down. Finally I asked him what was the matter and he told me he'd made a mistake that afternoon and wanted to go back to the field office to correct it before anyone discovered it. Patrick was so terribly conscientious about his work—please, I can't go on. Please. Oh Lord, help me—"

Very touching, Quinn thought. *But the fact remains, the children were asleep, and Martha and Patrick O'Gorman could have left the house together.*

No evidence was brought out about a heater in the car, although the piece of wool flannel with the bloodstains on it was discussed at length. The blood type was the same as O'Gorman's, and the flannel was part of a shirt O'Gorman frequently wore. Both Martha and two of O'Gorman's fellow clerks identified it. It was a bright yellow and black plaid, of the Macleod tartan, and his co-workers had kidded O'Gorman about an Irishman wearing a Scotch tartan.

"All right," Quinn said, addressing the blank wall. "Suppose I'm O'Gorman. I'm sick of being a little boy. I want to run away and see the world. But I can't face up to Martha so I have to disappear. I arrange to be in an accident while I'm wearing a shirt that will be identified as mine by a lot of people. I choose the time carefully, when the river is high and it's still raining. Okay, I rig the accident and the piece of flannel with my own blood on it. Then what? I'm left standing in my underwear in a heavy rainstorm three miles from town with only two bucks to my name. Great planning, O'Gorman, really great."

By nine o'clock he was more than willing to believe in Ronda's hitchhiking stranger.

4

QUINN ATE A late dinner at El Bocado, a bar and grill across the street from his motel. Entertainment facilities in Chicote were limited and the place was crowded to the doors with ranchers in ten-gallon Stetsons and oil workers in their field clothes. There weren't many women: a few wives already worried at nine about driving home at twelve; a quartet of self-conscious girls celebrating a birthday and acting a good deal noisier than the two prostitutes at the bar; a prim-faced woman about thirty standing near the door. She wore a blue turban, horn-rimmed spectacles and no make-up. She looked as if she had entered the place thinking it was the YWCA, and was now trying to muster the courage to walk out.

She spoke briefly to one of the waitresses. The waitress glanced around the room, her eyes finally settling on Quinn.

She approached him without hesitation. "Would you mind sharing your table, mister? There's a lady that has to eat before she catches the bus to L.A. Those bus stops serve lousy food."

So did El Bocado, but Quinn said politely, "I don't mind." Then, to the woman in the turban, "Please sit down."

"Thank you very much."

She sat down opposite him as if she expected to find a bomb under the seat.

"This is very kind of you, sir."

"Not at all."

"It is, though." She added, with an air of disdain, "In *this* town a lady never knows what to expect."

"You don't like Chicote?"

"Does anyone? I mean, it's terribly uncouth. That's why I'm leaving."

She herself looked a bit too couth, Quinn decided. Some lipstick and a less severe hat that showed a little of her hair would have improved her. Even without them she was pretty, with the kind of earnest anemic prettiness Quinn associated with church choirs and amateur string quartets.

Over fish and chips and cole slaw, she told Quinn her name, Wilhelmina de Vries, her occupation, typist, her ambition, to be a private secretary to an important executive. Quinn told her his name, his occupation, security officer, and his ambition, to retire.

"A security officer," she repeated. "You mean a policeman?"

"More or less."

"Isn't that simply fascinating? My goodness, are you here working on a case?"

"Let's just say I'm having a little holiday."

"No one comes to Chicote for a holiday. It's the kind of place people are always trying to get out of, like me."

"I'm interested in California history," Quinn said. "Where towns like this got their names, for instance."

She looked disappointed. "Oh, that's easy. Some man came out here from Kentucky for his health in the late 1890's. He was going to grow tobacco, fields and fields of the world's finest tobacco for the world's finest cigars. That's what Chicote means, cigar. Only the tobacco didn't grow, and the ranchers switched to cotton, which did. Then oil was discovered and that was the end of Chicote as an agricultural center. But here I am, doing all the talking, and you just sit there." Her smile revealed a dimple in her left cheek. "Now it's your turn. Where do you come from?"

"Reno."

"What are you doing here?"

"Learning some California history," Quinn said with considerable truth.

"That's a funny way for a policeman to be spending his time."

"*Chacun à son gout*, as they say in Hoboken."

"How true," she murmured. "Just as true here, I suppose, as it is in Hoboken."

Although her face didn't change expression, Quinn had a feeling that he was being kidded, and that, if Miss Wilhelmina de Vries sang in a church choir or played in a string quartet, some of the notes she produced would he intentionally off-key just for the hell of it.

"Please tell me really and truly and honestly," she said, "why you're visiting Chicote."

"I like the climate."

"It's miserable."

"The people."

"Uncouth."

"The cuisine."

"A starving dog would turn up his nose at this awful stuff. You know something? I'll bet a dollar to a doughnut you're working on a case."

"I'm a betting man but I'm fresh out of doughnuts."

"No, seriously, you really *are* here on a case, aren't you?" Her blue-green eyes glistened behind the thick lenses of her spectacles. "There hasn't been anything interesting happening lately so it has to be an old case . . . Does it involve money, a lot of money?"

It was one question Quinn could answer without hesitation. "Nothing I do involves a lot of money, Miss de Vries. What did you have in mind?"

"Nothing."

"So you're going down to Los Angeles to find a job?"

"Yes."

"Where's your suitcase?"

"Suit—oh, I checked it. At the bus depot. So I wouldn't have to carry it around. It's heavy, since all my clothes are in it and everything. And it's a terribly big suitcase in the first place."

If she'd simply claimed to have checked the suitcase, he might have believed her, having no reason not to. But she'd elaborated too much, as though she'd been trying to make the suitcase real to herself as well as Quinn.

The waitress brought Quinn's check.

"I must be going," he said, rising. "Nice to have met you, Miss de Vries. And good luck in the big city."

He paid the cashier and walked across the street to his motel. The garage belonging to the first unit was open. He stepped inside, watching the door of El Bocado café.

He didn't have long to wait. Miss Wilhelmina de Vries came out, stood hesitantly on the curb, and looked up and down the street. A wind had started blowing, brisk but very warm, and she was attempting to hold down her skirt and her turban at the same rime. Modesty finally won out. She unwound the turban, which turned out to be a long blue scarf, and stuffed it into her purse. Under the street lamp her hair, released from its confinement, sprung up in all directions and shone in the light, the color of persimmons. She walked half a block down the street, climbed into a small dark sedan, and drove off.

Quinn had no chance to follow her. By the time he could get his own car out of the garage and on the road, she would be home, or at the bus depot or wherever else young ladies like Miss de Vries went after an unsuccessful attempt to pump information out of a stranger. She was, obviously, an amateur at the game, and the turban, and probably the spectacles, too, were a crude disguise. Quinn wondered why she'd bothered with a disguise when he didn't even know her. Then he remembered sitting in John Ronda's office at the *Beacon* and seeing through the glass partition the tops of three heads. One of them had had hair the color of persimmons.

All right, assume she was there, Quinn thought. Ronda had a loud, distinct voice, and the walls of his office were only six feet high. Miss de Vries could have overheard something of sufficient interest to her to make her assume a disguise and arrange a pick-up in the El Bocado café, maybe with the collaboration of the waitress. But exactly what had she heard? The only subject he and Ronda had discussed was the O'Gorman case, the details of which were common knowledge in Chicote, the evidence a matter of public record available to anyone.

Miss de Vries had made what could be construed as a reference to O'Gorman—"it has to be an old case"—and then practically nullified it by adding, "Does it involve a lot of money?" There was no money connected with the O'Gorman business except the two one-dollar bills O'Gorman was carrying when he left the house for the last time.

Ronda's only mention of a subject unconnected with O'Gorman was his brief remark about a nice little lady embezzler caught with her fingers in the till. Quinn wondered what had happened to the nice little lady, and the money, and who else had been involved.

He crossed the driveway and went into the motel office to pick up his key. The night clerk, an old man with arthritis-swollen hands, looked up from the movie magazine he was reading. "Yes, sir?"

"The key to number seventeen, please."

"Seventeen, yes, sir. Just a minute." He shuffled over to the key rack. "Ingrid's not about to make a go of it with Lars any more than Debbie will with Harry. And you can quote me."

"Oh, I will," Quinn said. "Daily."

"What's that number again?"

"Seventeen."

"It's not here." The old man peered at Quinn over the top of his bifocals. "Why, I gave you number seventeen not more than an hour ago. You told me your name and gave me the license number of your car like it's written right here in the book."

"I wasn't here an hour ago."

"You must of been. I gave you the key. Only you had a hat on, a grey fedora, and you were wearing a topcoat. Maybe you been drinking and don't remember? Liquor befogs the memory something fierce. They say Dean has trouble with his lines on account of belting too many."

"At nine o'clock," Quinn said wearily, "I turned my key in to the girl who was here in the office."

"My granddaughter."

"All right, your granddaughter. I haven't been back since. Now, if you don't mind, I want into my room, I'm tired."

"Been carousing around, eh?"

"That's right. Carousing around trying to forget Ingrid and Debbie. Now find your pass-keys and let's get going."

Grumbling, the old man led the way outside and down the driveway. The air was still hot and dry, and not even the brisk wind could dispel the faint odor of oil that hung over the city.

Quinn said, "Pretty warm night for a hat and topcoat, isn't it?"

"I ain't wearing a hat and a topcoat."

"The man you gave my key to was."

"All that carousing's befogged your memory." They had reached the door of Quinn's room and the old man let out a sudden cry of triumph. "Lookie here, will you? See, the key's right in the lock where you left it. I told you. I gave it to you and you forgot about it. Now what do you think of that, eh?"

"Very little."

"You traveling fellows get careless, belting the booze and all."

There didn't seem to be any way of convincing the old man he was wrong, so Quinn said good night and locked himself in the room.

It looked, at first glance, exactly the way he'd left it, the bed rumpled, the pillows propped against the headboard, the gooard, the goosenecked lamp switched on. The two cardboard boxes containing Ronda's file on O'Gorman were still on the desk. It was impossible for Quinn to tell whether anything had been removed from them. Even Ronda, who had collected the material, might find it difficult, since he probably hadn't looked through it for years.

Quinn removed the lid from the first box. In a large manila envelope were the pictures of O'Gorman which Martha had given to Ronda: one formal photograph, obviously very old, since O'Gorman looked about twenty at the time; the rest snapshots, O'Gorman with the children, with a dog and cat, with Martha; O'Gorman changing a tire, standing beside a bicycle. In every case O'Gorman looked like a part of the background, and it was the dog and cat, the children, Martha, the bicycle, which seemed the real subjects of the pictures. Only the formal photograph showed O'Gorman's face clearly. He'd been a handsome young man with curly black hair and large gentle eyes with a faint expression of bafflement in them, as though he found life puzzling and not quite what he'd been led to expect. It was the kind of face that would appeal to a lot of women, especially the ones who might think they could solve life's puzzles for him and, motherlike, kiss away the hurts and bruises it inflicted.

Quinn returned the pictures to the envelope, his movements slowed by a sudden feeling of depression. Until he studied the portrait, O'Gorman had seemed unreal to him. Now O'Gorman had become a human being, a man who loved his wife and children and house and dog, who worked hard at his job, a man too soft-hearted to leave a hitchhiker standing on the road on a stormy night yet brave enough to resist a robber.

He had two bucks in his pocket, Quinn thought as he took off his clothes and got into bed. *Why did he put up a fight for a lousy two bucks? It doesn't make sense. There must have been something else, something no one has mentioned . . . I must talk to Martha O'Gorman again tomorrow. Maybe Ronda can arrange it for me.*

He didn't remember, until just before he fell asleep, that he had planned on driving back to the Tower in the morning, and from there to Reno. Both places were beginning to seem remote to him, dream stuff compared to the blunt and solid reality of Chicote. He couldn't even conjure up a clear picture of Doris, and Sister Blessing was no more than a bulky grey robe with a faceless head sticking out of one end and two large bare feet out of the other.

5

EARLY THE NEXT morning Quinn returned to the motel office. A middle-aged man, with a bald, sunburned pate, was untying a bundle of Los Angeles papers.

"What can I do for you, Mr.—ah—Quinn, isn't it? Seventeen?"

"Yes."

"I'm Paul Frisby, owner and manager, with the aid of my family. Is anything the matter?"

"Someone got into my room last night when I went across the road to have dinner."

"I did," Frisby said coldly.

"Any particular reason why?"

"Two of them. It's our policy that when a guest checks in without any luggage, we give his room the once-over when he goes out to eat. In your case there was an additional reason: the name on your car registration isn't Quinn."

"The car was lent to me by a friend."

"Oh, I believe you. But in this business it pays to be careful."

"Granted," Quinn said. "Only why the cloak-and-dagger routine?"

"Pardon?"

"The business of disguising yourself with a hat and topcoat and getting the key from the old man."

"I don't know what you're talking about," Frisby said, narrowing his eyes. "I have my own set of keys. Now what's this about grandpa?"

Quinn explained briefly.

"Grandpa has trouble with his eyes," Frisby said. "Glaucoma. You mustn't blame—"

"I'm not blaming anybody. I'd just like to know how someone else could walk in here, ask for my key and get it."

"We try to prevent things like that happening. But in the motel business they happen occasionally, especially if the impostor knows the name and car license number of the guest. Was anything taken?"

"I'm not sure. There were two boxes on the desk containing documents lent to me to examine. You must have seen the boxes when you were in the room, Frisby."

"Well. Well, as a matter of fact, yes."

"Did you open either of them?"

Frisby's face turned as red as the sunburn on his pate. "No. No, I didn't have to. I saw the label, O'Gorman. Everybody in Chicote knows all about that case. Oh certainly, I was curious about why a stranger should suddenly appear in town with a lot of stuff about O'Gorman."

There was a long uneasy silence.

"Just how curious were you?" Quinn said finally. "Did you tell your wife, for instance?"

"Well, I sort of mentioned it to her, yes."

"Anyone else?"

"Mister. Put yourself in my place for a minute—"

"Who else?"

After another silence Frisby said nervously, "I phoned the sheriff, I thought there might be some hanky-panky going on that he ought to know about, maybe something real serious. I can see now I was wrong."

"Can you?"

"I'm a pretty good judge of character and you don't act like a man who's got anything much to hide. But yesterday it was different. You check in with no luggage, driving a car with someone else's name and address on it and you're toting around a lot of stuff about O'Gorman. You can't blame me for being suspicious."

"So you called the sheriff."

"I just talked to him. He promised he'd keep his eye out for you."

"Would keeping his eye out extend to tricking an old man into giving him the key to number seventeen?"

"Great Scott, no," Frisby said vigorously. "Besides, Grandpa's known the sheriff since he was a little boy."

"Everybody in Chicote seems to know everybody else."

"It's a fact. There's no metropolis anywhere near, we're not on a main highway and it's rugged country. Here we all are, dependent on each other for survival, so naturally we get to know each other."

"And naturally you're suspicious of strangers."

"It's a close community, Mr. Quinn. When something like the O'Gorman affair happens, it affects every one of us. Most of us knew him, went to school with him or worked with him or met him at church and civic gatherings and the P.T.A. Not that O'Gorman was much for getting involved with community business, but Mrs. O'Gorman was, and he tagged along." A small grim smile moved across Frisby's face. "You might say that's a fitting epitaph for O'Gorman: 'He tagged along.' What's your interest in the case, Mr. Quinn? You going to write it up, maybe, for one of those true-crime magazines?"

"Maybe."

"Be sure to let me know when it's published."

"I'll do that," Quinn said.

He ate breakfast in a coffee shop, sitting at a front table so he could watch his car parked across the road with the O'Gorman file locked in the trunk. Although Frisby had given him no lead about the intruder of the previous night, he'd given him something else for which Quinn was grateful: an excuse to go around asking questions. He was, hereafter, an amateur writer looking for a new angle on the disappearance of O'Gorman.

He bought a pocket-sized notebook and a couple of ball point pens at a drug store before he drove to the *Beacon* office on Eighth Avenue. As soon as he opened the door he could hear John Ronda's voice distinctly above the clatter of typewriters and the ringing of a telephone. The red-haired Miss de Vries would have had no trouble at all eavesdropping even if she'd worn earmuffs.

Ronda said, "Good morning, Quinn. I see you've brought my file back safely."

"I'm not sure how safely." Quinn told him about the man with the topcoat and fedora.

Ronda listened, frowning and drumming his fingers on the desk. "Maybe he was just a petty thief after something else in the room."

"There wasn't anything else. I left my stuff in Reno, I intended to be back there by now."

"Why aren't you?"

"I got interested in O'Gorman," Quinn said easily. "I thought it might make an interesting article for one of the true-crime magazines."

"It already has, about a dozen times in the past five and a half years."

"Maybe I'll find a new angle. I started off on the wrong foot with Mrs. O'Gorman yesterday but I thought you might be able to fix that for me."

"How?"

"Call her, give me a little build-up."

Ronda looked pensively up at the ceiling. "I guess I could try it, but I'm not sure I want to. I know nothing about you."

"Ask questions, we'll get acquainted."

"All right. First, I'd better warn you, however, that I talked to Martha O'Gorman last night and she told me about your phone call and subsequent visit to her house. What interested me is that when you telephoned Martha at noon you apparently weren't aware that O'Gorman was dead."

"That's right, I wasn't."

"Why did you want to see him?"

"Professional ethics—"

"Which," Ronda interrupted, "obviously doesn't include telling whoppers to widows."

"—forbids me to name names, so I'll call my client Mrs. X. Mrs. X paid me to find out if a man named Patrick O'Gorman lived in Chicote."

"And?"

"That's all. I was merely to find out if he was still here, not talk to him or give him any message or contact him."

"Oh, come off it, Quinn," Ronda said brusquely. "All Mrs. X had to do was write a letter to the city authorities, the mayor, the sheriff, even the Chamber of Commerce. Why should she hire you to drive all the way up here?"

"She did."

"How much did she pay you?"

"A hundred and twenty dollars."

"For the love of heaven, she must be off her rocker."

"That's a good way of putting it," Quinn said. "For the love of heaven, she is."

"A nut, eh?"

"A lot of people would say so. By the way, all this is in confidence."

"Certainly. What's Mrs. X's connection with O'Gorman?"

"She didn't tell me, if there is one."

"It seems," Ronda said, "a funny job for a man like you to take."

"When I'm broke I take funny jobs."

"What broke you?"

"Roulette, dice, blackjack, casino."

"You're a professional gambler?"

Quinn's smile was humorless. "Amateur. The professionals win. I lose. This time I lost everything. Mrs. X's money looked nice and green and crisp."

"Telling whoppers to widows," Ronda said, "and taking money from nutty old women doesn't make you exactly a hero, Quinn."

"Not exactly. Mrs. X isn't old, by the way, and except for some rather obvious eccentricities, she's an intelligent woman."

"Then why didn't she simply write a letter, or make a phone call?"

"Neither is allowed where she lives. She's a member of an obscure religious cult which forbids unnecessary contact with the outside world."

"Then how," Ronda said dryly, "did she come across you?"

"She didn't. I came across her."

"How?"

"You probably won't believe me."

"I haven't so far. Keep trying, though."

Quinn kept trying and Ronda listened, shaking his head now and then in incredulity.

"It's crazy," he said when Quinn had finished. "The whole thing's crazy. Maybe you are, too."

"I'm not ruling out the possibility."

"Where is this place, anyway, and what's it called?"

"I can't tell you that. It's one of a number of cults, not uncommon in Southern California, made up of misfits, neurotics, the world's rejects. For the most part they mind their own business and stay out of trouble except for some brushes with the local authorities about schooling for the children."

"All right," Ronda said with a vague gesture. "Suppose I believe the whole implausible story, what do you want me to do?"

"Try and square me with Martha O'Gorman, for one thing."

"That may not be easy."

"And for another, tell me the name of the red-haired woman who was in your outer office yesterday afternoon when you went to get the file on O'Gorman."

"Why do you want to know that?"

"She picked me up in the El Bocado café last night," Quinn said, "at the same time that the man in the fedora was searching my room."

"You think there's a connection?"

"When do you expect Mrs. King to be back?" Quinn said.

"Any time. And I mean just that, any time. People get away with murder in a place like this. There are no *rules*. Are you a businessman, Mr.—?"

"Quinn. I'm in business, yes."

"Then you know that a business can't operate properly without hard and fast rules strictly adhered to by its employees. Without rules, what have we? Chaos."

Quinn glanced around the almost empty office. "Nice quiet kind of chaos."

"Chaos doesn't always show on the surface," Perkins said sourly. "For instance, my lunch hour is from twelve to one. It is now almost one, and I haven't eaten yet. A trivial example to you, perhaps, but not to me. I could have shown that property and been back here by eleven o'clock, because I don't fool around and then try to make up for it by buttering up the boss."

"How long has Mrs. King worked for Mr. Haywood?"

"I don't know. I was just hired last January."

"Is there a Mr. King?"

"Not in evidence," Perkins said with satisfaction. "She's a divorcée."

"Have you lived in Chicote very long?"

"All my life except for the two years I spent at San Jose State College. Can you beat that, two whole years of college and I end up—well. *Well*, it's about *time*."

The door opened with a blast of hot, dry air and Willie King came in, wearing a white sleeveless dress and a wide-brimmed straw hat. Because of the hat she didn't notice Quinn at first.

"I'm sorry I'm late, Earl."

"Well, I should *think* so," Perkins said. "My ulcer—"

"The place is as good as sold. I had to lie a little about the climate, though." She put her handbag on one of the desks, removed her hat, and saw Quinn. Except for a brief tightening of the mouth, her face didn't change expression. "I—I'm sorry, I didn't realize we had a client. Can I help you, sir?"

"Oh, I think so," Quinn said.

"I'll be with you in a minute. You'd better go and have your lunch now, Earl. And remember, no pepper, no ketchup."

"It's not pepper that's eating away my insides," Perkins said. "It's lack of *rules*."

"All right, you go and think up some good rules. Make a list."

"I already made a list."

"Make another one."

"By God, I will," Perkins said and slammed the door after him.

"He's only a boy," Willie King said in a maternal tone. "Much too young to have ulcers. I don't suppose you have ulcers, Mr. Quinn?"

"I might acquire a few if I try to swallow some of the stories you tell, Mrs. King. With or without pepper and ketchup. Did you enjoy your trip to L.A.?"

"I changed my mind."

"You decided Chicote was couth enough for you after all?"

"What I said about Chicote still goes. It's a hole."

"Then crawl out of it."

"I might fall in a worse one," she said with a shrug of her bare shoulders. "Besides I have ties here. Connections."

"Such as Mr. Haywood."

"Mr. Haywood, naturally. He's my boss."

"Off the job as well as on?"

"I don't know what you're talking about," she said blandly. "Unless you could be referring to last night?"

"I could be, yes."

"As a matter of fact, that was entirely my own idea. I heard you talking to Mr. Ronda in his office when I went in with our ads for the next issue of the *Beacon*. You were discussing the O'Gorman case. Naturally my curiosity was aroused. To the people of Chicote the word O'Gorman is what the word *earthquake* is to San Franciscans. Everybody's got a story about it, or a theory. Everybody knew O'Gorman or claimed to have known him. So"—she paused and took a deep breath— "so I got this idea, that maybe you were working on the case and that you might have found a new lead, and that you and I—"

"You and I what?"

"We could solve the case together. Make a scoop. Become famous."

"That was your idea, eh? Dreams of glory?"

"Oh, it sounds kind of silly when I say it in cold blood like this, but that's the honest truth about why I picked you up and tried to pump you last night."

"And who," Quinn said, "was your friend?"

"What friend?"

"The man who searched my room."

"I know nothing about that," she said, frowning. "Maybe you're just making it up to confuse me."

"Where was George Haywood last night?"

"In bed with a cold, I guess. He's been away from the office all week, he has bronchitis . . . Good heavens, you don't think for a minute that Mr. Haywood—"

"Yes, I think for a minute that Mr. Haywood got into my motel room while you were putting on your little act at El Bocado."

"Why, that's terrible," Willie King said vehemently. "That's just a terrible thing to think, it really is. Mr. Haywood is one of the most respected and well-liked businessmen in the whole community. He's a wonderful person."

"Chicote seems to have more wonderful people in it than heaven. But one of them got into my room by tricking an old man out of the key and I still think it was Haywood and that you helped him."

"That's libel. Or is it slander? I get them mixed up."

"You get a lot of things mixed up, Mrs. King. Now why don't you try telling the truth for a change? What's George Haywood's interest in me? What did he want from my room, and, more important, what did he get?"

"You'd realize how ridiculous all this is if you met Mr. Haywood."

"I'm trying to."

"Why?" Her face had turned almost as white as her dress.

"So I can ask him why he used you as a decoy to—"

"No. Please. You *can't* do that. He doesn't know anything about my picking you up in that awful place. He'd be mad if he found out about it, he might even fire me."

"Come off it, Mrs. King."

"No, I mean it. He's a stickler for conventions, especially since that business about his sister, Alberta. Because she did something wrong, he feels he's got to avoid the slightest hint of nonconformity or even bad taste. And that goes for his employees, too. Do you want to get me fired?"

"No."

"Then please don't tell him about last night. He'd never understand that I was just sort of playing a game—you know, Willie King, girl detective. Mr. Haywood isn't the type for games, he's too sober-minded. Promise you won't tell on me?"

"I might," Quinn said, "in return for a few favors."

Willie King studied him thoughtfully for a minute. "If you mean the kind I think you mean—"

"You read me wrong, Mrs. King. I only want to ask you a few questions."

"Ask ahead."

"Do you know Haywood's mother?"

"Do I not," Willie King said grimly. "What about her?"

"She had two daughters, didn't she?"

"Not to hear her tell it. George—Mr. Haywood isn't even allowed to mention their names, especially Alberta's."

"What happened to the other one?"

"Ruth? She ran away and got married to a man her mother didn't approve of, a fisherman from San Felice named Aguila. That was the end of her as far as the old girl was concerned."

"Where is Mrs. Aguila now?"

"In San Felice, I guess. Why?"

"Just checking."

"But why are you checking the Haywood family?" she said sharply. "Why aren't you talking to the people who knew O'Gorman?"

"Mr. Haywood knew him."

"Only very briefly, and in the line of business."

"So did Alberta Haywood."

"She may have met him, but I'm not even sure of that."

"George Haywood," Quinn said, "was very fond of his sister, is that right?"

"Yes, I suppose so."

"So fond, in fact, that after her embezzlement was discovered George himself had to answer a lot of questions from the police?"

It was only a guess on Quinn's part, and he was surprised by the vehemence of her reaction. "They were more than questions, I can tell you. They were downright accusations with question marks. Where was the money? How much of it had Alberta lent or given to George? How could George have lived in the same house with her and not have guessed that she was up to something? Didn't he see the racing forms she brought home every day?"

"Well, didn't he?"

"No. She didn't take them home. Not a single copy was found in her room or anywhere else in the house."

"A careful lady, Alberta. Or else someone took the trouble to clean up after her. Did you know her, Mrs. King?"

"Not very well. Nobody did. I mean, she was one of those background people you see every day but you don't think of as a person until something happens."

"'You don't think of as a person until something happens,'" Quinn repeated. "Perhaps that was her main motive, getting some attention."

"You're wrong," Willie King said with a brisk shake of her head. "She suffered horribly, incredibly. I went to the trial. It was terrible, it was like watching an animal that's been badly injured and can't tell you where it hurts so you can help."

"Yet George Haywood turned his back on her?"

"He had to. Oh, it must seem inhuman to you. You weren't there. I was. The old lady threw a fit every hour on the hour to prevent George from having anything to do with Alberta."

"Why all the vindictiveness on Mrs. Haywood's part?"

"It's in her nature, for one thing. For another, Alberta was always a disappointment to her mother. She was shy and plain, she didn't have boyfriends, she didn't get married and produce children, she wasn't even interesting to live with. Years and years of disappointment to a woman like Mrs. Haywood—well, I got the impression she used the embezzlement as an excuse to do what she'd always wanted to do to Alberta, kick her out and have done with her, forget her." Willie King looked down at her hands, slim and pale, bare of rings. "Then there was George, of course, the apple of her eye. When his first wife died I think Mrs. Haywood would have danced in the streets if it hadn't been for the neighbors. It meant

George belonged entirely to her again, head, heart and gall bladder. That woman is a monster. But don't let me go on about that, I could talk for weeks."

She didn't have to talk for weeks to make one point clear: the old lady and Willie King were fighting for the same man.

The telephone rang and Mrs. King answered it in a crisp, professional voice: "Haywood Realty Company. Yes . . . I'm sorry, the house across from Roosevelt Park didn't meet FHA specifications. We're going to work on another loan for you . . . Yes, as soon as possible." She put down the phone and made a little grimace in Quinn's direction. "Well, it's back to work for me. I hate to break this up, I've enjoyed talking to you, Mr. Quinn."

"Maybe you'd like to talk some more, say this evening?"

"I really couldn't."

"Why not? Taking a bus to L. A.?"

"Taking my kid sister to a movie."

"I'm sorry," Quinn said, rising. "Perhaps next time I come to town?"

"Are you leaving?"

"There's nothing to keep me here since you have a date with your kid sister."

"When are you coming back?"

"When do you want me to come back?"

Willie gave him a long, direct stare. "Stop kidding around. I know when a man's serious about wanting a date with me and when he's not. You're not. And I'm not."

"Then why are you interested in when I'm coming back?"

"I was merely being polite."

"Thanks," Quinn said. "And thanks for the information."

"You're welcome. Good-bye."

Quinn walked down the street to his car, drove a block west, made a U-turn and parked in the parking lot of a supermarket. From there he had a view of the Haywood Realty Company and the clock on top of the city hall.

At 1:30 Earl Perkins returned from lunch, looking as if it hadn't agreed with him. Two minutes later Willie King came out wearing the wide-brimmed straw hat and clutching her handbag. She looked flustered but determined as she climbed into her car and headed south.

Quinn followed her at a distance. Judging from the direct route she took to her destination, Quinn surmised that either she considered herself secure or she was in too much of a hurry to care.

She pulled into the driveway of an old frame house bearing a Haywood Realty "For Sale" sign on a porch pillar, unlocked the front door and went inside. For a minute Quinn thought he'd been mistaken about her after all—she was apparently doing just what she said she was going to do, get back to work. The house faced Roosevelt Park and was without doubt the one she had referred to on the telephone.

He was on the point of leaving when a green Pontiac station wagon stopped in front of the house and a man got out. In spite of the heat he wore a dark grey suit and a matching fedora. He was tall and thin and he walked with slow deliberation as if he'd been told not to hurry. Halfway up the porch steps he was seized by a fit of coughing. He leaned on the railing, holding one hand to his mouth and the other against his chest. When he had finished coughing he let himself into the house, using a key from a large key ring he pulled from his pocket.

Neat, safe and simple, Quinn thought. *When George and Willie want to get together without the old lady or anyone else knowing about it, they meet by prearrangement in one of Haywood Realty's vacant houses. Maybe a different house each time. And Willie's impassioned plea for me not to go to George and get her fired was just an attempt to prevent me from seeing him and asking questions. Well, it was a good performance, I almost fell for it. In fact, I almost fell for Willie.*

Quinn stared at the old frame house as if he were expecting one of the blinds to snap up and reveal some secrets. Nothing happened. It was a dead end and he knew it. Even if he waited and accosted George Haywood, he couldn't force any information out of him, he had no authority to ask him questions, and no proof that Haywood had been the man who had searched his motel room.

He turned on the ignition and pulled the car away from the curb. It was nearly two o'clock, checking-out time at the motel. By sticking to the mountain roads and by-passing San Felice, he figured he could reach the Tower by five.

Willie heard George's key in the lock and the front door open and close again. She wanted to run out into the hall and fling herself into his arms. Instead she waited, motionless, in the darkened living room, wondering whether the time would ever come when she would be able to act the way she felt in George's presence. Lately he seemed to discourage her enthusiasm as if he had too many serious problems on his mind to endure any extra demands on him.

"I'm in here, George." The empty room amplified her voice like an echo chamber. It sounded too hearty. She must remember to speak low.

George came in from the hall. He had taken off his hat and was holding it across his chest as if he were hearing the strains of "The Star-Spangled Banner." She felt a giggle tickling her throat and swallowed hard to suppress it.

"You were followed," he said.

"No. I swear I didn't see—"

"Quinn's car is parked across the street."

She raised a corner of one of the shades and looked out.

"I don't see any car."

"It was there. I told you to be careful."

"I tried." The giggle in her throat had been replaced by a lump she couldn't do anything about except pretend it wasn't there. "Are you feeling better today, George?"

He shook his head impatiently as if there was no time to be bothered by such trivialities. "Quinn's on to something. He called the office and then the house. Mother brushed him off as I asked her to."

At the mere mention of Mrs. Haywood, Willie's body began to stiffen. "I could have done the same thing."

"I'm afraid you've lost his confidence."

"I don't think so. He asked me for a date tonight."

"Did you accept?"

"No."

"Why not?"

"I—didn't think you'd want me to."

"You might have gotten some useful information."

She stared at the old brick fireplace. She thought of all the fires that had been built there and left to die and she wondered if there'd ever be another one.

"If I've hurt your feelings," he said in a gentler voice, "I'm sorry, Willie."

"Don't be. Obviously you have more important matters on your mind than my feelings."

"I'm glad you see that."

"Oh, I do. You've made it quite clear."

He put his hands on her shoulders. "Willie, don't. Please. Be patient with me."

"If you'd only tell me what all this is about—"

"I can't. It's a serious business, though. A lot of people are involved, good people."

"Does it matter what kind of people they are? And how do you tell the difference between good people and bad people? Do you ask your mother?"

"Leave her out of it, please. She hasn't the faintest idea what's going on."

"I'll leave her out if she'll leave me out." She turned to face him, ready for a fight. But he looked too tired and pale to endure a fight. "Forget it, George. Let's go out and come in again, shall we?"

"All right."

"Hello, George."

He smiled. "Hello, Willie."

"How are you?"

"Fine. And you?"

"I'm fine, too." But she turned her face away from his kiss. "This isn't much better than the first time, is it? You're not really thinking of me, you're thinking of Quinn. Aren't you?"

"I'm forced to."

"Not for long."

"What do you mean, not for long?"

"He's leaving town."

George's hands dropped to his sides as if she'd slapped them down. "When?"

"This afternoon, I guess. Maybe right this minute."

"Why? Why is he leaving?"

"He said he had no reason to stay since I wouldn't go out with him tonight. Naturally he was joking."

She waited, hoping George would deny it: *Of course Quinn wasn't joking, my dear. You're a very attractive woman. He's probably leaving town to avoid a broken heart.*

"He was joking," she repeated.

But George didn't even hear her this time. He was crossing the room, putting on his hat as he moved.

"George?"

"I'll call you in the morning."

"Where are you going? We haven't even talked yet, George."

"I haven't time right now. I'm showing a client the Wilson house out in Greenacres."

She knew the Wilson property was being handled by Earl Perkins and that George wouldn't interfere, but she didn't argue.

At the archway that led into the hall he turned and looked back at her. "Do me a favor, will you, Willie?"

"Certainly. You're the boss."

"Tell my mother I won't be home for dinner and not to wait up for me."

"All right."

It was a big favor and they both knew it.

Willie stood, listening to the front door open and close, then the sound of the station wagon motor and the squeaking of tires as the car made too quick a start. Head bowed, she walked over to the old fireplace. The inside was charred by the heat of a thousand fires. She stretched her hands out in front of her as if one of the fires might have left a little warmth for her.

After a time she went outside, locking the house behind her, and drove to the post office. Here, from a pay phone, she called George's house.

"Mrs. Haywood?"

"Yes."

"This is Willie King."

"Mrs. King, yes, of course. My son is not at home."

Willie clenched her jaws. In all their conversations Mrs. Haywood never referred to George as anything but *my son,* with a distinct emphasis on the *my.* "Yes, I know that, Mrs. Haywood. He asked me to tell you he'll be away for the evening."

"Away where?"

"I don't know."

"Then he won't be with you?"

"No."

"He's been away a great many evenings lately, and days, too."

"He has a business to run," Willie said.

"And of course you're a big help to him?"

"I try to be."

"Oh, but you are. He tells me you're a most *aggressive* salesman—or is it saleswoman? One thing baffles me about my son's business. I find it quite extraordinary the number of real estate deals that are consummated at night—the word *is* consummated, isn't it?"

"The word is whatever you want to make it, Mrs. Haywood."

There was a brief silence during which Willie put her hand over the receiver so that Mrs. Haywood wouldn't hear her angry breathing.

"Mrs. King, you and I are both fond of George, aren't we?"

I am, Willie thought. *You're not fond of anything.* But she said, "Yes."

"Has it occurred to you to wonder, perhaps, exactly where he's going tonight?"

"That's his business."

"And not yours?"

"No." *Not yet,* she added silently.

"Dear me, I think it should be your business if you're as interested in my son as you appear to be. He is, of course, a man of fine character, but he's human and there are temptresses around."

"Are you urging me to spy on him, Mrs. Haywood?"

"Using one's eyes and ears is not spying, surely." There was another silence, as if Mrs. Haywood was taking time out to plan a more devastating attack. But when she spoke again her voice sounded curiously broken. "I have this feeling, this very terrible feeling, that George is in trouble . . . Oh, you and I have never been friendly, Mrs. King, but I haven't considered you a real threat to George's welfare."

"Thank you," Willie said dryly. She was puzzled by Mrs. Haywood's sudden change of voice and attitude. "I have no reason to believe George is in trouble he can't handle."

"He is. I feel it, I know it. It involves a woman."

"A woman? I'm sure you're mistaken."

"I wish I were but I'm not. There have been too many things recently, too many unexplained out-of-town trips. Where does he go? What does he do? Whom does he see?"

"Have you asked him?"

"Yes. He told me nothing, but he couldn't hide his guilt. And what else besides a woman would he be feeling guilty about?"

"I'm quite sure you're mistaken," Willie said again. But this time she could hear the doubt in her own voice, and for a long time after she'd hung up she remained in the cramped, airless booth, her forehead resting against the telephone.

8

FINDING THE DIRT lane that led to the Tower was more difficult than Quinn thought it was going to be. He went two or three miles beyond it before he realized he had missed it. He made a precarious turn, and driving very slowly, in low gear, he tried to spot the only landmark he could recall, the grove of eucalyptus trees. The piercing sun, the strain of driving around endless blind curves, the utter desolation of the country, were beginning to fray his nerves and undermine his confidence. Ideas that had seemed good in Chicote, decisions that had seemed right, looked frail and foolish against the bleak, brown landscape; and the search for O'Gorman seemed unreal, absurd, a fox hunt without a fox.

A young doe bounded out from a clump of scrub oak and leaped gracefully across the road in front of him, avoiding the bumper of the car by inches. She looked healthy and well-nourished. Quinn thought, *She didn't get that way on the food supply she'd find around here at this time of year. I must be near irrigated land.*

He stopped the car at the top of the next hill and looked around. In the distance, to the east, he saw something glisten in the slanting rays of the sun. It was his first view of the Tower itself, a mere reflection of light from glass.

He released the brake and the car rolled silently down the hill. Half a mile farther on he spotted the grove of eucalyptus trees and the narrow dirt lane. Once he was on it he had a strange feeling of returning home. He was even a little excited at the prospect of being greeted, welcomed back. Then he saw one of the Brothers plodding along the road ahead of him. He honked the horn as he came alongside.

It was Brother Crown of Thorns, who had driven him to San Felice the previous morning.

"One good lift deserves another," Quinn said, leaning across the seat to open the door. "Get in, Brother."

Brother Crown stood rigid, his arms folded inside his robe. "We been expecting you, Mr. Quinn."

"Good."

"Not good, not good at all."

"What's the matter?"

"Pull your car off the road and leave it here," Brother Crown said shortly. "I got orders to take you to the Master."

"Good." Quinn parked the car and got out. "Or isn't that good, either?"

"A stranger snooping around inside the Tower is tempting the devil to destroy us all, but the Master says he wants to talk to you."

"Where is Sister Blessing?"

"In torment for her sins."

"Just what does that mean, Brother?"

"Money is the source of all evil." Brother Crown turned, spat on the ground, and wiped his mouth with the back of his hand before adding, "Amen."

"Amen. But we weren't talking about money."

"You were. Yesterday morning. I heard you say to her, 'About the money . . .' I heard it and I had to tell the Master. It is one of our rules, the Master's got to know everything so's he can protect us against ourselves."

"Where is Sister Blessing?" Quinn repeated.

Brother Crown merely shook his head and started walking up the dusty road. After a moment's hesitation Quinn followed him. They passed the communal dining hall, the storage shed where Quinn had spent the night, and a couple of small buildings which he hadn't seen before. Fifty yards beyond, the path rose sharply, and the steepness of the ascent and the unaccustomed altitude made Quinn breathe heavily and rapidly.

Brother Crown paused for a minute and looked back at him with contempt. "Soft living. Weak constitution. Flabby muscles."

"My tongue's not flabby, though," Quinn said. "I don't tattle to the teacher."

"The Master's got to be told everything," Brother Crown said, flushing. "I acted for Sister Blessing's own good. We got to be saved from ourselves and the devil that's in us. We all carry a devil around inside us gnawing our innards."

"So that's it. I thought my liver was acting up again."

"Have your jokes. Laugh on earth, weep through eternity."

"I'll buy that."

"Buy," Brother Crown said. "Money. Hell-words leading to everlasting damnation. Take off your shoes."

"Why?"

"This here's consecrated ground."

In a clearing, on top of the hill, the Tower rose five stories into the sky. It was made of glass and redwood in the shape of a pentagon surrounding an inner court.

Quinn left his shoes outside the entrance arch which bore an engraved inscription: THE KINGDOM OF HEAVEN IS WAITING FOR ALL TRUE BELIEVERS, REPENT AND REJOICE. From the inner court scrubbed wooden steps with a rope guardrail led up the five levels of the Tower.

"You're supposed to go up alone," Brother Crown said.

"Why?"

"When the Master gives an order or makes a suggestion, it don't pay to ask why."

Quinn started up the stairs. At each level heavy oak doors led into what he decided must be the living quarters of the cultists. There were no windows opening onto the court except at the fifth level. Here Quinn found the door open.

A deep, resonant voice said, "Come in. Please close the door behind you, I feel a draft."

Quinn went inside, and in that first instant he realized why the Tower had been built there in the wilderness and why the old lady whose money had built it felt that she was getting closer to heaven. The expanse of light and sky was almost too much for the eye to take in. Windows on all five sides revealed mountains beyond mountains, and three thousand feet below lay a blue lake in a green valley like a diamond on a leaf.

The scenery was so overpowering that the people in the room seemed of no importance. There were two of them, a man and a woman wearing identical white wool robes loosely belted with scarlet satin. The woman was very old. Her body had shriveled with the years until it was no larger than a little girl's, and her face was as creased and brown as a walnut. She sat on a bench looking up at the sky as if she expected it to open for her.

The man could have been anywhere from fifty to seventy years old. He had a gaunt, intelligent face, and eyes that burned like phosphorus at room temperature. Sitting cross-legged on the floor, he was working on a small hand loom.

"I am the Master," he said easily and without self-consciousness. "This is Mother Pureza. We bid you welcome and wish you well."

"*Buena acogida*," the woman said as if she were translating the words to a fourth person present who couldn't understand English. "*Salud*."

"We bear you no malice."

"*No estamos malicios*."

"Mother Pureza, it is not necessary for you to translate for Mr. Quinn."

The woman turned and gave him a stubborn look. "I like to hear my native tongue."

"And so do I, at the proper time and place. Now if you will kindly excuse us, Mr. Quinn and I have some matters to discuss."

"I want to stay and listen," she said querulously. "It gets lonely waiting all by myself for the doors of the Kingdom to open and receive me."

"God is always with you, Mother Pureza."

"I wish He'd say something. I get so lonely, waiting, watching . . . Who is that young man? Why is he here in my Tower?"

"Mr. Quinn has come to see Sister Blessing."

"Oh, oh, oh, he can't do that!"

"That is what I must explain to him, in private." The Master put a firm hand on her elbow and guided her to the steps. "Be careful going down, Pureza. It is a long fall to the inner court."

"Tell the young man that if he wants to visit my Tower he must wait for an engraved invitation from my secretary, Capirote. Send for Capirote immediately."

"Capirote isn't here, Pureza. That was a long time ago. Now take hold of the guardrail and walk slowly."

The Master closed the door quietly and returned to his position at the loom.

"Her Tower?" Quinn said.

"She commissioned it to be constructed. Now it belongs to us all. There is no private property in our community unless someone commits a material sin like our poor Sister Blessing." He held up one hand in a silencing gesture. "Please make no denials, Mr. Quinn. Sister Blessing has confessed in full and is repenting in full."

"I want to see her. Where is she?"

"What you want doesn't carry much weight with us. When you trespassed upon our property, you were, in a sense, entering another country with a different constitution, a different set of laws."

"I gather it's still part of the Union," Quinn said. "Or is it?"

"There has been no formal secession, that is true. But we do not accept as law what we do not believe to be right."

"By 'we' you mean 'I,' don't you?"

"I have been chosen to receive revelations and visions beyond the others. However, I am only an instrument of the divine will, a mere servant among its other servants . . . I can see I am not convincing you."

"No." Quinn wondered what the man had been in real life besides a failure. "You wanted to talk to me. What about?"

"Money."

"I thought that was a dirty word around here."

"It is sometimes necessary to use dirty words to describe dirty transactions, such as accepting a large sum of money from a woman for performing a very small service." He touched his forehead with his right hand while his left pointed to the sky. "You see, I know everything."

"You didn't get it in a vision," Quinn said. "And accepting a large sum of money from a woman doesn't seem to have bothered you much. This place wasn't built with green stamps."

"Hold your vicious tongue, Mr. Quinn, and I shall hold my temper, which can be equally vicious, I assure you. Mother Pureza is my wife, dedicated to my work, sharing my visions of the glory that awaits us. Oh, the glory, oh, if you could see the glory, you would understand why we are all here." The Master's face underwent an abrupt, unexplained change. The visionary suddenly became the realist. "You wish to make your report to Sister Blessing about the man O'Gorman?"

"I not only wish to, I intend to."

"That will be impossible. She is in isolation, renewing her vows of renunciation, a trivial punishment considering the magnitude of her sins, concealing money, withholding it from the common fund, trying to reestablish contact with the world she promised to leave behind her. These are grave infractions of our laws. She could have been banished from our midst entirely but the Lord told me in a vision to spare her."

The Lord, Quinn thought, *plus a little common sense. Sister Blessing's too useful to banish. There wouldn't be anybody left to keep the rest of them healthy while waiting to die.*

"You are to make your report to me," the Master said. "I will see that she gets it."

"Sorry, my instructions were specific. No Sister, no report."

"Very well. No report, no money. I demand an immediate return of what is left of the sum Sister Blessing gave you. That seems to me quite a fair and just idea."

"There's only one thing the matter with it," Quinn said. "The money's gone."

The Master pushed the loom aside with a sweep of his hand. "You spent a hundred and twenty dollars in a day and a half? You're lying."

"Living costs have gone up in my part of the Union."

"You gambled it away, is that it? Gambled and boozed and debauched—"

"Yes, I had a pretty busy time what with one thing and another. Now I'd like to do what I was paid to do and get out of here. The climate in your country doesn't agree with me, there's too much hot air."

A rush of blood stained the Master's face and neck but he said in a controlled voice, "I have long since been accustomed to the gibes of the ignorant and the unbelievers. I can only warn you that the Lord will smite you with the sword of His wrath."

"Consider me smote." Quinn's tone was considerably lighter than his feelings. The place was beginning to oppress him, the glorification of death hung over it as the smell of oil hung over Chicote. He thought, *Once you get the idea that dying is great, it's an easy step up to thinking you're doing someone a favor by helping him die. The old boy's been harmless so far but his next vision might have me in a featured role.*

"Let's quit playing games," Quinn said. "I came to see Sister Blessing. Aside from the fact that she paid me to do a job, I happen to like her, and I want to make sure she's all right. Now it's no secret that you've had some trouble with the law—the law of my part of the Union, of course—and you just might be asking for more."

"Is that a threat?"

"That's exactly what it is, Master. I'm not leaving here until I assure myself that Sister Blessing is alive and in good health, as she was yesterday morning when I left here."

"Why shouldn't she be alive? What kind of nonsense is this? You talk as if we were barbarians, savages, maniacs—"

"You're close."

The Master got clumsily to his feet, kicking aside the loom. It crashed against the wall. "Leave. Leave here immediately, or I will not be responsible for what happens to you. Get out of my sight."

Suddenly the door opened and Mother Pureza came in making little clucking noises with her tongue. "Oh, that's not polite, Harry. It really isn't polite after I sent him an engraved invitation through Capirote."

"Oh God," the Master said and covered his face with his hands.

"And you needn't scold me for eavesdropping, either. I told you I was lonely, *triste, desamparada*—"

"You have not been abandoned, Pureza."

"Then where *is* everybody? Where is Mama, and Dolores who brought my breakfast, and Pedro who polished my riding boots, and Capirote? Where *is* everybody? Where have they all gone, Harry? Why didn't they take me with them? Oh Harry, why didn't they wait for me?"

"Hush now, Pureza. You must be patient." He crossed the room and took her in his arms and patted her thinning hair, her emaciated shoulders. "You must not lose courage, Pureza. Soon you will see them all again."

"Will Dolores bring me breakfast in bed?"

"Yes."

"And Pedro, may I hit him with my riding crop if he doesn't listen to me?"

"Yes." The Master's voice was an exhausted whisper. "Whatever you like."

"I might hit you too, Harry."

"All right."

"Not hard, though. Just a tap on the dome to sting a little and let you know I'm alive . . . But I won't *be* alive then, Harry. I won't *be* alive. Oh, I'm so confused. How can I give you a little tap on the dome to let you know I'm alive when I won't *be* alive?"

"I don't know. Please stop it. Please be quiet and go to your room."

"You never help me think anymore," she said, moving her head back and forth. "You used to help me think, you used to explain everything to me. Now you tell me to be quiet, to go to my room, to watch the sky and wait. Why did we come here, Harry? I know there was a reason."

"For eternal salvation."

"Is that all? . . . Oh, oh, oh, there's a strange young man standing over there, Harry. Tell Capirote to show him out, and in the future not to admit anyone without a proper calling card. And hurry up about it. My orders are to be obeyed immediately, I am Dona Isabella Consrancia Querida Felicia de la Guerra."

"No, no, you are Mother Pureza," the Master said softly. "And you are going to your room to take a rest."

"But why?"

"Because you are tired."

"I am not tired. I am lonely. You're the one who's tired, aren't you, Harry?"

"Perhaps."

"So tired. Poor Harry, *muy amado mio.*"

"I'll help you, Pureza. Hang onto my arm."

Over the old woman's head he beckoned to Quinn to follow, and the three of them started off down the stairs. At the fourth level the Master opened the door and Mother Pureza went inside with just one small moan of protest. The Master leaned against the door and closed his eyes. A minute went by, two minutes. Quinn was beginning to think the man was in a trance or had gone to sleep standing up.

Suddenly his eyes opened. He touched his forehead. "I feel your pity, Mr. Quinn. I do not accept it, you are wasting your time and energy on pity as I wasted mine on anger. You observe I am no longer angry? Kicking a loom, how trivial it was, how small it will look in eternity. I am purified, I am cleansed."

"Good for you," Quinn said. "Now I'd like to see Sister Blessing."

"Very well, you'll see her. You'll regret your evil thoughts and dark suspicions. She is in spiritual isolation. Did I put her there? No, she went of her own accord. She is renewing her vows of renunciation. At my insistence? No, no, Mr. Quinn. At her own. Your simple mind cannot grasp the situation."

"It can try."

"In spiritual isolation, the senses do not exist. The eyes do not see, the ears do not hear, the flesh cannot feel. Perhaps, if the isolation is complete, she will not even know you are there."

"Then again perhaps she will. Especially if I can see her alone."

"Of course. I have total faith in the Sister's devotion to the spirit."

She was in a small square room on the ground floor. It contained no furniture but the wooden bench she sat on, facing the window, in a shaft of sunlight. Sweat, or tears, had streaked her forehead and cheeks, and there were moist patches on her robe. When Quinn spoke her name she didn't answer but her hunched shoulders twitched and her eyelids blinked.

"Sister Blessing, you asked me to come back and I did."

She turned and looked at him, mute and suffering. The fright in her eyes was so intense that Quinn felt like shouting at her: *Snap out of it, get away from this bughouse before you're as nutty as the old woman, recognize the Master for what he is, a schizo and a fear peddler. His racket's as old as the hills. It doesn't take the curse off it because he believes in it himself, it only makes it doubly dangerous.*

He said, in a conversational tone, "Remember those pink fuzzy slippers you told me you saw in a Sears catalogue? There was a pair just like that in a store window in Chicote."

For a moment something besides fear showed in her eyes, interest, curiosity. Then it was gone, and she was speaking in a listless monotone: "I have renounced the world and its evils. I have renounced the flesh and its weakness. I seek the solace of the spirit, the salvation of the soul."

"It's lucky you don't lisp," Quinn said, trying to coax a smile out of her. "I didn't find O'Gorman, by the way. He disappeared five and a half years ago. His wife thinks she's a widow, so do a lot of other people. What do you think?"

"Having done without comfort, I will be comforted by the Lord. Having hungered, I will feast."

"Did you know O'Gorman? Was he a friend of yours?"

"Having trod the rough earth, my feet uncovered, I will walk the smooth and golden streets of heaven."

"Maybe you'll meet O'Gorman," Quinn said. "He seems to have been a good man, no enemies, nice wife and kids. In fact, a very nice wife, it's too bad she's wasting her life in uncertainty. I think if she knew definitely that O'Gorman wasn't coming back, she could start living again. You're listening, Sister. You're hearing me. Answer just one question, will O'Gorman be coming back?"

"Having here forsaken the pride of ornament, I will be of infinite beauty. Having humbled myself in the fields, I will walk tall and straight in the hereafter, which does belong to the True Believers. Amen."

"I'm going back to Chicote, Sister. Have you any message for Martha O'Gorman? She deserves a break. Give it to her if you can, Sister. You're a generous woman."

"I have renounced the world and its evils. I have renounced the flesh and its weakness. Having done without comfort—"

"Sister, listen to me."

"—I will be comforted by the Lord. Having hungered, I will feast. Having trod the rough earth, my feet uncovered, I will walk the smooth and golden streets of heaven. Having here forsaken the pride of ornament, I will be of infinite beauty."

Quinn went out and closed the door quietly. Sister Blessing was as far beyond reach as O'Gorman.

9

THE INNER COURT contained rows of crude wooden benches placed around a stone shrine that reminded Quinn of a barbecue pit. The Master was standing in front of the shrine, head bowed, arms folded across his chest.

He said, without turning, "Well, Mr. Quinn? You found Sister Blessing alive and in good health?"

"I found her alive."

"And you are still not satisfied?"

"No," Quinn said. "I'd like to know a lot more about this place and the people in it, their names, occupations, where they came from."

"And what, pray, would you do with such information?"

"Try to solve the O'Gorman case."

"You're a stranger to me, Mr. Quinn. I have no obligations to you, but purely out of generosity I'll tell you one thing. The name O'Gorman is unknown here."

"Sister Blessing just picked it out of a hat?"

"Out of a dream," the Master said quietly. "Or you would call it a dream. I do not. I think the spirit of Patrick O'Gorman is wandering in hell, seeking salvation. He spoke to Sister, he asked her help because that is her name, Sister Blessing of the Salvation. Otherwise he would have chosen me to help him since I am the Master."

Quinn stared at him. The man obviously believed what he was saying. It would be useless to argue with him, possibly dangerous. "Why is O'Gorman in hell, Master? All indications are that he led an exemplary life, according to his lights."

"He was not a True Believer. Now, of course, he repents, he pleads for a second chance. He calls out to the Sister while she is asleep and her mind is receptive to his vibrations. The good Sister was both curious and afraid. The combination dulled her wits and made her do a very foolish thing."

"Hiring me."

"Yes." There was a trace of pity in the Master's faint smile. "You see, Mr. Quinn, you were asked to find someone who is wandering through the eternal abysses of hell. A formidable task, even for a brash young man like you, don't you agree?"

"If I accepted your premise, I'd have to agree."

"But you don't."

"No."

"You have a better premise, Mr. Quinn?"

"I think Sister Blessing may have known O'Gorman years ago, before she came here."

"You are quite wrong," the Master said calmly. "The good Sister never even heard the name until O'Gorman communicated with her from the depths of hell, seeking salvation. My heart bleeds for that poor miserable wretch, but what can I do? His repentance came too late, he will suffer throughout eternity for his ignorance and self-indulgence. Beware, Mr. Quinn, beware. It will happen to you unless you change your ways and renounce the world and its evils, the flesh and its weakness."

"Thanks for the advice, Master."

"It is not advice. It is a warning. Renounce and be saved. Repent and rejoice . . . You see Mother Pureza as an old woman, frail of body and sick of mind. I see her as a creature of God, one of the Chosen."

"Also one of the taken," Quinn said. "Just how much of her money was spent on this place?"

"You cannot make me angry again, Mr. Quinn. I regret that you are trying to. Have I not treated you with consideration? Answered your questions? Allowed you to see Sister Blessing? And still you are not satisfied? You are a greedy man."

"I want to find out what happened to O'Gorman so I can tell his wife the truth."

"Tell her Patrick O'Gorman is wandering in hell, suffering the torments of the forever damned. That is the truth."

Outside, Quinn put his shoes back on and straightened his tie while the Master watched from the arched doorway. The sun was beginning to set and smoke was rising from the chimney of the dining hall straight into the windless air. The only members of the cult in sight were Sister Contrition's two smaller children sliding on flattened cardboard boxes down an incline slippery with pine needles, and Brother Tongue of Prophets approaching the entrance of the Tower carrying his little bird in a cage. Behind him, puffing and red-faced, trotted Brother of the Steady Heart, who had shaved Quinn the previous morning.

The Brothers greeted the Master by touching their foreheads and bowing. Then they nodded politely in Quinn's direction.

"Peace be with you, Brothers," the Master said.

"Peace be with you," Brother Heart echoed.

"What brings you here?"

"Brother Tongue thinks his parakeet is sick. He wants Sister Blessing to look at it."

"Sister Blessing is in isolation."

"The parakeet is acting very funny," Brother Heart said apologetically. "Show the Master, Brother Tongue."

Brother Tongue put his head on his shoulder and pressed his hand against his mouth.

"The bird no longer speaks," Brother Heart translated, "and sits with his head hidden."

Brother Tongue pointed to his chest and moved his hand rapidly back and forth.

"The bird's pulse is very fast," Brother Heart said. "It has palpitations. Brother Tongue is very worried, he wants the Sister to—"

"Sister Blessing is in isolation," the Master repeated sharply. "The bird looks perfectly all right to me. Perhaps it's as tired of talking as I am of listening. Place a cover over its cage and let it rest. All birds have accelerated heartbeats, it's quite normal, nothing to worry about."

Brother Tongue's mouth quivered and Brother Heart emitted a long deep sigh, but neither of them put up an argument. They disappeared around the corner of the building, their bare feet leaving little puffs of dust.

The brief encounter puzzled Quinn. The bird had looked to him, as well as to the Master, in good health, and he wondered if it had been used as an excuse to obtain permission to see Sister Blessing. *Or perhaps,* he thought, *to take another look at me. No, I'm getting too suspicious. Another couple of hours in this place and I'll be receiving O'Gorman's vibrations from hell. I'd better flake off.*

The Master had the same idea at the same time. "I can waste no more of my strength on you, Mr. Quinn. You must leave now."

"All right."

"Tell Mrs. O'Gorman my prayers are being offered to ease her husband's agony."

"I don't think that will be much of a consolation."

"It is not my fault he went to hell. If he had come to me I would have saved him . . . Peace be with you, Mr. Quinn. I shall not expect you back, unless you come humbly and penitently as a convert."

"I'd prefer an engraved invitation from Capirote," Quinn said, but the Master had already closed the door.

Quinn walked back to the dirt lane. About a dozen Brothers and Sisters were standing in front of the dining hall when he passed but none of them greeted him. Only one glanced curiously in his direction, and Quinn recognized the leather-skinned face of Brother Light of the Infinite, the man who'd come to the storage shed to rid the mattress of fleas. It was as if the whole colony had been warned to ignore Quinn's presence because he was a threat to them. But as soon as he walked past he could feel a dozen pairs of eyes on the back of his neck.

The feeling persisted even after he'd reached his car and there was no one in sight. Each tree looked as if it had a Brother or Sister stationed behind it to watch him.

He released the brake and the car started coasting down the dirt lane. His mind went back to his first departure from the Tower, with Brother Crown driving the dilapidated truck before the sun came up. There had been, he recalled, a reason for the timing: to get the truck away from the place before Sister Contrition's oldest daughter, Karma, tried to hitch a ride to the city.

Quinn broke out in a sweat. The eyes on the back of his neck felt like crawling insects. His hand reached up to rub them off and found nothing but his own cold damp skin.

He said aloud, "Karma?"

There was no answer.

He had reached the main road by this time. He stopped the car, turned off the ignition and got out. Then he opened the back door. "This is the end of the line, friend."

The grey bundle on the floor stirred and whimpered.

"Come on," Quinn said. "You can make it back to the Tower before it gets dark if you start now."

Karma's long black hair appeared, then her face, blotched with pimples, sullen with resentment. "I'm not going back."

"A little bird tells me you are."

"I hate little birds. I hate Brother Tongue. I hate the Master and Mother Pureza and Brother Crown and Sister Glory. Most of all I hate my own mother and those awful yapping children. Yes, and I even hate Sister Blessing."

"That's a heap of hate," Quinn said.

"There's more. I hate Brother Behold the Vision because his teeth click when he eats and I hate Brother Light because he called me lazy, and I hate—"

"All right, all right, I'm convinced you're a first-class hater. Now get out of there. Start moving."

"Please, please take me with you. I won't be a nuisance, I won't even speak. You can pretend I'm not here. When we reach the city I'll find a job. I'm not lazy the way Brother Light claims I am . . . You're going to say no, aren't you?"

"Yes, I'm going to say no."

"Is it because you think I'm just a child?"

"There are other reasons, Karma. Now be a good girl, save us both a lot of trouble—"

"I'm already in trouble," she said calmly. "So are you. I hear things."

"What things?"

She sat up on the back seat, tucking her long hair behind her ears. "Oh, things. They talk in front of me as if I were too young to understand."

"Did Sister Blessing talk in front of you?"

"All of them."

"It's Sister Blessing in particular that I'm interested in," Quinn said.

"She talks plenty."

"About me?"

"Yes."

"What did she tell you?"

"Oh, things."

He gave her a hard look. "You're giving me the run-around, Karma, stalling for time. It won't do any good. Come out of there before I drag you out by the hair."

"I'll scream. I'm a good screamer and sounds carry in the mountains. They'll all hear me, they'll think you tried to kidnap me. The Master will be furious, he may even kill you. He has a terrible temper."

"He may also kill you."

"I don't care. I have nothing to live for."

"All right, you asked for it."

Quinn reached into the back seat to grab her. She took a long deep breath and opened her mouth to scream. He cut off the sound by pressing his hand against her mouth.

"Listen, you crazy kid. You'll get us both in a mess. I can't possibly take you with me to San Felice. You're going to need money, clothes, someone to look after you. You may not like it here but at least you're protected. Wait until you're older, then you can leave under your own power. Are you listening to me, Karma?"

She nodded.

"If I take my hand away, will you promise to be quiet and discuss this in a reasonable way?"

She nodded again.

"All right." He removed his hand from her mouth and leaned wearily against the back of the seat. "Did I hurt you?"

"No."

"How old are you, Karma?"

"Going on twenty-one."

"Sure, but how far have you got to go? Come on, the truth."

"I'm sixteen," she said, after a time. "But I could easily find a job in the city and earn money to buy some stuff for my face so I'll look like other girls."

"You have a very pretty face."

"No, it's terrible, all these terrible red things that they say I'll grow out of but I don't. I never will. I need money for the stuff to make them go away. One of my teachers told me about it last year when I went to school, acne ointment she called it. She was real nice, she said she used to have acne herself and she knew how I felt."

"And that's the reason you want to go to the city, to buy acne ointment?"

"Well, that's what I'd do first," she said, running her hands along her cheeks. "I need it very bad."

"Suppose I promise you that I'll buy some for you and see that you get it? Will you postpone your trip to the city until you're a little more capable of looking after yourself?"

She thought about it for a long time, twisting and untwisting a strand of her hair. "You're just trying to get rid of me."

"That's true. But I'd also like to help you."

"When could you get it for me?"

"As soon as possible."

"How would you know it's the right stuff?"

"I'll ask the pharmacist, the man who sells it."

She turned and looked up at him, very earnestly. "Do you think I will be pretty, as pretty as the girls at school?"

"Of course you will."

It was getting quite dark but she made no move to get out of the car and go back to the Tower. "Everyone here is so ugly," she said. "And dirty. The floors are cleaner than we are. At school there were showers with hot water and real soap, and each of us had a big white towel all to ourselves."

"How long have you been here at the Tower, Karma?"

"Four years, since it was built."

"And before then?"

"We were at some place in the mountains, the San Gabriel Mountains down south. It was just a lot of wooden shacks. Then Mother Pureza came along and we got the Tower."

"She was a convert?"

"Yes, a rich one. We don't get many rich ones. I guess the rich ones are too busy having fun spending their money to worry about the hereafter."

"Are you worried, Karma?"

"The Master scares me with his funny eyes," she said. "But with Sister Blessing I'm not scared. I don't really hate her the way I said I did. She prays every day for my acne."

"Do you know where she is now?"

"Everyone does. She's in isolation."

"For how long?"

"Five days. Punishment always lasts five days."

"Do you know the reason she's being punished?"

Karma shook her head. "There was a lot of whispering I couldn't hear, between her and the Master and Brother Crown. Then when my mother and I went to make dinner yesterday at noon, Sister Blessing was gone and Brother Tongue was crouched by the stove, crying. He just worships Sister Blessing because she babies him and makes a big fuss over him when he's sick. The only one that acted glad was Brother Crown and he's meaner than Satan."

"How long has Brother Crown been a convert?"

"He came about a year after the Tower was built. That would be three years ago."

"What about Sister Blessing?"

"She was with us in the San Gabriel Mountains. Nearly all the rest were, too, including a lot that have gone away since because they quarreled with the Master, like my father."

"Where's your father now, Karma?"

"I don't know," she said in a whisper. "And I can't ask. When someone is banished his name can never be mentioned again."

"Have you ever heard anyone here refer to a man called Patrick O'Gorman?"

"No."

"Can you remember that name, Patrick O'Gorman?"

"Yes. Why?"

"I'd appreciate it if you'd keep your ears open for it," Quinn said. "You needn't tell anyone I asked you to do this, it's strictly between you and me, like the ointment. Is it a bargain?"

"Yes." She touched her cheeks, her forehead, her chin. "Do you really and honestly think I will be pretty when my acne goes away?"

"I know it."

"How will you send me the ointment? The Master opens all the mail packages and he'd just throw something out if he thought it was drugs. He doesn't believe in drugs or doctors, only faith."

"I'll bring the stuff to you myself."

It was too dark now to see her face but Quinn felt her little movement of protest or dissent. "They don't want you to come here anymore, Mr. Quinn. They think you're trying to make trouble for the colony."

"I'm not. The colony, as such, doesn't interest me."

"You keep on coming."

"My first visit was an accident, my second was to give Sister Blessing the information she asked for."

"Is that the honest truth?"

"Yes," Quinn said. "It's getting late, Karma. You'd better start back before they send out a lynching party for me."

"I won't be missed. I told mother I was going to bed because I had a sore throat. She'll be busy in the kitchen until late. By that time," she added bitterly, "I expected to be half-way to the city. Only I'm not. I'm right here. I'll be right here until I die. I'll be old and ugly, and dirty like the rest of them. Oh, I wish I could die this very minute and go to heaven before I commit all the sins I'll probably commit when I get the chance, like having beautiful dresses and shoes and talking back to the Master and washing my hair every day in perfume."

Quinn got out of the car and held the door open for her. She climbed out slowly and awkwardly.

"Can you find your way in the dark?" Quinn said.

"I've been up and down this road a million times."

"Good-bye for now, then."

"Are you really coming back?"

"Yes."

"And you won't forget the stuff for my acne?"

"No," Quinn said. "And you won't forget your part of the bargain?"

"I'm to keep my ears open if anyone mentions Patrick O'Gorman. I don't think they will, though."

"Why not?"

"We're not allowed to talk about the people we knew before we were converted, and there's no one in the colony called O'Gorman. When I'm looking after Mother Pureza I often read the book the Master keeps with our other-world names in it. There's no O'Gorman in it. I have a very good memory."

"Can you remember Sister Blessing's name?"

"Naturally. Mary Alice Featherstone and she lived in Chicago."

Quinn asked her about some of the others but none of the names she mentioned meant any more to him than Mary Alice Featherstone did.

In the light of the rising moon he watched Karma walk back toward the Tower. Her step was brisk and buoyant as if she had forgotten all about wanting to die and was concentrating instead on the sins she intended to commit when her chance came.

Quinn drove to San Felice, checked in at a motel on the waterfront and went to sleep to the intermittent croaking of a foghorn and the sound of surf crashing against the breakwater.

10

By NINE O'CLOCK in the morning the sun had burned off most of the fog. The sea, calm at low tide, was streaked with colors, sky-blue on the horizon, brown where the kelp beds lay, and a kind of grey-green in the harbor itself. The air was warm and windless. Two children, who looked barely old enough to walk, sat patiently in their tiny sailing pram waiting for a breeze.

Quinn crossed the sandy beach and headed for the breakwater. Tom Jurgensen's office was padlocked but Jurgensen himself was sitting on the concrete wall talking to a grey-haired man wearing a yachting cap and topsiders and an immaculate white duck suit. After a time the grey-haired man turned away with an angry gesture and walked down the ramp to the mooring slips.

Jurgensen approached Quinn, unsmiling. "Are you back, or haven't you left?"

"I'm back."

"You didn't give me much chance to raise the money. I said a week or two, not a day or two."

"This is a social call," Quinn said. "By the way, who's your friend in the sailor suit?"

"Some joker from Newport Beach. He wouldn't know a starboard tack from a carpet tack but he's got a seventy-five-foot yawl and he thinks he's Admiral of the fleet and Lord of the four winds . . . How broke are you, Quinn?"

"I told you yesterday. Flat and stony."

"Want a job for a few days?"

"Such as?"

"The Admiral's looking for a bodyguard," Jurgensen said. "Or, more strictly, a boat guard. His wife's divorcing him and he got the bright idea of cleaning everything out of his safe deposit boxes and taking it aboard the *Briny Belle* before his wife could get a court order restraining him from disposing of community property. He's afraid she'll find out where he is and try to take possession of the *Briny* and everything on it."

"I don't know anything about boats."

"You don't have to. The *Briny's* not going anywhere until the next six-foot tide can ease her past the sand bar. That will be in four or five days. Your job would be to stay on board and keep predatory blondes off the gangplank."

"What's the pay?"

"The old boy's pretty desperate," Jurgensen said. "I think maybe you could nick him for seventy-five dollars a day, and that's not seaweed."

"What's the Admiral's name?"

"Alban Connelly. He married some Hollywood starlet, which doesn't mean much, since every female in Hollywood under thirty is a starlet." Jurgensen paused to light a cigarette. "Think of it, loafing all day in the sun, playing gin rummy over a few beers. Sound good?"

"Neat," Quinn said. "Especially if the Admiral's luck isn't too good."

"With ten million dollars, who needs luck? You want me to go and tell him about you, give you a little build-up?"

"I could use the money."

"Fine. I'll skip down to the *Briny* and talk to him. I suppose you can start work any time?"

"Why not?" Quinn said, thinking, *I have nothing else to do: O'Gorman's in hell, Sister Blessing's in isolation, Alberta Haywood's in jail. None of them is going to run away.* "Do you know many of the commercial fishermen around here?"

"I know all of them by sight, most of them by name."

"What about a man called Aguila?"

"Frank Aguila, sure. He owns the *Ruthie K.* You can see her from here if you stand on the sea wall." Jurgensen pointed beyond the last row of mooring slips. "She's an old Monterey-type fishing boat, anchored just off the port bow of the black-masted sloop. See it?"

"I think so."

"Why the interest in Aguila?"

"He married Ruth Haywood six years ago. I just wondered how they were getting along."

"They're getting along fine," Jurgensen said. "She's a hardworking little woman, often comes down to the harbor to spruce up the boat and help Frank mend his nets. The Aguilas don't socialize much, but they're pleasant, unassuming people . . . Come along, you can wait in my office while I go out to the *Briny Belle* to see Connelly."

Jurgensen unlocked his office and went inside. "There's the typewriter, you can write yourself a couple of references to make Connelly feel he's getting a bargain. And you don't have to bother with details. By ten o'clock Connelly will be too cockeyed to read anyway."

When Jurgensen had gone Quinn looked up Frank Aguila's number in the telephone directory and dialed. A woman who identified herself as the babysitter said that Mr. and Mrs. Aguila were down in San Pedro for a couple of days attending a union meeting.

When Quinn reached the *Briny Belle* a young man in overalls was painting out the name on her bow while Connelly leaned over the rail urging him to hurry.

Quinn said, "Mr. Connelly?"

"Quinn?"

"Yes."

"You're late."

"I had to check out of my motel and make arrangements for my car."

"Well, don't just stand there," Connelly said. "You're not about to be piped aboard if that's what you're waiting for."

Quinn walked up the gangplank, already convinced that the job wasn't going to be as pleasant as Jurgensen had let on.

"Sit down, Quinn," Connelly said. "What's-his-name, that jackass who sells boats—did he tell you my predicament?"

"Yes."

"Women don't know anything more about a boat than its name, so I'm having the *Briny's* name changed. Pretty clever, no?"

"Fiendishly."

Connelly leaned back on his heels and scratched the side of his large red nose. "So you're one of those sarcastic bastards that likes to make funnies, eh?"

"I'm one of those."

"Well, I make the funnies around here, Quinn, and don't you forget it. I make a funny, everybody laughs, see?"

"You can buy it cheaper in a can."

"I don't think I'm going to like you," Connelly said thoughtfully. "But for four or five days I'll go through the motions if you will."

"That sounds fair."

"I'm a fair man, very fair. That's what that little blonde tramp, Elsie, doesn't understand. If she hadn't grabbed for it, I'd have thrown it to her. If she hadn't gone around bleating about her career, I'd have bought her a career like some other guy'd buy her a bag of peanuts . . . What's-his-name said you play cards."

"Yes."

"For money?"

"I have been known to play for money," Quinn said carefully.

"Okay, let's go below and get started."

That first day established the pattern of the ones that followed. In the morning Connelly was relatively sober and he talked about what a good guy he was and how badly Elsie had treated him. In the afternoon the two men played gin rummy until Connelly passed out at the table; then Quinn would deposit him on a bunk and go up on deck with a pair of binoculars to see if there was any sign of activity on Aguila's fishing boat, the *Ruthie K.* In the evening Connelly started in drinking again and talking about Elsie, what a fine woman she was and how badly he had treated her. Quinn got the impression that there were two Elsies and two Connellys. The evening Elsie who was a fine woman should have married the morning Connelly who was a good guy, and everything would have turned out fine.

On the fourth afternoon Connelly was snoring on his bunk when Quinn went on deck with the binoculars. The Captain, a man named McBride, and two crewmen Quinn hadn't seen before had come aboard with their gear, and there was a great deal of quiet activity.

"We get under way at midnight tomorrow," McBride told Quinn. "There's a 6.1 tide. Where's Nimitz?"

"Asleep."

"Good. We can get some work done. You coming with us, Quinn?"

"Where are you going?"

"Nimitz is dodging the enemy," McBride said briskly. "My orders are top-secret. Also our friend has an engaging little habit of changing his mind in mid-channel."

"I like to know where I'm going."

"What does it matter? Come on along for the ride."

"Why the sudden burst of friendship, Captain?"

"Friendship, hell," McBride said. "I hate gin rummy. When you play with him, I don't have to."

Quinn focused the binoculars on the *Ruthie K.* He couldn't see anyone on board but a small skiff was tied up alongside that hadn't been there on the previous days. After about fifteen minutes a woman in jeans and a T-shirt appeared on the bridge and hung what looked like a blanket over the railing. Then she disappeared again.

Quinn approached Captain McBride. "If Connelly wakes up tell him I had to go ashore on an errand, will you?"

"I just took a look at him. He'd sleep through a typhoon."

"That's fine with me."

He went back to Jurgensen's office, borrowed a skiff and rowed out to the *Ruthie K.* The woman was on deck, and the railing by this time was lined with sheets and blankets airing in the sun.

Quinn said, "Mrs. Aguila?"

She stared down at him suspiciously like an ordinary housewife finding a salesman at her front door. Then she pushed back a strand of sun-bleached hair. "Yes. What do you want?"

"I'm Joe Quinn. May I talk to you for a few minutes?"

"What about?"

"Your sister."

An expression of surprise crossed her face and disappeared. "I think not," she said quietly. "I don't discuss my sister with representatives of the press."

"I'm not a reporter, Mrs. Aguila, or an official. I'm a private citizen interested in your sister's case. I know her parole hearing is coming up soon and the way things are she's pretty sure to be turned down."

"Why? She's paid her debt, she's behaved herself. Why shouldn't they give her another chance? And how did you find me? How did you know who I was?"

"I'll explain if you'll let me come aboard."

"I haven't much time," she said brusquely. "There's work to be done."

"I'll try to be brief."

Mrs. Aguila watched him while he tied the skiff to the buoy and climbed awkwardly up the ladder. The boat was a far cry from the spit and polish of the *Briny Belle* but Quinn felt more at home on it. It was a working boat, not a plaything, and the deck glistened with fish scales instead of varnish, and Elsie and the Admiral wouldn't have been caught dead in the cramped little galley.

Quinn said, "Mrs. King, an associate of your brother, told me your married name and where you lived. I was in Chicote the other day talking to her and a few other people like Martha O'Gorman. Do you remember Mrs. O'Gorman?"

"I never actually *met* her."

"What about her husband?"

"What is this anyway?" Mrs. Aguila said sharply. "I thought you wanted to discuss my sister, Alberta. I'm not interested in the O'Gormans. If there's a way I can help Alberta I'm willing to do it, naturally, but I don't see how the O'Gormans come into it. All three of them lived in Chicote, that's the only connection."

"Alberta was a bookkeeper. So, in a sense, was O'Gorman."

"And a few hundred other people."

"The difference is that nothing spectacular happened to the few hundred other people," Quinn said. "And within a month both Alberta and O'Gorman met up with quite unusual fates."

"Within a month?" Mrs. Aguila repeated. "I'm afraid not, Mr. Quinn. Alberta met up with her fate years and years before that, when she first started tampering with the books. Not to mince words, she was stealing from the bank before Patrick O'Gorman even came to Chicote. God knows what made her do it. She didn't need anything, she didn't seem to want anything more than she had except possibly a husband and children, and she never mentioned even that. I often think back to the four of us, Alberta, George and Mother and I, eating our meals together, spending the evenings together, behaving like any ordinary family. And all that time, all those years, Alberta never gave the slightest hint that anything was wrong. When the crash came I was already married to Frank and living here in San Felice. One evening I went out to pick up the newspaper from the driveway and there it was on the front page, Alberta's picture, the whole story . . ." She turned her head away as if the memory of that day was too painful to face again.

"Were you close to your sister, Mrs. Aguila?"

"In a way. Some people have described Alberta as cold but she was always affectionate towards George and me in the sense that she liked to buy us things, arrange surprises for us. Oh, I realize now the money she was spending didn't belong to her and that she was using it to try and purchase what she didn't have: love. Poor Alberta, she reached out for love with one hand and pushed it away with the other."

"She had no serious romance?" Quinn said.

"She had dates occasionally but men always seemed puzzled by Alberta. There were few repeats."

"How did she occupy her spare time?"

"She did volunteer work and went to movies, lectures, concerts."

"Alone?"

"Usually. She didn't seem to mind going places alone, although Mother always made a fuss about it. She considered it a reflection on her that Alberta didn't have lots of friends and a busy social life. The truth is, Alberta didn't want a social life."

"Didn't want one, or despaired of her ability to get one?"

"She showed no signs of despair. In fact, during my last year at home, she seemed quite contented. Not in the happy, fulfilled sense, but as if she'd resigned herself to her life and intended to make the best of it. She settled for spinsterhood is what it amounted to, I suppose."

"How old was she then?"

"Thirty-two."

"Isn't that a little early to settle for spinsterhood?" Quinn said.

"Not to a woman like Alberta. She was always very realistic about herself. She didn't dream, the way I did, of an ideal lover tooling up to the front door in a red convertible." She laughed self-consciously and put her hand on the rail of the boat in a gesture that was both proud and protective. "I never thought I'd be happy in an old tub that smells of fish scales and mildew."

She paused as if she expected Quinn to contradict her, and Quinn obliged by stating that the *Ruthie K* was not an old tub but a fine seaworthy craft. "But to return to Alberta, Mrs. Aguila. In view of her years of embezzling, I can't agree with your description of her as 'realistic.' She must have known that one day she'd be caught. Why didn't she stop? Or run away while she had the chance?"

"She may have wanted to be punished. This will sound funny to you, I guess, but Alberta had a very strict, stern conscience. She was highly moral in everything she did. If she made a promise she kept it, no matter how long it took or what lengths she had to go to. I remember when we got into trouble as children Alberta was the first to admit guilt and accept punishment. She had a lot more courage than I. She still has."

"Still has," Quinn repeated. "Does that mean you visit her in prison?"

"Whenever I can, which isn't often. Seven or eight times so far, I guess."

"Do you write to her?"

"Once a month."

"And she writes back?"

"Yes."

"Do you have any of her letters, Mrs. Aguila?"

"No," she said, flushing. "I don't keep them. None of my children can read yet, but they have older friends, and then there are babysitters and Frank's relatives. I'm not ashamed of Alberta but for the children's sake and Frank's I don't advertise the fact that she's my sister. It wouldn't do her any good."

"What kind of letters does she write?"

"Brief, pleasant, polite. Exactly the kind I'd expect from her. She doesn't seem unhappy. Her only complaint isn't about the prison at all, it's about George."

"Because she doesn't hear from him?"

Ruth Aguila stared up at Quinn, her mouth open a little in surprise. "What on earth gave you that idea?"

"I understood that George, at the insistence of his mother, cut off all relations with Alberta."

"Who told you?"

"John Ronda, the editor of the Chicote *Beacon,* and Mrs. King, who's an associate of George's."

"Well, I don't know them so I can't call them liars. But I never heard such nonsense in my life. George is utterly incapable of turning his back on a member of his family. He's absolutely devoted to Alberta. To him she's not a woman nearly forty who's been convicted of a major crime, she's still the little sister he has to protect, see to it that she gets a square deal. I'm his little sister, too, but George knows I'm married and being looked after so I'm not really important to him anymore. It's Alberta he adores and worries about and fusses over. Why should those two people have told you such a lie?"

"I'm pretty sure," Quinn said, "that they both believed it themselves."

"Why should they? Where would they get a story like that?"

"Obviously from George, since they're friends of his, Mrs. King a particularly close one."

Ruth Aguila's protest was immediate and firm. "That's really absurd. George wouldn't deliberately make himself out to be a heel when the truth is he's done everything possible for Alberta, more than she wants him to. That's what she complains about in her letters. George's visits every month distress her because he's so emotional. He keeps trying to help her and she refuses. She says she's old enough to carry her own burden and the sight of George's suffering only aggravates hers. She's told him she doesn't want to see him, at least not so often, but he keeps right on going anyway."

"People in prison are usually very eager, pathetically eager, to have visitors."

"I repeat, Alberta is realistic. If seeing George's suffering only aggravates her own, then it makes sense that she shouldn't want him to visit her very often."

"It may make sense, in a way," Quinn said. "But to me it sounds like the kind of explanation she might use to cover up the real one."

"And just what might the real one be?"

"I don't know. Perhaps she's afraid George might break down the defenses she's constructed in order to adjust to and accept her present environment. You said she doesn't seem unhappy. Is that what you want to believe, Mrs. Aguila, or the truth?"

"It happens to be both."

"Yet she spoke of her suffering," Quinn said. "Is there such a thing as happy suffering?"

"Yes. If you want punishment and are getting it. Or if you have something good to look forward to at the end of a bad time."

"Say, for instance, a large sum of money?"

She looked down at the oil-stained water lapping at the *Ruthie K's* grey hull. "The money's all gone, Mr. Quinn. Some of it she gave away, most of it she gambled away. She told me in a letter that she used to spend weekends in Las Vegas when George and Mother thought she'd gone to Los Angeles or San Francisco to shop and see the shows. It's funny, isn't it?—Alberta is the last woman on earth I'd suspect of gambling."

"Las Vegas is full of the last women on earth anyone would suspect of gambling."

"It must be a very peculiar compulsion, especially when someone keeps losing week after week."

"When you keep losing," Quinn said, "is when you don't think of stopping."

Mrs. Aguila was shaking her head in sorrow. "To think of all the trouble she went to year after year to steal that money, and then all she did was throw it away—it doesn't make sense to me, Mr. Quinn. Alberta never acted on impulse like that. She was a planner, a methodical, minute-by-minute planner. Everything she did was well thought out in advance, from her wardrobe budget to the route she drove to and from her office. Even a simple business like attending a movie, she conducted like a campaign. If the feature picture began at 7:30, dinner had to be served at exactly six, the dishes washed and put away by seven, and so on. It wasn't much fun going any place with her because all the time she was doing one thing you could practically feel her planning the next move."

Quinn thought, *She's doing one thing now, staying in jail, what next move has she planned? If Ronda is correct, she won't even be free for years.*

He said, "I understand that the mistake that tripped Alberta up at the bank was a very trivial one."

"Yes."

"I recall another trivial mistake that had consequences even more drastic than Alberta's did."

"What was it?"

"The night O'Gorman disappeared he was on his way back to his office to correct a mistake he'd made during the day. Two bookkeepers, two trivial errors, two disastrous fates within a month in one small city. Add these to the fact that O'Gorman worked for George Haywood at one time and that he probably knew Alberta, at least by sight. Add still another fact, that when I went to Chicote to ask questions about O'Gorman, George's curiosity was aroused to the extent that he broke into my motel room and searched it."

"You'd realize what a fantastic story that is if you knew George."

"I'm trying to know George," Quinn said. "So far I haven't had much of a chance."

"As for your other suspicions, and that's all they are, you seem to forget that the authorities went into every possible angle when O'Gorman disappeared. There was hardly a person in Chicote who wasn't questioned. George sent me every copy of the *Beacon*."

"Why?"

"He thought I'd be interested since I came from Chicote and knew O'Gorman slightly."

"How much is slightly?"

"I saw him in the office a couple of times. A good-looking man, though there was something effeminate about him that repelled me. Maybe that's too strong a word but it's how he affected me."

"That type can be very appealing to certain women," Quinn said. "You told me you haven't met Martha O'Gorman."

"She was pointed out to me on the street once."

"By whom?"

She hesitated for a moment. "George. He thought she was a very attractive woman and he wondered why she'd thrown herself away on a man like O'Gorman."

Quinn wondered, too, in spite of all the good things Martha O'Gorman had said about her marriage. "Was George interested in her?"

"I think he could have been if she hadn't already been married. It's a shame she was. George needed, and still needs, a wife. His own died when he was barely thirty. The longer he waits, the more he lives at home alone with Mother, the harder it will be for him to break away. I know how hard it is, I had to do it, break away or be broken."

It seemed to Quinn that whenever he turned another corner, he met up with George Haywood, and that the connection between the two cases, which he'd suspected from the beginning, was not Alberta Haywood as he'd once thought, but George. George and Martha O'Gorman, the respectable businessman and the grieving widow. And maybe the reason Martha hadn't remarried had nothing to do with her devotion to O'Gorman's memory; she was waiting for George to break away from his mother. *That would make two of them,* he thought. *Martha O'Gorman and Willie King, and I wouldn't bet a nickel on Willie's chances.*

He said, "You've spoken of George's loyalty to and fondness for his sister. Did it work both ways?"

"Yes. Too much so."

"Too much?"

Twin spots of color appeared on her cheeks and her hands gripped the railing tightly as if she were afraid of falling overboard. "I shouldn't have said that, I guess. I mean, I'm no psychologist, I have no right to go around analyzing people. Only—well, I can't help thinking George made a mistake going back home after his wife died. George used to be a warm, affectionate man who could give love and accept it—I mean real love, not the neurotic kind like my mother's and Alberta's. Perhaps it's uncharitable of me to talk this way about them, and I probably wouldn't do it if they'd acted decent about my marriage to Frank. That's a long answer to a short question, isn't it?

"More briefly, yes, Alberta was very fond of George. Without him around, her whole life might have been different, more satisfactory to her, so that she wouldn't have had to steal and gamble, she'd have gotten married like any ordinary woman. I think George understands this, in a way, and is ridden by guilt because of it. And so he goes to visit her, and they watch each other suffer, and—oh, it's such a rotten mess it makes me sick. I suppose what I'm trying to say is that I hate them. I hate all three of them. I don't want Frank or my children to be forced to have anything to do with any of them."

Quinn was surprised by the violence of her feelings, and he guessed that she was, too. She looked anxiously around at the boats moored nearby as if to make sure nobody had overheard her outburst. Then she turned back to Quinn with a sheepish little smile. "Frank says this always happens when I talk about my family. I start out by being very unemotional and detached, and end up in hysterics."

"I wish all the hysterics I had to deal with were as quiet."

"The fact is, the only thing I want from my family is to be let alone. When I watched you climbing up that ladder, knowing you were going to talk about Alberta, I felt like pushing you overboard."

"I'm glad you didn't," Quinn said. "This is my only suit."

When he returned to the *Briny Belle* it was five o'clock. The Admiral was pacing up and down the bull run, wearing a new white outfit and the same old dirty expression. "Where the hell you been, you lazy bum? You're supposed to stay on board twenty-four hours a day."

"I saw this fancy blonde on the breakwater. She looked like Elsie, so I thought I'd better check. It was Elsie all right—"

"Weeping Jesus! Let's get out of here. Call the Captain. Tell him we're leaving immediately."

"—Elsie Doolittle from Spokane. Nice girl."

"Why, you lousy bum," Connelly said. "You can't help making funnies, eh? At my expense, eh? I ought to kick your teeth in."

"You might mess up your sailor suit."

"By God, if I were twenty years younger—"

"If you were twenty years younger you'd be the same as you are now, a knuckle-headed lush who couldn't beat a cocker spaniel at gin rummy without cheating."

"I didn't cheat!" Connelly shouted. "I never cheated in my life. Apologize this instant or I'll sue you for libel."

Quinn looked amused. "I caught on to you halfway through the first game. Either stop cheating or take lessons."

"You won. How could I have been cheating if you won?"

"I took lessons."

Connelly's mouth hung open like a hooked halibut's. "Why, you double-crossed me. You're nothing but a thief."

He began screaming for Captain McBride, the crew, the police, the harbor patrol. About a dozen people had gathered around by this time. Quinn went quietly down the gangplank, without waiting for his salary. In his pocket he had about three hundred dollars of Connelly's money, the equivalent of four days' pay at seventy-five a day. He felt better about it than if he'd accepted it from Connelly's hand.

Take a long walk on a short deck, Admiral.

11

THE TECOLOTE PRISON for Women was a collection of concrete buildings built on a two-hundred-acre plateau above Deer Valley. Quinn guessed that the site had been chosen to discourage escapees, since there was no place to escape to. The countryside was more bleak than that which surrounded the Tower. There were no towns within fifty miles, and the stony soil and sparse rainfall had discouraged farmers and ranchers. The paved road that led to Tecolote stopped at the prison gates as if the engineers who built it had quit and gone home in despair.

At the administration building Quinn told the woman in charge that he wanted to see Alberta Haywood, and presented the private detective's license issued to him by the State of Nevada. After half an hour's questioning he was taken across a paved courtyard and left in one of the ground-floor rooms of a three-storied concrete building. The room looked as though someone had once started to decorate it. Half the windows were curtained and several oil paintings hung on the walls. There were two or three upholstered chairs, but most of the seating space was provided by wooden benches similar to the benches in the community dining hall at the Tower.

Other people were waiting: an elderly couple who stood close together beside the doorway exchanging anxious whispers; a young woman whose identity was hidden, or lost, under layers of make-up; a man Quinn's age, with dull eyes and sharp clothes; three blue-uniformed women with the artificial poise and nervous group-gaiety of volunteer social workers; a man and his teen-aged son who looked as though they'd had an argument about coming, not their first, not their last; a grey-haired woman carrying a paper bag with a split in it. Through the split Quinn could see the red sheen of an apple.

Names were called by a guard and people were led away until only Quinn and the father with the teen-aged boy were left in the room.

The man began to talk in a low intense voice. "You're to be more polite to your mother this time, you hear me? None of this sullen stuff. She's your own mother."

"Don't I know it? I get it rubbed in my face every day at school."

"None of that now. Put yourself in her shoes. She's lonely, she looks forward to seeing you. The least you can do is smile, be pleasant, tell her she's looking good and we miss her."

"I can't. I can't do it. None of it's true."

"Shut up and listen to me. You think I'm enjoying myself? You think everybody else is having fun? You think your mother likes being locked in a cage?"

"I don't think anything," the boy said listlessly. "I don't want to think anything."

"Don't make things any tougher for us than they are, Mike. There's a limit to what I can take."

The guard reappeared. "You can come along now, Mr. Williams. How are you doing, Mike? Still getting those fancy grades of yours in school?"

When the boy didn't answer, his father said, "He's doing great in school. Doesn't take after me, I can tell you. His mother's got the brains in the family. She passed them along to him. He ought to be grateful."

"I'm not. I don't want any brains from her, I don't want anything."

The three of them went out into the corridor.

Quinn waited another ten or fifteen minutes. He studied the paintings on the walls, the upholstery on the chairs, and the view from the windows of a three-storied concrete structure identical to the one he was in. Quinn wondered how many of its occupants would be rehabilitated. The same people who were building spaceships to reach the moon were sending their fellow human beings to eighteenth-century penal colonies, and more money was spent on seven astronauts than on the quarter of a million people confined to prisons.

A heavy-set woman in a blue serge uniform appeared at the door. "Mr. Quinn?"

"Yes."

"Your name isn't on Miss Haywood's approved visiting list."

"I explained that to the people in the administration building."

"Yes. Well, it's entirely up to Miss Haywood whether she'll talk to you or not. Come this way, please."

The visiting room was buzzing with conversation and nearly every cubicle was filled. Alberta Haywood sat behind the wire screen with as much composure as if she were still at her desk in the bank. Her small hands were loosely clasped on the counter in front of her and her blue eyes had an alert, kindly expression. Quinn half expected her to say, *Why, of course, we'd be delighted to open an account for you . . .*

Instead, "My goodness, you do stare. Is this your first visit to a prison?"

"No, it's not."

"The matron said your name is Quinn. Several of my old customers were named Quinn and I thought you might be one of them. I see now, of course, that you're not. We've never met before, have we?"

"No, Miss Haywood."

"Then why did you come here?"

"I'm a private detective," Quinn said.

"Really? That must be very interesting work. I don't recall ever having met a private detective before. What exactly do they do?"

"What they're paid to do."

"One naturally assumes that," she said with a hint of rebuff in her voice. "It fails to shed any light on why you should want to see me. My world has been rather limited these past few years."

"I was hired to find Patrick O'Gorman."

Quinn wasn't prepared for her reaction. A look of fury crossed her face, and her mouth opened as if she was struggling to catch her breath. "Then find him. Don't waste your time here, go and find him. And when you do, give him what's coming to him. Show him no mercy."

"You must have known him pretty well to feel so strongly about him, Miss Haywood."

"I don't feel strongly about *him*. I barely knew him. It's what he did to me."

"And what was that?"

"I wouldn't be here in this place if he hadn't disappeared like that. For a month the whole town did nothing else but talk about him, O'Gorman this, O'Gorman that, why, how, who, when, on and on and on. I would never have made that silly error in the books if my mind hadn't been distracted by all the shenanigans over O'Gorman. It made me so nervous I couldn't concentrate. Such incredible fussing over one ordinary little man, it was quite absurd. Naturally my work suffered. It required a great deal of concentration and careful planning."

"I'm sure it did," Quinn said.

"Some fool of a man decides to run away from home and I end up serving a prison term— I, a perfectly innocent bystander."

She sounded as if she really thought she was a perfectly innocent bystander and Quinn wondered whether she had always thought so or whether the years at Tecolote, the hours of boredom, of waiting, had made her slightly, perhaps more than slightly, paranoid. She was the martyr, O'Gorman the villain. The white and the black.

She was staring at Quinn through the wire mesh, her eyes narrowed. "Give me your honest opinion, was that fair?"

"I'm not well enough acquainted with the details to form an opinion."

"No further details are necessary. O'Gorman put me behind these bars. It may even have been deliberate on his part."

"That hardly seems likely, Miss Haywood. He couldn't have anticipated the results of his disappearance on your powers of concentration. You were only slightly acquainted with him anyway, weren't you?"

"We nodded," she said, as if she regretted doing even that much for the man responsible for her predicament. "If our paths should cross in the future, of course, I intend to cut him dead, shun him like a rattlesnake."

"I don't think your paths will cross again, Miss Haywood."

"Why not? I'm not going to be stuck in this place forever."

"No, but O'Gorman may very well be stuck in his," Quinn said. "The majority of people believe he was murdered."

"Who'd go to the trouble of murdering O'Gorman? Unless, of course, he pulled the same kind of dirty trick on somebody else as he did on me."

"There was no evidence of anyone bearing a grudge against him."

"Anyway, he wasn't murdered. He's not dead. He *can't* be."

"Why not?"

She half rose as if she were going to run away from the question. Then she realized that the matron was watching her, and sat down again. "Because then I wouldn't have anyone to blame. Somebody's got to be blamed. Somebody's responsible. It must be O'Gorman. He did it to me deliberately. Perhaps he thought I acted too snobbish towards him? Or he was angry because George fired him?"

"What happened to O'Gorman wasn't intended to involve you at all, Miss Haywood."

"It *did* involve me."

"It wasn't planned that way, I'm sure," Quinn said.

"They keep telling me that, too, only they don't know everything."

She didn't explain who "they" were, but Quinn assumed she was referring to the prison psychologists and perhaps George as well.

"Your brother George comes to visit you quite frequently, Miss Haywood?"

"Every month." She pressed her finger tips hard against her temples as if she felt a sudden intense pain. "I wish he wouldn't. It's too sad. He talks of old friends, old places, that I can't afford to think about anymore or I'd lose my—I would get overly emotional. Or else he talks of the future and that's even worse. In this place, though you realize there will be a future, you can't feel it inside you because every day is like a year. By my estimate," she added with a small bitter smile, "I'm now about 1,875 years old and it's a little late to be thinking of futures. I don't say things like this to them, naturally. They'd call it depression, melancholia, they'd have some name for it, any name but the right one: prison. Prison. It's funny how they try to avoid that word around here and substitute 'Correctional Institution' or 'Branch of the Adult Authority.' Fancy terms that fool no one. I'm a prisoner in a prison, and listening to George prattle merrily on about a trip to Europe and a job in his office makes me sick. How can a trip to Europe seem real to someone who's locked in a cell and hasn't been further than the canteen for over five years? Why am I here? Why are we all here? There must be, there has to be, a better method. If society wants revenge for our crimes why don't they flog us in front of the city hall? Why don't they torture us and get it over with? Why do they leave us here to pass endless unproductive hours when we might be doing something useful? We're like vegetables, only vegetables grow and get eaten and we don't even have that much satisfaction. We're not wanted even for dog food." She held out her hands. "Put me in a meat grinder, chop me up, let me feed some hungry dog, some starved cat!"

Her voice had risen, and people in the adjoining cubicles were standing and peering over the partitions at her.

"Let me be useful! Grind me up! Listen to me, all of you! Don't you want to be ground up to feed the starving animals?"

The matron hurried over, her keys jangling against her blue serge thighs. "Is anything the matter, Miss Haywood?"

"Prison. I'm in prison and the animals are starving."

"Hush, now. They're not starving."

"You don't care about them!"

"I care more about you," the matron said pleasantly. "Come along, I'll take you back to your room."

"Cell. I am a prisoner in a prison and I live in a cell, not a room."

"Whatever it is, you're going back to it and I don't want any fussing and carrying-on. Now be a good girl, eh?"

"I am not a good girl," Miss Haywood said distinctly. "I am a *bad woman* who lives in a *cell* in a *prison*."

"Good grief."

"And watch your language."

The matron put a firm hand on Alberta Haywood's elbow and guided her out. The conversations in the room began again but the voices were quieter, more guarded, and when Quinn got up to leave, the eyes that followed him seemed full of accusations: *You didn't answer her question, mister. Why are we all here?*

Quinn returned to the administration building, and after another series of delays was given permission to see the psychiatric social worker who counseled the inmates due for parole hearings.

Mrs. Browning was young, earnest, baffled. "This is a period of great strain for all of them, naturally. Still, the report of Miss Haywood's crack-up surprises me. I suppose it shouldn't. I've had very little actual contact with her." She adjusted her spectacles as if she hoped to bring Miss Haywood into clearer focus. "In an institution like this, where the psychology department is understaffed, it's the squeaky wheel that gets the grease, and heaven knows we have enough squeaky wheels without bothering about the quiet ones like Miss Haywood."

"She's never caused any trouble?"

"Oh no. She does her work well—in the prison library—and she teaches a couple of courses in bookkeeping." To Quinn it was a nice piece of irony, but Mrs. Browning seemed unaware of it as she continued, "She has a natural talent for figures."

"So I gathered."

"I've frequently noticed that among women there is a correlation between mathematical ability and a lack of warmth and emotion. Miss Haywood is respected by the other inmates but she's not well liked and she has no special friends or confidantes. This must have been true of her before she was sent here because only one person comes to visit her, a brother, and his visits are anything but satisfactory."

"In what sense?"

"Oh, she seems to look forward to them, yet she's upset for a long time afterwards. And by upset I don't mean the way she acted today. Miss Haywood withdraws, becomes completely silent. It's as if she has so very much to say, to get off her chest, that she can't allow herself to begin."

"She began today."

"Yes, perhaps it's a breakthrough." But Mrs. Browning's eyes were strained as if the silver lining they saw was very faint and far away. "There's another odd thing about Miss Haywood, at least it's odd to me when I consider her circumstances: she's nearly forty, she has a prison record, she's without a husband and family to return to, she can hardly get another job in the only field she's trained in; in other words, her future appears pretty black, and she herself claims she's only waiting to die. Yet she takes extraordinarily good care of herself. She diets, and to diet in a place like this which has to serve a lot of cheap starchy food requires a great deal of will power. She exercises in her cell, half an hour in the morning, half an hour at night, and the eighteen dollars she's permitted to spend in the canteen every month—supplied by her brother—goes for vitamin pills instead of cigarettes and chewing gum. I can only presume that if she's waiting to die she's determined to die healthy . . ."

12

QUINN SPENT THE night in San Felice, and by noon the following day he was back in Chicote. The weather had not improved during the week and neither had Chicote. It lay parched and prosperous under the relentless sun, a city of oil that needed water.

He checked in at the same motel downtown.

Mr. Frisby, on duty in the office, looked a little surprised. "My goodness, it's you again, Mr. Quinn."

"Yes."

"I'm glad you're not bearing a grudge about that little episode in your room a week ago. I've warned Grandpa to be more careful in the future, and it won't happen a second time, I can assure you."

"No, I don't think it will."

"Any luck yet with your story about O'Gorman?"

"Not much."

Frisby leaned across the counter. "I wouldn't want this to get around—the sheriff's a friend of mine, sometimes he appoints me special deputy—but in my opinion the case was bungled."

"Why?"

"Civic pride, that's why. None of the authorities would admit we've got juvenile delinquency around here same as the big cities or, maybe even worse. Now according to my way of thinking, here's what happened: O'Gorman was on his way back to his office at the oil field when an earful of young punks spotted him and decided to have a little fun and games. They forced him right off the road. They did the same thing to me last year, I ended up in a ditch with two broken ribs and a concussion. Just kids they were, too, and with no motive at all except they wanted to raise hell. Some of the kids around here, especially on the ranches, learn to drive when they're ten, eleven years old. By the time they're sixteen they know everything about a car except how to behave in it. Well, I was luckier than O'Gorman. I ended up in a ditch, not a river."

"Was there any evidence that O'Gorman was forced off the road?"

"A big dent in the left side of the bumper."

"Surely the sheriff must have noticed it."

"You bet he did," Frisby said. "I pointed it out to him myself. I was there when they pulled the car out of the river and the first thing I looked for were marks like were found on my car last year. That dent was in the very same spot and there was a faint trace of dark green paint in it. Maybe not enough to take any scrapings for scientific tests, but enough so you could see if you looked real close and knew exactly what to look for."

Reliving the excitement had sent the blood rushing up into Frisby's face. It seemed to be increasing in size and getting ready to explode like a bright pink balloon. But even as Quinn watched, the balloon began diminishing and its color began fading.

"Everything was there to support my theory," Frisby said with a sudden deep sigh. "Except for one thing."

"And that was?"

"Martha O'Gorman."

The name struck Quinn's ears like a discord he'd been expecting to hear and was trying to avoid. "What about Mrs. O'Gorman?"

"Now I don't claim the lady was lying. What I've seen of her, she seems a nice, quiet-spoken young woman, not like some of these overpainted floozies you meet on the street."

"What did Martha O'Gorman say about the dent in the bumper?"

"Said she'd put it there herself a week beforehand. She claimed she backed into a lamppost while she was trying to park on the left side of a one-way street. What street and what lamppost she couldn't remember, but everybody believed her."

"Except you."

"It seemed a peculiar thing to forget, to my mind." Frisby glanced uneasily out of the window as if he half expected the sheriff to be lurking outside. "Let's suppose for a minute that I was right in thinking O'Gorman was forced off the road by another car, only this car contained not a bunch of juveniles but somebody who had reason to hate O'Gorman and want him dead. In that case Mrs. O'Gorman's story would make a pretty good cover-up, wouldn't it?"

"For herself?"

"Or a—well, a friend, say."

"You mean a boyfriend?"

"Well, it happens every day," Frisby said defensively. "Heck, I don't want to cast aspersions on an innocent woman, but what if she's not innocent? Think about that dent, Mr. Quinn. Why didn't she remember where she got it so her story could be checked?"

"There's a point in her favor you seem to have overlooked. The lampposts in Chicote are all dark green."

"So were about fifteen percent of the cars that year."

"How do you know that?"

"I did my own checking," Frisby said. "For a whole month I kept track of the cars that came here. Out of nearly five hundred, over seventy of them were dark green."

"You went to a lot of trouble to try and prove Mrs. O'Gorman was lying."

Frisby's soft round face was swelling and getting pink again. "I *wasn't* trying to prove she was lying. I wanted to find out the truth, that's all. Why, I even went around examining lampposts on one-way streets to see if I could locate the one she hit, or said she hit."

"Any luck?"

"They were all pretty beat-up, as a matter of fact. They were put in too close to the curbs. That was a long time ago, before somebody dreamed up those crazy tailfins."

"So you proved nothing."

"I proved," Frisby said brusquely, "that fifteen percent of the cars on the road that year were dark green."

From a drug store Quinn telephoned the hospital where Martha O'Gorman worked and was told that she had taken the day off because of illness. When he called her at home the O'Gorman boy said his mother was in bed with a migraine and couldn't come to the phone.

"Give her a message, will you please?"

"Sure thing."

"Tell her Joe Quinn is staying at Frisby's Motel on Main Street. She can get in touch with me there if she wants to."

She won't want to, he thought, hanging up the phone. *O'Gorman's more real to her than I am. She's still waiting for him to walk in the door—or is she?*

Or is she? The little question with the big answer echoed and reechoed in his mind.

Martha O'Gorman called out from the bedroom, "Who was that on the phone, Richard? And don't yell, the windows are open. Come right in here and tell me."

Richard came in and stood at the foot of the bed. The shades were drawn and the room was so dark his mother was merely a white shapeless lump. "He said his name was Joe Quinn and I was to tell you he was staying at Frisby's Motel on Main Street."

"Are you—are you sure?"

"Yes."

There was a long silence, and the lump on the bed remained motionless, but the boy could sense the tension in the air. "What's the matter, Mom?"

"Nothing."

"You've been acting kind of funny lately. Are you worrying about money again?"

"No, we're doing fine." Martha sat up suddenly and swung her legs over the side of the bed in an attempt at vivacity. The movement brought a spasm of pain to the entire left side of her head. Pressing her hand tight against her neck to lessen the pain, she said in a falsely cheerful voice, "As a matter of fact, my headache's much better. Perhaps we should do something to celebrate."

"That'd be great."

"It's too late for me to go to work now and tomorrow's my day off and the next day's Sunday. We'd have time to take a little camping trip. Would you and Sally like that?"

"Gosh, yes. It'd be super."

"All right, you get the sleeping bags out of the storeroom and tell Sally to start fixing some sandwiches. I'll pack the canned goods."

The mere act of standing up was agonizing to her but she knew it had to be done. She had to get out of town. It was easier to face physical pain than it would be to face Quinn.

After lunch Quinn drove over to the office of the Haywood Realty Company. Earl Perkins, the young man he'd met before, was talking on the telephone at the rear of the room. His facial contortions indicated that either his stomach was bothering him again or he was having trouble with a client.

Willie King sat behind her desk, elegant and cool in a silk sundress the same green as her eyes. She didn't seem overjoyed at Quinn's return. "Well, what are you doing back here?"

"I've grown very fond of Chicote."

"Baloney. Nobody's fond of this place. We're just stuck here."

"What's sticking you? George Haywood?"

She looked as if she wanted to get angry and couldn't quite make it. "Don't be silly. Haven't you heard about me and Earl Perkins? I'm madly in love with him. We're going to get married and live happily ever after, all three of us, Earl and I and his ulcer."

"Sounds like a great future," Quinn said. "For the ulcer."

She flushed slightly and stared down at her hands. They were large and strong, and, except for the orange polish on the fingernails, they reminded Quinn of Sister Blessing's. "Go away and leave me alone, will you please? I have a headache."

"This seems to be headache day for the ladies of Chicote."

"I mean it. Just go away. I can't answer any of your questions. I don't really know how I got into all this—this mess."

"What mess, Willie?"

"Oh, everything." She watched her hands wrestle each other as if they were separate entities over which she had no control. "Have you heard about Jenkinson's law? It says, everybody's crazy. Well, you can add Willie King's law, everything's a mess."

"No exceptions?"

"I don't see any from where I sit."

"Change seats," Quinn said.

"I can't. It's too late."

"What brought on all the gloom, Willie?"

"I don't know. The heat, maybe. Or the town."

"It's the same heat you've had all summer in the same town."

"I need a vacation, I guess. I'd like to take a trip some place where it's cold and foggy and rains every day. A couple of years ago I drove up to Seattle thinking that would be the right place. And you know what happened? When I got there Seattle was having the worst heat wave and the worst drought in its history."

"Which goes to prove Willie King's law all over again?"

She stirred restlessly in her chair as if she was having a delayed reaction to Quinn's suggestion about changing seats. "You never give a straight or serious answer to anything, do you?"

"Not if I can help it. That's Quinn's law."

"Break it for once and tell me why you've come back here?"

"To talk to George Haywood."

"About what?"

"His visits to his sister Alberta in Tecolote prison."

"Where on earth did you get a crazy idea like that?" she said impatiently. "You know perfectly well George broke off all connections with Alberta years ago. I told you."

"What you tell me isn't necessarily the truth."

"All right, so I've lied a little here and there, off and on, but not about that."

"Maybe you didn't lie about it, Willie," Quinn said. "But you were certainly misinformed. George goes to see his sister once a month."

"I don't believe it. What reason would he have for pretending?"

"That's one of the questions I intend to ask him, right this afternoon if I can arrange it."

"You can't."

"Why not?"

She bent forward in the chair, her hands clasped tight against her stomach as if to ease the sharp pain of a cramp. "He's not here. He left the day before yesterday."

"For where?"

"Hawaii. He's been having a bad time with bronchial asthma for the past couple of months and the doctor thought a change of climate would help."

"How long will he be away?"

"I don't know. Everything happened so suddenly. He came into the office three days ago and out of the blue he announced he was flying to Hawaii the next morning for a vacation."

"Did he ask you to make a reservation for him?"

"No. He said he'd made it himself." She groped in her pocket for a handkerchief and held it against her forehead. "It was quite a—a shock. I had done a lot of planning—or dreaming I guess you'd call it—about George and me spending our vacation together this year. Then suddenly I get the whammy, he's flying to Hawaii. Alone. Period."

"So that's what's causing your glooms?"

"Well, at least he could have said something, sorry you're not coming along, Willie, some little thing like that. He didn't, though. I'm afraid. I'm afraid this is the end of the line."

"You're over-imagining, Willie."

"No, I don't think so. God knows I'd like to, but I can't. George acted like a different man. He wasn't *George* anymore. The real George, my George, wouldn't go on a trip like that without careful planning in advance about where he'd stay and what he'd do and how long he'd be gone. He didn't tell me a single detail beyond the fact that he was leaving the next morning. So you see, I have reason to be afraid. I've got this terrible feeling he's not coming back. I keep thinking of O'Gorman."

"Why O'Gorman?"

She pushed the handkerchief across her forehead again. "Endings can happen so suddenly. I should have argued with George, begged him to take me along. Then if the plane crashed, at least we'd have died together."

"You're getting morbid, Willie. I didn't hear of any plane crash day before yesterday. Right this minute George is probably surrounded by a bevy of sun-browned maidens who are teaching him the hula."

She stared up at Quinn coldly. "If that was intended to cheer me up, I assure you it didn't. Sun-browned maidens, hell."

"With hibiscus in their hair."

"I have a hibiscus growing in my own backyard. Any time I want to put one in my hair, I can. I can also get a tan *and* do the hula, if I have to."

"I'd bet on you any day, Willie."

"Would you?"

"Try me."

"Oh, stop kidding around, Quinn," she said with a brisk shake of her head. "I'm not your type, and you're not mine. I like older, more mature men, not the kind who know where they're going, but the kind who are already there. I've been through that stardust and baked beans routine once. Never again. I want security. I don't think you even know what you want."

"I'm beginning to find out."

"Since when?"

"Since I hit rock-bottom a couple of weeks ago."

"How far down is rock-bottom for you, Quinn?"

"Far enough," he said, "so there's no direction to go but up. Have you ever heard of the Tower of Heaven?"

"I had a very religious aunt who was always using phrases like that in her conversation."

"This isn't a phrase, it's a real place in the mountains behind San Felice. I've been there twice and I've promised to go back a third time. Which reminds me, did you ever have acne?"

Her precisely plucked brows moved up her forehead. "Say, are you losing your marbles?"

"I may be. I'd like an answer to my question anyway."

"I never had acne, no," she said carefully, as though she were humoring an idiot. "My kid sister did when she was in high school. She got rid of it by washing her face six or seven times a day, using Norton's drying lotion, and not eating any sweets or oils. Is that what you want to know?"

"Yes. Thank you, Willie."

"I suppose if I asked *why* you wanted to know, you wouldn't—"

"I wouldn't."

"You're a very peculiar man," Willie said thoughtfully. "But I'm sure that's already been pointed out to you?"

"At my mother's knee. Besides, we can't all be perfect like George."

"I didn't claim he was perfect." There was a sharp note in her voice as if she had suddenly had too vivid a picture of George surrounded by the sun-browned maidens. "He's headstrong like his mother, for one thing. When he gets an idea, he goes right ahead and acts on it, without consulting anyone else or caring what I—what someone else might think."

"Like the sudden trip to Hawaii?"

"It's a good example."

"You're sure he went to Hawaii?"

"Why, I—of course. Of course I'm sure."

"Did you see him off?"

"Naturally."

"Where?"

"He came to my apartment to say good-bye," she said. "He was going to drive to San Felice, catch a plane there, and then transfer at Los Angeles to a jet liner for Honolulu."

"Leaving his car at San Felice airport?"

"Yes."

"They don't have a garage at San Felice airport."

"There must be garages nearby," she said anxiously. "Aren't there?"

"I guess so. What kind of car was he driving?"

"His own. A green Pontiac station wagon, last year's. Why are you asking me all these questions? I don't like it. It makes me nervous. You seem to be implying that George didn't go to Hawaii at all."

"No. I just want to make sure he did."

"Why, it never even occurred to me to doubt it until you started hinting around," she said in an accusing voice. "Maybe you're deliberately trying to cause trouble between George and me for reasons of your own."

"There's already been trouble between George and you, hasn't there, Willie?"

Her jaws tightened, giving her face a strong sinewy look Quinn hadn't seen before. "None that I couldn't handle. His mother has been, well, rather difficult."

"Last time you talked about her she was an old harridan. Is she improving, or are you?" When she didn't answer, Quinn went on. "I heard an interesting rumor a few days ago from what I consider a reliable source. It concerns George."

"Then I don't care to hear it. A man in George's position, especially after what happened to Alberta, becomes the target for all kinds of rumors and gossip. He's borne up under it the only way he could, by living a clean, decent, exemplary life. There's something about George you couldn't know since you haven't met him—he's an extraordinarily brave man. He could easily have left town to avoid the scandal. But he didn't. He stayed here and fought it."

"Why?"

"I told you. He's a brave man."

"Maybe he had ties in Chicote, the same kind that keep you here."

"You mean his mother? Or me?"

"Neither," Quinn said. "I mean Martha O'Gorman."

Willie's face looked ready to fall apart, but she caught it in time and held it together by sheer will power. The effort left her trembling. "That's ridiculous."

"I don't see why. She's an attractive woman and she has class."

"Class? So that's what you call it when someone acts as though she's better than the rest of us. I know all about Martha O'Gorman. My best friend works with her at the hospital lab and she says Martha throws a fit if anyone makes the least little mistake."

"The least little mistake in a hospital lab can be pretty big."

Quinn realized that Willie, not for the first time, had quite neatly turned the conversation away from George. *There are certain kinds of birds,* he thought, *that protect their nests, when they're threatened, by pretending the nest is someplace else. The maneuver involves a lot of squawking and wing-beating; Willie's good at both, but she's a little too obvious, and she suffers from the current disadvantage of not being entirely sure where her nest is and what's going on inside it.*

Willie kept right on squawking, anyway. "She's a cold, hard woman. You've only to look at that frozen face of hers to figure out that much. The girls at the lab are all scared of her."

"You seem pretty scared of her yourself, Willie."

"Me? Why should I be?"

"Because of George."

She began, once again, telling Quinn how ridiculous the idea was, how absolutely absurd to think of George paying attention to a woman like that. But her words had a hollow ring, and Quinn knew she wasn't even convincing herself. He knew another thing, too: Willie King was suffering from a severe case of jealousy, and he wondered what had caused it. A week ago she had seemed a great deal more sure of herself, and the only fly in her amber was George's mother. Now the amber was polished and other flies had become visible. Martha O'Gorman and the sun-browned maidens with hibiscus in their hair, and perhaps still others Quinn hadn't yet discovered.

13

IT WAS AN old white-brick three-storied house, a Victorian dowager looking down her nose and trying to ignore the oil-rich newcomers she was forced to associate with. Behind thick lace curtains and bristling turrets she brooded, pondered, disapproved, and fought a losing battle against the flat-roofed ranch-styles and stucco and redwood boxes. Quinn expected that the woman who answered the door would match the house.

Mrs. Haywood didn't. She was slim and stylish in beige-colored linen. Her hair was dyed platinum pink, and her face bore the barely visible scars of a surgical lifting. She looked as youthful as her son George, except for the ancient griefs that showed in her eyes.

Quinn said, "Mrs. Haywood?"

"Yes." No amount of surgery could disguise her voice; it was the cracked whine of an old woman. "I buy nothing from peddlers."

"My name is Joe Quinn. I'd like to discuss some business with Mr. Haywood."

"Business should be confined to the office."

"I called his office and was told he wasn't in. I took a chance on his being home."

"He's not."

"Well, I'm sorry to have bothered you, Mrs. Haywood. When your husband gets home, please tell him to get in touch with me, will you? I'm at Frisby's Motel on Main Street."

"Husband?" She pounced on the word like a starving cat. Quinn could almost feel the sting of her claws. He was both repelled and moved to pity by the desperate hunger in her eyes and the coy girlish smile that failed to hide it. "You've made a mistake, Mr. Quinn, but what a very nice one. It's too bad all the mistakes we humans make can't be so pleasant. George is my son."

Quinn was sorry he'd had to use such raw bait but it was too late now to snatch it away. "That's hard to believe."

"Quite frankly, I adore flattery, so I'm not going to argue with you."

"I'm sure the mistake's been made before, Mrs. Haywood."

"Oh yes, on a number of occasions, but it never fails to astonish and amuse me. I'm afraid poor George isn't quite so amused. Perhaps this time I won't tell him about it; it will remain our little secret, Mr. Quinn, just between you and me."

And the next hundred people she meets, Quinn thought.

Now that he had come face to face with Mrs. Haywood, he was no longer surprised by her complete rejection of her two daughters. There was no room in the house for younger females who might invite comparisons. Mrs. Haywood's maternal instinct was a good deal weaker than her instinct for self-preservation. She meant to survive, on her own terms, and she couldn't afford the luxury of sentiment. *Poor Willie, her road to security has more chuckholes and detours than she's equipped to handle. If there was no room in the house for Alberta and Ruth, there will certainly be none for Willie.*

Mrs. Haywood had assumed a picturesque, fashion-magazine pose against the doorjamb. "Of course, I've always kept fit. I see no reason why people should let themselves go after fif—forty. I've always tried to impress upon my family my own axiom: you *are* what you *eat*."

If Mrs. Haywood subsisted on gall and wormwood, then her axiom was undoubtedly true. Quinn said, "I'm sorry to have missed Mr. Haywood. Will he be in his office later this afternoon?"

"Oh no. George is in Hawaii." She obviously didn't like either the change of subject or the idea of George being in Hawaii. "Doctor's orders. It's absurd, of course. There's nothing the matter with George that good cold showers and hard exercise won't cure. But then, doctors are all alike, aren't they? When they have no real cure to offer they recommend a change of climate and scene. Are you a friend of George's?"

"I have some business to discuss with him."

"Well, I don't know when he'll be back. The trip came as a complete surprise to me. He didn't even mention it to me until after he'd bought his ticket. Then it was too late for me to do anything about it. It seems terribly foolish and extravagant to spend all that money because some incompetent doctor suggests it. George could just as easily have gone to stay in San Felice, the climate's the same as Hawaii. I have my own share of aches and pains but I don't take off for exotic places. I simply increase my wheat germ and tiger's milk and do a few extra knee bends. Do you believe in vigorous exercise, Mr. Quinn?"

"Oh yes. Yes, indeed."

"I thought so. You seem very fit."

She changed her pose from fashion magazine to Olympic champion, and looked hopefully at Quinn as if she expected another compliment. Quinn couldn't think of any he could offer without gagging. He said instead, "Do you happen to know what airline Mr. Haywood took?"

"No. Should I?"

"You said he'd bought his ticket. I thought he might have showed it to you."

"He brandished an envelope under my nose but I knew he was only doing it to annoy me so I pretended complete indifference. I will not be provoked into a common quarrel, it's too hard on the heart and the arteries. I simply express my viewpoint and refuse to discuss the matter any further. George was quite aware how I felt about this trip of his. I considered it unnecessary and extravagant, and I told him point-blank that if he was really concerned about his health he'd stay home more in the evenings instead of chasing around after women."

"Mr. Haywood isn't married?"

"He was. His wife died many years ago. It was hardly unexpected. She was a poor spiritless little thing, life was too much for her. Since her death, of course, every woman in town has set her cap for George. Fortunately, he has me to point out to him some of their wiles and pretenses. He'd never see through any of them himself, he's hopelessly naive. A very good example of this happened a few days ago. A woman called and said she had to see George about a mysterious letter she'd received—I heard her because I had picked up the extension phone, quite by accident. Mysterious letter, indeed. Why, a child could have seen through a ruse like that. But George, no. In spite of his cough, off he went before I had a chance to tell him that even if she was speaking the truth she was up to no good. The *right* people just do not receive mysterious letters. When I asked him about it later he blew up at me. I tell you, it's not easy to be a mother in this age of hard liquor and harder women." She smiled with a flash of teeth too white and perfect to have been around as long as the rest of her. "I find you restful and *simpatico,* Mr. Quinn. Do you live in Chicote?"

"No."

"What a shame. I was hoping you could come to dinner one night with George and me. We eat simple, healthful food, but it's quite tasty, nevertheless."

"Thank you for the offer," Quinn said. "You know, you've aroused my curiosity, Mrs. Haywood."

She looked flattered. "I have? How?"

"That mysterious letter. Did it really exist?"

"Well, I can't be sure because George wouldn't tell me. But I think, personally, that she invented it. It was merely an excuse to get George to go over to her house and see her in her own setting, with the two children, and a fire in the fireplace, and something bubbling on the stove, that sort of thing. Deliberate domesticity, if you follow me."

I follow you, Quinn thought, *right up to Martha O'Gorman's front door.*

There was no fire in the fireplace, and if something was bubbling on the stove, none of its aroma was escaping through the locked windows and drawn blinds. The brass lion's-head knocker on the front door looked as if it hadn't been used since Quinn's first visit a week ago. From the yard next door a girl about ten years old, wearing shorts and a T-shirt, watched Quinn curiously as he waited for someone to answer his knock.

After a time she said in a dreamy voice, "They're not home. They left about an hour ago."

"Do you happen to know where they went?"

"They didn't tell me, but I saw Richard putting the sleeping bags in the car so I guess they went camping. They do a lot of camping."

The girl chewed reflectively on her gum for a minute. Quinn said, by way of encouragement, "Have you been a neighbor of the O'Gormans very long?"

"Practically forever. Sally's my best friend. Richard I hate, he's too bossy."

"Have you ever gone camping with them?"

"Once, last year. I didn't like it."

"Why not?"

"I kept thinking of big black bears. Also, rattlesnakes, on account of that was where we were camping, on the Rattlesnake River. It was real scary."

"What's your name, young lady?"

"Miranda Knights. I hate it."

"I think it's very pretty," Quinn said. "Do you remember exactly where you camped on the Rattlesnake River, Miranda?"

"Sure. Paradise Falls, where the Rattlesnake flows into the Torcido River. It's not really a falls, though; it's just some big boulders with trickles of water falling down. Richard likes it because he hides behind the boulders and makes noises like a bear and jumps out to scare Sally and me. Richard's ghastly."

"Oh, I can see that."

"My brothers are ghastly, too, but they're smaller than I am so it's not such a terrible problem."

"I'm sure you can handle it," Quinn said. "Tell me, Miranda, do the O'Gormans usually camp at Paradise Falls?"

"I never heard Sally talk about any other place except that."

"Do you know how to get there?"

"No," Miranda said. "But it doesn't take long, less than an hour."

"Are you sure of that?"

"Naturally. Last year when I was with them and I got homesick and scared of black bears and rattlesnakes, Mrs. O'Gorman kept telling me I was less than an hour from home."

"Thank you, Miranda."

"You're welcome."

Quinn returned to his car. He thought of asking directions at a gas station and setting out immediately for Paradise Falls. But the mid-afternoon heat was so intense that it rose in waves from the streets and sidewalks, and the whole town had a blurry look as if it had grown fuzz.

He went back to his motel room, turned the air-conditioner on full, and lay down on the bed. The more he learned of Martha O'Gorman, the less he felt he knew her. Her image, like the town shimmering in the heat, had become blurred. It had been clear enough at first: she was a woman devoted to her family and still in mourning for a beloved husband, a woman of both sense and sensitivity who dreaded the thought that the inquiry into her husband's disappearance might be reopened. The dread was natural enough, she'd been through a bad time, harassed by gossip, rumors and publicity. They had all died down now and Quinn could understand why she was reluctant to start them up again. What bothered him was the fact that at the coroner's inquest Martha O'Gorman had had a chance to resolve the whole case and she had refused it. If she had not claimed that she had put the dent in the rear bumper of the car by backing into a lamppost, the coroner's jury would probably have decided that O'Gorman's car had been forced off the road. There could be only one of two reasons behind her claim: either it was the truth, or she couldn't afford to leave open that particular area of investigation: *gentlemen of the jury, I put that dent in the bumper, you needn't look any further.* Apparently they hadn't looked any further, and only a few skeptics like Frisby still believed Martha had lied, to save her own skin, or somebody else's.

A dent and a few traces of dark green paint—small things in themselves, made larger in Quinn's eyes by the contradictions in Martha's character and behavior. She was too ill to work, yet she went on a camping trip. And the spot she chose, and, according to the girl Miranda, always chose, was not just any old campground. It was the place which, if the police and John Ronda were correct, her husband's body had floated by. Quinn remembered John Ronda telling him about it: a few miles beyond the bridge where O'Gorman's car went over, the Rattlesnake River joined the Torcido, which at that time was a raging torrent fed by mountain streams and melting snow.

Why did she keep returning to the same place? Quinn wondered. Did she hope to find him, after all these years, wedged between a couple of boulders? Or was she motivated by guilt? And what did she tell the kids?—*Let's all go out and look for Daddy.*

The boy, Richard, had gathered driftwood and pine cones for the campfire and he was itching to light it. But his mother told him it wasn't cool enough yet and it would be better to wait.

His mother and sister Sally were cooking supper on the charcoal grill, beans and corn on the cob and spareribs. Sometimes the ribs caught fire and Sally would put out the flames by squirting them with a plastic water pistol. She didn't handle the pistol the way a boy would have, pretending to shoot something or someone. She was very solemn about it, using the child's toy like an adult, for practical reasons.

Richard wandered off by himself. Some day he wanted to come to this place all alone, without two females around to spoil the illusion that he was a man and that this was a very dangerous spot and he was not in the least afraid of it. Yet he was afraid, and it was not of the place itself but of the change that came over his mother as soon as they arrived. It was a change he didn't understand and couldn't put his finger on. She talked and acted the same as she did at home and she smiled a lot, but her eyes often looked sad and strange, especially when she thought no one was watching her. Richard was always watching. He was too alert and intelligent to miss anything, but still too much of a child to evaluate what he noticed.

He had been seven when his father disappeared. He still remembered his father, though he wasn't sure which were real memories and which were things his mother often talked about: *Do you remember the funny little car you and Daddy made with the wheels from your old scooter?* Yes, he remembered the car, and the scooter wheels, but he couldn't remember his father working with him to build anything; and Martha's continued references, intended to create in him a strong father-picture, confused the boy and made him feel guilty about his memory lapses.

He crawled to the top of a boulder and lay down on his stomach, as still and silent as a lizard in the sun. From here he could see the road that led into the campgrounds. Pretty soon other people would start arriving for the weekend and by dusk the campsites would all be taken and the air would be filled with the smell of woodfires and hamburgers cooking, and the shriek of children's voices. But right now he and his mother and Sally were the only ones; they had the choicest campsite, right beside the river, and the best stone barbecue pit and picnic table, and the tallest trees.

Do you remember the first time Daddy brought us here, Richard? You were halfway up a pine tree before we missed you. Daddy had to climb up and bring you down. He could remember climbing the pine tree but not being brought down by anyone. He'd always been a good climber—why hadn't he come down by himself? As he lay on the boulder, it occurred to him for the first time in his life that his mother's memories might be as tenuous as his own and that she was only pretending they were vivid and real.

He heard a car in the distance and raised his head to listen and to watch for it. A couple of minutes later it was visible on the road into camp, a blue and cream Ford Victoria with a man at the wheel. There was no one else in the car and no camping equipment strapped to the roof or piled in the back seat. Richard noticed these details automatically, without being especially curious. It was a few moments before he realized he had seen the car before. About a week ago it had been pulling away from the curb in front of his own house when he had returned home from the Y. When he went inside, he found his mother in the kitchen, white-faced and silent.

14

SHE SAW QUINN getting out of the car and she said to Sally in a carefully casual voice, "Why don't you go and find Richard? Supper won't be ready for another half-hour. You could collect more pine cones so we'll have some to gild for Christmas."

"Are you trying to get rid of me?" The girl glanced thoughtfully at Quinn approaching from the road. "So you can talk to him?"

"Yes."

"Is it about money?"

"Perhaps. I don't know."

Money, or lack of it, was a key word in the O'Gorman household, and the children had learned to respect it. Sally walked briskly away in search of her brother and pine cones.

Martha turned to face Quinn. She stood at rigid attention like a soldier confronted with a surprise inspection. "How did you find me? What do you want?"

"Let's call this a friendly visit."

"Let's not. I can put up with your hounding me personally, but why do you have to bring my children into it?"

"I'm sorry, that's the way things worked out. May I sit down, Mrs. O'Gorman?"

"If you feel you must."

He sat on one of the benches attached to the redwood picnic table, and after a moment's hesitation she walked over to the other bench and sat down, too, as if she were agreeing to a kind of truce. It reminded Quinn of the last time they had met, in the hospital cafeteria. Then, too, there had been a table between them, and that table, like this one, had been invisibly loaded with questions, doubts, suspicions, accusations. Quinn would have liked to brush them all off with his hand and start over again. He knew, from the hostility on her face, that she did not share this feeling.

He said quietly, "You're not obliged to answer any of my questions, Mrs. O'Gorman. I have no official authority to ask them."

"I'm aware of that."

"You can, in fact, order me off the premises."

"The premises belong to the county," she said with a vague gesture. "You're as welcome as anyone else on public camping grounds."

"You like this place?"

"We've been coming here for many years, since Sally was born."

The statement caught Quinn by surprise. He had assumed that Martha O'Gorman had begun coming to the campsite after her husband's disappearance. As it was, she had merely continued a practice started years before. It fitted in with what he already knew about her character: she was still trying to carry on her life, as much as possible, in the same way as she had before O'Gorman disappeared or died, as if, by repeating the pattern, she could magically invoke O'Gorman's spirit.

Quinn said, "Then your husband was familiar with the surrounding area, the river and so forth?"

"He'd explored every inch of the river—both rivers—a dozen times, as I have."

She looked as though she was daring him to make something of it. Quinn didn't have to, the point was already made. If O'Gorman had planned his own disappearance, his plans had been based on knowledge of, and perhaps experiments on, both rivers involved.

"I know what you're thinking," she said. "You're wrong."

"Am I?"

"My husband was murdered."

"A week ago you were claiming he died in an accident, you were very sure of it, in fact."

"I've had reason to change my mind."

"What reason, Mrs. O'Gorman?"

"I can't tell you that."

"Why not?"

"I don't trust you," she said bluntly, "any more than you trust me. That's not very much, is it?"

Quinn was silent for a minute. "I don't know exactly how much it is, Mrs. O'Gorman. I only know I wish it were more. On both sides."

"Well, it's not."

She got up and went over to the grill and removed the ribs from the heat. They were almost as black as the charcoal they had been cooked over.

"I'm sorry if I've ruined your dinner, Mrs. O'Gorman."

"You haven't," she said crisply. "Richard's like his father, he has to have all meat burned so it's less likely to remind him of—well, the source of it. He loves animals, as Patrick did."

"You're sure now that your husband's dead?"

"I was always sure of that. It was how he died that I couldn't make up my mind about."

"But you have recently, in fact just this week, decided he was murdered?"

"Yes."

"Have you told the authorities?"

"No." There was a brief flash of temper in her eyes. "And I'm not going to. My children and I have suffered enough. The O'Gorman case is closed and it will remain closed."

"Even though you have evidence to reopen it?"

"What gave you that idea?"

"A conversation I had this afternoon with George Haywood's mother," Quinn said. "Mrs. Haywood can't resist an extension phone when other people are on the line."

"Well."

"Is that all you have to say, well?"

"That's all."

"Mrs. O'Gorman, it's not good enough. If you've received concrete evidence of the murder of your husband, it's your duty to hand it over to the police."

"Is it really?" she said with an indifferent shrug. "I guess I should have thought of that before I burned it."

"You burned the letter?"

"I did."

"Why?"

"Both Mr. Haywood and I thought it was the most practical course to take."

"Mr. Haywood and you," Quinn repeated. "How long have you been asking for, and following, George's advice?"

"Is that any of your business, Mr. Quinn?"

"In a way, yes."

"What way?"

"I want to find out what the competition is because I think I've fallen for you."

Her laugh was brief and brittle. "Think again, Mr. Quinn."

"Well, I'm glad I amuse you, anyway."

"You don't. I'm not amused, I'm amazed that you'd consider me naive enough to swallow such an obvious line of flattery. Did you expect me to believe you? Did you imagine I'd be so swept off my feet that—"

"Stop it," he said sharply.

She stopped, more from surprise than because he had ordered her to.

"I made a statement, Mrs. O'Gorman. Be amused, amazed, or anything else, but I'm sticking by it. Now you can forget it, if you like."

"I think we'd both better forget it."

"All right."

"You—well, you confuse me. You're so unpredictable."

"Nobody's unpredictable," Quinn said, "if someone takes the time and trouble to predict him."

"I wish you'd—we'd stop talking personally like this. It upsets me. I don't know what to think anymore."

"Well, don't ask George. His advice hasn't been too good up to now. Was it his idea to burn the letter?"

"No, my own. He agreed with me, because he thought the letter was merely a hoax or a bad joke. He didn't take it seriously the way I did."

"Who wrote it, Mrs. O'Gorman?"

She stared up at the sky. The sun was beginning to set and its golden-red rays were reflected in her face. "There was no signature and I didn't recognize the handwriting. But it was from a man who said he'd murdered my husband five years ago last February."

She looked as though she would burst into tears at the least sign or word of sympathy, so Quinn offered none. "Was it a local letter?"

"No. The postmark was Evanston, Illinois."

"And the contents?"

"He said he'd just been informed that he had cancer of the lung and before he died he wanted to make peace with God and his conscience by confessing all his sins."

"Did he give the actual details of the murder?"

"Yes."

"And his motive?"

"Yes."

"What was it?"

She shook her head slowly, wincing as if the movement pained her. "I simply can't tell you. I'm—ashamed."

"You weren't too ashamed to call George Haywood and invite him over to see the letter."

"I needed his advice, the advice of a man of experience."

"John Ronda's a man of experience. He's also a good friend of yours."

"He's also," she said grimly, "the editor of a newspaper and an incurable talker. Mr. Haywood isn't. I was sure I could trust his discretion. I had another reason, too. Mr. Haywood knew my husband. I thought he could evaluate the charge made against him in the letter."

"The charge against your husband, you mean?"

"Yes. It was a—a terrible thing. I couldn't believe it, of course. No wife could, about her husband. And yet—" Her voice, which had been barely more than a whisper, now faded out entirely.

"And yet you did, Mrs. O'Gorman?"

"I didn't want to, God knows. But for some time before my husband's death I'd been aware of a darkness in our lives. I kept trying to act as though it didn't exist. I couldn't force myself to turn on the lights and find out what the darkness was hiding. Then this letter came and the lights were on, whether I wanted them to be or not." She rubbed her eyes, as if to rub away the memory. "I panicked and called George Haywood. I realize now that it was a mistake, but I was desperate. I had to talk to someone who'd known Patrick and worked with him. A man. It had to be a man."

"Why?"

Her mouth moved in a bitter little smile. "Women are easily fooled, even the smart ones, perhaps especially the smart ones. Mr. Haywood came over to the house right away. I guess I was hysterical by that time. He acted very calm, though I had the impression he was quite excited underneath."

"What was his opinion of the letter?"

"He said it was a lot of hogwash, that every murder attracts false confessions from emotionally disturbed people. I knew that was true, of course, but there was something so real and poignant about the letter, and every detail of the murder was correct. If the person who sent it was disturbed, then the disturbance certainly hadn't affected his memory or his ability to express himself."

"It often doesn't."

"I even considered the possibility that Patrick was alive and had written it himself. But there were too many discrepancies. First of all, it wasn't his style. The envelope was addressed to Mrs. Patrick O'Gorman, Chicote, California. Patrick would surely have remembered his own street and house number. Then, too, the writing wasn't Patrick's. He was left-handed and wrote with an extreme slant towards the left. The handwriting in the letter slanted in the opposite direction and it was very awkward and childish, more like a third-grader's than a grown man's. But the overwhelming reason Patrick couldn't have written the letter was the accusation against him. No man would admit such a thing about himself."

"Did the writer claim to have known your husband well?"

"No. He'd never seen him until that night. He was a hobo who'd been camping out by the river. When the weather got too bad he decided to move on to Bakersfield. He was standing on the side of the road waiting to hitch a ride. Patrick stopped and picked him up. Then Patrick—oh, my God, I can't believe it, I won't!"

Quinn knew she did, though, and no amount of tears would wash away the belief. She was weeping, almost without sound, her hands covering her face, the tears slithering out between her fingers, down her wrists, into the sleeves of her denim jacket.

"Mrs. O'Gorman," he said. "Martha. Listen to me, Martha. Perhaps Haywood was right and the letter was a sadistic joke."

She raised her head and stared at him, looking like a forlorn child. "How could anyone hate me that much?"

"I don't know. But a twisted person can hate anyone, with or without reason. What was the general tone of the letter?"

"Sorrow and regret. Fear, too, fear of dying. And hatred, but not directed against me. He seemed to loathe himself for what he'd done, and Patrick for making him do it."

"Your husband made an improper advance, is that what you've been trying to say, Martha?"

"Yes." It was hardly more than a sigh of admission.

"That's why you burned the letter instead of showing it to the authorities?"

"I had to destroy it, for the sake of my children, myself—yes, and for Patrick's sake, too. Don't you see that?"

"Yes, of course I do."

"There was nothing to be gained by going to the police, and everything to be lost. A great deal's been lost already, but it's my own private personal loss, and I can stand that as long as my children are protected and Patrick's good name is kept intact. As it will be. Even if you went to the police and told them everything I've said this afternoon, they couldn't do a thing. I would deny every word of it, and so would Mr. Haywood. I have his promise. The letter never existed."

"I suppose you realize that suppressing evidence about a murder is very serious?"

"Legally, I guess it is, but that doesn't concern me right now. It's funny, I've always been a law-abiding citizen but at the moment I couldn't care less about the legal technicalities. If a murderer goes unpunished because of me, I won't regret it. Too many innocent people would be punished along with him. Justice and the law don't always amount to the same thing—or are you still too young and starry-eyed to have found this out?"

"Not young," Quinn said. "Definitely not starry-eyed."

She was studying him intently, her face grave and a little sad. "I think you're both."

"That's your privilege."

"You'd like me to go running to the police, wouldn't you?"

"No. I just—"

"Yes, you would. You really believe that when the law demands an eye for an eye, that's what it gets. Well, you're wrong. The mathematics involved becomes amazingly intricate and somehow the law ends up with a dozen eyes. Six of them are *not* going to belong to me and my children. If necessary, I would swear on a stack of Bibles in front of the Supreme Court that no letter concerning my husband's death was ever delivered to me."

"Would George be willing to do the same?"

"Yes."

"Because he's in love with you?"

"You seem to have romance on your mind," she said coldly. "I hope it's just a phase. No, Mr. Haywood is not in love with me. He happens to view the situation in the same light as I do. Whether the letter was a hoax, as he believes, or the truth, as I do, we both agreed that it would be disastrous to publicize it. And that's exactly what handing it over to the police would have meant, so I burned it. Do you want to know where I burned it? In the incinerator in the backyard, so that every single ash of it would be blown away by the wind. It exists now only in the mind of the man who wrote it, and Mr. Haywood's, and my own."

"And mine."

"Not yours, Mr. Quinn. You never saw it. You can't be sure there ever was such a thing. I could have invented it, couldn't I?"

"I don't think so."

"I wish I had invented it. I wish—"

Whatever wishes she had were blown away by the wind like the ashes of the letter. Even though she was looking at Quinn he had the feeling he was invisible to her, that her eyes were focused on some point in the past, some happier and more innocent place than this.

"Martha—"

"Please, I don't want you to call me Martha."

"It's your name."

She raised her head. "I am Mrs. Patrick O'Gorman."

"That was a long time ago, Martha. Wake up. The dream's over, the lights are on."

"I don't want them to be on."

"But they are. You said so yourself."

"I can't bear it," she whispered. "I thought we were so happy, such a happy family . . . And then the letter came and suddenly everything turned to garbage. And it was too late to clean it up, get rid of it, so I had to pretend, I must go on pretending—"

"Pretend yourself right into a butterfly net. I can't stop you. I can warn you, though, that you're making too much of everything. Your life didn't change from moonlight and roses to garbage just because O'Gorman made a pass at another man. It was always some moonlight, some roses, some garbage, like anyone else's life. You're not a tragic heroine picked out for special glory and special disaster, and O'Gorman wasn't a hero or a villain, just an unfortunate man. You told me the last time we talked that you were very realistic. Do you still believe that?"

"I don't know. I—I thought I was. I managed things so that they worked out."

"Including O'Gorman."

"Yes."

"You knocked yourself out covering up O'Gorman's mistakes and weaknesses. Now that you've come to realize you knocked yourself out for nothing, you can't face it. One minute you stick your chin in the air and announce proudly that you're Mrs. Patrick O'Gorman, and the next minute you're squawking about garbage. When are you going to reach a compromise?"

"That's no concern of yours."

"I'm making it my concern, as of now."

She looked a little frightened. "What are you going to do?"

"Do? What can I do?" he said wearily. "Except wait around for you to get tired running from one extreme to another. Maybe eventually you'll settle for something worse than paradise but better than hell. Do you think it's possible?"

"I don't know. And I can't talk about it here, now."

"Why not?"

"It's getting dark. I must call the children." She stood up. The movement seemed uncertain and so did her voice. "I—will you stay for supper?"

"I'd like to, very much. But I'm afraid the timing's wrong. I don't want to be presented to your children as a surprise intruder on their campout. This place belongs to you and them and O'Gorman. I'll wait until I can offer a place the three of you can share with me."

"Please don't talk like that. We barely know each other."

"When we last met, you told me something I believed at the time. You said I was too old to learn about love. I no longer believe that, Martha. What I think is that, until now, I've been too young and scared to learn about it."

She had turned away, bowing her head, so that he could see the white nape of her neck that contrasted with the deep tan on her face. "We have nothing in common. Nothing."

"How do you know?"

"John Ronda told me something about you, how you lived, where you worked. I could never adjust to such a life, and I'm not foolish enough to think I could change you."

"The change has already started."

"Has it?" Her mouth smiled but her voice remained sad. "I said before that you were starry-eyed. You are. People don't change just because they want to."

"You've had too much trouble, Martha. You're disillusioned."

"And how does one go about getting re-illusioned?"

"I can't answer that for anyone else. I only know it happened to me."

"When?"

"Not long ago."

"How?"

"I'm not sure how." He could remember the exact moment, though, the pungent smell of pine, the moon growing in the trees like a golden melon, the stars bursting out all over the sky like popping seeds. And Sister Blessing's voice, tinged with impatience: *"Haven't you ever seen a sky before?" "Not this one." "It's the same as always." "It looks different to me." "Do you suppose you're having a religious experience?" "I am admiring the universe."*

Martha was watching him with a mixture of interest and anxiety. "What happened to you, Joe?"

"I guess I fell back in love with life, I became a part of the world again after a long exile. The funny thing is that it happened in the most unworldly place in the world."

"The Tower?"

"Yes." He stared at the last faint glow in the sky. "After I left you last week, I went back to the Tower."

"Did you see Sister Blessing? Did you ask her why she hired you to find Patrick?"

"I asked her. She didn't answer, though. I doubt if she even heard me."

"Why? Was she sick?"

"In a sense, yes. She was sick with fear."

"Of what?"

"Not getting into heaven. By hiring me, by having anything to do with me in fact, she'd committed a grave sin. Also she'd withheld money from the communal fund and the word 'money' to the Master is both sacred and dirty. He's a queer man; compelling, forceful, and quite insane. He has a strangle hold on his flock, and the smaller the flock becomes, the more desperate the strangle hold gets and the more extreme his proclamations and edicts and punishments. Even his old followers, like his own wife and Sister Blessing, show signs of restlessness. As for the younger ones, it's only a matter of time until they escape from the Tower."

He thought of the tortured face of Sister Contrition as she led her three docile, rebellious-eyed children into the living room, and of the querulous voice of Mother Pureza who had already escaped from the Tower and was living in the brighter rooms of her childhood with her beloved servant, Capirote.

Martha said, "Are you going back there?"

"Yes, I made a promise to go back. I must also tell Sister Blessing that the man she hired me to find is dead."

"You won't mention the letter?"

"No."

"To anyone?"

"To anyone." Quinn stood up. "Well, I'd better be going."

"Yes."

"When will I see you again, Martha?"

"I don't know. I'm very confused right now because of the letter and—and the things you've said."

"Did you come here today to run away from me?"

"Yes."

"Are you sorry I found you?"

"I can't answer that. Please don't ask me."

"All right."

He walked over to his car and got in. When he glanced back Martha was lighting the campfire and the mounting flames made her quiet face seem vivacious and warm, the way it had looked in the hospital cafeteria when she had first talked about her marriage to O'Gorman.

"We came back as soon as we heard the car leave," Richard said. He had smelled some mystery in the air as distinctly as he had smelled the first puffs of smoke from the campfire. "Who was the man?"

"A friend of mine," Martha said.

"You don't have many boyfriends."

"No, I don't. Would you like me to?"

"I guess it'd be okay."

"No, it *wouldn't*," Sally said earnestly. "*Mothers* don't have boyfriends."

Martha put her hand on the girl's shoulder. "Sometimes they do, when they no longer have a husband of their own."

"Why?"

"Men and women are meant to become interested in each other and get married."

"And have children?"

"Sometimes, yes."

"How many children do you think you'll have?"

"Of all the stupid questions I ever heard in my life," Richard said with contempt. "You don't have children when you're old and grey."

Martha's tone was sharper than she intended. "That's not very complimentary, is it, Richard?"

"Gosh, no. But you're my mother. Mothers don't expect compliments."

"It would be nice to be surprised for a change. My hair, by the way, is brown, not grey."

"Gee whiz, old and grey is just an expression."

"Well, it's an expression I don't care to hear until it's literally true. Perhaps not even then, is that clear?"

"Boy, are you touchy tonight! A guy can't say anything around here without getting ranked. When do we eat?"

"You may serve yourselves," Martha said coldly. "I'm feeling far too decrepit to lift anything."

Richard stared at her, wide-eyed and open-mouthed. "Well, boy oh boy, you're not even acting like a *mother* anymore."

After the children were settled for the night in their sleeping bags, Martha took the mirror out of her handbag and sat down to study her face by the light of the fire. It seemed a very long time since she had looked at herself with any real interest, and she was depressed by what she saw. It was an ordinary, healthy, competent face, the kind that might appeal to a widower with children, seeking someone to run his house, but would have no attraction for an unattached young man like Quinn.

I acted like an idiot, she thought. *I almost believed him for a while. I should have believed Richard instead.*

15

ON HIS WAY back to the motel Quinn passed the stucco building occupied by the staff of the *Beacon*. The lights were still on.

He wasn't anxious to meet Ronda again since there were too many things he couldn't afford to tell him. But he was pretty sure Ronda would find out he was in town and be suspicious if no contact was made. He parked the car and went into the building.

Ronda was alone in his office, reading a San Francisco *Chronicle* and drinking a can of beer. "Hello, Quinn. Sit down, make yourself at home. Want a beer?"

"No thanks."

"I heard you were back in our fair city. What have you been doing all week, sleuthing?"

"No," Quinn said. "Mostly acting as nursemaid to an ersatz admiral in San Felice."

"Any news?"

"News like what?"

"You know damned well like what. Did you come across anything more about the O'Gorman case?"

"Nothing you could print. A lot of rumors and opinions, but no concrete evidence. I'm beginning to go along with your theory about the hitchhiking stranger."

Ronda looked half-skeptical, half-pleased. "Oh, you are, eh? Why?"

"It seems to fit the facts better than any other."

"Is that your only reason?"

"Yes. Why?"

"Just checking. I thought you might have latched onto something you prefer to keep secret." Ronda tossed the empty can into a wastebasket. "Since you got most of your information from me in the first place, it wouldn't be sporting of you to withhold anything now, would it?"

"Definitely not," Quinn said virtuously. "I'd take a dim view of such unsportsmanlike conduct."

"I'm quite serious, Quinn."

"So am I."

"Then *sound* it."

"All right."

"Now we'll start over again. What have you been doing all week?"

"I answered that before. I had a job in San Felice." Quinn knew he'd have to tell Ronda something of his activities in order to allay suspicion. "While I was there I talked to Alberta Haywood's sister, Ruth. I didn't learn anything about O'Gorman, but I found out a few things about Alberta Haywood. I found out more when I went to see her in Tecolote prison."

"You *saw* her? Personally?"

"Yes."

"Well, I'll be damned. How did you manage that? I've been trying to get an interview for years."

"I have a private detective's license issued in Nevada. Law enforcement officials are usually glad to cooperate."

"Well, how is she?" Ronda said, leaning excitedly across the desk. "Did she tell you anything? What did she talk about?"

"O'Gorman."

"O'Gorman. Well, I'll be damned. This is just what—"

"Before you go off the deep end I might as well tell you that her references to O'Gorman weren't very rational."

"What do you mean?"

"She's under the delusion that the uproar over O'Gorman's disappearance caused her to lose her powers of concentration and make the mistake that sent her to jail. She even tried to convince me that O'Gorman planned it deliberately to get back at her for snubbing him or for being fired by her brother, George."

"She blames O'Gorman for everything?"

"Yes."

"That's nutty," Ronda said. "It would mean, among other things, that O'Gorman knew about her embezzlements a month before the bank examiners, and that he calculated both the uproar over his disappearance and its effect on her. Doesn't she realize how impossible that is?"

"She's dealing with her own guilt, not the laws of possibility. She completely rejects the idea that O'Gorman's dead, because, in her words, if he was murdered, she has no one to blame for her predicament. She's got to cling to the delusion that O'Gorman planned his disappearance in order to avenge himself on her. Without O'Gorman to blame, she'd have to blame herself, and she can't face that yet. Perhaps she never will."

"How far gone is she?"

"I don't know. Too far to follow, anyway."

"What made her crack up like that?"

"Five years in a cell would do it for me," Quinn said. "Maybe they did it for Alberta."

The memory of the scene in the penitentiary filled him with contempt and disgust, not at Alberta's sickness but at the sickness of a society which cut off parts of itself to appease the whole and then wondered why it was not feeling well.

Ronda was pacing up and down the office as if he himself were confined in a cell. "I can't print what you've just told me. A lot of people would disapprove."

"Naturally."

"Does George Haywood know all this?"

"He should. He visits her once a month."

"How did you find that out?"

"Several people told me, including Alberta. George's visits are painful to her, and presumably to George, too, yet he keeps on making them."

"Then his split with her was just a phony to fool the old lady?"

"The old lady, and perhaps other people."

"George is an oddball," Ronda said, frowning up at the ceiling. "I can't understand him. One minute he's so secretive he wouldn't give you the time of day, and the next he's in here pumping my hand like a long-lost brother and telling me about his trip to Hawaii. Why?"

"So you'd print it in the *Beacon*. That's my guess."

"But he's never given us any society-page material before. He even squawks like hell if his name is included in a guest list at a party. Why the sudden change of policy?"

"Obviously he wants everyone to know he's gone to Hawaii."

"Social butterfly stuff, and the like? Nonsense. That doesn't fit George."

"A lot of things don't fit George," Quinn said. "But he's wearing them anyway, and probably for the same reason I wore my brother's cast-off clothes when I was a kid—because he has to. Well, I'd better shove off. I've taken enough of your time."

Ronda was opening another can of beer. "There's no hurry. I had a little argument with my wife and I'm staying away from the house for a while until she cools off. Sure you won't join me in a beer?"

"Reasonably sure."

"By the way, have you seen Martha O'Gorman since you got back?"

"Why?"

"Just wondering. My wife called her at the hospital this afternoon to invite her over for Sunday dinner. They said she'd taken the day off because of illness, but when my wife went over to the house to offer to help her, Martha wasn't there and the car was gone. I thought you might know something about it."

"You give me too much credit. See you later, Ronda."

"Wait just a minute." Ronda was hunched over the can of beer, staring into it. "I have a funny feeling about you, Quinn."

"A lot of people have. Don't worry about it."

"Oh, but I *am* worried. This funny feeling tells me you're holding something back, maybe something very important. Now that wouldn't be nice, would it? I'm your friend, your pal, your buddy. I gave you the low-down on the O'Gorman case, I lent you my personal file."

"You've been true-blue," Quinn said. "Good night, friend, pal, buddy. Sorry about that funny feeling of yours. Take a couple of aspirin, maybe it'll go away."

"You think so, eh?"

"I could be wrong, of course."

"You could be and you are, dammit. You can't fool an old newspaperman like me. I'm intuitive."

When Ronda got up to open the door he stumbled against the corner of the desk. Quinn wondered how long he'd been drinking and how much the beer had to do with his powers of intuition.

He was glad to get back out to the street. A fresh breeze was blowing, bringing with it half the population of Chicote. The town, deserted at noon, had come to life as soon as the sun went down. All the stores on Main Street were open and there were line-ups in front of the movie theaters and at the malt and hamburger stands. Cars full of teenagers cruised up and down the street, horns blasting, radios blaring, tires squeaking. The noise eased their restlessness and covered up their lack of any real activity.

At the motel Quinn parked his car in the garage for the night and was closing the door when a voice spoke from the shrubbery: "Mr. Quinn. Joe."

He turned and saw Willie King leaning against the side of the garage as if she had been, or was going to be, sick. Her face was as white as the jasmine blossoms behind her and her eyes looked glassy and not quite in focus.

"I've been waiting," she said. "Hours. It seems hours. I didn't—I don't know what to do."

"Is this another of your dramatic performances, Willie?"

"No. *No!* This is *me.*"

"The real you, eh?"

"Oh, stop it. Can't you tell when someone's acting and when she isn't?"

"In your case, no."

"Very well," she said with an attempt at dignity. "I won't— I shan't bother you any further."

"Shan't you."

She started to walk away and Quinn noticed for the first time that she was wearing a pair of old canvas sneakers. It seemed unlikely that she would put on sneakers before giving a performance. He called her name, and after a second's hesitation she turned back to face him.

"What's the matter, Willie?"

"Everything. My whole life, everything's ruined."

"Do you want to come in my room and talk about it?"

"No."

"You don't want to talk about it?"

"I don't want to come in your room. I mean, it wouldn't be proper."

"Perhaps not," Quinn said, smiling. "There's a little courtyard where we can sit, if you prefer."

The courtyard consisted of a few square yards of grass around a brightly lit bathtub-sized swimming pool. No one was in the pool, but the wet footprints of a child were visible on the concrete and one tiny blue swim fin floated on the surface of the water. Hiding the courtyard from the street and from the motel units was a hedge of pink and white oleanders, heavy with blossoms.

The furniture had all been put under cover for the night, so they sat on the grass which was still warm from the sun. Willie looked embarrassed, and sorry that she had come. She said lamely, "The grass is very nice. It's very hard to keep it that way in this climate. You have to keep the hose running practically all the time and even then the soil gets too alkaline—"

"So that's what's on your mind, grass?"

"No."

"What is it then?"

"George," she said. "George is gone."

"You've known that for some time."

"No. I mean, he's really *gone*. And nobody knows where. Nobody."

"Are you sure?"

"I'm sure of one thing, he didn't take any trip to Hawaii." Her voice broke and she pressed one hand against her throat as if she were trying to mend the break. "He lied to me. He could have told me anything about himself, anything in this world, and I would still love him. But he deliberately lied, he made a fool of me."

"How do you figure that, Willie?"

"This afternoon after you left the office, I began to get suspicious—I don't know why, it just sort of came over me that maybe I'd been a patsy. I phoned all the airlines in Los Angeles long distance. I told them a story about an emergency in the family and how I had to contact George Haywood and wasn't sure whether he'd gone to Hawaii or not. Well, they checked their passenger lists for Tuesday and Wednesday and there was no George Haywood on any of them."

"They could have made a mistake," Quinn said. "Or George might be traveling under another name. It's possible."

She wanted to believe it, but couldn't. "No. He's run away, I'm sure of it. From me and from his mother and the two of us fighting over him. Oh, not fighting physically or even outwardly, but fighting all the same. I guess he couldn't stand it anymore; he couldn't make a decision either in her favor or mine so he had to escape from both of us."

"That would be a coward's decision, and from everything I've heard about George, he's no coward."

"Maybe I've made him into one without realizing what I was doing. Well at least I have one satisfaction—he didn't tell *her* the truth either. I wish now I had gone to her house instead of telephoning her. I'd like to have seen the expression on the old biddy's face when she found out her darling Georgie hadn't taken the trip to Hawaii after all."

"You called her?"

"Yes."

"Why?"

"I *wanted* to," she said harshly. "I wanted her to suffer the way I was suffering—to wonder, as I'm wondering, whether George will ever come back."

"Aren't you being a little dramatic? What makes you think he won't come back?"

She shook her head helplessly.

"Do you know more than you're telling me, Willie?"

"Only that he's had something on his mind lately that he wouldn't talk about."

"By 'lately' do you mean since I arrived in Chicote?"

"Even before that, though it's been worse since you started prying around and asking questions."

"Perhaps he was afraid of my questions," Quinn said. "And the reason he left town is to get away from me, not you and his mother."

She was silent for a minute. Then, "Why should he be afraid of you? George has nothing to hide except—well, except that business the first night when I picked you up in the café."

"That was George's idea?"

"Yes."

"What was the reason behind it?"

"He said"—her emphasis on the word seemed involuntary—"He *said* you might be a cheap crook planning an extortion racket. He wanted me to keep you occupied while he searched your room."

"How did he know where my room was, or even that I existed?"

"I told him. I overheard you talking to Ronda in the office that first afternoon. I heard you mention Alberta Haywood and I thought I'd better call George right away. I did, and he asked me to follow you and find out who you were and where you were staying."

"Then it wasn't the name O'Gorman that caught your attention, it was Alberta's?"

"Her actual name wasn't mentioned, but Ronda referred to a local embezzlement and a nice little lady and I knew it had to be Alberta."

"Do you run to the phone and call George every time someone mentions Alberta?"

"No. But I was suspicious of you. You had a look about you, a what's-in-it-for-me look that I didn't trust. Also, I guess I used the occasion to seem important in George's eyes. I don't," she added somberly, "very often get the chance. I'm just an ordinary woman. It's hard to compete with all that wheat germ and tiger's milk and the other stuff Mrs. Haywood goes in for to attract attention and make other women seem dull by comparison."

"You're developing a real complex about the old lady, Willie."

"I can't help it. She bugs me. Sometimes I almost think that the reason I fell in love with George was because she was so dead set against it. Maybe that's a terrible thing to say, but she's a monster, Joe, I mean it. More and more every year I can understand why Alberta committed those crimes. She was defying her mother. Alberta knew she'd be caught someday. Perhaps she deliberately arranged to be caught to punish and disgrace the old lady. Mrs. Haywood's not stupid—this is as close to a compliment as she'll ever get from me—and I think she understands Alberta's underlying motive, and that's why she cast her off completely and insisted George do the same."

But Quinn couldn't bring himself to believe it. "There were a hundred other ways Alberta could have punished her mother without going to jail herself and without dragging George into it."

Willie was plucking blades of grass one by one, like a young girl playing he-loves-me, he-loves-me-not, with daisy petals. "Where do you think he's gone, Joe?"

"I don't know. It would help if I could find out why he left."

"To get away from me and his mother."

"He could have done that some time ago."

It was the timing that interested Quinn. Martha O'Gorman had shown George the letter from her husband's murderer, and, although George professed to consider the letter a hoax, it had excited him, according to Martha. Immediately afterward he had arranged to have it known all over town that he was taking a trip to Hawaii for his health. He had even made a point of having the news published in the local paper.

Quinn said, "Wasn't it unusual on George's part to make his plans public?"

"A little. It surprised me."

"Why do you think he did it?"

"I have no idea."

"I have. But you're not going to like it, Willie."

"I don't like things the way they are now, either. Could they be worse?"

"A lot worse," Quinn said. "All the noise George made about the trip might mean that he was trying to establish an alibi in advance for something that has happened, or is going to happen, right here in Chicote."

She kept plucking away at the grass with a grim determination intended to conceal her fear. "Nothing's happened so far."

"That's right. But I want you to be careful, Willie."

"Me? Why me?"

"You were George's confidante. He might have told you things he now regrets telling you."

"He told me nothing," she said roughly. "George never had a confidante in his life. He's a loner, like Alberta. The way those two can clam up, it's not—not human."

"Maybe clams have a way of communicating with each other. Or do you still refuse to believe he went to visit Alberta every month?"

"I believe it now."

"Think back, Willie. Was there ever a time when you were with George that he was off guard?—say he was in a state of extreme anxiety, or he'd had too much to drink, or he was heavily sedated."

"George didn't discuss his worries with me, and he very seldom drinks. Once in a while he has to take a lot of stuff for his asthma."

"Did you ever see him on those occasions?"

"Sometimes. But he never seemed to act any different. Oh, maybe a little dopey, you know, not quite with it." She hesitated, her hands quiet now, as if she was channeling all her energies into the task of remembering. "Then there was the time he had his appendix out, about three years ago. I went up to the hospital to be with him because Mrs. Haywood refused. She was at home throwing fits about how George's appendix would have been perfectly all right if he'd eaten his wheat germ and molasses. I was in the room when he was coming out of the anesthetic.

"He was a scream. Afterwards he wouldn't believe he'd said some of the things he did. The nurses were practically hysterical because he kept telling them to put on their clothes, that it was no proper way to run a hospital, with naked nurses."

"Was he aware of your presence?"

"Sort of."

"What do you mean, sort of?"

"He thought I was Alberta," she said. "He called me by her name and told me I was a silly old spinster who should know better."

"Know better than to do what?"

"He didn't explain. He was mad at her, though, boiling mad."

"Why?"

"Because she'd given away some of his clothes to a transient who'd come to the house. He called her a gullible, soft-hearted fool. Which made about as much sense as the naked nurses. Alberta might be a fool but she's neither gullible nor softhearted. If there really was a transient, and if she gave him some of George's clothes, she must have had a reason besides simple generosity. I mean, the Haywoods aren't the kind who give handouts at the door. They might contribute to various organized charities but they're not impulsive off-the-cuff givers. So I don't believe it really happened, any more than the nurses had done a striptease."

"Did you ask George about it later?"

"Well, I told him some of the things he said."

"What was his reaction?"

"He laughed, not very comfortably. George is terribly dignified, he hated the idea that he'd made a fool of himself. Yet he has a sense of humor, too, and he couldn't help laughing about the naked nurses."

"Was he equally amused by his references to Alberta?"

"No, I think he felt guilty over calling her those names even when he wasn't responsible for his words."

Willie had lost interest in the grass and the little game of he-loves-me, he-loves-me-not. She had transferred her attention to a hole in the toe of her left sneaker and was picking at the frayed canvas like a bird gathering lint for its nest. Beyond the oleander hedge the city noise seemed remote and meaningless.

"What's George's financial status, Willie?"

She looked surprised that anyone should question it. "He's no millionaire, he works for his money. And though business isn't as good as it was a few years ago, it's good enough. He doesn't spend much except on his mother. She's pretty extravagant. The last face job she had done in Los Angeles cost a thousand dollars and naturally she had to buy a new wardrobe to match the quote new unquote face."

"Does George do much gambling, like his sister?"

"No."

"Sure of that?"

"How can I be sure of anything at this point?" she said in a tired voice. "All I know is that he never talked about it and he hasn't the temperament of a gambler. George plans things, he doesn't like to take chances. He nearly blew a fuse when I bought a ticket on the Irish Sweepstakes last year. He said I was a sucker. Well, I didn't win, so maybe he was right."

George and Alberta, Quinn thought. *The two planners, the two clams who could communicate with each other through closed shells. What had they communicated, a new plan? Alberta's parole hearing is coming up soon, it seems a funny time for George to disappear. Unless that's part of the new plan.*

Willie's elaborate beehive coiffure had come undone and was sagging to one side like a real hive deserted by its bees and exposed to the weather. It gave her a slightly tipsy look that suited her; Willie's judgments weren't entirely sober.

"Joe."

"Yes."

"Where do you think George is?"

"Perhaps right here in Chicote."

"You mean living under an assumed name in a hotel or boarding house or something? He couldn't get away with that. Everyone in town knows him. Besides, why would he have to hide out?"

"He might be waiting."

"For what?"

"God knows. I don't."

"If he'd only confided in me, if he'd only asked my advice—" Her voice started to break again but she caught it in time. "But that's silly, isn't it? George doesn't ask, he tells."

"You think you're going to change him after you're married?"

"I don't want to change him. I *like* to be told." Her mouth was set in a thin, obstinate line. "I really do."

"All right, all right, you like to be told, so I'll tell you. Go home and get a good night's rest."

"That isn't the kind of thing I meant."

"Let's face it, Willie. You don't like to be told one darned thing."

"I do so. By the right person."

"Well, the right person's not here. You'll have to accept a substitute."

"You're a lousy substitute," she said softly. "You're not sure enough of yourself to give orders. You couldn't fool a dog."

"Oh, I don't know. A few lady dogs have taken me quite seriously."

She turned away, flushing. "I'll go home, but not because you told me to. And don't worry about George and me. I can handle him—after we're married."

"Those are famous last words, Willie."

"I guess they are, but I've got to believe them."

He went with her to her car. They walked apart and in silence, like strangers who happened to be going in the same direction, absorbed by their own problems. When she got into the car he touched her shoulder lightly and she gave him a brief, anxious smile.

"Drive carefully, Willie."

"Oh, sure."

"Everything's going to be all right."

"Want to give me a written guarantee of that?"

"Nobody gets a written guarantee in this world," Quinn said, "so don't sit around waiting for one."

"I won't."

"Good night, Willie."

He passed the motel office on his way back to his room. The entire Frisby clan was gathered around the desk, Grandpa, Frisby and his wife, the daughter and her husband, and several people Quinn hadn't seen before. They were all talking at once and the radio was going full blast. It was as noisy as a revival meeting. The hand-clapping, foot-stamping music from the radio suited the occasion perfectly.

Frisby saw Quinn through the window and came sprinting out of the door, his bathrobe flapping around his legs, his face glistening with sweat and excitement.

"Mr. Quinn! Wait a minute, Mr. Quinn!"

Quinn waited. A sense of foreboding shook his body, and he wasn't quite sure whether it was imagination or whether he'd experienced the shockwaves of an actual earthquake. He said, "I have my key, thanks, Mr. Frisby."

"I know that. But I figured, being as the radio in your room is on the blink, you maybe missed the big news." The words tumbled moistly around Frisby's mouth like clothes in a washing machine. "You'll never believe it."

"Try me."

"Such a nice quiet little woman, the last person in the world you'd expect to pull a stunt like that."

It's Martha, Quinn thought, *something's happened to Martha.* He wanted to reach out and put his hand over Frisby's mouth to prevent him from saying any more, but he forced himself to stand still, to listen.

"You could have knocked me over with a feather when I heard about it. I yelled to the wife and she came running in, thinking I was having a fit. Bessie, I told her, Bessie, you'll never guess what's happened. 'The Martians have landed,' said she. 'No,' I said, 'Alberta Haywood has escaped from prison."

"God." The word was not an expression of surprise but of gratitude and relief. For a minute he couldn't even think about the news of Alberta Haywood, his mind refused to go beyond Martha. She was safe. She was sitting, as he had last seen her, in front of the campfire, and she was safe.

"Yes, sir, Miss Haywood escaped clean as a whistle in a supply truck that was servicing the candy machines in the canteen."

"When?"

"This afternoon some time. The prison authorities didn't release the details, but she's gone all right. Or all wrong, as the case may be, ha ha." Frisby's laugh was more like a nervous little hiccup. "Anyway, the police haven't been able to find her yet because the supply truck stopped at three or four other places and she could have gotten off at any one of them with nobody the wiser. Maybe it was all planned ahead of time and she had a friend waiting for her in a car. That's my story. What do you think of it, eh?"

"It sounds reasonable," Quinn said. *Except for two possible errors. Instead of a friend in a car, it might have been a brother in a green Pontiac station wagon.*

The clams had communicated, the planners were at work.

"Maybe," Frisby said, "she's coming back here."

"Why?"

"On television, when someone escapes from prison, they always return to the scene of the crime to straighten out a miscarriage of justice. It could be she's innocent and she's going to try and prove it."

"Whatever she's trying to prove, Mr. Frisby, she's not innocent. Good night."

For a long time after he went to bed Quinn lay awake listening to the whine of the air-conditioner and the loud angry voices of the couple in the next room quarreling over money.

Money, Quinn thought suddenly. Sister Blessing's money had come from her son in Chicago, and the letter Martha O'Gorman had destroyed had been postmarked Evanston, Illinois. A son in Chicago, a letter from Evanston. If there was a connection, the only person to ask about it was Sister Blessing.

16

EVEN WHILE THE new day was still no more than a barely perceptible lightening of the sky, Sister Blessing knew it was going to be a good one. Her bare feet sped down the dark path to the shower room, and she sang as she washed herself, unmindful of the coldness of the water and the grittiness of the grey homemade soap: "There's a good day coming, yes, Lord, there's a good day coming, yes, Lord."

"Peace be with you," she called out when Sister Contrition came in, carrying a kerosene lantern. "A fine morning, is it not?"

Sister Contrition put the lantern down with a clank of disapproval. "And pray, what's the matter with you all of a sudden?"

"Nothing, Sister. I am well, I am happy."

"You'd think a person would have more to do in this world than going around being happy."

"You can be happy and do things, too, can't you?"

"I don't know, I've never tried."

"Poor Sister, is your head bothering you again?"

"You attend to your head, I'll attend to mine." Sister Contrition poured a little water into a basin, rinsed her face and dried it on a scrap of wool salvaged from a worn-out robe. "You'd think a person would take a more sober viewpoint, especially after the Punishment."

"The Punishment's over." But she became a little less cheerful at the memory of it. It had been a black time for her, in spite of her satisfaction in knowing that things had not been easy in the colony while she was gone. The Master was finally forced to cut her isolation to three days instead of five because he couldn't manage Mother Pureza without her and because Brother Crown had sprained his ankle falling off the tractor. *They need me,* she thought, and her spirits soared again, beyond the dark grimy room and above the disgruntled face of Sister Contrition, still oily after its brief bath. *They need me and I am here.* She hung on to the words like a child to the string of a kite riding a high wind.

She began singing again. "There's a good day coming, yes, Lord."

"Well, it's about time," Sister Contrition said irritably. "I've had enough of the other kind lately, what with Karma acting up. I hear there's a new convert."

"It's too early to tell but I have hopes, very high hopes. It may be a whole new beginning for the colony. Perhaps it's a sign from Heaven that we are to prosper again like in the old days."

"Is it a man?"

"Yes. His soul is very troubled, I hear."

"Is he young? I mean, is he young enough so I'll have to keep an eye on Karma every minute she's awake?"

"I haven't seen him."

"God grant he's old and feeble," Sister Contrition said, sighing. "And poor eyesight wouldn't hurt, either."

"Haven't we enough old and feeble ones as it is? The Tower needs youth, strength, vitality."

"That's all very well, in theory. In practice, I have Karma to consider. Oh, what a terrible problem it is to be a mother."

Sister Blessing nodded soberly. "Yes. Yes, it is."

"At least it's over for you. My worries are just beginning."

"About Karma, Sister. Perhaps she should go away for a while."

"Where?"

"You have a sister in Los Angeles. Karma could live with her—"

"She'd never come back here once she got away. Worldly pleasures look good to her because she's never known them, how trivial they are, how treacherous. To send her to my sister's would be consigning her to hell. How could you even suggest such a thing? Has the Punishment caused you to lose your senses?"

"I don't think so," Sister Blessing said. She wasn't sure, though. It was certainly very odd to feel so good after so much suffering, but then the punishment had ended nearly a week ago and it was becoming blurred in her mind like an image in a cracked and dirty mirror.

Outside she began to sing again, pausing only to call out a greeting to the people she passed on her way to the kitchen. "Good morning, Brother Heart . . . Peace be with you, Brother Light. How is the new wee goat?"

"She's a frisky one, fat as butter."

"Is she now."

A new dawn, a new goat, a new convert. *"Yes, Lord, there's a good day coming.* Good morning, Brother Tongue of Prophets. How are you feeling?"

Brother Tongue smiled and nodded.

"And your little bird is all better?"

Another nod, another smile. She knew he could talk if he wanted to, but perhaps it was just as well that he didn't. *"Yes, Lord . . ."*

She made a fire in the kitchen stove with the wood Brother Tongue brought in from the shed. Then she helped Sister Contrition fry ham and eggs, hoping that the Master would appear for breakfast and announce the admission of the new convert. So far only the Master and Mother Pureza had seen him: he spent his time in the Tower, observing the colony at work, talking to the Master, asking questions and answering them. It was a difficult period of testing for both of them. Sister Blessing knew it was no easy matter to qualify for entrance and she hoped the Master would be a little lenient with the man and not scare him off. The colony needed new blood, new strength. There had been too much sickness lately among the Brothers and Sisters because they were overworked. How welcome an extra pair of hands would be to help with the milking and the gardening and the wood-chopping, an extra pair of good strong legs to herd the cattle—

"You are dreaming again. Sister," Brother Crown said in an accusing voice. "I've asked you three times to slice a little more bread. My ankle will not heal on an empty stomach."

"It's practically healed already."

"No, it's not. You're just saying that because you're holding a grudge against me for reporting your sins to the Master."

"Nonsense. I don't have time for grudges. Your ankle doesn't show the faintest trace of swelling. Let's look at it."

Brother Tongue had been listening to the exchange, jealous of the attention Sister Blessing was giving someone else. He put his hand on his chest and coughed loud and hard, but the Sister was onto his tricks and pretended not to hear.

"It's as good as new," she said, touching Brother Crown's ankle lightly.

New ankle, new dawn, new goat, new convert. "*Yes, Lord—*"

But the Master didn't appear and Sister Contrition took breakfast for three over to the Tower while Sister Blessing helped Karma clear the table and wash the dishes.

To the banging of tin plates and cups Sister Blessing resumed her singing. "*There's a good day coming, yes, Lord.*" It was music strange to the Tower, whose only songs were old somber hymns with new words written by the Master. They all sounded alike and cheered and comforted no one.

"Why are you making so much noise?" Karma said, clearing the crumbs from the table with a disdainful air, as if each and every one of them was personally offensive to her.

"Because I feel full of life and hope."

"Well, I don't. All the days are the same around here. Nothing changes except we get older."

"Hush now, and stop copying your mother. Crankiness is a habit hard to break."

"I don't care. What reason have I got for not being cranky?"

"You mustn't let the rest of them hear you speak such words," Sister Blessing said, trying to sound very severe. "It would hurt me deeply to see you punished again."

"I'm being punished twenty-four hours a day just by having to stay here. I hate it. When I get another chance I'm going to run away."

"No, Karma, no. It's hard to think of eternity when you're young, but you must try. Having trod the rough earth, your feet uncovered, you will walk the smooth and golden streets of heaven. Remember that, child."

"How do I know it's true?"

"It is. It *is* true." But her own voice echoed falsely in her ears: *Isn't it?* "You must fill your mind with visions of glory, Karma." *Mustn't you?*

"I can't. I keep thinking of the boys and girls at school, and their pretty clothes, and the way they laughed a lot, and all the books they had to read. Hundreds of books about things I never heard of before. Just touching them and knowing they were there—oh, it was such a wonderful feeling." Karma's face was pale under the bright red pimples that spotted it like a clown's make-up. "Why can't we have books here, Sister?"

"How could the colony survive with everyone's noses buried in books? There's work to be—"

"That's not the real reason."

Sister Blessing looked uneasy. "Now, now, this isn't a safe subject. The rules clearly state—"

"No one's listening. I know the real reason. If we find out from books how other people live, we might not want to stay here and there wouldn't be any colony."

"The Master is the best judge of our welfare, you must understand that."

"Well, I don't."

"Oh, Karma, my child, what are we to do with you?"

"Let me go."

"The outside world is a cruel place."

"Crueler than this?"

There was no answer. Sister Blessing had turned away and was scrubbing a tin plate she had already scrubbed twice in the past minute. *It is time,* she thought, *time for Karma to leave and for me to help her. I would give the breath in my body to help her but I don't know how. Oh Lord, give me guidance.*

"Mr. Quinn doesn't think the world's such a cruel place," Karma said.

The name caught Sister Blessing by surprise. She had been deliberately suppressing it for days now. When it popped up in her mind like a jack-in-the-box, she forced it down again, pressed the lid over it and held it tight. But the lid was slippery and her hand not always strong and quick enough, and out he would come, the young man she wished she had never seen. She said sharply, "What Mr. Quinn thinks is of no importance. He has gone out of our lives completely and forever."

"No, he hasn't."

"What do you know about it?"

"I'm not telling if I don't want to."

Sister Blessing turned away from the tubful of dishes and, her hands still wet, grasped Karma by the shoulders. "You saw him? You talked to him?"

"Yes."

"When?"

"When you were in isolation," Karma said. "I told him about my acne and he promised to come back and bring me some lotion for it. And he will."

"No, he won't."

"He promised."

"He is not coming back," Sister Blessing said, pressing the lid down, holding it tight. "He must let us alone. He is our enemy."

Malice spread over Karma's face like a blush she couldn't prevent. "The Master says we don't have any enemies, only friends who have not yet seen the light. What if Mr. Quinn comes back to be shown the light?"

"Mr. Quinn has returned to the gambling tables of Reno where he belongs. If he gave you any promise he was foolish, and you're even more foolish to believe him. Listen, Karma, I made a bad mistake which involved Mr. Quinn and I have been punished for it severely. Now that must be the end of it. We won't see him again and there'll be no more talk about him, is that clear?" She paused, then added in a quieter, more reasonable voice, "Mr. Quinn's intentions were all right but he has caused trouble."

"Trouble over Patrick O'Gorman?"

"Where did you get that name?"

"I—I just sort of heard it," Karma said, frightened by the Sister's intensity which she couldn't understand. "It just— floated through the air, I guess, into my ears."

"That's a lie. You heard it from Mr. Quinn."

"No. I swear, it just sort of floated through the air into my ears."

Sister Blessing's hand dropped from Karma's shoulders in a gesture of futility. "I despair of you, Karma."

"I wish everybody did," Karma said in a soft, stubborn voice. "Then they'd banish me and I could go away with Mr. Quinn when he comes with the lotion."

"He is not coming. He performed the service I paid him for in my moment of weakness and indiscretion, and there is no good reason for him to return. A promise to a child means nothing to a man like Mr. Quinn. You were very naive to take him seriously."

"You must take him seriously, too, or you wouldn't act so scared."

"Scared?" The word fell into the middle of the room like a stone thrown through the skylight. Sister Blessing attempted to hide the stone by surrounding it with camouflage: "You are a dear girl, Karma, but what a flighty imagination you have. And I strongly suspect you developed a bit of a crush on Mr. Quinn."

"I don't know what that means, a crush."

"It means you're indulging in a silly dream about his coming back here to rescue you, to make you beautiful with a magic lotion. That's all it is, Karma, a dream."

The Sister returned to the tub of dishes. The water was cold by this time, grease floated on top of it and the harsh soap would not lather. As she forced her hands into the dirty

245

water she tried to resume her song but she couldn't remember the music, the words no longer seemed prophetic, only wistful: *Isn't there, surely, a good day coming, Lord?*

At noon the official announcement was made in the shrine in the inner court. A tall, thin, bespectacled man, already shaved and robed, was introduced briefly by the Master: "It is with humble rejoicing that I acquaint you with Brother Faith of Angels who has come to share our lives in this world and our salvation in the next. Amen."

"Amen," said Brother Faith, and the others echoed, "Amen."

There was an undercurrent of excitement among the brethren but they dispersed quickly and quietly and returned to their jobs. Brother Light trudged back to the barn, thinking, with satisfaction, of the new convert's soft white hands and how soon they would be changed; and Sister Contrition ran toward the kitchen, her face contorted by anxiety and lack of breath: *He is not old but he is certainly not young, either, and perhaps his eyesight is failing and he will not notice Karma. How cruelly fast she has developed into a woman.*

Brother Crown headed for the tractor, whistling jubilantly through the gap between his two front teeth. He had seen the new convert's car, and oh, what a beauty it was, and how the engine's purr grew into a deep, powerful roar. He pictured himself behind the wheel, foot hard on the accelerator, taking the curves of the mountain road with a shrieking of tires. *Zoom, zoom, here I come. Zoom, zoom, zoom.*

Brother Steady Heart and Brother Tongue resumed hoeing weeds in the vegetable garden.

"Does he have a strong back, that's the important thing," Brother Heart said. "Arms, legs, hands, these you can strengthen by work and exercise, but a strong back is a gift of God. Isn't that so?"

Brother Tongue nodded agreeably, wishing that Brother Heart would shut up, he was becoming a terrible old bore.

"Yes sir, a strong back in a man, and fine, delicate limbs in a woman, these are the gifts of God, eh, Brother Tongue? Oh, the ladies, I miss them. Shall I tell you a secret? I was never much to look at, but I used to be a great hit with the ladies, would you believe it?"

Brother Tongue nodded again. *Somebody shut this bastard up before I kill him.*

"You appear a mite peaked today, Brother Tongue. Are you feeling all right? Your pleurisy may be acting up again, maybe you'd better take a rest. Sister Blessing says you must not overdo. Go on now and have yourself a nice little nap."

The Master climbed the stairs to the top of the Tower and looked down at the blue lake in the green valley, and up at the green mountains in the blue sky. Ordinarily, the view inspired him, but now he felt old and tired. It had been a difficult period, testing Brother Faith of Angels and being tested in return, and at the same time trying to handle Mother Pureza, to keep her quiet and contented. Her flights into the past were becoming wilder as her body grew feebler. She gave orders to her servant, Capirote, who had been dead for thirty years, and became violent when her orders were not obeyed. She called out to her parents and her sisters and wept bitterly when they did not answer. Sometimes she fingered the rosary no one had ever been able to take from her, and in spite of the Master's efforts to stop her she said the Hail Marys she had learned as a child. She had disliked the new Brother on sight, cursed him in Spanish, accused him of trying to rob her and threatened him with a flogging. The Master knew the time was approaching when he would have to send her away. He hoped she would die before it became necessary.

He had left her resting in her room when he went down to make the announcement. Now he knocked softly on her door, and, pressing his lips against the crack, whispered, "Dear love, are you asleep?"

There was no answer.

"Pureza?"

When there was still no answer, he thought, *She is asleep, God be merciful and grant she dies before she wakes.*

He bolted her door so she couldn't get out, and went back to his own room to pray.

Mother Pureza, hiding behind the stone shrine in the inner court below, watched the futile bolting of her door and giggled until she was out of breath and her eyes watered.

She stayed there a long time. It was cool and quiet. Her chin tipped forward on her scrawny breast and her eyelids drooped, and with a great rush of air Capirote flew down at her from the sky.

17

QUINN FOUND HER wandering up the dirt lane. She was walking stiffly, holding her hands straight out from her sides, like a little girl who had disobeyed orders and got herself dirty. Even from a distance Quinn could see that the dirt was blood. Her robe was covered with it.

He stopped the car and got out and ran over to her. "Mother Pureza, what are you doing?"

Although she didn't recognize him, she seemed neither frightened nor curious. "I am looking for the washroom. My hands are soiled. They feel sticky, it's quite unpleasant."

"Where did they get sticky?"

"Oh, back there. Away back there."

"The washroom's in the opposite direction."

"Fancy that. I'm turned around again." She peered up at him, her head on one side like an inquisitive bird. "How do you know where the washroom is?"

"I've been here before. You and I talked, you promised you'd send me an engraved invitation through Capirote."

"I shall have to cancel that. Capirote is no longer in my employ. He's carried his play-acting too far this time. I have ordered him off the premises by nightfall . . . I suppose *you* think this is real blood?"

"Yes," Quinn said gravely. "Yes, I think it is."

"Nonsense. It's juice. It's some kind of juice Capirote thickened with cornstarch to play a trick on me. I wasn't fooled for a minute, of course. But it was a cruel joke, wasn't it?"

"Where is he now?"

"Oh, back there."

"Where?"

"If you shout at me, young man, I shall have you flogged."

"This is very important, Mother Pureza," Quinn said, trying to keep his voice under control. "It's not a joke. The blood's real."

"I'm onto him and his tricks—real?" She looked down at the stains on her robe, already darkening and stiffening. "Real blood? Are you sure?"

"Yes."

"Well, dear me, I didn't think he'd go so far as to collect real blood and pour it all over himself. One must really admire such thoroughness. Where do you suppose he got it, from a goat or a chicken? Ah, now I have it, he's pretending that he sacrificed himself in front of the shrine—young man, where are you going? Don't run away. You promised to show me where the washroom is."

She stood and watched him until he disappeared among the trees. The sun beat down on her withered face. She closed her eyes and thought of the vast old house of her youth, with its thick adobe walls and heavy tiled roof to keep out the sun and the noises of the street. How orderly everything had been, how quiet and clean, there had been no need to think of dirt or blood. She had never even seen blood until Capirote —"*You must prepare yourself for a shock, Isabella. Capirote has been thrown from his horse and he is dead.*"

She opened her eyes and cried out in despair, "Capirote? Capirote, you are dead?"

She saw the Master coming toward her, and the fat, cranky little woman who brought her meals, and Brother Crown with his cruel eyes. They were calling out to her, "Pureza!" which wasn't her name. She had many names, Pureza was not one of them.

"I am Dona Isabella Constancia Querida Felicia de la Guerra. I wish to be correctly addressed."

"Isabella," the Master said, "you must come with me."

"*You* are giving *me* orders, Harry? Aren't you forgetting you were nothing but a grocery clerk? Where did you get all your fine visions, Harry, from hauling around cans of soup and baked beans?"

"Please be quiet, Pur—Isabella."

"I have nothing further to say." She drew herself up, glanced haughtily around. "Now if you will kindly direct me to the washroom? I have somebody's blood on my hands. I wish to be rid of it."

"Did you see it happen, Isabella?"

"See what happen?"

"Brother Faith of Angels has killed himself."

"Of course he killed himself. Did the silly idiot think he could fly by flapping his arms?"

The body lay where Mother Pureza had indicated, in front of the shrine like a sacrifice. The man's face had struck one of the protruding stones of the shrine, and it was crushed and bloodied beyond recognition. But Quinn had seen the car parked beside the barn, a green Pontiac station wagon, and he knew he was looking at the body of George Haywood. His throat thickened with grief, both for Haywood and for the two women who had fought over him and lost, and would never forgive each other either the fight or the loss.

Although the blood had stopped flowing, the body was still warm and Quinn guessed that death had occurred no more than half an hour before. The shaved head, the bare feet and the robe made it clear that Haywood had come to the Tower as a convert. But how long had he been here? Had he come directly after saying good-bye to Willie King in Chicote? If that was the case, who had engineered Alberta Haywood's escape? Was it possible that the two of them had planned to meet at the Tower and hide out there?

Quinn shook his head, as if responding to a question spoken aloud by someone else. *No, George would never have chosen the Tower as a hiding place. He must have heard, from Willie, from John Ronda or from Martha O'Gorman, that this was the place where the investigation into O'Gorman's death started all over again. He wouldn't pick a hideout I knew about and visited. In fact, why hide out at all?*

The death, the strangeness of its setting, and the sight and smell of the fresh blood were making him sick. He went outside, gulping in air like a swimmer exhausted from fighting a heavy surf.

Mother Pureza was coming up the path supported by Sister Contrition and Brother Crown, and chattering in Spanish. Behind the trio the Master walked, his head down, his face grey and gaunt.

He said, "Take her up to her room and see that she is cleansed. Be gentle. Her bones are brittle. Where is Sister Blessing? You'd better fetch her."

"She is ill," Sister Contrition said. "A touch of indigestion."

"All right, do the best you can by yourselves." When they had gone, he turned to Quinn. "You have arrived at an inopportune time, Mr. Quinn. Our new Brother is dead."

"How did it happen?"

"I was in my quarters meditating, I was not a witness to the event. But surely it's obvious?—Brother Faith was a troubled man with many problems. He chose a way to solve them that I cannot condone, though I must accept it with pity and understanding."

"He jumped from the top of the Tower?"

"Yes. Perhaps it is my fault for underestimating the degree of his spiritual despair." His deep sigh was almost a groan. "If this be true, God forgive me and grant our Brother eternal salvation."

"If you didn't see him jump, what brought you to the scene so fast?"

"I heard Mother Pureza scream. I came rushing out and saw her bending over the body, shouting at it to get up and stop play-acting. When I called to her, she ran away. I stopped long enough to see if there was anything I could do to help our Brother, then I went after her. I met Sister Contrition and Brother Crown on the way and asked them for their assistance."

"Then the others don't know yet about Haywood?"

"No." He paused to wipe the sweat off his face with the sleeve of his robe. "You—you called him Haywood?"

"It's his name."

"He was a—friend of yours?"

"I know his family."

"He told me he no longer had a family, that he was alone in the world. Are you saying he lied to me?"

"I'm saying he has a mother, two sisters and a fiancée."

The Master looked shocked, not by the existence of Haywood's family but by the fact that he'd been deceived. It was a blow to his pride. After a minute's thought he said, "I am sure it was not a deliberate lie. He *felt* alone in this world, and so he claimed to be. That is the explanation."

"You believe he came here as a true convert?"

"Of course. Of course he did. What other reason would he have that he should want to share our humble life? It is not easy, to live as we do."

"What are you going to do now?"

"Do?"

"About his death."

"We look after our own dead," the Master said, "as we look after our own living. We shall give him a decent burial."

"Without notifying the authorities?"

"I am the authority here."

"Sheriff, coroner, judge, jury, doctor, mortician, dog-catcher, soul saver?"

"All of those, yes. And please spare me your petty irony, Mr. Quinn."

"You have a big job, Master."

"God has granted me the strength to do it," he said quietly, "and the ability to see how it must be done."

"The sheriff might be a little hard to convince of that."

"The sheriff can take care of his own, I will take care of mine."

"There are laws, and you're living within their jurisdiction. Haywood's death must be reported. If you don't do it, I'll have to."

"Why?" the Master said. "We are a peace-loving community. We harm no one, we ask no favors from the outside world beyond the favor of being allowed to live as we see fit."

"All right, let's put it this way: a member of the outside world wandered in here and got himself killed. That's the sheriff's business."

"Brother Faith of Angels was one of *us*, Mr. Quinn."

"He was George Haywood," Quinn said. "A real estate man from Chicote. And whatever his reasons for coming here, I know saving his soul wasn't one of them."

"God forgive you for your blasphemy, and your lies. Brother Faith was a True Believer."

"You were the believer, not Haywood."

"His name was not Haywood. It was Martin. He was a banker in San Diego, a widower alone in the world, a troubled man."

For a moment Quinn was almost convinced he'd made a mistake, and that the green Pontiac station wagon was merely a coincidence. Then he saw the uncertainty growing in the Master's eyes and heard the doubt in his voice even while he was denying it.

"Hubert Martin. His wife died two months ago—"

"Ten years ago."

"He was desolate and lonely without her."

"He had a red-headed girlfriend named Willie King."

The Master leaned heavily against the archway as if the sudden burden of the truth was too great for him. "He was— he was not seeking salvation?"

"No."

"Why, then, did he come here? To rob us, to cheat us? We have nothing to be robbed or cheated of, only the car that he himself gave to our common fund. We possess no money."

"Maybe he thought you did."

"How could he? I explained in detail how the colony operates on a self-sufficient basis. I even showed him our account books to prove how little use we have for money here, when there is nothing we must buy except gasoline and a few spare parts for the tractor and the odd pair of spectacles for one of our Brothers whose sight is failing."

"Did Haywood seem interested?"

"Oh yes, very. You see, being a banker, I suppose he—"

"A real estate agent."

"Yes. I keep forgetting. I—it's been a very confusing day. You must excuse me now, Mr. Quinn. I have to inform the others of the sad news and arrange with Sister Blessing to take care of the body."

Quinn said, "You'd better leave everything as it is until the sheriff gets here."

"The sheriff, yes. You're going to tell him, I suppose."

"I have no choice."

"Please do me a favor and refrain from mentioning Mother Pureza. It would frighten her to be questioned. She is like a child."

"Children can be violent, too."

"There is violence in her, but only in her talk. She is too frail to have pushed him over the handrail. God forgive me the very thought of it."

He reached inside the folds of his robe and brought out a set of keys. Quinn recognized them, with a shock, as the keys to the ignition of his car. He said, "You intended to keep me here?"

"No. I merely wished to be able to control the time of your departure. I didn't realize then that Haywood had a family and friends, and that his death would have to be investigated by someone from the outside. You're free to leave now, Mr. Quinn. But before you do, I want you to realize that you are doing us an incalculable amount of damage, and we, on our part, have offered you nothing but kindness, food and drink when you were hungry and thirsty, shelter when you were homeless, and prayers though you were an infidel."

"I'm not entirely responsible for the course of events. I didn't intend to make trouble for anyone."

"That's a matter you will have to settle with your own conscience. Your lack of intention changes nothing. A flooding river does not intend to overflow its banks, nor an iceberg to ram a ship, yet the farmlands are ruined by flood and the ship sinks. Yes, the ship sinks . . . And the people on it, they all die. Yes, yes, I see it quite clearly in my mind."

"I'd better leave now."

"They are screaming for me to help them. The ship is broken in two, the sea is boiling with anger . . . Don't be afraid, my children. I am coming. I will open the gates of heaven for you."

"Good-bye, Master."

Quinn walked away, his heart pounding against his rib cage as if it were trying to escape. His throat felt swollen and there was a taste of old vomit in his mouth, shreds and pieces of the past too fibrous to be swallowed.

He saw Karma running toward him between the trees awkwardly, as if she had not yet become accustomed to her new body.

She shouted at him, "Where's Master?"

"I left him at the Tower."

"Sister Blessing's sick. Oh, she's terrible sick. And Brother Tongue is crying and I can't find my mother and I don't know what to do. I don't know what to *do.*"

"Take it easy. Where's the Sister?"

"In the kitchen. She fell on the floor. Oh, she looks bad, she looks dying. Please don't let her die. She promised to help me get away, she promised just this morning. Please, please don't let her die."

Quinn found Sister Blessing on the floor, doubled up with pain. Her mouth was drawn back from her teeth, and a thick colorless fluid flowed from both corners, too much of it to be ordinary saliva. Brother Tongue was trying to hold a wet cloth against her forehead but she kept twitching her head away and moaning.

Quinn said, "How long has she been like this, Karma?"

"I don't know."

"Was it before lunch, after lunch?"

"After. Maybe half an hour after."

"What did she complain of?"

"Cramps. Very bad cramps, and a burning in her throat. She went outside and vomited and then she came back and fell on the floor, and I screamed for help and Brother Tongue was in the washroom and he heard me."

"We'd better get her to a hospital."

Brother Tongue shook his head, and Karma cried out, "No, no. We can't. The Master won't let us. He doesn't believe in—"

"Be quiet." Quinn knelt beside Sister Blessing and felt the pulse in her wrist. It was feeble, and her hands and forehead were hot and dry as if she had lost a great deal of body fluid. "Can you hear me, Sister? I am going to drive you to the hospital in San Felice. Don't be frightened. They'll take good care of you. Remember that hot bath you told me you wanted? And the fuzzy pink slippers? Well, you'll be able to have all the hot baths you like, and I'll buy you the fuzziest pink slippers in the country. Sister?"

She opened her eyes slightly but there was no recognition in them, and a moment later the lids dropped shut again.

Quinn got to his feet. "I'll bring the car as close to the door as I can."

"I'm coming with you," Karma said.

"You'd better stay here. See if you can get her to swallow a little water."

"I tried to and so did Brother Tongue, only it didn't work." She followed Quinn outside and down the path, talking nervously and glancing over her shoulder as if afraid someone was watching. "She was so happy this morning. She kept singing about how there was a good day coming. She couldn't have felt sick or she wouldn't have been singing like that. Why, she even said she—she felt full of life and hope. Only then she got mad at me because I told her you were coming back to bring the lotion for my acne . . . Did you?"

"Yes, it's in the car. She didn't like the idea of me coming back?"

"Oh no. She acted scared, sort of, and she said you were our enemy."

"But I'm not your enemy, or hers. In fact, Sister Blessing and I got along very well together."

"*She* didn't think so. She said you were back at the gambling tables in Reno where you belonged and I wasn't to take your promise seriously."

"Why was she scared, Karma?"

"Maybe because of O'Gorman. When I mentioned his name she looked ready to throw a fit. It seemed like she didn't want to be reminded of you or O'Gorman—you know, like she thought things had been settled and didn't want to hear about them anymore."

"Like things had been settled," Quinn repeated, frowning. Only one thing had been settled, the fact that O'Gorman had been murdered. "Is mail delivered to the Tower, Karma?"

"Three miles down the main road, where you turn off to the neighboring ranch, there are two mailboxes. One of them is ours, but the Master only goes to it about once a week since nothing important ever comes."

"If mail is delivered, it must also be picked up."

"We're not allowed to write a letter unless it's real important, such as to right a wrong we committed."

To right a wrong, Quinn thought. *To confess a murder and make peace with God and conscience.* He said, "Did Sister Blessing ever talk about her son?"

"Not to me. I know she has one, though."

"What's his name?"

"I guess the same as hers used to be, Featherstone. Maybe Charley Featherstone."

"Why maybe?"

"Well, when Brother Tongue came in after she'd fallen on the floor she looked at him and said 'Charley,' like she meant him to tell Charley she was sick. That's how it sounded to me."

"Could she have been addressing Brother Tongue as Charley?"

"That wouldn't make sense. She knows as well as I do that his name's Michael. Michael Robertson."

"You have a good memory, Karma."

She blushed and made an awkward attempt to hide the blush with her hands. "I don't have much to remember. The only reading I do is the Master's record book when I'm looking after Mother Pureza. I read it aloud to her sometimes like I would a story. It keeps her quiet except when she interrupts to ask if the people lived happily ever after. I always tell her yes."

It was to Quinn a strange and touching picture, the girl earnestly reading a list of names and the deranged old woman listening, hearing a fairy tale: *"Once upon a time there was a woman called Mary Alice Featherstone and a man called Michael Robertson—" "And did they live happily ever after?" "Oh yes, happily ever after."*

He said, "Is Charles the real name of any of the Brothers who are here now?"

"No. I'm sure of that."

They had almost reached the car. The girl ran ahead of Quinn and opened the door. With a cry of triumph she picked up the bottle of lotion that was lying on the front seat and held it against her face as if it could work its magic even through glass.

She whispered, half to herself, half to Quinn, "Now I will look like other girls. And I'll go to Los Angeles and live with my aunt, Mrs. Harley Baxter Wood. Isn't that a beautiful name? And I'll go back to school, and I'll—"

"Live happily ever after?"

"Yes, I will. *I will.*"

Although Quinn was able to maneuver the car between the trees right up to the kitchen door, it took all three of them, Karma and Brother Tongue and himself, to get Sister Blessing into the back seat. Brother Tongue put a folded blanket under her head and a moist cloth across her forehead. This time she didn't twitch away or moan in protest. She had lost consciousness.

Both men realized it was a bad sign but Karma didn't. "She's gone to sleep. That means the pain must be better and she's going to be all right, doesn't it? She'll live happily ever after, won't she?"

Quinn was too busy to answer, and Brother Tongue said, "Shut up," in a voice that had a squawk in it, like a door hinge long unused, unoiled.

The unexpected sound, and the fury behind it, shocked Karma into silence.

Quinn said to Brother Tongue, who was wiping his eyes with the sleeve of his robe, "Do you think there's any danger of her falling off the seat?"

"Not if you drive slowly."

"I can't afford to drive slowly."

"The gates of heaven are opening for her? Is that what you're saying?"

"She's very ill."

"Oh God. Please God, grant an easy end to her suffering."

Quinn got into the car and started down the slope to the dirt lane. In the rear-view mirror he could see Brother Tongue down on his knees praying, his hands lifted toward the sky in supplication. A moment later the Brother was swallowed up by trees, and nothing of the Tower or its outbuildings was visible to Quinn.

He came to the end of the irrigated land, and the trees became gradually more stunted and misshapen. The bleak brown countryside, that could support so little life, seemed a fitting place to die.

"Sister? Can you hear me, Sister? If someone did this to you, it's my fault. I disobeyed your orders. You told me not to try and contact O'Gorman, that it might do a lot of harm. Just find out where he is, you said, and report to you. I should have listened to you. I'm sorry. Please hear me, Sister. I'm sorry."

Sorry. The word echoed from the sheer walls of rock that lined parts of the road, *I'm sorry*, and the grey inert mass on the back seat stirred slightly. Quinn's eye caught the movement in the mirror.

"Why did you hire me to find a dead man, Sister?"

There was no response.

"When you ordered me not to contact him, you couldn't have known he was dead. Yet you must have guessed there was something peculiar going on that involved O'Gorman. Who could have told you except the murderer? And why after all these years did he decide to confess the crime in a letter? Was it because I asked you last week to give Martha O'Gorman a break, put an end to her uncertainty? . . . Was the letter of confession forced on the murderer by you? And why have you been trying to protect him?"

She let out a sudden cry of pain or protest.

"Did you believe he was penitent, Sister, and would never kill again?"

Another cry, more vehement than the first, like a child's wail of rage at an injustice. The rage was unmistakable, but Quinn wasn't sure whether it was directed at him for his questions, or at the killer for his betrayal, or at still a third person.

"Who killed O'Gorman, Sister?"

18

THROUGH THE EMERGENCY entrance of the San Felice hospital, Sister Blessing was carried on a stretcher. A young intern led Quinn into a waiting room hardly larger than a piano crate, and the questions began.

What was the name of the sick woman? Who was her closest relative? How old was she? Was she under treatment for any chronic disease or infection? What were the initial signs of her present illness? When had she last eaten, and what? Did she vomit? Was the vomitus discolored? Did it have an odor? Did she have difficulty speaking? Breathing? Had she passed any bloody urine or bloody stools? Was there rigidity of the muscles? Twitching? Face livid or flushed? Hands cold or warm? Was she delirious? Drowsy? Were the pupils of her eyes expanded or contracted? Were there burn marks around her mouth and chin?

"I'm sorry, I can't answer all those questions," Quinn said. "I'm not a trained medical observer."

"You did all right. Wait here, please."

For almost half an hour he was left alone in the room. It was stifling hot and smelled of antiseptic and something sour, the sweat and fear of all the people who had waited in this room before him, and watched the door and prayed. The smell seemed to become stronger until he could taste it in the back of his throat.

He got up to open the door and almost collided on the threshold with a tall, thickset man. He looked like a rancher. He wore a broad-brimmed Stetson hat, a rumpled Western-style suit and, in place of a tie, a leather thong fastened with a large turquoise and silver clip. He had an air of wary cynicism about him, as if he'd spent too much time in places like emergency wards and no good had come out of any of them.

"Your name's Quinn?"

"Yes."

"May I see your identification, please?"

Quinn took the papers out of his wallet. The man glanced at them briefly and without much interest, as though obeying a rule he had little use for.

"I'm Sheriff Lassiter." He returned the papers. "You brought a woman in here about an hour ago?"

"Yes."

"Friend of yours?"

"I met her ten or eleven days ago."

"Where?"

"At the Tower of Heaven. It's a religious cult located in the mountains about fifty miles east of here."

Lassiter's expression suggested that he had had dealings at the Tower, and not very pleasant ones. "How come you got mixed up with an outfit like that?"

"By mistake."

"You haven't been living there?"

"No."

"This is going to take all night if you just stand there saying yes and no. Can't you volunteer some information?"

"I don't know where to begin."

"Begin somewhere, that's all I ask."

"I drove to the Tower this morning from Chicote." He went on to explain his meeting Mother Pureza on the road, and his subsequent discovery of the dead man. He described the construction of the inner court, the position of the body in relation to it and the circumstances of the death.

The sheriff listened, his only sign of interest a slight narrowing of the eyes. "Who was the man?"

"George Haywood. He owned a real estate business in Chicote."

"He fell or was pushed from the top level, no way of knowing which?"

"None that I could see."

"This is a bad day for your friends, Mr. Quinn."

"I saw Haywood only once before in my life, you could hardly call him a friend."

"You saw him only once," Lassiter repeated, "and yet you identified the body immediately, even though the face was battered in and covered with blood? You must have more highly developed eyesight than the rest of us."

"I recognized his car."

"By the license plates?"

"No."

"The registration on the steering wheel?"

"No. By the make and model."

"That's all?"

"Yes."

"Now wait a minute, Mr. Quinn. You saw a car in the vicinity, the same make and model as Haywood's, and you immediately assumed it was his?"

"Yes."

"Why? There are hundreds of identical cars on the roads."

"Haywood left Chicote a few days ago under peculiar circumstances," Quinn said. "He told his mother and friends he was flying to Hawaii, but one of his associates checked the airlines and discovered his name wasn't on any of the flight lists."

"That's still a pretty thin reason for jumping to the conclusion that the dead man is Haywood. Unless, of course, you *expected* to find him at the Tower?"

"I didn't."

"You didn't go there looking for him?"

"No."

"His presence was a complete surprise to you?"

"It was a surprise."

"Even in these parts very few people have ever heard of the Tower, let alone know its location. What would a real estate agent from Chicote be doing there?"

"He was dressed as a convert. He wore the regulation robe and his head was shaved."

Lassiter assumed an expression of exaggerated concern. "You found this body in a strange place, wearing strange clothes, head shaved and face battered to a pulp, and you identified it positively as belonging to a man you'd seen only once?"

"Not positively. But if you're a betting man, Sheriff, I'll give you odds."

"Officially, I'm not a betting man. Unofficially, what odds?"

"Ten to one."

"Those are very good odds," Lassiter said, nodding gravely. "Very good indeed. Makes me kind of wonder what you base them on. Is it possible you haven't been entirely frank with me, Mr. Quinn?"

"I can't be entirely frank about Haywood. I know very little about him."

Someone knocked on the door and Lassiter went out into the corridor for a minute. When he came back his face was flushed and beaded heavily with sweat.

He said, "There was an item in this afternoon's newspaper about a woman named Haywood. Did you see it?"

"No."

"She escaped from Tecolote prison yesterday in a supply truck. Early this morning she was picked up wandering around the hills about fifteen miles north of Tecolote. She was suffering from shock and exposure and could give no explanation of her actions. Are the two Haywoods related, by any chance?"

"They're brother and sister."

"Now isn't that interesting. Maybe Miss Haywood was also a friend of yours?"

"I saw her once," Quinn said wearily. "Which happens to be the same number of times I saw her brother, which doesn't make either of them exactly a pal of mine."

"Have you any reason for believing the two Haywoods planned a rendezvous at the Tower?"

"No."

"It seems a funny coincidence, though, doesn't it? Haywood disappears, and a couple of days later his sister tries to. Were they pretty chummy?"

"Yes, I think so."

"You're a great disappointment to me, Mr. Quinn. I assumed that since you're a licensed detective you'd be brimming with information which you would naturally pass on to me. But I expect it's easier to get a license in Nevada than in California?"

"I wouldn't know."

"Well, maybe you'll find out if you try to get one here," Lassiter said. "Now about this woman you brought in, what's her connection with Haywood?"

"I have no idea."

"I presume she has a name other than Sister Blessing of the Salvation?"

"Mrs. Featherstone. Mary Alice Featherstone."

"Any close relatives that you know of?"

"A son living in or near Chicago. His name may be Charlie."

"Is that another of your hunches, Mr. Quinn?"

"Not one I'd care to lay odds on."

Lassiter went back to the door and addressed someone standing in the corridor outside: "Send Sam over here with the lab car, will you, Bill? And get in touch with the Chicago police, see if they can locate a man called Featherstone, first name possibly Charlie, and tell him his mother's dead. Somebody fed her enough arsenic to kill a horse."

In spite of the heat in the room, Quinn had begun to shiver and his throat felt as though a hand had seized it. *She was a nurse,* he thought. *Perhaps she knew right away that she'd been poisoned and who had done it, yet she made no attempt to accuse anyone, or to save her own life by taking an antidote.*

He remembered the first night he had talked to her. She had stood in front of the stove rubbing her hands together as if she felt the chill of death in the air: "*I am getting old . . . Some of the days are hard to face. My soul is at peace but my body rebels. It longs for some softness, some warmth, some sweetness. Mornings when I get out of bed my spirit feels a touch of heaven, but my feet—oh, the coldness of them, and the aches in my legs. Once in a Sears catalogue I saw a picture of a pair of slippers . . . They were the most beautiful slippers I ever did see, but of course an indulgence of the flesh . . .*"

"Come on, Quinn," Lassiter said. "You're about to take another trip to the Tower."

"Why?"

"You seem to know your way around the place. You can act as our guide and interpreter."

"I prefer not to."

"I'm not offering you a preference. What's the matter, feeling a little nervous? Something on your mind?"

"A pair of fuzzy pink slippers."

"Sorry, we're fresh out of fuzzy pink slippers. How about a nice cuddly Teddy bear instead?"

Quinn took a long deep breath. " 'Having trod the rough earth, my feet uncovered, I will walk the smooth and golden streets of heaven.' . . . I'd like to see Sister Blessing, if I may."

"You'll have plenty of time to see her later. She's not going anywhere." Lassiter's mouth stretched in a mirthless smile. "You don't like that kind of talk, eh, Quinn? Well, here's my advice, learn to like it. In this business, if you start thinking too seriously about death, you end up cutting out paper dolls at the funny farm."

"I'll take that chance, Sheriff."

Quinn rode in the back seat with Lassiter while a deputy in uniform drove the car. A second car followed, containing two more deputies and portable lab equipment.

It was four o'clock and still very warm. As soon as they were outside the city limits Lassiter took off his hat and coat and unbuttoned his shirt collar.

"How well did you know this Sister Blessing, Quinn?"

"I talked to her a couple of times."

"Then how come you got all choked up at her death?"

"I liked her very much. She was a fine, intelligent woman."

"Somebody evidently didn't share your high opinion of her. Any idea who?"

Quinn looked out of the window, wishing there was a way he could tell the sheriff about O'Gorman's murder without bringing in the letter to Martha O'Gorman. He had promised Martha never to mention it to anyone, but he was beginning to realize that his promise might be impossible to keep.

"I have reason to believe," he said carefully, "that Sister Blessing was acting as the friend and confidante of a murderer."

"Someone inside the colony?"

"Yes."

"A stupid and reckless position for a woman you describe as intelligent."

"In order to understand the situation, you have to understand more about the colony itself. It operates as a unit almost entirely separated from the rest of the country. The True Believers, as they call themselves, do not feel bound to obey our laws or follow our customs. When a man enters the Tower he sheds his other life completely, his name, his family, his worldly goods, and, last but not least, his sins. Under our system it's illegal to harbor a murderer. But look at it from the viewpoint of the sect: the victim belonged to a world they no longer recognized, the crime is punishable under laws they don't believe in or consider valid. In her own eyes Sister Blessing was not acting as an accessory after the fact of murder. Neither were the others, *if* they knew about the murder, and that's a big if."

"You're making a lot of excuses for her, Quinn."

"She doesn't need my excuses," Quinn said. "I'm only trying to help you realize that in a short time you'll be dealing with people whose attitudes are vastly different from your own. You're not going to change them, so you might as well understand them."

"You sound like a member of the Peace Corps making a report on Cuckooland."

"Cuckooland may not be quite as cuckoo as you think."

"All right, all right, I get the message." Lassiter yanked irritably at his collar as if he were being choked by new ideas. "So how do you fit into the picture?"

"I'd lost my shirt in Reno and was hitchhiking a ride to San Felice to collect a debt. The driver, a man named Newhouser, works on a ranch near the Tower. He was in a hurry to get home and couldn't take me all the way to San Felice. I went to the Tower for food and water. During the course of my overnight stay there, Sister Blessing asked me to find a man called Patrick O'Gorman. Just find him, that's all. I have the impression now that at the time she hired me she wasn't even sure O'Gorman had ever existed. It's possible that, when the murderer confessed killing O'Gorman, Sister Blessing didn't quite believe it, she thought the whole business might be a delusion. Naturally she wanted to find out the truth, although it meant breaking the rules of the colony and subsequent punishment. As it turned out, no delusion was involved. O'Gorman had existed all right. He was murdered near Chicote five and a half years ago."

"You told the Sister this?"

"Yes, a week ago."

"Did it frighten her?"

"No."

"She wasn't afraid that the murderer might regret confessing his crime and make sure she didn't inform anyone else?"

"Apparently not. According to Karma, the girl who was with her this morning, Sister Blessing was in high spirits, singing about a good day coming."

"Well, it didn't get here," Lassiter said grimly. "Not for her, anyway. What made her imagine there was a good day coming?"

"I don't know. Perhaps she was thinking not of herself but of the colony as a whole. It's been going downhill for a number of years and the appearance of a new convert must have been encouraging."

"Meaning George Haywood, or the man you think is George Haywood?"

"Yes. She had no reason that I know of to suspect Haywood wasn't a genuine convert."

"Someone else obviously had," Lassiter said. "Now that's a funny thing, isn't it?—Sister Blessing knew a week ago that the murder was no delusion, it had happened, and yet it wasn't until Haywood appeared on the scene that the murderer made sure she wouldn't talk. How do you figure it, Quinn?"

"I don't."

"What's the present size of the colony?"

"There are twenty-seven people, including two children and the sixteen-year-old girl, Karma."

"Can you eliminate any of them as suspects?"

"The children, certainly, and Karma. Sister Blessing was Karma's only hope of getting away from the colony and going to live with her aunt in Los Angeles. The Master himself would probably have to be eliminated—at the time of O'Gorman's murder he was in charge of the colony when it was still located in the San Gabriel Mountains. His wife, Mother Pureza, is both frail and senile, which makes her an unlikely prospect."

"Poisoning doesn't require brawn or brains."

"I don't believe any female members of the colony are involved in the murder."

"Why?"

Quinn knew the answer but he couldn't say it aloud: *The letter to Martha O'Gorman was written by a man.* "It seems improbable to me. Sister Blessing's role in the community was almost as vital as the Master's. She was the nurse, the manager, the housekeeper. The mother figure, I guess the psychologists would call her. Pureza's title of mother is purely nominal. She doesn't, and probably never did, function in that capacity."

"Tell me about some of the men in the group."

"Brother Crown of Thorns is the mechanic, a bad-tempered semiliterate, and probably the most fanatic believer of them all. Since he reported Sister Blessing's infringement of the rules and caused her punishment, she had reason to dislike him and quite probably he didn't like her, either. But I can't see him committing a murder unless he received his instructions in a vision. Brother Tongue of Prophets is a timid neurotic suffering from partial aphasia."

"What the hell's aphasia?"

"Inability to talk. He is, or was, as dependent on Sister Blessing as a little boy, and for that reason an unlikely suspect. Brother of the Steady Heart, the barber, poses as a jolly fat man, but I'm not sure he is. Brother Light of the Infinite, who looks after the livestock, is humorless and hard-working. Perhaps he works to the point of exhaustion in order to purge himself of guilt. At any rate he had access to poison in the form of sheep dip. Brother Behold the Vision is the butcher and the cheesemaker. I saw him only briefly, at a distance. I don't know any of the others by name."

"It seems to me you know quite a lot for a man who allegedly spent only a short time at the Tower."

"Sister Blessing was a good talker, I'm a good listener."

"Are you now," Lassiter said dryly. "Well, listen to this: I don't believe a word you've told me."

"You're not trying, Sheriff."

The car had started to climb and the altitude was already having an effect on Lassiter. Even the slight exertion of talking made him breathe faster and more heavily, and, although he was not tired or bored, he yawned frequently.

"Slow down on the curves, Bill. These bloody mountains give me the heaves."

"Think about something else, Sheriff," the deputy said earnestly. "You know, nice things. Trees. Music. Food."

"Food, eh?"

"Roast prime ribs, medium rare, baked potatoes—"

"Forget the whole thing, will you?"

"Yes, sir."

Lassiter leaned his head against the back seat and closed his eyes. "Do they know I'm coming, Quinn?"

"I told the Master I intended to report Haywood's death."

"What kind of reception do you think I'll get?"

"Don't expect a brass band."

"Damn it, I don't like these cases involving a bunch of nuts. Sane people are bad enough, but at least you can predict how they're about to act. Like you said, this is practically going into a foreign country where they don't speak our language, observe our laws—"

"Welcome to the Peace Corps," Quinn said.

"Thanks, but I'm not joining."

"You've been drafted, Sheriff."

In the front seat the deputy's shoulders shook in silent laughter. The sheriff leaned forward and spoke softly into his ear: "What's so funny, Bill?"

"Nothing, sir."

"That's how I figure it. Nothing's funny. So I'm not laughing."

"Neither am I, sir. It's just the altitude, it gives me hiccups."

Lassiter turned his attention back to Quinn. "Think they'll try and keep us out? I'd like to be forewarned if there's going to be any violence."

"Theoretically they don't believe in violence."

"Theoretically neither do I. But I sometimes have to use it."

"They have no weapons that I know of. Unless you count sheer force of numbers."

"Oh, I count it all right."

Lassiter's right hand moved instinctively toward the gun in his holster. Quinn noticed the gesture and felt a protest rising inside him. He thought of Mother Pureza the way he had first seen her, looking up at the sky as if she expected it to open for her, and the Master, torn between pity and duty, trying to guide her back from her wanderings through the halls of her childhood . . . Brother Tongue with the little bird on his shoulder to speak for him . . . Brother of the Steady Heart plying his razor, and like any barber anywhere, talking about anything: "In my day, the ladies were fragile, and had small, delicate feet." . . .

He remembered the harassed voice of Brother Light as he brought the can of sheep dip into the storage shed: "I have a hundred things to do, but Sister says I must fix the mattress or the stranger will be eaten alive by fleas." . . . And Brother Crown, the prophet of doom: "We all carry a devil around inside us, gnawing our innards."

Quinn said, in a voice that sounded ragged, gnawed by his own devil, "There must be no violence."

"Tell them that."

"I'm telling you first. By your own aggression, you might scare them into acts of destruction."

"More Peace Corps stuff, Quinn?"

"Call it that if you like."

"You suddenly bucking for sergeant in the army of the Lord? Maybe you're hearing voices, too, eh?"

"That's right," Quinn said. "I'm hearing voices."

One, in particular: "*I have renounced the world and its evils. I have renounced the flesh and its weakness. I seek the solace of the spirit, the salvation of the soul. Having done without comfort, I will be comforted by the Lord. Having hungered, I will feast. Having trod the rough earth, my feet uncovered, I will walk the smooth and golden streets of heaven. Having here forsaken the pride of ornament, I will be of infinite beauty. Having humbled myself in the fields, I will walk tall and straight in the hereafter, which does belong to the True Believers."*

Quinn looked out at the desolate landscape. *I hope you've made it, Sister. I hope to God you've made it.*

19

NOTHING SEEMED TO have changed since Quinn's first visit. The cattle grazed in the pasture, tails to the wind; the goats were still tethered to the manzanita tree, and the sheep in their log pen stared incuriously at the car as it passed. Even the spot on the path where Quinn had met Mother Pureza earlier in the day bore no traces of the encounter, no drops of blood, no footprints. Oak leaves and pine needles had drifted over it and the dark orange flakes of madrone bark that looked like cinnamon. The forest had hidden its records as effectively as the sea.

Sheriff Lassiter got out of the car, glancing around uneasily as though he half expected to be ambushed from behind a tree. He gave orders for the deputies in the second car to stay where they were until he had a chance to inspect the place, then he and Bill, the driver, followed Quinn up the sharp ascent of the path.

There was no sound. No wind moved the quiet trees, the birds had not yet started to forage for their evening meal, and if the three men were observed as they approached the dining building, the observer gave no audible alarm. Now and then a tired little wisp of smoke climbed out of the chimney and disappeared.

"Damn it, where is everybody?" Lassiter said. His voice sounded so loud in the thin air that he flushed with embarrassment and looked ready to apologize if anyone had appeared to accept the apology.

No one did.

He knocked on the kitchen door, waited, knocked again. "Hello in there!"

"They may all be at prayer in the Tower," Quinn said. "Try the door."

It wasn't locked. When he opened it, a draft of hot dry air struck Lassiter's face, and the sun pouring in through the enormous skylight almost blinded him.

The long wooden table was set for the next meal, tin plates and cups and stainless steel utensils. The kerosene lamps were filled, ready to be lit; the fire in the wood stove was going and more logs lay piled neatly on the floor beside it, to be added later when Sister Contrition arrived to start supper.

The place on the stone floor where Sister Blessing had fallen had been scrubbed clean, and there was an acrid smell in the air like burning wool. Lassiter went over to the stove and lifted the lid with the handle. The charred remnants of the cloths used to clean the floor were still smoking.

"They've burned the evidence," Lassiter said in helpless fury. "Well, by God, they're not going to get away with this if I have to lock every one of them behind bars. Put *that* in your peace pipe, Quinn."

He made several futile attempts to retrieve some of the remnants of cloth with a poker, but they fell apart at a touch. He threw the poker down. It barely missed his foot and he glowered at Quinn as if Quinn had been the one who had thrown it. "All right, where's the Tower? I want to ask these buddies of yours a few questions."

Bill was watching his boss anxiously. "Take it easy, Sheriff. Like Mr. Quinn says, this is foreign territory. Maybe we sort of need an interpreter, somebody can talk their language. What I mean is, sure, you have a viewpoint, but maybe they have a viewpoint, too, and if we kind of go easy at first—"

"What's happened to you?" Lassister said. "You getting soft in the head like Quinn here?"

"No. But—"

"Okay, then. No buts, Billy-boy."

The only sounds as they walked were the occasional crunch of an oak leaf underfoot and the squawk of a scrub jay sensing danger and giving the alarm. In silence, the three men passed under the entrance arch of the Tower into the inner courtyard. The dead man lay where he had fallen, in front of the shrine.

The body had been covered with a blanket, and on a bench nearby sat Mother Pureza, clutching a rosary and watching the intruders with unblinking eyes. She had been washed and wore a clean white robe.

Quinn spoke to her softly. "Mother Pureza?"

"Dona Isabella, if you please."

"Of course. Where are the others, Dona Isabella?"

"Gone."

"Where?"

"Away."

"They left you here all alone?"

"I'm not alone. There's Capirote—" She pointed a bony forefinger at the dead man, then at Quinn. "And you. And you. And you. That's four, and I make five. I'm not nearly as alone as I was when I had to sit up in my room with no one to talk to. Five is a good little conversational group. What shall we choose as an opening topic?"

"Your friends. The Master, Sister Contrition, Karma—"

"They are all gone. I told you that."

"Are they coming back?"

"I don't think so," she said with an indifferent shrug. "Why should they?"

"To take care of you."

"Capirote will take care of me when he wakes up."

Lassiter had removed the blanket from the dead man and was bending down, examining the head wounds. Quinn said to him, "I can't believe her husband would have left her like this to fend for herself."

Lassiter straightened up, his face grim. "Can't you?"

"He seemed very fond of her."

"This is another country, remember? Maybe fondness isn't a word in their language."

"I think it is."

"All right, what do you suggest? That they haven't really gone away, they're out there playing hide-and-seek in the trees?"

"No."

"What then?"

"Either the Master plans to return, or else he left his wife here deliberately, realizing the time had arrived when he could no longer care for her properly. He knew we'd be coming, that she wouldn't be alone for any length of time."

"You mean he felt the old lady would be a hindrance while he and the rest of them were on the run?"

"No. I think he intended her to be found and to be put in an institution. She needs custodial care."

"Your interpretation of the Master's motives are pretty charitable," Lassiter said. "It doesn't change the facts: a murder has been committed, perhaps two, and an old lady sick in the head has been abandoned."

"He would never have abandoned her for purely selfish reasons."

"You're having another peace-pipe dream, Quinn, and the smoke's gotten in your eyes."

"I can't hear you," Mother Pureza interrupted sharply. "Are you saying anything interesting? Speak up, speak up. What's the good of conversation that can't be heard?"

"For Pete's sake, keep her quiet," Lassiter said. "She gives me the creeps. I can't think."

Bill, who had gone on a brief inspection of the upper levels of the Tower, returned with the news that the place was empty. He glanced sympathetically at Mother Pureza. "I have a grandmother like that."

"So what do you do to keep her quiet?" Lassiter said.

"Well, she likes to suck Life Savers."

"Then for Pete's sake give her a Life Saver, will you?"

"Sure. Come on, Grandma. Let's go sit outside. I've got something nice for you."

"Are you a good conversationalist?" Mother Pureza said, frowning. "Can you quote poetry?"

"You bet." Bill helped her to her feet and led her slowly toward the archway. "How's this? 'Open your mouth and close your eyes, and I'll give you something to make you wise.'"

"I've never heard that before. Who wrote it?"

"Shakespeare."

"Fancy that. It must have been during one of his lighter moments."

"It was."

"Do you know any stories?"

"Some."

"Will you tell me the one about how they all lived happily ever after?"

"Sure."

Mother Pureza's eyes brightened and she clapped her hands in delight. "Start right now. 'Once upon a time there was a woman'—Go on, say it."

"'Once upon a time there was a woman,'" Bill repeated.

"'Named Mary Alice Featherstone.'"

"'Named Mary Alice Featherstone.'"

"'And she lived happily ever after.'"

Lassiter watched them leave, wiping the sweat off his face with his shirt sleeve. "We'll have to take her back to San Felice with us, County General Hospital, I guess. A hell of a thing, leaving an old lady alone like that."

The immediate problem of Mother Pureza had overshadowed the fact of Haywood's death. His body seemed hardly more than a prop of scenery against which real, live people were acting out their personal dramas.

"Are there any other buildings?" Lassiter said.

"A barn, a couple of washrooms, a storage shed."

"Take a look around, will you? I'll radio headquarters to send an ambulance and put out an A.P.B."

Quinn went to the barn first. The lone occupant was a mother goat suckling her new kid. The truck and the green station wagon were gone. The washrooms were empty, too; the only sign of recent occupancy was a bar of grey gritty soap lying in a couple of inches of water in a tin basin. The pieces of wool used for towels were all dry, an indication to Quinn that the colonists had abandoned the place shortly after his departure. They had stayed long enough to clean up the kitchen, burn the evidence, cover Haywood's body, then they had taken off.

The big question was, where could they have gone? Whatever their destination, they could hardly hope to escape notice, all of them robed and barefooted and the Brothers with their heads shaved. To avoid attracting immediate attention they must have changed to ordinary clothes, perhaps the very clothes they had worn when they first came to the Tower. It wasn't like the Brothers to throw anything away.

Quinn walked quickly along the path to the storage shed. The small room where he had spent the night at the Tower seemed to be in the same condition as he had left it. The two blankets were still on the iron cot, and underneath them was Karma's old school book which Sister Blessing had given him to read. The window was still open, the padlocks on the doors leading to the other compartments still in place. But on closer examination he saw that he was mistaken. One of the padlocks had been too carelessly or too hastily closed and had failed to snap shut. Quinn removed it and opened the door.

It was a small, square, windowless room that smelled of must and mildew. When his eyes adjusted to the dimness he could see that the place was filled with cardboard cartons of all sizes, some with lids, some without, some empty, some stuffed with clothing, books, handbags, hats, bundles of letters, hand mirrors, wallets, hair brushes, bottles of medicine, boxes of pills. There was a fan made of peacock feathers, an old-fashioned hand-crank phonograph, a miniature outrigger canoe constructed of matchsticks, a red velvet pillow pitted with holes, an abalone shell, a pair of hockey skates, a lamp with a tattered silk shade, a framed reproduction of Custer's last stand, a headless doll and an oversized coffee mug with DAD on it. Each of the cartons was labeled with the name of a member of the colony, printed in crayon.

One of the cartons looked new and bore the brand name of a detergent that had only recently been put on the market. It was labeled Brother Faith of Angels. Quinn carried it out, put it on the iron cot and opened the lid.

The dark grey fedora on top was identical to the hat he had seen George Haywood wearing when he had met Willie King at the empty house in Chicote. Both the hat and the dark grey suit underneath it came from Hadley & Son, Chicote, California. The white shirt, undershirt, shorts and two handkerchiefs carried the same laundry mark, HA 1389X. The black oxfords and striped blue tie were made by nationally known manufacturers and could have been bought anywhere. There was no wallet or personal papers of any kind.

He was in the act of replacing the clothes in the carton when Sheriff Lassiter appeared in the doorway.

"Find anything?" Lassiter said.

"George Haywood's clothes, I think."

"Let's have a look." He examined the items carefully, holding each one up to the light, squinting against the slanting rays of the sun. "Are there any more of these cartons?"

"Dozens."

"Okay, we'd better get going on them."

Sister Blessing's was brought out first. A thick layer of dust on the lid indicated that it had not been opened for some time. It contained a black wool coat, some white uniforms, a flowered crepe dress, underclothes, two pairs of white nurses' shoes, a calfskin handbag, a few pieces of costume jewelry, a man's gold watch and chain, and a sheaf of letters, some very old, signed your loving husband, Frank, and a few more recent, signed Charlie. The last one was dated the previous December:

> *Dear Mother:*
>
> *Once again I am writing to wish you a Merry Christmas from Florence and the two boys and myself. I only wish it could be a Merry Christmas for you. When are you going to come to your senses and leave that place? Surely there's enough misery in the world without the extra you're deliberately inflicting on yourself, for no sane reason. There's plenty of room for you here, if you choose to reconsider.*
>
> *Flo and the boys had the flu last month but we are all well now. I enclose twenty dollars. Spend it, save it, tear it up, but for the love of heaven don't hand it over to that doom-spouting madman who seems to have you mesmerized.*
>
> *Merry Christmas,*
> *Charlie*

Not even by reading between the lines could Quinn detect any sign of love or affection in the letter. Charles had written it in anger, and if he intended it as a real invitation for his mother to come and share his house, it was poorly expressed. Four words would have done the trick: *We need you here.*

"There's no time to read letters now," Lassiter said sharply.

"You'd better glance at it. It's from her son, Charlie."

"So?"

"You'll probably have to phone him and break the news."

"That will be pleasant. 'Hello, Charlie, your old lady's just been done in!'" He took the letter Quinn handed him and put it in his pocket. "Okay, let's bring out the rest of the junk. I don't want to be stuck in this joint all night."

The hockey skates belonged to Brother Light of the Infinite, the abalone shell to Brother Behold the Vision, the lamp and coffee mug to Sister Contrition. It was Brother of the Steady Heart who had cranked the phonograph, Brother Tongue of Prophets who had glued together the outrigger, and Karma who had cherished the headless doll and the velvet pillow.

Underneath the pillow Quinn found several sheets of paper filled on both sides with single-spaced typing. It had obviously been done by someone just learning to type, on a machine whose ribbon was running out of ink. There were sentences, half-sentences, numbers, letters of the alphabet in order and in reverse order, lines of semicolons and punctuation marks, and, interspersed here and there, the name Karma.

Some of the sentences were factual, others adolescent fantasy:

> *My name is name is Karma; which I hate.*
> *Because of my of my great beuaty beauty they are holding me prisoner in the tower in the forest. It is a sad fate for a princess.*
> *Quin said ge he would bring me a magic presnt presant for my face but I don't think ge he will.*
> *Today I said hell hell hell 3 times out loud.*
> *The princess made a brade of her long hair and strangled all her enemies and got loose and re turned to the kingdom.*

"What's that?" Lassiter said.

"Some of Karma's doodling on the typewriter."

"There's no typewriter here."

"Whoever it belonged to must have taken it along."

It seemed a logical conclusion and the subject was dropped.

The carton labeled Brother Crown of Thorns contained no sentimental mementos of the past, only a few pieces of clothing: a tweed suit and a sweater, both riddled by moths; a broadcloth shirt, a pair of shoes, and some woolen socks so full of holes they were barely recognizable. All of the articles had been lying undisturbed in the carton for a long time.

Quinn said suddenly, "Wait a minute."

"What's the matter?"

"Hold one of those shirts up against your chest as if you were measuring it for size."

Lassiter held the shirt up. "Pretty good fit."

"What size do you take?"

"Sixteen and a half."

"Try the suit coat on, will you?"

"Just what are you getting at, Quinn? I don't like messing around other people's clothes." But he tried the coat on anyway. It was too tight around the shoulders and the sleeves were too long.

"Now the sweater, I suppose?"

"If you don't mind."

The sweater was a fairly good fit except that once again the sleeves were too long.

"All right, Quinn." Lassiter tossed the sweater back into the carton. "What's the pitch?"

"A real sinker," Quinn said. "Those clothes don't belong to Brother Crown. He's a man of medium build, a little on the short side even."

"Maybe he's lost weight since he arrived here—"

"His legs and arms didn't shrink."

"—Or the carton was mislabeled. There could be a dozen explanations."

"There could be, yes. But I want the right one."

Quinn carried the sweater, the coat and one of the shirts over to the doorway and examined them in sunlight. Neither the sweater nor the coat bore a manufacturer's label. Inside the collar of the shirt there was a label, Arrow, 16Vz, 100% pure cotton, Peabody & Peabody, and the barely distinguishable remains of a laundry mark.

"Have, you got a magnifying glass, sheriff?"

"No, but I have twenty-twenty vision."

"Try it on this laundry mark."

"Looks like an H to begin with," Lassiter said, blinking. "HR. Or maybe HA. That's it, HAI or HAT."

"How about HA one?"

"You may be right. HA one. The next looks like a three or a two. Then an eight."

"HA 1389X," Quinn said.

Lassiter sneezed, partly from annoyance, partly from the dust hanging in the air like fog. "If you knew it already, why did you ask me?"

"I wanted to be sure."

"You think it's important?"

"That's George Haywood's laundry mark."

"Well, I'll be damned." Lassiter sneezed again. "Judging from the amount of moth damage and dust, I'd say these things had been in here for years. What's it add up to?"

"When Brother Crown first came to the Tower he was apparently wearing George Haywood's clothes."

"Why? And how did he get hold of them?"

Quinn wasn't quite ready to answer the question though he was pretty sure he knew the answer. Willie King had given it to him the previous night in the courtyard motel. Of George, coming out of the anesthetic, she had said. "He was a scream . . . He thought I was Alberta . . . and told me I was a silly old spinster who should know better . . . He was mad at her . . . because she'd given away some of his clothes to a transient who'd come to the house. He called her a gullible, soft-hearted fool . . . Alberta might be a fool but she's neither gullible nor soft-hearted. If there really was a transient, and if she gave him some of George's clothes, she must have had a reason besides simple generosity."

Quinn felt a painful triumph rising inside him. The connection he'd been searching for, between Alberta Haywood and the murder of Patrick O'Gorman, was gradually becoming clear. The transient to whom she had given George's clothes, the hitchhiker O'Gorman had picked up in his car, the writer of the confession letter to Martha O'Gorman, had all been the same man, Brother Crown of Thorns.

Questions still unanswered raced around in Quinn's mind. Where was Brother Crown now? How had he managed to persuade the entire colony to disperse in order to save him from arrest? Was it George Haywood's sudden appearance at the Tower that made Sister Blessing's death necessary? And what reason besides simple generosity had prompted Alberta Haywood to hand over her brother's clothes to a stranger? Suppose, though, that he was not a stranger, or didn't remain one very long. Suppose Alberta, on opening the door to him, had sensed in him a desperation that matched her own and had offered him money to kill O'Gorman.

Quinn had been considering for some time the idea that O'Gorman had had a connection with, or at least knowledge of, Alberta's embezzlements. It was impossible to believe O'Gorman had used his knowledge to blackmail her but he might have tried to talk to her, to reason with her: *Now see here, Miss Haywood, you really shouldn't be taking money from the bank, it's not a nice thing to do. I think you ought to stop. You're putting me in an awkward position. If I keep quiet about it, I'm condoning your crime—*

Alberta was such a timid little creature it probably didn't occur to O'Gorman that she might be capable of hiring a man to kill him.

Yes, it all fitted together, Quinn thought. Even now, back in her jail cell, Alberta was blaming O'Gorman for her plight. Her irrational claims that he was not dead might be caused by her inability to face her guilt, a refusal to admit that she had been responsible for his death. Then where did George fit into the picture? How long had he suspected his sister of planning O'Gorman's murder? And were his regular visits to her intended to get at the truth or to conceal it?

"Give me a hand with these cartons," Lassiter said. "We'd better take them along in case any of the Brothers gets the notion of coming back for them."

"I don't think they'll be back."

"Nor do I. But there are always buts. Where do you suppose they're headed?"

"South, probably. The original colony was in the San Gabriel Mountains."

Lassiter lit a cigarette, put out the match and broke it in two before tossing it out the door. "Now if I were the Master, which God forbid, that's the last thing I'd do, unless I wanted to be caught. Even though they've all put on ordinary clothes, twenty-five people in a truck and a station wagon are pretty likely to attract attention."

"So what would you do?"

"Disperse. Drive to the nearest big city, L.A., and separate completely. They don't stand a chance in the mountains."

"They don't stand much of a chance in the city, either," Quinn said. "They have no money."

In the back seat, lulled by the motion of the car, Mother Pureza went to sleep sucking a Life Saver. With her legs drawn up and her chin dropped on her chest, she looked like a very old fetus.

Lassiter rode in the front. When they reached the main road he turned around to frown at Quinn. "You said there was a ranch near here?"

"Yes. The turn-off's a couple of miles down the road."

"We'll have to stop by and get some help."

"What kind of help?"

"Only a city boy would ask that," Lassiter said with a grunt. "The livestock has to be looked after. Cows can't milk themselves. It's a funny darn thing, the Brothers walking off and leaving behind a valuable herd like that."

"With only a truck and a station wagon, they had no alternative."

"I wonder if there's any possibility that they're hiding out in the hills near here and intend to come back for the cattle, perhaps during the night. Being a city boy, you wouldn't understand how much a colony like the Tower depends on its livestock. The herd looked healthy and well-tended."

"It was," Quinn said, remembering the intensity of Brother Light's voice as he had spoken of the cattle, the sheep, the goats. Wherever Brother Light was now, in the hills nearby, in the San Gabriel Mountains, or in the city, Quinn knew what he would be thinking of as the sun set.

The turn-off to the ranch was marked by a wooden sign, Rancho Arido, decorated with horseshoes. Half a mile up the road they were met by a man driving a jeep with a couple of collies in the back seat, barking and wagging their tails furiously.

At the approach of the sheriff's car the man stopped the jeep and climbed out.

"What's up, Sheriff?"

"Hello, Newhouser," Quinn said.

Newhouser leaned over and peered through the window. "Well, I'll be a monkey's uncle, it's you again, Quinn."

"Yes."

"Thought you'd be back in Reno by this time."

"I hit a detour."

"You know, Quinn, it's been kind of on my conscience, my leaving you on the road like I did. I'm glad you're okay. You never can tell what'll happen."

Quinn's sudden deep breath was like the gasp of a man drowning in a flash flood of memories. Riding the crest of the flood was Sister Blessing, smiling a greeting to him: "*Welcome, stranger . . . We never turn away the poor, being poor ourselves.*"

"No," he said quietly, "you never can tell what will happen."

20

AT NINE O'CLOCK Quinn was still in the sheriff's office waiting for the operator to put through a call to Charlie Featherstone on the sheriff's private phone. When the phone finally rang, Lassitter glanced first at it, then at Quinn:

"I'm no good at this kind of thing. You answer it."

"It's not my duty."

"You knew his mother, I didn't. Answer it."

"All right," Quinn said. "But I prefer speaking to him alone."

"This is my office."

"It's also your phone."

"Oh, for Pete's sake," Lassiter said and went out, slamming the door behind him.

Quinn picked up the phone. "Hello."

"Yes."

"Mr. Featherstone?"

"Yes. Who's this?"

"My name is Quinn. I'm calling from San Felice, California. I've been trying to reach you for some time."

"I was out."

"I'm afraid I have some bad news for you."

"I'm not surprised." Featherstone's voice had the whine of a chronic complainer. "I never get any *good* news from that part of the country."

"Your mother died this afternoon."

For a long time there was no response. Then, "I warned her, I told her she was a fool to stay there, neglecting her health, never looking after herself properly."

"She didn't die of neglect, Mr. Featherstone. She was poisoned."

"Good God, what are you saying? Poisoned? My mother poisoned? How? Who did it?"

"I'm not sure of the details yet."

"If that hell-ranting maniac is responsible, I'll tear that holy carcass of his apart."

"It was not his fault."

"Everything's his fault." Featherstone was shouting now, translating his grief into anger. "If it weren't for him and that line of bull he shoots, she'd have been here, leading a decent life."

"Her life was decent, Mr. Featherstone. She did what she wanted to do, serve others."

"And these *others* were so full of gratitude that they poisoned her? Well, it figures, from what I know of the place, it really figures. I should have suspected something funny was going on when I had a letter from her last week. I should have—should have acted."

He must have broken down at this point: Quinn could hear muffled sobs and a woman's voice pleading, "Charlie, please don't take it so hard. You did everything you could to reason with her. Please, Charlie."

After a time Quinn said, "Mr. Featherstone? Are you still there?"

"Yes. Yes, I— Go on."

"Before she died, she spoke your name. I thought you'd want to know that."

"I don't. I *don't* want to know it."

"Sorry."

"She was my mother. It was my duty to look after her, and I couldn't do a thing once that madman got to her with a line that wouldn't fool a two-year-old child. Other women lose their husbands, it doesn't mean they have to stop wearing shoes."

"About that letter she wrote you—"

"There were two letters," Featherstone said. "One was a short note telling me she felt well and happy and not to worry about her. The other letter was in a sealed envelope which I was to post here in Evanston as a favor to her."

"Did she explain why?"

"Only that the letter would clear up a situation that was making someone unhappy. I thought it was just some more of her religious nonsense so I posted it. It was an air-mail letter addressed to a woman named Mrs. O'Gorman, in Chicote, California."

"What about the handwriting?"

"It wasn't my mother's. It looked more like a kid's, third- or fourth-grade level, or perhaps it was other-handed writing."

"Other-handed?"

"Written left-handed by a right-handed person, or vice versa. Or else whoever wrote it was semiliterate."

He was, Quinn thought. It must have been a chore for Brother Crown to have written the letter at all. Why had he done it? Fear of dying before receiving absolution? It hardly seemed possible. He appeared to be in excellent health, much better than any of the rest of them. If fear hadn't motivated his confession, what had? Or who had?

Quinn recalled his second visit to the Tower when he had gone to see Sister Blessing, in isolation for her sins. He had told her about Martha O'Gorman and her uncertainty over her husband's death: "*She deserves a break. Give it to her if you can, Sister. You're a generous woman.*" He had thought Sister Blessing wasn't listening to him, but she must have heard, must have considered Martha O'Gorman's plight and then gone to Brother Crown, demanding that he write the letter and set the record straight. She was a persuasive, strong-minded woman, and Brother Crown had agreed to her demand.

That's how it must have happened, yet the situation did not seem to Quinn either real or plausible. He could believe Sister Blessing's part of it, but not Brother Crown's. Brother Crown had made no secret of his antipathy toward the Sister; he was not dependent on her, like some of the others; he was stubborn and he was self-righteous. Such a man would be unlikely to write a letter confessing a murder, at the request of one woman, on behalf of another. *No,* Quinn thought, *it's not the situation that's unreal, it's the cast of characters. I can see Sister Blessing giving Crown an order, but I can't see Crown obeying her. In their relationship the balance of power was in his hands, not hers.*

Featherstone had returned to his favorite subject: his mother had been duped by a maniac, the man should be arrested, the whole colony taken to a booby hatch, and the buildings burned to the ground.

Quinn finally interrupted him. "I can understand your feelings, Mr. Featherstone, but—"

"You can't. She wasn't your mother. You don't know what it's like to watch a member of your own family being hypnotized by a madman into leading a life not fit for a dog."

"I'm sorry you didn't have a chance to see your mother before she died. Her life was a lot happier than you seem to realize. If she made sacrifices, she also had compensations. She told me that she had at last found her place in the world and that she would never leave it."

"That wasn't *her* talking, it was *him*."

"It was your mother, telling me quite seriously what she really believed."

"The poor, crazy fool. A *fool*, that's what she was."

"At least she was a fool in her own way."

"Are you sticking up for him?"

"No, for her, Mr. Featherstone."

There was a groan on the other end of the line, then a woman's voice: "I'm sorry, my husband can't talk about this anymore, he's too upset. I'll have to make the arrangements about the—the body. There'll be an autopsy?"

"Yes."

"When it's over, when she can be shipped here for burial, will you let me know?"

"Of course."

"Then I guess there's nothing more to say right now except—well, please excuse Charlie."

"Yes. Good-bye, Mrs. Featherstone."

Quinn replaced the phone. His hands were shaking, and though the room was cold, sweat slithered down behind his ears into his collar. He wiped it off and went out into the corridor.

Lassiter was standing just outside the door, talking to a severe-looking young man in a policeman's uniform.

He said to Quinn, "Okay for Charlie?"

"Okay for Charlie."

"Thanks. This is Sergeant Castillo. He's been working on those cartons we found in the storage shed. Tell him, Sergeant."

Castillo nodded. "Yes, sir. Well, the clothes contained in the first one, labeled Brother Faith of Angels, have not been in there more than a week, perhaps much less."

"We know that," Lassiter said impatiently. "They belonged to George Haywood. Go on, Sergeant."

"Yes, sir. The contents of the carton labeled Brother Crown of Thorns haven't been touched for several years. My estimate would be six years, based mainly on the amount of moth damage. Entomology is one of my hobbies. If you'd like me to go into detail about the life cycle of this particular kind of moth and how each generation—"

"That won't be necessary. We'll take your word for it. Six years it is."

"Another interesting point concerns Brother Crown's name on the carton. I'd say it was pasted on quite recently. When I removed it, there was evidence underneath that another label had been there previously and torn off. Only a trace of it remained."

"Any letters visible?"

"No."

"All right. Thanks." Lassiter waited for the sergeant to get out of earshot. "Six years. What does it prove, Quinn?"

"That the clothes didn't belong to Brother Crown. He joined the colony only three years ago."

"How do you know that?"

"Karma told me. She's the young daughter of the cook, Sister Contrition."

"So we've tabbed the *wrong* man," Lassiter said harshly. "Not that it makes any difference. No one's seen hide or hair of any of them. The whole damn caboodle has disappeared, leaving me with a herd of cattle, a flock of sheep, five goats and some chickens. How do you like that?"

Quinn liked it quite well, in a way, though all he said was, "Am I free to go now?"

"Go where?"

"To a restaurant for some dinner and a motel for some sleep."

"And after that?"

"After that I don't know. I have to find a job. Maybe I'll head for L.A."

"Then again, maybe you won't," Lassiter said. "Why not stick around here for a while?"

"Is that an order?"

"It's a nice little city, San Felice. Mountains, ocean, parks, beaches, harbor."

"And no jobs."

"You have to look for them, I'll admit that. But the place is gradually opening up to a few smokeless industries. Try applying."

"Is that an order?" Quinn repeated. "I hope not, Sheriff. I can't stay here. I have to go back to Chicote, for one thing . . . Has anyone broken the news to George Haywood's mother?"

"I called the Chief of Police there. He'll have done it by this time."

"Somebody had better tell Alberta, too," Quinn said. "She might have something to tell in return."

"For example?"

"Why she hired one of the Brothers to kill O'Gorman and how Haywood found out about it."

21

ALBERTA HAYWOOD LAY staring up through black thoughts at the white ceiling. It was no ordinary ceiling, though. Sometimes it receded until it seemed as far away as the sky, and sometimes it closed in on her, its soft satin whiteness touching her face until she thought she was in a coffin. But even in her coffin she had no more privacy than she had had in prison. People moved around her, poked her in the chest and back, stuck tubes in her nose and needles in her arm, talked. If what they said was interesting, she responded; if not, she pretended to have heard nothing.

Occasionally she asked a question of her own, "Where is George?"

"Now, Miss Haywood, we told you that several days ago."

"I don't remember."

"Your brother George is dead."

"Really? Well, he'll have to find his own coffin. There certainly isn't any room in this one. I'm quite cramped as it is."

A medley of voices: "She's still delirious." . . . "But the pneumonia's clearing up, her white count's practically back to normal." . . . "It's been nearly a week now." . . . "Continue the glucose." . . . "Wish we could get a decent x-ray." . . . "She keeps trying to take the tube out of her nose." . . . "Apathy." . . . "Hysteria." . . . "Delirium." . . .

The voices came and went. She took out the tube and it was replaced. She pulled off the blankets and they were put back. She fought and was beaten.

"Miss Haywood, there's a man here to ask you some questions."

"Tell him to go away."

But the man did not go away. He stood beside the bed, looking down at her with strange, sad eyes. "Did you hire anyone to kill O'Gorman, Miss Haywood?"

"No."

"Did you give your brother's clothes to a transient?"

"No."

It was absolutely true. She'd done neither of those things. The man who asked such absurd questions must be an idiot. "Who are you?"

"Joe Quinn."

"Well, you're an idiot, Joe Quinn."

"Yes, I guess I am."

"I don't answer the door to transients, let alone arrange murders. Ask George."

"I can't ask George. He was killed six days ago."

"Of course."

"Why do you say, 'Of course,' Miss Haywood?"

"George interfered with people's lives. Quite natural someone should kill him."

"Did he interfere with yours?"

"Every time he came here he tormented me with questions. He shouldn't have done that."
Tears, some for George, some for herself, squeezed out from under her closed eyelids. "He shouldn't have done it. Why couldn't he let people alone?"

"What people, Miss Haywood?"

"Us."

"Who is 'us'?"

"Us people. All us people of the world."

She could sense, from the sudden quietness in the room, that she had made a bad mistake. To distract attention from it, she reached up and wrenched the feeding tube out of her nose. It was replaced. She threw off the blankets from the bed, and they were put back. She fought, even in her sleep, and even in her sleep she was beaten. There were no fresh sweet dreams left for her.

It was the first time Willie King had appeared at the office since George's funeral. Nothing in it had changed. On the floor, desks and chairs and wastebaskets were in the same position, and on the walls, Washington was still crossing the Delaware, and young Lincoln was still smiling inscrutably.

She stared around her, filled with resentment that nothing had changed. She wanted to take a crowbar and vandalize the place, smash the windows and ashtrays and telephone, demolish the chairs and desks, then everything would look the way she felt inside.

Earl Perkins, hanging up his coat on the rack, gave her a small tentative smile. "Hello, Willie. You all right?"

"Fine. Just fine, thanks."

"Gosh, Willie, I'm sorry. I mean, gosh, what can I say?"

"Try shutting up." She glanced at the pile of mail on Earl's desk, some of it already opened. "Business as usual, eh?"

"Mrs. Haywood's orders were to keep going just as if George hadn't died."

"That's a laugh. She's a very funny woman. I get hysterics when I think about her."

"Now don't start that again, Willie."

"Why not?"

"It won't do any good. And after all, maybe in her own way she's not as bad as you think."

"She's worse."

"So all right, she's worse," Earl said in a resigned voice. "There's nothing you can do about it."

"Yes, there is." She went over to her desk and picked up the telephone. "I can call her, tell her a few of the things I couldn't tell her when George was alive."

"You don't want to do that, Willie."

"Oh, but I do. I've been planning it for days. Listen, you old harridan, I'll say. Listen, you selfish, conniving old woman. You want to know who killed George? You did. Not last week, or last month, but years ago, years and years. You choked the life out of him with those scrawny claws of yours—"

"Give me that phone," Earl said.

"Why should I?"

"Stop arguing and give it to me."

She shook her head stubbornly and began to dial. George was dead. She didn't care what happened now, there was no future for her. "Hello?"

"Hello."

"Mrs. Haywood?"

"Yes, this is Mrs. Haywood speaking."

How old she sounds, Willie thought with surprise. *How very old and sick and defeated.*

"This is Willie, Mrs. Haywood. I'm sorry I haven't called sooner. How are you getting along?"

"Adequately, thank you."

"Perhaps you'd like me to come over one of these nights. We could keep each other company. I'm lonely, too."

"Indeed? Well, you cope with your loneliness, I'll cope with mine."

"If you change your mind, let me know."

Willie put the receiver back on the hook and turned to face Earl. She had not particularly noticed him before except as a kid who shared the same office and had trouble with his digestion. He was a little young, perhaps, but he had a nice appearance and he worked hard. And if she could keep him on his ulcer diet—

She said, "Thanks, Earl. I'm really grateful to you."

"What for? I didn't do anything except stand here."

"Maybe that's enough. You just keep standing there, will you?"

"Well, sure. Only I don't know what in heck you're talking about."

"You will."

From the telephone in the hall, Mrs. Haywood went back to the kitchen and resumed her preparation of breakfast. Celery stalks, spinach, carrots, a head of lettuce, wheat germ, powdered protein and two eggs went into the blender and came out the thick grey-green mixture which started Mrs. Haywood's dietary day.

So far she hadn't admitted to herself or to anyone else that George had been murdered. In her reconstruction of his death, George, standing at the top of the Tower, had suffered an attack of vertigo and fallen, due to poor eating habits and lack of proper exercise and rest. To Quinn, to Sheriff Lassiter, to the police officials of Chicote, to John Ronda, the local publisher, she had reiterated this belief without attempting to explain why George had gone to the Tower in the first place or what he had hoped to accomplish there. On the subject of Alberta, she was silent.

"Lonely, are you, Willie?" she said aloud. "Well, you deserve to be. Who kept George out at nights so he didn't get his eight hours of sleep? Who made him eat restaurant dinners high in cholesterol and low in calcium and riboflavin? Who persuaded him to sit for hours at a movie when he should have been using his muscles at the Y?"

In the past two weeks she had begun to talk to herself and to people who were not there and never would be. Much of what she said consisted of excerpts and homilies from her collection of self-help books on nutrition, positive thinking, dynamic living, health and happiness through concentration, peace of mind, and the uses and development of will power. She took all the self-styled authorities with utter seriousness, even though they frequently contradicted themselves and each other. It kept her busy and prevented her from thinking.

"The authorities are too stupid to recognize a simple truth. First, there was the exertion of climbing the stairs when his system was not prepared for it. His heart muscles were flabby, his arteries choked with cholesterol. Then, too, he should have had at least eighty-five grams of protein that day, and one full gram of calcium, and of course he didn't."

She poured the mixture from the blender into a glass and held it up to the window over the sink. In the opaque greyness she could see youth and health and vigor, will power, happiness, peace of mind, free-flowing arteries, firm abdominal muscles, a fortune in real estate and eternal life.

She took a sip of her dream cocktail.

"If George had started his day with this, he'd be alive right now. The vertigo would never have happened."

The first sip had tasted bitter and the texture was wrong. She took a second and it was the same, bitter, too thin to eat, too thick to drink.

"I must have left something out. What did I leave out?"

September came. The O'Gorman children went back to school and every night Martha helped them with their homework. Richard had written a theme on "How I Spent My Summer Vacation" and given it to her to check for spelling and grammatical errors.

"This handwriting is terrible," Martha said. "Don't they teach handwriting in school anymore?"

"Sure they teach it," Richard said cheerfully. "I guess I just don't learn it."

"I don't think I'll be able to read it."

"Just keep trying, Mom."

"Oh, I'll keep trying, all right, but will the teacher?" Martha returned to the theme. According to Richard's version of the summer, he had done more work than a company of Seabees. "This *is* you you're writing about?"

"Sure. That's the title, isn't it? How *I* Spent *My* Summer. Listen, Mom. Do you know what a lot of the kids are doing this year?"

"I certainly do," Martha said dryly. "I've been told often enough. Some of them are driving their own Cadillacs. Others get fifty a week allowance, are allowed to stay out until midnight—"

"No, I'm serious, Mom. Some of the kids—one of them, anyway, does his homework on a typewriter."

"At your age?"

"Sure. Why not?"

"If you use a typewriter for everything now, by the time you're ready for college you'll have forgotten how to write by hand."

"You said I couldn't anyway."

Martha looked at him coolly. "Well, what I didn't say, but what I'm saying right now, smarty pants, is that you'd better pay stricter attention to your handwriting. Is that clear?"

Richard groaned, twitched and rolled his eyes, but he said, "Yes, ma'am."

"Beginning now. You should copy this theme over before you give it to the teacher, if you're interested in a decent grade on it."

"Didn't we have a typewriter once? A long time ago?"

"Yes."

"What happened to it?"

Martha hesitated before she answered, "I don't really know."

"Gosh, maybe it's still around some place in the storeroom or the garage. I'm going to look for it."

"No. You won't find it, Richard."

"I might. You said you didn't really know where it is."

"I *do* know where it isn't. There's no need to ransack the storeroom and the garage looking for something that doesn't exist. Now please don't start telling me what the other kids are allowed to do. Just accept the fact that you're underprivileged, abused, neglected and short-changed, and carry on from there. Will you do that?"

"Well, gee whiz."

"That just about sums it up, friend. Gee whiz."

She kept her tone light so the boy wouldn't suspect how much the sudden mention of the typewriter had shaken her. It had been Patrick's, an old portable he had bought secondhand, and which had never worked properly. The keys stuck together, the margin regulators were temperamental, and the bell rang only when it wanted to. She remembered how earnestly and patiently Patrick had hunched over it, trying to teach himself the touch system and never succeeding at that any more than he had at all the other things he had tried. *I encouraged him too much,* she thought. *I let him climb too high and when he fell I provided too soft a cushion so he never broke a bone or learned his own limitations.*

When Richard went back to his room to rewrite his theme, Martha picked up the telephone and put in a long-distance call to San Felice.

Quinn answered on the second ring. "Hello."

"This is Martha, Joe."

"I was just sitting here wondering whether I should make a nuisance of myself by calling you again. I have some news for you. One of the members of the Tower, Brother Crown, has been picked up in San Diego, working at a garage. Sheriff Lassiter and I drove down yesterday to question him but we didn't get any answers. Even when he confronted me, Crown wouldn't admit his identity, so it looks like another dead end. I thought you would like to know about it anyway."

"Thank you," Martha said. "How's the new job?"

"Fine. I haven't sold any boats yet but it's fun trying."

"Will you be up this weekend?"

"I can't promise. I have to go to L.A. and make another attempt to contact Mrs. Harley Baxter Wood."

"Karma's aunt?"

"Yes."

"You said the house was all closed up."

"Yes, but I figure she'll be opening it again now that school's started. She has a couple of children, she can't afford to keep on the run."

"Why do you think she went away?"

"If I'm right, Karma's with her, and the aunt's taking no chances on any members of the colony getting to her again."

For a minute there was the kind of awkward silence that occurs between people who are talking about one thing and thinking about another.

"Joe—"

"Do you miss me, Martha?"

"You know I do . . . Listen, Joe, I've got something to tell you. I'm not sure it's important. It didn't come out at the inquest into Patrick's death because I simply didn't remember it then, and later, when I did, it seemed too slight a matter to bring to anyone's attention. Richard mentioned it a few minutes ago."

"Mentioned what?"

"Patrick's typewriter. He'd put it in the car a week before, intending to take it into the repair shop. But he kept forgetting about it. I think it was in the back seat when he picked up the hitchhiker that night."

22

QUINN HAD BEEN waiting in his car outside Mrs. Wood's house for half an hour. When he had pressed the door chime, no one had answered, but he was pretty sure there was someone inside. Drapes were pulled back, windows were open, a radio was playing.

He looked at his watch. Ten o'clock. The tree-lined street was quiet except for an occasional car and the ringing of distant church bells. After a time he became aware that someone was watching him from one of the second-floor windows. There was no breeze to account for the sudden twitching of the pink net curtain.

He went back to the front door and pressed the chime again. A cat meowed softly in reply.

"Mrs. Wood?" he called out. "Mrs. Wood—"

"And where did it come from?"

"Alberta Haywood's embezzlements."

"For Pete's sake." Lassiter whirled around impatiently. "*You* were the one who convinced me she was telling the truth about not paying anyone to murder O'Gorman, not knowing the transient, not giving him George Haywood's clothes—"

"I still think it was the truth."

"You're contradicting yourself."

"No," Quinn said. "I don't believe she gave a lot of money and George's clothes to a transient. I believe she gave them to somebody else."

23

HE HAD BECOME part of the forest.

Even the birds were used to him by now. The mourning doves waddling around outside their sloppy nests or paired in swift whistling flights, the towhees foraging noisily with both feet in the dry leaves, the goshawks waiting in ambush to pounce on a passing quail, the chickadees clinging upside down on the pine branches, the phainopeplas, scraps of black silk basted to the grey netting of Spanish moss, the tanagers, quick flashes of yellow and black among the green leaves, none of them either challenged or acknowledged the presence of the bearded man. They ignored his attempts to lure them by imitating their calls and offering them food. They were not fooled by his coos and purrs and warbles, and there was still food enough in the forest: madrone berries and field mice, insects hiding beneath the eucalyptus bark, moths in the oaks at dusk, slugs in the underbrush, cocoons under the eaves of the Tower.

The birds were, in fact, better fed than he. What cooking he did was hurried and at night, so the smoke of his fire wouldn't be seen by rangers manning the lookout station. Even at best, the supplies at the Tower were meager and now they were also stale. He ate rice with weevils in it, he fought the cockroaches for the remains of the wheat and barley, he trapped bush bunnies and skinned them with a straight razor. What saved him was the vegetable garden. In spite of the weeds and the depredations of deer and rabbits and gophers, there were tomatoes and onions to be picked, and carrots and beets and potatoes to be dug up and cooked, or half cooked, depending on how long he felt it was safe to keep the fire going.

The fawns, the only wild creatures willing to make friends with him, were, of necessity, his enemies. When they came to the vegetable garden, at dawn and at dusk, he threw stones to chase them away, feeling sick at heart when they fled.

Sometimes he apologized to them and tried to explain: "I'm sorry. I like you, but you're stealing my food and I need it. You see, someone is coming for me but I'm not sure how much longer I have to wait. When she comes, I'll go away with her and the vegetables will all be yours. I have been through a great deal. You wouldn't want me to starve now, just at the point where our plan is working out . . ."

He still called it "our plan," though it had been hers from the beginning. It had started with such innocence, a meeting on a street corner, an exchange of tentative smiles and good mornings: "I'm afraid it's going to be another hot day." "Yes ma'am, I'm afraid it is."

After that he ran into her unexpectedly at all sorts of places, a supermarket, the library, a parking lot, a coffee house, a movie, a laundromat. By the time he was beginning to suspect that these meetings were not entirely accidental, it no longer mattered because he was sure he was in love with her. Her quietness made him feel like talking, her gentleness made him bold, her timidity brave, her lack of criticism self-confident.

Their private meetings were, necessarily, brief and in places avoided by other people, like the dry, dusty river bed. Here, without even touching each other, they voiced their love and despair until the two seemed inseparable, one word, love-despair. Their mutual suffering became a neurotic substitute for happiness until a point of no return was reached.

"I can't go on like this," he told her. "All I can think of is chucking everything overboard and running away."

"Running away is for children, dearest."

"Then I'm childish. I want to take off and never see anyone again, not even you."

She knew the time had come when his misery was so great that he would accept any plan at all. "We must make long-term arrangements. We love each other, we have money, we can start a whole new life together in a different place."

"How, for God's sake?"

"First we must get rid of O'Gorman."

He thought she was joking. He laughed and said, "Oh, come now. Poor O'Gorman surely doesn't deserve that."

"I'm serious. It's the only way we can be sure we'll always remain together, with no one trying to separate us or interfere with us."

During the next month she worked out every detail down to the very clothes he would wear. She bought, and stocked with supplies, an old shack in the San Gabriel Mountains where he was to hide out while waiting for her. His nearest neighbors were members of an obscure religious cult. It was with the children that he first became acquainted, the oldest a girl about ten. She was fascinated by the sound of his typewriter, peering at him from behind trees and bushes as he sat on the back porch typing because there was nothing else to do.

She was a timid little creature with odd flashes of boldness. "What's that thing?"

"A typewriter."

"It sounds like a drum. If it was mine I'd hit it harder and make more noise."

"What's your name?"

"Karma."

"Don't you have another name, too?"

"No. Just Karma."

"Would you like to try the typewriter, Karma?"

"Does it belong to the devil?"

"No."

"All right."

He used Karma as an excuse for his first visit to the colony. As his loneliness grew more unbearable, there were other visits. Excuses became unnecessary. The Brothers and Sisters asked him no questions: they accepted it as perfectly natural that he, like themselves, should have turned his back on the world and sought refuge in the mountains. In turn, he appreciated their community life. There was always someone around, always some chore to be done which kept him from brooding, and their rigid rules gave him a sense of security.

He had been in the mountains for over a month when the bad news came in a letter:

> Dearest, I have only a minute now to write, I've made a mistake and they're onto me. I'll be gone for a while. Please wait. This is not the end for us, it is just a postponement, dear one. We must not try and contact each other. Have faith in me as I have in you. I can endure anything knowing you'll be waiting for me. I love you, I love you . . .

Before he burned it, he read the brief note a dozen times, whimpering like an abandoned child. Then he took the blade out of his safety razor and cut both his wrists.

When he returned to consciousness he was lying on a cot in a strange room. Both his wrists were heavily bandaged and Sister Blessing was bending over him: "You are awake now, Brother?"

He tried to speak and couldn't, so he nodded.

Her plan seemed crazy to him at first, but eventually he came to accept it because he had no better one to offer her; in fact, he had no plan at all, he was not used to doing his own thinking.

He insisted on one promise from her, that after O'Gorman was out of the picture, she would take no more chances at the bank. She would stop falsifying the books and wait for the time when it would be safe for her to leave Chicote without anyone connecting her with O'Gorman's disappearance. She had broken the promise and made the mistake that sent her to prison. It wasn't like Alberta to make mistakes. Had she been thinking too much of him and of their future together? Or had she acted out of an unconscious desire to be caught and punished not only for her embezzlements but for her relationship with him? Though she had never voiced her feelings of sexual guilt, he was aware that they were strong in her, and aware, too, that she had known no other man.

His own feelings of guilt were strong, too, but they were assuaged by the hardships and austerity of the life he led. Occasionally, in rare moments of insight, he wondered whether he had chosen such a life in order to make his guilt more bearable. On being awakened each morning by the scurrying rats in the hay or the sharp bite of a flea, the sting of cold or the pangs of hunger, he did not resent any of these things, he used them as excuses to an unseen, unheard accuser: *See me, how miserable I am, see the circumstances I live under, the pain, the hunger, the loneliness, the privation. I have nothing, I am nothing. Isn't this penance enough?*

His long wait for the future had become a way of life to such an extent that he was afraid to think beyond it and reluctant to repeat the past. Though desperate for companionship, he didn't want the members of the colony to come back. The only ones he had really liked would not be coming back anyway: Mother Pureza, whose wild flights of fancy amused him, and Sister Blessing, who had looked after him when he was ill. He did not miss Sister Contrition's querulous whining, Brother Steady Heart's boasts of his success with the ladies, Brother Crown's sour self-righteousness, or the Master's harangues with the devil.

As time passed, his memory began to fail about certain events. He had only a dim recollection of the colony's last day at the Tower. His mind had been numbed by the sudden shock of seeing Haywood again and realizing that all the careful planning and the long wait had been for nothing. He had not intended to kill Haywood, only to reason with him.

But Haywood wasn't reasonable. "I'm going to stay here, I'm going to hound your footsteps every minute of every day until I discover where you've hidden the money."

He was too dazed even to attempt a denial. "How—how did you find me? Alberta told you?"

"I followed Quinn's car from Chicote. No, Alberta didn't tell me, lover-boy. I give her credit for one thing, anyway, obstinacy. Once a month for over five years I've coaxed and bullied and nagged her to tell me the truth so I could help her. I suspected something right from the first, ever since she told me she'd given some of my clothes to a transient. She gave them to you, didn't she?"

"Yes."

"You couldn't take the chance of buying a new set of clothes that might later be reported as missing from your wardrobe. Oh, you two were very careful, all right. Everything was thought out in advance, everything went into the great scheme except plain ordinary common sense. Her planning must have begun months in advance. She started going out alone every night, to the movies, lectures, concerts, so that when she went out in her car that particular night no one would think anything of it. She started to buy the Racing Form, always from the same newsstand, laying the groundwork for the gambling story in case she was ever caught embezzling and questioned about where the money went. All that planning, and for what? The poor woman sits in a prison cell, still dreaming great dreams. Only they're not going to come true."

"Yes they are. I love her, I'll wait for her forever."

"You may have to."

"What does that mean?"

"It means," Haywood said, "that when her parole hearing comes up in a few weeks, some people aren't going to believe her story of gambling away the money any more than I believe it. And if they don't believe it, if they consider her uncooperative, she'll have to serve her full term. This is where I enter the picture. I want that money. Now."

"But—"

"All of it. When I have it, Alberta will know the game's up and she'll be forced to tell the parole board the truth and make restitution to the bank. Then she'll be a free woman, free of prison and free of you, too, I hope to God."

"You don't understand. Alberta and I—"

"Don't start prattling about love and romance. Big romance. Big deal. Hell, I don't even think you're a man. Maybe that's the reason behind the whole thing: Alberta isn't quite a woman and you're not quite a man, so you decided to play the star-crossed lovers' game. The game had a big advantage for both of you. It kept you apart for the present while allowing you to believe in a future of togetherness."

He couldn't remember pushing Haywood over the railing, but he remembered the sight and sound of him as he fell, a great grey flapping bird uttering its final cry. He didn't wait to see Haywood land. He hurried back to his room at the third level of the Tower where Brother Steady Heart had sent him to rest after hoeing in the vegetable garden. He waited until Mother Pureza ran out and the Master went after her. Then, walking like a robot that had been given orders, he went directly to the barn to get the rat poison.

He had only one vivid recollection of Sister Blessing's death, her scream as the first pain struck her. Sometimes a bird made a noise like it and the bearded man would turn numb and fall to the ground, as though he believed Sister Blessing had returned to life as a bird to haunt him. These were the worst times, when he doubted his own sanity and imagined that the creatures of the forest were human beings. The mockingbird, arrogant and loud-mouthed, was Brother Crown. The tiny green-backed finch, clowning among the tall weeds, was Mother Pureza. The crow, strong and hungry, was Brother Light. The band-tailed pigeon, haughty in a treetop, was the Master. The mourning dove, sounding the sorrows of the world, was Sister Contrition, and the scrub jay was Haywood, criticizing him, taunting him.

"Creep!" it squawked.

"Shut up."

"Cheap creep."

"I am a man."

"Cheap creep."

"I am a man! I am a man! I am a man!"

But the jay always had the last word, *creep.*

One morning he was awakened in the hayloft by the rustling of wood rats on the roof. Even before he opened his eyes he was aware that during the night a change had taken place: the colony had returned.

He lay still and listened. He heard no voices, no bustle of activity or familiar coughing of the truck engine, but there was another sound he used to know well, a quick, spasmodic drumming. It was Karma playing with the typewriter in the storage shed.

Forgetting for once his ritual of self-effacement, he climbed down the crude ladder and ran between the trees toward the storage shed. He was halfway there when the noise stopped and an acorn woodpecker flapped out of a sugar pine with a flash of black and white.

He shook his fist at it and cursed it, but his rage was for himself and the trick his mind had played on him. He realized the typewriter wasn't in the shed, the sheriff's men had taken it away along with a lot of other stuff. Well, it wouldn't do them any good, they couldn't prove it belonged to him, they still didn't know he was the one they were looking for, they still—

"Karma."

He spoke the name aloud and there was more of a curse in it than what he had screamed at the woodpecker because this time the anger was aggravated by fear.

He went numb as he remembered something he had forgotten about the last day at the Tower, Karma following him out to the shed.

"Are you taking the typewriter with you, Brother?"

"No."

"May I have it?"

"Stop bothering me."

"Please, may I have it?"

"No. Now leave me alone. I'm in a hurry."

"When I go to my aunt's house, I can get it all fixed up good as new. Please let me have it, Brother."

"All *right,* if you'll shut up about it."

"Thank you very much," she said solemnly. "I'll never forget this, never in my whole life."

I'll never forget this. They were simple words of gratitude, at the time. Now, recurring to his mind, they were enlarged and distorted. *I'll never forget this* had become *I'll tell everyone the typewriter belonged to you.*

"Karma!"

The name rang through the trees, and through the trees he followed it.

24

THE LONG-DISTANCE call came just before noon on Saturday. Quinn was puttering around his apartment waiting for Martha to arrive from Chicote. He had arranged to spend the day on the beach with her and the two children, swimming and sunning. But a high thin fog obscured the sun as efficiently as a layer of steel, and from his window Quinn looked out on a deserted beach and a grim grey sea. He was trying to decide on an alternate plan when the phone rang.

Half expecting that Martha had changed her mind about coming, he picked up the phone. "Hello."

"I have a person-to-person call for Mr. Joe Quinn."

"Quinn speaking."

"Here's your party. Go ahead, please."

Then Karma's voice, tremulous and quick. "I said I wasn't ever going to phone you, Mr. Quinn. I even tore up your card, but I remembered the number on it and—well, I'm scared. And I can't tell my aunt because she's not here, and even if she were I couldn't tell her because I want the message from my mother and my aunt won't let me have anything to do with her anymore."

"Take it easy, Karma. Now what's this about a message from your mother?"

"Brother Tongue called me a few minutes ago and said he had a very important message for me from my mother and that he wanted to deliver it in person."

"Where?"

"Here at the house."

"How did he find out where you were?"

"Oh, he knows about my aunt. I often mentioned her. Anyway, I told him he couldn't come here because my aunt was home, which was a lie, she's working on her garden-club display for the flower show. Chrysanthemums and pampas grass with a hidden electric fan to keep the grass blowing. It's going to be very pretty."

"I'm sure it is," Quinn said. "Why didn't Brother Tongue just give you the message over the telephone?"

"He said he promised my mother he'd see me personally. To report on how I am, etcetera, I guess, though he didn't say that."

"Was his call a local one?"

"Yes, he's in town. He's coming to the house this afternoon at four o'clock; I told him my aunt would be away by that time. I thought I'd better phone you about it because you said if anything at all happened involving any member of the colony I was to let you know."

"I'm glad you did. Listen carefully now, Karma. Does it seem likely to you that your mother would choose Brother Tongue to deliver an important message to you?"

"No." After a moment she added, with a child's candor, "I always thought they hated each other. Naturally we weren't supposed to hate, but some of us did anyway."

"All right, let's assume there is no message, that Brother Tongue has an entirely different reason for wanting to see you. Can you guess what it might be?"

"No."

"Perhaps it's something quite trivial to you but not to him."

"I can't think of anything," she said slowly. "Unless he wants his silly old typewriter back. Well, he can have it. My aunt bought me a brand new portable for my birthday last month. It's a grey and pink—"

"Wait a minute. Brother Tongue gave you an old typewriter?"

"Not exactly *gave* it to me. I talked him out of it."

"It belonged to him?"

"Yes."

"And he kept it in the storage shed?"

"Yes. I used to go out there and fool around with it until the ink dried up and the ribbon broke and I didn't have any more paper anyway. I was a mere child then."

"Why are you so sure it belonged to Brother Tongue?"

"Because it was how I first met him. We were living in the San Gabriel Mountains and I was exploring around when I heard a funny noise like a drum. Brother Tongue was on the back porch of his shack, typing, only he wasn't Brother Tongue then. It's funny, if it hadn't been for me hearing his typewriter he would never have become Brother Tongue."

Quinn heard the front door of his apartment open and Martha's quick light step as she crossed the room, he spoke hurriedly into the phone: "Listen, Karma. Stay right where you are. Lock the doors and don't open any of them until I get there. I'm driving right down."

"Why?"

"I have some questions to ask Brother Tongue."

"Do you think that maybe my mother really gave him a message for me?"

"No, I think he wants his typewriter back."

"Why should he? It's so old and broken-down, he couldn't use it for anything."

"No, but the police could. That typewriter was in the back seat of O'Gorman's car the night he was murdered. I'm telling you this because I want you to realize he's a dangerous man."

"I'm scared."

"You don't have to be scared, Karma. When he comes at four o'clock I'll be in the house with you."

"Promise?"

"Promise."

"I believe you," she said gravely. "You kept your other promise about the acne lotion."

It seemed to Quinn, as he hung up, a very long time ago, in a different world.

He went into the front room. Martha was standing at the window, looking out at the sea the way she always did when she came to the apartment, as though the sea was a miracle to her after the parched earth of Chicote.

She said, without turning, "So it's not ended yet."

"No."

"Will it go on forever, Joe?"

"Don't talk like that." He put his arms around her and pressed his mouth against her neck. "Where are the kids?"

"Staying with the neighbors."

"They didn't want to see me?"

"Yes, they did. It was a real sacrifice for them to miss a day with you on the beach."

"And just what was the sacrifice for?"

"Us," she said with a faint smile. "Richard got the idea I would like to be alone with you for a change."

"And would you?"

"Yes."

"He's a very perceptive boy, our Richard."

She turned and gazed earnestly up into his eyes. "Do you really feel that way, that he's our Richard?"

"Yes. Our Richard, our Sally."

"You make it sound as though we'll all live happily ever after—"

"We will."

"—without any problems."

"With lots of problems," he said. "But with lots of solutions, too, if we love and respect each other. And I think we do, don't you?"

"Yes." Doubt was evident in her voice, it always was, but each time they met, the doubt was becoming weaker, and he believed that eventually it would disappear entirely.

"There are times," he added, "when you'll think of O'Gorman and I won't measure up."

"That's not true."

"Yes. And other times when the children will resent any discipline or advice from me because I'm not their real father. There will be disagreements, money problems—"

"Don't go on." She pressed her fingertips against his mouth. "I've thought of all those things, Joe."

"All right then, we both have. We won't be walking into marriage with our eyes closed. Why do you hesitate?"

"I don't want to make another mistake."

"Are you telling me O'Gorman was a mistake?"

"Yes."

"Because it's true or because you think I want to hear it?"

"It's true," she said, and her shoulders beneath his hand went suddenly tense. "Hindsight's not as good as foresight but it serves a purpose. The marriage was my idea, really, not Patrick's. My nesting instinct was so strong that it smothered my rationality. I married Patrick in order to raise a family, he married me because—well, I suppose there were lots of reasons but the main one was that he didn't have the strength to oppose or displease me. Now that I know he's dead, I can be more objective, not only about him but about myself. The basic fault of our marriage was too much interdependence on each other. He was dependent on me and I was dependent on his dependence. No wonder he loved birds, he must often have felt like a caged bird himself . . . What's the matter, Joe?"

"Nothing."

"But there is, I can feel it. Please tell me."

"I can't. Not right now, anyway."

"All right," she said lightly. "Some other time."

He wished some other time would be a long way off, but he knew it wouldn't. It was waiting around the corner and he could already see its shadow.

He said, "I just made a pot of coffee. Would you like some?"

"No thanks. If we're to be in L.A. by four o'clock, we'd better start now in case we run into a traffic tie-up."

"We?"

"Well, I didn't drive all the way down here just to see you for ten minutes."

"Listen, Martha."

"I'll be listening but I won't hear, not if you're going to try to stand me up."

"It's not a question of standing you up. Karma's phone call took me by complete surprise. I don't know what's behind it. Perhaps nothing, perhaps Brother Tongue actually has a message for her from her mother. But in case things aren't going to be that simple, I'd prefer not to have you around."

"I'm pretty good in an emergency."

"Even ones involving yourself?"

"Especially those," she said with a tinge of bitterness. "I've had a lot of experience."

"Then you've made up your mind to come with me."

"If you don't object."

"And if I do?"

"Please don't. Please."

"I have to," he said patiently. "Because I love you, I must steer you away from trouble when I can."

"I thought we were going to share trouble, going to have lots of problems but lots of solutions, too. Was that all just so much talk, Joe?"

"I'm trying to warn you, Martha, I'm trying to tell you something and you won't listen."

"Don't be afraid for me. It makes me feel like half a woman, the way my fears for Patrick must have made him feel like half a man. If you see me walking in front of a speeding bus, by all means yell a warning or pull me back. But this—this is wispy, unreal. What harm will it do me to go to Karma's house with you? The girl might need looking after, she's only a child and in a frightening situation. Don't shut me up in a closet when I could be of some use."

"All right," he said with a noise that was almost a groan, "step out of the closet, ma'am."

"Thank you, sir. You'll never regret this decision."

"Won't I."

"You sound so funny, Joe. What's really the matter? What's on your mind?"

"I'm wishing," he said, "that it was a larger closet so there'd be room for both of us."

25

HE WALKED ALONG the city streets stopping every now and then to focus his eyes on the sky as if he expected to see some of his companions from the forest, the bold black and white flash of an acorn woodpecker, the blurry blue of a band tail, the rufous flapping of a flicker. But all he saw was an occasional sparrow on a telephone wire or a pigeon on a rooftop.

He had an intermittent fantasy about all the city people turning into birds. On the roads and freeways cars would stop, suddenly and forever, and birds would fly up out of the windows. From factories, office buildings, houses, hotels, apartments, from doorways, chimneys, patios, gardens, sidewalks, the birds would come soaring, gliding, fluttering, swooping, trilling, twittering, whistling, whooping, in a riot of color and movement and sound. One bird was larger, grander, louder than all the rest. It was a golden eagle, himself.

The fantasy grew in his mind like a bubble, and burst. No cars stopped on the freeway. People remained people, wingless, hapless, and the golden eagle was grounded on the sweltering sidewalk, no different from the rest, at the mercy of the tyrant gravity.

For too long he had been out of contact with human beings. Even the old ones frightened him and the young ones he hurried past, expecting them to jeer at his robe and shaved head and bare feet. Then he caught sight of himself in the window of a little neighborhood grocery store and he realized they would have no reasons to jeer at him now. He looked like any ordinary man. During his weeks in the forest his hair had grown in, curly and black with touches of grey. He had had it trimmed in a barber shop and his beard shaved off, and bought the clothes he was wearing in a men's wear store, grey suit and tie, white shirt, and black leather moccasins which were beginning to pinch his toes. He was no longer Brother Tongue. He was a nameless man walking along a city street, his image unreflected in the blank eyes of strangers, his presence unmarked by any show of interest or curiosity. He was nobody, noticed by nobody.

He went into the grocery store to ask how to get to Greengrove Avenue where Karma lived. The proprietress told him, without looking up from her paper.

He said, "Thank you very much, ma'am."

"Huh."

"I'm sure I'll be able to find it. Hot day, isn't it?"

"Huh."

"Do you happen to have the time?"

"Hapestry."

"I beg your pardon. I didn't quite catch—"

"You deaf? You for'n? It's hapestry."

"Thank you." *No, I am neither deaf nor foreign. I am a golden eagle in disguise, you fat-bellied pigeon.*

Half-past three. He had plenty of time. As he turned the next corner he put his right hand in his pocket and felt the warm smooth bone of the razor handle. The razor was no longer sharp enough to shave with, but a man's whiskers were tougher than a girl's throat. Which was a funny thing, so funny that, before he could swallow it or choke it back, a titter escaped his mouth. It was the sound of a little bird, not the animal bark of a golden eagle, and he wished he had not heard it. It shook his confidence, drained the strength out of his legs, so that he had to stop and lean against a lamppost for a moment to steady himself.

From the bench at the bus stop nearby, three young girls eyed him suspiciously as if they saw, sticking out from under his new suit, the tattered grey robe of Brother Tongue. Although he hated them, he felt he had to appease them in some way, make them accept him.

He said, "Hot day, isn't it?"

One of them stared at him, one giggled, one turned away.

"On a hot day like this it pays to have cool thoughts."

There was another silence. Then the tallest of the girls said primly, "We're not allowed to speak to strange men."

"But I'm not a strange man. Do I look strange? Why, no, I look quite ordinary, common. That's who I am, the common man. There are thousands of me—"

"Come on, Laura, Jessie. Member what mom said."

"—going to work every day, never having quite enough money, never sure, never safe, never free like the birds, but always hoping things will be evened up a little in heaven. Only it's a long wait, a very long wait."

He knew the girls were gone by now and he was addressing an empty bench, but he knew, too, that this must be a common procedure for the common man: when no one would listen to him he had to talk to empty benches, to silent walls and ceilings, deaf trees, blank mirrors, closed doors.

He started walking again. The neighborhood grew richer, the lawns greener, the fences higher, yet the houses were more deserted-looking, as if the wealthy had built them for show and then gone somewhere else to live. Only now and then did a door slam, a voice speak, a curtain move. *They're in there*, he thought. *They're in there, all right, but they're hiding. They're afraid of me, the common man.*

When he reached Greengrove Avenue he stopped for a minute, standing on his right foot to ease his left, then on his left to ease his right. It seemed to him that he had been walking all day and with each step his shoes had shrunk a little. He wondered how many common men had been walking all day in shrinking shoes on their way to commit a murder. Probably quite a few. Probably a lot more than people realized. He was doing nothing really unusual. Besides, Karma had taken her vows of poverty and renunciation; rich living would ruin her chances of walking the smooth and golden streets of heaven. He would be doing her a favor by saving her from her own folly.

Sometimes, when he thought of his years of listening to and obeying the Master, his mind rebelled and dismissed the Master as a fraud and the Brothers and Sisters as his dupes, but these occasions were infrequent. Constant repetition had left a deep imprint on him. He couldn't efface it as he had effaced the imprint of his body in the hayloft, he couldn't bury it as he had buried his garbage, or cover it with pine needles like the ashes of his fires. Especially here in the city, the material world looked evil to him, the gaudy men and painted women wore the brand of the devil. Rich houses contained sick souls, and unbelievers rode in big cars on wide streets to a large hell.

The Master's brand was on him, and he realized, in the back of his mind, that this was what the girls on the bench had seen, not the grey robe of Brother Tongue sticking out from under the new suit. They had spotted the Master's brand, and, while not recognizing it, they had become instantly aware that he was not a common man at all but a strange one on a strange mission. Although the girls had been gone for some time, he quickened his pace as if to get away from their critical eyes.

The minutes passed, and the houses. Some bore numbers only, others had numbers and names. Number 1295 was identified by a name plate on a miniature wrought iron lamppost: Mrs. Harley Baxter Wood. Like many of the other houses it looked deserted, but he knew it was not. On the telephone Karma had sounded suspicious at first, but her suspicion had turned into curiosity, and her curiosity into eagerness. He knew she had a deep attachment to her mother, in spite of their skirmishes; she would be waiting for a message from her.

He ignored the door chime and tapped lightly on the diamond-shaped panes of glass with his knuckles. It was more like the signal of a friend than the knock of a stranger. It remained unanswered, and yet he had a strong feeling that Karma was there, on the other side of the door. He even fancied he could hear her breathing, very quickly and nervously and vulnerably, the way his little bird had breathed just before it dropped its head and closed its eyes and died in his hand. Later he had dug a grave for it under a manzanita tree and then he had taken an axe and smashed its cage into pieces. He could remember his wild excitement as the axe fell on the wire bars, as if it had been he himself who had been a prisoner inside them and the blows he struck were for freedom. When his excitement had passed he threw the remnants of the cage into a ravine, like a murderer trying to conceal the evidence of his violence.

"Karma?"

Yes, he could hear her breathing.

"It's me, Brother Tongue. You don't recognize me, is that the trouble? Don't be concerned over a few outward changes. It's really me. Come, take a look, see for yourself, you silly girl."

He pressed his mouth against the crack of the door.

"Come on out, Karma. I have a very important message for you from your mother."

She spoke finally, in a thin, quavering voice. "You can tell it to me from there."

"No, I can't."

"I don't want to—to come out."

"Are you afraid, is that it? Bless my soul, you have nothing to fear from poor old Brother Tongue. Why, we've been friends for years, Karma. I'm like an uncle to you. Didn't I give you my most prized possession, the typewriter?"

"It wasn't yours to give," she said. "You stole it from O'Gorman's car."

"You're calling me a thief? It was *mine*, I tell you. It belonged to *me*."

"I know where it came from."

"Someone's been feeding you lies, you stupid girl, and you've been swallowing them like candy. Nobody knows the truth except me, and of course I can't tell you with a door between us. Open it, Karma."

"I can't. My aunt's here. She's upstairs in her room."

It was such a feeble story he almost laughed out loud, and even if it were true, what help would an aunt be, with her woman's throat softer than a man's whiskers?

He said softly, "What a little liar you are, and a mischief-maker. When I think of the times you teased me, tried to goad me into talking—Brother Tongueless, you called me, Tongue, Tongue, who's got your tongue?—remember that, Karma? But I didn't break down, did I? I couldn't afford to. People with secrets must learn not to talk, and I learned. I learned, and then I betrayed myself in sleep. I have always betrayed myself in some way. What irony that I should do it in sleep, when the issue was life itself."

She said nothing, and for a moment he had the sensation of being back in the forest, alone, trying to explain himself to all the living things that couldn't or didn't care to hear.

A police patrol car cruised by the house. He stood up straight, and tried to look grave and dignified like a minister paying a Sunday afternoon call on a member of the church. He had always fancied himself as a minister. How easy it would be, advising other people what to do and how to act, obeying a few simple rules of conduct for yourself and memorizing the odd text or two.

The police car worried him, though. He wondered whether the three young girls he had met at the bus stop had gone home and told their mother about him and the mother had phoned the police. Then the two men in the patrol car might be looking for him. Perhaps this time they had not noticed him, but if they came around again— No, that was nonsense. Why should they come around again? The girls' mother had no reason to report him. It was not as if he had accosted them or tried to pick them up or offered them candy. The silly girls, their silly mother, they had no reason, no reason—

"The first patrol car's spotted him," Quinn said. "Stall him a few minutes more, Karma."

"I can't." Even with Quinn beside her and Martha's supporting arm around her shoulders, the girl was afraid because she knew they were afraid, too, and she could not understand their fear. It seemed much deeper and more terrible than the fear they would have of a mere man, however dangerous. She looked at the white line around Quinn's mouth and the desperation in Martha's eyes and she repeated, "I can't. I don't know what to say."

"Encourage him to talk."

"What about?"

"Himself."

Karma raised her voice. "Where have you been hiding, Brother Tongue?"

The question annoyed him. It implied that he was a criminal, forced to hide out, instead of an intelligent man who had chosen the forest of his own free will as the best place to live.

"I can't stand here all afternoon," he said irritably. "Your mother's waiting for us."

"Where?" Karma said.

"At a friend's house. She's very ill, she may be dying. She asked me to bring you to her."

"What's the matter with her?"

"Nobody knows. She refuses to call a doctor. If you come with me, perhaps you can persuade her to seek medical attention. Will you?"

"How far are we going?"

"Practically just around the corner." *Not a street corner, though. A corner of time you pass only once. For you there will be no return.* "Your mother's illness is critical, child. You'd better hurry."

"All right. I'll be ready in a minute."

"Aren't you going to ask me to step inside to wait?"

"I can't. You might wake my aunt, and she wouldn't let me go with you because she hates the Tower people, she thinks they might try and take me away. She says they might—"

"Stop chattering, girl, and get ready."

He waited, watching the street for the return of the police car, counting off the seconds as they passed through his mind's eye like little toy soldiers, saluting, calling out their names to him: one, sir, two, sir, three, sir, four, sir, five, sir, six, sir, seven, sir.

Respectful creatures. Always called him sir, briskly but affectionately. Yes, they liked their genial general. They knew he had once been a common man, had risen from the ranks to become the commander of time and wear stars on his sleeves. But of course the stars were invisible, it was still light, still afternoon. It was only at night that the stars swooped down from the sky to perch on his sleeves.

A hundred and fourteen, sir. A hundred and fifteen, sir. A hundred and—

Suddenly an alarming change took place. The toy soldiers switched uniforms and became policemen in blue serge. They were no longer saluting him, no longer calling out their names, they were demanding his name, instead, in coarse disrespectful voices.

"What's your name?"

"Commander," he said.

"Commander what?"

"I am the commander of time."

"You are, eh?"

"It's a specialized job. I decide on the times that things are to happen to people, to animals and birds, to the trees of the forest—"

"Okay, Commander. Let's go and review some troops."

"This isn't the proper time."

"I think it is."

"But that's *my* decision."

"Let's go, Commander. We've got a real mixed-up clock down at the station. We want you to talk to it, straighten it out, see?"

It struck him suddenly then, the realization that these men were not policemen at all. They were agents of a foreign power sent to take over the country by disrupting the time schedule and kidnapping the commander.

The door of the house opened and a man he recognized as Quinn came out, and a woman who looked familiar to him although he couldn't remember her name.

He called out to Quinn, "Don't let them take me away! They're enemy agents, I tell you. They're going to overthrow the government!"

Quinn stepped back, as if the words had hit him in the stomach and knocked him off-balance, and the woman with him began to scream, "Patrick, Patrick! Oh, my God, Patrick!"

He stared at her, wondering why she looked so familiar to him and who Omigod Patrick was.

THE FIEND

For Jewell and Russ Kriger,
with deep affection, as always

The fiend with all his comrades
Fell then from heaven above,
Through as long as three nights and days . . .

Caedmon

1

IT WAS THE end of August and the children were getting bored with their summer freedom. They had spent too many hours at the mercy of their own desires. Their legs and arms were scratched, bruised, blistered with poison oak; sea water had turned their hair to straw, and the sun had left cruel red scars across their cheekbones and noses. All the trees had been climbed, the paths explored, the cliffs scaled, the waves conquered. Now, as if in need and anticipation of the return of rules, they began to hang around the school playground.

So did the man in the old green coupé. Every day at noon Charlie Gowen brought his sandwiches and a carton of milk and parked across the road from the playground, separated from the swings and the jungle gym by a steel fence and some scraggly geraniums. Here he sat and ate and drank and watched.

He knew he shouldn't be there. It was dangerous to be seen near such a place.

"—where children congregate. You understand that, Gowen?"

"I think so, sir."

"Do you know what *congregate* means?"

"Well, not exactly."

"Don't give me that dumb act, Gowen. You spent two years at college."

"I was sick then. You don't retain things when you're sick."

"Then I'll spell it out for you. You are to stay away from any place frequented by children—parks, certain beach areas, Saturday afternoon movies, school playgrounds—"

The conditions were impossible, of course. He couldn't turn and run in the opposite direction every time he saw a child. They were all over, everywhere, at any hour. Once even at midnight when he was walking by himself he'd come across a boy and a girl, barely twelve. He told them gruffly to go home or he'd call the police. They disappeared into the darkness; he never saw them again even though he took the same route at the same time every night after that for a week. His conscience gnawed at him. He loved children, he shouldn't have

295

threatened the boy and girl, he should have found out why they were on the streets at such an hour and then escorted them home and lectured their parents very sternly about looking after their kids.

He started on his second sandwich. The first hadn't filled the void in his stomach and neither would the second. He might as well have been eating clouds or pieces of twilight, though he couldn't express it that way to his brother, Benjamin, who made the lunches for both of them. He had to be very careful what he said to Benjamin. The least little fanciful thought or offbeat phrase and Ben would get the strained, set look on his face that reminded Charlie of their dead mother. Then the questions would start: Eating clouds, Charlie? Pieces of twilight? Where do you get screwy ideas like that? You're feeling all right, aren't you? Have you phoned Louise lately? Don't you think she might want to hear from you? Look, Charlie, is something bothering you? You're sure not? . . .

He knew better, by this time, than to mention anything about clouds or twilight. He had said simply that morning, "I need more food, Ben."

"Why?"

"Why? Well, because I'm hungry. I work hard. I was wondering, maybe some doughnuts and a couple of pieces of pie—"

"For yourself?"

"Sure, for myself. Who else? Oh, now I see what you're thinking about. That was over two years ago, Ben, and the Mexican kid was half starved. Everything would have been fine if that busybody woman hadn't interfered. The kid ate the sandwich, it filled him up, he felt good for a change. My God, Ben, is it a crime to feed starving children?"

Ben didn't answer. He merely closed the lid of the lunchbox on the usual two sandwiches and carton of milk, and changed the subject. "Louise called last night when you were out. She's coming over after supper. I'll slip out to a movie and leave you two alone for a while."

"Is it? Is it a crime, Ben?"

"Louise is a fine young woman. She could be the making of a man."

"If I were a starving child and someone gave me food—"

"Shut up, Charlie. You're not starving, you're overweight. And you're far from being a child. You're thirty-two years old."

It was not the command that shut Charlie up, it was the sudden cruel reference to his age. He seldom thought about it on his own because he felt so young, barely older than the little girl hanging upside down from the top bar of the jungle gym.

She was about nine. Having watched them all impartially now for two weeks, Charlie had come to like her the best.

She wasn't the prettiest, and she was so thin Charlie could have spanned her waist with his two hands, but there was a certain cockiness about her that both fascinated and worried him. When she tried some daring new trick on the jungle gym she seemed to be challenging gravity and the bars to try and stop her. If she fell—and she often did—she bounced up off the ground as naturally as a ball. Within five seconds she'd be back on the top bar of the jungle gym, pretending nothing had happened, and Charlie's heart, which had stopped, would start to beat again in double time, its rhythm disturbed by relief and anger.

The other children called her Jessie, and so, inside the car with the windows closed, did Charlie.

"Careful, Jessie, careful. Self-confidence is all very well, but bones can be broken, child, even nine-year-old bones. I ought to warn your parents. Where do you live, Jessie?"

The playground counselor, a physical education major at the local college, was refereeing a sixth-grade basketball game. The sun scorched through his crew cut, he was thirsty, and his eyes stung from the dust raised by scuffling feet, but he was as intent on the game as though it were being played in the Los Angeles Coliseum. His name was Scott Roberts, he was twenty, and the children respected him greatly because he could chin himself with one hand and drove a sports car.

He saw the two little girls crossing the field and ignored them as long as possible, which wasn't long, since one of them was crying.

He blew the whistle and stopped the game. "Okay, fellas, take five." And, to the girl who was crying, "What's the matter, Mary Martha?"

"Jessie fell."

"It figures, it figures." Scott wiped the sweat off his forehead with the back of his hand. "If Jessie was the one who fell, why isn't she doing the crying?"

"I couldn't be bothered," Jessie said loftily. She ached in a number of places but nothing short of an amputation could have forced her to tears in front of the sixth-grade boys. She had a crush on three of them; one had even spoken to her. "Mary Martha always cries at things, like sad events on television and people falling."

"How are your hands? Any improvement over last week?"

"They're okay."

"Let me see, Jessie."

"Here, in front of everybody?"

"Right here, in front of everybody who's nosy enough to look."

He didn't even have to glance at the sixth-graders to get his message across. Immediately they all turned away and became absorbed in other things, dribbling the ball, adjusting shoelaces, hitching up shorts, slicking back hair.

Jessie presented her hands and Scott examined them, frowning. The palms were a mass of blisters in every stage of development, some newly formed and still full of liquid, some open and oozing, others covered with layers of scar tissue.

Scott shook his head and frowned. "I told you last week to get your mother to put alcohol on your hands every morning and night to toughen the skin. You didn't do it."

"No."

"Don't you have a mother?"

"Of course. Also a father, and a brother in high school, and an aunt and uncle next door— they're not really blood relations but I call them that because they give me lots of things, etcetera —and heaps of cousins in Canada and New Jersey."

"The cousins are too far away to help," Scott said. "But surely one of the others could put alcohol on your hands for you."

"I could do it myself if I wanted to."

"But you don't want to."

"It stings."

"Wouldn't you prefer a little sting to a big case of blood poisoning?"

Jessie didn't know what blood poisoning was, but for the benefit of the sixth-grade boys she said she wasn't the least bit scared of it. This remark stimulated Mary Martha to relate the entire plot of a medical program she'd seen, in which the doctor himself had blood poisoning and didn't realize it until he went into convulsions.

"By then it was too late?" Jessie said, trying not to sound much interested. "He died?"

"No, he couldn't. He's the hero every week. But he suffered terribly. You should have seen the faces he made, worse than my mother when she's plucking her eyebrows."

Scott interrupted brusquely. "All right, you two, knock it off. The issue is not Mother's eyebrows or Dr. Whoozit's convulsions. It's Jessie's hands. They're a mess and something has to be done."

Flushing, Jessie hid her hands in the pockets of her shorts. While she was playing on the jungle gym she'd hardly noticed the pain, but now, with everyone's attention focused on her, it had become almost unbearable.

Scott was aware of this. He touched her shoulder lightly and the two of them began walking toward the back-exit gate, followed by an excited and perspiring Mary Martha. None of them noticed the green coupé.

"You'd better go home," Scott said. "Take a warm bath, put alcohol on your hands with a piece of cotton, and stay off the jungle gym until you grow some new skin. You'd better tell your mother, too, Jessie."

"I won't have to. If I go home at noon and take a bath she'll think I'm dying."

"Maybe you are," Mary Martha said in a practical voice. "Imagine me with a dying best friend."

"Oh, shut up."

"I'm only trying to help."

"That's the kind of help you ought to save for your best enemy," Scott said and turned to go back to the basketball game.

Out of the corner of his eye he noticed the old green coupé pulling away from the curb. What caught his attention was the fact that, although it was a very hot day, the windows were closed. They were also dirty, so that the driver was invisible and the car seemed to be operating itself. A minute later it turned onto a side street and was out of sight.

So were the two girls.

"We could stop in at my house," Mary Martha said, "for some cinnamon toast to build your strength up."

"My strength is okay, but I wouldn't mind some cinnamon toast. Maybe we could even make it ourselves?"

"No. My mother will be home. She always is."

"Why?"

"To guard the house."

Jessie had asked the same question and been given the same answer quite a few times. She was always left with an incongruous mental picture of Mary Martha's mother sitting large and formidable on the porch with a shotgun across her lap. The real Mrs. Oakley was small and frail and suffered from a number of obscure allergies.

"Why does she have to stay home to guard the house?" Jessie said. "She could just lock the doors."

"Locks don't keep him out."

"You mean your father?"

"I mean my ex-father."

"But you can't have an ex-father. I asked my Aunt Virginia and she said a wife can divorce her husband and then he's an ex-husband. But you can't divorce a father."

"Yes, you can. We already did, my mother and I."

"Did he want you to?"

"He didn't care."

"It would wring my father's heart," Jessie said, "if I divorced him."

"How do you know? Did he ever tell you?"

"No, but I never asked."

"Then you don't know for sure."

The jacaranda trees, for which the street was named, were in full bloom and their falling petals covered lawns and sidewalks, even the road itself, with purple confetti. Some clung to Jessie's short dark hair and to Mary Martha's blonde ponytail.

"I bet we look like brides," Jessie said. "We could pretend—"

"No." Mary Martha began brushing the jacaranda petals out of her hair as if they were lice. "I don't want to."

"You always like pretending things."

"*Sensible* things."

Jessie knew this wasn't true, since Mary Martha's favorite role was that of child spy for the FBI. But she preferred not to argue. The lunch she'd taken to the playground had all been eaten by ten o'clock and she was more than ready for some of Mrs. Oakley's cinnamon toast. The Oakleys lived at 319 Jacaranda Road in a huge redwood house surrounded by live oak and eucalyptus trees. The trees had been planted, and the house built, by Mr. Oakley's parents. When Jessie had first seen the place she'd assumed that Mary Martha's family was terribly rich, but she discovered on later visits that the attic was just full of junk, the four-car garage contained only Mrs. Oakley's little Volkswagen and Mary Martha's bicycle, and some of the upstairs rooms were empty, with not even a chair in them.

Kate Oakley hated the place and was afraid to live in it, but she was even more afraid that, if she sold it, Mr. Oakley would be able by some legal maneuver to get his hands on half of the money. So she had stayed on. By day she stared out at the live oak trees wishing they would die and let a little light into the house, and by night she lay awake listening to the squawking and creaking of eucalyptus boughs, and hoping the next wind would blow them down.

Mary Martha knew how her mother felt about the house and she couldn't understand it. She herself had never lived any other place and never wanted to. When Jessie came over to play, the two girls tried on old clothes in the attic, put on shows in the big garage, rummaged through the cellar for hidden treasure, and, when Mrs. Oakley wasn't looking, climbed the trees or hunted frogs in the creek, pretending the frogs were handsome princes in disguise. None of the princes ever had a chance to become undisguised since Mrs. Oakley always made the girls return the frogs to the creek: *The poor little creatures . . . I'm ashamed of you, Mary Martha, wrenching them away from their homes and families. How would you like it if some enormous giant picked you up and carried you away?"*

The front door of the Oakley house was open but the screen was latched and Mary Martha had to press the door chime. The sound was very faint. Mrs. Oakley had had it muted shortly after Mr. Oakley moved out because sometimes he used to come and stand at the door and keep pressing the chime, demanding admittance.

"If she's not home," Jessie said hopefully, "we could climb the sycamore tree at the back and get over on the balcony of her bedroom and just walk in . . . What's the matter with your doorbell?"

"Nothing."

"Ours is real loud."

"My mother and I don't like loud noises."

Mrs. Oakley appeared, blinking her eyes in the light as if she'd been taking a nap or watching television in a darkened room.

She was small and pretty and very neat in a blue cotton dress she had made herself. Her fair hair was softly waved and hung down to her shoulders and she wore high-heeled shoes without any backs to them. Sometimes, when Jessie was angry at her mother, she compared her unfavorably with Mrs. Oakley: her mother liked to wear sneakers and jeans or shorts, and she often forgot to comb her hair, which was as dark and straight as Jessie's own.

Mrs. Oakley kissed Mary Martha on the forehead. "Hello, lamb." Then she patted Jessie on the shoulder. "Hello, Jessie. My goodness, you're getting big. Each time I see you, I truly swear you've grown another inch."

Whenever Mrs. Oakley said this to her, which was at least once a week, Jessie felt highly complimented. Her own mother said, "Good Lord, do I have to buy you another pair of shoes *already*?" And her brother called her beanpole or toothpick or canary legs.

"I eat a lot," Jessie said modestly. "So does my brother, Mike. My father says he should get double tax exemptions for us."

As soon as she'd made the remark Jessie realized it was a mistake. Mary Martha nudged her in the side with her elbow, and Mrs. Oakley turned and walked away, her sharp heels leaving little dents in the waxed linoleum.

"You shouldn't talk about fathers or taxes," Mary Martha whispered. "But it's okay, because now we won't have to tell her about your hands. She hates the sight of blood."

"I'm not bleeding."

"You might start."

Charlie wrote the name and address on the inside cover of a book of matches: Jessie, 319 Jacaranda Road. He wasn't sure yet what he intended to do with the information; it just seemed an important thing to have, like money in the bank. Perhaps he would find out Jessie's last name and write a letter to her parents, warning them. Dear Mr. and Mrs. X: I have never written an anonymous letter before, but I cannot stand by and watch your daughter take such risks with her delicate bones. Children must be cherished, guarded against the terrible hazards of life, fed good nourishing meals so their bones will be padded and will not break coming into contact with the hard cruel earth. In the name of God, I beg you to protect your little girl . . .

2

FOR MANY YEARS the Oakley house had stood by itself, a few miles west of the small city of San Félice, surrounded by lemon and walnut groves. Most of the groves were gone now, their places taken by subdivisions with fanciful names and low down payments. Into one of these tract houses, a few blocks away from the Oakleys, Jessie had moved a year ago with her family. The Brants had been living in an apartment in San Francisco and they were all delighted by the freedom of having their own private house and plot of land. Like most freedoms, it had its price. David Brant had been forced to renew his acquaintance with pliers and wrenches and fuse boxes, the children were expected to help with the housework, and Ellen Brant had taken over the garden. She bought a book on landscaping and another on Southern California flowers and shrubs, and set out to show the neighbors a thing or two.

Ellen Brant was inexperienced but obstinate. Some of the shrubs had been moved six or seven times and were half dead from too much attention and overfeeding. The creeping fig vine, intended to cover the chimney of the fireplace, refused to creep. The leaves of the jasmine yellowed and dropped from excess dampness, and Ellen, assuming their wilting was due to lack of water, turned on the sprinkling system. Bills from the nursery and the water department ran high but when Dave Brant complained about them Ellen pointed out that she was actually increasing the value of the property. In fact, she didn't know or care much about property values; she simply enjoyed being out-of-doors with the sun warm on her face and the wind smelling mysteriously of the sea.

She was busy snipping dead blossoms off the rosebushes when Jessie arrived home at one o'clock.

Ellen stood up, squinting against the sun and brushing dirt off her denim shorts and bare knees. She was slim and very tanned, like Jessie, and her eyes were the same unusual shade of greyish green.

"What are you doing home so early?" she said, pushing a strand of moist hair off her forehead with the pruning shears. "By the way, you didn't straighten up your room before you left. You know the rules, you helped us write them."

It seemed to Jessie a good time to change the subject as dramatically as possible. "Mary Martha says I may be dying."

"Really? Well, you wouldn't want to be caught dead in a messy room, so up you go. Start moving, kiddo."

"You don't even believe me."

"No."

"I bet if Mary Martha went home and told *her* mother she was dying, there'd be a terrible fuss. I bet there'd be ambulances and doctors and nurses and people screaming—"

"If it will make you feel any better I'll begin screaming right now."

"No! I mean, somebody might hear you."

"That's the general purpose of screaming, isn't it?" Ellen said with a smile. "Come on, let's have it, old girl—what's the matter?"

Jessie exhibited her hands. A dusting of cinnamon hadn't improved their appearance but Ellen Brant showed neither surprise nor dismay. She'd been through the same thing with Jessie's older brother, Mike, a dozen times or more.

She said, "I have the world's climbingest children. Where'd you do this?"

"The jungle gym."

"Well, you go in and fill the washbasin with warm water and start soaking your hands. I'll be with you in a minute. I want to check my record book and see when you had your last tetanus booster shot."

"It was the Fourth of July when I stepped on the stingray at East Beach."

"I hope to heaven you're not going to turn out to be accident-prone."

"What's that?"

"There were at least a thousand people on the beach that afternoon. Only you stepped on a stingray."

Although Jessie knew this was not intended as a compliment, she couldn't help taking it as such. Being the only one of a thousand people to step on a stingray seemed to her quite distinctive, the sort of thing that could never happen to someone like Mary Martha.

Half an hour later she was ensconced on the davenport in the living room, watching a television program and drinking chocolate milk. On her hands she wore a pair of her mother's white gloves, which made her feel very sophisticated if she didn't look too closely at the way they fitted.

The sliding glass door was partly open and she could see her mother out on the lawn talking to Virginia Arlington, who lived next door. Jessie was quite fond of Mrs. Arlington and called her Aunt Virginia, but she hoped both women would stay outside and not interrupt the television movie.

Virginia Arlington's round pink face and plump white arms were moist with perspiration. As she talked she fanned herself with an advertisement she'd just picked up from the mailbox.

Even her voice sounded warm. "I saw Jessie coming home early and I was worried. Is anything the matter?"

"Not really. Her hands are sore from playing too long on the jungle gym."

"Poor baby. She has so much energy she never knows when to stop. She's like you, Ellen. You drive yourself too hard sometimes."

"I manage to survive." She dropped on her knees beside the rosebush again, hoping Virginia would take the hint and leave. She liked Virginia Arlington and appreciated her kindness and generosity, but there were times when Ellen preferred to work undisturbed and without someone reminding her she was driving herself too hard. Virginia had no children, and her husband, Howard, was away on business a great deal; she had a part-time gardener and a cleaning woman twice a week, and to open a can or the garage doors or the car windows, all she had to do was press a button. Ellen didn't envy her neighbors. She knew that if their positions were reversed, she would be doing just as much as she did now and Virginia would be doing as little.

Virginia lingered on, in spite of the sun which she hated and usually managed to avoid. Even five minutes of it made her nose turn pink and her neck break out in a rash. "I have an idea. Why don't I slip downtown and buy Jessie a couple of games?—you know, something absorbing that will keep her quiet."

"I thought Howard was home today."

"He is, but he's still asleep. I could be back by the time he wakes up."

"I appreciate your offer, naturally," Ellen said, "but you've already bought Jessie so many toys and books and games—"

"That won't spoil her. I was reading in a magazine just this morning that buying things for children doesn't spoil them unless those things are a substitute for something else."

Ellen had read the same magazine. "Love."

"Yes."

"Jessie gets plenty of love."

"I know. That's my whole point. If she's already loved, the little items I buy her can't harm her."

Ellen hesitated. Some of the items hadn't been so little—a ten-gear Italian bicycle, a cashmere sweater, a wristwatch—but she didn't want to seem ungrateful. "All right, go ahead if you like. But please don't spend too much money. Jessie might get the idea that she deserves an expensive gift every time something happens to her. Life doesn't work out that way."

There was a minute of strained silence between the two women, like the kind that comes after a quarrel over an important issue. It bothered Ellen. There had been no quarrel, not even a real disagreement, and the issue was hardly important, a two-dollar game for Jessie.

Virginia said softly, "I haven't offended you, have I, El? I mean, maybe you think I was implying that Jessie didn't have enough toys and things." Virginia's pale blue eyes were anxious and the tip of her nose was already starting to turn red. "I'd feel terrible if you thought that."

"Well, I don't."

"You're absolutely sure?"

"Don't go on about it, Virginia. You want to buy Jess a game, so buy it."

"We could pretend it was from you and Dave."

"I don't believe in pretending to my children. They're subjected to enough phoniness in the ordinary course of events."

From one of the back windows of the Arlington house a man's voice shouted, "Virgie! Virgie!"

"Howard's awake," Virginia said hastily. "I'll go and make his breakfast and maybe slip downtown while he's eating. Tell Jessie I'll be over later on."

"All right."

Virginia walked across the lawn and down her own driveway. It was bordered on each side with a low privet hedge and small round clumps of French marigolds. Everything in the yard, as in the house, was so neat and orderly that Virginia felt none of it belonged to her. The house was Howard's and the cleaning woman's, and the yard was the gardener's. Virginia was a guest and she had to act like a guest, polite and uncritical.

Only the dog, a large golden retriever named Chap, was Virginia's. She had wanted a small dog, one she could cuddle and hold on her lap, and when Howard brought Chap home from one of his trips she had felt cheated. Chap was already full-grown then and weighed ninety pounds, and the first time she was left alone with him she was frightened. His bark was loud and ferocious; when she fed him he nearly gobbled her hand; when she took him out on a leash he'd dragged her around the block like a horse pulling a wheelless carriage. She had gradually come to realize that his bark was a bluff, and that he had been underfed by his previous owners and never taught to obey any orders.

From the beginning the dog had attached himself to Virginia, as if he knew she needed his company and protection. He was indifferent to Howard, despised the cleaning woman, and held the gardener in line with an occasional growl. He slept inside at night and kept prowlers away not only from Virginia but from the immediate neighbors as well.

Howard had gotten up and let the dog out. Chap came bounding down the driveway, his plumed tail waving in circles.

Virginia leaned down and pressed her cheek against the top of his huge golden head. "You silly boy, why the big greeting? I've only been away for ten minutes."

Through the open kitchen window Howard overheard her and said, "A likely story. You've probably been over at the Brants' gabbing with Ellen all morning."

She knew he intended it mainly, though not entirely, as a joke. Without replying, she went in the back door, through the service porch to the kitchen. The dog followed her, still making a fuss, as if she were the one, not Howard, who'd been gone for two weeks.

Howard had made coffee and was frying some bacon on the grill in the middle of the stove. When he was home he liked to mess around the kitchen because it was a pleasant contrast to sitting in restaurants, being served food he didn't enjoy. He was a fussy eater for such a large man.

A head taller than Virginia, he had to lean way down to kiss her on the mouth. "You're a sight for sore eyes, Virgie."

"Am I?" Virginia said. "The bacon's burning."

"Let it. Did you miss me?"

"Yes."

"Is that all, yes?"

"I missed you very much, Howard."

He flipped the bacon expertly with a spatula, all four slices at once. "Still want me to quit my job, Virgie?"

"I haven't brought that subject up for over a year."

"I know. It makes me wonder how you've been spending your time while I'm away."

"If you want to know, ask me."

"I'm asking you."

"All right." Virginia sat down at the kitchen table, her pale pretty hands folded in her lap. "I start off each day with a champagne breakfast. After that, it's luncheon with the girls, with plenty of drinks, of course. We play bridge for high stakes all afternoon and end up at a cocktail party. Then I have dinner at a nightclub and carouse until dawn with a group of merry companions."

"Sounds rigorous," Howard said, smiling. "How do you manage to stay so beautiful?"

"Howard—"

"Put a couple of slices of bread in the toaster, will you?"

"Howard, were you serious when you asked me how I spent my time?"

"No."

"I think you were. Perhaps you'd like me to keep a diary. It would make fascinating reading. Juicy items like how I took some clothes to the cleaners, borrowed a book from the library, bought groceries—"

"Cut it out, will you, Virgie? Something popped into my head and I said it and I shouldn't have. I'm sorry. Let's forget it."

"I'll try."

He brought his plate of bacon to the table and sat down opposite her. "I hope I didn't wake you when I came in this morning. Chap made a hell of a fuss, he almost convinced me I had the wrong house. You'd think he'd know me by this time."

"He's a good watchdog," she said, adding silently: *You'd think I, too, would know you by this time, Howard, but I don't.* "How was the trip?"

"Hot—103 degrees in Bakersfield, ninety-five in L.A."

"It's been hot here, too."

"I have an idea. Why don't we head for the beach this afternoon? We'll loll around on the sand, have a walk and a swim—"

"It sounds nice, Howard, but I'm afraid I can't. You know how badly I sunburn."

"You could wear a wide straw hat and we'll take along the umbrella from the patio table."

"No."

He stared at her across the table, his eyes puzzled. "That was a pretty definite no, Virginia. Are you still sore at me?"

"Of course not. It's just that—well, the umbrella's no good anymore. It was torn. I threw it away."

"It was practically brand-new. How did it get torn?"

"The wind. I intended to tell you. We had a big wind here Tuesday afternoon, a Santa Ana from the desert. I was downtown when it started and by the time I got home the umbrella was already damaged."

"Why didn't you take it to one of those canvas shops to have it repaired?"

"The spokes were bent, too. You should have seen it, Howard. It looked as if it had been in a hurricane."

"The bougainvillea beside the garage usually blows over in a Santa Ana. I didn't notice anything wrong with it."

"Salvador may have tied it up."

She knew this was safe enough. Salvador, who spoke or pretended to speak only Spanish, wasn't likely to deny or confirm anything. He would merely smile his stupid silver-toothed smile and crinkle up his wise old eyes and go right on working. *You speak, señor, but if I do not hear you, you do not exist.*

There had been no Santa Ana on Tuesday afternoon, just a fresh cool breeze blowing in from the ocean. Virginia had not been downtown, she'd been sitting on the front porch watching Jessie and Mary Martha roller-skate up and down the sidewalk. It was Jessie's idea to borrow the umbrella to use as a sail, and it had worked all too well. The two girls and the umbrella ended up against the telephone pole at the corner. Over cookies and chocolate malted milks Virginia told the girls, "There's no need to go blabbing to your parents about this. You know your mother, Jessie. She'd insist on paying for the umbrella and she can't really afford to. So let's keep this our secret, shall we?"

Virginia got up and poured Howard some coffee. Her hands were shaking and she felt sick with fear that Howard suspected her of lying. "I'm terribly sorry about the whole thing, Howard."

"Come on now. I hardly expect you to apologize for a Santa Ana. As for the umbrella, it was just an object. Objects can be replaced."

"I could go downtown right now and buy one, while you're reading the newspaper."

"Nonsense. We'll have one sent out."

"I'm going down anyway."

"Do you have to? We've hardly had a chance to talk."

We've had a chance, Howard, she thought, *we just haven't used it to very good advantage.* She said, "You'll be reading the paper anyway. It seems silly for me merely to sit and watch you when I could be accomplishing something."

"Since you put it like that," Howard said, taking her hand, "go ahead. Do you need money? What do you want to accomplish?"

"An errand."

"Ah, we're playing the woman of mystery today, are we?"

"There's no mystery about it," she said bluntly. "Jessie's sick. I want to buy her a little game or two to keep her quiet."

"I see."

She could tell from his tone that what he saw gave him little pleasure.

"I'm sorry the kid's sick," he added. "What's the matter with her?"

"According to Ellen, Jessie's hands are sore from playing on the jungle gym."

"It hardly sounds catastrophic."

"I know, but Ellen tends to minimize things like that. Sometimes I think she's not sympathetic enough with the child."

"Sympathy can be overdone and children can take advantage of it."

"Not Jessie. She's really a wonderful girl. You know, when she and I are alone together, I never have the least trouble with her. The problem of discipline doesn't even come up."

"Why should it?" Howard said dryly. "She calls the shots."

Virginia looked shocked. "That's not true."

"All right, it's not true. I'm just imagining that she comes barging in here without knocking, helps herself to whatever is in the refrigerator, bangs on the piano, feeds the dog until he's too stuffed to move—"

"It so happens that she has my permission to feed both the dog and herself and to come in here when she feels like it. She has no piano of her own so I'm giving her lessons on ours because I think she has talent."

"Listen, Virginia, I've wanted to say this before but I hated to cause trouble. Now that trouble's here anyway, I might as well speak my piece. You're getting too bound up with Jessie."

"I won't listen to you."

She put her hands over her ears and shook her head back and forth. After a moment's hesitation, Howard grabbed her by the wrists and forced her hands to her sides.

"You'll listen, Virginia."

"Let go of me."

"Later. It's natural enough for you to be fond of the kid since we don't have any of our own. What isn't natural is that she's taken everybody's place in your life. You don't see your friends anymore, you don't even seem to want to spend much time with me when I'm home."

"Why should I, when all you do is pick on me?"

"I'm not picking on you. I'm warning you for your own good not to make yourself vulnerable to a heartbreak. Jessie doesn't belong to you, you have no control over her. What if something happens to her?"

"Happens? What?"

"For one thing, Dave Brant could lose his job or be laid off and forced to move away from here."

Virginia was staring at him bleakly, her face white. "That would suit you fine, wouldn't it?"

"No. I happen to like the Brants and enjoy their company. They're not, however, my sole interest in life. I'm prepared to survive without them. Are you?"

"I think you're jealous," Virginia said slowly. "I think you're jealous of a nine-year-old girl."

He let go of her wrists as if the accusation had suddenly paralyzed him. Then, with a sound of despair, he walked away into the living room. She stood motionless in the middle of the kitchen, listening to the rustle of Howard's newspaper, the sighing of his leather chair as he sat down, and the rebellious beat of her own heart.

3

AT 12:50 CHARLIE Gowen went back to the wholesale paper supply company where he was employed. He was always punctual, partly by nature, partly because his brother, Benjamin, had been drumming it into him for years. "So you have your faults, Charlie, and maybe you can't help them. But you can be careful about the little things, like being on time and neat and keeping your hair combed and not smoking or drinking, and working hard— A bunch of little things like that, they all add up, they look good on a man's record. Employment record, I mean."

Charlie knew that he didn't mean employment record but he let it go and he listened to Ben's advice because it sounded sensible and because, since the death of his mother, there was no one else to listen to. He felt, too, that he had to be loyal to Ben; Ben's wife had divorced him on account of Charlie. She'd walked out leaving a note in the middle of the bed: "I'm not coming back and don't try to find me. I'm sick of being disgraced."

Charlie worked at the paper supply company as a stock boy. He liked his job. He felt at home walking up and down the narrow aisles with shelves, from floor to ceiling, filled with such a variety of things that even Mr. Warner, the owner, couldn't keep track of them: notebooks, pens, pencils, party decorations and favors, brooms and brushes and mops, typewriter ribbons and staplers and stationery, signs saying No TRESPASSING, FOR RENT, PRIVATE, WALK IN, erasers and bridge tallies and confetti and plastic lovers for the tops of wedding cakes, huge rolls of colored tickets to functions that hadn't even been planned yet, maps, charts, chalk, ink, and thousands of reams of paper.

The contents of the building were highly inflammable, which was one of the main reasons why Charlie had been hired. Though he carried matches for the convenience of other people, he hadn't smoked since the age of fourteen when Ben had caught him trying it and beaten the tar out of him. Mr. Warner, the owner, had been so delighted to find a genuine nonsmoker, not just someone who'd quit a few weeks or months ago, that he'd given Charlie the job without inquiring too closely into his background. He knew in a general way that Charlie had had "trouble," but there was never any sign of it at work. Charlie arrived early and stayed late, he was pleasant and earnest, always ready to do a favor and never asking any in return.

In the alley behind the building Charlie found one of his coworkers, a young man named Ed Hines, leaning against the wall with an unlit cigarette in his hand.

"Hey, Charlie, got a match?"

"Sure." Charlie tossed him a packet of book matches. "I'd appreciate having them back, if you don't mind. There's an address written on the cover."

Ed grinned. "And a phone number?"

"No. Not yet."

"You gay old dog, you!"

"No. No, it's not like that actually—" Charlie stopped, realizing suddenly that Ed wouldn't understand the truth, that there was a family at 319 Jacaranda Road who were neglecting their pretty little girl, Jessie.

Ed returned the matches. "Thanks, Charlie. And say, the old man's in a stew about something. You better check in at the front office."

Warner was behind his desk, a small man almost lost in the welter of papers that surrounded him: order forms, invoices, sales slips, bills, correspondence. Some of this stuff would be filed, some would simply disappear. Warner had started the business forty years ago. It had grown and prospered since then, but Warner still tried to manage the place as if he personally knew, as he once had, every customer by name, every order from memory. Many mistakes were made, and with each one, Warner got a little older and a little more stubborn. The business continued to make money, however, because it was the only one of its kind in San Félice.

Charlie stood in the doorway, trying to hold his head high, the way Ben kept telling him to. But it was difficult, and Mr. Warner wasn't watching anyway. He had the telephone perched on his left shoulder like a crow. The crow was talking, loud and fast, in a woman's voice.

Mr. Warner put his hand over the mouthpiece and looked at Charlie. "You know anything about some skeletons?"

"Skeletons?" The word emerged from Charlie's throat as if it had been squeezed out of shape by some internal pressure. Then he went dumb entirely. He couldn't even tell Mr. Warner that he was innocent, he had done nothing, he knew nothing about any skeletons. He could only shake his head back and forth again and again.

"What's the matter with you?" Warner said irritably. "I mean those life-size cardboard skeletons we have in stock around Halloween. Some woman claims she ordered a dozen for a pathologists' convention dance that's being held tomorrow night." Then into the telephone, "I can't find any record of your order, Miss Johnston, but I'll check again. I promise you you'll get your skeletons even if I, ha ha, have to shoot a couple of my employees. Yes, I'll call you back." He hung up, turning his attention to Charlie. "And believe me, I meant everything but the ha ha. Now let's start searching."

Charlie was so dizzy with relief that he had to hold on to the doorjamb to steady himself. "Yes, sir. Right away. If I knew exactly what to search for—"

"A package from Whipple Novelty in Chicago."

"That came in this morning, Mr. Warner."

"It did? Well, I'll be damned." Warner looked pleasantly surprised, like a man who doesn't expect or deserve good news. "Well, I hand it to you, Charlie. You're getting to know the business. I ask for skeletons, you produce skeletons."

"No. No, I—"

"I saw you at the drive-in the other night, by the way. You were with a nice-looking young woman. Funny thing, I could have sworn I've seen her before. Maybe she's one of our customers, eh?"

"No, sir. She works at the library, in the reference department."

"That explains it, then," Warner said. "So she's a librarian, eh? She must be pretty smart."

"Yes, sir."

"It pays to have a smart wife."

"No, no. She's not—I mean, we're not—"

"Don't fight it, Charlie. We all get hooked sooner or later."

Charlie would have liked to stay and explain to Mr. Warner about his relationship with Louise, but Mr. Warner had picked up the phone and was dialing, and Charlie wasn't sure he could explain it anyway.

He felt sometimes that he had known Louise all his life and at other times that he didn't know her at all. In fact, he had met her about a year ago at the library. Charlie was there at Ben's insistence: "You don't want to be a stock boy forever, Charlie. I bet there are careers you never even heard about. One of them might be just down your alley but you've got to investigate, look around, find out what's available."

And so, night after night, Charlie went to the library and read books and magazines and trade journals about electronics, photography, turkey farming, real estate, personnel management, mining engineering, cartooning, forestry, interior design, cabinet-making, raising chinchillas, mathematics. He barely noticed the woman who helped him locate some of this material until one night she said, "My goodness, you certainly have a wide range of interests, Mr. Gowen."

Charlie merely stared at her, shocked by the sudden attention and the fact that she even knew his name. He thought of a library as a warm, safe, quiet place where people hadn't any names or faces or problems. The woman had no right to spoil it, no right—

But the next time he went, he wore a new shirt and tie, and a very serious expression which befitted a man with a wide range of interests. He took out an imposing book on architecture and sat with it open on the table in front of him and watched Louise out of the corner of his eye as if he had never seen a woman before and wasn't sure what to expect from the strange creature.

He guessed, from the way her colleagues deferred to her, that she was head of the department and so must be at least in her late twenties. But she had a tiny figure like a girl's with the merest suggestion of hips and breasts, and her movements were quick and light as if she weighed scarcely anything at all. Every time Charlie caught her glancing at him, something expanded inside of him. He felt larger and stronger.

He was only vaguely aware that it was getting late and people were leaving the library.

Louise came from behind the desk and approached the table where he was sitting. "I hate to disturb you, Mr. Gowen, but we're getting ready to lock up."

Charlie rose awkwardly to his feet. "I'm terribly sorry, I didn't notice. I—I was absorbed."

"You must have great powers of concentration to study in a noisy place like this."

"No. No, I really haven't."

"I wish I could let you take this book home but it's from the reference shelves and isn't allowed out. Unless, of course, there are special circumstances—"

"No. No, there aren't." Charlie hung his head and stared down at the floor. He could almost feel Ben behind him, telling him to square his shoulders and keep his head up and look proud. "I mean, I'm not an architect or anything. I don't know anything about architecture."

He hadn't planned on telling her this, or, in fact, talking to her at all. He'd intended to let her think he was a man of some background and education, a man to be respected. Now he could hear his own voice ruining everything, and he was powerless to stop it.

"Not a thing," he added.

"Neither do I," Louise said cheerfully. "Except about this building, and here I qualify as an expert. I can predict just where the roof will be leaking, come next January."

"You can? Where?"

"The art and music department. You see, last year it was the children's wing, they patched that up. And the year before, it was here, practically above my desk. So next time it's art and music's turn."

"I'll have to come back in January and find out if you were right."

There was a brief silence; then Louise said quietly, "That sounds as if you're going away some place. Will you be gone long, Mr. Gowen?"

"No."

"We'll miss you."

"No. I mean, I must have given you the wrong impression. I'm not going anywhere."

"You didn't give me the wrong impression, Mr. Gowen. I simply jumped to a wrong conclusion. My dad says I'm always doing it. I'm sorry."

"Even if I wanted to, I couldn't go anywhere."

Charlie could feel Ben behind him again: *Stop downgrading yourself, Charlie. Give people a chance to see your good side before you start blabbing. You've got to put up a front, develop a sense of self-preservation.*

"In fact," Charlie said, "I can't even leave the county without special permission."

Louise smiled, thinking it was a joke. "From whom?"

"From my parole officer."

He didn't wait to see her reaction. He just turned and walked away, stumbling a little over his own feet like an adolescent not accustomed to his new growth.

For the next three nights he stayed home, reading, watching television, playing cards with Ben. He knew Ben was suspicious and Charlie tried to allay the suspicion by talking a lot, reminiscing about their childhood, repeating jokes and stories he heard at work.

Ben wasn't fooled. "How come you don't go to the library anymore, Charlie?"

"I've been a little tired this week."

"You don't act tired."

"A man needs a change now and then. I've been getting into a rut spending every night at the library."

"You call this a nonrut?" Ben gestured around the room. Since their mother's death nothing in the house had been moved. It was as if the chairs and tables and lamps were permanently riveted in place. "Listen, Charlie, if anything happened, I have a right to know what it was."

"Why?"

"Because I'm your older brother and I'm responsible for you."

"No. No, you're not," Charlie said, shaking his head. "I'm responsible for myself. You keep telling me to grow up. How can I, with you breathing down my neck? You won't allow me to do anything on my own."

"I won't allow you to make a fool of yourself if I can help it."

"Well, you can't help it. It's over. It's done." Charlie began pacing up and down the room, his arms crossed on his chest in a despairing embrace. "I made a fool of myself and I don't care, I don't give a damn."

"Tell me about it, Charlie."

"No."

"You'd better. If it's not too serious I may be able to cover up for you."

"I keep uncovering and you keep covering up. Back and forth, seesaw, where will it end?"

"That's up to you."

Charlie paused at the window. It was dark outside, he could see nothing on the street, only himself filling the narrow window frame like a painting that had gotten beyond control of the artist and outgrown its canvas. A layer of greasy film on the glass softened his image. He looked like a very young man, broad-shouldered, slim-waisted, with a lock of light brown curly hair falling over his forehead and twin tears rolling down his cheeks.

Ben saw the tears, too. "My God, what have you done this time?"

"I—I ruined something."

"You sound surprised," Ben said bitterly, "as if you didn't know that ruining things was your specialty in life."

"Don't. Don't nag. Don't preach."

"Tell me what happened."

Charlie told him, while Ben sat in the cherrywood rocking chair that had belonged to his mother, rocking slowly back and forth the way she used to when she was worried over Charlie.

"I don't know why I said it, Ben, I just don't *know*. It popped out, like a burp. I had no control over it, don't you understand?"

"Sure, I understand." Ben said wearily. "I understand you've got to put yourself in a bad light. Whenever things are going all right you've got to open your big mouth and wreck them. Who knows? This woman might have become interested in you, a nice relationship might have developed. God help you, you could use a friend. But no, no, you couldn't keep your trap shut long enough even to find out her name . . . Don't you *want* a friend, Charlie?"

"Yes."

"Then why in hell do you do these things?"

"I don't know."

"Well, it's over with, it's finished. There's not much use discussing it." Ben rose, heavily, from the rocking chair. "I suppose this means you won't be going to the library anymore?"

"I can't."

"You could if you wanted to. If it were me, I'd just sail in there one of these nights with a smile on my face and pretend the whole thing was a joke."

"She knew it wasn't a joke."

"How can you be sure? You said you turned and walked out. If you didn't stick around to watch her reaction, you can't tell what it was. She might have gotten a big laugh out of it, for all you know."

"Stop it, Ben. It's no use."

"It's no use always looking on the black side, either. You're a good-looking man, Charlie. A woman could easily flip over you if you gave her a chance. If you held your head up, squared your shoulders, if you thought white instead of black for a change, if you put on a front—"

Charlie knew all the ifs, including the one that was never spoken: If you got married, Charlie, some of your weight would be lifted off my back.

The following afternoon, when Charlie got home from work, there was a letter waiting for him, propped up against the sugar bowl on the kitchen table. Charlie received few letters and he would have liked to sit with it in his hands for a few minutes, wondering, examining the small neat handwriting. But Ben came out of the bedroom where he had changed from his good gabardine suit into jeans and T-shirt.

"There's a letter for you."

"Yes."

"Aren't you going to open it?"

"If you want me to."

"If *I* want you to?" Ben said irritably. "For Pete's sake, what have *I* got to do with it? It's your letter."

Charlie didn't argue, though he knew the letter wasn't really his. He had nothing that was privately, exclusively his own, any more than a five-year-old child has. The letter might as well have been addressed to Ben, because Ben would read it anyway, just as if Charlie, in his times of trouble, had lost the ability to read.

Charlie slit the envelope open with a table knife and unfolded the small sheet of stationery:

> *Dear Mr. Gowen:*
>
> *I wanted to tell you this in person, but since you haven't appeared at the library, I must do it by letter. I was deeply moved by your courage and forthrightness on Monday evening. Very few people are capable of such honesty. Perhaps I'm being too presumptuous but I can't help hoping that what you did was an act of trust in me personally. If it was, I will try to deserve this trust, always.*
>
> *Very sincerely yours,*
> *Louise Lang*
>
> *P.S. About that reference book on architecture, I have arranged for you to borrow it for a month, if you'd like to.*

"Well," Ben said, "who's it from?"

"Her."

"Her?"

Charlie's left hand was clenched into a fist and he kept rubbing it up and down his jaw as if he were testing it for a vulnerable place to strike a blow. "She—she misunderstood. It wasn't like that. I'm not like that. I'm not any of those things she said."

"What in hell are you talking about?"

"I'm not, I'm not brave and forthright and honest."

Ben picked up the letter and read it, his eyebrows raised, one corner of his mouth tucked in. Charlie was watching him anxiously. "What's it mean, Ben?"

"It means," Ben said, "that she wants to see you again."

"But why?"

"Because she likes you. Don't try to figure it out. Just enjoy it. She likes you, she wants to see you again. You want to see her too, don't you?"

"Yes."

"All right, then. Go and do it. Right after supper."

"I will," Charlie said. "I have to set her straight. I can't let her go on thinking all those good things about me when they aren't true."

Ben took it very quietly, without arguing or making a fuss or giving a lecture. But after supper, when the dishes were done, he changed back into the brown gabardine suit he wore to the cafeteria he managed. Then he told Charlie, "It's such a nice night I think I'll take a little walk to the library."

"It's foggy out, Ben."

"I like fog."

"It's bad for your bronchial tubes."

"I'm going with you," Ben said heavily, "because I know that if I don't, you'll louse things up for yourself. You may, anyway; in fact, you probably will. But the least I can do is try and stop you."

The rest of that night was never quite clear in Charlie's mind. He remembered the fog and Ben walking gravely beside him, in absolute silence. He remembered how, at the library, he'd stood beside the newspaper rack while Ben and Louise talked at Louise's desk. Every now and then they would glance, sympathetically and kindly, over at Charlie, and Charlie knew that between the two of them they were creating a fictional character, a person who didn't exist, called Charlie Gowen; a brave, forthright, honest man, too modest to admit his good qualities; every maiden's dream, every brother's joy.

The scene in the library had taken place a year ago. Since then Louise had become almost part of the family, but Charlie often felt that there had been no real change during the year. He was still standing apart, across a room, unrecognized, unidentified, while Ben and Louise talked, adding more touches to their creation, the Charlie doll. They were so proud of their doll that Charlie did his best to copy it.

Charlie located the package of cardboard skeletons and took them up to the front of the building. Mr. Warner's secretary hadn't returned from her lunch hour and Warner had just left for his, so the office was empty. This was the first time Charlie had been in the office when it was empty and it gave him an odd but not unpleasant feeling that he was doing something wrong. It was like entering a private bedroom while the owner slept, exposed, defenseless, and searching through the contents of pockets and purses and bureau drawers and suitcases.

To make room for the package on Mr. Warner's desk, Charlie had to move the telephone. As he touched it, an impulse seized him to call Louise. He dialed the number of the library and asked for the reference department.

"Louise? It's me, Charlie."

"Hello, Charlie." She seemed, as she always did, very happy to hear his voice. "Your timing is good. I just this minute arrived at work."

"Louise, would you do me a small favor?"

"Consider it done."

"Would you look up an address in the city directory and tell me who lives there? It's 319 Jacaranda Road. You don't have to do it immediately. Just make a note of the name and give it to me tonight when you come over."

"What's the mystery?"

"Nothing. I mean, it's not a mystery, I'll tell you about it tonight."

"Are you feeling all right, Charlie?"

"Sure I am. Why?"

"You sound kind of excited."

"No. No, I don't," Charlie said, and hung up.

She must be crazy, he thought. *Why should I be excited? What have I got to be excited about?*

4

MARY MARTHA OAKLEY was on the window seat in the front room, playing with her cat, Pudding. Her feelings toward the cat were ambivalent. Sometimes she loved him as only a solitary child can love an animal. At other times she didn't want to see him because he symbolized all the changes that had taken place in her life during the last two years. Her mother had brought the cat home from the pet shop on the same day her father had moved out of the house.

"See, lamb? It's a real live kitten, just what you've always wanted."

Where had her father gone?

"Look at his adorable eyes and his silly little nose. Isn't he adorable?"

Was he coming back?

"Let's think of a real yummy name for him. How about Pudding?"

After the cat there were other changes: new locks on the doors and the downstairs windows and the garage, a private phone with an unlisted number that Mary Martha wasn't allowed to tell anyone, even her teachers at school or her best friend, Jessie. Furniture began to disappear from the upstairs rooms, silver and china from the dining room, pictures from the walls, and all the pretty bottles from the wine cellar. The cook and the gardener stopped coming, then the cleaning woman, the grocery boy, the once-a-month seamstress, the milkman. Kate managed everything herself, and did her own shopping at a cash-and-carry supermarket.

Pudding was the only one of these changes that Mary Martha liked. Into his furry and uncritical ear she whispered her confidences and her troubled questions, and if Pudding couldn't give her any answers or reassurance, he at least listened, blinking his eyes and now and then twitching his tail.

"Mary Martha, I've been calling you."

The child raised her head and saw her mother standing in the doorway looking hot and fretful as she always did when she worked in the kitchen. "I didn't hear you."

"It's all right, it's not important. I just—" *I just wanted to talk to somebody.* "I just wanted to tell you that dinner will be a little late. It's taking the hamburgers longer to thaw than I reckoned it would . . . Stop letting the cat bite your ponytail. It's not sanitary."

"He's as clean as I am."

"No, he isn't. Besides, he should go outside now. He doesn't get enough fresh air and sunshine."

Mrs. Oakley leaned over to pick up the cat and it was then that she saw the old green coupé parked at the curb across the street. At noon when she'd unlatched the front screen door to let the girls in, she'd seen it too, but this time she knew it couldn't be a coincidence. She knew who was behind the wheel, who was staring out through the closed, dirty window and what was going on in his closed, dirty mind.

Her hands tightened around the cat's body so hard that he let out a meow of pain, but she kept her voice very casual. "Mary Martha, I've been concerned about those book reports that were assigned to you for summer work. How many do you have to write?"

"Ten. But I've got a whole month left."

"A month isn't as long as you think, lamb. I suggest you go up to your room right now and start working on one. After all, you want to make a good first impression on your new teacher."

"She already knows me. It's just Mrs. Valdez."

"Are you going to argue with me, lamb?"

"I guess not."

"That's my angel. You may take Pudding up with you if you like."

Mary Martha went toward the hallway with the cat at her heels. Though she couldn't have put her awareness into words, she realized that the more pet names her mother called her, the more remote from her she actually was. Behind every lamb and angel lurked a black sheep and a devil.

"Mother—"

"Yes, sweetikins?"

"Nothing," Mary Martha said. "Nothing."

As soon as Kate Oakley heard Mary Martha's bedroom door slam shut, she rushed out to the telephone in the front hall. With the child out of the way she no longer had to exercise such rigid control over her body. It was almost a relief to let her hands tremble and her shoulders sag as they wanted to.

She dialed a number. It rang ten, twelve, fifteen times and no one answered. She was sure, then, that her suspicions were correct.

She dialed another number, her mouth moving in a silent prayer that Mac would still be in his office, detained by a client or finishing a brief. She thought of how many times she had been the one who detained him, and how many tears she had shed sitting across the desk from him. If they had been allowed to collect, Mac's office would be knee-deep in brine, yet they had all been in vain. She had been weeping for yesterday as though it were a person and would be moved to pity by her tears and would promise to return . . . *Don't cry, Kate. You will be loved and cherished forever, and forever young. Nothing will change for you.*

Mac's secretary answered, sounding as she always did, cool on the hottest day, dry on the wettest. "Rhodes and MacPherson. Miss Edgeworth speaking."

"This is Mrs. Oakley. Is Mr. MacPherson in?"

"He's just going out the door now, Mrs. Oakley."

"Call him back, will you? Please."

"I'll try. Hold on."

A minute later Mac came on the line, speaking in the brisk, confident voice that had been familiar to her since she was Mary Martha's age and her father had died. "Hello, Kate. Anything the matter?"

"Sheridan's here."

"In the house? That's a violation of the injunction."

"Not in the house. He's parked across the street, in an old green car he probably borrowed from one of his so-called pals. He won't use his own, naturally."

"How do you know it's Sheridan? Did you see him?"

"No, he's got the windows closed. But it couldn't be anyone else. There's nothing across the street except a vacant lot. Also, I called his apartment and he wasn't home. When you add two and two, you get four."

"Let's just add one and one first," Mac said. "Do you see anybody in the car?"

"No. I told you, the windows are closed—"

"So you're not sure that there's even anyone in it?"

"I *am* sure. I *know*—"

"It's possible the car stalled or ran out of gas and was simply abandoned there."

"No. I saw it at noon, too." Her voice broke, and when she spoke again, it sounded as if it had been pasted together by an amateur and the pieces didn't fit. "He's spying on me again, trying to get something on me. What does he hope to gain by all this?"

"You know as well as I do," Mac said. "Mary Martha."

"He can't possibly prove I'm an unfit mother."

"I'm aware of that, but apparently he's not. Divorces can get pretty dirty, Kate, especially if there's a child involved. When money enters the picture too, even nice civilized people often forget every rule of decency they ever knew."

Kate said coldly, "You're speaking, I hope, of Sheridan."

"I'm speaking of what happens when people refuse to admit their own mistakes and take cover behind self-righteousness."

"You've never talked to me like this before."

"It's been a long day and I'm tired. Perhaps fatigue works on me like wine. You and Sheridan have been separated for two years and you're still bickering over a financial settlement, you haven't come to an agreement about Mary Martha, there have been suits, countersuits—"

"Please, Mac. Don't be unkind to me. I'm distracted, I'm truly distracted."

"Yes, I guess you truly are," Mac said slowly. "What do you want me to do about it?"

"Tell Sheridan to get out of town and I'll settle for eight hundred dollars a month."

"What about Mary Martha? He insists on seeing her."

"He'll see her over my dead body and no sooner. I won't change my mind about that."

"Look, Kate, I can't tell a man that simply because his wife no longer loves him he has to quit his job, leave the city he was born and brought up in and give up all rights to his only child."

"He's always loathed this town and said so. As for that silly little job, he only took it to get out of the house. He has enough money from his mother's trust fund. He can well afford to pay me a thousand dollars—"

"His lawyer says he can't."

"Naturally. His lawyer's on his side." She added bitterly, "I only wish to God my lawyer were on mine."

"I can be on your side without believing everything you do is right."

"You don't know, you don't *know* what I've gone through with that man. He's tried everything—hounding me, holding back on support money so I've had to sell half the things in the house to keep from starving, following me around town, standing outside the door and ringing the bell until my nerves were shattered—"

"That's all over now. He's under a court order not to harass you."

"Then what's he doing parked outside right this minute? Waiting to see one of my dozens of lovers arrive?"

"Now don't work yourself up, Kate."

"Why can't he leave us alone? He's got what he wanted, that fat old gin-swilling whore who treats him like little Jesus. Does he actually expect me to allow Mary Martha to associate with *that?*"

Lying on her stomach on the floor of the upstairs hall, Mary Martha suddenly pressed her hands against her ears. She had eavesdropped on dozens of her mother's conversations with Mac and this was no different from the others. She knew from experience that it was going to last a long time and she didn't want to hear anymore.

She thought of slipping down the back stairs and going over to Jessie's house, but the steps creaked very badly. She got to her feet and tiptoed down the hall to her mother's room.

To Mary Martha it was a beautiful room, all white and pink and frilly, with French doors opening onto a little balcony. Beside the balcony grew a sycamore tree where she had once found a hummingbird's tiny nest lined with down gathered from the underside of the leaves and filled with eggs smaller than jelly beans.

It was the cat, Pudding, who had alerted Mary Martha to the possibilities of the sycamore tree. Frightened by a stray dog, he had leaped to the first limb, climbed right up on the balcony and sat on the railing, looking smugly down on his enemy. Mary Martha wasn't as fearless and adept a climber as either Pudding or Jessie, but in emergencies she used the tree and so far her mother hadn't caught her at it.

She stepped out on the balcony and began the slow difficult descent, trying not to look at the ground. The gray mottled bark of the tree, which appeared so smooth from a distance, scratched her hands and arms like sandpaper. She passed the kitchen window. The hamburger was thawing on the sink and the sight of it made her aware of her hunger but she kept on going.

She dropped onto the grass in the backyard and crossed the dry creek bed, being careful to avoid the reddening runners of poison oak. A scrub jay squawked in protest at her intrusion. Mary Martha had learned from her father how to imitate the bird, and ordinarily she would have squawked back at him and there would have been a lively contest between the two of them. But this time she didn't even hear the jay. Her ears were still filled with her mother's voice: *"He's got what he wanted, that fat old gin-swilling whore who treats him like little Jesus."* The sentence bewildered her. Little Jesus was a baby in a manger and her

314

father was a grown-up man with a mustache. She didn't know what a whore was, but she assumed, since her father was interested in birds, that it was an owl. Owls said, "Whoo," and were fat and lived to be quite old.

Mr. and Mrs. Brant were in the little fenced-in patio at the back of their house, preparing a barbecue. Mr. Brant was trying to get the charcoal lit and Mrs. Brant was wrapping ears of corn in aluminum foil. They both wore shorts and cotton shirts and sandals.

"Why, it's Mary Martha," Ellen Brant said, sounding pleased and surprised, as though Mary Martha lived a hundred miles away and hadn't seen her for a year. "Come in, dear. Jessie will be out in a few minutes. She's taking a bath."

"I'm glad she didn't get blood poisoning and convulsions," Mary Martha said gravely.

"So am I. Very."

"Jessie is my best friend."

"I know that, and I think it's splendid. Don't you, Dave?"

"You bet I do," Dave said, turning to give Mary Martha a slow, shy smile. He was a big man with a low-pitched, quiet voice, and a slight stoop to his shoulders that seemed like an apology for his size.

It was his size and his quietness that Mary Martha especially admired. Her own father was short in stature and short of temper. His movements were quick and impatient and no matter what he was doing he always seemed anxious to get started on the next thing. It was restful and reassuring to stand beside Mr. Brant and watch him lighting the charcoal.

He said, "Careful, Mary Martha. Don't get burned."

"I won't. I often do the cooking at home. Also, I iron."

"Do you now. In ten years or so you'll be making some young man a fine wife, won't you?"

"No."

"Why not?"

"I'm not going to get married."

"You're pretty young to reach such a drastic decision."

Mary Martha was staring into the glowing coals as if reading her future. "I'm going to be an animal doctor and adopt ten children and support them all by myself so I don't have to sit around waiting for a check in the mail."

Over her head the Brants exchanged glances, then Ellen said in a firm, decisive voice, "No loafing on the job, you two. Put the corn on and I'll get the hot dogs. Would you like to stay and eat with us, Mary Martha?"

"No, thank you. I would like to but my mother will be alone." *And she will have a headache and a rash on her face and her eyes will be swollen, and she'll call me sweetie-pie and lambikins.*

"Perhaps your mother would like to join us," Ellen said. "Why don't you call her on the phone and ask her?"

"I can't. The line's busy."

"How do you know that? You haven't tried to—"

"She wouldn't come, anyway. She has a headache and things."

"Well," Ellen said, spreading her hands helplessly. "Well, I'd better get the hot dogs."

She went inside and Dave was left alone with Mary Martha. He felt uneasy in her presence, as if, in spite of her friendliness and politeness, she was secretly accusing him of being a man and a villain and he was secretly agreeing with her. He felt heavy with guilt and he wished someone would appear to help him carry it, Jessie or Ellen from the house, Michael from the football field, Virginia and Howard Arlington from next door. But no one came. There was only Mary Martha, small and pale and mute as marble.

For a long time the only sound was an occasional drop of butter oozing from between the folds of the aluminum foil and sputtering on the coals. Then Mary Martha said, "Do you know anything about birds, Mr. Brant?"

"No, I'm afraid not. I used to keep a few homing pigeons when I was a boy but that's about all."

"You didn't keep any owls?"

"No. I don't suppose anyone does."

"My ex-father has one."

"Does he now," Dave said. "That's very interesting. What does he feed it?"

"Gin."

"Are you sure? Gin doesn't sound like a suitable diet for an owl or for anything else, for that matter. Don't owls usually eat small rodents and birds and things like that?"

"Yes, but not this one."

"Well," Dave said, with a shrug, "I don't know much either about owls or about your fath—your ex-father, so I'll just have to take your word for it. Gin it is."

Twin spots of color appeared on Mary Martha's cheeks, as if she'd been stung by bees or doubts. "I heard my mother telling Mac about it on the telephone. My ex-father has a fat old whore that drinks gin."

There was a brief silence. Then Dave said carefully, "I don't believe your mother was referring to an owl, Mary Martha. The word you used doesn't mean that."

"What does it mean?"

"It's an insulting term, and not one young ladies are supposed to repeat."

Mary Martha was aware that he had replied but hadn't answered. The word must mean something so terrible that she could never ask anyone about it. Why had her mother used it then, and what was her father doing with one? She felt a surge of anger against them all, her mother and father, the whore, David, and even Jessie who wasn't there but who had a real father.

Inside the kitchen the phone rang and through the open door and windows Ellen's voice came, clear and distinct: "Hello. Why yes, Mrs. Oakley, she's here . . . Of course I had no idea she didn't have your permission . . . She's perfectly all right, there's no need to become upset over it. Mary Martha isn't the kind of girl who'd be likely to get in trouble . . . I'll have Dave bring her right home . . . Very well, I'll tell her to wait here until you arrive. Good-bye."

Ellen came outside, carrying a tray of buttered rolls and hot dogs stuffed with cheese and wrapped in bacon. "Your mother just called, Mary Martha."

Mary Martha merely nodded. Her mother's excitement had an almost soothing effect on her. There would be a scene, naturally, but it would be like a lot of others, nothing she couldn't handle, nothing that hadn't been said a hundred times. *"If you truly love me, Mary Martha, you'll promise never to do such a thing again." "I truly love you, Mother. I never will."*

"She's driving over to get you," Ellen added. "You're to be waiting on the front porch."

"All right."

"Jessie will wait with you. She's just putting her pajamas on."

"I can wait alone."

"Of course you can, you're a responsible girl. But you came over here to see Jessie, didn't you?"

"No, ma'am."

"Why did you come, then?"

Mary Martha blinked, as if the question hurt her eyes. Then she turned and walked into the house, closing the screen door carefully and quietly behind her.

Dave Brant watched his wife as she began arranging the hot dogs on the grill. "Maybe you shouldn't question her like that, Ellen."

"Why not?"

"She might think you're prying."

"She might be right."

"I hope not."

"Oh, come on, Dave. Admit it—you're just as curious as I am about what goes on in that household."

"Perhaps. But I think I'm better off not knowing." He thought of telling Ellen about the fat old whore but he couldn't predict her reaction. She might be either quite amused by the story or else shocked into doing something tactless like repeating it to Mrs. Oakley. Although he'd been married to Ellen for eighteen years, her insensitivity to certain situations still surprised him.

"Dave—"

"Yes?"

"We'll never let it happen to our children, will we?"

"What?"

"Divorce," Ellen said, with a gesture, "and all the mess that goes with it. It would kill Michael, he's so terribly sensitive, like me."

"He's going to have plenty of reason to be sensitive if he's not home by 6:30 as he promised."

"Now, Dave, you wouldn't actually punish him simply for losing track of the time."

"He has 20/20 vision and a wristwatch," Dave said. But he wasn't even interested in Michael at the moment. He merely wanted to change the subject because he couldn't bear to talk or even think about a divorce. The idea of Jessie being in Mary Martha's place appalled him, Michael was sixteen, almost a man, but Jessie was still a child, full of trust and innocence, and the only person in the world who sincerely believed in him. She wouldn't always. Inevitably, the time would come when she'd have to question his wisdom and courage, perhaps even his love for her. But right now she was nine, her world was small, no more than a tiny moon, and he was the king of it.

The two girls sat outside the front door on the single concrete step which they called a porch. Jessie was picking at the loose skin on the palm of one hand, and Mary Martha was watching her as if she wished she had something equally interesting to do.

Jessie said, "You'll probably catch it when your mother comes."

"I don't care."

"Do you suppose you'll cry?"

"I may have to," Mary Martha said thoughtfully. "It's lucky I'm such a good crier."

Jessie agreed. "Maybe you should start in right now and be crying when she arrives. It might wring her heart."

"I don't feel like it right now."

"I could make up a real sad story for you."

"No. I know lots of real sad stories. My ex-father used to tell them to me when he was you-know-what."

"Drunk?"

"Yes."

It had been two years now since she'd heard any of these stories but she remembered them because they were all about the same little boy. He lived in a big redwood house which had an attic to play in and trees around it to climb and a creek at the back of it to hunt frogs in. At the end of every story the little boy died, sometimes heroically, while rescuing an animal or a bird, sometimes by accident or disease. These endings left Mary Martha in a state of confusion: she recognized the house the little boy lived in and she knew he must be her father, yet her father was still alive. Why had the little boy died? *"He was better off that way, shweetheart, much better off."*

"I wish you could stay at my house for a while," Jessie said. "We could look at the big new book my Aunt Virginia gave me. It's all about nature, mountains and rivers and glaciers and animals."

"We could look at it tomorrow, maybe."

"No. I have to give it back as soon as she gets home from the beach."

"Why?"

"It was too expensive, twenty dollars. My mother was so mad about it she made my father mad too, and then they both got mad at me."

Mary Martha nodded sympathetically. She knew all about such situations. "My father sends me presents at Christmas and on my birthday, but my mother won't even let me open the packages. She says he's trying to buy me. Is your Aunt Virginia trying to buy you?"

"That's silly. Nobody can buy children."

"If my mother says they can, they can." Mary Martha paused. "Haven't you even heard about nasty old men offering you money to go for a ride? Don't you even know about *them?*"

"Yes."

"Well, then."

She saw her mother's little Volkswagen rounding the corner. Running out to the curb to meet it she tried to make tears come to her eyes by thinking of the little boy who always died in her father's stories. But the tears wouldn't come. Perhaps her father was right and the little boy was better off dead.

Kate Oakley sat, pale and rigid, her hands gripping the steering wheel as if she were trying to rein in a wild horse with a will of its own. Cars passed on the road, people strolled along the sidewalk with children and dogs and packages of groceries, others watered lawns, weeded flower beds, washed off driveways and raked leaves. But to the woman and child in the car, all the moving creatures were unreal. Even the birds in the trees seemed made of plastic and suspended on strings and only pretending to fly free.

Mary Martha said in a whisper, "I'm sorry, Momma."

"Why did you do it?"

"I thought you'd be talking on the telephone for a long time and that I'd be back before you even missed me."

"You heard me talking on the telephone?"

"Yes."

"And you listened, deliberately?"

"Yes. But I couldn't help it. I wanted to know about my father, I just wanted to know, Momma."

Real tears came to her eyes then, she didn't have to think of the little dead boy.

"God forgive me," her mother said as if she didn't believe in God or forgiving. "I've tried, I'm still trying to protect you from all this ugliness. But how can I? It surrounds us like a lot of dirty water, we're in it right up to our necks. How can I pretend we're standing on dry land, safe and secure?"

"We could buy a boat," Mary Martha suggested, wiping her eyes.

There was a silence, then her mother said in a bright, brittle voice, "Why, lamb, that's a perfectly splendid idea. Why didn't I think of it? We'll buy a boat just big enough for the two of us, and we'll float right out of Sheridan's life. Won't that be lovely, sweetikins?"

"Yes, ma'am."

5

QUICKLY AND QUIETLY, Charlie let himself in the front door. He was late for supper by almost an hour and he knew Ben would be grumpy about it and full of questions. He had his answers ready, ones that Ben couldn't easily prove or disprove. He hated lying to Ben but the truth was so simple and innocent that Ben wouldn't believe it: he'd gone to 319 Jacaranda Road, where the child Jessie lived, to see if she was all right. She'd taken a bad fall at the playground, she could have injured herself quite seriously, her little bones were so delicate.

He knew from experience what Ben's reaction would be. Playground? What were you doing at a playground, Charlie? How did you learn the child's name? And where she lives?

And that her little bones are delicate? How did she fall, Charlie? Were you chasing her and was she running away? Why do you want to chase little girls, Charlie?

Ben would misunderstand, misinterpret everything. It was better to feed him a lie he would swallow than a truth he would spit out.

Charlie took off the windbreaker he always wore no matter what the weather and hung it on the clothes rack beside the front door. Then he went down the dark narrow hall to the kitchen.

Ben was standing at the sink, rinsing a plate under the hot-water tap. He said, without turning, "You're late. I've already eaten."

"I'm sorry, Ben. I had some trouble with the car. I must have flooded it again. I had to wait half an hour before the engine would turn over."

"I've told you a dozen times, all you've got to do when the engine's flooded is press the accelerator down to the floorboard and let it up again very slowly."

"Oh, I did that, Ben. Sometimes it doesn't work."

"It does for me."

"Well, you've got a real way with cars. You command their respect."

Ben turned. He didn't look in the least flattered, as Charlie had hoped he would. "Louise called. She'll be over early. She's getting off at seven because she's taking another girl's place tomorrow night. You'd better hurry up and eat."

"Sure, Ben."

"There's a can of spaghetti in the cupboard and some fish cakes."

Charlie didn't particularly like fish cakes and spaghetti but he took the two cans out of the cupboard and opened them. Ben was in a peculiar mood, it would be better not to cross him even about so minor a thing as what to have for supper. He wanted to cross him, though; he wanted to tell him outright that he, Charlie, was a grown man of thirty-two and he didn't have to account for every minute of his time and be told what to eat and how to spend the evening. So Louise was coming. Well, suppose he wasn't there when she arrived. Suppose he walked out right now . . .

No, he couldn't do that, not tonight anyway. Tonight she was bringing him something very important, very urgent. He didn't understand why he considered it so important but it was as if she were going to hand him a key, a mysterious key which would unlock a door or a secret box.

He thought of the hidden delights behind the door, inside the box, and his hands began to tremble. When he put the fish cakes in the frying pan, the hot grease splattered his knuckles. He felt no pain, only a sense of wonder that this grease, which had no mind or will of its own, should be able to fight back and assert itself better than he could.

"For Pete's sake, watch it," Ben said. "You're getting the stove dirty."

"I didn't mean to."

"Put a lid on the frying pan. Use your head."

"My head wouldn't fit, Ben. It's too small."

Ben stared at him a moment, then he said sharply, "Stop doing that. Stop taking everything literally. You know damned well I didn't mean for you to decapitate yourself and use your head as a lid for the frying pan. Don't you know that?"

"Yes."

"Damn it all, why do you do it then?"

Charlie turned, frowning, from the stove. "But you said, put a lid on the frying pan, use your head. You *said* that, Ben."

"And you think I meant it like that?"

"I wasn't really thinking. My mind was occupied with other things. Maybe with Louise coming and all like that."

"Look, Charlie, I'm only trying to protect you. You pull something like this at work and they'll consider you a moron."

"No," Charlie said gravely. "They just laugh. They think I'm being funny. Actually, I don't have much of a sense of humor, do I?"

"No."

"Did I ever? I mean, when we were boys together, Ben, before—well, before anything had happened, did I have a sense of humor then?"

"I can't remember."

"I bet you can if you tried. You've always had a good memory, Ben."

"Now I've got a good forgetter," Ben said. "Maybe that's more essential in this life."

"No, Ben, that's wrong. It's important for you to remember how it was with us when we were kids. Mother and Dad are dead, and I can't remember, so if you don't, it's like it never happened and we were never kids together—"

"All right, all right, don't get excited. I'll remember."

"Everything?"

"I'll try."

"Did I have a sense of humor?"

"Yes. Yes, you did, Charlie. You were a funny boy, a very funny boy."

"Did we do a lot of laughing together, you and I and Mom and Dad?"

"Sure."

"Louise laughs a lot. She's very cheerful, don't you think?"

"Louise is a very cheerful girl, yes."

Slowly and thoughtfully, Charlie turned the fish cakes. They were burned but he didn't care. It would only be easier to pretend they were small round tender steaks. "Ben?"

"Yes."

"She wouldn't stay cheerful very long if she married me, would she?"

"Stop talking like—"

"I mean, you haven't leveled with her, Ben. She doesn't realize what a drag I am and how she'd have to worry about me the way you do. I would hurt her. I would be hurting her all the time without meaning to, maybe without even knowing it. Would she be cheerful then? Would she?"

Ben sat down at the table, heavily and stiffly, as if each of the past five minutes had been a crippling year.

"Well? Would she, Ben?"

"I don't know."

Charlie looked dismayed, like a child who's been used to hearing the same story with the same happy ending, and now the ending has been changed. It wasn't happy anymore, it wasn't even an ending. Did the frog change into a prince? *I don't know.* Did he live happily ever after with his princess? *I don't know.*

Charlie said stubbornly, "I don't like that answer. I want the other one."

"There is no other one."

"You always used to say that marriage changed a man, that Louise could be the making of me and we could have a good life together if we tried. Tell it to me just like that all over again, Ben."

"I can't."

"All right then, give me hell. Tell me I'm downgrading myself, that I'd better look on the bright side of things, start putting on a front—that's all true, isn't it?"

"I don't know," Ben said. "Eat your supper."

"How can I eat, not knowing?"

"The rest of us eat, not knowing. And work and sleep, not knowing." He added in a gentler voice, "You're doing all right, Charlie. You're holding down a job, you've got a nice girlfriend, you're keeping your nose clean—you're doing fine, just fine."

"And you're not mad at me anymore for being late?"

"No."

"I flooded the engine, see. I had to wait and wait for the gas to drain out of it. I thought of calling you, but then I thought, Ben won't be worrying, he knows I'm behaving myself, keeping my nose clean . . ." *I watched from the road. The house is a long way back among the trees but I could see the child sitting at one of the front windows. Poor Jessie, poor sweetheart, resting her little bruised body. Why don't her parents protect her? If anything happens to the girl it will be their fault, and their fault alone.*

6

THE ARLINGTONS ARRIVED home from the beach at seven o'clock and Virginia went directly to her room, without saying a word. Howard was in the kitchen unpacking the picnic basket when the dog, Chap, began barking and pawing at the back door.

Howard called out, "Who's there?"

"It's me, Uncle Howard. Jessie."

"Oh. Well, come on in."

Jessie went in, wearing a robe over her pajamas and carrying the book that weighed nearly half as much as she did. "Is Aunt Virginia here?"

"Oh, she's here all right, but she's incommunicado."

"Does that mean in the bathroom?"

Howard laughed. "No, it means she's sore at me."

"Why?"

"A dozen reasons. She's sunburned, she's got sand in her hair, she doesn't like the way she looks in a bathing suit, a bee stung her on the foot—all my fault, of course." Howard put the picnic basket, now empty, on the top shelf of the broom closet, and closed the door. "When you grow up, are you going to fuss about things like that?"

"I don't think so."

"Atta girl."

Jessie put the book on the table, then leaned over to pet the dog. Chap, smelling the butter that had dribbled down her chin from an ear of corn, began licking it off. Jessie was so flattered she stood the tickling without a giggle, though it was almost unbearable. "Do you think Chap likes me, Uncle Howard?"

"Obviously."

"Does he like everybody?"

"As a matter of fact, no," Howard said dryly. "He doesn't even like me."

"Why? Is he afraid of you?"

"Afraid of me? Why should he be? What gave you that idea?"

"I don't know."

"Well, I don't beat him, kid, if that's what you mean. He's just been spoiled rotten by women. All he has to do is roll his eyes and he gets a T-bone steak. A little more," he added, "is required of the human male though God knows what it is."

Jessie wasn't sure what he was talking about but she realized he was in a bad mood and she wished Aunt Virginia would come out of communicado.

Howard said, "Who's the book for?"

"Aunt Virginia. She gave it to me this afternoon, only when my mother saw it she told me I had to give it back."

"Why?"

"It cost twenty dollars."

"Oh?" Howard opened the book and looked at the price on the inside back jacket. "So it did. Twenty dollars."

He sounded very calm but his hands were shaking and both the child and the dog sensed trouble.

"Virginia!"

There was no response from the bedroom.

"You'd better come out here, Virginia. You have a visitor, one I'm sure you wouldn't want to miss."

Virginia's voice answered, soft and snuffly, "I'm in bed."

"Then get out of bed."

"I—I can't."

"You can and you will."

The dog, tail between his legs, crawled under the table, his eyes moving from Howard to the bedroom door and back to Howard.

The door opened and Virginia came out, clutching a long white silk robe around her. All of her skin that was visible was a fiery red and her eyes were bloodshot. "I'm not feeling very well, Howard. I have a fever."

"You also have a visitor," Howard said in the same calm voice. "Jessie has come to return the book you gave her this afternoon. It seems her mother considered it too expensive a gift for her to accept. How much did it cost, Virginia?"

"Please, Howard. Not in front of the child. It's—"

"How much?"

"Twenty dollars."

"And where did you get the twenty dollars, Virginia?"

"From my—purse."

Howard laughed.

"Where did you get the money in your purse? Perhaps you've taken a job and the twenty came out of your salary?"

"You know I haven't, it didn't . . . Jessie, you'd better go home now. Right away, dear."

"Let her stay," Howard said.

"Please, Howard. She's only a little girl."

"Little girls can cause big troubles. And do. I want you to tell me, in front of Jessie, just where the twenty dollars came from."

"From you, Howard."

"That's right. From my paycheck. So that makes me the Santa Claus of the neighborhood, not you, Virginia. Right?"

"Yes."

He picked the book up from the table and held it out toward Jessie. "Here you are, kid. Take the book, it's all yours, with love and kisses from Santa Claus."

Jessie stared at him, wide-eyed. "I can't. My mother won't let—"

"Take it. Get it out of here. I'm sick of the sight of it."

"I don't want it."

"You don't want it. I see. Maybe you'd rather have the money, eh? All right."

He reached for his wallet, pulled out two ten-dollar bills and thrust them into her hand. Behind his back she saw Virginia nod at her and smile a shaky little smile that asked her to humor Howard. Jessie looked down at the bills in her hand, then she put them in the pocket of her bathrobe, quickly, as though she didn't like the feel of them. She remembered the conversation she'd had with Mary Martha about grownups buying children and she wondered if she had been bought and what buying and selling really meant.

Sex had no particular interest or mystery for Jessie. Her mother and father had explained it to her quite carefully. But nobody had ever explained money and why people were affected by it. To Jessie it seemed like black magic, nice when it was on your side and bad when it wasn't, but you couldn't tell in advance which it would be. Money was what bought things to make people happy, like the new house, but it was also what parents quarreled about when they thought the children were sleeping; it caused Virginia to cringe in front of Howard, and lie about the patio umbrella; it made her mother irritable when the mail arrived and made her brother Michael threaten to quit school and get a job. It was as mysterious as God, who had to be thanked for blessings but couldn't be blamed for their lack.

The pocket of her bathrobe felt heavy with power and with guilt. She could buy things now, but she had also been bought.

"What are you standing around for, kid?" Howard said. "You have your money and your earful. That's about all you can expect from one visit."

Virginia walked quickly to the back door and opened it. Her face appeared very peculiar because she was trying, with one part of it, to give Howard a dirty look, and with the other part, to smile reassuringly at Jessie. "Good night, dear. Don't worry. I'll explain things to your mother in the morning."

"I bet you will," Howard said when Jessie had gone. "The explanation should be a doozy. I wish I could stick around to hear it but I can't. I'm leaving."

"Why? Haven't you done enough damage for one night?"

"I'm afraid I might do more if I stay."

He went into the bedroom. His suitcase was lying on the floor, open but still unpacked except for his toothbrush and shaving kit. He gave it a kick and the lid fell shut.

Virginia said from the doorway, "You don't have to be childish."

"It's better than kicking you or the dog, isn't it?"

"Why do you have to kick anything?"

"Because I'm a bully, I'm the kind of guy who forces his sweet little wife to go out in the nasty sun and fresh air down to the nasty beach. That's your version of this afternoon, isn't it?"

"I can't help it if I sunburn easily."

"Well, here's my version. This is my first day at home in two weeks. I wanted to be with my wife and I also wanted to get some fresh air and exercise which I happen to need. That's all. Not exactly reaching for the moon, was I, Virginia?"

"No. But—"

"Let me finish. I realized my wife had delicate skin so I bought her a large straw hat and a beach umbrella. She decided the hat wasn't becoming enough, and after a while she got bored sitting under the umbrella so she went for a walk. The sun was strong, there was a wind and there was also, unfortunately, a half-dead bee which she stepped on. To complicate matters, she became conscious of all the young girls on the beach with young figures and by the time we were ready to eat she'd decided to go on a diet. She didn't eat anything. I did, though, the way any man would when he hasn't had a meal at home in two weeks. My wife sat and watched me. She was sunburned, hungry, nursing a sore foot and silent as a tomb. It was an interesting afternoon. I thank you for it, Virginia. It makes going back to work a real pleasure."

"Is that where you're going now, back to work?"

"Why not?"

He picked his suitcase up off the floor and tossed it on the bed. A sock and a drip-dry shirt fell out and Virginia went over to pick them up. The shirt was clean but wrinkled, as if Howard had laundered it himself and hung it up on the shower rod of any of a dozen anonymous motor courts or hotels.

Virginia held the shirt against her breasts as if it, more than the man who wore it, could move her to pity. "Did you wash this yourself, Howard?"

"Yes."

"Where? I mean, what city, what hotel?"

He looked at her, puzzled. "Why do you want to know that?"

"I just do."

"It was the Hacienda Inn in Bakersfield. There was an all-night party going on next door. Instead of taking a sleeping pill I got up and did some laundry."

"Howard, your job isn't much fun, is it?"

"Sometimes it is, in some ways," he said brusquely. "I don't expect to go around laughing all the time."

After a moment's hesitation Virginia went over to the bed and started taking the things out of his suitcase and putting them away in the clothes closet and the bureau drawers. She worked quickly and nervously as if she wanted to get it done before he had a chance to protest. Neither of them spoke until the suitcase was empty and snapped shut and hidden under the bed. Then Virginia said, "I'm sorry I was such a poor sport this afternoon."

"I knew you were a poor sport when I married you," Howard said quietly. "I should have had more sense than to plan a beach picnic."

"But you wanted one, you deserved one. You work hard at a difficult job and—"

"Come on now, don't go to extremes. I do a job, like any other man. I also get mad and lose my temper. Yes, and I guess I get jealous, too . . . I'm sorry I made an ass of myself in front of the kid. Giving her twenty dollars like that—God, what'll Dave and Ellen think when she tells them?"

"Nothing. She won't tell them."

"Why not?"

"Because they'd make her return the money and she doesn't want to."

Howard sat down on the edge of the bed, shaking his head ruefully. "I'm sorry. I'm very sorry."

"Stop thinking about it. We were both wrong and we're both sorry." Virginia sat down beside him and put her head on his shoulder. "I'm a poor sport and you're a jealous idiot. Maybe we deserve each other."

"Your sunburn—"

"It doesn't hurt so much anymore."

After a time he said, "I'll be very gentle with you, Virginia."

"I know."

"I love you."

"I know that, too."

She lay soft in his arms, her eyes closed, thinking that it had been exactly seven months and one week since she'd told Howard that she loved him.

7

LOUISE DRESSED CAREFULLY in a blue linen sheath with a Peter Pan collar, matching flat-heeled shoes that emphasized the smallness of her feet, and white gloves so tiny that she had to buy them in the children's department. At the last minute she pinned a bow in her short brown hair because Charlie liked girls to wear bows in their hair.

She went to the living room to say good night to her parents. Mr. Lang was doing the crossword puzzle in the evening newspaper, and Mrs. Lang was embroidering the first of a dozen pillow slips she would send to her relatives at Christmas.

"Well, I'm off," Louise said from the doorway. "I won't be late, but don't wait up."

Mrs. Lang peered at her over the top of her spectacles. "You look just lovely, dear. Doesn't she, Joe, look lovely?"

Mr. Lang put down his paper and stood up, as if Louise were a stranger he had to be polite to. Sitting, he had appeared to be of normal size, but when he stood up he wasn't much taller than Louise, though he held himself very straight. "You look very lovely indeed, my dear. Is this a special occasion?"

"No."

"Where are you going?"

"To Ben and Charlie's."

"It sounds like the name of a bar and grill on lower State Street."

"What a way to talk," Mrs. Lang said quickly. "You stop that, Joe, you just stop it. You know perfectly well who Ben and Charlie are. They're nice, respectable—"

Her husband silenced her with a gesture, then he turned his attention back to Louise. "Other girls seem to find satisfaction in dating only one gentleman at a time. They are also, I believe, called for at home by the gentleman. Are you different, Louise?"

"The situation is different."

"Exactly what is the situation?"

"One that I'm old enough to handle by myself."

"Old enough yes—at thirty-two, you should be—but are you equipped?"

"Equipped?" Louise looked down at her body as if her father had called attention to something that was missing from it, a part that had failed to grow, or one she had carelessly lost somewhere between the house and the library. She said, keeping her voice steady, "Daddy, I'm going over to play cards with two friends who happen to be male. Either one of them would be glad to pick me up here, but I have my own car and I enjoy driving it."

"Louise, honey, I'm not questioning your motives. I'm simply reminding you that you've had very little experience in—well, in keeping men in line."

"Haven't I just."

"I also remind you that appearances still count, even in this licentious world. It doesn't look right for a girl of your class and position to go sneaking off surreptitiously at night to visit two men in their house."

"Home, if you don't mind."

"Call it what you will."

"I'll call it what it is," Louise said sharply. "A *home,* where Charlie and Ben have lived since they were children. As for my sneaking off surreptitiously, that's some trick when you drive a sports car that can be heard a mile away. I must be a magician. Or are you getting deaf?"

Mrs. Lang moved her heavy body awkwardly out of her chair, grunting with the effort. She stood between her husband and daughter like a giant referee between two midget boxers who weren't obeying the rules. "Now I've heard just about enough from you two. Louise, you ought to be ashamed, talking fresh to your father like that. And you, Joe, my goodness, you've got to realize you're living in the modern world. People don't put so much stock in things like a man calling for his date at home. It's not as if Charlie was a stranger you didn't know. You've met him and talked to him. He's a nice, agreeable man."

"Agreeable, yes." Mr. Lang nodded dryly. "I said it was hot and he agreed. I said it was too bad about the stock market and he agreed. I—"

Louise interrupted. "He's shy. You embarrassed him by asking him personal questions about his background and his job."

"I don't mind people asking me about my job and my background."

"You're not shy like Charlie."

"What makes Charlie shy?"

"Sensitivity, *feeling*—"

"Which I don't have?"

Mrs. Lang put her hands, not too gently, on Louise's shoulders and pushed her out of the door into the hall. "You go along now, dear, or you'll be late. Don't pay too much attention to Dad tonight, he's having some trouble with his supervisor. Do you have your latchkey?"

"Yes."

"Enjoy yourself, dear."

"Yes." Slowly, Louise reached up and touched the bow in her hair. She could scarcely feel it through the fabric of her glove but it was still there, for Charlie. "Do I—look all right?"

"Just lovely. I told you that before, at least I think I did."

"Yes. Good night, Mother."

Mrs. Lang made sure the door was locked behind Louise, then she went back into the living room, panting audibly, as if it took more energy to be a referee than to be a contestant. She wished Joe would go to bed and leave her to dream a little: *Louise will be married in the church, of course. With a long-sleeved, floor-length bridal gown to hide her skinny arms and legs, and the right make-up to enlarge her eyes, she'll look quite presentable. She has a nice smile. Louise has a very nice smile.*

Joe was standing where she'd left him, in the middle of the room. "Sensitivity, feeling, my foot. He seemed plain ordinary stupid to me. Hardly opened his mouth."

"Oftentimes you don't bring out the best in people, Joe."

"Why shouldn't I ask him questions about his job? What's he got to hide?"

"Nothing," his wife said mildly. "Now stop carrying on, it's bad for your health. Charlie Gowen is a fine-looking young man with good manners and gainful employment. He probably has a wide choice of female companions. You should consider it a lucky thing that he picked Louise."

"Should I?"

"As for his being shy, I, for one, find it refreshing. There are so many smart-alecky young men going around tooting their own horn these days. That kind doesn't appeal to Louise. She has a spiritual nature." She added, without any change of tone, "I'm warning you, Joe. Don't ruin her chances or you'll regret it."

"Her chances for what? Becoming the talk of the town? Acquiring a bad reputation that might even cost her her job?"

"Louise and Charlie will be getting married."

For a moment Joe was stunned into silence. Then, "I see. Louise told you?"

"No."

"Charlie told you?"

"No. Nobody told me. Nobody had to. I can feel it in the air." She settled herself in the chair again and picked up her embroidery. "You may laugh at my intuition, but wasn't I right last fall when I said I could feel it in my bones that we'd have a wet winter? And about Mrs. Cudahy when I said she couldn't last more than a week and she died the next day? Wasn't I right?"

He didn't answer. It had been a wet winter, Mrs. Cudahy had died, Louise was marrying Charlie.

Ben met her at the door. He was freshly shaved—she could smell his shaving cream when they shook hands—and he had on a business suit, not the jeans and T-shirt he usually wore around the house.

"Well, you're all dressed up," Louise said, smiling. "Are we going out some place?"

Ben looked uneasy. "No. I mean, I'm going out. You and Charlie can do what you like, of course."

"But I thought we were all three of us going to play cards as usual. What made you change your mind? Has anything happened?"

"No. I just figured you and Charlie might want to be alone together for a change."

She was seized by a panic so severe that for several seconds her heart stopped. She could feel it in the middle of her chest, as heavy and silent as a stone. "If Charlie wanted to be alone with me, he'd arrange it that way, wouldn't he?"

"Not necessarily. Charlie may want something but he often doesn't know he wants it until I tell him."

"Until you tell him," she repeated. "Well, did you?"

"What?"

"Tell him he wanted to be alone with me tonight?"

"No. I just said I was going out."

"And he didn't run away," she said, "so that means he wants to be alone with me? How very romantic."

"Don't be childish, Louise. You know Charlie as well as I do. He doesn't spell romance for anyone."

A slight noise at the end of the hall made them both turn simultaneously. Charlie was standing at the door of his bedroom, coatless and with one hand on his tie as if he hadn't quite finished dressing.

"Why, I can so," he said with a frown. "I can spell *romance*. R-o-m-a-n-c-e."

Louise hesitated a moment, then gave him a quick little nod of approval. "That's very good, Charlie."

"Not really. It's an easy word. I bet I could spell it when I was nine years old."

"I bet you could."

"Maybe not, though. I can't remember much about when I was nine. Ben does my remembering for me. You know what he remembered tonight, Louise?"

"No. What?"

"That I had a nice sense of humor when I was young."

"I'm not surprised."

"I am." He turned to Ben. "I thought you were going out tonight. Didn't you tell me that?"

"Yes."

"You'd better hurry. Louise and I have something to talk about."

Louise flushed and stared down at the stained and worn carpet. One of the first things she'd do would be to replace it. She had money in the bank, she would use it to fix the place up before she invited anyone, even her parents, to visit her in her own home.

"Well, I can take a hint," Ben said, sounding very pleased. "I know when I'm not wanted. Good night, you two. Have fun."

He went outside, closing the door softly behind him, as if the slightest sound might change Charlie's mood. The night air was cool but sweat was running down behind his ears and under his collar like cold, restless worms. Before he got into his car he turned to glance back at the house. The drapes in the front room hadn't been drawn and he could see Louise sitting on the davenport and Charlie standing facing her, bending over a little, ready to whisper into her ear.

Ben let out his breath suddenly and violently, as if he'd been holding it for years. He stood on the driveway for a long time, not watching the house anymore, just breathing in and out, in and out, like any free man on a summer night.

Charlie said, "Are you comfortable, Louise?"

"Yes."

"If it's too cool for you in here, I could turn on the heater."

"I'm fine, I really am."

"You don't think I hurt Ben's feelings, practically ordering him to get out of the house like that?"

"I'm sure he's not hurt. Stop worrying and sit down."

He sat beside her and she leaned toward him a little so that their shoulders touched and she could feel the smoothness of his arm and the hardness of its muscle. She wanted to tell him how strong he was and how much she admired strength when it was combined with gentleness like his. But she was afraid he would become mute with embarrassment, or else claim, quite flatly, that he wasn't the way she imagined him at all, he was weak and brutal.

"I had to get rid of him," Charlie said, "so you and I could talk. Ben doesn't have to be in on everything, does he?"

"No."

"When he's around and I make a remark or ask a question, he always has to know why. Ben always has to know the why of things. Sometimes there *is* no why. You understand that, don't you?"

"Of course," Louise said softly. "It's that way with love."

"Love?"

"Nobody can explain what it is, what makes people fall in love with each other. Do you remember that first night when you were sitting in the library and I looked over and there you were with that book on architecture? I felt so strange, Charlie, as if the world had begun to move faster and I had to cling like mad to stay on it. It hasn't slowed down even for a minute, Charlie."

He stared down at the floor, frowning, as if he were trying to see it move in space. "I don't like that idea. It makes me dizzy."

"I'm dizzy, too. So we're two dizzy people. What's the matter with that?"

"It's not scientific. Nobody can feel the world move."

"I can."

He drew away from her as if she'd confessed having a disease he didn't want to catch. Then he got up entirely and walked over to the window. He could see the dark figure of a man standing in the driveway and he knew it must be Ben. It worried him. Ben didn't stand quietly in driveways, he was always busy, always moving like the world and making people dizzy, unsure of themselves, unable to figure out the why of anything even if there was one.

He said, "Did you tell Ben what we talked about on the telephone?"

"What we talked—?"

"The information I asked you to get for me. The house, who lives in the house on Jacaranda Road. You found out for me, didn't you?"

Louise was sitting so still he thought she'd suddenly gone to sleep with her eyes open, a dreamless sleep because her face held no expression whatever. In nice dreams you smiled, in bad ones you cried and woke up screaming and Ben came in and asked *why?*

He went over and put his hand on her shoulder to wake her up. "Louise? You didn't forget about it, did you? It's important to me. You see, these people—the people who live in the house—have a dog, a little brown dog. When I drove past there this morning on my way to work the dog chased my car and I nearly hit the poor creature. One inch closer and I would have killed it. I must tell those people they've got to take better care of their little dog unless they want it to be killed by a car or something. Isn't that the right thing for me to do?"

He knew she wasn't sleeping because she stirred and blinked her eyes, though she still didn't speak.

"Louise?"

"Is—this what you wanted to talk to me about, Charlie?"

"Why, yes. It may not seem important to you, but I love dogs. I couldn't bear to hurt one, see it all mangled and bloody."

She looked down at her blue dress. It was spotless, unwrinkled. It bore no sign that she had run out into the street after Charlie's car and been dragged under the wheels and lacerated; and Charlie, unaware that anything had happened, had driven on alone. He had seen nothing and felt little more. *Maybe I felt a slight bump but I thought it was a hole in the road, I certainly didn't know it was you, Louise. What were you doing out on the road chasing cars like a dog?*

"Oakley," she said in a high, thin voice. "Mrs. Cathryn Oakley."

"The little dog has no father?"

"I guess not."

"Do you spell her first name with a *C* or a *K*?"

"C-a-t-h-r-y-n."

"You must have looked it up in the city directory?"

"Yes. Mrs. Oakley is listed as head of the household, with one minor child."

Charlie's face was flushed, as if he'd come out of the cold into some warm place. "It's funny she'd want to live alone in that big house with just a little girl."

He knew, as soon as the words left his mouth, that he'd made a mistake. But Louise didn't seem to notice. She had stood up and was brushing off her dress with both hands. He could see the outline of her thighs, thin, delicate-boned, with hardly any solid flesh to protect them from being crushed under a man's weight. She wasn't wearing any garters and he would have liked to ask her how she kept her stockings up. It was a perfectly innocent question on his part, but he was afraid she would react the way Ben would, as if such thoughts didn't occur to normal men, only to him, Charlie. *"Why do you ask that, Charlie?" "Because I want to know." "But why do you want to know?" "Because it's interesting." "Why is it interesting?" "Because gravity is pulling her stockings down and she must be doing something to counteract it."*

Louise had taken her gloves out of her handbag and was putting them on, holding her fingers stiff and smoothing the fabric down over each one very carefully. Charlie looked away as if she were doing something private that he had no right to watch.

She said, "I'd better be going now."

"But you just got here. I thought you and I were going to have a talk."

"We already have, haven't we?"

"Not real—"

"I think we've covered the important thing, anyway—Mrs. Oakley and her dog and her child. That was the main item on tonight's agenda, wasn't it? Perhaps the only one, eh, Charlie?"

She sounded friendly and she was smiling, but he was suddenly and terribly afraid of her. He backed away from her, until his buttocks and shoulders touched the wall. It was a cool wall with hot red roses climbing all over it.

"Don't," he whispered. "Don't hurt me, Louise."

Her face didn't alter except that one end of her smile began to twitch a little.

"Louise, if I've done anything wrong, I'm sorry. I try to do what you and Ben tell me to because my own thinking isn't too good sometimes. But tonight nobody told me."

"That's right. Nobody told you."

"Then how was I to know? I saw you and Ben looking at each other in the hall and I could sense, I could feel, you were expecting me to do something, but I didn't understand what it was. You and Ben, you're my only friends. I'd do anything for you if you'd just tell me what you want."

"I won't do that."

"Why not?"

"You must figure it out for yourself, apart from Ben and me."

"I can't. I *can't.* Help me, Louise. Hold out your hand to me."

She walked toward him, her arms outstretched stiffly like a robot obeying an order. He took both her hands and pressed them hard against his chest. She could feel the fast, fearful beating of his heart and she wished it would stop suddenly and forever, and hers would stop with it.

"Oh God, Louise, don't leave me here alone in this cold dark."

"I can't make it any lighter for you," she said quietly. "Warmer, yes, because there would be two of us. I've had foolish dreams about you, Charlie, but I've never kidded myself that I could turn on any lights for you when other people, even professionals, have failed. I can share your darkness, though, when you need me. I know what darkness is, I have some of my own."

329

"For me to share?"

"Yes."

"And I can help you, too?"

"You already have."

He held her body close against his own. "It's warmer already, isn't it, Louise? Don't you feel it?"

"Yes."

"Imagine me helping anybody, that's a switch. I could laugh. I could laugh out loud."

"Don't."

She put one hand gently over his mouth, staring into his eyes as she would twin pools of water. On the surface she saw her own reflection, but underneath there were live creatures of every shape and size, moving mysteriously in and out, toward and past each other; arriving, departing, colliding, unconcerned with time or joy or grief. At the bottom of the cold, dark water lay the stones of death, but small green creatures clung to them and survived, unafraid. There was enough light to live by, even down there, and they had each other for comfort.

Charlie said, "Why—are you looking at me like that?"

"Because I love you."

"That's not a reason."

"It's reason enough for anything."

"You talk sillier than I do," he said, touching her hair and the ribbon in it. "I like silly girls."

"I've never been called a silly girl before. I'm not sure I approve."

"You do, though. I can tell."

He laughed, softly and contentedly, then he swooped her up in his arms and carried her over to the davenport. She sat on his lap with her face pressed against the warm moist skin of his neck.

"Louise," he said in a whisper, "I want you and me to be married in a church and everything, like big shots."

"I want that, too."

"You in a long fluffy dress, me in striped trousers and a morning coat. I can rent an outfit like that down at Cosgrave's. One of the fellows at work rented one for his sister's wedding and he said it made him feel like an ambassador. He hated to take it back because actually he's just a truck driver. I wouldn't mind feeling like an ambassador, for a few hours anyway."

"An ambassador to where?"

"Anywhere. I guess they all feel pretty much the same."

"I suppose I could stand being an ambassador's wife for a few hours," Louise said dreamily, "as long as I could have you back again exactly the way you are now."

"Exactly?"

"Yes."

"Now you're talking silly again. I mean, it's not sensible to want me just as I am, with all my—my difficulties."

"Shhh, Charlie. Don't think about the difficulties, think about us. We must start planning. First, we'll have to decide on a church and a date and make a reservation. Someone told me that autumn weddings are starting to outnumber June weddings."

"Autumn," he repeated. "It's August already."

"If that's too soon for you," she said quickly, "we'll postpone it. Is it too soon, Charlie?"

She knew the answer before she asked the question. The muscles of his arms had gone rigid and the pulse in his neck was beating fast and irregularly. It was as if he could picture her in a long fluffy dress and himself in a morning coat, looking like an ambassador, but he couldn't put the two of them together, at one time and in one place.

"Actually," she said, "when I consider it, it does seem like rushing things. There are so many plans to make, and as you said, it's August already."

"Yes."

"I've always thought Christmas would be a good time for a wedding. Things are so gay then, with all the pretty parcels and people singing carols. And the weather's usually good here at Christmas too. Sometimes it's the very best weather of the year. You wouldn't have to worry about rain getting your striped trousers wet. You couldn't very well feel like an ambassador with your trousers wet, could you?"

"I guess not."

"You like Christmas, don't you, Charlie? Opening packages and everything? Of course I don't want to rush you. If you'd rather wait until early spring or even June—"

"No," he said, touched by her desire to please him and wanting to please her in return. "I don't want to wait even until Christmas. I think we should be married right away. Maybe the first week of September, if you can be ready by then."

"I've been ready for a year."

"But we just met a year ago."

"I know."

"You mean you fell in love with me right away, just looking at me, not knowing a thing about me? That's funny."

"Not to me. Oh, Charlie, I'm so happy."

"Imagine me making anyone happy," Charlie said. "Ben will certainly be surprised."

Ben wouldn't be able to say *I don't know* anymore. He'd have to admit that the frog turned into a prince and lived happily ever after with his princess.

"Louise, I just thought, what if your parents don't approve? Your father doesn't seem to like me very much."

"Yes, he *does*. He told me tonight as I was leaving that you were a fine young man."

"Did he really?"

"It wouldn't matter anyway, Charlie."

"Yes, it would. I want everything to be right, everyone to be —well, on our side."

"Everything will be right," she said. "Everyone is on our side."

She thought of the small green creatures clinging to the stones at the bottom of the cold dark water. They survived, with nothing on their side but each other.

8

IT WAS THE following noon that Kate Oakley received the letter. She was alone in the house; Mary Martha had gone to the playground with Jessie and Jessie's brother, Mike, who was supposed to see to it that the girls stayed off the jungle gym and kept their clothes clean. Kate had promised to drive them to the Museum of Natural History right after lunch.

She liked to take the girls places and let people assume they were both her daughters, but she was dreading this particular excursion. The museum used to be—and perhaps still was—one of Sheridan's favorite hangouts. He hadn't seen Mary Martha for four months and Kate was afraid that if he ran into her now there would be a scene in front of everybody, quiet and sarcastic if he was sober, loud and weepy if he wasn't. Still, she had to risk it. There weren't many places she could take Mary Martha without having to pay, and money was very short.

She had received no check from Sheridan for temporary support for nearly two months. She knew it was Sheridan's way of punishing her for keeping him away from Mary Martha but she was determined not to give in. She was strong—stronger than he was—and in the end she would win, she would get the money she needed to bring Mary Martha up in the manner she deserved. Things would be as they were before. She would have a woman to do the cleaning and laundering, a seamstress to make Mary Martha's school clothes, a gardener to mow the vast lawn and cut the hedges and spray the poison oak. The groceries would be delivered and she would sign the bill without bothering to check it and tip the delivery boy with real money, not a smile, the way she had to tip everyone now.

These smile tips didn't cost her anything but they were expensive. They came out of her most private account, her personal capital. Nothing had been added to this capital for a long time; she had been neither loved nor loving, she offered no mercy and accepted none; hungry, she refused to eat; weary, she couldn't rest; alone, she reached out to no one. Sometimes at night, when Mary Martha was in bed asleep and the house seemed like a huge empty cave, Kate could feel her impending bankruptcy but she didn't realize that it had very little connection with lack of money.

She was vacuuming the main living room when she saw the postman coming up the flagstone walk. She went out into the hall but she didn't open the door to exchange greetings with him. She waited until he dropped the mail in the slot, then she scooped it up greedily from the floor. There was no check from Sheridan, only a couple of bills and a white envelope with her name and address printed on it. The contents of the envelope were squeezed into one corner like a coin wrapped in paper and her first thought was that Sheridan was playing another trick on her, sending her a dime or a quarter to imply she was worth no more than that. She ripped open the envelope with her thumbnail. There was no coin inside. A piece of notepaper had simply been folded and refolded many times, the way a child might fold a note to be secretly passed during class.

The note was neatly printed in black ink:

Your daughter takes too dangerous risks with her delicate body. Children must be guarded against the cruel hazards of life and fed good, nourishing food so their bones will be padded. Also clothing. You should put plenty of clothing on her, keep arms and legs covered, etc. In the name of God please take better care of your little girl.

She stood for a minute, half paralyzed with shock. Then, when her blood began to flow again, she reread the note, more slowly and carefully. It didn't make sense. No one—not even Sheridan, who'd accused her of everything else—had ever accused her of neglecting Mary Martha. She was well fed, well clothed, well supervised. She was, moreover, rather a timid child, not given to taking dangerous risks or risks of any kind unless challenged by Jessie.

Kate refolded the note and put it back in the envelope. She thought, *it can't be a mistake because it's addressed to me and my name's spelled correctly. Perhaps there's some religious crank in the neighborhood who's prejudiced against divorced women, but it hardly seems possible now that divorce is so common.*

Only one thing was certain: the letter was an attack, and the person most likely to attack her was Sheridan.

She went out into the hall and telephoned Ralph MacPherson's office. "Mac, I hate to bother you again."

"That's all right, Kate. Are you feeling better today?"

"I was, until the mail came. I just received an anonymous letter and I think I know who—"

"Don't think about it at all, Kate. Tear it up and forget it."

"No, I want you to see it."

"I've seen quite a few of them in my day," Mac said. "They're all the same, sick and rotten."

"I want you to see it," she repeated, "because I'm pretty sure it's from Sheridan. If it is, he's further gone than I imagined. He may even be—well, committable."

"That's a big word in these parts, Kate. Or in any parts, for that matter."

"People are committed every day."

"Not on the word of a disgruntled spouse . . . All right. Bring the letter down to my office. I'll be here until I leave for court at 1:30."

"Thank you, Mac. Thank you very much."

She dressed hurriedly but with care, as if she were going to be put on exhibition in front of a lot of people, one of whom had written her the letter.

Before leaving the house she made sure all the windows and doors on the ground floor were locked, and when she had backed her car out of the garage she locked the garage doors behind her. She had nothing left to steal, but the locking habit had become fixed in her. She no longer thought of doors as things to open; doors were to close, to keep people out.

She usually handled her small car without thinking much about it, but now she drove as she had dressed, with great care, as though a pair of unfriendly eyes was watching her, ready to condemn her as an unfit mother if she made the slightest mistake, a hand signal executed a little too slowly, a corner turned a little too fast.

She headed for the school playground, intending to tell the girls that she would be late picking them up. She had gone about three blocks when she stopped for a red light and saw, in the rear-view mirror, an old green coupé pull up behind her. Kate paid more attention to cars than most women, especially since she'd been living alone, and she recognized it instantly as the car she'd noticed parked outside her house the previous afternoon.

She tried to keep calm, the way Mac had told her to: *Don't jump to conclusions, Kate. If you thought Sheridan was driving that car, why didn't you go out and confront him, find out why he was there? If it happens again—*

Well, it was happening again.

She opened the door and had one foot on the road when the light changed. The left lane was clear and the green coupé turned into it and shot past her with a grinding of gears. Its grimy windows were closed and she could see only that a man was behind the wheel. It was enough. Sheridan was following her. He may even have been waiting outside the house while the postman delivered his letter, eager to watch its effect on her. She thought, *Well, here it is, Sheridan, here's the effect.*

She didn't hesitate even long enough to close the door. She pressed down on the accelerator and the door slammed shut with the sudden forward thrust of her car. For the next five minutes she was not in conscious control either of herself or of the car. It was as though a devil were driving them both and he was responsible to no one and for no one; he owned the roads, let others use them at their own risk.

Up and down streets, around corners, through a parking lot, down an alley, she pursued the green coupé. Twice she was almost close enough to force it over to the curb but each time it got away. She was not even aware of cars honking at her and people yelling at her until she ran a red light. Then she heard the shrieking of her own brakes as a truck appeared suddenly in front of her. Her head snapped forward until it pressed against the steering wheel. She sat in a kind of daze while the truck driver climbed out of the cab.

"For Chrissake, you drunk or something? That was a red light."

"I didn't—see it."

"Well, keep your eyes open next time. You damn near got yourself killed. You woulda spoiled my record, I got the best record in the company. How they expect a guy to keep his record with a lot of crazy women scooting around in kiddie cars?"

"Shut up," she said. "Please shut up."

"Well, well, now you're trying to get tough with me, eh? Listen, lady, you'll be damn lucky if I don't report you for reckless driving, maybe drunk driving. You been drinking?"

"No."

"They all say that. Where's your driver's license?"

"In my purse."

"Get it out."

"Please don't—"

"Lady, a near accident like this happens and I'm supposed to check on it, see? Maybe you've got some kind of restriction on your license, like you're to wear glasses when you're driving, or a hearing aid."

She fumbled around in her purse until she found her wallet with her driver's license in it. On the license there was a little picture of her, taken the day she'd passed her test. She was smiling confidently and happily into the camera.

She saw the truck driver staring at the picture in disbelief. "This is you, lady?"

She wanted to reach out and strike him between the eyes, but instead she said, "It was taken three years ago. I've been— things have happened to me. When you lose weight, it always shows in the face, it makes you appear—well, older. I was trying to think of a nicer word for it but there isn't one, is there? More aged? That's no improvement. More ancient, decrepit? Worn out? Obsolete?"

"Lady, I didn't mean it like that," he said, looking embarrassed. "I mean—oh hell, let's get out of here."

A crowd had begun to gather. The truck driver waved them away and climbed back into his cab. The green coupé had long since disappeared.

The two girls, on Mike's orders, were sitting on a bench in an area of the playground hidden from the street by an eight-foot oleander hedge. Mike was lying face down on the grass nearby, listening to a baseball game on a transistor radio. Every now and then he raised his head, consulted his wristwatch in an authoritative manner, and gave the girls what was intended to be a hypnotic glance.

They had both been absolutely silent and motionless for seven minutes except for the occasional blink of an eye or twitch of a nose. Mike was beginning to worry about whether he actually had hypnotized them and how he was going to snap them out of it, when Jessie suddenly jumped off the bench.

"Oh, I hate this game! It's not even a *game,* seeing who can stay stillest the longest."

"You're just sore because Mary Martha won," Mike said airily. "I was betting she would. You can't keep your trap shut for two seconds."

"I can if I want to."

"Yackety yak."

"Anyhow, I know why you're making us sit here."

"O clever one, do tell."

"So none of your buddies going past will see you babysitting. I heard you tell Daddy you'd never be able to hold up your head in public again if they saw you playing with two little girls. But Daddy said you had to play with us anyway. Or else."

"Well, I wish I'd taken the *or else,*" Mike said in disgust. "Anything'd be better than looking after a pair of dimwitted kids who should be able to look after themselves. *I* didn't need a babysitter at your age."

Jessie blushed, but the only place it showed was across the bridge of her nose where repeated sunburns had peeled off layers of skin. "I don't need one either except I've got sore hands."

"You're breaking my heart with your itty bitty sore hands. Man, oh man, you get more mileage out of a couple of blisters than I could get from a broken neck."

"If I won the game," Mary Martha said wistfully, "may I move now? There's a bee on my arm and it tickles me."

"So tickle it back," Mike said and turned up the volume of the radio.

"My goodness, he's mean," Mary Martha whispered behind her hand. "Was he born that way?"

"I've only known him for nine years, but he probably was."

"Maybe some evil witch put a curse on him. Do you know any curses?"

"Just g-o-d-d-a-m, which I never say."

"No, I mean real curses." Mary Martha contorted her face until it looked reasonably witchlike. Then she spoke in a high eerie voice:

"Abracadabra,
Purple and green,
This little boy
Will grow up mean."

"Did you just make that up?" Jessie asked.

"Yes."

"It's very good."

"I think so, too," Mary Martha said modestly. "We could make up a whole bunch of them about all the people we hate. Who will we start with?"

"Uncle Howard."

"I didn't know you hated your Uncle Howard."

Jessie looked surprised, as if she hadn't known it herself until she heard her own voice say so. She stole a quick glance at Mike to see if he was listening, but he was engrossed in the ball game, his eyes closed. She said, "You won't ever tell anyone, will you?"

"Cross my heart and hope to die. Now let's start the curse. You go first."

"No, you go first."

Mary Martha assumed her witchlike face and voice:

"Abracadabra,
Yellow and brown,
Uncle Howard's the nastiest
Man in town."

"I don't like that one very much," Jessie said soberly.

"Why not?"

"Oh, I don't know. Let's play another game."

From the street a horn began to blow, repeating a pattern of three short, two long.

"That's my mother," Mary Martha said. "We'd better wake Mike up and tell him we're leaving."

"I'm awake, you numbskull," Mike said, opening his eyes and turning down the volume of the radio. Then he looked at his watch. "It's only a quarter after twelve. She's not supposed to be here until one." He rolled over on his back and got up. "Well, who am I to argue with good fortune? Come on, little darlings. Off to the launching pad."

"You don't have to come with us," Jessie said.

"No kidding? You mean you can actually walk out of here without breaking both your legs? I don't believe it. Show me."

"Oh, shut up."

"Yes, you shut up," Mary Martha added loyally.

The two girls went out through the stone arch, arm in arm, as if to show their solidarity against the enemy.

Mike waited a couple of minutes before following them. He saw Mrs. Oakley standing on the curb talking to them, then Mary Martha and her mother got into the car and Jessie turned and walked back to the playground, alone. She was holding her head high and her face was carefully and deliberately blank.

Mike said, "What's the matter?"

"We're not going to the Museum today."

"Why not?"

"Mrs. Oakley has some errands to do in town. Mary Martha didn't want to go along but she had to."

"Why?"

"Mrs. Oakley won't leave her at the playground alone anymore."

"What does she mean, alone?" Mike said, scowling. "*I'm* here."

"I guess she meant without a grownup."

"For Pete's sake, what does she think I am? A two-year-old child? Man, oh man, women sure are hard to figure . . . Well, come on, no use hanging around here anymore. Let's go home."

"All right."

"Aren't you even going to argue?"

"No."

"You're sick, kid."

"I'm sorry," Kate Oakley repeated for the third or fourth time. "I hate to disappoint you and Jessie but I can't help it. Something unexpected came up and I must deal with it. You understand that, don't you?"

Mary Martha nodded. "But I could have stayed at the playground with Jessie while you were dealing."

"I want you with me."

"Why? To protect you?"

"No," Kate said with a sharp little laugh. "You've got it all wrong, sweetikins. *I'm* protecting *you*. What on earth gave you the silly idea that I need your protection?"

"I don't know."

"Sometimes your mind works in a way that truly baffles me. I mean, really, angel, it doesn't make sense that I need your protection, does it? I am a grownup and you're a little girl. Isn't that right?"

"Yes, ma'am," Mary Martha said politely. She would have liked to ask what her mother was protecting her from, but she was aware that Kate was already upset. The signs were all there: some subtle, like the faint rash that was spreading across her neck; some obvious, like the oversized sunglasses she was wearing. Mary Martha didn't understand why her mother put on these sunglasses when she was under pressure, she knew only that it was a fact. Even in the house on a dark day Kate sometimes wore them and Mary Martha had come to hate the sight of them. They were like a wall or a closed door behind which untold, untellable things were happening. If you threw questions at this wall they bounced back like ping-pong balls: *what on earth do you mean, lamb?*

They had reached the center of town by this time. Kate drove into the parking lot behind the white four-story building where Mac had his office. It was the first inkling Mary Martha had of where her mother was going and she dreaded the thought of waiting in Mac's outer office, listening to the rise and fall of voices, never hearing quite enough and never understanding quite enough of what she heard. If the voices became distinct enough, Miss Edgeworth, Mac's receptionist, started talking loudly and cheerfully about the weather and how Mary Martha was doing in school and what a pretty dress she was wearing.

When her mother got out of the car Mary Martha made no move to follow her.

"Well?" Kate said. "Aren't you coming?"

"I can wait here."

"No. I don't like the look of that parking-lot attendant. You can't trust these—"

"Or I could go to the library and maybe start on one of my book reports."

"I don't think a nine-year-old should be wandering around downtown by herself."

"The library's only a block away."

Kate hesitated. "Well, all right. But you've got to promise you'll go straight there, not loiter in the stores or anything. And once you're there, you're to stay. No matter how long I am, don't come looking for me, just wait right there."

"I promise."

"You're a good girl, Mary Martha."

Mary Martha got out of the car. She was glad that her mother called her a good girl but she couldn't understand why she said it in such a strange, sad voice, as if having a good child was somehow harder to bear than having a bad one. She wondered what would happen if she turned bad. Maybe Kate would give her to Sheridan and that would be the end of the fighting over the divorce terms. Or maybe Sheridan wouldn't want her either, and she'd have to go and live with a foster family like the Brants and be Jessie's almost-sister.

Once the idea occurred to her, the temptation to try being bad was irresistible. The problem was how to begin. She thought of loitering in the stores, but she wasn't sure what loitering was or if she could do it. Then she heard her mother say, "I don't know what I'd do without you, Mary Martha," and the temptation died as suddenly as it had been born. She felt rather relieved. Loitering in stores didn't sound like much fun and probably the Brants couldn't afford to feed another mouth anyway.

Kate went in the rear entrance of the building and up the service stairs to avoid meeting anyone. After the bright light of noon the stairway seemed very dark. She stumbled once or twice but she didn't remove her sunglasses, she didn't even think of it. By the time she reached Mac's office on the third floor she was breathing hard and fast and the rash on her neck had begun to itch.

Miss Edgeworth was out to lunch. Her typewriter was covered and her desk was bare of papers, as though she'd tidied everything up in case she decided never to come back.

The door of Mac's office was open and he was sitting at his desk with his chair swiveled around to face the window. He was eating a sandwich, very slowly, as if he didn't like it or else liked it so much he didn't want to reach the end of it. Kate had known him for over twenty years and it seemed to her that he hadn't changed at all since she first met him. He was still as thin as a rake, and his hair was still brown and curly and cut very short to deny the curl. He had the reddish tan and bleached eyes of a sailor.

"Mac?"

He turned in surprise. "I didn't hear the elevator."

"I used the back steps."

"Well, come in, Kate, if you don't mind watching me eat. There's extra coffee, would you like some?"

"Yes, please."

He poured some coffee into a plastic cup. "Sit down. You look a bit under the weather, Kate. You're not dieting, I hope."

"Not by choice," she said grimly. "The support check's late again. Naturally. He's trying to make me crawl. That I'm used to, that I can stand. It's these—these awful other things, Mac."

"Have you seen him today?"

"About half an hour ago, on my way here. He was driving that same old green car he drove yesterday when he was parked outside the house. When I saw it in the rear-view mirror, something terrible came over me, Mac. I—I just wanted to *kill* him."

"Now, now, don't talk like that."

"I mean it. All I could think of was chasing him, ramming his car, running him down, getting rid of him some way, any way."

"But you didn't."

"I tried."

"You tried," he repeated thoughtfully. "Tell me about it, Kate."

She told him. He listened, with his head cocked to one side like a dog hearing a distant sound of danger.

"You might have been killed or seriously injured," he said when she'd finished.

"I know that now. I may even have known it then, but it didn't matter. I wasn't thinking of myself, or even, God help me, of Mary Martha. Just of him, Sheridan. I wanted to—I *had* to get even with him. This time he went too far."

"This time?"

"The letter, the anonymous letter."

"Have you got it with you?"

"Yes."

"Show it to me."

She took the letter out of her handbag and put it on his desk.

He studied the envelope for a minute, then removed the wad of paper and began unfolding it. He read aloud: "Your daughter takes too dangerous risks with her delicate body. Children must be guarded against the cruel hazards of life and fed good, nourishing food so their bones will be padded. Also clothing. You should put plenty of clothing on her, keep arms and legs covered, etc. In the name of God please take better care of your little girl."

"Well?" Kate said.

He leaned back in his chair and looked up at the ceiling. "It's a curious document. The writer seems sincere and also very fond—if fond is the correct word—of children in general."

"Why in general? Why not Mary Martha in particular? Sheridan's never particularly liked children; he's crazy about Mary Martha because she's an extension of his ego, such as it is."

"This doesn't sound like Sheridan's style to me, Kate."

"Who else would accuse me of neglecting my daughter?"

"I don't read this as an accusation, exactly. It seems more like a plea or a warning, as if the writer believes he has advance knowledge that something will happen to Mary Martha unless you take preventative steps." Alarmed by her sudden pallor, he added quickly, "Notice I said he *believes* he has such knowledge. Beliefs often have little relationship to fact. My own feeling is that this is from some neighborhood nut. Have you or Mary Martha had any unpleasantness with any of your neighbors recently?"

"Of course not. We mind our own business and I expect other people to mind theirs."

"Perhaps you expect too much," Mac said with a shrug. "Well, I wouldn't worry about the letter if I were you. It's unlikely, though not impossible, that Sheridan wrote it. If he did, he's flipped faster and further than I care to contemplate."

"Will you find out the truth?"

"Naturally I'll try to contact him. If he's pulling these shenanigans he's got to be stopped, for his own sake as well as yours and Mary Martha's. Meanwhile I'll keep the letter, with your permission. I have a friend who's interested in such things. By the way, was it folded half a dozen times like this when it was delivered?"

"Yes."

"Kid stuff, I'd say. Just one more question, Kate. Did you manage to get the license number of the green car?"

"Yes. It's GVK 640."

"You're sure of that?"

"I should be," she said harshly. "I rammed his license plate."

"Kate. Kate, listen to me for a minute."

"No. I can't. I can't listen anymore. I want to talk, I've got to *talk* to somebody. Don't you understand, Mac? I spend all my time with a child. She's a wonderful girl, very bright and sweet, but she's only nine years old. I can't discuss things with her, I can't burden her with my problems or ask her for help or support. I've got to put up a front, pretend that everything's all right, even when I can feel the very earth crumbling under my feet."

"You've isolated yourself, Kate," he said calmly. "You used to have friends you could talk to."

"Friends are a luxury I can't afford anymore. Oh, people were very kind when Sheridan first moved out. They invited me over to cheer me up and hear all the gruesome details. One thing I learned, Mac, and learned well: the only people who really enjoy a divorce are your best friends. All that vicarious excitement and raw emotion, all the blood and guts spilled—why, it was almost as good as television."

"You're being unfair to them."

"Perhaps. Or perhaps I didn't have the right kind of friends. Anyway, I stopped accepting invitations and issuing them. I didn't want people coming over and feeling sorry for me because I was alone, and sorry for themselves because I couldn't afford to offer them drinks. You want to lose friends, Mac? Stop buying liquor. No money down, results guaranteed."

"What about Mary Martha?" Mac said.

"What about her?"

"She needs some kind of social environment."

"She has friends. One friend in particular, Jessie Brant. I don't especially care for the Brants—Ellen's one of these pushy modern types—but Jessie's an interesting child, free-wheeling and full of beans. I think she's a good influence on Mary Martha, who's inclined to be overcautious . . . That's another thing about the letter, Mac. It was inaccurate. Mary Martha doesn't take dangerous risks, and I certainly wouldn't call her delicate. She's the same age and height as Jessie but she outweighs her by eight or ten pounds."

"Perhaps the 'risks' mentioned didn't refer to a physical activity like tree-climbing, but to something else that Mary Martha did. Say, for instance, that she was a little reckless while riding her bike and one of the neighbors had to swerve his car to avoid hitting her—"

"Mary Martha is very careful on her bicycle."

"Yes. Well, it was only a suggestion."

She was silent for a minute. Then she said in a low bitter voice, "You see? It's happened the way it always does. I was talking about myself, and now we're suddenly talking about Mary Martha again. There is no me anymore. There's just the woman who lives in the big house who looks after the little girl. I've lost my personship. I might just as well have a number instead of a name."

"Calm down now, Kate, and get hold of yourself."

"I told you, myself doesn't exist anymore. There is no me, there's nothing to get hold of."

In the outer office Miss Edgeworth had come back from lunch. As soon as she'd found out that Mrs. Oakley had made an appointment with Mac, she'd gone out and bought two chocolate bars to give to Mary Martha. When she saw that Mrs. Oakley hadn't brought Mary Martha along after all, Miss Edgeworth was so relieved she ate both of the chocolate bars herself.

9

AFTER THE NOON lunchers departed and before the one o'clock lunchers arrived there was always a short lull in the cafeteria which Ben managed for the owner. Ben used this period to stand out in the alley behind the cafeteria and soak up a little sun and smoke his only cigarette of the day. Ben didn't enjoy smoking but he became sick of food odors and he believed that smoking would dull his sense of smell.

He watched a flock of seagulls circling overhead, waiting for a handout. He thought what a fine day it was for the beginning of his new life. Charlie was engaged. Charlie and Louise were going to be married. Ben had told the good news to his employees and some of his regular customers, and though most of them didn't even know Charlie, they were pleased because Ben was. The whole place seemed livelier. A wedding was in the air, it hardly mattered whose.

Ben leaned against the sunny wall, letting the smoke curl up through his nostrils like ether. He felt a little dizzy. He wasn't sure whether it was from the cigarette or from the surges of happiness that had been sweeping over him off and on all morning. *I'll let Louise and Charlie have the house, Mother always planned it that way. I'll get a little apartment down near the beach and buy a dog. I've always wanted a dog. I could have bought one years ago—Charlie would never have mistreated an animal, he's crazy about animals—but I never got around to it. I don't know the reason. Why, Charlie would cut off his right arm before he'd hurt a dog.*

"Ben."

At the sound of his name Ben turned, although he didn't recognize the voice. It was a little boy's voice, high and thin, not like Charlie's at all. Yet it was Charlie running toward him, down the alley from the street. His clothes were disheveled and he was clutching his stomach with both hands as though he were suffering an acute attack of cramps. Ben felt the happiness draining out of him. All the pores of his skin were like invisible wounds from which his life was spurting.

"What's—the matter, Charlie?"

"Oh God, Ben. Something terrible. She tried to kill me. A woman, a woman in a little blue car. I swear to God, Ben, she meant to kill me and I don't even know her, I never saw her before."

"Sshhh." Ben looked quickly up and down the alley. "Keep your voice down. Someone might hear you."

"But it's true! I didn't imagine it. I don't imagine things like that, ever. Other things, maybe, but not—"

"Calm down and tell me about it, quietly."

"Yes. Yes, I will, Ben. Anything you say."

"Take a deep breath."

"Yes."

"Now where did this happen?"

Charlie leaned against the wooden rubbish bin. His whole body was shaking and the more he tried to control it, the more violently it shook, as though the lines of communication between his brain and his muscles had been cut. "I d-don't remember the name of the street but it was over on the north side. I'd gone to Pinewood Park to eat my lunch."

"Why?"

"Why?" Charlie repeated. "Well, for the fresh air. Sun and fresh air, they're nice, they're good for you. Didn't you tell me that, Ben?"

"Yes. *Yes.* Now go on."

"I was driving back to work and this little blue car was in front of me, with a lady at the wheel. She was going real slow like maybe she was drunk and trying to be extra careful to avoid an accident. Well, I passed her. That's all I did, Ben, I just passed her."

"You didn't honk your horn?"

"No."

"Or look at her in a way that she might have—well, misinterpreted?"

"*No.* I swear to you, Ben, I just *passed* her. Then I heard this terrible sound of gears and I looked around and she was after me. I stepped on the gas to get away from her."

"Why?"

"What else could I have done? What would you have done?"

"Pulled over to the curb, or into a gas station, and asked the lady what the hell she thought she was doing."

"I never thought of that," Charlie said earnestly. "When someone chases me, I run."

"Yes, I guess you do." Ben wiped the sweat off his forehead with the back of his hand. Only a few minutes ago the sun had been like a warm, kindly friend. Now it was his enemy. It stabbed his eyes and temples and burned the top of his head where his hair was thinning, and the dry tender skin around his mouth. It imprisoned him in the alley with the smell of cooking food and the smell of Charlie's fear.

He lit another cigarette and blew the smoke out through his nostrils to deaden them. It was when he threw away the spent match that he noticed the little plant growing out of a crack in the concrete a yard or so from where Charlie was standing. It was about six inches high. It was covered with city dust and some of its leaves had been squashed by the wheel of a car, but it was still growing, still alive. He was filled with a sense of wonder. The little plant had nothing going for it at all: seeded by accident out of garbage, driven over, walked on, unwatered, with no rain since March, it was still alive.

He said, "Everything's going to be okay, Charlie. Don't worry about it. Things work out one way or another."

"But what do I do now, Ben?"

"Get back on the job or you'll be late."

"I can't use my own car."

"What's the matter with it?"

"Nothing," Charlie said. "The engine's running fine, only—well, here's how I figure it, Ben. That woman, she couldn't have anything against me when I don't even know her. So it must be the car. She has a grudge against the former owner and she thought he was driving, not me. So it seems obvious what I've got to do now."

"To you, perhaps. Not to me."

"Don't you see, Ben? Everything will be solved if I buy a new car. Oh, not a brand-new one but a different one so that woman won't chase me again."

If there was a woman, Ben thought, *and if there was a chase. Maybe he invented the whole thing as an excuse to change cars again.* "You can't afford to buy a car now," he said bluntly, "with the wedding coming up so soon."

Charlie looked surprised as if he'd forgotten all about the wedding. "I have money in the bank."

"You'll be needing it to buy Louise's ring, pay for the honeymoon, buy yourself some new clothes—"

"I'm old enough to make my own decisions," Charlie said, kicking the side of the rubbish bin. "I'm an engaged man. An engaged man has to plan things for himself."

Ben looked down at the little tomato plant growing out of the crack in the concrete. "Yes. Yes, I suppose he does."

"Thank you, Ben. I really do thank you."

"What for?"

"For everything. Even just for being around."

"You're an engaged man now, Charlie. I'm not going to be around much longer. You and Louise will be making a life of your own."

One of the Mexican busboys came out into the alley and said something to Ben in Spanish. The boy spoke softly, smiled softly, moved softly. Ben gave him fifty cents and the boy went back inside.

Charlie had paid no attention to the interruption. His eyes were fixed on Ben's face and his thin silky brows were stitched together in a frown. "You talk as if everything's going to change between us. But it's not. You'll be living with Louise and me, we'll be eating our meals together and playing cards in the evening the way we used to. Why should we let things change?"

"Things change whether we let them or not. And that's good—it keeps us from getting bored with life and with each other."

"But I'm *not* bored."

"Listen to me, Charlie. I won't be living with you and Louise, first because I don't want to, and second, because Louise wouldn't want me to, and third be—"

"Louise wouldn't mind. She's crazy about you, Ben. Why, I bet when you come right down to it, she'd just as soon marry you as marry me."

Ben reached out and grabbed him by the shoulder. "Goddam it, don't you talk like that. It's not fair to Louise. Do you hear me?"

"Yes," Charlie said in a whisper. "But I was only—"

"Sure, you were *only*. You're always *only*. You know what happens when you're *only*? Things get so fouled up—"

"I'm sorry, Ben."

"Yeah. Sure. Well."

"I only meant it as a compliment, to show you how much Louise likes you and that she wouldn't mind at all if you lived with us."

Ben took a deep drag on his cigarette. "I have to go back inside."

"You're not really mad at me?"

"No."

"And it's okay if I buy another car, say right after work?"

"It's your money."

"Wouldn't you like to come along and give me advice on what make and model to get and things like that?"

"Not this time."

Charlie heard the finality in his voice and he knew Ben meant *not this time and not any time ever again.*

He watched Ben go back into the cafeteria kitchen and he felt like a child abandoned in the middle of a city, in a strange noisy alley filled with the clatter of dishes and the clanking of pots and pans, and voices shouting, in Spanish, words he couldn't understand.

I'm frightened. Help me, Ben!

Not this time. Not any time ever again.

The two Charlies walked, together but not quite in step, down the alley and into the street, the engaged man about to buy a new car, and the little boy looking for a little girl to play with.

10

MISS ALBERT FIRST noticed the child because she was so neat and quiet. Most of the children who came to the library during summer vacation wore jeans or shorts with cotton T-shirts, as if they were using the place as a rest stop between beach and ball game, movie and music lesson. In groups or alone, they were always noisy and always chewing something—chocolate bars, bubble gum, peanut brittle, apples, ice cream cones, bananas, occasionally even cotton candy. Miss Albert had a recurrent nightmare in which she opened up one of the valuable art books and found all the pages glued together with cotton candy.

The little girl with the blonde ponytail was not chewing anything. She wore a pink dress with large blue daisies embroidered on the patch pockets. Her shoes had the sick-white color that indicated too many applications of polish to cover too many cracks in the leather. The child's expression was blank, as if her hair was drawn back and fastened so tightly that her facial muscles couldn't function. *It must be just like having your hair pulled all the time,* Miss Albert thought. *I wouldn't like it one bit. She probably doesn't either, poor child.*

The girl picked a magazine from the rack and sat down. She opened it, turned a few pages, then closed it again and sat with it on her lap, her eyes moving from the main door to the clock on the mezzanine and back again. The obvious conclusion was that the girl was waiting for someone. But Miss Albert didn't care for the obvious; she preferred the elaborate, even the bizarre. The child's family had just arrived in town, possibly to get away from a scandal of some kind—what kind Miss Albert would decide on her lunch hour—and the girl, alone and friendless, had come to the library for the children's story hour at half past one. But Miss Albert was not satisfied with this explanation. The girl had no look of anticipation on her face, no look of anything, thanks to that silly hair-do. *She'd be cute as a bug with her hair cut just below her ears and a fluffy bang. Or maybe with an Alice-in-Wonderland style like Louise, except on Louise it looks ridiculous at her age. Imagine Louise getting married, I think it's just wonderful. It shows practically anything can happen if you wait long enough.*

Half an hour passed. Miss Albert's stomach was rumbling and her arms were tired from taking books from her metal cart and putting them back on their proper shelves. From the children's section adjoining the main reading room, she could hear a rising babble of voices and the scrape of chairs being rearranged. In ten minutes the story hour would begin and Mrs. Gambetti, with nothing to do at children's checkout, would come and relieve Miss Albert for lunch. And Miss Albert would take her sandwich and thermos of coffee over to Encinas Park to watch the people with their sandwiches and their Thermoses of coffee.

But I really can't leave the child just sitting there, she thought. *Very likely she doesn't know where to go and she's probably too timid to ask, having been through all that scandal whatever it was but I'm sure it was quite nasty.*

Miss Albert pushed her empty cart vigorously down the aisle like a determined weekend shopper. At the sound of its squeaking wheels, Mary Martha turned her head and met Miss Albert's kindly and curious gaze.

Miss Albert said, "Hello."

Mary Martha had been instructed not to speak to strangers but she didn't think this would apply to strangers in a library, so she said, "Hello" back.

"What's your name?"

"Mary Martha Oakley."

"That's very pretty. You're new around here, aren't you, Mary?"

The child didn't answer, she just looked down at her shoes. Her toes had begun to wiggle nervously like captive fish. She didn't want the lady to notice so she attempted to hide her feet under the chair. During the maneuver, the magazine slid off her lap onto the floor.

Miss Albert picked it up, trying not to look surprised that a child so young would choose *Fortune* as reading material. "Did you move to town recently, Mary?"

"I'm not supposed to answer when people call me Mary because my name is Mary *Martha*. But I guess it's all right in a library. We didn't move to town, we've always lived here."

"Oh. I thought—well, it doesn't matter. The story hour is beginning in a minute or two. You just go through that door over there"—Miss Albert pointed—"and turn to the right and take a seat. Any seat you like."

"I already have a seat."

"But you can't hear the story from this distance."

"No, ma'am."

"You don't want to hear the story?"

"No, ma'am, I'm waiting for my mother."

Miss Albert concealed her disappointment behind a smile. "Well, perhaps you'd like something to read that would be a little more suitable for your age bracket."

Mary Martha hesitated, frowning. "Do you have books about everything?"

"Pretty nearly everything, from aardvarks to Zulus. What kind of book are you interested in?"

"One about divorce."

"Divorce?" Miss Albert said with a nervous little laugh. "Goodness, I'm not sure I— Wouldn't you like a nice picture book to look at instead?"

"No, ma'am."

"Well, I'm afraid I don't—that is, perhaps we'd better ask Miss Lang in the reference department. She knows more about such situations than I do. Come on, I'll take you over and introduce you."

Behind the reference desk Louise was acting very busy but Miss Albert wasn't fooled. Checking the number of sheep in Australia or the name of the capital of Ghana hadn't put the color in her cheeks and the dreamy, slightly out-of-focus look in her eyes.

"I hope I'm not interrupting anything," Miss Albert said, knowing very well she was, but feeling that it was the kind of thing that should be interrupted, especially during working hours. "This is Mary Martha Oakley, Louise. Mary Martha, this is Miss Lang."

Louise stared at the girl and said, "Oh" in a cold way that puzzled Miss Albert because Louise was usually very good with children.

"Mary Martha," Miss Albert added, "wants a book on divorce."

"Does she, indeed," Louise said. "Am I to gather, Miss Albert, that you've encouraged the child in her request by bringing her over here?"

"Not exactly. My gosh, Louise, I thought you'd get a kick out of it, a laugh."

"You know the rules of the library as well as I do, or you should. You're excused now, Miss Albert."

"Good," Miss Albert said crisply. "It happens to be my lunch hour."

Over Mary Martha's head she gave Louise a dirty look, but Louise wasn't even watching. Her eyes were still fixed on Mary Martha, as if they were seeing much more than a little girl in a pink dress with daisies.

"Oakley," she said in a thin, dry voice. "You live at 319 Jacaranda Road?"

"Yes, ma'am."

"With your mother."

"Yes."

"And your little dog."

"I don't have a little dog," Mary Martha said uneasily. "Just a cat named Pudding."

"But there's a dog in your neighborhood, isn't there? A little brown mongrel that chases cars?"

"I never saw any."

"Never? Perhaps you don't particularly notice dogs."

"Oh yes, I do. I always notice dogs because they're my favorites even more than cats and birds."

"So if you had one, you'd certainly protect it, wouldn't you?"

"Yes, ma'am."

Louise leaned across the desk and spoke in a smiling, confidential whisper. "If I had a dog that chased cars, I wouldn't be anxious to admit it, either. So of course I can't really blame you for fibbing. Just between the two of us, though—"

But there was nothing between the two of them. The child, wary-eyed and flushed, began backing away, her hands jammed deep in her pockets as if they were seeking the roots of the embroidered daisies. Ten seconds later she had disappeared out the front door.

Louise watched the door, in the wild hope that the girl would decide to come back and change her story—yes, she had a little dog that chased cars; yes, one of the cars was an old green Ford coupé.

There was a dog, there had to be, because Charlie said so. It had chased his car and Charlie, afraid for the animal's safety, felt that he should warn the owner. That's why he wanted to find out who lived at 319 Jacaranda Road. What other reason could he possibly have had?

He's not a liar, she thought. *He's so devastatingly honest sometimes it breaks my heart.*

She rubbed her eyes. They were dry and gritty and in need of tears. It was as if dirt, blowing in from the busy street, had altered her vision and blurred the distinctions between fact and fantasy.

"Don't talk so fast, lamb," Kate Oakley said. "Now let me get this straight. She asked you if you had a little brown dog that chased cars?"

Mary Martha nodded.

"And she wouldn't believe you when you denied it?"

"No, ma'am."

"It's crazy, that's what it is. I declare, I think the whole world has gone stark staring mad except you and me." She spoke with a certain satisfaction, as if the world was getting no more than it deserved and she was glad she'd stepped out of it in time and taken Mary Martha with her. "You'd expect a librarian, of all people, to be sensible, with all those books around."

Immediately after Kate's departure, Ralph MacPherson made two telephone calls. The first was to the apartment where Sheridan Oakley claimed to be living. He let the phone ring a dozen times, but, as on the previous afternoon and evening, there was no answer.

The second call was to Lieutenant Gallantyne of the city police department. After an exchange of greetings, Mac came to the point:

"I'm in the market for a favor, Gallantyne."

"That's no switch," Gallantyne said. "What is it?"

"A client of mine claims that her husband, from whom she's separated, is harassing her and her child. She says he's driving around town in a green Ford coupé, six or seven years old, license GVK 640."

"And?"

"I want to know if he is."

"All I can do is check with Sacramento and find out who owns the car. That may take some time, unless you can come up with a more urgent reason than the one you've given me, say like murder, armed robbery—"

"Sorry, no armed robbery or murder. Just a divorce, with complications."

"I think your cases are often messier than mine are," Gallantyne said with a trace of envy.

"Could be. We'll have to get together on one sometime."

"Let's do that. Now, you want us to contact Sacramento about the green Ford?"

"Yes, but meanwhile pass the license number around to the traffic boys. If they spot the car anywhere I'd like to hear about it, any time of the day or night. I have an answering service."

"What's that license again?"

"GVK, God's Very Kind, 640."

11

HE BOUGHT THE new car right after work, a three-year-old dark, inconspicuous sedan. As soon as he got behind the wheel he felt safe and secure as though he'd acquired a whole new body and nobody would recognize the old Charlie anymore. He felt quite independent, too. He had chosen the car by himself, with no help from Ben, and he had paid for it with his own money. The used-car salesman had taken his check without hesitation as if he couldn't help but trust a man with such an honest face as Charlie's. And Charlie, inspired by this trust, was absolutely convinced that the car had been driven only 10,000 cautious miles by one owner and a Detroit-trained garage mechanic at that. A man so skillful, Charlie reasoned, would have practically no spare time and that would account for the extremely low mileage on the car.

It seemed to him that the salesman, who had paid little attention to him when he first started browsing around the lot, noticed the change in him, too. He started to call him sir.

"I hope you'll be very happy with your car, sir."

"Oh, I will. I already am."

"There's no better advertising than a satisfied customer," the salesman said. "The only trouble with selling a man a good car like this is that we don't see him around for a long time. Good luck and safe driving to you, sir."

"Thank you very much."

"It was a pleasure."

Charlie eased the car out into the street. It was getting quite late and he knew Ben would be starting to worry about him, but he didn't want to go home just yet. He wanted to drive around, to get the feel of his new car and test the strength of his new body before he exposed either to Ben or Louise. They would both be suspicious, Ben of the car and the salesman and the garage mechanic, Louise of the change in him. He realized, in a vague way, that Louise didn't really want him to change, that she was dependent on his weakness though he couldn't understand why.

When he started out, he had, at the conscious level, no destination in mind. At crossroads he made choices seemingly unconnected with what he was thinking. He turned left because the car in front of him did; he turned right to watch a flock of blackbirds feeding on a lawn; he went straight because the road crossed a creek and he liked bridges; he turned left again because the setting sun hurt his eyes. The journey took on an air of adventure, as if the streets, the bridge, the blackbirds, the setting sun were all strange to him and he was a stranger to them. He wasn't lost—nobody could get lost in San Félice where the mountains were to the east and the sea to the west, with one or the other, or both, always visible—he was deliberately misplaced, as if he were playing a game of hide-and-seek with Ben and Louise. An hour must have passed since the game started. *Ready or not, you must be caught, hiding around the goal or not.*

The sun had gone down. Wisps of fog were floating in from the sea and gathering in the treetops like spiders' webs. It was time to turn on the headlights but he wasn't sure which button to press, there were so many of them on the dashboard. He pulled over to the curb and stopped the car about fifty feet from an intersection. The intersection looked familiar to him although he didn't recognize it. It wasn't until he switched on the headlights and their beam caught the street sign and held it, that he knew where he was. Jacaranda Road, 300 block.

He felt a sudden and terrible pain in his head. He heard his own voice in his ears but he couldn't tell whether it was a whisper or a scream.

"Ben! Louise! Come and find me, I'm not hiding. It's not a game anymore. Help me. Come and take me home, Louise, don't leave me in this bad place. You don't know, nobody knows, how bad—dirty—dirty bad—"

At 8:30 the phone rang and Ben, who'd been sitting beside it for a long time, answered on the first ring.

"Hello."

"Ben, this is Louise. Charlie was supposed to pick me up half an hour ago. He may have forgotten, so I thought I'd call and jog his memory a bit."

"He's not here."

"Well, he's probably on his way then. I'll just go wait on the steps for him. It's a nice night."

"It's cold."

"No, it's not," Louise said, laughing. "You know how it is when you're in love, Ben. All the weather is wonderful."

"You'd better stay in the house, Louise. I don't think he's on his way over."

"Why not? Is something the matter?"

"I'm not sure," Ben said in his slow careful voice. "He came to the cafeteria at noon with some crazy—a far-fetched story about a strange woman trying to kill him with her car. I didn't know how much of it, if any, to believe. He may have invented the whole thing as an excuse to buy a new car. You know Charlie, he can't just go ahead and do something; he has to have a dozen reasons why, no matter how nutty some of them are. Anyway, he told me he was going to buy a new car after work."

"He got off work three and a half hours ago. How long does it usually take him to buy a car?"

"Judging from past performance, I'd say five minutes. He sees one he likes the look of, kicks a couple of the tires, sounds the horn, and that's it. It can be the worst old clunker in town but he buys it."

"Then he should be home by now."

"Yes."

"Ben, I'm coming over."

"What good will that do? It will simply mean two of us sitting around worrying instead of one. No, you stay where you are, Louise. Get interested in something. Read a book, wash your hair, call a girlfriend, anything."

"I can't. I won't."

"Look, Louise, I don't want to be brutal about this, but waiting for Charlie is something you must learn to handle gracefully. You may be doing quite a bit of it. Ten chances to one, he's okay, he's just gotten interested in something and—"

"I can't afford to bet on it, even at those odds," Louise said and hung up before he could argue any further.

She went down the hall toward her bedroom to pick up a coat. All the weather was wonderful, but sometimes it paid to carry a coat.

She walked quickly and quietly past the open door or the shoebox-sized dining room where her parents were still lingering over coffee and the evening paper, going line by line over the local news, the obituaries and divorces and marriages, the water connections and delinquent tax notices and building permits and real estate transfers. But she didn't move quietly enough. *No one could,* she thought bitterly. *Not even the stealthiest cat, not even if the carpet were velvet an inch thick.*

"Louise?" her father called out. "Are you still here, Louise?"

"Yes, Daddy."

"I thought you were going out tonight."

"I am. I'm just leaving now."

"Without saying good-bye to your parents? Has this great romance of yours made you forget your manners? Come in here a minute."

Louise went as far as the door. Her parents were seated side by side at the table with the newspaper spread out in front of them, like a pair of school children doing their homework together.

Mr. Lang rose to his feet and made a kind of half-bow in Louise's direction. For as long as Louise could remember he had been doing this whenever she entered a room. But his politeness was too elaborate, as if, by treating her like a princess, he was actually calling attention to her commonness.

Louise stared at him, wondering how she could ever have been impressed by his silly posturings or affected by his small, obvious cruelties. She said nothing, knowing that he hated silence because his weapon was his tongue.

"I understood," he said finally, "that this was the night your mother and I were to congratulate our prospective son-in-law. Am I to assume the happy occasion has been postponed?"

"Yes."

"What a pity. I had looked forward to some of his stimulating conversation: yes, Mr. Lang; no, Mr. Lang—"

"Good night."

"Wait a minute. I haven't finished."

"Yes, you have," Louise said and walked down the hall and out the front door. For once, she was grateful for her father's cruelty. It had saved her from trying to explain where Charlie was and why he hadn't kept their date.

Ben must have been watching for her from the front window because as soon as she pulled up to the curb in front of the house he came out on the porch and down the steps.

To the question in her eyes he shook his head. Then, "You might as well go home, Louise."

"No."

"All right. But it's silly to start driving around looking for him when I haven't the slightest idea where he is."

"I have," she said quietly. "It's just a feeling, a hunch. It may be miles off but it's worth trying. We've got to find him, Ben. He needs us."

"He needs us." Ben got in the car and slammed the door shut. "Where have I heard that before? Charlie needs this, Charlie needs that, Charlie needs, period. Some day before I die, *I'm* going to have a need. Just once somebody's going to say, *Ben* needs this or that. Just once— Oh, what the hell, forget it. I don't really need anything."

"I do."

"What?"

"I need Charlie."

"Then I'm sorry for you," Ben said, striking his thigh with his fist. "I'm so sorry for you I could burst into tears. You're a decent, intelligent young woman, you deserve a life. What you're getting is a job."

"Don't waste any pity on me. I'm happy."

"You're happy even now, with Charlie missing and maybe in the kind of trouble only Charlie can get into?"

"He's alive—you'd have been notified if he'd been killed in an accident or anything—and as long as Charlie's alive, I'm happy."

"I'm not," he said bluntly. "In fact, there have been times, dozens, maybe hundreds of times, when I've thought the only solution for Charlie would be for him to step in front of a fast-moving truck. Before this is all over, you might be thinking the same thing."

"That's a—a terrible thing to say to me."

"I'm sorry, I had to do it. I didn't want to hurt you, but—"

"Isn't it funny how many times people don't want to hurt you, *but?*"

"I suppose it's pretty funny, yes."

She was staring straight ahead of her into the darkness but her eyes were squinting as if they were exposed to too much light. "Stop worrying about Charlie and me. If you want us to get married, give us your blessing and hope we'll muddle through all right. If you don't want us to get married, say so now, tonight."

"You have my blessing and my hope. I'm not much of a hoper, or a blesser either, but—"

"Sssh, no buts. They ruin everything." She smiled and touched his arm. "You see, Ben, you've been very good to Charlie. I think, though, that I'll be better *for* him."

"I hope so."

"Thanks for talking to me, and letting me talk. I feel calmer and more sure of myself, and of Charlie, than I ever have before. Good night, Ben."

"Good night? I thought we were going out to look for Charlie."

"You're not, I am. Looking for Charlie is my job now."

"All right." He got out of the car and stood on the curb with the door open, trying to decide whether to get back in. Then he leaned down and shut the door very firmly, as if this was a door he'd had trouble with in the past and he knew it needed a good slam to stay closed. "Good night, Louise."

If she said good night to him again he didn't hear it above the roar of the engine. She was out of sight before he reached the top of the steps.

He felt no sharp, sudden pain, only a terrible sadness creeping over him like fog over the city. He thought, *she's driving blind, following a wild hunch,* and he wondered how many hunches she would have before she gave up. One in twenty might be correct and she'd bank on that one, believing that she finally understood Charlie, that she'd pressed the right button and come up with the right answer. It would take her a long time to realize that with Charlie the buttons changed position without reason, and yesterday's answer was gibberish and today's only a one-in-twenty hunch.

Ben remembered the document word by word, though it had been years since he'd seen it:

> We are recommending the release of Charles Edward Gowen into the custody and care of his brother. We feel that Gowen has gained insight and control and is no longer a menace to himself or to others. Further psychiatric treatment within the closed environment of a hospital seems futile at this time. Gainful employment, family affection and outside interests are now necessary if he is to become a useful and self-sufficient member of society.

12

THE FOG THICKENED as she drove. Trees lost their tops, whole sections of the city disappeared, and street lights were no more than dim and dirty halos. But inside her mind everything was becoming very clear, as if the lack of visibility around her had forced her to look inward.

What she had called a hunch to Ben was now a conclusion based on a solid set of facts. Charlie was frightened beyond the understanding of anyone like Ben or herself; he was running away from Ben, from her, from marriage, from the responsibility of growing up. He must be treated like a scared boy, shown the dark room and taught that it had no more terrors than when it was light; he must be trusted even when trust was very difficult. But first he must be found because he was trying to escape into a world that seemed safe to him, that seemed to present no challenge. Yet it was a dangerous place for Charlie, this world of children.

Her hands were gripping the steering wheel so tightly that the muscles of her forearms ached, but she felt compelled to go on thinking calmly and reasonably, like a mathematician faced with a very long and difficult equation. *If I am to deal with this thing, if I am to help Charlie deal with it, I must know what it is. I must know . . .*

Charlie had never even mentioned children to her, he never looked at them passing on the street or watched them playing in the park. Yet somehow, somewhere, he had seen the girl, Mary Martha, and found out where she lived. Louise remembered his excitement the previous night when he was talking about 319 Jacaranda Street and the little dog that chased cars. Well, there was no little dog; there was a child, Mary Martha. Charlie had said so himself and though Louise had deafened her ears at the time, his words rang in them now like the echo of tolling bells: *"It's funny she'd want to live alone in the big house with just a little girl."*

She wondered whether it had been a slip of the tongue or whether Charlie, in some corner of his mind, wanted her to know about it and was asking for her help.

"Oh God," she said aloud, "how do you help someone like Charlie?"

She found him at the corner of Toyon Drive and Jacaranda Road. He was leaning against the hood of a dark car she didn't recognize, his hands folded across his stomach, his head sunk low on his chest. A passing stranger might think he'd had engine trouble, had lifted the hood and discovered something seriously wrong and given up in despair.

Although he must have heard her car stop and her footsteps as she approached, he didn't move or open his eyes. Jacaranda petals clung thickly to his hair and his windbreaker. They looked very pale in the fog, like snowflakes that couldn't melt because they'd fallen on something as cold as they were.

She spoke his name very softly so she wouldn't startle him.

He opened his eyes and blinked a couple of times. "Is that— is that you, Louise?"

"Yes."

"I was calling you. Did you hear me?"

"No. Not in the way you mean. I heard, though, Charlie. I'll always hear you."

"How can you do that?"

"It's a secret."

He stood up straight and looked around him, frowning. "You shouldn't be here, Louise. It's a bad place for women and children. It's—well, it's just a bad place."

"The children are all safe in bed," she said with calm deliberation. "And, as a woman, I'm not afraid because I have you to look after me. It's awfully cold, though, and I'll admit I'd feel more comfortable at home. Will you take me home, Charlie?"

He didn't answer. He was staring down at the sidewalk, mute and troubled.

"You've bought a new car, Charlie."

"Yes."

"It's very sleek and pretty. I'd like a ride in it."

"No."

"You were calling me, Charlie. Why did you call me if you didn't want to see me?"

"I did, I do want to see you."

"But you won't drive me home?"

"No," he said, shaking his head. "It would be too complicated."

"Why?"

"Well, you see, there are two cars and two people, so each of the cars has to be driven by one person. That's just plain arithmetic, Louise."

"I suppose it is."

"If I take you home, your car will be left sitting here alone, and I told you what kind of place this is."

"It looks like a perfectly nice residential neighborhood to me, Charlie."

"That's on the surface. I see what's underneath. I see things so terrible, so—" He began to grind his fists into his eyes, as though he were trying to smash the images he saw into a meaningless pulp.

She caught his wrists and held them. "Stop it. Stop it, please."

"I can't."

"All right," she said steadily. "So you see terrible things. Perhaps they exist, in this neighborhood and in yourself. But you mustn't let them blind you to the good things and there are more of them, many more. When you take a walk in the country, you can't stop and turn over every stone. If you did, you'd miss the sky and the trees and the flowers and the birds. And to miss those would be a terrible thing in itself, wouldn't it?"

He was watching her, earnest and wide-eyed, like a child listening to a story. "Are there good things in me, Louise?"

"Too many for me to tell you."

"That's funny. I wonder if Ben knows."

"Ben knows."

"Is that why he never tells me about them? Because there are too many?"

"Yes."

"That's nice, that's very nice," he said, nodding. "I like that about the stones, Louise. Ben and I used to turn over a lot of stones when we went hiking in the mountains. We used to find some very interesting things under stones. No birds, naturally, but sow bugs and lizards and Jerusalem crickets . . . I made a crazy mistake the first time I ever saw a young Jerusalem cricket. It lay there on its back in the ground, flesh-colored and wriggling its—well, they looked like arms and legs. And I thought it was a real human baby and that that was where they came from. When I asked Ben about it he told me the truth, but I didn't like it. It didn't seem nearly so pleasant or so natural as the idea of babies growing in the ground like flowers.

If I could start all over again, I'd want to start like that, growing up out of the ground like a flower . . . You're shivering, Louise. Are you cold?"

"Yes."

"I'll take you home."

"That's a good idea," she said soberly, as if it had not occurred to her before.

He opened the door for her and she got into the car. The seat covers felt cold and damp like something Charlie had found under a stone.

He walked around the front of the car. The headlights were still on and as he passed them he shielded his entire face with his hands like a man avoiding a pair of eyes too bright and knowing. But as soon as he got behind the wheel of the car and turned on the ignition, he began to relax and she thought, *the crisis is over. At least, one part of one crisis is over. That's all I dare ask right now.*

She said, "The engine sounds very smooth, Charlie."

"It does to me, too, but of course I'm not an expert like Ben. Ben will probably find a dozen things the matter with it."

"Then we won't listen to him."

"I don't have enough courage not to listen to Ben. In fact, I just don't have enough courage, period."

"That's not true," she said, thinking, *for people with problems, like Charlie, just to go on living from day to day requires more courage than is expected of any ordinary person.* "Does the fog bother you, Charlie?"

He gave a brief, bitter laugh. "Which fog, the one out there or the one in here?"

"Out there."

"I like it. I'd like to lose myself in it forever and that'd be the end of me, and good riddance."

"It would be the end of me, too, Charlie. And I don't want to end yet. I feel I only began after I met you."

"Don't say that. It scares me. It makes me feel responsible for you, for your life. I'm not fit for that. Your life's too valuable and mine's not worth a—"

"All lives are valuable."

"Oh God, I can't *explain* to you. You won't *listen.*"

"That's right, I won't listen."

"You're stubborn like Ben."

"No," she said, smiling. "I'm stubborn like myself."

For the next few blocks he didn't speak. Then, stopping for a red light, he blurted out, "I didn't mean it to be like this, Louise."

"Mean what to be like what?"

"Tonight, our date, the car. I was—I was going to come to your house and surprise you with the new car. But I decided I'd better drive around a bit first and get used to the motor so I wouldn't make any mistakes in front of you. I started out, not thinking of where or why, not thinking of anything. Then I stopped, I just stopped, I don't even remember if I had a reason. And there I was, in that place I hate. I hate it, Louise, I hate that place."

"Then you mustn't go there anymore," she said calmly. "That makes sense, doesn't it, Charlie? To avoid what makes you feel miserable?"

"I didn't *go* there. I was led, I was driven. Don't you understand that, Louise?"

"I'm trying."

She watched the streetlights step briskly out of the fog and back into it again like sentries guarding the greatness of the night. She wondered how much she could afford to understand Charlie and whether this was the time to try. Perhaps she might never have a better opportunity than now, with Charlie in a receptive mood, humble, wanting to change himself, and grateful to her for finding him.

She bided her time, saying nothing further until they arrived at her apartment house and Charlie parked the car at the curb. He reached for her hands and held them tightly in his own, against his chest. She almost lost her nerve then, he looked so tired and defenseless. She had to remind herself that it wasn't enough just to get by, to smooth things over for one day when there were thousands of days ahead of them. *I must do it,* she thought. *I can't hurt him any more than he's already hurting himself.*

"To me," she said finally, "Jacaranda Road is like any other. Why do you hate it, Charlie? Why do you call it a bad place?"

"Because it is."

"The whole street is?"

He let go of her hands as if they'd suddenly become too personal. "I don't want to dis—"

"Or just one block? Or perhaps one house?"

"Please stop. Please don't."

"I have to," she said. "The bad part, is it the house where the little Oakley girl lives with her mother?"

He kept shaking his head back and forth as though he could shake off the pain like a dog shaking off water. "I don't—don't know any Oakley girl."

"I think you do, Charlie. It would help you, it would help us both, if you'd tell me the truth."

"I don't know her," he repeated. "I've seen her, that's all."

"You've never approached her?"

"No."

"Or talked to her?"

"No."

"Then nothing whatever has happened," she said firmly. "You have no reason to feel so bad, so guilty. Nothing's *happened,* Charlie, that's the important thing. It doesn't make sense to feel guilty about something that hasn't even happened."

"Do you think it's that simple, Louise?"

"No. But I think it's where we have to start, dividing things into what's real and what isn't. You haven't harmed anyone. The Oakley girl is safe at home, and I believe that even if I hadn't found you when I did, she'd still be safe at home."

He was watching her like a man on trial watching a judge. "You honest to God believe that, Louise?"

"Yes, I do."

"Tell it to me again. Say it all over again."

She said it over again and he listened as if he'd been waiting all of his life to hear it. It wasn't like anything he would have heard from Ben: *"Can't you use your head for a change? You've got to avoid situations like that. God knows what might have happened."*

"Nothing happened," he said. "Nothing happened at all, Louise."

"I know."

"Will you—that is, I suppose you'll be telling Ben about all this business tonight."

"Not if you don't want me to."

"He wouldn't understand. Not because he's dumb or anything, but because I've disappointed him so often, he can't help expecting the worst from me . . . You won't tell him where you found me?"

"No."

"How did you find me, Louise? Of all the places in the city, what made you go there?"

"A lucky guess based on a lucky coincidence," she said, smiling. "The little Oakley girl was in the library this afternoon. She wanted a special book and Miss Albert brought her to my department and introduced her to me. Since I'd just looked up who lived at

319 Jacaranda Road for you, I asked her if that was her address and she said yes. It was that simple."

"No, it couldn't have been. You couldn't have even guessed anything from just that much."

"Well, we talked a little."

"Not about me. She's never even seen me."

"We talked," Louise said, "about her cat. She doesn't own a dog."

He turned away from her and looked out the window though there was nothing to see but different shades of greyness. "That wasn't a very good lie about the little dog that chased cars, I guess."

"No, it wasn't."

"It's a funny thing, her coming to the library like that. It's as if someone planned it, God or Ben or—"

"Nobody planned it. Kids go to libraries and I work in one, that's all . . . You see lots of little girls, Charlie. What made you—well, take a fancy to that particular one?"

"I don't know."

"Was it because she reminded you of me, Charlie? She reminded me of me right away, with those solemn eyes and that long fine blonde hair."

"Blonde?"

"Don't sound so incredulous. I used to be a regular towhead when I was a kid."

He put his hands on the steering wheel and held on tight like a racing driver about to reach a dangerous curve. *Blonde,* he thought. *That crazy mother has dyed Jessie's hair blonde. No, it's impossible. Jessie's hair is short, it couldn't have grown long in a day. A wig, then. One of those new wigs the young girls are wearing now—*

"There must be trouble in the family," Louise said. "Mary Martha wanted a book on divorce."

"Who?"

"The Oakley girl, Mary Martha . . . You look upset, Charlie. I shouldn't go on talking about her like this, and I won't. I promise not to say another word." She pressed her cheek against his shoulder. "I love you so much, Charlie. Do you love me, too?"

"Yes."

"You're tired, though, aren't you?"

"Yes."

"Do you want to go home?"

"Yes," he said. "*Yes.* I—it's late, it's cold."

"I know. You go home and get a good night's sleep and you'll feel much better in the morning."

"Will I?" He looked straight ahead of him, his eyes strained, as if he was trying to make out the outlines of the morning through the fog. But all he could see was Jessie coming out of the playground with Mary Martha. Their heads were together and they were whispering, they were planning to trick him. All the time he thought they hadn't noticed him and they'd been on to him right from the start. They'd looked at him and seen even through the dirty windows of the old green car, something different about him, something wrong. And Jessie—it must have been Jessie, she was always the leader—had said, *"Let's fool him. Let's pretend I live in your house."*

Children were subtle, they could see things grownups couldn't. Their attention wasn't divided between past and present, it was focused on the present. But what was there about him that had made Jessie notice him? How had she found out he was different?"

Louise said, "Good night, Charlie."

Although he said, "Good night," in return, he was no longer even aware of Louise except as a person who'd come to bring him bad news and was now leaving. *Good riddance, stranger.*

The car door opened and closed again. He turned on the ignition and pulled out into the street. Somewhere in the city, in some house hidden now by night and fog, a little girl knew he was different—no, she was not a little girl, she was already a woman, devious, scheming, provocative. She was probably laughing about it right at this minute, remembering how she'd tricked him. He had to find her.

Reasons why he had to find her began to multiply in his mind like germs. *I'll reprimand her, without scaring her, of course, because I'd never scare a child no matter how bad. I'll ask her what there was about me she noticed, why I looked different to her. I'll tell her it's not nice, thinking such terrible thoughts . . .*

13

JESSIE CALLED OUT from her bedroom, "I got up for a glass of water and now I'm ready to be tucked in again, somebody!"

She didn't especially need tucking in for the third time but she could hear her parents arguing and she wanted to stop the sound which was keeping her awake. She thought the argument was probably about money, but she couldn't distinguish any particular words. The sound was just a fretful murmur that crept in through the cracks of her bedroom door and made her ears itch. It wasn't a pleasant tickle like the kind she got when she hugged the Arlingtons' dog, Chap; it was like the itch of a flea bite, painful, demanding to be scratched but not alleviated by scratching.

She called again and a minute later her father appeared in the doorway. He had on his bathrobe and he looked sleepy and cross. "You're getting away with murder, young one. Do you realize it's after ten?"

"I can't help it if time passes. I couldn't stop it if I wanted to."

"No, but you might make its passing a little more peaceful for the rest of us. Mike's asleep, and I hope to be soon."

She knew from his tone that he wasn't really angry with her. He even sounded a little relieved that his conversation with Ellen had been interrupted.

"You could sit on the side of my bed for a minute."

"I think I will," he said, smiling slightly. "It's the best offer I've had today."

"Now we can talk."

"What about?"

"Oh, everything. People can always find something to talk about."

"They can if one of the people happens to be you. What's on your mind, Jess?"

She leaned against the headboard and gazed up at the ceiling. "Are Ellen and Virginia best friends?"

"If you're referring to your mother and your Aunt Virginia, yes, I suppose you'd call them best friends."

"Do they tell each other everything?"

"I don't know. I hope not."

"I mean, like Mary Martha and me, we exchange our most innermost secrets. Did you ever have a friend like that?"

"Not since I was old enough to have any secrets worth mentioning," he said dryly. "Is something worrying you, Jessie?"

She said, "No," but she couldn't prevent her eyes from wandering to the closed door of her closet. A whole night and day had passed since she'd taken back the book Virginia had given her and Howard had pressed the twenty dollars into her hand. The money was out of sight now, hidden in the toe of a shoe, but she might as well have been still carrying it around in her hand. She thought about it a good deal, and always with the same mixture of power and guilt; she had money, she could buy things now, but she had also been bought. She wondered what grownups did with children they bought. Did they keep them? Or did they sell them again, and to whom? Perhaps if she returned the twenty dollars to Howard and

Virginia, they would give her back to her father and everything would be normal again. She hadn't wanted the money in the first place, Howard had forced it on her; and she had a strong feeling that he would refuse to take it back.

She said in a rather shaky voice, "Am I *your* little girl?"

"That's an odd question. Whose else would you be?"

"Howard and Virginia's."

He frowned slightly. "Where'd you pick up this idea of calling adults by their first names?"

"All the other kids do it."

"Well, you don't happen to be all the other kids. You're my special gal." He added casually, "Were you over at the Arlingtons' today?"

"No."

"You seem to be doing a lot of thinking about them."

"I was wondering why they don't have children of their own."

"I'm afraid you'll have to go on wondering," he said. "It's not the kind of question people like being asked."

"They could *buy* some of their own, couldn't they? They have lots of money. I heard Ellen say—"

"Your mother."

"—my mother say that if she had a fraction of Virginia's money, she'd join a health club and get rid of some of that fat Virginia carries around. Do you think Virginia's too fat? Howard doesn't. He likes to kiss her, he kisses her all the time when he's not mad at her. Boy, he was mad at her last night, he—"

"All right, that's enough," Dave said brusquely. "I don't want to hear any gossip about the Arlingtons from a nine-year-old."

"It's not gossip. It really happened. I wanted to tell you about the twenty dollars he—"

"I don't want to listen, is that clear? Their private life isn't my business or yours. Now you'd better settle down and go to sleep before your mother comes charging in here and shows you how mad someone can really get."

"I'm not afraid of her. She never *does* anything."

"Well, *I* might do something, kiddo, so watch it. No more drinks of water, no more tucking in, and no more gossip. Understand?"

"Yes."

"Lie down and I'll turn out your light."

"I haven't said my prayers."

"Oh, for heaven's sa—okay. Okay, say your prayers."

She closed her eyes and folded her hands.

> "Dear Jesus up in heaven,
> Like a star so bright,
> I thank you for the lovely day,
> Please bless me for the night.

"Amen. I don't really think it's been such a lovely day," she added candidly. "But that's in the prayer so I have to say it. I hope God won't consider me a liar."

"I hope not," her father said. His hand moved toward the light switch but he didn't turn it off. Instead, "What was the matter with your day, Jessie?"

"Lots of things."

"Such as?"

"I was treated just like a child. Mike even went to the school with me and Mary Martha to make sure I didn't play on the jungle gym because of my hands. He acted real mean. I'm thinking of divorcing him."

"Then you'd better think again," Dave said. "You can't divorce a brother or any blood relative."

"Mary Martha did. She divorced Sheridan."

"That's silly."

"Well, she never ever sees him, so it's practically the same thing as divorce."

"Why doesn't she ever see him?"

Jessie looked carefully around the room as if she were checking for spies. "Can you keep a secret even from Ellen?"

Although he smiled, the question seemed to annoy him. "It may be difficult but I could try."

"Cross your heart."

"Consider it crossed."

"Sheridan went to live with another woman," Jessie whispered, "so he can't see Mary Martha ever again. Not ever in his whole life."

"That seems a little unreasonable to me."

"Oh no. She's a very bad woman, Mary Martha told me this morning. She looked up a certain word in the dictionary. It took her a long time because she didn't know how to spell it but she figured it out."

"She figured it out," Dave repeated. "Yes, that's Mary Martha all right."

"Naturally. She's the best speller in the school."

"And you, my little friend, are about to become the best gossip."

"Why is it gossip if I'm only telling the truth?"

"You don't know it's the truth, for one thing." He paused, rubbing the side of his neck as if the muscles there had stiffened and turned painful. "The woman involved might not be so bad. Certainly Mrs. Oakley's opinion of her is bound to be biased." He paused again. "How on earth I get dragged into discussions like this, I don't know. Now you settle down and close your eyes and start thinking about your own affairs for a change."

She lay back on the pillow but her eyes wouldn't close. They were fixed on Dave's face as if she were trying to memorize it. "If you and Ellen got divorced, would I ever see you again?"

"Of course you would," he said roughly and turned out the light. "I want no more nonsense out of you tonight, do you hear? And kindly refer to your mother as your mother. This first-name business is going to be nipped in the bud."

"I wish the morning would hurry up and come."

"Stop wishing and start sleeping and it will."

"I hate the night, I just hate it." She struck the side of the pillow with her fist. "Nothing to do but just lie here and sleep. When I'm sleeping I don't feel like me, myself."

"You're not supposed to feel like anything when you're sleeping."

"I mean, when I'm sleeping and wake up real suddenly, I don't feel like me. It's different with you. When you wake up and turn on the light, you see Ellen in the other bed and you think, that's Ellen over there so I must be Dave. You know right away you're Dave."

"Do I?" His voice was grave and he didn't rebuke her for using first names. "Suppose I woke up and Ellen wasn't in the other bed?"

"Then you'd know she was just in the kitchen getting a snack or making a cup of tea. Ellen's always around some place. I never worry about her."

"That sounds as if you worry about me, Jess. Do you?"

"I guess not."

"But you're not sure?"

She put one hand over her eyes to shade them from the hall light coming through the door. "Well, fathers are different. They can just move out, like Sheridan, and you never see them anymore."

"That's nonsense," he said sharply. "The Oakley case is a very special one."

"Mary Martha says it always happens the same way."

"If it makes Mary Martha feel better to believe that, let her. But you don't have to." He leaned over and smoothed her hair back from her forehead. "I'll always be around, see? In fact, I'll be around for such a long time that you'll get mighty sick of me eventually."

"No, I won't."

"Wait until the young men start calling on you and you want the living room to entertain them in. You'll be wishing dear old Dad would take a one-way trip to the moon."

She let out a faint sound which he interpreted as a giggle.

"There now," he added. "You're feeling better, aren't you? No more worrying about me and no more thinking about the Oakleys. They're in a class by themselves."

"No, there are others."

"Now what do you mean by that, if anything? Or are you just trying to prolong the conversation by dreaming up—"

"No. I heard with my own ears."

"Heard what?"

"You might call it gossip if I tell you."

"I might. Try me."

She spoke in a whisper as if the Arlingtons might be listening at the window. "Howard is moving out, exactly the way Sheridan did. He told Virginia last night, right in front of me. 'I'm leaving,' he said, and then he stomped away."

"He didn't stomp very far," Dave said dryly. "I saw him outside helping the gardener this morning. Look, Jessie, married people often say things to each other that they don't mean. Your mother and I do it sometimes, although we shouldn't. So do you and Mike, for that matter. You get mad at each other or your feelings are hurt and you start making threats. You both know very well they won't be carried out."

"Howard *meant* it."

"Perhaps he did at the time. But he obviously changed his mind."

"He could change it back again, couldn't he?"

"It's possible." He stared down at her but he could tell nothing from her face. She had averted it from the shaft of light coming from the hall. "You sound almost as if you wanted Howard to leave, Jessie."

"I don't care."

"The Arlingtons have always been very nice to you, haven't they?"

"I guess so. Only it would be more fun if somebody else lived next door, a family with children of their own."

"What makes you think the Arlingtons are going to sell their house?"

"If Howard leaves, Virginia will have to because she'll be without money like Mrs. Oakley."

He stood up straight and crossed his arms on his chest in a gesture of suppressed anger. "I'm getting pretty damned tired of the Oakleys. Best friend or no best friend, I may have to insist that you see less of Mary Martha if you're going to let her situation dominate your thinking."

She sensed that his anger was directed not against the Oakleys, whom he didn't even know except for Mary Martha, but against the Arlingtons and perhaps even Ellen and himself. One night she had overheard him telling Ellen he wanted to move back to San Francisco and Ellen had appeared at breakfast the next morning with her eyes swollen. Nobody questioned her story about an eye allergy but nobody believed it either. For a whole week afterward Dave had acted very quiet and allowed Mike and Jessie to get away with being late for meals and fighting over television programs.

"Did you hear me, Jessie?"

"Yes. But I'm getting sleepy."

"Well, it's about time," Dave said and went out and shut the door very quickly as if he were afraid she might start getting unsleepy again.

357

Left alone, Jessie closed her eyes because there was nothing to see anyway. But her ears wouldn't close. She heard the Arlingtons arriving home in Howard's car—it was noisier than Virginia's—the barking of their dog Chap, the squawk of the garage door, the quick, impatient rhythm of Howard's step, the slow one of Virginia's that sounded as if she were being dragged some place she didn't want to go.

"The Brants' lights are still on," Virginia said, her voice slurred and softened by fog. "I think I'll drop over for a minute and say good night."

"No you won't," Howard said.

"Are you telling me I *can't?*"

"Try it and see."

"What would you do, Howard? Embarrass me in front of the Brants? That's old stuff, and I don't embarrass so easily anymore. Or perhaps you'd try and bring Jessie into the act. It's funny you can't solve your problems without dragging in the neighbors. You're such a big, clever man. Can't you handle one wife all by yourself?"

"I could handle a wife. I can't handle an enemy."

Jessie tiptoed over to the window and looked out through the slats of the Venetian blind. The floodlight was turned on in the Arlingtons' yard and she could see Howard bending over unlocking the back door. Virginia stood behind him holding her purse high against her shoulder as if she intended to bring it down on the back of Howard's neck. For a moment everything seemed reversed to Jessie: Howard was the smaller, weaker of the two and Virginia was the powerful one, the boss. Then Howard stood up straight and things seemed normal again.

Howard opened the door and said, "Get inside," and Virginia walked in quickly, her head bowed.

The floodlight went off, leaving the yard to the fog and the darkness, and the only sound Jessie heard was the dripping of moisture among the loquat leaves.

14

THE FOLLOWING MORNING Ralph MacPherson rose, as usual, at 5:30. Since his wife had died he found it possible to fill his days, but the nights were unbearably lonely. He minimized them by getting up very early and going to bed when many lawyers were just finishing dinner. His matchmaking friends disapproved of this routine but Mac thrived on it. It was a healthy life.

Before breakfast he took his two dogs for a run, worked in the garden and put out food and water for the wild birds and mammals. After breakfast he read at the dining-room window, raising his head from time to time to watch the birds swooping down from the oaks and pines, the bush bunnies darting out of poison oak thickets at the bottom of the canyon and the chipmunks scampering up the lemon tree after the peanuts he'd placed in an empty coconut shell. Helping the wild creatures survive made him feel good, like a secret conspirator against the depredations and greed of man.

He reached his office at 8:30. Miss Edgeworth was already at her desk, looking fresh and crisp in a beige silk suit. Although he'd never accused her of it—Miss Edgeworth didn't encourage personal conversation—Mac sometimes had the notion that she was making a game out of beating him to the office, no matter how early he arrived, and that winning this game was important to her; it reinforced her low opinion of the practicality and efficiency of men.

There was always a note of triumph in her "Good morning, Mr. MacPherson."

"Good morning, Miss Edgeworth."

Her name was Alethea and she had worked for him long enough to be on a first-name basis. But it seemed to him that "Good morning, Alethea" was even more formal than "Good morning, Miss Edgeworth." He was afraid the day would come when he would accidentally call her what the girls in the office called her behind her back—Edgy.

He said, "Any calls for me?"

"Lieutenant Gallantyne wants you to contact him at police headquarters. It's about a car. Shall I get him for you?"

"No. I'll do it."

"Mrs. Oakley also—"

"That can wait."

He went into his office, closed the door and dialed police headquarters.

"Gallantyne? MacPherson here."

"Hope I didn't wake you up," Gallantyne said in a tone that hoped the opposite. "You lawyers nowadays keep bankers' hours."

"Do we. Any line on the green coupé?"

"One of the traffic boys spotted it an hour ago. It's standing in Jim Baker's used-car lot on lower Bojeta Street near the wharf."

"How long has it been there?"

"Garcia didn't ask any questions. He wasn't instructed to."

"I see. Well, thanks a lot, Gallantyne. I'll check it out myself."

He hung up, leaned back in the swivel chair and frowned at the ceiling. The fact that the green car had been sold made it more likely that Kate was right in claiming that the man behind the wheel had been Sheridan. Ordinarily Mac took her accusations against Sheridan with a grain of salt. A number of them were real, a number were fantasy, but most of them fell somewhere in the middle. If she walked across a room and stubbed her toe she would blame Sheridan even if he happened to be several hundred miles away. On the other hand, Sheridan had pulled some pretty wild stuff. It was quite possible that he'd tried to frighten her into coming to terms over the divorce and had ended up being frightened himself when she pursued him with her car.

Mac thought, as he had a hundred times in the past, that they were people caught like animals in a death grip. Neither was strong enough to win and neither would let go. The grip had continued for so long that it was now a way of life. It was not the sun that brightened Kate's mornings or the sea air that freshened Sheridan's. It was the anticipation, for each of them, of a victory over the other. They could no longer live without the excitement of battle. Mac remembered two lines from the children's poem about a gingham dog and a calico cat who had disappeared simultaneously:

> "The truth about the cat and pup
> Is this: they ate each other up."

It hardly mattered now who took the first bite, Kate or Sheridan. The important thing was how to prevent the last bite, and so far Mac hadn't found any way of doing it. With the idea that perhaps someone else could, he had tried many times to persuade Kate to engage another lawyer. She always had the same answer: *"I couldn't possibly. No other lawyer would understand me." "I don't understand you either, Kate." "But you must, you've known me since I was a little girl."*

Kate's attitude toward men was one of unrealistic expectation or unjustified contempt, with nothing in between. If they behaved perfectly and lived up to the standards she set, they were god figures. When they failed as gods, they were immediately demoted to devils. Mac had avoided demotion simply by refusing either to accept her standards or to take her expectations seriously.

Sheridan's demotion had been quick and thorough, and there was no possibility of a reversal. Sheridan was aware of this. One of the main reasons why he went on fighting her was his knowledge that no matter how generous a settlement he made or how many of her demands he satisfied, he could never regain his godship.

Mac was sorry for them both and sick of them both. He almost wished they would move away or finish the job of eating each other up. Mary Martha might be better off in a foster home.

He told Miss Edgeworth he'd be back in an hour, then he drove down to the lower end of Bojeta Street near the wharf. It was an area of the city that was doomed now that newcomers from land-locked areas were moving in and discovering the sea. Real estate speculators were greedily buying up ocean-front lots and razing the old buildings, the warehouses and fish-processing plants and shacks for Mexican agricultural workers. All of these had been built in what the natives considered the damp and undesirable part of town.

Jim Baker's used-car lot was jammed between a three-story motel under construction and a new restaurant and bar called the Sea Aira Club. A number of large signs announced bargains because Baker was about to lose his lease. Baker himself looked as if he'd already lost it. He was an elderly man with skin wrinkled like an old paper bag and a thick, husky voice that sounded as if he'd swallowed too many years of fog.

He came out of his oven-sized office, chewing something that might have been gum or what was left of his breakfast, or an undigested fiber of the past. "Can I do anything for you?"

"I'm interested in the green coupé at the rear of the lot."

"Interested in what way?" Baker said with a long, deliberate look at Mac's new Buick. "Something fishy about the deal?"

"Not that I'm aware of. My name is Ralph MacPherson, by the way. I'd like to know when the car was sold to you."

"Last night about six o'clock. I didn't handle the transaction —my son, Jamie, did—but I was in the office. I'd brought Jamie's dinner to him from home. We're open fourteen hours out of the twenty-four, and Jamie and I have to spell each other. He sold the young man a nice clean late-model Pontiac that had been pampered like a baby. I hated to see it go, frankly, but the young man seemed anxious and he had the cash. Sooo—" Baker shrugged and spread his hands.

"How young a man was he?"

"Oh, about Jamie's age, thirty-two, thirty-five, maybe." Sheridan was thirty-four. "Do you remember his name?"

"I never knew it. It's in the book but I'm not sure I ought to look it up for you. I wouldn't want to cause him any trouble."

"I'm trying to prevent trouble, Mr. Baker. A client of mine—I'm a lawyer—is convinced that the husband she's divorcing has been using the green coupé to spy on her. I've been a family friend for many years and I'm simply trying to find out the truth one way or the other. Even a description of the man would be a big help."

Baker thought about it. "Well, he was nice, clean-cut, athletic-looking. Tall, maybe six feet, with kind of sandy hair and a smile like he was apologizing for something. Would that be the husband?"

Sheridan was short and dark and wore glasses, but Mac said, "I'm not sure. Perhaps you'd better look up the name."

"I guess it'd be all right, being as it's just a divorce case and nothing criminal. I don't want to get caught up in anything criminal. It plays hell with business."

"To the best of my knowledge, nothing criminal is involved."

"Okay, wait here."

Baker went into the office and returned in a few minutes with a name and address written on an old envelope: Charles E. Gowen, 495 Miria Street.

"Is that the man?" Baker asked.

"I'm glad to say it's not." Mac returned the envelope. "This will be good news to my client."

"Women get funny ideas sometimes."

"Do they not."

If it was good news to Kate, she didn't show it. She met him at the front door, wearing a starched cotton dress and high-heeled shoes. Her face was carefully made up and her hair neat. It seemed to Mac that she was always dressed for company but company never came. He knew of no one besides himself who any longer got past the front door.

They went into the smaller of the two living rooms and she sat on the window seat while he told her what he'd found out. With her face in shadow and the sun at her back illuminating her long, fair hair, she looked scarcely older than Mary Martha. *She's only thirty,* Mac thought. *Her life has been broken and she's too brittle to bend down and pick up the pieces.*

"You can stop worrying about the green car," he told her. "Sheridan wasn't in it."

She didn't look as if she intended or wanted to stop worrying. "That hasn't been proved."

"The car was registered to Charles Gowen. He traded it in last night."

"Funny coincidence, don't you think?"

"Yes. But coincidences happen."

"A lot of them can be explained. I told you from the beginning that Sheridan was too crafty to use his own car. Obviously, he borrowed the green coupé from this man Gowen. The kind of people Sheridan runs around with nowadays exchange cars and wives and mistresses as freely as they exchange booze. Sheridan's moved away down in the world, farther than you think."

"I haven't time to go into that now, Kate. Let's stick to the point."

"Very well. He used Gowen's car to harass me. Then when I fought back, when I chased him, he got scared and told Gowen to sell it."

"Why? Why didn't he simply return it to Gowen and let the matter drop? Selling the car was what led me to Gowen."

"Sheridan's mind is usually, I might say always, befuddled by alcohol. He probably considered the gambit quite a cunning one."

"What about Gowen?"

"I don't know about Gowen," she said impatiently. "I've never heard of him before. But if he's typical of Sheridan's current friends, he'll do anything for a few dollars or a bottle of liquor. Don't forget, Sheridan has money to fling around. It makes him pretty popular, and I suppose powerful, in certain circles." She paused, running her hand along her left cheek. The cheek was bright red as though it had been slapped. "You asked, 'What about Gowen?' Well, why don't you find out?"

"I don't think there's enough to warrant an investigation."

She looked at him bitterly. "Not *enough?* I suppose you think I've imagined the whole thing?"

"No, Kate. But—"

"I didn't imagine that car parked outside my house, watching me. I didn't imagine an anonymous letter accusing me of neglecting my daughter. I didn't imagine that chase around town yesterday. Would an innocent man have fled like that?"

"Perhaps there are no innocent men," Mac said. "Or women."

"Oh, stop talking like a wise old philosopher. You're not old, and you're not very wise either."

"Granted."

"If you had been in that car, would you have run away like that? Answer me truthfully."

"You seem concerned only with the fact that he ran away. I'm more concerned with the fact that you chased him."

"I was upset. I'd just received that letter."

"Perhaps he had had a disturbing experience, too, and was reacting in an emotional rather than a logical manner."

She let out a sound of despair. "You won't *listen* to me. You won't take me seriously."

"I do. I am."

"No. You think I'm a fool. But I feel a terrible danger, Mac, I know it's all around me. Something awful is waiting to happen, it's just around the corner, waiting. It can't be seen or heard or touched, but it's as real as this house, that chair you're sitting on, the tree outside the window."

"And you think Sheridan is behind this danger?"

"He must be," she said simply. "I have no other enemies."

Mac thought what a sad epitaph it made for a marriage: *I have no other enemies.* "I'll try again to contact Sheridan. As you know, he hasn't been answering his telephone."

"Another sign of guilt."

"Or a sign that he's not there," Mac said dryly. "As for Charles Gowen, I can't go charging up to him with a lot of questions. I haven't the legal or moral right. All I can do is make a few discreet inquiries, find out where he lives and works, and what kind of person he is, whether he's likely to be one of Sheridan's cronies, and so on. I may as well tell you now, though: I don't expect anything to come of it. If Gowen had a guilty reason for not wanting the green coupé found, it seems to me he'd have taken a little more trouble in disposing of it. There are at least a hundred used-car dealers between here and Los Angeles, yet Gowen sold it right here, practically in the center of town."

"He may simply be stupid. Sheridan's friends nowadays are not exactly intellectual giants."

Mac's smile was more pained than amused. "One of the things a lawyer has to learn early in his career is not to assume that the other guy is stupid."

He rose. His whole body felt heavy, and stiff with tension. He always felt the same way when he was in Kate's house, that he couldn't move freely in any direction because he was under constant and judgmental surveillance. He could picture Sheridan trying, at first anyway, to conform and to please her, and making mistakes, more and more mistakes every day, until nothing was possible but mistakes.

He knew he was not being fair to her. To make amends for his thoughts, he crossed the room and leaned down and kissed her lightly on the top of her head. Her hair felt warm to his lips, and smelled faintly of soap.

She looked up at him, showing neither surprise nor displeasure, only a deep sorrow, as if the show of tenderness was too little and too late and she had forgotten how to respond. "Is that a courtesy you extend to all your clients?"

"No," he said, smiling. "Only the ones I like and have known since they were freckle-faced little brats."

"I never had freckles."

"Yes, you did. You were covered with them every summer. You probably still would be if you spent any time in the sun. Listen, Kate, I have an idea. Why don't you and Mary Martha come sailing with me one of these days?"

"No. No, thank you."

"Why not?"

"I wouldn't be very good company. I've forgotten how to enjoy myself."

"You could relearn if you wanted to. Perhaps you don't want to."

Her sorrow had crystallized into bitterness, making her eyes shine hard and bright like blue glass. "Oh, stop it, Mac. You're offering me a day of sailing the way you'd throw an old dog a bone. Well, I'm not that hungry. Besides, I can't afford to leave the house for a whole day."

"You can't afford not to."

"Sheridan might force his way in and steal something. He's done it before."

"Once."

"He might do it ag—"

"He was drunk," Mac said, "and all he took was a case of wine which belonged to him anyway."

"But he broke into the house."

"You refused to admit him. Isn't that correct?"

"Naturally I refused. He was abusive and profane, he threatened me, he—" She stopped and took a long, deep breath. "You're always making excuses for him. Why? You're supposed to be on my side."

"I'm a man. I can't help seeing things from a man's point of view occasionally."

"Then perhaps," she said, rising, "I'd better hire a woman lawyer."

"That might be a good idea."

"You'd like to get rid of me, wouldn't you?"

"Let's put it this way: I'd like for us both to be rid of your problems. My going along with you and agreeing with everything you say and do is not a solution. It gets in the way of a solution. Your difficulties can't just be dumped in a box labeled Sheridan. You had them before Sheridan, and you're having them now, after Sheridan. I'd be doing you no favor by pretending otherwise."

"I was a happy, healthy, normal young woman when I married him."

"Is that how you remember yourself?"

"Yes."

"My memory of you is different," he said calmly. "You were moody, selfish, immature. You flunked out of college, you couldn't hold on to a job, and your relationship with your mother was strained. You tried to use marriage as a way out of all these difficulties. It put a very heavy burden on Sheridan, he wasn't strong enough to carry it. Can you see any truth in what I'm saying, Kate? Or are you just standing there thinking how unfair I'm being?"

They were face to face, but she wasn't looking at him. She was staring at a piece of the wall beyond his left shoulder, as if to deny his very presence. "I no longer expect fairness, from anyone."

"You're getting it from me, Kate."

"You call that fairness—that repulsive picture of me when I was nineteen?"

"It's not repulsive, or even particularly unusual. A great many girls in the same state go into marriage for the same reason."

"And what about Sheridan's reasons for getting married?" she said shrilly. "I suppose *they* were fine, *he* was mature, *he* got along great with *his* mother, *he* was a *big* success in the world—"

He took hold of her shoulders, lightly but firmly. "Keep your voice down."

"Why should I? Nobody will hear. Nobody can. The Oakleys were very exclusive, they liked privacy. They had to build the biggest house in town on the biggest lot because they didn't want to be bothered by neighbors. I could scream for help at the top of my lungs and not a soul would hear me. I've got enough privacy to be murdered in. Sheridan knows that. He's probably dreamed about it a hundred times: *wouldn't it be nice if someone came along and murdered Kate?* He may even have made or be making some plans of his own along that line, though I don't believe he'd have enough nerve to do it himself. He'd probably hire someone, the way he hired Gowen."

Her quick changes of mood and thought were beginning to exhaust Mac. Trying to keep track of them was like following a fast rat through a tortuous maze: Sheridan had borrowed the car from Gowen, who was one of his drunken friends—Sheridan had been at the wheel—Sheridan hadn't been at the wheel— Gowen wasn't his friend, he'd been hired—Gowen had driven the car himself. At this point Mac might have dismissed her whole story as fictional if she hadn't produced the real license number of a real car. The car existed, and so did Gowen. They were about the only facts Mac had to go on.

"Now you're suggesting," he said, "that Gowen was hired by Sheridan to intimidate you."

"Yes. He's probably some penniless bum that Sheridan met in a bar."

He didn't point out that penniless bums didn't pay cash for late-model sedans. "That should be easy enough to check."

"Would you, Mac? Will you?"

"I'll try my best."

"You're a dear, you really are."

She seemed to have forgotten her ill-feeling toward him. She looked excited and flushed as if she'd just come in from an hour of tennis in the sun and fresh air. But he knew the game wasn't tennis and the sun wasn't the same one that was shining in the window. What warmed her, brightened her, made her blood flow faster, was the thought of beating Sheridan.

15

CHARLIE HAD LAIN awake half the night making plans for the coming day, how he would spend his free hour at noon and where he'd go right after work. But before noon Louise phoned and invited him to meet her for lunch, and at five o'clock his boss Mr. Warner asked him to take a special delivery to the Forest Service ten miles up in the mountains. He couldn't refuse either of these requests without a good reason. His only reason would have seemed sinister to Louise and peculiar to Mr. Warner, but to Charlie himself it made sense: he had to find a little girl named Jessie to warn her not to play any more tricks on him because it was very naughty.

It was six o'clock before he arrived back at the city limits. He drove to the school grounds as fast as he could without taking any chances on being stopped by the police. The mere sight of a police car might have sent him running home to Ben, but he saw none.

At the rear of the school the parking lot, usually empty at this time, contained half a dozen cars. Charlie's first thought was that an accident had happened, Jessie had taken another fall and hurt herself very seriously and would be in the hospital for a long period; she would be safe in a hospital with all the doctors and nurses around; no stranger could reach her, a stranger would be stopped at the door and sent packing. Alternate waves of relief and despair passed over him like cold winds and hot winds coming from places he had never visited.

He drove around to the side of the school and saw that no accident had happened. A group of older boys were playing baseball and a few spectators were watching the game, including a man and woman who acted like parents. There were no young children in sight.

Charlie pulled over to the curb and turned off the ignition. He had no reason to stay there, with Jessie gone, but he had no reason to go home either. He had called Ben from work and told him that he was going on an errand for the boss and not to expect him home until seven or later. Though Ben had sounded suspicious at first, the words "special delivery" and "Forest Service" seemed to convince him not only that Charlie was telling the truth but that Mr. Warner trusted him enough to send him on an important mission.

Charlie watched the game for a few minutes without interest or attention. Then one of the players he hadn't noticed before came up to bat. He was a boy about sixteen, tall and thin as a broom handle. Even from a distance his cockiness was evident in every movement he made. He tapped the dirt out of his cleats, took a called strike, swung wildly at the second pitch and connected with the third for a home run that cleared the fence. With a little bow to his teammates he began jogging nonchalantly around the bases. As he rounded second base Charlie recognized him as the boy he'd seen several times with Jessie. There was no doubt about his identity: he even looked like Jessie, dark, with thin features and bright, intense eyes.

Charlie sat motionless, hardly even breathing. This was Jessie's brother. The phrase kept running through his head like words on a cracked record: *Jessie's brother, Jessie's brother, Jessie's brother.* Jessie's brother would live in the same house as Jessie, so it was now simply a question of following him, cautiously so the boy wouldn't get suspicious, but keeping him in sight at all times until he stopped at a house and went inside. Charlie's throat felt so thick that he had to touch it with his fingers to make sure he was not swelling up like a balloon. *The house he goes into will be Jessie's house. If I'm lucky there'll be a name on the mailbox and I won't have to ask Louise to help me. I'll be on my own, I'll do it all by myself.*

The home run had broken up the game. There was a round of cheers and applause, with the man and woman deliberately abstaining. They walked onto the field and started talking to the pitcher, who turned his back on them. Players and spectators were dispersing, toward the parking lot and the side gate. Within five minutes the playground was empty of victors and vanquished alike, and a flock of blackbirds were walking around in the dust, nodding their heads as if they'd known right from the beginning how it would all end: someone would win, someone would lose. Charlie had done both.

The boys drifted off in twos and threes, wearing their uniforms but carrying their cleated shoes and bats and baseball mitts. Some of them passed Charlie's car, still discussing the game, but Jessie's brother and two of his teammates went out the gate on the other side of the school.

Charlie drove around the block, passed them, and parked in front of a white stucco house. As they went by the car Charlie pretended to be searching for something in the glove compartment in order to keep his face hidden from them. Their voices were so loud and clear that he had a moment's panic when he thought they were talking directly to him. They knew all about him, they were baiting him—

"—four o'clock in the morning, man, she'll have a fit," Jessie's brother said. "She's always grouching about me waking everybody up too early when I go fishing."

"We could all stay at my house overnight. My folks sleep like they're in a coma."

"Good thinking, man. I'll just check in at the house and check right out again."

"Maybe we should leave even earlier than four. We'll catch the fish before they've got their eyes open—"

The boys passed out of earshot. Cautiously, Charlie raised his head. The snatch of conversation he'd overheard worried him. He couldn't shake off the feeling that Jessie had told her brother about him and the brother had told his two friends and the three of them were taunting him: he was the fish who would be caught before he opened his eyes. They had found out from some secret source that he always woke up at four o'clock in the morning. Or was it five? Or six?

The ordinary facts of his existence were all crowding together in one part of his mind and trampling each other like frightened horses in the corner of a corral. Some died, some were mutilated beyond recognition, some emerged as strange, unidentifiable hybrids. Four and five and six were all squashed together; he didn't know what time it was now or what time he woke in the morning. The setting sun could have been a rising moon or the reflected glow of a fire or a lighted spaceship about to land. Jessie and her brother merged into a single figure, a half-grown boy-girl. Louise and Ben had faces but they wouldn't let him see; they kept their backs to him because he'd done something they didn't like. He couldn't remember what it was he'd done but it must have been terrible, their backs were rigid with disapproval and Louise had deliberately let her hair grow long and braided it around her head the way his mother used to. He hated it. He wanted to take a pair of scissors and cut it off. But the scissors wasn't in the kitchen drawer where it was always kept, and the drawer had lost its handle. It didn't even open like a drawer. It sprung out when he pushed a little silver button, like the glove compartment in a car.

Glove compartment. Car. He blinked his eyes painfully, as though he were emerging from a long and dreadful sleep. The sun was beginning to set. It was a quarter to seven by his watch. Three boys were walking up the street. He followed them.

Ralph MacPherson worked at the office until nearly seven o'clock. He felt too weary to contact Kate again but he could picture her waiting at the telephone for his call, getting herself more and more worked up, and he knew he couldn't postpone it any longer.

She answered before the second ring, in the guarded half-disguised voice she always used before he identified himself.

"Hello."

"Kate, this is Mac."

"Have you found anything out about Gowen?"

"Yes."

"Well? Was I right? He's some bum Sheridan picked up in a bar and hired to do his dirty work for him."

"I hardly think so," Mac said as patiently as he could. "I went over to Miria Street this afternoon and dropped in at a drugstore around the corner from Gowen's house. I pretended I'd lost the address. Not very subtle, perhaps, but it worked. The druggist knows the Gowen family, they've been his customers for years. It didn't take much to start him talking. Business was slow."

She made an impatient sound. "Well, what did he *say?*"

"Charles Gowen lives with his brother Ben. Ben manages a downtown cafeteria, Charles has a job with a paper company. They're both hard-working and clean-living. They don't smoke or drink, they pay their bills on time, they mind their own business. There's a neighborhood rumor that Charles is going to marry one of the local librarians, a very nice woman who is also hard-working and clean-living, etcetera, etcetera. In brief, Gowen's not our man."

"But he must be," she said incredulously. "He ran away from me. He acted guilty."

"It's possible that you scared the daylights out of him. He may not be used to strange women chasing him around town. Not many of us are. Make me a promise, will you, Kate?"

"What is it?"

"That you'll stop thinking about Sheridan's machinations just for tonight and get yourself a decent rest."

She didn't argue with him but she didn't promise either. She simply said she was sorry to have bothered him and hung up.

Parked half a block away, Charlie watched the three boys turn in the driveway of a house on Cielito Lane. Only a difference in planting and a ribbon of smoke rising from a backyard barbecue pit distinguished it from its neighbors, but to Charlie it was a very special house.

He drove past slowly. The mailbox had a name on it: David E. Brant.

16

IT WAS HOWARD Arlington's last night in the city for two weeks and he and Virginia had been invited to a farewell barbecue on the Brants' patio. They didn't want to go but neither of them indicated this in any way. Ever since their unpleasant scene the previous night, they'd been excessively polite to each other, to Dave and Ellen and Jessie, even to the gardener and the cleaning woman. It was as if they were trying to convince everyone, including themselves, that they were not the kind of people who staged domestic brawls—not they.

This new formal politeness affected not only their speech and actions but their style of dress. They both knew that Ellen and Dave would be in jeans and sneakers, but Howard had put on a dark business suit, white shirt and a tie, and Virginia wore a pink-flowered silk dress with a stole and matching high-heeled sandals. They looked as though they were going out to dinner and a symphony instead of to the neighbors' backyard for hamburgers and hi-fi, both of which would be overdone.

The hi-fi was already going and so was the fire. Smoke and violins drifted into the Arlingtons' kitchen window. Normally, Howard would have slammed the window shut and made some caustic remark about tract houses. Tonight he merely said, "Dave's sending out signals. What time does Ellen want us over there?"

Virginia wasn't sure Ellen wanted them over there at all but the invitation had been extended and accepted, there was nothing to be done about it. "Seven o'clock."

"It's nearly that now. Are you ready?"

"Yes."

"Perhaps we'd better leave Chap in the house."

"Yes, perhaps we'd better." Her voice gave no hint of the amused contempt she felt. The big retriever was already asleep on the davenport and it would have taken Howard a long time to wake him up, coax, bribe, push and pull him outside. Chap would not be mean about it, simply inert, immovable. Sometimes she wondered whether the dog had learned this passive resistance from her or whether she'd learned it from him. In any case the dog seemed just as aware as Virginia that the technique was successful. Inaction made opposing action futile; Howard was given no leverage to work with.

They went out the rear door, leaving a lamp in the living room turned on for Chap, and the kitchen light for themselves. At the bottom of the stairs, Howard suddenly stopped.

"I forgot a handkerchief. You go on without me, I'll join you in a minute."

"I'd rather wait, thank you. We were invited as a couple, let's go as a couple."

"A couple of what?" he said and went back in the house.

Virginia's face was flushed with anger, and the rush of blood made her sunburn, now in the peeling stage, begin to itch painfully. She no longer blamed the sun as the real culprit, she blamed Howard. It was a Howardburn and it itched just as painfully inside as it did outside. There was a difference, though: inside, it couldn't be scratched, no relief was possible.

When Howard returned, he was holding the handkerchief to his mouth as if to prove to her that he really needed it. His voice was muffled. "Virginia, listen."

"What is it?"

"You don't suppose the kid told her parents about that twenty dollars I gave her?"

"I talked to Ellen today, nothing was mentioned about it. By the way, Jessie has a name. I wish you'd stop referring to her as 'the kid.'"

"There's only one kid in our lives. It hardly seems necessary to name her."

"I thought we'd agreed to be civil to each other for the rest of your time at home. Why do you want to start something now? We've had a pleasant day, don't ruin it."

"You think it's been a pleasant day, do you?"

"As pleasant as possible," Virginia said.

"As pleasant as possible while I'm around, is that what you mean? In other words, you don't expect much in my company."

"Perhaps I can't afford to."

"Well, tomorrow I'll be back on the road. You and the kid can have a real ball."

"Let's stop this right now, Howard, before it goes too far. We're not saying anything new anyway. It's all been said."

"And done," Howard added. "It's all said and done. Amen." He looked down at her with a smile that was half-pained, half-mocking. "The problem is, what do people do and say after everything's said and done? Where do we go from here?"

"To the Brants' for a barbecue."

"And then?"

"I can't think any further than that now, Howard. I can't think."

She leaned against the side of the house, hugging her stole around her and staring out at the horizon. Where the sea and sky should have met, there was a grey impenetrable mass of fog between them. She dreaded the time when this mass would begin to move because nothing, no one, could stop it. The sea would disappear, then the beaches, the foothills, the mountains. Streets would be separated from streets, houses from houses, people from people. Everyone would be alone except the women with a baby growing inside them. She saw them nearly every day in stores, on corners, getting into cars. She hated and envied the soft, confident glow in their eyes as if they knew no fog could ever be thick enough to make them feel alone.

Howard was watching her. "Let me get you a sweater, Virginia."

"No, thank you."

"You look cold."

"It's just nerves."

They crossed the lawn and the concrete driveway and Ellen's experimental patch of dichondra with a Keep Off sign in the middle. From the beginning, neither the dichondra nor the sign had stood much of a chance. The sign had been bumped or kicked or blown to a 45° angle, and between the dichondra plants were the marks of bicycle tires and children's sneakers. The sneaker marks were about the size that Jessie would make, and Virginia had an impulse to lean down and push some dirt over them with her hand so that Jessie wouldn't be blamed. But she realized she couldn't do such a thing in front of Howard; it would only aggravate his jealousy of the child. So, instead, she stepped off the flagstone path into the dichondra patch, putting her feet deliberately over the imprints of Jessie's.

Howard opened his mouth to say something but he didn't have time. Mike was coming out of the gate of the patio fence, carrying some fishing tackle, a windbreaker, and three hamburgers still steaming from the grill.

Mike grinned at Howard and Virginia but there was impatience behind the grin, as though he suspected they would try to keep him there talking when he had other and more interesting things to do.

Howard said formally, "Good evening, Michael."

"Oh hi, Mr. Arlington, Mrs. Arlington. If you'll excuse me now, I've got some of the gang waiting for me. We're going fishing at two o'clock in the morning."

"That's pretty early even for fish, isn't it?"

"Maybe. I'm not sure whether fish sleep or not."

"I'm not, either. Well, good luck anyway."

"Thanks, Mr. Arlington. So long."

Virginia hadn't spoken. She was still standing in the dichondra patch looking vague and a little puzzled, as if she was wondering how she got there, and whether fish slept or not. Her high heels were sinking further and further into the ground like the roots of a tree seeking nourishment and moisture. For a moment she imagined that she was a tree, growing deeper, growing taller, putting out new leaves and blossoms, dropping fertile seeds into the earth.

Then Howard grasped her by the arm and it was an arm, not a branch, and it would never grow anything but old.

"For heaven's sake, what are you doing, Virginia?"

"Would you really like to know?"

"Yes."

She let out a brief, brittle laugh. "I'm pretending to be a tree."

"You're acting very peculiar tonight."

"I'm a very peculiar woman. Hadn't you noticed that before, Howard? Surely those sharp eyes of yours couldn't miss anything so obvious. I'm not like other women, I'm a freak. There's something missing in me."

"Take my hand and I'll help you out of there."

"I don't want to get out. I *like* being a tree."

"Stop playing games. Are you going to let me help you?"

"No."

"All right." Without further argument he picked her up and lifted her out of the dichondra patch. He had to exert all his strength to do it because she'd made herself limp—arms, legs, waist, neck. "Okay, tree, you've just been uprooted."

"Damn you. *Damn* you."

"That's better. Now suppose we go inside and you can start pretending you're a person." He opened the gate for her. "Coming?"

"I have no choice."

"You'd have even less choice if you were a tree."

They went into the patio and Howard closed the gate behind them with unnecessary force. The loud bang seemed to Virginia to be a warning, like a shot fired over her head.

"Come in, come in," Dave said. "Welcome to Brants' Beanery."

He was standing at the barbecue grill wearing an apron over his Bermuda shorts and T-shirt, and drinking a can of beer. Ellen sat barefoot at the redwood picnic table, slicing an onion. Neither of them looked as though they expected company or particularly wanted any.

Even though Virginia had known this was how it was going to be, she felt a stab of resentment, aggravated by a feeling, a hangover from her childhood, that she was the one who was wrong, and no matter how hard she tried, she always would be. She had spent an hour dressing and fixing her hair but Dave didn't even look at her. He had opened a can of beer for Howard and the two men were already deep in conversation, one on each side of the barbecue pit.

Virginia sat down beside Ellen. "Anything I can do to help?"

"It's all done, thanks. I wouldn't allow you to touch a thing in that dress, anyway. I'd feel so guilty if you spilled something on it. It's simply gorgeous."

Virginia had to take it as a compliment but she knew it wasn't. Ellen's voice was too objective, as though the dress had nothing to do with Virginia personally; a gorgeous dress was a gorgeous dress and it didn't matter who wore it or who owned it.

"It's not new," Virginia said. "I mean, it's just been lying around." For a whole week it had been lying around, waiting for an occasion. Now the occasion had arrived, hamburger and onions and baked beans in the next-door neighbors' backyard. She thought wildly and irrationally, *damn you, Howard. You didn't have to bring me here.*

"I thought perhaps it was the one you bought last week at Corwin's," Ellen said. "You told me about it."

"No, no, I took that back. I've had this dress since—well, since before you even moved here. That seems ages ago, doesn't it? I feel so close to you and Dave and Mike and, of course, Jessie." She glanced hastily in Howard's direction to make sure he hadn't overheard the name. He was still engrossed in his conversation with Dave. "Where is Jessie?"

"In the front room watching television."

"I'll go in and say hello. I have a little something for her."

"Virginia, you shouldn't, you'll—"

"It's nothing at all, really, just a piece of junk jewelry. I saw it in a store window this afternoon and I thought Jessie would like it."

"She's too young to wear jewelry."

"It's only a small ring with an imitation pearl. I had one exactly like it when I was six years old. I remember it so clearly. My hands grew too fast and it had to be filed off."

"It won't have to be filed off Jessie," Ellen said dryly. "She'll lose it within a week."

"Then you don't mind if I give it to her?"

"I suppose not."

Virginia rose and crossed the patio, moving with unaccustomed agility as though she wanted to get away before she could be called back.

Jessie was curled up in a corner of the davenport, her chin resting on her knees, her arms hugging her legs. Her eyes widened a little when she saw Virginia in the doorway but it was the only sign of recognition she gave.

"Hello, Jessie." Virginia went over to the television set. "May I turn this down a minute?"

"I—yes, I guess."

"I haven't seen you for two days."

"I've been busy," Jessie said, looking down at the floor as if she were talking to it and not Virginia. "My mother took me swimming this afternoon. To see if the salt water would hurt my hands."

"And did it?"

"Not much."

Virginia sat down on the davenport beside her. "You know what I did this afternoon? I went downtown shopping."

"Did you buy something?"

"Yes."

"Was Howard with you to pay for it?"

Virginia sucked in her breath as though the question had knocked it out of her. "No, no, he wasn't. I paid for it myself."

"But the other night he said—"

"The other night he said a lot of things he didn't mean. He was tired and out of sorts. We all get like that sometimes, don't we?"

"Yes, sometimes."

"When two people are married, they share whatever money comes into the house, whether it's the man's salary or the woman's or both. If I see something I want and can afford, I buy it. I don't need Howard's permission." *But it helps,* she added bitterly to herself. *He likes to play Big Daddy, spoiling his foolish and extravagant little girl, as long as the little girl is duly appreciative.*

Jessie was considering the subject, her mouth pursed, her green eyes narrowed. "I guess Howard gives you lots of money, doesn't he?"

"Yes."

"Every month my daddy gives money to the bank for this house. In nineteen more years we're going to own it. When is Howard going to own you?"

"Never," Virginia said sharply. Then, seeing Jessie's look of bewilderment, she added in a softer voice, "Look, dear, I'm not a house. Howard isn't making payments on me."

"Then why does he give you money?"

"He doesn't exactly give it to me. We share it. If Howard didn't have me to look after the house for him, he'd have to hire someone else to perform the same services for him."

"If he hires you, that makes him the boss."

"*No.* I mean—how on earth did we get off on this subject? You're too young to understand."

"Will I understand when I'm older?"

"Yes," Virginia said, thinking, *I hope you never grow up to understand what I do. I hope you die before your innocence is torn away from you.*

Jessie was frowning and biting the nail of her left thumb. "I certainly have tons of stuff to learn when I grow up. I wish I could start right now."

"No. No, don't wish that. Stay the way you are, Jessie. Just stay, stay like this, like tonight."

"I can't," Jessie said in a matter-of-fact voice. "Mary Martha would get way ahead of me. She's already taller and spells better. Mary Martha knows a lot."

"Some of them are things I couldn't bear having you know, Jessie."

"Why not? They're not bad, they don't hurt her."

"They hurt. I see her hurting."

Jessie shook her head. "No. If she was hurting, she'd cry. She's an awful sissy sometimes, she can't stand the sight of blood or anything oozing."

"Do you ever see me cry, Jessie?"

"No."

"Well, I hurt. I hurt terribly."

"Because of your sunburn?"

Virginia hesitated a moment, then she laughed, the harsh, brief laugh she heard herself utter so often lately. It was like the distress signal of an animal that couldn't communicate in words. "Yes, of course. Because of my sunburn. I must be as big a sissy as Mary Martha."

"She's not a sissy about everything."

"Perhaps I'm not either, about everything. I don't know. Not everything's been tried on me yet. Not quite."

Jessie would have liked to ask what had or had not been tried, but Virginia had averted her face and was changing the subject, not very subtly or completely, by opening her purse. It was a pink silk pouch that matched her dress. Inside the pouch was a tiny box wrapped in white paper and tied with a miniature golden rope.

Jessie saw the box and immediately and deliberately turned her head away. "Your shoes are dirty."

"I stepped off the path. Jessie, I have a little pres—"

"You're not supposed to step off the path."

Virginia's face was becoming white even where she was sunburned, on her cheekbones and the bridge of her nose, as though whiteness was not a draining away of blood but a true pigmentation that could conceal other colors. "Jessie, dear, you're not paying attention to what I'm telling you. I said, I have a little present for you. It's something I'm sure you'll love."

"No, I won't. I *won't* love it."

"But you don't even know what it is yet."

"I don't care."

"You don't want it, is that it?"

"No."

"You won't—won't even open it?"

"No."

"That's too bad," Virginia said slowly. "It's very pretty. I used to have one exactly like it when I was a little girl and I was so proud of it. It made me feel grown-up."

"I don't want to feel grown-up anymore."

"Oh, you're quite right, of course. You're really very sensible. If I had it to do over again, I wouldn't choose to grow up either. To live the happy years and die young—"

"I'm going to watch television." Jessie's lower lip was quivering. She had to catch it with her teeth to hold it still so that Virginia wouldn't see how frightened she was. She wasn't sure what had caused the sudden, overwhelming fear but she realized that she had to fight it, with any weapon at all that she could find. "My—my mother doesn't like you."

Virginia didn't look surprised, her eyes were merely soft and full of sadness. "I'm sorry to hear that because I like her."

"You're not supposed to like someone who doesn't like you."

"Really? Well, I guess I do a lot of things I'm not supposed to. I step off paths and get my shoes dirty, I buy presents for little girls—Perhaps some day I'll learn better."

"I'm going to watch television," Jessie repeated stubbornly. "I want to see the ending of the program."

"Go ahead."

"You turned it off. When company turns it off my mother makes me keep it that way."

"Turn it on again. I'm not company."

Awkwardly, Jessie unfolded her arms and legs and went over to the television set. Her head felt heavy with what she didn't yet recognize as grief: something was lost, a time had passed, a loved one was gone. "You—you could watch the ending with me, Aunt Virginia."

"Perhaps I will. That's the nice part about television programs, they start with a beginning and end with an ending. Other things don't. You find yourself in the middle and you don't know how you got there or how to get out. It's like waking up in the middle of a water tank with steep, slippery sides. You just keep swimming around and around, there's no ladder to climb out, nobody flings you a rope, and you can't stop swimming because you have this animal urge to survive . . . No television program is ever like that, is it, Jessie?"

"No, because it has to end to make room for another program. Nobody can be left just swimming around."

"How would it end on television, Jessie?"

Jessie hesitated only long enough to take a deep breath. "A dog would find you and start barking and attract a lot of people. They'd tie all their jackets and sweaters and things together to make a rope and they'd throw it to you and lift you out. Then you'd hug the dog and he'd lick your face."

"Thanks for nothing, dog," Virginia said and got up and went over to the doorway. "I'll see you later."

"Aren't you going to stay for the ending?"

"You've already told me the ending."

"That's not *this* program. *This* is about a horse and there's no water tank in it, just a creek like the one behind Mary Martha's house."

But Virginia had already gone. Jessie turned up the sound on the television set. Horses were thudding furiously across the desert as if they were trying to get away from the loud music that pursued them. Above the horses' hoofs and trumpets, Jessie could hear Virginia laughing out on the patio. She sounded very gay.

17

THE PAIN BEGAN, as it usually did, when Charlie was a couple of blocks away from his house. It started in his left shoulder and every heartbeat pushed it along, down his arm and up his neck into his head until he was on fire. Alone in his room with no one to bother him, he could endure the pain and even derive some satisfaction from not taking anything to relieve it. But tonight Ben was waiting for him. Questions would be asked— some trivial, some innocent, some loaded—and answers to them would be expected. It would be at least an hour before he was allowed to go into his room and be by himself to plan what he would say to Jessie.

He stopped for a red light and was reaching into the glove compartment for the bottle of aspirin he kept there when he remembered that he wasn't driving the green coupé anymore. There was no bottle of aspirin in this one, only a map of Los Angeles, unfolded and torn, as if someone had crammed it into the glove compartment in a fit of impatience.

The light turned green. He drove past the house. Ben's car was parked in the driveway, looking, to Charlie, exactly like its owner, not new anymore but sturdy and clean and well taken care of, with no secret trouble in the engine.

The drugstore was around the corner, one block down. There was no one in the store but Mr. Forster, the owner, who was behind the prescription counter reading the evening newspaper.

"Well, it's you, Charlie." Mr. Forster took off his spectacles and tucked them in the pocket of his white jacket. "Long time no see. How are you?"

"Not so good, Mr. Forster."

"Yes, I see that. Yes, indeed." Mr. Forster was the chief diagnostician of the neighborhood, even for people who had their own doctors. Out of respect for his position his customers always addressed him as Mr. Forster and so did his wife. He took his responsibilities very seriously, subscribing to the A.M.A. journal and *Lancet*, and reading with great care the advertising material that accompanied each new drug sample.

"A bit feverish, aren't you, Charlie?"

"I don't think so. I have a headache. I'd like some aspirin."

"Any nausea or vomiting?"

"No."

"What about your eyes? Are they all right?"

"Yes."

"Had your blood pressure checked recently?"

"No. I just want some—"

"It sounds like a vascular headache to me," Forster said, nodding wisely. "Maybe you should try one of the new reserpine compounds. By the way, did the man find your house?"

"What—what man?"

"Oh, he was in here a while ago, nice-looking grey-haired fellow around fifty. Said he'd lost your address."

"I haven't been home yet tonight."

"Well, he may be there right now, waiting for you."

"Not for me," Charlie said anxiously. "For Ben. People come to the house to see Ben, not me."

"Isn't your name Charles Gowen?"

"You know it is, Mr. Forster."

"Well, Charles Gowen is who he wanted to see." Forster took a bottle of aspirin off a shelf. "Shall I put this in a bag for you?"

"No. No, I'll take one right away." Charlie reached for the bottle. His hands were shaking, a fact that didn't escape Forster's attention.

"Yes, sir, if I were you, Charlie, I'd have my blood pressure checked. A niece of mine had a vascular headache and reserpine fixed her up just like magic. She's a different woman."

Charlie unscrewed the cap of the bottle, removed the cotton plug and put two aspirins in his mouth. The strong bitter taste spread from his tongue all the way to his ears and his forehead. His eyes began to water so that Mr. Forster's face looked distorted, like a face in a fun-house mirror.

"Let me get you a glass of milk," Forster said kindly. "You should always take a little milk with aspirin, it neutralizes the stomach acids."

"No, thank you."

"I insist."

Forster went into the back room and came out carrying a paper cup full of milk. He stood and watched Charlie drink it as though he were watching a stomach fighting a winning battle over its acids.

"I can understand your being nervous," Forster said, "at this stage of the game."

"What game?"

"The marriage game, of course. The word's gotten out how you're engaged to a nice little woman that works in the library. Marriage is a great thing for a man, believe me. You might have a few qualms about it now but in a few years you'll be glad you took the big step. A man stays single just so long, then people begin to talk." Forster took the empty paper cup from Charlie's hand and squeezed it into a ball. "Mind if I say something personal to you, Charlie?"

Charlie didn't speak. The milk seemed to have clotted in his throat like blood.

Forster mistook silence for assent. "That old trouble of yours, you mustn't let it interfere with your happiness. It's all over and done with, people have forgotten it. Why, it was so long ago you were hardly more than a boy. Now you're living a clean, decent life, you're just as good as the next man and don't you be thinking otherwise."

Please stop, Charlie thought. *Please stop him, God, somebody, anybody, make him be quiet. It's worse than listening to Ben. They don't know, neither of them, they don't know—*

"Maybe it's not in such good taste, dragging it up like this, but I want you to understand how I feel. You're going to do fine, Charlie. You deserve a little happiness. Living with a brother is all right when it's necessary, but what the heck, a man needs a wife and family of his own. When's the big day?"

"I don't know. Louise—it's her decision."

"Don't leave all the deciding to the lady, Charlie. They like to be told once in a while, makes them feel feminine. You want me to charge the aspirin?"

"Yes."

"Right. Well, all the best to you and the little lady, Charlie."

"Thank you, Mr. Forster."

"And bear in mind what I said. The town's getting so filled up with strangers that only a few old-timers like myself know you ever had any trouble. You just forget it, Charlie. It's water under the bridge, it's spilled milk. You ever tried to follow a drop of water down to the sea? Or pour spilled milk back into the bottle?"

"No. I—"

"Can't be done. Put that whole nasty business out of your head, Charlie. It's a dead horse, bury it."

"Yes. Good-bye, Mr. Forster."

Charlie began moving toward the door but Forster moved right along beside him. He seemed reluctant to let Charlie go, as if Charlie was a link with the past, which for all its cruelties was kinder than this day of strangers and freeways and super drugstores in every shopping center.

"I've got to go now, Mr. Forster. Ben's waiting for me."

"A good man, that Ben. He was a tower of strength to you in your time of need, always remember that, Charlie. He's probably quite proud of you now, eh? Considering how you've changed and everything?"

Charlie was staring down at the door handle as though he wished it would turn of its own accord and the door would open and he could escape. *Ben's not proud of me. I haven't changed. The horse isn't dead, the milk is still spilling, the same drop of water keeps passing under the bridge.*

Forster opened the door and the old-fashioned bell at the top tinkled its cheerful warning. "Well, it's been nice talking to you, Charlie. Come in again soon for another little chat. And say hello to Ben for me."

"Yes."

"By the way, that man who was in here asking for your address, he had an official bearing like he was used to ordering people around. But don't worry, Charlie. I didn't tell him a thing about that old trouble of yours. I figured it was none of his business if he wasn't an official, and if he was he'd know about it anyway. It's all on the record."

The same drop of water was passing under the bridge, only it was dirtier this time, it smelled worse, it carried more germs. Charlie leaned forward as if he meant to scoop it up with his hand and throw it away, so far away it would disintegrate, and all the dirt and smell and germs with it. But Mr. Forster was watching him, and though his smile was benevolent his eyes were wary. *You can never tell what these nuts are going to do, no matter how hard you try to be kind to them.*

"You," Charlie said, "you look like Ben, Mr. Forster."

"What?"

"You look exactly like Ben. It shows up real clear to me."

"It does, eh? You'd better go home and get some sleep. You're tired."

He was tired but he couldn't go home. The man might be there waiting for him, ready to ask him questions. He had done nothing wrong, yet he knew he wouldn't be believed. He couldn't say it with absolute conviction, the way Louise had the night she found him on Jacaranda Road: "*Nothing's happened, Charlie . . . You haven't harmed anyone. The Oakley girl is safe at home, and I believe that even if I hadn't found you when I did, she'd still be safe at home.*"

The Oakley girl was safe at home. So was the Brant girl, Jessie. Or was she? He hadn't seen her at the playground, or outside her house when he drove past. Perhaps something had happened to her and that was why the man wanted to question him. He might even have to take a lie-detector test. He had heard once that real guilt and feelings of guilt showed up almost the same on a lie-detector test. If he were asked whether he knew Jessie Brant he would say no because this was the truth. But his heart would leap, his blood pressure would rise, his voice would choke up, he would start sweating, and all these things would be recorded on the chart and brand him a liar. Even Ben would think he was lying. Only Louise would believe him, only Louise. He felt a terrible need to hear her say: "*Nothing happened, Charlie. The Oakley girl is safe at home, and the Brant girl and the other little girls, all safe at home, all snug in their beds, nothing to fear from you, Charlie. I love you, Charlie . . .*"

He left his car in the parking lot behind the library. The lot was almost filled, mainly with cars bearing high school and city college stickers. The back door of the library was marked EMPLOYEES ONLY, but he used it anyway because it was the shortest way to Louise.

He found himself in the filing and catalogue room, lined with steel drawers and smelling of floor wax. An old man with a push broom looked at him curiously but offered no challenge; libraries were for everybody.

"Could you," Charlie said and stopped because his voice sounded peculiar. He cleared his throat, swallowing the last of the clotted milk. "Could you tell me if Miss Lang is here?"

"I don't know one from the other," the old man answered with a shrug. "I only been on the job three nights now."

Nodding his thanks, Charlie walked the length of the room and through a corridor with an open door at the end of it. From here he could see Louise's desk behind the reference counter but Louise wasn't there. A woman about thirty was sitting in her chair. She looked familiar to Charlie though he wasn't sure he'd ever met her.

A sixth sense seemed to warn her she was being watched. She turned her head and spotted Charlie standing in the doorway. She got up immediately, as though she was expecting his arrival and had planned a welcome for him. She came toward him, smiling.

"Mr. Gowen?"

"Yes, I—yes."

"I'm Betty Albert. Louise introduced us a couple of weeks ago. Are you looking for her?"

"Yes. I thought she was working tonight."

"She was," Miss Albert said in a confidential whisper, "but some teenagers gave her a bad time. Oh, she handled it beautifully, it was as quiet as church within ten minutes, but the strain upset her. She went home. The public doesn't realize yet that we have quite a policing problem in the library, especially on Friday nights when school's not in session and the kids don't have a football or basketball game to go to. I claim the schools should be open all year, it would give the little darlings something to do. Bored teenagers running around loose act worse than maniacs, don't you think? . . . Mr. Gowen, wait. You're really not supposed to use that back exit. It's just for employees. Mr. Gowen—?"

Miss Albert returned to her desk, her step light, her eyes dreamy. *He must be madly in love with her,* she thought as she lowered herself into the chair, lifting her skirt a few inches at the back to prevent seat-sag. *Why, the instant he heard she'd had a bad time and gone home, he looked sick with worry, then off he tore out the wrong exit. He's probably speeding to her side right now. Louise doesn't realize how lucky she is to have a man speeding to her side. When there isn't a thing the matter with her except nerves.*

Miss Albert sat for a while, her emotions swinging between wonder and envy. When the pendulum stopped, she found herself thinking in a more practiced and realistic manner. Louise was her superior in the library, it wouldn't hurt to do her a favor and warn her that Charlie was coming. It would give her a chance to pretty up, she'd looked awfully ratty when she left.

Louise's number was listed on a staff card beside the telephone. Miss Albert dialed, humming softly as if inspired by the sound of the dial tone.

Louise herself answered. "Yes?"

"This is Betty Albert."

"Oh. Is anything wrong?"

"No. Mr. Gowen was just here asking for you. When I told him you'd gone home he rushed right out. He should be there any minute. I thought—"

"Did he tell you he was coming here?"

"Why, no. But—well, it seemed obvious from the way he tore out and used the wrong exit and everything. I thought I'd tell you so you'd have a chance to pretty up before he arrived."

"Thanks, I'll do that," Louise said. "Good night, Miss Albert."

She hung up and went back down the hall toward her bedroom. Through the open door of the kitchen she could see her parents, her father watching something boiling on the stove, her mother getting the company dinnerware out of the top cupboard. She remembered that it was her father's birthday, and to celebrate the occasion he was preparing a special potato dish his grandmother used to cook for him in Germany when he was a boy. The thought of having to eat and pretend to enjoy the thick grey gluey balls nauseated Louise.

She spoke from the doorway. "I'm going out for a drive, if you don't mind."

He father turned around, scowling. "But I do mind. The *kloessen* are almost done and I've gone to a great deal of trouble over them."

"Yes, I know."

"You know but you don't care. Well, that's typical of the younger generation, lots of knowledge, no appreciation. When my grandmother was making *kloessen* you couldn't have dragged any of us away from the house with wild horses. I don't understand you, Louise. One minute you're lying down half-dead and the next minute you're going out. You're not consistent this last while."

"I guess I'm not."

"It's that man who's responsible. He's no good for you. He's blinded you to—"

"A lot of blind people do very well," Louise said. "With luck, so will I."

"So now the man isn't enough. You're demanding luck too, are you?"

"No, I'm praying for it."

"Well, I hope you get it."

"Then *sound* as if you hope it, will you? Just for once, *sound* as if you believed in me, as if you wanted me to have a life of my own, independent of you, unprotected by you."

"Oh, do hush up, both of you," Mrs. Lang said, brushing some dust off a plate with her apron. "It's hot in here. Open another window, will you, Joe? And Louise, don't forget to take a coat. You never can tell when the fog might come in."

The sun had gone down and stars were bursting out all over the sky like fireworks that would burn themselves out by morning and begin their infinite fall.

Charlie leaned against the side of the building. Of all the things Miss Albert had said to him, only one had registered in his mind: Louise had gone home. When he desperately needed her reassurance, she had gone where he was afraid to follow.

Home was where people went who had never done anything wrong—like Ben and Louise. For the others—the ones like him, Charlie—there wasn't any room, no matter how large the world. There wasn't any time to rest, no matter how long the night. Whatever their course of action or inaction they were always wrong. If they called out for help they were cowards, if they didn't call they were fools. If they stayed in one place they were loitering; if they moved they were running away. "We, the jury, find the defendant guilty of everything and sentence him to a life of nothing—" And all the people in the crowded courtroom, all the people in the world, broke into applause.

He knew it hadn't really occurred like that. No jury would say such a thing even though it might be what they meant. Besides, there'd been no jury, only a judge who kept leaning his head first on one hand and then on the other, as if it were too heavy for his neck. And the courtroom wasn't crowded. There were just the lawyers and bailiffs and reporter and Ben and his mother sitting near Charlie, and on the other side of the room, the child's parents, who didn't even glance at him. The girl herself wasn't brought in. Charlie never saw her again. When it was all over, Charlie rode in the back of the Sheriff's car to the hospital with two other men, and Ben took his savings and his mother's, and borrowed money from the bank, and gave it to the girl's parents, who'd sued for damages. They left town and Charlie never saw them again either.

That time it had happened. Even Louise couldn't have said it didn't, that it wasn't real, that the girl was at home safe in her bed. Perhaps she would have said it anyway, knowing it wasn't true. He couldn't afford to believe her ever again. He had to find out for himself what was real and what wasn't and which children were safe at home in their beds.

18

ELLEN HAD EXPECTED a dull evening because the Arlingtons were usually tense and quiet the night before Howard was to leave on another business trip. She was pleasantly surprised by Virginia's show of vivacity and by the sudden interest Howard was taking in Jessie.

While the others ate at the redwood picnic table, Howard sat with Jessie on the lawn swing, asking her all about school and what she was doing during the holidays. Jessie, who'd been taught to answer adults' questions but not to speak with her mouth full, compromised by keeping her answers as brief as possible. School was okay. Natural history was best. During the holidays she played. With Mary Martha. On the jungle gym. Also climbing trees. Sometimes they went swimming.

"Oh, come now," Howard said. "Aren't you forgetting Aunt Virginia? You visit her every day, don't you?"

"I guess."

"Do you like to visit her?"

"Yes."

"You go downtown shopping with her and to the movies and things like that, eh?"

"Not often."

"Once or twice a week?"

"Maybe."

Howard took a bite of hamburger and chewed it as if his teeth hurt. Then he put his plate down on the grass, shoving it almost out of sight under the swing. "Does anyone else go along on these excursions of yours?"

"No."

"Just the two of you, eh?"

Jessie nodded uncomfortably. She didn't know why Howard was asking so many questions. They made her feel peculiar, as if she and Virginia had been doing wrong things.

"It's nice of you to keep Virginia company," Howard said pleasantly. "She's a very lonely woman. You eat quite a few meals with her, don't you?"

"Not so many."

"When you've finished eating, what then? She reads to you, perhaps, or tells you stories?"

"Yes."

"She tells me some, too. Do you believe her stories?"

"Yes, unless they're fairy tales."

"How can you be sure when they're fairy tales?"

"They begin 'Once upon a time.'"

"Always?"

"They have to. It's a rule."

"Is it now," Howard said with a dry little laugh. "I'll remember that. The ones that begin 'Once upon a time,' I won't believe. Do I have to believe all the others?"

"You should. Otherwise—"

"Otherwise, she'd be telling fibs, eh?"

"I don't think so. Grownups aren't supposed to tell fibs."

"Some of them do, though. It's as natural to them as breathing."

Although Virginia was talking to Dave and Ellen and hadn't even glanced in Howard's direction, she seemed to be aware of trouble. She rose and came toward the swing, her stole trailing behind her like some pink wisp of the past.

"Have you finished eating, Jessie?"

"Yes."

"It's getting close to your bedtime, isn't it?"

"The kid has parents," Howard said. "Let them tell her when to go to bed. It's none of your business."

"I don't *have* to be told," Jessie said with dignity, and slid off the swing, glad for once to be getting away from the company of adults. She wished Michael were at home so she could ask him why Howard and Virginia were acting so peculiar lately.

"Well," Howard said, "I suppose now the party's over for you, Virginia. Not much use sticking around after the kid goes to bed. Shall we leave?"

"I'm warning you. Don't make a scene or you'll regret it."

"Your threats are as empty as your promises. Try another approach."

"Such as begging? You'd like that, wouldn't you? The only time you ever feel good anymore is when I come crawling to you for something. Well, you're going to have to think of other ways to feel good because from now on I'm not crawling and I'm not begging."

"Three days." Howard said bitterly, "I've been home three days and not for one minute have I felt welcome. I'm just a nuisance who appears every two or three weeks and disrupts your real life. The hell of it is that I don't understand what your real life is, so I can't try to fit into it or go along with it. I can only fight it because it doesn't include me. I want, I need, a place in it. I used to have one. What went wrong, Virginia?"

Dave and Ellen exchanged embarrassed glances like two characters in a play who found themselves on stage at the wrong time. Then Ellen put some dishes on a tray and started toward the house and after a second's hesitation Dave followed her. Their leaving made no more difference to the Arlingtons than their presence had.

"What's the matter, Virginia? If it's my job, I can change it. If it's the fact that we have no family, we can change that, too."

"No," she said sharply. "I no longer want a family."

"Why not? You've wept for one often enough."

"We no longer have anything to offer a child." She stared out beyond the patio walls to the horizon. The wall of fog had begun to expand. Pretty soon the city would disappear, streets would be separated from streets and people from people and everyone would be alone. "Yes, Howard, I wept, I wept buckets. I was young then. I didn't realize how cruel it would be to pass along such an ugly thing as life. Poor Jessie."

He frowned. "Why? Why poor Jessie?"

"She's only nine, she's still full of innocence and high hopes and dreams. She will lose her innocence and high hopes and dreams; she will lose them all. By the time she's my age she will have wished a thousand times that she were dead."

Twice Louise covered the entire length of Jacaranda Road, driving in second gear, looking at every parked car and every person walking along the street or waiting at bus stops. There was no sign of Charlie or his car, and the Oakley house at 319 was dark as if no one lived in it anymore. She was encouraged by the dark house. If anything had happened, there would be light and noise and excitement. *Nothing's happened. Nothing whatever—*

She drove to Miria Street. Ben let her in the front door. "Hello, Louise. I thought you were working tonight."

"I was."

"Charlie's not here but come in anyway. I'm making a fresh pot of coffee. Would you like some?"

"Please." She followed him down the hall to the kitchen. He walked slowly as though his back ached, and for the first time she thought of him not as one of the Gowen brothers but as a middle-aged man.

She accepted the cup of coffee he poured her and sat down at the table. "Are you tired, Ben?"

"A little. It was Dollar Day in most of the stores downtown. What the ladies saved on hats and dresses they came in and spent on food." He sat down opposite her. "I think I've found the right place."

"Place?"

"The apartment I wanted down near the breakwater. It's furnished, so I wouldn't have to take a thing out of the house here, and the landlord told me I could keep a dog if it wasn't too big. I'll sign the lease as soon as you and Charlie name the wedding day . . . You don't look very pleased. What's the matter?"

"I was trying to imagine this house without you in it. It's very—difficult."

"This house has seen enough of me. And vice versa."

"Charlie would like you to stay with us."

"He'd soon get over that idea. He's nervous, that's all. He's like a kid, dreading any change even if it's a good one."

"Maybe I'm a little like that, too."

"Come off it, Louise. Why, I'll bet after you've been married a few weeks you'll meet me on the street and think, *that guy looks familiar, I must have seen him before some place.*"

"That could never happen."

"A lot of things are going to happen. Good things, I mean, the kind you and Charlie deserve."

She took a sip of coffee. It was so strong and bitter she could hardly swallow it. "Did—did Charlie come home after work?"

"No. But don't worry about it. He had to go on an errand for the boss. It was an important errand, too—making a delivery to the Forest Service up the mountain. It shows the boss is beginning to trust him with bigger things. Charlie told me on the phone not to expect him before seven o'clock."

"It's nearly nine."

"He may have had some trouble with his car. I've had trouble up there myself on hot days. The engine started to boil—"

"He was at the library about an hour ago."

"There's more to this, I suppose?"

"Yes."

Ben's face didn't change expression but suddenly he pushed his chair away from the table with such violence that his coffee cup fell into the saucer. Brown fluid oozed across the green plastic cloth like a muddy stream through a meadow. "Well, don't bother telling me.

I won't listen. I want one night, just this one night, to think about my own future, maybe even dream a little. Or don't I deserve a dream because I happen to be Charlie's older brother?"

"I'm sorry, Ben. I guess I shouldn't have come running to you." She rose, pulling her coat tightly around her body as if the room had turned cold. "I must learn to deal with situations like this on my own. Don't come with me, Ben. I can let myself out."

"Situations like what?"

"You don't want to hear."

"No, but you'd better tell me."

"I think I can handle it myself."

"By crying?"

"I'm not crying. My eyes always water when—when I'm under a strain. There's a certain nerve that runs from the back of the ear to the tear ducts and—"

"We'll discuss the structure of the nervous system some other time. Where is Charlie?"

"I don't know," she said, wiping her eyes with the back of one hand. "I've been looking for him ever since Miss Albert called to tell me he'd been at the library."

"You've been looking where?"

"Up and down Jacaranda Road."

"Why Jacaranda Road? You must have had a reason. What is it?"

She took a step back, as if dodging a blow.

"You've got to answer me, Louise."

"Yes. I'm trying—trying to say it in the right way."

"If it's a wrong thing, there's no right way to say it."

"I'm not sure that it's wrong. There may be nothing to it except in Charlie's imagination and now mine. I mean, he gets so full of worry that I start to worry, too."

"What about?"

She hesitated for a long time, then she spoke quickly, slurring her words as if to make them less real. "There's a child living at 319 Jacaranda Road, a little girl named Mary Martha Oakley. Charlie swears he's never even talked to her and I believe him, but he's afraid. So am I. I think he's been watching her and—well, fantasying about her. I know this isn't good because a fantasy that gets out of control can become a fact."

"How long have you known about the girl?"

"Two days."

"And you didn't level with me."

"Charlie asked me not to."

"But you're leveling now, in spite of that. Why?"

"I want you to tell me how it was the—the other time. I've got to know all about it, how he acted beforehand, if he was quiet or moody or restless, if he stayed away from the house on nights like this without telling anyone. Did he talk about the girl a lot, or didn't he mention her? How old was she? What did she look like? How did Charlie meet her?"

Ben went over to the sink and tore off a couple of sheets of paper toweling. Then he wiped the coffee off the table, slowly and methodically. His face was blank, as if he hadn't heard a word she'd said.

"Aren't you listening, Ben?"

"Yes. But I won't do what you're asking me to. It would serve no purpose."

"It might. Everybody has a pattern, Ben. Even strange and difficult people have one if you can find it. Suppose I learned Charlie's pattern so I could be alert to the danger signals—"

"It happened a long time ago. I don't remember the details, the fine points." Ben threw the used towel in the wastebasket and sat down again, his hands pressed out flat on the table in front of him, palms down. "If there were danger signals, I didn't see them. Charlie was just a nice, quiet young man, easy to have around, never asking much or getting much. He'd had two years of college. The first year he did well; the second, he had trouble concentrating—my mother suspected a love affair but it turned out she was wrong. He didn't go back for the third year because my father died. At least that was the accepted reason. After that he went to work. He held a succession of unimportant jobs. One of them was at a veterinary hospital and boarding kennels on Quila Street near the railroad tracks. Every day the girl walked along the tracks on her way to and from school. Charlie used to chase her away because he was afraid she'd get hurt by a train or by one of the winos who hung around the area. That's how it began, with Charlie trying to protect her."

Louise listened, remembering the reason Charlie had given her for wanting to find out the name of the people who lived at 319 Jacaranda Road: *"I must tell those people they've got to take better care of their little dog unless they want it to be killed by a car or something."*

She said, "How old was the girl?"

"Ten. But she looked younger because she was so small and skinny."

"Was she pretty?"

"No."

"What color was her hair, and was it short or long?"

"Dark and short, I think. I only saw her once, but I remember one of her front teeth was chipped from a fall."

"Though it may seem like a terrible thing to say, Ben, all this sounds very promising."

"Promising?"

"Yes. You see, I've met Mary Martha. She's a plump, pretty child with a long blonde ponytail, quite mature-looking for her age. She's not a bit like that other girl. Isn't that a good sign? She doesn't fit the pattern at all, Ben." Louise's pale cheeks had taken on a flush of excitement. "Now tell me about Charlie, how he acted beforehand, everything you can think of."

"I saw no difference in him," Ben said heavily. "But then I wasn't looking very hard, I'd just gotten married to Ann. Charlie could have grown another head and I might not have noticed."

"You'd just gotten married," Louise repeated. "Now Charlie's about to get married. Is this just a coincidence or is it part of the pattern?"

"Stop thinking about patterns, Louise. A whole battery of experts tried to figure out Charlie's and got nowhere."

"Then it's my turn to try. Where did you live after the wedding?"

"Here in this house. It was only supposed to be a temporary arrangement, we were going to buy a place of our own. Then Charlie was arrested and everything blew up in our faces. I didn't have enough money left to buy a tent, but by that time it didn't matter because I had no wife either."

"And now Charlie and I will be living in this house, too." Louise was looking around the room as if she were seeing it for the first time as a place she would have to call her home. "You still don't notice any pattern, Ben?"

"What if I say yes? What do I do then?"

"You mean, what do *we* do? I'm in it with you this time."

"Don't say this time. There isn't going to be a this time. It happened once, and it's not going to happen again, by God, if I have to keep him in sight twenty-four hours a day, if I have to handcuff him to me."

"That won't be much of a life for Charlie. He'd be better off dead."

"Do you suppose I haven't thought of that?" he said roughly. "A hundred times, five hundred, I've looked at him and seen him suffering, and I've thought, this is my kid brother. I love him, I'd cut off an arm for him, but maybe the best thing I could do for him is to end it all."

"You mean, kill him."

"Yes, kill him. And don't look at me with such horror. You may be thinking the same thing yourself before long."

"If you feel like that, your problems may be worse than Charlie's." She looked a little surprised at her own words as if they had come out unplanned. "Perhaps yours are much worse because you're not aware of them. When something happens to you, or inside yourself, you've always had Charlie to blame. It's made you look pretty good in the eyes of the world but it hasn't helped Charlie. He's already had more blame than he can handle. What he needs now is confidence in himself, a feeling that he'll do the right thing on his own and not because you'll force him to. You spoke a minute ago of handcuffing him to you. That might work, up to a point. Perhaps it would prevent him from doing the wrong thing but it wouldn't help him to do the right one."

"Well, that was quite a speech, Louise."

"There's more."

"I'm not sure I want to hear it."

"Listen anyway, will you, Ben?"

"Since when have you become an authority on the Gowen brothers?"

She ignored the sarcasm. "I've been trying to do some figuring out, that's all."

"And you've decided what?"

"Charlie's problem wasn't born inside him. It doesn't belong only to him, it's a family affair. Some event, some relationship, or several of both, made him not want to grow up. He let you assume the grown-up role. He remained a child, the kid brother, the baby of the family. He merely went through the motions of manhood by imitating you and doing what you told him to."

She lapsed into silence, and Ben said, "I hope you've finished."

"Almost. Did you and Ann go on a honeymoon?"

"We went to San Francisco for a week. I can't see what that—"

"How soon after you got back did the trouble happen between Charlie and the girl?"

"A few days. Why?"

"Perhaps," she said slowly, "Charlie was only trying, in his mixed-up way, to imitate you by 'marrying' the girl."

Jessie had turned off her light and closed her door tightly to give her parents the impression that she'd gone to sleep. But both her side and back windows were wide open and she missed very little of what was going on.

She heard Virginia and Howard quarreling in the patio, and later, the gate opening and slamming shut again, and Howard's car racing out of the driveway and down the street. Virginia started to cry and Dave took her home and then set out in his car to look for Howard. Jessie lay in the darkness, staring up at the ceiling and wondering how adults could get away with doing such puzzling things without any reason. She herself had to have at least one good reason, and sometimes two, for everything she did.

Shortly before ten o'clock Ellen paused outside Jessie's door for a few seconds, then continued on down the hall.

Jessie called out, "I'm thirsty."

"All right, get up and pour yourself a glass of water."

"I'd rather you brought me one."

"All *right*." Ellen's voice was cross, and when she came into the bedroom with the glass of water she looked tired and tense. "Why aren't you ever thirsty during the day?"

"I don't have time then to think about it."

"Well, drink up. And if you need anything else get it *now*. I have a headache, I'm going to take a sleeping capsule and go to bed."

"May I take one, too?"

"Of course not. Little girls don't need sleeping capsules."

"Mrs. Oakley gives Mary Martha one sometimes."

"Mrs. Oakley is a—Well, anyway, you close your eyes and think pleasant thoughts."

"Why did Howard and Virginia have a fight?"

"That's a good question," Ellen said dryly. "If, within the next fifty years, I come up with a good answer, I'll tell it to you. Have you finished with the water?"

"Yes."

Ellen reached for the glass, still nearly full. "Now this is the final good night, Jessie. You understand that? Absolutely *final*." When she went out she shut the door in a way that indicated she meant business.

Jessie closed her eyes and thought of butterscotch sundaes and Christmas morning and flying the box kite with her name printed in big letters on all sides. Her name was away up in the air and she was flying up in the air to join it, carried effortlessly by the wind, higher and higher. She had almost reached her name when she heard a car in the driveway. She came to earth with a bang. The descent was so real and sudden and shocking that her arms and legs ached and she lay huddled in her bed like the survivor of a plane wreck.

She heard a man's footsteps across the driveway, then Virginia's voice, sounding so cold and hard that Jessie wouldn't have recognized it if it hadn't been coming from Virginia's back porch.

"You didn't find him, I suppose."

"No," Dave said.

"Well, that suits me. Good riddance to bad rubbish, as we used to say in my youth, long since gone, long since wasted on a—"

"Talk like that will get you nowhere. Be practical. You need Howard, you can't support yourself."

"That's a wonderful attitude to take."

"It's a fact, not an attitude," Dave said. "You seem ready to quarrel with anyone tonight. I'd better go home."

"Do that."

"Virginia, listen to me—"

The voices stopped abruptly. Jessie went over to the window and peered out through the slats of the Venetian blinds. The Arlingtons' porch was empty and the door into the house was closed.

Jessie returned to bed. Lying on her back with her hands clasped behind her head, she thought about Virginia and how she needed Howard because she couldn't support herself. She wondered how much money Virginia would require if Howard never came back. Virginia had a car and a house with furniture and enough clothes to last for years and years. All she'd really have to buy would be food.

Without moving her head Jessie could see the half-open door of her clothes closet. In the closet, in the toe of one of her party shoes, were the two ten-dollar bills Howard had pressed into her hand. Although she would miss the money if she gave it back to Virginia, it would be a kind of relief to get rid of it and to be doing Virginia a favor at the same time. Twenty dollars would buy tons of food, even the butterscotch sundaes Virginia liked so much.

Once the decision was made, Jessie wasted no time. She put on a bathrobe and slippers, fished the two bills from the toe of her party shoe and tiptoed down the hall, through the kitchen and out the back door.

Moving through the darkness in her long white flowing robe, she looked like the ghost of a bride.

19

THE ILLUMINATED DIAL on his bedside clock indicated a few minutes past midnight when Ralph MacPherson was awakened by the phone ringing. He picked up the receiver, opening his eyes only the merest slit to glance at the clock.

"Yes?"

"It's Kate, Mac. Thank heaven you're there. I need your help."

"My dear girl, do you realize what time it is?"

"Yes, of course I realize. I should, I was asleep, too, when the pounding woke me up."

"All right, I'm hooked," Mac said impatiently. "What pounding?"

"At the front door. There's a man out there."

"*What* man?"

"I don't know. I came downstairs without turning on any lights. I thought that it was Sheridan, and I was going to pretend I wasn't home."

"You're sure it's not Sheridan?"

"Yes. I can see his shadow. He's too big to be Sheridan. What will I do, Mac?"

"That will depend on what the man's doing."

"He's just sitting out there on the top step of the porch making funny sounds. I think—I think he's crying. Oh God, Mac, so many crazy things have happened lately. I feel I'm lost in the middle of a nightmare. Why should a strange man come up on my front porch to cry?"

"Because he's troubled."

"Yes, but why my porch? Why here? Why *me*?"

"It's probably just some drunk on a crying jag who picked your house by accident," Mac said. "If you want to get rid of him, I suggest you call the police."

"I won't do that." There was a silence. "It gives a place a bad reputation to have police arriving with their sirens going full blast and all."

"They don't usually—Never mind. What do you want me to do, Kate?"

"If you could just come over and talk to him, Mac. Ask him why he came here, tell him to leave. He'd listen to you. You sound so authoritative."

"Well, I don't feel very authoritative at this hour of the night but I'll try my best. I'll be there in about ten minutes. Keep the doors locked and don't turn on any lights. Where's Mary Martha?"

"Asleep in her room."

"See that she stays that way," he said and hung up. One Oakley female was enough to cope with at one time.

In the older sections of town the streetlights were placed only at intersections, as if what went on at night between corners was not the business of strangers or casual passers-by. The Oakley house was invisible from the road. Mac couldn't even see the trees that surrounded it but he could hear them. The wind was moving through the leaves and bough rubbed against bough in false affection.

From the back seat Mac took the heavy flash-and-blinker light he'd kept there for years in case of emergency. A lot of emergencies had occurred since then but none in which a flashlight was any use. He switched it on. Although the beam wasn't as powerful as it had been, it was enough to illumine the flagstone path to the house.

The steps of the front porch were empty and for one very bad moment he thought Kate had imagined the whole thing. Then he saw the man leaning over the porch railing. His head was bent as though his neck had been broken. He turned toward the beam of the flashlight, his face showing no reaction either to the light or to Mac's presence. He was a tall, heavily built man about forty. He wore blue jeans and a sweatshirt, both stained with blood, and he kept one hand pressed against his chest as if to staunch a wound.

Mac said, "Are you hurt?"

The man's mouth moved but no sound came out of it.

Mac tried again. "I'm Ralph MacPherson. Mrs. Oakley, who lives in this house, called me a few minutes ago to report a man pounding on her door. That was you?"

The man nodded slightly though he looked too dazed to understand the question. "What are you doing here?"

"My dau—dau—"

"Your dog? You've lost your dog, is that it?"

"Dog?" He covered his face with his hands and Mac saw that it was his right hand that was bleeding. "Not dog. Daughter. *Daughter.*"

"You're looking for your daughter?"

"Yes."

"What makes you think she might be here?"

"Her best—best friend lives here."

"Mary Martha?"

"Yes."

Mac remembered his office conversation with Kate about Mary Martha's best friend. "You're Jessie Brant's father?"

"Yes. She's gone. Jessie's gone."

"Take it easy now, Brant. How did you hurt yourself?"

"Don't bother about me. Jessie—"

"You're bleeding."

"I was running and I fell. I don't care about me. Don't you understand? My daughter is missing. *She is missing from her bed.*"

"All right, don't get excited. We'll find her."

Mac crossed the porch and rapped lightly on the front door. "Kate, turn on the light and open the door."

The porch light went on and the door opened almost instantly as if Kate had been standing in the hall waiting for someone to tell her what to do. She had on fresh make-up that seemed to have been applied hastily and in the dark. It didn't cover the harsh lines that scarred her face or the anxiety that distorted her eyes.

"Mac?"

"Kate, you remember Mr. Brant, don't you?"

She glanced briefly at Dave and away again. "We're acquainted. That hardly gives him the right to come pounding at—"

"Be quiet and pay attention, Kate. Mr. Brant is here looking for Jessie. Have you seen her?"

"Why no, of course not. It's after midnight. What would Jessie be doing out at a time like this? He has blood on him," she added, staring up into Mac's face. "Tell him to go away. I hate the sight of blood. I won't allow him inside my house."

Dave pressed his hands together tightly to prevent them from reaching out and striking her. His voice was very quiet. "I won't come inside your house, Mrs. Oakley. I wouldn't be here at all if I could have gotten you on the phone."

"I have an unlisted number."

"Yes. I tried to call you."

"People have no right to call others at midnight," she said, as if she herself wouldn't dream of doing such a thing. "Mary Martha and I keep early hours. She was asleep by 8:30 and I shortly afterward."

"Your daughter is in bed asleep, Mrs. Oakley?"

"Why yes, of course."

"Well, *mine isn't.*"

"What do you mean?" She turned to Mac, touching his coat sleeve with her hand like a child pleading for a favor. "What does he mean, Mac? All little girls ought to be in bed at this time of night."

"Jessie is missing," Mac said.

"I'm sure she won't be missing for long. She's probably just playing a trick on her parents. Jessie's full of ideas and she truly loves to be the center of attention. She'll turn up any minute with one of her preposterous stories and everything will be fine. Won't it? Won't it, Mac?"

"I don't know. When did you see her last?"

"This afternoon. She dropped in to invite Mary Martha to go swimming with her. I didn't allow Mary Martha to go. I've been supervising her extra carefully ever since I received that anonymous letter."

Mac had forgotten the letter. He put his hand in the left pocket of his coat. There were other papers in the pocket but the letter was unmistakable to the touch. One corner of the envelope bulged where the paper had been folded and refolded until it was no more than an inch square. Mac remembered enough of the contents of the letter to make him regret not taking it immediately to his friend, Lieutenant Gallantyne. Gallantyne had a collection of anonymous letters that spanned thirty years of police work.

Mac said, "Will you describe Jessie to me, Mr. Brant?"

"I have pictures of her at home." He almost broke down at the word *home*. His face started to come apart and he turned it toward the darkness beyond the porch railing. "I must get back to my wife. She's expecting me to—to bring Jessie home with me. She was so sure Jessie would be here."

Kate was clutching her long wool bathrobe around her as though somebody had just threatened to tear it off. "I don't know why she was sure Jessie would come here. I'm the last person in the world who'd be taken in by one of Jessie's fancy schemes. I would have telephoned Mrs. Brant immediately. Wouldn't I, Mac?"

"Of course you would, Kate," Mac said. "You'd better go back in the house now and see if you can get some sleep."

"I won't be able to close my eyes. There may be some monster loose in the neighborhood and no child is safe. He won't stop with just Jessie. Mary Martha might be next."

"Shut up, Kate."

"Oh, Mac, please don't go. Don't leave me alone."

"I have to. I'm driving Mr. Brant home."

"Everybody leaves me alone. I can't stand—"

"I'll talk to you in the morning."

The door closed, the porch light went off. The two men began walking in slow, silent unison down the flagstone path, following the beam of Mac's flashlight as if it were a dim ray of hope.

Inside the car Mac said, "Where do you live, Brant?"

"Cielito Lane."

"That's in the Peppertree tract, isn't it?"

"Yes."

The car pulled away from the curb.

"Have you called the police?"

"Virginia—Mrs. Arlington did. She lives next door. She and Jessie are very good friends. My wife thought that if Jessie were in any kind of trouble or even just playing a trick on us, she'd go to the Arlingtons' house first. We searched all through it and the garage twice. Jessie wasn't there. Virginia called the police and I set out for Mrs. Oakley's. I couldn't think of any other place Jessie would go late at night. We haven't lived in town long and we have no relatives here."

"You'll forgive me for asking this," Mac said, "but is Jessie a girl who often gets into trouble?"

"No. She never does. Leaving her bicycle in the middle of the sidewalk, coming home late for meals, things like that, yes, but nothing more serious."

"Has she ever run away from home?"

"Of course not."

"Runaways are picked up by the police every day, Brant."

"She didn't run away," Dave said hoarsely. "I wish to God I could believe she had."

"Why can't you?"

"She had no money, and the only clothes missing from her closet are the pajamas she wore to bed and a bathrobe and a pair of slippers. Jessie's a sensible girl, she'd know better than to try and run away without any money and wearing an outfit that would immediately attract everybody's attention."

That might be the whole point, Mac thought, but all he said was, "Can you think of any recent family scene or event that might make her want to run away?"

"No."

"Has she been upset about something lately?"

Dave turned and looked out the window. The night seemed darker than any he could ever remember. It wasn't the ordinary darkness, an absence of light; it was a thick, soft, suffocating thing that covered the whole world. No morning could ever penetrate it.

"Has something upset her?" Mac repeated.

"I'm trying to answer. I—she's been talking a lot about divorce, fathers deserting their families like Sheridan Oakley. Obviously Mary Martha's fed her a lot of stuff and Jessie's taken it perhaps more seriously than it deserves. She's a funny kid, Jessie. She puts on a big front about not caring but she feels everything deeply, especially where Mary Martha is concerned. The two girls have been very close for almost a year now, in fact almost inseparable."

Mac remembered the opening sentence of the letter he was carrying in his pocket: *Your daughter takes too dangerous risks with her delicate body.* He said, "Do you consider Jessie a frail child, that is, delicate in build?"

"That's an odd question."

"I have good reasons for asking it which I can't divulge right now."

"Well, Jessie might look delicate to some people. Actually, she's thin and wiry like her mother, and extremely healthy. The only times she's ever needed a doctor were when she's had accidents."

"Accidents such as?"

"Falls, stings, bites. The normal things that happen to kids plus a few extra. Right now her hands are badly blistered from overuse of the jungle gym at the school playground."

"Does she often play at the school playground?"

"I don't know. I'm at work all day."

"Would you say she goes there twice a week? Five times? Seven?"

"All the neighborhood kids go there. Why shouldn't they?" Dave added defensively, "It's well supervised, there are organized games and puppet shows and things not available in the ordinary backyard. Just what were you implying?"

"Nothing. I was merely—"

"No. I think you know something that you're not telling me. You're holding out on me. Why?"

"I have no knowledge at present," Mac said, "that would be of any value or comfort to you."

"That's only a fancy way of saying you won't tell me." There was a silence, filled with sudden distrust and uneasiness. "Who are you, anyway? What are you? How did you get into this?"

"I gave you my name, Ralph MacPherson. I'm a lawyer and an old friend of Mrs. Oakley's."

"She didn't waste much time contacting a lawyer. Why?"

"She called me as a friend, not a lawyer. I've known her since she was Jessie's age . . . Let's see, I take the next turn, don't I?"

"Yes."

All the houses in the block were dark except for two. In the driveway that separated the two, a black Chrysler sedan was parked. Mac recognized it as one of the unmarked police cars used for assignments requiring special precautions.

Except for the number of lights burning in the two houses, there was no sign that anything had happened. The streets were deserted, and if the immediate neighbors were curious, they were keeping their curiosity behind closed drapes in dark rooms.

Mac braked the car, leaving the engine running. "I'd be a damned fool if I said I'm glad to have met you, Brant. So I'll just say I hope we meet again under more pleasant circumstances."

"Aren't you coming inside?"

"It didn't occur to me that you might want me to."

"I can't face Ellen alone."

"I don't see that I'll be of much help. Besides, you won't be alone with her, the police are there."

"I won't—I can't walk into that house and tell her I didn't find Jessie. She was so full of hope. How can I go in there and take it all away from her?"

"She has to be told the truth, Brant. Come on, I'll go with you."

The two men got out of the car and began walking toward the house. Mac had no thought of involving himself in the situation. He felt that he was merely doing his duty, helping a person in trouble, and that the whole thing—or at least his part in it— would be over in a few minutes. He could afford a few minutes, some kind words.

Suddenly the front door opened and a woman rushed out. It was as if a violent explosion had taken place inside the house and blown the door open and tossed the woman out.

She said, "Jessie?" Then she stopped dead in her tracks, staring at Mac. "Where's Jessie?"

"Mrs. Brant, I—"

"I know. You must be the doctor. It happened the way I thought. Jessie was on her way to Mary Martha's by the short cut and she fell crossing the creek. And she's in the hospital and you've come to tell me she'll be all right, it's nothing serious, she'll be home in a—"

"Stop it, Mrs. Brant. I'm a lawyer, not a doctor."

"Where is Jessie?"

"I'm sorry, I don't know."

Dave said, "She didn't go to Mary Martha's, Ellen. I haven't found her."

"Oh God. Please, God, help her. Help my baby."

Dave took her in his arms. To Mac it was not so much an embrace as a case of each of them holding the other up. He felt a deep pity but he realized there was nothing further he could do for them now. He started back to his car. The letter in his pocket seemed to be getting heavier, like a stone to which things had begun to cling and grow and multiply.

He had almost reached the curb when a voice behind him said, "Just a minute, sir."

Mac turned and saw a young man in a dark grey suit and matching fedora. The fedora made him look like an undergraduate dressed up for a role in a play. "Yes, what is it?"

"May I ask your name, sir?"

"MacPherson."

"Do you have business here at this time of night, Mr. MacPherson?"

"I drove Mr. Brant home."

"I'm sure you won't mind repeating that to the lieutenant, will you?"

"Not," Mac said dryly, "if the lieutenant wants to hear it."

"Oh, he will. Come this way, please."

As they walked down the driveway Mac saw that there was another police car parked outside the garage, its searchlight had been angled to shine on the window of a rear bedroom. A policeman was examining the window; a second one stood just outside the periphery of the light. All Mac could see of him was his grey hair, which was cut short and stood up straight on his head like the bristles of a brush. It was enough.

"Hello, Gallantyne."

Gallantyne stepped forward, squinting against the light. He was of medium height with broad, heavy shoulders, slightly stooped. His posture and his movements all indicated a vast impatience just barely kept under control. He always gave Mac the impression of a well-trained and very powerful stallion with one invisible saddle sore which mustn't be touched. No one knew where this sore was but they knew it was there and it paid to be careful.

"What are you doing here, Mac?" Gallantyne said.

"I was invited. It seems I come under the heading of suspicious characters seen lurking in the neighborhood."

"Well, were you?"

"I was seen, I don't believe I was lurking," Mac said. "Unless perhaps I have a natural lurk that I'm not aware of. May I return the question? What are you doing here, Gallantyne? I thought you were tied to a desk."

"They untie me once in a while. Salvadore's on vacation and Weber has bursitis. Come inside. I want to talk to you."

For reasons he didn't yet understand, Mac felt a great reluctance to enter the house. He didn't want the missing child to seem any more real to him than she did now; he didn't want to see the yard where she played, the table she ate at, the room she slept in. He wanted her to remain merely a name and a number, Jessie Brant, aged nine. He said, "I'd prefer to stay out here."

"Well, I prefer different."

Gallantyne turned and walked through an open gate into a patio. He didn't bother looking back to see if he was being followed. It was taken for granted that he would be, and he was.

The back door of the house had been propped open with a flowerpot filled with earth containing a dried-out azalea. A policeman in uniform was dusting the door and its brass knob for fingerprints. There was no sign that the door had been forced or the lock tampered with.

The kitchen contained mute evidence of a family going through a crisis: cups of half-consumed coffee, overflowing ashtrays, a bottle of aspirin with the top off, a wastebasket filled with used pieces of tissue and the empty box they'd come in.

Gallantyne said, "Sit down, Mac. You look nervous. Are you the family lawyer?"

"No."

"An old friend, then?"

"I've known Brant about an hour, his wife for five minutes." He explained briefly about responding to Kate's phone call and meeting Brant on the porch of her house.

"It sounds crazy," Gallantyne said.

"Anything involving Mrs. Oakley has a certain amount of illogic in it. She's a nervous woman and she's been under a great strain, especially for the past few days."

"Why the past few days?"

"Two reasons that I know of, though there may be more. She thinks the husband she's divorcing has hired someone to spy on her. And this week she received an anonymous letter warning her to take better care of her daughter."

Gallantyne's thick grey eyebrows leaped up his forehead. "Have you read it?"

"Yes. Mrs. Oakley brought it to my office right away. She'd pretty well convinced herself that Mr. Oakley had written it to harass her. I didn't believe it. In fact, I didn't really take the whole thing seriously. Now I'm afraid, I'm very much afraid, that I made a bad mistake."

"Why?"

"Here, see for yourself." Mac took the envelope out of his pocket. He was appalled at the severe trembling of his hands. It was as if his body had acknowledged his feelings of guilt before his mind was conscious of them. "I realize now that I should have shown this to you right away. Oh, I have the customary excuses: I was busy, I was fed up with Kate Oakley's shenanigans, and so on. But excuses aren't good enough. If I—"

"You're too old for the if-game," Gallantyne said and took the letter out of the envelope. "Was it folded like this when Mrs. Oakley received it?"

"Yes."

"Well, that's a switch anyway." He read the letter through, half aloud. "'Your daughter takes too dangerous risks with her delicate body. Children must be guarded against the cruel hazards of life and fed good, nourishing food so their bones will be padded. Also clothing. You should put plenty of clothing on her, keep arms and legs covered, etc. In the name of God please take better care of your little girl.'"

Gallantyne reread the letter, this time silently, then he tossed it on the table as though he wanted to get rid of it as quickly as possible. The grooves in his face had deepened and drops of sweat appeared on his forehead, growing larger and larger until they fell of their own weight and were lost in his eyebrows. "All I can say is, I'm damn glad this wasn't sent to the Brants. As it is, I figure the kid decided to throw a scare into her parents by running away. Probably one of the patrol cars has picked her up by now . . . Why the hell are you staring at me like that?"

"I think the letter was intended for Mrs. Brant."

"You said it was addressed to Mrs. Oakley."

"Jessie Brant and the Oakley girl, Mary Martha, are best friends. According to Brant, they're inseparable, which no doubt involves a lot of visiting back and forth in each other's houses. Mary Martha's a tall girl for her age, a trifle overweight, and inclined to be cautious. The writer of the letter wasn't describing Mary Martha. He, or she, was describing Jessie."

"You can't be sure of that."

"I can be sure of two things. Mary Martha's at home with her mother and Jessie isn't."

Gallantyne stood in silence for a minute. Then he picked up the letter, refolded it and put it in his pocket. "We won't tell anybody about this right now, not the parents or the press or anyone else."

20

HOWARD ARLINGTON WOKE up at dawn in a motel room. Seen through half-closed eyes the place looked the same as a hundred others he'd stayed in, but gradually differences began to show up: the briefcase Virginia had given him years ago was not on the bureau where he always kept it, and the luggage rack at the foot of the bed was empty. When he turned his head his starched collar jabbed him in the neck and he realized he was still fully dressed. Even his tie was knotted. He loosened it but the tightness in his throat didn't go away. It was as if, during the night, he'd tried to swallow something too large and too fibrous to be swallowed.

He got up and opened the drapes. Fog pressed against the window like the ectoplasm of lost spirits seeking shelter and a home. He closed the drapes again and turned on a lamp. Except for the outline of his body on the chenille bedspread, the room looked as though it hadn't been occupied. The clothes closet was empty, the ashtrays unused, the drinking glasses on the bureau still wrapped in wax paper.

He couldn't remember checking into the motel; yet he knew he must have registered, given his name and address and car license number, and paid in advance because he had no luggage. His last clear recollection was of Virginia standing in the Brants' patio saying she didn't want a child anymore: "We no longer have anything to offer a child . . . How cruel it would be to pass along such an ugly thing as life. Poor Jessie . . . She will lose her innocence and high hopes and dreams; she will lose them all. By the time she's my age she will have wished a thousand times that she were dead."

He'd quarreled with Virginia and he was in a motel. These were the only facts he was sure of. Where the motel was, in what city, how he'd reached it and why, he didn't know.

He spent so much of his life driving from one city to another and checking in and out of motels that he must have acted automatically.

He left the room key on top of the bureau and went out to his car. On the front seat there was an empty pint bottle of whiskey and a hole half an inch wide burned in the upholstery by a cigarette. *Fact three,* he thought grimly, *I was drunk.* He put the bottle in the glove compartment and drove off.

The first street sign he came to gave him another fact: he was still in San Félice, down near the breakwater, no more than four miles from his own house.

The lights in the kitchen were on when he arrived. It was too early for Virginia to be awake and he wondered whether she'd left them on, expecting him home, or whether she'd forgotten to turn them off. She often forgot, or claimed to have forgotten. Sometimes he thought she kept them on deliberately because she was afraid of the dark but didn't want to admit it. He parked his car beside hers in the garage, then crossed the driveway and walked up the steps of the back porch. The door was unlocked.

Virginia was sitting at the kitchen table with the big retriever lying beside her chair. Neither of them moved.

Howard said, "Virginia?"

The dog opened his eyes, wagged his tail briefly and perfunctorily, and went back to sleep.

"At least the dog usually barks when I get home," he said. "Don't I even rate that much anymore?"

Virginia turned. Her eyes were bloodshot, the lids blistered by the heat of her tears and surrounded by a network of lines Howard had never seen before. She spoke in a low, dull voice.

"The police are looking for you."

"The police? Why in heaven's name did you call them in? You knew I'd be back."

"I didn't. Didn't know, didn't call them."

"What's going on around here anyway? What have the police got to do with my getting drunk and spending the night in a motel?"

"Is that what you did, Howard?"

"Yes."

"Can you prove it?"

"Why should I have to prove it?"

She covered her face with her hands and started to weep again, deep, bitter sobs that shook her whole body. The dog rose to a sitting position and put his head on her lap, watching Howard out of the corner of his eye, as if he considered Howard responsible for the troubled sounds.

He blames me for everything, Howard thought, *just the way she does. Only this time I don't even know what I'm being blamed for. Did I do something while I was drunk that I don't remember? I couldn't have been in a fight. There are no marks on me and my clothes aren't torn.*

"Virginia, tell me what happened."

"Jessie—Jessie's gone."

"Gone where?"

"Nobody knows. She—she just disappeared. Ellen took her a glass of water about ten o'clock and that's the last anyone saw of her except—" She stopped, pressing the back of her hand against her trembling mouth.

"Except who?" Howard said.

"Whoever made her disappear."

Howard stared at her, confused and helpless. He wasn't sure whether she was telling the truth or whether she'd imagined the whole thing. She'd been acting and talking peculiarly last night, standing in the dichondra patch saying she was a tree.

She saw his incredulity and guessed the reason for it. "You think I've lost my mind. Well, I wish I had. It would be easier to bear than this, this terrible thing." She began to sob again, repeating Jessie's name over and over as if Jessie might be somewhere listening and might respond.

Howard did what he could, brought her two tranquilizer pills and poured her some ice water from the pitcher in the refrigerator. She choked on the pills and the water spilled down the front of her old wool bathrobe. Its coldness was stinging and shocking against the warm skin between her breasts. She let out a gasp and clutched the bathrobe tightly around her neck. Her eyes were resentful but they were no longer wild or weeping.

"So the police are looking for me," Howard said. "Why?"

"They're questioning everyone, friends, neighbors, anyone who knew—who knows her. They said in cases like this it's often a relative or a trusted friend of the family."

"Cases like what?"

She didn't answer.

"When did she disappear, Virginia?"

"Between ten and eleven. Ellen tucked her in bed at ten o'clock, then she took a sleeping capsule and went to bed herself. Dave was out looking for you. Ellen said she'd locked the back door but when Dave came back it was unlocked. He checked Jessie's bedroom to see if she was sleeping. She was gone. He searched the house, calling for her, then he woke Ellen up. They came here to our house. We looked all over but we couldn't find Jessie. I called the police and Dave set out for Mary Martha's house, using the path along the creek that the girls always took."

"Kids have run away before."

"The only clothes missing are the pajamas she was wearing, a bathrobe and a pair of slippers. Besides, she had no motive and no money."

"She had the twenty dollars I gave her the other night."

"Why, of course." Virginia's face came alive with sudden hope. "Why, that would seem like a fortune to Jessie. We've got to tell—"

"We tell no one, Virginia."

"But we must. It might throw a whole new light on everything."

"Including me," Howard said sharply. "The police will ask me why I gave the kid twenty dollars. I'll tell them because I was sore at you and wanted to get back at you. But will they believe it?"

"It's the truth."

"It might not strike them that way."

She didn't seem to understand what he was talking about. When he spelled it out for her, she looked appalled. "They couldn't possibly think anything like that about you, Howard."

"Why not?"

"You're a respectable married man."

"Coraznada State Hospital is full of so-called respectable married men." He took out a handkerchief and wiped his neck. "Did the police question you?"

"Yes. A Lieutenant Gallantyne did most of the talking. I don't like him. Even when I was telling the truth he made me feel that I was lying. There was another man with him, a Mr. MacPherson. Every once in a while they'd put their heads together and whisper. It made me nervous."

"Who's MacPherson?"

"Dave said he's a lawyer."

"Whose lawyer?"

"Mrs. Oakley's."

"How did Mrs. Oakley get into this?"

"I don't *know*. Stop bullying me, I can't stand it."

She seemed on the verge of breaking up again. Howard got up, put some water and coffee in the percolator and plugged it in. After a time he said, "I'm not trying to bully you, Virginia. I simply want to find out what you told the police about last night so I can corroborate it. It wouldn't be so good—for either of us—if we contradicted each other."

She was looking at him, her eyes cold under their blistered lids. "You don't care that Jessie has disappeared, do you? All you care about is saving your own skin."

"And yours."

"Don't worry about mine. Everybody knows how I love the child."

"That's not quite accurate, Virginia," he said quietly. "Everybody knows that you love her, but not how you love her."

The coffee had begun to percolate, bubbling merrily in the cheerless room. Virginia turned and looked at the percolator as if she hoped it would do something unexpected and interesting like explode.

She said, "Where did you go after you left the Brants' last night?"

"To a liquor store and then down to the beach. I ended up at a motel."

"You were alone, of course?"

"Yes, I was alone."

"What motel?"

"I don't remember, I wasn't paying much attention. But I could find it again if I had to."

"Ellen told the police," she said, turning to face him, "that you were jealous of my relationship with Jessie."

"That was neighborly of her."

"She had to tell the truth. Under the circumstances you could hardly expect her to lie to spare your feelings."

"It's not my feelings I'm worried about. It is, as you pointed out, my skin. What else was said about last night?"

"Everything that happened, how we quarreled, and the funny way you talked to Jessie as if you were half-drunk when you only had two beers; how you tore off in the car and Dave tried to find you and couldn't."

"I didn't realize what loyal friends I had. It moves me," he added dryly. "It may move me right into a cell. Or was that the real objective?"

"You don't understand. We were forced to tell the whole truth, all of us. A child's life might be at stake. Gallantyne said every little detail could be vitally important. He made us go over and over it. I couldn't have lied to protect you even if I'd wanted to."

"And the implication is, you didn't particularly want to?"

She was staring at him in incredulity, her mouth partly open. "It still hasn't come through to you yet, has it? A child is missing, a nine-year-old girl has disappeared. She may be dead, and you don't seem to care. Don't you feel *anything*?"

"Yes. I feel somebody's trying to make me the goat."

Between four and seven in the morning Ellen Brant slept fitfully on the living-room couch beside the telephone. She'd dreamed half a dozen times that the phone was ringing and had wakened up to find herself reaching for it. She finally got up, washed her face and ran a comb through her hair, and put on a heavy wool coat over her jeans and T-shirt. Then she went into the bedroom to see if Dave was awake and could hear the telephone if it rang.

He was lying on his back, peering up at the ceiling. He turned and looked at her, the question in his eyes dying before it had a chance to be born. "There's been no news, of course."

"No. I'm going over to the Oakleys'. I want to ask Mary Martha some questions."

"The lieutenant will do that."

"She might talk to me more easily. She and her mother freeze up in front of strangers."

"What's it like outside?"

"Cold and foggy."

She knew he was thinking the same thing she was, that somewhere in that cold fog Jessie might be wandering, wearing only her cotton pajamas and light bathrobe. Biting her underlip hard to keep from breaking into tears again, she went out to the garage and got into the old Dodge station wagon. The floorboard of the front seat was covered with sand from yesterday's trip to the beach. It seemed to have happened a long time ago and in a different city, where the sun had been shining and the surf was gentle and the sand soft and warm. She had a feeling that she would never see that city again.

She backed out of the driveway, tears streaming down her face, warm where they touched her cheeks, already cold when they reached the sides of her neck. She brushed them angrily away with the sleeve of her coat. She couldn't afford to cry in front of Mary Martha, it might frighten her into silence, or worse still, into lying. She had seen Mary Martha many times after an emotional scene at home. The effect on her was always the same—blank eyes, expressionless voice: no, nothing was the matter, nothing had happened.

Mary Martha answered the door herself, first opening it only as far as the chain would allow. Then, recognizing Ellen, she unfastened the chain and opened the door wide. In spite of the earliness of the hour she was dressed as if for a visit to town in pink embroidered cotton and newly whitened sandals. Her pony-tail was neat and so tightly fastened it raised her eyebrows slightly. She looked a little surprised to see Ellen, as though she might have been expecting someone else.

She said, "If you want my mother, she's in the kitchen making breakfast."

"I prefer to talk to you alone, Mary Martha."

"I'd better get my mother's permission. She's kind of nervous this morning, I don't know why. But I have to be careful."

"She hasn't told you anything?"

"Just that Mac was coming over with a soldier and we were all going to have a chat."

"A soldier?"

"He's a lieutenant. I'm supposed to remember to call him that so I'll make a good impression." Mary Martha looked down at her dress as if to reassure herself that it was still clean enough to make a good impression. "Do you want to come in?"

"Yes."

"I guess it'll be all right."

She was just closing the door when Kate Oakley's voice called out from the kitchen, "Mary Martha, tell Mac I'll be there in a minute."

"It's not Mac," the child said. "It's Jessie's mother."

"Jessie's—?" Kate Oakley appeared at the far end of the hall. She began walking toward them very rapidly, her high heels ticking on the linoleum like clocks working on different time schedules, each trying to catch up with the other. Her face was heavily made up to look pink and white but the grey of trouble showed through. She placed one arm protectively around Mary Martha's shoulders. "You'd better go and put the bacon in the warming oven, dear."

"I don't care if it gets cold," Mary Martha said. "It tastes the same."

"You mustn't be rude in front of company, lamb. That's understood between us, isn't it?"

"Yes, ma'am."

"Off you go."

Mary Martha started down the hall.

"But I want to talk to her," Ellen said desperately. "I've got to. She might know something."

"She knows nothing. She's only a child."

"Jessie's *only* a child, too."

"I'm sorry. I really am sorry, Mrs. Brant. But Mary Martha isn't supposed to talk to anyone until our lawyer arrives."

"You haven't even told her about Jessie, have you?"

"I didn't want to upset her."

"She's got to be told. She may be able to help. She might have seen someone, heard something. How can we know unless we ask her?"

"Mac will ask her. He can handle these—these situations better than you or I could."

"Is that all it is to you, a situation to be handled?"

Kate shook her head helplessly. "No matter what I said to you now, it would seem wrong because you're distraught. Further conversation is pointless. I must ask you to leave." She opened the heavy oak door. "I'm truly sorry, Mrs. Brant, but I think I'm doing the right thing. Mac will talk to Mary Martha. She feels freer with him than she would with you or me."

"Even though he has a policeman with him?"

"Did she tell you that?"

"I figured it out."

"Well, it won't make any difference. Mary Martha adores Mac and she's not afraid of policemen."

But the last word curled upward into a question mark, and when Ellen looked back from the bottom of the porch steps, Kate was hanging on to the oak door as if for support.

When breakfast was over, Mary Martha sat on the window seat in the front room with the cat, Pudding, on her lap. She wasn't supposed to get her hands dirty or her dress wrinkled but she needed the comfort of the cat, his warm body and soft fur, his bright eyes that seemed to be aware of so many things and not to care about any of them very much.

In a little while she saw Mac and the lieutenant emerge from the fog and come up the front steps. She heard her mother talking to them in the hall, at first in the low, careful voice she used when meeting strangers, later in a higher, less restrained and more natural voice. She sounded as if she was protesting, then arguing, and finally, losing. After a time the two men came into the front room alone, and Mac closed the door.

"Hello, Mary Martha," Mac said. "This is Lieutenant Gallantyne."

Still holding the cat, Mary Martha got up and executed a brief, formal curtsy.

Gallantyne bowed gravely in return. "That's a pretty cat you have there, Mary Martha. What's his name?"

"Pudding. He has other names too, though."

"Really? Such as?"

"Geronimo, sometimes. Also King Arthur. But when he's bad and catches a bird, I call him Sheridan." She switched the cat from her left shoulder to her right. It stopped purring and made a swift jab at her ponytail. "Do you have any medals?"

Gallantyne raised his bushy eyebrows. "Well now, I believe I won a few swimming races when I was a kid."

"I mean real medals like for killing a hundred enemies."

The men exchanged glances. It was as if they were both thinking the same thing, that it seemed a long and insane time ago that men were given medals for killing.

"Lieutenant Gallantyne is not in the army," Mac said. "He's a policeman. He's also a good friend of mine, so you needn't be afraid of him."

"I'm not. But why does he want to see me instead of my mother?"

"He'll talk to your mother later. Right now you're more important."

She seemed pleased but at the same time suspicious. "Why am I?"

"We hope," Gallantyne said, "that you'll be able to help us find your friend, Jessie."

"Is she hiding?"

"We're not sure."

"She's an awfully good hider. Being so skinny she can squeeze behind things and under things and between."

"You and Jessie play together a lot, do you?"

"All the time except when one of us is being punished."

"And you tell each other secrets, I suppose?"

"Yes, sir."

"Do you promise each other never to reveal these secrets to anyone else?"

Mary Martha nodded and said firmly, "And I'm not going to, either, because I crossed my heart and hoped to die."

"Oh, I'm sure you can keep a secret very well," Gallantyne said. "But I want you to imagine something now. Suppose you, Mary Martha, were in a dangerous situation in a place nobody knew about except you and Jessie. You're frightened and hungry and in pain and you want desperately to be rescued. Under those circumstances, wouldn't you release Jessie from her promise to keep the name of that place a secret?"

"I guess so, only there isn't any place like that."

"But you have other secrets."

"Yes."

Gallantyne was watching her gravely. "I believe that if Jessie could communicate with you right now, she'd release you from all your promises."

"Why can't she *comm*—communicate?"

"Nobody's seen her since last night at ten o'clock. We don't know where she is or why she left or if she left by herself or with someone else."

In a spasm of fear Mary Martha clutched the cat too tightly. He let out a yowl, unsheathed his claws and fought his way out of her grasp, onto the floor. She stood, very pale and still, one hand pressed to her scratched shoulder. "He hurt me," she said in a shocked voice. "Sheridan hurt me."

"I'm sure he didn't mean to."

"He always means to. I hate him."

"You can cry if you like," Gallantyne said. "That might help."

"*No.*"

"All right, then, we'll go on. Is that okay?"

"I guess so."

"Did you and Jessie ever talk about running away together? Perhaps just in fun, like, *let's run away and join the circus.*"

"That would be plain silly," she said in a contemptuous voice. "Circuses don't even come here."

"Times have changed since I was a boy. The only thing that made life bearable when I was mad at my family was the thought of running away and joining the circus. Did Jessie often get mad at her family?"

"Sometimes. Mostly at Mike, her older brother. He bosses her around, he's awfully mean. We think a bad witch put a curse on him when he was born."

"Really? What kind of curse?"

"I'm not sure. But I made one up that sounds as if it might work."

"Tell it to me."

> "'Abracadabra,
> Purple and green,
> This little boy
> Will grow up mean.'"

"It should be said in a more eerie-like voice, only I don't feel like it right now."

Gallantyne pursed his lips and nodded. "Sounds pretty authentic to me just the way it is. Do you know any more?"

"'Abracadabra,
Yellow and brown,
Uncle Howard's the nastiest
Man in town.'"

"That one," she added anxiously, "isn't so good, is it?"

"Well, it's not so much a curse as a statement. Uncle Howard's the nastiest man in town, period. By the way, who's Uncle Howard?"

"Mr. Arlington."

"Why do you think he's so nasty, Mary Martha?"

"I don't. I only talked to him once and he was real nice. He gave me fifty cents."

"Then why did you make up the curse about him?"

"Jessie asked me to. We were going to make up curses about all the people we hate and she wanted to start with Uncle—with Mr. Arlington."

"Who was next on the list?"

"Nobody. We got tired of the game, and anyway my mother came to pick me up."

"I wonder," Gallantyne said softly, "why Jessie felt that way about Mr. Arlington. Do you have any idea?"

"No, sir. That was the first day she ever told me, when we were at the playground with Mike."

"What day was that?"

"The day my mother and I went downtown to Mac's office."

"Thursday," Mac said.

Gallantyne thanked him with a nod and turned his attention back to Mary Martha. "Previous to Thursday, you thought Jessie and the Arlingtons were good friends?"

"Yes, on account of the Arlingtons were always giving her presents and making a big fuss over her."

"Both of the Arlingtons?"

"Well—" Mary Martha studied the toes of her shoes. "Well, I guess it was mostly Aunt Virginia, him being away so much on the road. But Jessie never said anything against him until Thursday."

"Let's assume that something happened, on Wednesday perhaps, that changed her opinion of him. Did you see Jessie on Wednesday?"

"Yes, I went over to her house and we sat on the porch steps and talked."

"What about?"

"Lots of things."

"Name one."

"The book Aunt Virginia gave her. It was all about glaciers and mountains and rivers and wild things. It sounded real interesting. Only Jessie had to give it back because it cost too much money and her parents wouldn't let her keep it. *My* mother," she added virtuously, "won't let me accept anything. When Sheridan sends me parcels, I'm not even allowed to peek inside. She sends them right back or throws them away, bang, into the garbage can."

Gallantyne looked at the cat. "I gather you're referring to another Sheridan, not this one."

"Cats can't send parcels," Mary Martha said with a faint giggle. "That's silly. They don't have any money and they can't wrap things or write any name and address on the outside."

Gallantyne thought, wearily, of the anonymous letter. He'd been up all night, first with the Brants and Mrs. Arlington, and later in the police lab examining the letter. He was sure now that it had been written by a man, young, literate, and in good physical health. The description fitted hundreds of men in town. The fact that Howard Arlington was one of them meant nothing in itself.

He said, "Mary Martha, you and Jessie spend quite a lot of time at the school grounds, I'm told."

"Yes. Because of the games and swings and jungle gym."

"Have you ever noticed anyone watching you?"

"The coach. That's his job."

"Aside from the coach, have you seen any man hanging around the place, or perhaps the same car parked at the curb several days in a row?"

"No." Mary Martha gave him a knowing look. "My mother told me all about men like that. They're real nasty and I'm supposed to run home right away when I see one of them. Jessie is, too. She's a very good runner."

Perhaps not quite good enough, Gallantyne thought grimly. "How are you going to recognize these men when you see them?"

"Well, they offer you things like gum or candy or even a doll. Also, a ride in their car."

"And nothing like this ever happened to you and Jessie?"

"No. We saw a mean-looking man at the playground once, but it was only Timmy's father, who was mad because Timmy missed his appointment at the dentist. Timmy wears braces."

One corner of Gallantyne's mouth twitched impatiently. *So Timmy wears braces, and he has a mean-looking father and I am getting exactly nowhere.* "Do you know the story of Tom Sawyer, Mary Martha?"

"Our teacher told us some of it in school."

"Perhaps you remember the cave that was the secret hideout. Do you and Jessie have somewhere like that? Not a cave, particularly, but a special private place where you can meet or leave notes for each other and things like that?"

"No."

"Think carefully now. You see, I and a great many other people have been searching for Jessie all night."

"She wouldn't hide all night," Mary Martha said thoughtfully. "Not unless she took lots of sandwiches and potato chips along."

"There's no evidence that she did."

"Then she's not hiding. She'd be too hungry. Her father says he should get a double tax exemption for her because she eats so much. What's a tax exemption?"

"You'll find out soon enough." Gallantyne turned to Mac, who was still standing beside the door as if on guard against a sudden intrusion by Kate Oakley. "Have you any questions you'd like to ask her?"

"One or two," Mac said. "What time did you go to bed last night, Mary Martha?"

"About eight o'clock."

"That's pretty early for vacation time and daylight saving."

"My mother and I like to go to bed early and get up early. She doesn't—we don't like the nights."

"Did you go to sleep right away?"

"I must have. I don't remember doing anything else."

"That seems like logical reasoning," Mac said with a wry smile. "Did you get up during the night?"

"No."

"Not even to go to the bathroom?"

"No, but you're not supposed to talk about things like that in front of strangers," Mary Martha said severely.

"Lieutenant Gallantyne is a friend of mine."

"Well, he's not mine or my mother's."

"Let's see if we can change that," Gallantyne said. "Ask your mother to come in here, will you?"

"Yes, sir. Only—well, you better not keep her very long."

"Why not?"

"She might cry, and crying gives her a headache."

"We mustn't let that happen, must we?"

"No, sir." Mary Martha executed another of her stiff little curtsies, picked up the cat and departed.

"She's a funny kid," Gallantyne said. "Is she always like that?"

"With adults. I've never seen her in the company of other children."

"That's odd. I understand you're the old family friend."

"I'm the old family friend when things go wrong," Mac said dryly. "When things are going right, I think I must be the old family enemy."

"Exactly why did you invite yourself to come with me this morning, Mac?"

"Oh, let's just say I'm curious."

"Let's not."

"All right. The truth is that Kate Oakley's a very difficult and very vulnerable woman. Because she is difficult, she can't ask for or accept help the way an ordinary vulnerable person might. So I'm here to lend her moral support. I may criticize her and give her hell occasionally but she knows I'm fond of her."

"How fond?"

"She's twenty years younger than I am. Does that answer your question?"

"Not quite."

"Then I'll lay it on the line. There's no secret romance going on between Kate Oakley and myself. I was her father's lawyer when he was alive, and when he died I handled his estate, or rather the lack of it. I am officially Mary Martha's godfather, and unofficially I'm probably Kate's, too. That's the whole story."

"The story hasn't ended yet," Gallantyne said carefully. "Surely you're not naïve enough to believe we can write our own endings in this world."

"We can do a little editing."

"Don't kid yourself."

Mac wanted to argue with him but he heard Kate's footsteps in the hall. He wondered what her reaction would have been to Gallantyne's insinuations: shock, displeasure, perhaps even amusement. He could never tell what she was actually thinking. When she was at her gayest, he could feel the sadness in her, and when she was in despair he sensed that it, too, was not real. Everything about her seemed to be hidden, as if at a certain period in her life she had decided to go underground where she would be safe.

He thought about the wild creatures in the canyon behind his house. The foxes, the raccoons, the possums, the chipmunks, they could all be lured out of their winter refuge by the promise of food and the warmth of a spring sun. There was no spring sun for Kate, no hunger that could be satisfied by food. He watched her as she came in, thinking, *what do you want, Kate? Tell me what you want and I'll give it to you if I can.*

She hesitated in the doorway, looking as though she were trying to decide how to act.

Before she had a chance to decide, Gallantyne spoke to her in a quiet, confident manner, "Please sit down, Mrs. Oakley. We're hoping you'll be able to help us."

"I hope so, too. I was—I'm very fond of Jessie. If anything's happened to her, it will be a terrible blow to Mary Martha. Do you suppose it could have been a kidnapping?"

"There's no evidence of it. The Brants are barely getting by financially, and they've received no ransom demand. We're pretty well convinced that Jessie walked out of the house voluntarily."

"How can you know that for sure?"

"There were no signs of a struggle in Jessie's bedroom, the Arlington's dog didn't bark as he certainly would have if he'd heard a stranger, and the back door was unlocked. It's one of the new kinds of lock built into the knob—push the knob and it locks, pull and it unlocks.

We think Jessie unlocked the door, accidentally or on purpose, when she went out. I'm inclined to believe that she unlocked it deliberately with the intention of returning to the house. Someone, or something, interfered with that intention."

He paused to light a cigarette, cupping his hands around the match as though he were outside on a windy day. "We'll assume, then, that she left the house under her own power and for a reason we don't know yet. The two likeliest places she might have gone are the Arlingtons' next door, or this house. Mrs. Arlington claims she didn't see her and you claim you didn't."

"Of course I didn't," she said stiffly. "I would have phoned her mother immediately."

"What I want you to consider now is the possibility that she might somehow have gotten into the house without your seeing her, that she might have hidden some place and fallen asleep."

"There's no such possibility."

"You seem very sure."

"I am. This house is Sheridan-proof. My ex-husband acquired the cunning habit of breaking in during my absences and helping himself to whatever he fancied—liquor, furniture, silver, and more liquor. I had a special lock put on every door and window. When I go out or retire for the night, I check them all. It would be as much as my life is worth to miss any of them."

"Jessie knew about these locks, of course?"

"Yes. She asked me about them. It puzzled her that a house should have to be secured against a husband and father . . . No, Lieutenant, Jessie could never have entered this house without my letting her in."

That leaves the Arlingtons, he thought, *or someone on the street between here and the Arlingtons' house.* "Would you call Jessie a shy child, Mrs. Oakley?"

"No. She has—had quite a free and easy manner with people."

"Does that include strangers?"

"It included everyone."

"Have you had any strangers hanging around here recently?"

She gave Mac a quick, questioning look. He responded with a nod that indicated he'd already told Gallantyne about the man in the green coupé.

"Yes," she said, "but I never connected him with Jessie or Mary Martha."

"Do you now?"

"I don't know. It seems odd that he'd show himself so openly if he were planning anything against Jessie or Mary Martha."

"Perhaps he wasn't actually planning anything, he was merely waiting. And when Jessie walked out of that house by herself, she provided what he was waiting for, an opportunity."

A spot of color, dime-sized, appeared suddenly on her throat and began expanding, up to her ear tips, down into the neckline of her dress. The full realization of Jessie's fate seemed to be spreading throughout her system like poison dye. "It could just as easily have been Mary Martha instead of Jessie. Is that what you're telling me?"

"Think about it."

"I won't. It's unthinkable. Mary Martha wouldn't leave the house without my permission, and she'd certainly never enter the car of a strange man."

"Some pretty powerful inducements can be offered a child her age who's lonely and has affection going to waste. A puppy, for instance, or a kitten—"

"No, no!" But even the sound of her own voice shouting denials could not convince her. She knew the lieutenant was right. She knew that Mary Martha had left the house without permission just a few nights before. She'd run over to Jessie's using the short cut across the creek. Suppose she'd gone out the front, the way she often did. The man had been parked across the street at that very moment. "No, no," she repeated. "I've taught Mary Martha what it took me years of torment to learn, that you can't trust men, you can't believe them.

They're liars, cheats, bullies. Mary Martha already knows that. She won't have to find it out the hard way as I did, as Jessie—"

"Be quiet, Kate," Mac said in a warning tone. "The lieutenant is too busy to listen to your theories this morning."

She didn't even glance in his direction. "Poor Jessie, poor misguided child with all her prattle about her wonderful father. She believed it, and that fool mother of hers actually encouraged her to believe it even though she must have been aware what was going on."

Gallantyne raised his brows. "And what was going on, Mrs. Oakley?"

"Plenty."

"Who was involved?"

"I must caution you, Kate," Mac said, "not to make any statements you're not able and willing to substantiate."

"In other words, I'm to shut up?"

"Until you've consulted your attorney."

"All my attorney ever does for me is tell me to shut up."

"Rumors and gossip are not going to solve this case."

"No, but they might help," Gallantyne said mildly. "Now, you were going to give me some new information about Jessie's father."

Kate looked from Gallantyne to Mac, then back to Gallantyne, as if she were trying to decide which one of them was the lesser evil. "It can hardly be called new. It goes back to Adam. Brant's a man and he's been availing himself of the privilege, deceiving his wife, cheating his children out of their birthright. Oh, he puts on a good front, almost as good as Sheridan when he's protesting his great love for Mary Martha."

"You're implying that Brant is having an affair with another woman?"

"Yes."

"Who is she?"

"Virginia Arlington."

Both men were watching her, Mac painfully, Gallantyne with cool suspicion.

"It's true," she added, clenching her fists. "I can't prove it, I don't have pictures of them in bed together. But I know it's a fact."

"Facts, Mrs. Oakley, are often what we choose to believe."

"I have nothing against Mrs. Arlington, I have no reason for wanting to believe bad things about her. She's probably just a victim like me, hoodwinked by a man, taken in by his promises. Oh, you should have heard Sheridan in the heyday of his promises . . . But then you very likely know all about promises, Lieutenant. I bet you've made lots of them."

"A few."

"And they weren't kept?"

"Some weren't."

"That makes you a liar, doesn't it, Lieutenant? No better than the rest of them—"

"Please be quiet, Kate," Mac said. "You're not doing yourself any good or Jessie any good."

He touched Gallantyne lightly on the arm and the two men walked over to the far corner of the room and began talking in whispers. Though she couldn't distinguish any words, she was sure they were talking about her until Gallantyne finally raised his voice and said, "I must ask you not to mention Charlie Gowen to anyone, Mrs. Oakley."

"Charlie Gowen? I don't even know who—"

"The man in the green coupé. Don't tell anyone about him, not your friends or relatives or reporters or any other policeman. As far as you're concerned, Charlie Gowen doesn't even exist."

21

WHEN CHARLIE ARRIVED home at 5:30, he was so tired he could hardly get out of his car and cross the patch of lawn that separated the driveway from the house. He had worked very hard all day in the hope that his boss, Mr. Warner, would notice, and approve of him. He especially needed Mr. Warner's approval because Ben was angry with him for staying out too late the previous night. Although he knew Mr. Warner and Ben were entirely different people, and pleasing one didn't necessarily mean placating the other, he couldn't keep from trying. In his thoughts they weighed the same, and in his dreams they often showed up wearing each other's faces.

At the bottom of the porch steps he stooped to pick up the evening *Journal.* It lay under the hibiscus bush, fastened with an elastic band and folded so he could see only the middle third of the oversized headline: U SEEN THE

Usually, Charlie waited for the *Journal* until after Ben had finished with it because Ben liked to be the first to discover interesting bits of news and pass them along. But tonight he didn't hesitate. He tore off the elastic band and unfolded the paper. Jessie's face was smiling up at him. It didn't look the way it had the last time he'd seen her, shocked and frightened, but she was wearing the same clothes, a white bathrobe over pajamas.

The headline said HAVE YOU SEEN THIS GIRL?—and underneath the picture was an explanation of it: "This is a composite picture made from a snapshot of Jessie Brant's face superimposed on one of a child of similar height and build wearing clothes similar to those missing from Jessie's wardrobe. The *Journal* is offering $1,000 reward for information leading to the discovery of Jessie Brant's whereabouts."

For a long time Charlie stood looking at the girl who was half-Jessie, half-stranger. Then he turned and stumbled up the porch steps and into the house, clutching the newspaper against his chest as though to hide from the neighbors an old wound that had reopened and started to bleed again. In his room, with the door locked and the blinds drawn, he read the account of Jessie's disappearance. It began with a description of Jessie herself; of her father, a technician with an electronics firm; her brother, Michael, who hadn't learned the news until he'd been picked off a fishing boat by the Coast Guard cutter; her mother, the last member of her family to see Jessie alive at ten o'clock.

The official police announcement was issued by Lieutenant D. W. Gallantyne: "The evidence now in our possession indicates that Jessie departed from her house voluntarily, using the back door and leaving it unlocked so she would be able to return. What person, or set of circumstances, prevented her return? We are asking the public to help us answer that question. There is a strong possibility that someone noticed her leaving the house or walking along the street, and that that person can give us further information, such as what direction she was going and whether she was alone. Anyone who saw her is urged to contact us immediately. Jessie's grief-stricken parents join us in this appeal."

The light in the room was very dim. Narrowing his eyes to keep them in focus, Charlie reread the statement by Gallantyne. It was wrong, he knew it was wrong. It hadn't happened like that. Somebody should tell the lieutenant and set him straight.

He lay down on the bed, still holding the newspaper against his chest. The ticking of his alarm clock sounded extraordinarily loud and clear. He'd had the clock since his college days. It was like an old friend, the last voice he heard at night, the first voice in the morning: *tick it, tick it, tick it.* But now the voice began to sound different, not friendly, not comforting.

Wicked wicked, wicked sicked, wicked sicked.

"I'm not," he whispered. "I'm not. I didn't touch her."

Wicked sicked, pick a ticket, try and kick it, wicked wicked, buy a ticket, buy a ticket, buy a ticket.

Ben called out, "Charlie? You in there?" When he didn't get an answer he tried the door and found it locked. "Listen, Charlie, I'm not mad at you anymore. I realize you're a grown man now and if you want to stay out late, well, what the heck, that's your business. Right?"

"Yes, Ben."

"I've got to stop treating you like a kid brother who's still wet behind the ears. That's what Louise says and by golly, it makes sense, doesn't it?"

"I guess so."

"She'll be over pretty soon. You don't want her to catch you sulk—unprepared."

"I'm preparing, Ben."

"Good. I couldn't find the *Journal,* by the way. Have you got it in there?"

"No."

"The delivery boy must have missed us. Well, I hate to report him so I think I'll go pick one up over at the drugstore. I'll be back in a few minutes."

"All right."

"Charlie, listen, you're okay, aren't you? I mean, everything's fine?"

"I am not sicked."

"What? I didn't hear what you—"

"I am not sicked."

The unfamiliar word worried Ben. As the worry became larger and larger, chunks of it began dropping off and changing into something he could more easily handle—anger. By the time he reached the drugstore he'd convinced himself that Charlie had used the word deliberately to annoy him.

Mr. Forster was standing outside his drugstore. Though his face looked grave, there was a glint of excitement in his eyes as though he'd just found out that one of his customers had contracted a nonfatal illness which would require years of prescriptions.

"Well, well, it's Benny Gowen. How's the world treating you, Benny?"

"Fine. Nobody calls me Benny anymore, Mr. Forster."

"Don't they now. Well, that puts me in a class by myself. What can I do for you?"

"I'd like a *Journal.*"

"Sorry, I'm all sold out." Mr. Forster was watching Ben carefully over the top of his spectacles. "Soon as I put them out here on the stand this afternoon people began picking them up like they were ten-dollar bills. Nothing sells papers like a real nasty case of murder or whatever it was. But I guess you know all about it, being you work downtown in the hub of things."

"I don't have a chance to read when I'm on the job," Ben said.

"Who was murdered?"

"The police don't claim it was murder. But I figure it must have been. The kid's gone, nobody's seen hide nor hair of her since last night."

"Kid?"

"A nine-year-old girl named Jessie Brant. Disappeared right from in front of her own house or thereabouts. Now, nobody can tell me a nine-year-old kid wearing nightclothes wouldn't have been spotted by this time if she were still alive. It's not reasonable. Mark my words, she's lying dead some place and the most they can hope for is to find the body and catch the man responsible for the crime. You agree, Benny?"

"I know nothing about it."

Mr. Forster took off his spectacles and began cleaning them with a handkerchief that was dirtier than they were. "How's Charlie, by the way?"

He is not sicked. "He's all right. He's been all right for a long time now, Mr. Forster."

"Reason I asked is, he came in here yesterday with a bad headache. He bought some aspirin, but shucks, taking aspirin isn't getting to the root of anything. A funny thing about headaches, some doctors think they're mostly psychological, you know, caused by emotional problems. In Charlie's case I'm inclined to agree. Look at the record, all that trouble he's had and—"

"That's in the past."

"Being in the past and being over aren't necessarily the same thing." Mr. Forster replaced his spectacles with the air of a man who confidently expected new knowledge from increased vision. "Now don't get me wrong. *I* think Charlie's okay. But I'm a friend of his, I'm not the average person reading about the kid and remembering back. There's bound to be talk."

"I'm sure you'll do your share of it." Ben turned to walk away but Mr. Forster's hand on his arm was like an anchor. "Let go of me."

"You must have misunderstood me, Ben. I *like* Charlie, I'm on his side. But I can't help feeling there's something wrong again. It probably doesn't involve the kid at all because it started yesterday afternoon before anything happened to her. Are you going to be reasonable and listen to me, Ben?"

"I'll listen if you have anything constructive to say."

"Maybe it's constructive, I don't know. Anyhow, a man came in here yesterday asking where Charlie lived. He gave me a pretty thin story about forgetting to look up the house number. I pretended to go along with it but I knew damned well he was trying to pump me."

"About Charlie?"

"Yes."

"What'd you tell him?"

"All the right things. Don't worry about that part of it, I gave Charlie a clean bill of health, 100 percent. Only—well, it's been on my mind ever since. The man looked like an official of some kind, why was he interested in Charlie?"

"Why didn't you ask him?"

"Heck, it would have spoiled the game. I was supposed to be taken in, see. I was playing the part of—"

"Playing games isn't going to help Charlie."

Mr. Forster's eyes glistened with excitement. "So now you're leveling with me, eh, Ben? There *is* something wrong, Charlie needs help again. Is that it?"

"We all need help, Mr. Forster," Ben said and walked away, this time without interference. He knew Mr. Forster would be watching him and he tried to move naturally and easily as though he couldn't feel the leaden chains attached to his limbs. He had felt these chains for almost his entire life; attached to the other end of them was Charlie.

He stopped at the corner, aware of the traffic going by, the people moving up and down and across the streets, the clock in the courthouse tower chiming six. He wanted to quiet the clock so he would lose consciousness of time; he wanted to join one of the streams of strangers, anonymous people going to unnamed places. Whoever, wherever, whenever, was better than being Ben on his way home to Charlie to ask him about a dead child.

Louise's little sports car was parked at the curb in front of the house. Ben found her in the living room, leafing through the pages of a magazine. She smiled when she looked up and saw him in the doorway, but he could tell from the uneasiness in her eyes that she'd read about the child and had been silently asking the same questions that Mr. Forster was asking out loud.

He said, trying to sound cheerful and unafraid, "Hello, Louise. When did you arrive?"

"About ten minutes ago."

"Where's Charlie?"

"In his room getting dressed."

"Oh. Are you going out some place? I thought—well, it's turning kind of cold out, it might be a nice night to build a fire and all three of us sit around and talk."

Louise smiled again with weary patience as if she was sick of talk and especially the talk of children, young or old. "I don't know what Charlie has in mind. When he answered the door he simply told me he was getting dressed. I'm not even sure he wanted me to wait for him. But I'm waiting, anyway. It's becoming a habit." She added, without any change in tone, "What time did he come home last night?"

"It must have been pretty late. I was asleep."

"You went to *sleep* with Charlie still out wandering around by himself? How could you have?"

"I was tired."

"You led me to understand that you'd go on looking for him. You said if I went home for some rest that you'd take over. And you didn't."

"No."

"Why not?"

"Because I started thinking about the conversation we had earlier," Ben said with deliberation. "You gave me the business about how I should trust Charlie, let him have a chance to grow up, allow him to reach his own decisions. You can't have it both ways, Louise. You can't tell me one minute to treat him like a responsible adult and the next minute send me out chasing after him as if he was a three-year-old. You can't accuse me of making mistakes in dealing with him and then an hour later beg me to make the same mistakes. Be honest, Louise. Where do you stand? What do you really think of Charlie?"

"Keep your voice down, Ben. He might hear you."

"Is that how you treat a responsible adult, you don't let him overhear anything?"

"I meant—"

"You meant what you said. The three-year-old shut up in the bedroom isn't supposed to hear what Mom and Pop are talking about in the living room."

"I wouldn't want Charlie to think we're quarreling, that's all."

"But we *are* quarreling. Why shouldn't he think so? If he's a responsible adult—"

"Stop repeating that phrase."

"Why? Because it doesn't fit him, and you can't bear listening to the truth?"

"Stop it, Ben, please. This isn't the time."

"This is the very time," he said soberly. "Right now, this minute, you've got to figure out how you really feel about Charlie. Sure, you love him, we both do. But you're not committed to him the way I am, or to put it bluntly, you're not stuck with him. You still have a chance to change your mind, to get away. Do it, Louise."

"I can't."

"For your own sake, you'd better try. Walk out of here now and don't look back. For nearly a year you've been dreaming, and I've been letting you. Now the alarm's ringing, it's time to wake up and start moving. Beat it, Louise."

"You don't know what you're asking."

"I'm asking," he said, "that one out of this trio gets a chance to survive. It won't be Charlie and it can't be me. That leaves you, Louise. Use your chance, for my sake if not your own. I'd like to think of you as being happy in the future, leading a nice, uncomplicated life."

"There's no such thing."

"You won't leave?"

"No."

"Then God help you." He went over to the window and stood with his back to Louise so she wouldn't see the tears welling in his eyes. "A little girl disappeared last night. One person in this neighborhood has already mentioned Charlie in connection with the crime. There'll be others, not just common gossips like Forster, but men with authority. Whatever Charlie has or hasn't done, it's going to be rough on him, and on you, too, if you stick around."

"I'm sticking."

"Yes, I was afraid you would. Why? Do you want to be a martyr?"

"I want to be Charlie's wife."

"It's the same thing."

"Don't try to destroy my confidence completely, Ben," she said. "It would be easy, I don't have very much. But what I have may help Charlie and perhaps you, too, in the days to come."

"Days? You're thinking in terms of *days*? What about the months, years—"

"They're composed of days. I choose to think of them in that way. Now," she added in a gentler voice, "do I get your blessing, Ben?"

"You get everything I have to offer."

"Thank you."

She turned toward the doorway, hearing Charlie's step in the hall. It sounded brisk and lively as if he'd had an abrupt change of mood in the past ten minutes. When he came in she noticed that he was freshly shaved and wearing his good suit and the tie she'd given him for his birthday. He looked surprised when he saw that she was still there, and she wondered whether he'd expected her to leave, and if so, why he'd taken the trouble to get all dressed up. He was carrying the evening newspaper. It was crumpled and torn as though it had been used to swat flies.

He put it down carefully on the coffee table, his eyes fixed on Ben. "I found it after all, Ben. Right after you left to buy one I decided to go out and search for it again, and sure enough there it was, hidden behind that shrub with the pink flowers. Remember what we used to call it when we were kids, Ben? High biscuits. I used to think that it actually had biscuits on it but they were up so high I couldn't see them."

"I looked under the hibiscus," Ben said.

"You must have missed it. It was there."

"It wasn't there."

"You—you could have made a mistake, Ben. You were complaining about your eyes last week. Anyway, it's such a small thing, we shouldn't be raising all this fuss about it in front of Louise."

"Louise better get used to it. And if it's such a small thing, why are you lying about it?"

"Well, I—well, maybe it didn't happen *exactly* like that." The muscles of Charlie's throat were working, as if he was trying to swallow or unswallow something large and painful and immovable. "When I got home I picked up the paper and took it into my room to read."

"Why? You're not usually interested."

"I saw the headline about the little girl, and the picture. I wanted to study it, to make sure before—before going to the police."

Ben stared at him in silence for a moment, then he repeated, "Before going to the police. Is that what you said?"

"Yes. I'm sure now—the face, the clothes, her name and address. I'm very sure. That's why I got dressed up, so I'll make a good impression at headquarters. You've always told me how necessary a good impression is. Do I look okay?"

"You look dandy. You'll make a dandy impression . . . Jesus Godalmighty, what are you trying to do to me, to yourself? It isn't enough that—"

"But I'm only doing what I have to, Ben. The paper said any witnesses should come forward and tell what they know. And I'm a witness. That's funny, isn't it? I always wanted to be somebody and now I finally am. I'm a witness. That's pretty important, according to the paper. I may even be the only one in the whole city, can you beat that?"

"No. I don't think anyone can. This time you've really done it, you've set a new high."

Charlie's smile was strained, a mixture of pride and anxiety.

"Well, I didn't actually *do* anything, I just happened to be there when she came out of the house. The police are wrong about which house she came out of. It wasn't her own, the way the paper said. It was the one—"

"You just happened to be there, eh, Charlie?"

"Yes."

"In your car?"

"Yes."

"Was the car parked?"

"I—I'm not sure but I think I may have been only passing by, very slowly."

"Very, *very* slowly?"

"I think so. I may have stopped for a minute when I saw her on account of I was surprised. It was so late and she shouldn't have been out. Her parents should have taken better care of her, not letting her run wild on the streets past ten o'clock, no one to protect her."

"Did you offer to protect her, Charlie?"

"Oh no."

"Did you talk to her at all?"

"No. I may have sort of spoken her name out loud because I was so surprised to see her, it being late and cold and lonely." He broke off suddenly, frowning. "You're mixing me up with your questions. You're getting me off the subject. That's not the important part, how I happened to be there and what I did. The important thing is, she didn't come out of her own house. The police think she did, so it's my duty to straighten them out. I bet they'll be very glad to have some new evidence."

"I just bet they will," Ben said. "Go to your room, Charlie."

"What?"

"You heard me. Go to your room."

"I can't do that. I'm a witness, they need me. They *need* me, Ben."

"Then they'll have to come and get you."

"You're interfering with justice. That's a very wrong thing to do."

"Justice? What kind of justice do you think is in store for you, when you can't even tell them what you were doing outside the girl's house, or whether you were parked there or just passing by?"

"You've got it all wrong, Ben. They're not after me, I didn't do anything."

Ben turned away. He wanted to hit Charlie with his fist, he wanted to weep or to run shrieking out into the street. But all he could do was stand with his face to the wall, wishing he were back on the street corner where he could pretend he was anyone, going any place, at any hour of the day or night.

The only sound in the room was Charlie's breathing. It was ordinary breathing, in and out, in and out, but to Ben it was the sound of doom. "Maybe I ought to go ahead and let you ruin yourself," he said finally. "I can't do that, though. Not yet, anyway. So I'm asking you to stay in your room for tonight and we'll discuss this in the morning."

"Ben may be right, Charlie," Louise said. It was the first time she'd spoken since Charlie came into the room. She used her library voice, very quiet but authoritative. "You need time to get your story straight."

Charlie shook his head stubbornly. "It's not a story."

"All right then, you need time to remember the facts. You can't claim to have been at the scene without giving some plausible reason why you were there and what you were doing."

"I wanted some fresh air."

"Other streets, other neighborhoods, have fresh air. The police will ask you why you picked that one."

"I didn't. I was driving around everywhere, just driving around, breathing the free—the fresh air."

"The way you did the other night?"

"Other night?"

"When I found you on Jacaranda Road."

"Why do you bring that up?" he said violently. "You know nothing happened that night. You told me, you were the one who convinced me. You said, *nothing's happened, Charlie. Nothing whatever has happened, it's all in your mind.* Why aren't you saying that now, Louise?"

"I will, if you want me to."

"Not because you believe it?"

"I—believe it." She clung to his arm, half-protectively, half- helplessly.

He looked down at her as if she were a stranger making an intimate demand. "Don't touch me, woman."

"Please, Charlie, you mustn't talk to me like that. I love you."

"No. You spoil things for me. You spoiled my being a witness."

He jerked his arm out of her grasp and ran toward the hall. A few seconds later she heard the slam of his bedroom door. There was a finality about it like the closing of the last page of a book.

It's over, she thought. *I had a dream, the alarm rang, I woke up and it's over.*

She could still hear the alarm ringing in her ears, and above it, the sound of Ben's voice. It sounded very calm but it was the calmness of defeat.

"I should have forced you to leave. I would have, if I'd known what was going on in his mind. But this witness bit, how could I have called that?" He looked out the window. It was getting dark and foggy. The broad, leathery leaves of the loquat tree were already dripping and the streetlights had appeared wearing their gauzy grey nightgowns. "Either the whole thing's a fantasy, or he's telling the truth but not all of it."

"All of it?"

"That he attacked the child and killed her."

"Stop it. I'll never believe that, never."

"You half believed it when you walked in this door. You came here for reassurance. You wanted to be told that Charlie arrived home early last night, that he and I had a talk and then he went to bed. Well, he didn't, we didn't. This isn't a very good place to come for reassurance, Louise. It's a luxury we don't keep in stock."

"I didn't come here for reassurance. I wanted to see Charlie, to tell him that I love him and I trust him."

"You trust him, do you?"

"Yes."

"How far? Far enough to allow him to go to the police with his story?"

"Naturally I'd like him to get the details straight first, before he exposes himself to—to their questions."

"You make it sound very simple, as if Charlie's mind is a reference book he can open at will and look up the answers. Maybe you're right, in a way. Maybe his mind is a book, but it's written in a language you and I can't understand, and the pages aren't in order and some of them are glued together and some are missing entirely. Not exactly a perfect place to find answers, is it, Louise?"

"Stop badgering me like this," she said. "It's not fair."

"If you don't like it, you can leave."

"Is that all I ever get from you anymore, an invitation to leave, walk away, don't come back?"

"That's it."

"Why?"

"I told you before, one of the three of us should have a chance, just a chance." He was still watching the fog pressing at the window like the grey facelessness of despair. "Charlie's my problem, now more than ever. I'll look after him. He won't go to the police tonight or any other night. He'll do what I tell him to do. I'll see that he gets to work in the morning and that he gets home safely after work. I'll stay with him, talk to him, listen to him, play the remember-game with him. He likes that— *remember when we were kids, Ben?*—he can play it for hours. It won't be a happy life or a productive one, but the most I can hope for Charlie right now is that he's allowed to survive at all. He's a registered sex offender.

Sooner or later he's bound to be questioned about the child's disappearance. I only hope it's later so I can try and push this witness idea out of his head."

"How will you do that?"

"I'll convince him that he wasn't near the house, he didn't see the child, he didn't see anything. He was at home with me, he dozed off in an armchair, he had a nightmare."

"Don't do it, Ben. It's too risky, tampering with a mind that's already confused about what's real and what isn't."

"If he doesn't know what's real," Ben said, "I'll have to tell him. And he'll believe me. It will be like playing the remember-game. *Remember last night, Charlie, when you were sitting in the armchair? And you suddenly dozed off, you cried out in your sleep, you were having a nightmare about a house, a child coming out of a house . . .*"

He had to write the letter very quickly because he knew Ben would be coming in soon to talk to him. He folded the letter six times, slipped it into an envelope, addressed the envelope to Police Headquarters and put it in the zippered inside pocket of his windbreaker. Then he returned to his desk. The desk had been given to him when he was twelve and it was too small for him. He had to hunch way down in order to work at it but he didn't mind this. It made him feel big, a giant of a man; a kindly giant, though, who used his strength only to protect, never to bully, so everyone respected him.

When Ben came in, Charlie pretended to be studying an advertisement in the back pages of a magazine.

"Dinner's ready," Ben said. "I brought home some chicken pies from the cafeteria and heated them up."

"I'll eat one if you want me to, Ben, but I'd just as soon not."

"Aren't you hungry?"

"Not very. I had chicken pie last night."

"We had ravioli last night. Don't you remember? I cut myself opening the can. Look, here's the cut on my finger."

Charlie looked at the cut with polite interest. "That's too bad. You must be more careful. I wasn't here last night for dinner."

"Yes, you were. You ate too much and later you dozed off in Father's armchair in the front room."

"No, Ben, that was a lot of other nights. Last night was different, it was very different. First I took that delivery to the Forest Service. All that heat and dust up in the mountains gave me a headache so I went to the drugstore for some aspirin."

"The aspirin made you sleepy. That's why you dozed—"

"I wasn't a bit sleepy, I was hungry. I was going to take Louise some place to eat—I don't mean eat *her*," he added earnestly. "I mean, where we could both eat some food. Only she wasn't at the library so I went by myself and had a chicken pie."

"Where?"

"The cafeteria you manage. It wouldn't be loyal to go anywhere else."

"You picked a hell of a time to be loyal," Ben said. "Did anyone see you?"

"They must have. There I was."

"Did you speak to anyone?"

"The cashier. I said hello."

"Did she recognize you?"

"Oh yes. She made a joke about how everyone had to pay around that joint, even the boss's brother."

That fixes it, Ben thought. *If he'd planned every detail in advance he couldn't have done a better job of lousing things up.* "What time were you there?"

"I don't know. I hate watching the clock, it watches me back."

"What did you do after you finished eating?"

"Drove around, I told you that. I wanted some fresh air to clear the dust out of my sinuses."

"You were home by ten o'clock."

"No, I couldn't have been. It was after ten when I saw—"

"You saw nothing," Ben said harshly. "You were home with me by ten o'clock."

"I don't remember seeing you when I came in."

"You didn't. I was in bed. But I knew what time it was because I'd just turned out the light."

"You couldn't be mistaken, like about the ravioli?"

"The ravioli business was simply a device to get at the truth. I knew you'd been to the drugstore and the library but I wanted you to recall those things for yourself. You did."

"Not this other, though."

"You were home by ten. I wasn't asleep yet, I heard you come in. If anyone asks you, that's what you're to say. Say it now."

"Please leave—leave me alone, Ben."

"I can't." Ben leaned over the desk, his face white and contorted. "You're in danger and I'm trying to save you. I'm going to save you in spite of yourself. Now say it. Say you were home by ten o'clock."

"Will you leave me alone, then?"

"Yes."

"You promise?"

"*Yes.*"

"I was home by ten o'clock," Charlie repeated, blinking. "You cut yourself opening a can of ravioli. You were bleeding, you were bleeding all over the bloody kitchen. Let me see your cut again. Does it still hurt, Ben?"

"No."

"Then what are you crying for?"

"I have a—a pain."

"You shouldn't eat highly spiced foods like ravioli."

"No, that was a mistake." Ben's voice was a rag of a whisper torn off a scream. "I'll try to make it up to you, Charlie."

"To me? But it's your pain."

"We share it. Just like in the old days, Charlie, when we shared everything. Remember how my friends used to kid me about my little brother always tagging along? I never minded, I liked having you tag along. Well, it will be like that again, Charlie. I'll drive you to work in the morning, you can walk over to the cafeteria and have lunch with me at noon—"

"I have my own car," Charlie said. "And sometimes Louise and I prefer to have lunch together."

"Louise's lunch hour is going to be changed. It probably won't jibe with yours anymore."

"She didn't tell me that."

"She will. As for the car, it seems wasteful to keep two of them running when I can just as easily drive you wherever you want to go. Let's try it for a while and see how it works out. Maybe we can save enough money to take a trip somewhere."

"Louise and I are going to take a trip on our honeymoon."

"That might not be for some time."

"Louise said September, next month."

"Well, things are a little hectic at the library right now, Charlie. There's a chance she might not—she might not be able to get away."

"Why does Louise tell you stuff before she tells me? Explain it to me, Ben."

"Not tonight."

"Because of your pain?"

"Yes, my pain," Ben said. "I want you to give me your car keys now, Charlie."

Charlie put his left hand in the pocket of his trousers. He could feel the outline of the keys, the round one for the trunk, the pointed one for the ignition. "I must have left them in the car."

"I've warned you a dozen times about that."

"I'm sorry, Ben. I'll go and get them."

"*No.* I will."

Charlie watched him leave. He hadn't planned it like this, in fact he had planned nothing beyond the writing of the letter. But now that he saw his opportunity he couldn't resist it any more than a caged animal could resist an open gate. He picked up his windbreaker and went quietly through the kitchen and out of the back door.

22

RALPH MACPHERSON WAS preparing for an early bedtime when the telephone rang. He reached for it quickly, afraid that it would be Kate calling and afraid that it wouldn't. He hadn't heard from her all day and her parting words that morning had been hostile as if she hadn't forgiven him for doubting her story about Brant and Mrs. Arlington.

"Hello."

"This is Gallantyne, Mac."

"Don't you ever sleep?"

"I had a couple of hours this afternoon. Don't worry about me."

"I'm worried about me, not you. I was just going to bed. What's up?"

"I'm calling to return a favor," Gallantyne said. "You let me read the anonymous letter Kate Oakley received, so I'll let you read one that was brought to me tonight if you'll come down to my office."

"I've had more tempting offers."

"Don't bet on it. The two letters were written by the same man."

"I'll be right down," Mac said and hung up.

Gallantyne was alone in the cubicle he called an office. He showed no signs of the fatigue that Mac felt weighing down his limbs and dulling his eyes.

The letter was spread out on the desk with a goosenecked lamp turned on it. It was printed, like the one Kate Oakley had received, and it had been folded in the same way, many times, as though the writer was unconsciously ashamed of it and had compressed it into as small a package as possible. An envelope lay beside it, with the words Police Department printed on it. It bore no stamp.

Mac said, "How did you get hold of this?"

"It was dropped in the mail slot beside the front door of headquarters about two hours ago. The head janitor was just coming in to adjust the hot-water heater and he saw the man who put the letter in the slot. He gave me a good description."

"Who was it?"

"Charles Gowen," Gallantyne said. "Surprised?"

"I'm surprised at the crazy chances he took, delivering the letter himself, making no effort to alter his printing or the way he folded the paper."

"What kind of people take chances like that, Mac?"

"The ones who want to be caught."

Gallantyne leaned back in his chair and looked up at the ceiling. In the center of it, the shadow of the lampshade was like a black moon in a white sky. "I checked his record. It goes back a long way and he's been treated since then, both at Coraznada State Hospital and privately. But a record's a record. When a man's had cancer, the doctors can't ignore his medical history. Well, this is cancer, maybe worse. Gowen's had it, and I think he has it again. Read the letter."

It was briefer than the first one.

To the Police:

*I was driving along Cielito Lane last night at 10:30 and
I know you are Bad about which house Jessie came out of. It was the house
next door on the west side. They will keep me a prisoner now so I can never tell
you this in person but it is True.*

A Witness
P.S. Jessie is my fiend.

Mac read it again, wondering who "they" were; the brother, probably, and the woman Mr. Forster the druggist had mentioned, Gowen's fiancée.

Gallantyne was watching him with eyes as hard and bright as mica.

"Interesting document, wouldn't you say? Notice the capitalizations, Bad and True. And the postscript."

"I suppose he intended to write 'friend' and omitted the 'r.'"

"I think so."

"And by 'Bad' I gather he means wrong."

"Yes. The house next door on the west side belongs to the Arlingtons." Gallantyne leaned forward and moved the lamp to one side, twisting the shade. The black moon slid down the white sky and disappeared. "As soon as the letter came, I sent Corcoran over to Gowen's house. The brother was there, Ben, and Gowen's girlfriend, Louise Lang. Gowen was missing. The brother and girlfriend claimed they didn't know where he'd gone, but according to Corcoran, they were extremely nervous and what they weren't saying, they were thinking. Anyway, I gave the word for Gowen to be picked up for questioning."

"Do you believe what he said in his letter about Jessie coming out of the Arlingtons' house?"

"Well, it seems to fit in with Mrs. Oakley's story that Mrs. Arlington and Brant were something more than neighbors."

"I've told you before, you can't afford to take Kate too seriously. She frequently thinks the worst of people, especially if they have any connection in her mind with Sheridan."

"The letter tends to support her statement."

"I don't see it."

"Then you're not looking. And the reason you're not looking is obvious—Kate Oakley. You're doing your best, in a quiet way, to keep her out of this case."

"That's a false conclusion," Mac said. "When a statement in a letter showing certain signs of disturbance is supported by the word of a woman who shows similar signs, it doesn't mean both are right because they agree. It could mean that neither is right."

"You want more evidence? Okay, let's gather some." Gallantyne got up, the swivel chair squawking in protest at the sudden, violent movement. "I'm going to talk to Brant. Coming with me?"

"No. I prefer to get some sleep."

"Sleep is for babies."

"Look, I don't want to be dragged into this thing any further."

"You dragged yourself in, Mac. You didn't come here tonight out of idle curiosity or because anyone forced you. You're here on the chance that you might be able to help Kate Oakley. Why don't you admit it? Every time you mention her name, I see it in your face and hear it in your voice, that anxious, protective—"

"It's none of your business."

"Maybe not, but when I'm working with somebody I want to be sure he's working with me and not against me on behalf of a woman he's in love with."

"Now you're telling me I'm in love with her."

"I figure somebody should. You're a little slow about some things, Mac. No hard feelings, I hope?"

"Oh no, nothing like that."

"Then let's go."

The Brant house was all dark except for a light above the front door and a lamp burning behind the heavily draped windows of the living room.

Gallantyne pressed the door chime and waited. For the first time since Mac had known him, he looked doubtful, as if he'd just realized that he was about to do something he wouldn't approve of anyone else doing, dealing another blow to a man already reeling.

"Sure, it's a dirty business," he said, as much to himself as to Mac. "But it's got to be done. It's my job to save the kid, not spare the feelings of the family and the neighbors. And by God, I think the whole damn bunch of them have been holding out on me."

"If the only way you can handle this situation is to get mad," Mac said, "all right, get mad. But watch your step. The fact that Brant's daughter is missing doesn't deprive him of his rights, both legal and human."

"How I feel now is nobody has any rights until that kid is found alive and kicking."

"That's dangerous talk coming from a policeman. If you ignore Brant's rights, or Gowen's, you're giving people an invitation to ignore yours."

Gallantyne pressed the door chime again, harder and longer this time, although the answering tinkle was no louder and no faster. "I'm sick of a little lie here and a little lie there. Gowen's in the picture all right, but he's only part of it. I want the rest, the whole works in living color. Why did Mrs. Arlington claim the kid didn't go to her house?"

"Gowen might be the one who's lying, or mistaken."

"I repeat, his statement jibes with Kate Oakley's."

"It's not necessary to drag Kate into—"

"Mrs. Oakley dragged herself in, the same way you did. She volunteered that information about Brant. Nobody asked her, nobody had to pump it out of her. She's in, Mac, and she's in because she wanted to be in."

"Why?"

"Who knows? Maybe she needs a little excitement in her life—though that should be your department, shouldn't it?"

"That's a crude remark."

"So I'm having a crude night. It happens in my line of work, you get a lot of crude nights."

A light went on in the hall and a few seconds later Dave Brant opened the door. He was still wearing the clothes he'd had on the previous night, jeans and a sweatshirt, dirty and covered with bloodstains now dried to the color of chocolate. The hand he'd injured in a fall was covered with a bandage that looked as though he'd put it on himself.

He was grey-faced, grey-voiced. "Is there any news?"

Gallantyne shook his head. "Sorry. May we come in?"

"I guess so."

"You remember Mr. MacPherson, don't you?"

"Yes."

"I'd like to talk to you for a few minutes, Mr. Brant."

"I've told you everything."

"There may be one or two little items you forgot." Gallantyne closed the door. "Or overlooked. Are you alone in the house?"

"I sent my son Michael to spend the night with a friend. My wife is asleep. The doctor was here half an hour ago and gave her a shot."

"Did he give you anything?"

"Some pills. I didn't take any of them. I want to be alert in case—in case they find Jessie and she needs me. I may have to drive somewhere and pick her up, perhaps several hundred miles away."

"I suggest you take the pills. Any picking up can be done by the police—"

"No. I'm her father."

"—in fact, must be done by the police. If Jessie turns up now, at this stage, it won't simply be a matter of putting her to bed and telling her to forget the whole thing."

"You mean she will be questioned?"

"She will be questioned if she's physically and mentally able to answer."

"Don't say that, don't—"

"You asked."

Gallantyne hesitated, glancing uneasily at Mac. The hesitation, and the doubt in his eyes, made it clear to Mac why he'd been invited to come along. Gallantyne needed his support; he was getting older, more civilized; he'd learned to see both sides of a situation and the knowledge was destroying his appetite for a fight.

"Perhaps we'd all better go in the living room and sit down," Mac said. "You must be tired, Mr. Brant."

"No. No, I'm alert, I'm very alert."

"Come on."

The single lamp burning in the living room was behind an imitation leather chair. On the table beside the chair, pictures of Jessie were spread out: a christening photograph taken when she was a baby, classroom pictures, snaps of Jessie with Michael, with her parents, with the Arlingtons' dog; Mary Martha and Jessie, arms self-consciously entwined, standing on a bridge; Jessie on the beach, on her bicycle, in a hammock reading a book.

Silently, Dave bent down and began gathering up the pictures as if to shield Jessie from the eyes of strangers. Gallantyne waited until they were all returned to their folders. Then he said, "You asked me before, Mr. Brant, if I had any news. I told you I hadn't, and that's true enough. I do have something new, though. A man claims to have seen Jessie at 10:30 last night."

"Where?"

"Coming out of the Arlingtons' house. Would you know anything about that, Mr. Brant?"

"Yes."

"What, for instance?"

"It's not—not true."

"Now why do you say that? You weren't anywhere around at that time, were you? I understand you were out searching for Mr. Arlington, who'd left here after a quarrel with his wife."

"Yes."

"Where did you go?"

"A few bars, some cafés."

"And after that?"

"Home."

"Whose home?"

Dave turned his head away. "Well, I naturally had to check in at Virg—at Mrs. Arlington's house to tell her I hadn't been able to find Howard."

"This checking in," Gallantyne said softly, "was it pretty involved? Time-consuming?"

"I told her the places where I had looked for Howard."

"It took you exactly two seconds to tell me."

"We discussed a few other things, too. She was worried about Howard, he'd been acting peculiarly all evening."

"In what way?"

"He seemed jealous of the attention Virginia paid to Jessie."

"Did he have any other cause for jealousy?"

"I don't know what you're getting at."

"It's a simple enough question, surely."

"Well, I can't answer it. I don't know what was going on in Howard's mind."

"I'm talking about *your* mind, Mr. Brant."

"I've—I've forgotten the question. I'm—you're confusing me."

"Sorry," Gallantyne said. "I'll put it another way. How did you feel when Mr. Arlington walked out of here last night?"

"We were all upset by it. Howard had never done anything like that before."

"What time did he leave?"

"Between 9:30 and ten."

"What happened after that?"

"I took Virginia home. Then I decided I'd better try and find Howard."

"You decided, not Mrs. Arlington?"

"It was my idea. She was too depressed to be thinking clearly."

"Depressed. I see. Did you attempt to cheer her up in any way?"

"I went looking for her husband."

"And you returned to her house at what time?"

"I'm not sure. I wasn't wearing a watch."

"Well, let's try and figure it out, shall we? You know what time you discovered Jessie missing from her room."

"Eleven. She has a clock beside her bed."

"Very well. At ten, your wife retired for the night. Half an hour later Jessie was seen leaving the Arlington house."

Dave kept shaking his head back and forth. "No, I told you that's not true. It's a—a terrible impossibility."

"Impossibilities can't be terrible, Mr. Brant. By definition, they don't exist. Possibilities are a different matter. They can happen, and they can be quite terrible, like the one you're seeing now."

"No. I don't, I *won't*."

"You have to," Gallantyne said. "I suggest that Jessie went over to the Arlingtons' place between ten and 10:30. The house was always open to her, she could come and go as she liked, according to Mrs. Arlington. She entered by the back door —"

"No. It was locked, it must have been locked."

"Did you lock it yourself?"

"No."

"That was a pretty serious mistake, wasn't it, Brant? Or are you so casual about that sort of thing you don't mind an onlooker?"

"She didn't see us, she couldn't—"

"I think she did. She saw her father, and the woman she called her aunt, in an attitude that shocked and frightened her so badly that she dashed out into the street. I don't know what was in her mind, perhaps nothing more than a compulsion to escape from that scene. I do know there was a man waiting for her in a car. Perhaps he'd been waiting a long time, and for many nights previously, but that was the night that counted because Jessie's guard was down. She was in a highly emotional state, she didn't have sense enough to cry out or to run away when the man accosted her."

Dave's body was bent double, his forehead touching his knees, as though he was trying to prevent himself from fainting.

Mac crossed the room and leaned over him. "Are you all right, Brant?"

"Aaah." It was not a word, merely a long, painful sigh of assent: he was all right, he wished he were dead but he was all right.

"Listen, Brant. It didn't necessarily happen the way Lieutenant Gallantyne claims it did."

"Yes. My fault, all my fault."

"Tell him, Gallantyne."

Gallantyne raised his eyebrows in a show of innocence. "Tell him what?"

"Can't you see he's in a bad way and needs some kind of reassurance?"

"All right, I'll give him some." Gallantyne's voice was quiet, soothing. "You're a real good boy, Brant. You had nothing to do with your daughter's disappearance. A little hanky-panky with the dame next door; well, Jessie was nine, old enough to know about such things. She shouldn't have been shocked or scared or confused. Don't they teach these matters in the schools nowadays? The birds and the bees, Daddy and Aunt Virginia . . . Now, you want to tell me about it?"

Slowly and stiffly, Dave raised his head. "There's nothing to tell except it—it happened."

"Not for the first time?"

"No, not for the first time."

"Did you plan on divorcing your wife and marrying Mrs. Arlington?"

"I had no plan at all."

"What about Mrs. Arlington?"

"If she had one, I wasn't the important part of it."

"Who was?"

"Jessie. Jessie seems to be a projection of herself. She's the child Virginia was and all the children Virginia will never have."

"When did you find this out?"

"Today. I started thinking about it today."

"A bit late, weren't you?" Gallantyne said. "Too late to do Jessie any good."

"You—are you trying to tell me Jessie is—that she's dead?"

"The man who was waiting for her in the car has a history of sexual psychopathy. I can't offer you much hope, Brant." *Not any hope except that the other child in his history managed to survive.*

23

HE WAS MOVING toward the sea as inevitably as a drop of water. There were stops for traffic lights, detours to avoid passing places where Ben or Louise sometimes went; there were backtrackings when he found himself on a strange street. These things delayed him but they didn't alter his destination.

He passed the paper company where he worked. A light was burning in the office and he went over and peered into the window, hoping to see Mr. Warner sitting at his desk. But the office was empty, the light burning only to discourage burglars. Charlie was disappointed. He would have liked to talk to Mr. Warner, not about anything in particular, just a quiet, calm conversation about the ordinary things which ordinary people discussed. To Mr. Warner he wasn't anyone special; such a conversation was possible. But Mr. Warner wasn't there.

Charlie went around the side of the building to the loading zone, which was serviced by a short spur of railroad track. He followed the spur for no reason other than that it led somewhere. He took short, quick steps, landing on every tie and counting them as he moved. At the junction of the spur and the main track he stopped, suddenly aware that he was not alone. He raised his head and saw a man coming toward him, walking in the dry, dusty weeds beside the track. He looked like one of the old winos who hung around the railroad jungle, waiting for a handout or an empty boxcar or an even break. He was carrying a paper bag and an open bottle of muscatel.

He said, "Hey, chum, what's the name of this place?"

"San Félice."

"San Félice, well, what do you know? I thought it seemed kinda quiet for L.A. It's California, though, ain't it?"

"Yes."

"Not that it matters none. I been in them all. They're all alike, except California has the grape." He touched the bottle to his cheek. "The grape and me, we're buddies. Got a cigarette and a light?"

"I don't smoke but I think I have some matches." Charlie rummaged in the pocket of his windbreaker and brought out a book of matches. On the outside cover an address was written: 319 Jacaranda Road. He recognized the handwriting as his own but he couldn't remember writing it or whose address it was or why it should make him afraid, afraid to speak, afraid to move except to crush the matches in his fist.

"Hey, what's the matter with you, chum?"

Charlie turned and began to run. He could hear the man yelling something after him but he didn't stop until the track rounded a bend and a new sound struck his ears. It was a warning sound, the barking of dogs; not just two or three dogs but a whole pack of them.

The barking of the dogs, the bend in the tracks, the smell of the sea nearby, they were like electric shocks of recognition stinging his ears, his eyes, his nose. He knew this place. He hadn't been anywhere near it for years, but he remembered it all now, the boarding kennels behind the scraggly pittosporum hedge and the grade school a few hundred yards to the south. He remembered the children taking the back way to school because it was shorter and more exciting, teetering along the tracks with flailing arms, waiting until the final split second to jump down into the brush before the freight train roared past. It was a game, the bravest jumped last, and the girls were often more daring than the boys. One little girl in particular seemed to have no fear at all. She laughed when the engineer leaned out of his cab and shook his fist at her, and she laughed at Charlie's threats to report her to the principal, to tell her parents, to let some of the dogs loose on her.

"You can't, ha ha, because they're not your dogs and they wouldn't come back to you and a lot of them would have babies if they got away. Don't you even know that, you dumb old thing?"

"I know it but I don't talk about it. It's not nice to talk about things like that."

"Why not?"

"You get off those tracks right away."

"Come and make me."

For nearly an hour Virginia had been standing at the window with one corner of the drape pulled back just enough so that she had a view of the front of the Brant house and the curb where the black Chrysler was parked. She had seen Gallantyne and the lawyer getting out of it and had stayed at the window watching hopefully for some sign of good news. Minute by minute the hope had died but she couldn't stop watching.

She could hear Howard moving around in the room behind her, picking up a book, laying it down, straightening a picture, lighting a cigarette, sitting, standing, making short trips to the kitchen and back. His restless activity only increased her feeling of coldness and quietness.

"You can't stand there all night," Howard said finally. "I've fixed you a hot rum. Will you drink it?"

"No."

"It might help you to eat something."

"I don't want anything."

"I can't let you starve."

For the first time in an hour she turned and glanced at him. "Why not? It might solve your problems. It would certainly solve mine."

"Don't talk like that."

"Why not? Does it hurt your ego to think that your wife would rather die than go on living like this?"

"It hurts me all over, Virginia. Without you I have nothing."

"That's nonsense. You have your work, the company, the customers—you see more of them than you do of me."

"I have in the past. The future's going to be different, Virginia."

"Future," she repeated. "That's just a dirty word to me. It's like some of the words I picked up when I was a kid. I didn't know what they meant but they sounded bad so I said them to shock my aunt. I don't know what future means either but it sounds bad."

"I promise you it won't be. I called the boss in Chicago this morning while you were still in bed. I didn't mention it to you because I would have liked the timing to be right but I guess I can't afford to wait any longer. I resigned, Virginia. I told him my wife and I were going to—to adopt a baby and I wanted to spend more time at home with them."

"What made you say a crazy thing like that?"

"I hadn't planned to, it just popped out. When I heard myself saying it, it didn't seem crazy. It seemed right, exactly right, Virginia."

"No. You mustn't—"

"He offered me a managerial position in Phoenix. I'd be on a straight salary, no bonuses for a big sale or anything like that, so it would mean less money actually. But I'd be working from nine to five like anybody else and I'd be home Saturdays and Sundays. I told him I'd think about it and let him know by the end of the week."

She had turned back to the window so he couldn't see her face or guess what was passing through her mind.

"Maybe you wouldn't like Phoenix, Virginia. It's a lot bigger than San Félice and it's hot in the summers, really hot, and of course there's no ocean to cool it off."

"No—no fog?"

"No fog."

"I'd like that part of it. The fog makes me so lonely. Even when the sun's shining bright I find myself looking out towards the sea, wondering when that grey wall will start moving towards me."

"I guarantee no fog, Virginia."

"You sound so hopeful," she said. "Don't. Please don't."

"What's wrong with a little hope?"

"Yours isn't based on anything."

"It's based on you and me, our marriage, our life together."

She took a long, deep breath that made the upper part of her body shudder. "We don't have a marriage anymore. Remember the nursery rhyme, Howard, about the young woman who 'sat on a cushion and sewed a fine seam, and fed upon strawberries, sugar and cream'? Well, the sitting bored her, the cream made her fat, the strawberries gave her hives and her fine seams started getting crooked. Then Jessie came to live next door. At first her visits were a novelty to me, a break in a dull day. Then I began to look forward to them more and more, finally I began to depend on them. I was no longer satisfied to be the friend next door, the pseudo-aunt. I wanted to become her mother, her legal mother . . . Do you understand what I'm trying to tell you, Howard?"

"I think so."

"I saw only one way to get what I wanted. That was through Dave."

"Don't say anymore."

"I have to explain how it happened. I was—"

"Even if Phoenix is hot in the summer, we can always buy an air-conditioned house. We could even build one from scratch if you'd like."

"Howard, listen—"

"We'll look around for a good-sized lot, make all our own blueprints or hire an architect. They say it's cheaper in the long run to hire an architect and let him decide what we need on the basis of what kind of life we want and what kind of people we are."

"And what kind of people are we, Howard?"

"Average, I guess. Luckier than most in some things, not so lucky in others. We can't ask for more than that . . . I've forgotten exactly what the phoenix was. Do you recall, Virginia?"

"A bird," she said. "A bird with gorgeous bright plumage, the only one of his kind. He burned himself to death and then rose out of his own ashes as good as new to begin life again." She turned away from the window, letting the drape fall into place. "Lieutenant Gallantyne is leaving the Brants' house. Ask him to come in here, will you, Howard?"

"Why?"

"I want to tell him everything I didn't tell him before, about Jessie and my plans for her, about Dave, even about the twenty dollars you gave Jessie. We can't afford to hide things anymore, from other people or each other. Will you ask the lieutenant to come in, Howard?"

"Yes."

"It will be a little bit like burning myself to death but I can stand it if you can."

She sat down on the davenport to wait, thinking how strange it would be to get up every morning and fix Howard's breakfast.

The girl was coming toward him around the bend in the tracks. She was taller than Charlie remembered, and she wasn't skipping nimbly along on one rail in her usual manner. She was walking on the ties between the rails slowly and awkwardly, pretending the place was strange to her. She had a whole bundle of tricks but this was one she'd never pulled before. The night made it different, too. She couldn't be on her way to or from school; she must have come here deliberately looking for him, bent on mischief and not frightened of anything—the dark, the dogs, the winos, the trains, least of all Charlie. She knew when and where the trains would pass, she knew the dogs were confined and the winos wanted only to be left alone and Charlie's threats were as empty as the cans and bottles littering both sides of the tracks. She always had an answer for everything: he didn't own the tracks, he wasn't her boss, it was a free country, she would do what she liked, so there, and if he reported her to the police she'd tell them he'd tried to make a baby in her and that would fix him, ha ha.

He was shocked at her language and confounded by her brashness, yet he was envious too, as if he wanted to be like her sometimes: *It's a free country, Ben, and I'm going to do what I like. You're not my boss, so there—* He could never speak the words, though. They vanished on his tongue like salt, leaving only a taste and a thirst.

He stood still, watching the girl approach. He was surprised at how fast she had grown and how clumsy her growth had made her. She staggered, she stumbled, she fell on one knee and picked herself up. No, this could not be pretense. The nimble, fearless, brash girl was becoming a woman, burdened by her increasing body and aware of what could happen. Danger hid in dark places, winos could turn sober and ugly dogs could escape, trains could be running off schedule and Charlie must be taken seriously.

"Charlie?"

During her time of growing she had learned his name. He felt pleased by this evidence of her new respect for him, but the change in her voice disquieted him. It sounded so thin, so scared.

He said, "I won't hurt you, little girl. I would never hurt a child."

"I know that."

"How did you find out? I never told you."

"You didn't have to."

"What's your name?"

"Louise," she said. "My name is Louise."

Gallantyne let Mac off in the parking lot behind police headquarters.

Mac unlocked his car and got in behind the wheel. The ugliness of the scene with Brant, followed by Virginia Arlington's completely unexpected admissions, had left him bewildered and exhausted.

"Go home and get some sleep," Gallantyne said. "I don't think you were cut out for this line of work."

"I prefer to function in the more closely regulated atmosphere of a courtroom."

"Like a baby in a playpen, eh?"

"Have it your way."

"The trouble with lawyers is they get so used to having everything spelled out for them they can't operate without consulting the rule book. A policeman has to play it by ear."

"Well, tonight's music was lousy," Mac said. "Maybe you'd better start taking lessons."

"So you don't approve of the way I handled Brant."

"No."

"I got through to him, didn't I?"

"You broke him in little pieces. I suggest you buy yourself a rule book."

"I have a rule book. I just keep it in my Sunday pants so it doesn't get worn out. Now let's leave it like that, Mac. We're old friends, I don't want to quarrel with you. You take things too seriously."

"Do I."

"Good night, Mac. Back to the playpen."

"Good night." Mac yawned, widely and deliberately. "And if you come up with any more hot leads, don't bother telling me about them. My phone will be off the hook."

He pulled out of the parking lot, hoping the yawn had looked authentic and that it wouldn't enter Gallantyne's head that he was going anywhere but home.

The clock in the courthouse began to chime the hour. Ten o'clock. Kate would be asleep inside her big locked house from which everything had already been stolen. He would have to awaken her, to talk to her before Gallantyne had a chance to start thinking about it: how could she have known about the affair between Brant and Virginia Arlington? She didn't exchange gossip with the neighbors, she didn't go to parties or visit bars, she had no friends. That left one way, only one possible way she could have found out.

He expected the house to be dark when he arrived, but there were lights on in the kitchen, in one of the upstairs bedrooms and in the front hall. He pressed the door chime, muted against Sheridan as the doors were locked against Sheridan and the blinds pulled tight to shut him out. *Yet he's here,* Mac thought. *All the steps she takes to deny his existence merely reinforce it. If just once she would forget to lock a door or pull a blind, it would mean she was starting to forget Sheridan.*

Mary Martha's voice came through the crack in the door. "Who's there?"

"Mac."

"Oh." She opened the door. She didn't look either sleepy or surprised. Her cheeks were flushed, as if she'd been running around, and she had on a dress Mac had never seen before, a party dress made of some thin, silky fabric the same blue as her eyes. "You're early. But I guess you can come in anyway."

"Were you expecting me, Mary Martha?"

"Not really. Only my mother said I was to call you at exactly eleven o'clock and invite you to come over."

"Why?"

"I didn't ask her. You know what? I never stayed up until eleven o'clock before in my whole, entire life."

"Your mother must have had a reason, Mary Martha. Why didn't you ask her?"

"I couldn't. She was nervous, she might have changed her mind about letting me stay up and play."

"Where is she now?"

"Sleeping. She had a bad pain so she took a bunch of pills and went to bed."

"When? When did she take them? What kind of pills?"

The child started backing away from him, her eyes widening in sudden fear. "I didn't do anything, I didn't do a single thing!"

"I'm not accusing you."

"You are so."

"No. Listen to me, Mary Martha." He forced himself to speak softly, to smile. "I know you didn't do anything. You're a very good girl. Tell me, what were you playing when I arrived?"

"Movie star."

"You were pretending to be a movie star?"

"Oh no. I was her sister."

"Then who was the movie star?"

"Nobody. Nobody real, I mean," she added hastily. "I used to have lots of imaginary playmates when I was a child. Sometimes I still do. You didn't notice my new dress."

"Of course I noticed. It's very pretty. Did your mother make it for you?"

"Oh no. She bought it this afternoon. It cost an enormous amount of money."

"How much?"

She hesitated. "Well, I'm not supposed to broadcast it but I guess it's okay, being as it's only you. It cost nearly twenty dollars. But my mother says it's worth every penny of it. She wanted me to have one real boughten dress in case a special occasion comes up and I meet Sheridan at it. Then he'll realize how well she takes care of me and loves me."

In case I meet Sheridan. The words started a pulse beating in Mac's temple like a drumming of danger. He knew what the special occasion would have to be, Kate had told him a dozen times: *"He'll see Mary Martha over my dead body and not before."*

"Louise?" Charlie peered at her through the darkness, shielding his eyes with one hand as though from a midday sun. "No. You don't look like Louise."

"It's dark. You can't see me very well."

"Yes, I can. I know who you are. You get off these tracks immediately or I'll tell your parents, I'll report you to the school principal."

"Charlie—"

"Please," he said. "Please go home, little girl."

"The little girls are all at home, Charlie. I'm here. Louise."

He sat down suddenly on the edge of one of the railroad ties, rubbing his eyes with his fists like a boy awakened from sleep. "How did you find me?"

"Is that important?"

"Yes."

"All right then. I could see you were troubled, and sometimes when you're troubled you go down to the warehouse. You feel secure there, you know what's expected of you and you do it. I saw you looking in the window of the office as if you wanted to be inside. I guess the library serves the same purpose for me. We're not very brave or strong people, you and I, but we can't give up now without a fight."

"I have nothing to fight for."

"You have life," she said. "Life itself."

"Not for long."

"Charlie, please—"

"Listen to me. I saw the child last night, I spoke to her. I don't—I can't swear what happened after that. I might have frightened her. Maybe she screamed and I tried to shut her up and I did."

"We'll find out. In time you'll remember everything. Don't worry about it."

"It seemed so clear to me a couple of hours ago. I was the witness then. It felt so good being the witness, with the law on my side, and the people, the nice people. But of course that couldn't last."

"Why not?"

"Because they're not on my side and never will be. I can hear them, in my ears I can hear them yelling, *get him, get him good, he killed her, kill him back.*"

She was silent. A long way off a train wailed its warning. She thought briefly of stepping into the middle of the tracks and standing there with Charlie until the train came. Then she reached down and took hold of his hand. "Come on, Charlie. We're going home."

Even before Mac opened the door he could hear Kate's troubled breathing. She was lying on her back on the bed, her eyes closed, her arms outstretched with the palms of her hands turned up as if she were begging for something. Her hair was carefully combed and she wore a silky blue dress Mac had never seen before. The new dress and the neatness of the room gave the scene an air of unreality as if Kate had intended at first only to play at suicide but had gone too far. On the bedside table were five empty bottles, which had contained pills, and a sealed envelope. The envelope bore no name and Mac assumed the contents were meant for him since he was the one Mary Martha had been told to call at eleven o'clock.

"Kate. Can you hear me, Kate? There's an ambulance on the way. You're going to be all right." He pressed his face against one of her upturned palms. "Kate, my dearest, please be all right. Please don't die. I love you, Kate."

She moved her head in protest and he couldn't tell whether she was protesting the idea of being all right or the idea of his loving her.

She let out a moan and some words he couldn't understand.

"Don't try to talk, Kate. Save your strength."

"Sheridan's—fault."

"Shush, dearest. Not now."

"Sheridan—"

"I'll look after everything, Kate. Don't worry."

The ambulance came and went, its siren loud and alien in the quiet neighborhood. Mary Martha stood on the front porch and watched the flashing red lights dissolve into the fog. Then she followed Mac back into the house. She seemed more curious than frightened.

"Why did my mother act so funny, Mac?"

"She took too many pills."

"Why?"

"We don't know yet."

"Will she be gone one or two days?"

"Maybe more than that. I'm not sure."

"Who will take care of me?"

"I will."

She gave him the kind of long, appraising look that he'd seen Kate use on Sheridan. "You can't. You're only a man."

"There are different kinds of men," Mac said, "just as there are different kinds of women."

"My mother doesn't think so. She says men are all alike. They do bad things like Sheridan and Mr. Brant."

"Do you know what Mr. Brant did?"

"Sort of, only I'm not supposed to talk about the Brants, ever. My mother and I made a solemn pact."

Mac nodded gravely. "As a lawyer, I naturally respect solemn pacts. As a student of history, though, I'm aware that some of them turn out badly and have to be broken."

"I'm sleepy. I'd better go to bed."

"All right. Get your pajamas on and I'll bring you up some hot chocolate."

"I don't like hot chocolate—I mean, I'm allergic to it. Anyway, we don't have any."

"When someone gives me three reasons instead of one, I'm inclined not to believe any of them."

"I don't care," she said, but her eyes moved anxiously around the room. "I mean, it's okay to tell a little lie now and then when you're keeping a solemn and secret pact."

"But it isn't a secret anymore. I know about it, and pretty soon Lieutenant Gallantyne will know and he'll come here searching for Jessie. And I think he'll find her."

"No. No, he won't."

"Why not?"

"Because."

"He's a very good searcher."

"Jessie's a very good hider." She stopped, clapping both hands to her mouth as if to force the words back in. Then she began to cry, watching Mac carefully behind her tears to see if he was moved to pity. He wasn't, so she wiped her eyes and said in a resentful voice, "Now you've spoiled everything. We were going to be sisters. We were going to get a college education and good jobs so we wouldn't always be waiting for the support check in the mail. My mother said she would fix it so we would never have to depend on bad men like Sheridan and Mr. Brant."

"Your mother wasn't making much sense when she said that, Mary Martha."

"It sounded sensible to me and Jessie."

"You're nine years old." *So is Kate,* he thought, picturing the three of them together the previous night: Jessie in a state of shock, Mary Martha hungry for companionship, and Kate carried away by her chance to strike back at the whole race of men. That first moment of decision, when Jessie had appeared at the house with her story about Virginia Arlington and her father, had probably been one of the high spots in Kate's life. It was too high to last. Her misgivings must have grown during the night and day to such proportions that she couldn't face the future.

There was, in fact, no future. She had no money to run away with the two girls and she couldn't have hidden Jessie for more than a few days. Even to her disturbed mind it must have been clear that when she was caught, Sheridan would have enough evidence to prove her an unfit mother.

The three conspirators, Kate, Mary Martha, Jessie, all innocent, all nine years old; yet Mac was reminded of the initial scene of the three witches in *Macbeth*—*When shall we three meet again?*—and he thought, with a terrible sorrow, *Perhaps never, perhaps never again.*

He said, "You'd better go and tell Jessie I'm ready to take her home."

"She's sleeping."

"Wake her up."

"She won't want to go home."

"I'm pretty sure she will."

"You," she said, "you spoil everything for my mother and me."

"I'm sorry you feel that way. I would like to be your friend."

"Well, you can't be, ever. You're just a man."

When she had gone, he took out the letter he'd picked up from Kate's bedside table before the ambulance attendants had arrived. She had written only one line: "You always wanted me dead, this ought to satisfy you."

He realized immediately that it was intended for Sheridan, not for him. She hadn't even thought of him. First and last it was Sheridan.

He stood for a long time with the piece of paper in his hand, listening to the old house creaking under the weight of the wind. Over and beyond the creaking he thought he heard the sound of Sheridan's footsteps in the hall.

BEYOND THIS POINT ARE MONSTERS

For Judge John A. Westwick

IN DEVON'S DREAM they were searching the reservoir again for Robert. It was almost the way it had happened the first time, with the Mexican policeman, Valenzuela, shouting orders to his men, and the young divers standing around in rubber suits with aqualungs strapped to their backs.

In the dream Devon watched, mute and helpless, from the ranch house. The real Devon had gone out to protest to Estivar, the foreman: "Why are they looking for him in there?"

"They have to look every place, Mrs. Osborne."

"The water's so dirty. Robert's a very clean person."

"Yes, ma'am."

"He would never have gone in such dirty water."

"He might not have had much to say about it, ma'am."

The water, used only for irrigation, was too murky for the divers to work, and in the end the police used a giant scoop and strainer. They spent hours dragging the bottom. All they found were rusting pieces of machinery and old tires and pieces of lumber and the muddy bones of a newborn baby. Finding the nameless, faceless child had upset the policeman, Valenzuela, more than finding a dozen Roberts. It was as if the Roberts of this world always did something to deserve their fate, however bloody or wet or feverish. But the child, the baby— "*Goddamn*," Valenzuela said, crossing himself, and took the little pile of bones away in a shoe box.

She woke up to the sound of Dulzura knocking on the bedroom door.

"Mrs. Osborne? You awake?" The door opened no more than a crack. "You better get up now. Breakfast is on the stove."

"It's early," Devon said. "Only six-thirty."

"But this is the *day.* Have you forgot?"

"No." Not very likely. She'd signed the petition herself while the lawyer watched, looking relieved that she'd finally consented.

Dulzura's small fat hand trembled on the door. "I'm scared. Everybody will be staring at me."

"You only have to tell the truth."

"How am I sure of the truth after all this time? And if I lie after swearing on the Bible, Estivar says they'll put me in jail."

"He was joking."

"He didn't laugh."

"They won't put you in jail," Devon said. "I'll be ready for breakfast in ten minutes."

But she lay still, listening to Dulzura's leaden step on the stairs and the grumbling of the wind as it went round and round the house trying to get in. The autumn night had been warm. Devon's short brown hair was moist and her nightgown clung damply to her body, as though she herself had been fished out of the reservoir and stretched on the bed to dry, a half-drowned mermaid.

Dulzura would tell the truth, of course, because it was too simple to distort: after dinner Robert had gone out to look for his dog and on the way he'd stopped in the kitchen to see Dulzura. He wished her a happy birthday, kidded her about getting to be a big girl and went out the back door toward the garage.

Robert's car was still there, the top down, the key in the ignition. Estivar said it was bad policy to leave the car like that, it was too much of a temptation to the Mexican migrant workers who came to harvest lemons in the spring and crate tomatoes in the summer and pick cantaloupe in the fall. Every group of migrants that had arrived and departed during the past year undoubtedly knew about the car, but no attempt had ever been made to steal it. Perhaps Estivar had warned them severely or perhaps they thought such a car would have a curse on it. Whatever the reason, it lay dead and undisturbed under its shroud of dust.

The tides of migrants that came and went were governed by the sun the way the ocean tides were governed by the moon. It was now October, the peak season of the year, and the bunkhouse was full. Devon had no personal connection with the migrant workers. They spoke no English, and Estivar discouraged her from trying to communicate with them in her high school Spanish. She didn't know their names or where they came from. Small and hungry, they moved across her fields like rodents. "Must have been a couple of wetbacks," one of the deputies said. "Must have robbed and killed him and buried him some place." "We have no wetbacks here," Estivar said sharply. Later Estivar told Devon that the deputy was a very ignorant man because the term wetbacks, *mojados*, was applicable only in Texas where the U.S.-Mexican border was the Rio Grande River; here, in California, where the border was marked by miles of barbed-wire fence, the illegal entrants were properly called *alambres*, wires.

Devon got out of bed and went over to the window to pull aside the drapes. She had long since moved out of the bedroom she'd shared with Robert into the smallest room on the second floor of the ranch house. Small rooms were less lonely, easier to fill. This one, which faced south, had a sweeping view of the river valley, and in the distance the parched hills of Tijuana with its wooden shacks and its domed cathedral the same color as the mustard they sold for hot dogs at the race track and the bull ring. Tijuana looked best at night when it became a cluster of starry lights on the horizon, or at dawn when the cathedral dome turned pink and the shacks were still hidden by darkness.

Through the open window Devon could hear the phone ringing in the kitchen below and Dulzura answering it, her voice shrill as a parrot's because telephones made her nervous. A minute later she was at the bedroom door again, breathing heavily from exertion and resentment.

"It's his mother, says it's important."

"Tell her I'll call her back."

"She don't like to wait."

No, Devon thought, Robert's mother didn't like to wait. But she had waited, the same as the rest of them, for the sound of a doorbell, a phone, a car in the driveway, a step in the hall; she had waited for a letter, a telegram, a postcard, a message from a friend or a stranger.

"Tell her I'll call her back," Devon said.

From the window she could see, too, the rows of tamarisks planted to break the wind and protect the reservoir from blowing sand. To the east was the dry riverbed and to the west the fields of tomatoes, already harvested. The fields were alive with small birds. They swooped between the rows of plants, fluttered among the yellowing leaves, pecked at the rotting remains of fruit and searched the ground for fallen seeds and insects. Estivar could identify every one of them. He called them by their Mexican names, which made them all seem foreign and exotic to Devon until she found out that many of them were birds she'd known back home. The *chupamirto* was just a hummingbird, the *cardelina* a goldfinch, the *golondrina* a swallow.

Other things which had familiar names were not familiar at all. To Devon, born and brought up on the East Coast, rain was what spoiled a picnic or a trip to the zoo, not something people measured in tenths of inches like misers with molten gold. And a river had always been a permanent thing, like the Hudson or the Delaware or the Potomac. The river she watched now from her bedroom window was bone-dry most of the year, yet sometimes it turned into a rampaging torrent strong enough to carry a truck downstream. There were few bridges. It was generally assumed that when it rained hard, people would have sense enough to stay home or stick to the main highway; and when it was dry, they simply drove or walked across the riverbed as if it were a special road, untaxed and maintenance-free.

The far side of the river marked the boundary line of the next ranch, which belonged to Leo Bishop. When Robert brought her home as his bride a year and a half ago, Leo Bishop was the first neighbor she'd met. Robert asked her to be especially nice to him because he'd lost his wife suddenly and tragically during the winter. Devon had done her best, but there were still times when he seemed as foreign to her as any of the *alambres*.

Devon showered and began to dress. The clothes she was to wear had been hanging ready for a week. She had driven into San Diego to meet Robert's mother and Robert's mother had picked the outfit, a brown sharkskin suit a shade lighter than Devon's hair and a shade darker than her tanned skin. It made her look as though she and the suit had come out of the same dye vat, but she didn't argue with the choice. Brown seemed as good a color as any for a young woman about to become a widow on a sunny day in autumn.

She went down the back stairs that led directly into the kitchen.

Dulzura was at the stove, stirring something in a skillet with her left hand and fanning herself with her right. She was not yet thirty years old, but her youth, like the stool she sat on, was camouflaged by folds of fat.

She said, without looking around, "I'm making some scrambled eggs to go with the chorizo."

"I'll just have orange juice and coffee, thanks."

"Mr. Osborne used to be crazy about chorizo, he had a real Mexican stomach . . . You should anyway try the eggs. See how nice they look."

Devon glanced briefly at the moist yellow mass rusted with chili powder and turned away. "They look very nice."

"But you don't like."

"Not this morning."

"No Mrs. Osborne, no little dog, I will have to eat everything myself. Obalz."

It was Dulzura's favorite expression and for a long time Devon had assumed it was a Spanish word indicating displeasure. She'd finally asked the foreman, Estivar, about it.

"There is no such word in my language," Estivar said.

"But it must mean something, Dulzura uses it all the time."

"Oh, it means something all right, you can bet on that."

"I see. It's English."

"Yes, ma'am."

Dulzura was one of Estivar's so-called cousins. He had great numbers of them. If they spoke English, he claimed they were from the San Diego or Los Angeles branch of the family; if they spoke only Spanish, they were from the Sonora branch, or the Sinaloa or Jalisco or Chihuahua, whichever word suited his fancy if not the facts. At times of peak employment Estivar's cousins swarmed over the valley like an army of occupation. They planted, cultivated, irrigated; they pruned, thinned, stripped, sprayed; they picked, sorted, baled, boxed and bunched. Then suddenly they would disappear, as if the earth from which such an abundance of produce had been taken had absorbed the workers themselves like fertilizer.

Dulzura scraped the eggs out of the skillet into a bowl. "His mother on the phone, she said I better wear stockings. I only got the pair I'm saving for my brother's wedding."

"You can wear them more than once, surely."

"Not if I have to kneel when I swear on the Bible."

"Nobody kneels in a courtroom." Devon had never been in a courtroom but she spoke with conviction because she knew Dulzura was watching for any sign of uncertainty, her eyes dark and moist as ripe olives. "The women will be wearing stockings, and all the men coats and ties."

"Even Estivar and Mr. Bishop?"

"Yes."

The phone began ringing again and Devon went down the hall to answer on the extension in the study.

The study had been Robert's room. For a long time it had remained, like his car in the garage, exactly the way he left it. It was too painful for Devon to go inside or even to pass the closed door. Now the room was altered. As soon as the date for the hearing had been set, Devon began packing Robert's things in cardboard cartons, planning to store them in the attic—his tennis rackets and the trophies he'd won, his collection of silver coins, the maps of places he'd wanted to go, the books he'd intended to read.

Devon had cried so hard over the task that Dulzura began crying, too, and they wailed together like a couple of old Irishwomen at a wake. After it was over and Devon could see again out of her swollen eyes, she took a marking pencil and printed Salvation Army on each of the cartons. Estivar was carrying the last of them into the front hall when Robert's mother arrived from the city, as she sometimes did, without warning.

Devon expected Mrs. Osborne to be disturbed by the sight of the cartons or at least to argue about their disposition. Instead, Mrs. Osborne calmly offered to deliver them to the Salvation Army herself. She even helped Estivar load the trunk of her car and the back seat. She was half a head taller than Estivar and almost as strong, and the two of them worked together quickly and efficiently and in silence as though they'd been partners on many such jobs in the past. Mrs. Osborne was seated behind the wheel ready to leave when she turned to Devon and said in her soft, firm voice: "Robert always intended to clean up his study. He'll be glad we saved him the trouble."

Devon closed the door of the study and picked up the phone. "Yes?"

"Why didn't you call me back, Devon?"

"There was no hurry. It's still very early."

"I'm well aware of it. I spent the night watching the clock."

"I'm sorry you couldn't sleep."

"I didn't want to," Mrs. Osborne said. "I was trying to reason things out, to decide whether this is the right step to take."

"We must take it. Mr. Ford and the other lawyers told you that."

"I don't necessarily have to believe what people tell me."

"Mr. Ford is an expert."

"On legal matters, yes. But where Robert is concerned, I am the expert. And what you're going to do today is wrong. You should have refused to sign the papers. Perhaps it's still not too late. You could call Ford and ask him to arrange a postponement because you need more time to think."

"I've had a whole year to think. Nothing has changed."

"But it could, it might. Any day now the phone might ring or there'll be a knock at the door and there he'll be, good as new. Maybe he was kidnapped and is being held captive somewhere across the border. Or he had a blow on the head the night he disappeared and he's suffering from amnesia. Or—"

Devon held the telephone away from her ear. She didn't want to hear any more of the maybes Mrs. Osborne had dreamed up during the long nights and elaborated on during the long days.

"Devon? *Devon.*" It was the closest thing to a scream Mrs. Osborne ever permitted herself except when she was alone. "Are you listening to me?"

"The hearing will be held today. I can't stop it now and wouldn't if I could."

"But what if—"

"There isn't going to be a knocking at the door or a ringing of the phone. There isn't going to be anything."

"It's cruel, Devon, it's cruel to destroy someone's hope like this."

"It would be crueler to encourage you to wait for something that can't happen."

"Can't? That's a strong word. Even Ford doesn't say can't. Miracles are happening every day. Look at the organ transplants they're doing all over the country. Suppose Robert was found dying and they gave his heart to someone else. That would be better than nothing, wouldn't it?—knowing his heart was alive—wouldn't it?"

Mrs. Osborne went on, repeating the same things she'd been saying throughout the year, not even bothering anymore to make it seem new by altering a word here, a phrase there.

Two clocks at opposite ends of the house began sounding the hour: the grandfather clock in the living room, and in the kitchen the cuckoo clock Dulzura kept on the wall above the stove. Dulzura claimed it was a present from her husband, but nobody believed she ever had a husband, let alone one that gave her presents. The grandfather clock belonged to Mrs. Osborne. Carved at the base were the words meant to accompany its chimes:

God Is With You,
Doubt Him Never,
While the Hours
Leave Forever.

When Mrs. Osborne moved out of the ranch house to let Devon and Robert occupy it alone, she'd taken along her antique cherrywood desk and mahogany piano, her silver tea service and collection of English bone china, but she left the clock behind. She no longer believed that God was with her and she didn't want to be reminded that the hours left forever.

Seven o'clock.

The Mexican workers were coming out of the bunkhouse and out of the old wooden building, formerly a barn, that was now equipped as a mess hall. Quickly and quietly they piled into the back of the big truck that would drop them off in whatever fields were ready for harvesting. There was little in their lives except hard work, and the food that made work possible.

At noon they would sit in the bleachers built by Estivar's sons beside the reservoir and eat their lunch in the shade of the tamarisks. At five they would have tortillas and beans in the mess hall and by nine-thirty all the bunkhouse lights would be out. The hours that left forever were good riddance.

Agnes Osborne was still talking. Between the time Devon had stopped listening and the time she started again, Mrs. Osborne had somehow reconciled herself to the fact that the hearing would be held as scheduled, beginning at ten o'clock. "It will probably be better if we met right in the courtroom so we won't miss each other. Do you remember the number?"

"Five."

"Will you be bringing your own car into town?"

"Leo Bishop asked me to ride with him."

"And you accepted?"

"Yes."

"You'd better call and tell him you've changed your mind. Today of all days you don't want to start people gossiping about you and Leo."

"There's nothing to gossip about."

"If you're too nervous to drive yourself, come with Estivar in the station wagon. Oh, and make sure Dulzura wears hose, will you?"

"Why? Dulzura's not on trial. We're not on trial."

"Don't be naive," Mrs. Osborne said harshly. "Of course we're on trial, all of us. Ford tried to keep everything as quiet as possible, naturally, but witnesses had to be subpoenaed and many people had to be given legal notice of the time and place of the hearing, so it's not exactly a secret. It won't be exactly a picnic, either. Signing a piece of paper is one thing, it's quite another to get up in a courtroom and relive those terrible days in public. But it's your decision, you're Robert's wife."

"I'm not his wife," Devon said. "I'm his widow."

2

THE TWO CARS moved slowly along the dirt road, the dust rising in the air behind them like smoke signals.

In the lead was the station wagon driven by Estivar. He was nearly fifty now, but his hair was still dark and thick, and from a distance his quick wiry body looked like a boy's. He had dressed for the occasion in the only suit he possessed, a dark blue gabardine which he kept for the yearly banquets of the Agricultural Association and for his appearances before the immigration authorities when some of his men were picked up by the border patrol for having entered the country illegally.

The blue suit, which was intended to make him appear respectable and, hopefully, beyond reproach, merely emphasized his uneasiness, his mistrust of this latest turn of events. If there was to be official recognition of Robert Osborne's death, it should take place not in court but in church, with prayers and pleadings and long somber words intoned by grey-faced priests.

Estivar had brought his wife, Ysobel, with him for moral support and because she refused to stay home. She was a *mestiza*, half-Indian, with high red-bronze cheekbones and flat black eyes that looked blind and missed nothing. She held her neck rigid and her body erect, refusing to surrender to the motion of the car.

In the seat behind Ysobel, Dulzura sat sideways and stretched her legs out straight in front of her in order to save her stockings at the knees. She wore a giant of a dress, with dwarf horses galloping around the hem and across the pockets. She'd purchased the dress for a weekend trip to the races in Agua Caliente, but the man who proposed the trip failed to show up. The only time Dulzura felt bitter about his defection was when she thought of the money she might have won.

"Five hundred pesos, maybe," she said aloud to no one in particular. "That's forty dollars."

Beside Dulzura sat Lum Wing, the elderly Chinese who cooked for the men. He never associated with them, he merely arrived when they did, carrying a bag with his clothes in it and a padlocked wooden case containing his collection of knives, his whetstone sharpener and a chess set; and when the men left, he left, but not with them or even in the same direction if he could help it.

Lum Wing sucked on the stem of an unlit corncob pipe, wondering what exactly was expected of him. A man in uniform had handed him a piece of paper and told him he'd better show up, by God, or else. He had a premonition, based on some facts he thought no one else knew, that he would end up in jail. And when a good cook landed in jail, no one was ever in a hurry to set him free, that much he'd learned from experience. Out of nervousness he'd been swallowing air all morning and every now and then the excess would escape in a long loud burp.

Ysobel spoke to her husband in Spanish. "Tell him to stop making those disgusting noises."

"He can't help it."

"Do you suppose he's sick?"

"No."

"It seems to me he looks more yellow than the last time I saw him. Perhaps it's contagious. I'm beginning not to feel so well myself."

"Me, too," Dulzura said. "I think we should stop off at a place in Boca de Rio and have something to steady our nerves."

"You know what she means by something. Not coffee, I can tell you. And wouldn't it look splendid to have us walk into the courthouse with her reeling drunk."

Estivar braked the car sharply and ordered them both to keep quiet, and the journey continued for a while in silence. Past the lemon groves sweet with the scent of blossoms, past the acres of stubble where the alfalfa had been cut, and the field of ripening pumpkins which Estivar's youngest son, Jaime, had grown to take into Boca de Rio for Halloween jack-o'-lanterns and Thanksgiving pies.

Jaime was fourteen. He lay now on his stomach in the back of the station wagon, gnawing his right thumbnail and wondering if the kids at school knew where he was and what he had to do. Maybe they were already blowing it up into something wild like he was a friend of the fuzz. Word like that could put a guy down for the rest of his life.

It was the pumpkins that had done it to him. During the last week in October he had delivered some of them to school for the fair and the rest to a grocery store in Boca de Rio. The following Saturday Jaime was ordered by his father to take one of the small tractors and plow the pumpkin vines under. The machine turned up the butterfly knife in the southeast corner of the field. It was an elegant little knife with a double handle which opened like a pair of wings and folded back to reveal the blade in the middle. One of Jaime's friends owned a butterfly knife. If you got the hang of it and practiced a lot in your spare time, the blade could be brought into striking position almost as fast as a switchblade, which was illegal.

Jaime was delighted with his find until he noticed the brownish crust around the hinges. He put the knife carefully down on the ground, wiped his hands on his jeans and went to tell his father.

SOUTH OF BOCA DE RIO the road met the main highway that connected San Diego and Tijuana. The two cities, so dissimilar in sight and sound and atmosphere, were bound together by geography and economics, like stepsisters with completely different backgrounds forced to live together under the same roof.

Within a matter of minutes Estivar and the station wagon were lost in the heavy flow of traffic. Leo Bishop drove in the slow lane, both hands so tight on the steering wheel that his knuckle bones seemed ready to force their way out of his skin. He was a tall thin man in his early forties. There was about him an air of defeat and bewilderment, as though all the rules he'd learned in life were, one by one, being reversed.

If Dulzura's youth was camouflaged by fat, Leo's age was exaggerated by years of sun and wind. His red hair was bleached to the color of sand, his face was scarred over his cheekbones and across the bridge of his nose by repeated burns. He had light green eyes which he protected from the sun by squinting, so that when he moved into the shade and his facial muscles relaxed, fine white lines appeared below and at the corners of his eyes where the ultraviolet rays hadn't reached. These lines gave him a curiously intense expression, which made some of the Mexicans whisper about *mal ojo*, evil eye, and *azar*, bad luck.

After his wife drowned in the river the whispers increased, he had trouble with his crews, equipment broke down, frost killed the grapefruit and damaged the date palms . . . *mal ojo . . . demonios del muerte.* He suspected Estivar of encouraging the rumors, but he never mentioned his suspicions to Devon. She would have trouble believing that evil eyes and demons were still part of Estivar's world.

"Devon."

"Yes?"

"It will soon be over."

She stirred, unbelieving. "What time is it?"

"Ten after nine."

"Mr. Ford said nothing would be settled today. Even if he manages to question all the witnesses, there'll still be a delay while the judge goes over the evidence. He may not announce his decision for a week, it depends on how much other work he has."

"At least your part will be over."

She wasn't sure what her part was going to be. The lawyer had instructed her not only to answer questions but to volunteer information whenever she felt like it, small personal things, homely things, that would help to show Robert as he really was. "We want to make him come alive," Ford said. He did not apologize for the ill-chosen phrase; he seemed to be testing her composure to see if it would hold up in court.

The road had turned west toward San Diego Bay. Sail boats moved gently in the water like large white butterflies that had dipped down to drink. At the edge of the bay a thin strand of beach, wet from the ebbing tide and silvered by the sun, held back the open sea.

"You'd better let me off half a block or so from the courthouse," Devon said. "Mrs. Osborne thinks we shouldn't be seen together."

"Why?"

"People might talk."

"Would that matter?"

"It would to her."

They drove for a while without speaking. In the bay the sailboats gave way to navy vessels, the white butterflies to grey steel waterbugs with ferocious-looking antennae and weird superstructures.

"After this is over," Leo said, "you won't have to be quite so concerned about Agnes Osborne's opinions. She'll be your ex-mother-in-law. Tomorrow, the day after, next week, you'll be a free agent."

She repeated the phrase to herself, liking the sound of it. Widow was a word of loss and sorrow. Free agent suggested the future. "And what do free agents do, Leo?"

"They make choices."

For Devon it had been a year without choices, a year when all decisions were made by other people. She had paid the bills Estivar told her to, signed the papers the lawyer, Ford, put in front of her, answered the questions asked by Valenzuela, the policeman, eaten what Dulzura cooked, worn what Agnes Osborne suggested.

Soon the year would be officially over and the decisions would be hers. There would be no more brown sharkskin suits, no more chorizo and scrambled eggs hidden by chili powder; Valenzuela wasn't even on the police force any longer; after the conclusion of probate there would be no reason to see Ford; she might sell the ranch, and then Estivar, too, would become part of the past.

YSOBEL LEANED FORWARD to stare at the speedometer. "So we are in a race." Her voice was heavy with irony. "It is news to me that they hold races on the highway."

"The speed limit is sixty-five," Estivar said. "I have to keep up with the traffic."

"You'd think we were going to something nice like a fiesta the way you're in such a hurry to arrive. Mr. Bishop has more sense. He is miles behind us, and why not? He knows there's no prize waiting at the other end."

Estivar, who'd been in a sour mood all morning, suddenly let out a harsh, brief laugh. "You could be wrong about that."

"Hush. Someone might hear you and start putting two and two together."

She was not worried about Jaime, who seemed most of the time to be stone-deaf, or about Lum Wing, whose only Spanish, as far as she knew, consisted of some dirty words and a few seldom-used amenities like *buenos dias.*

"You should be careful to guard your tongue when Dulzura is listening," Ysobel added. "She is a born gossip."

Dulzura opened her mouth in exaggerated amazement. It was not true she was a gossip, born or otherwise. She told nobody nothing, mainly because in such a godforsaken place there was nobody to tell except the people who already knew. She wondered what prize could be waiting for Mr. Bishop and how much it was worth and whether she should ask young Mrs. Osborne about it.

"The little Señora," Ysobel said more softly. "Is that what you mean by prize?"

"What else?"

"She would never marry him. He is too old."

"There isn't exactly a line-up at her door."

"Not yet. She is still by law a married woman and cultivated people are very particular about such things. Just wait, after today there will be men enough, young men, too. But she'll have none of them. She'll sell the ranch and go back to the city."

"How do you know?"

"I dreamt it last night. In color. When I went to the fortune teller in Boca de Rio, she said to pay strict attention to all dreams in color because good or bad they would come true . . . Have you been dreaming in color, Estivar?"

"No."

"Oh well, it's no matter. This is how it will be: the little Señora will sell the ranch and return to her own part of the country."

"What about me?"

"The new owner will naturally be delighted to get a foreman with nearly twenty-five years of experience."

"Was that in the dream too, about the new owner?"

"No. But maybe I didn't watch closely enough. Tonight I will keep a sharp lookout for him standing in some corner."

"If he looks like Bishop," Estivar said grimly, "wake up fast."

"Bishop has no money to buy the ranch."

"He can marry it."

"No, no, no. The Señora is sick of the place. She will go back to the city, like in my dream. I saw her walking between tall grey buildings, wearing a purple dress and flowers in her hair."

Estivar's bad mood was aggravated by the exchange with his wife. The next time Lum Wing burped, Estivar shouted at him to stop making those damned noises or get out and walk.

Lum Wing would have preferred to get out and walk, but the car didn't stop to allow him to leave, and besides, there was that ominous piece of paper in his shirt pocket, *you better show up, by God, or else* . . . The old man was well aware that he had no control over his own fate. When other people were around, they decided what he should do. It was only when he was by himself that he had choices: solitaire or chess, lime in his gin or lemon, or no gin at all but a dozen or so jimsen seeds. To ensure his privacy, and his times of choice, he had fixed up a corner of the building which was used as a mess hall when the workers were in residence. Between the stove and the cupboard he'd hung a double flannelette sheet borrowed from one of the bunks. After his day's work was done he retired to his corner to play chess with imaginary partners who were very shrewd and merciless though not quite as shrewd and merciless as Lum Wing himself.

Half of the stove used butane as fuel, the other half used wood or coal. Even on warm nights Lum Wing kept a small fire going with bits of old lumber, or limbs pruned from the trees or blown off in windstorms. He liked the busy but impersonal noise of the burning wood. It helped cover what came out of the darkness on the other side of his flannelette wall—whispers, grunts, snatches of conversation, laughter.

Lum Wing tried to ignore these common sounds of common people and to keep his mind fixed on the ivory silence of kings and queens and knights. But there were times when in spite of himself he recognized a voice in the dark, and when this happened he made tiny plugs out of pieces of paper and pushed them as far into his ears as he could. He knew curiosity killed more men than cats.

He swallowed and regurgitated another mouthful of air.

". . . probably his liver," Ysobel said. "I have been told there are many contagious diseases of the liver." She took a handkerchief out of her purse and held it tight against her nose and mouth. Her sharp voice was muffled: "Jaime! Do you hear me, Jaime? Answer your mother."

"Answer your mother, Jaime," Dulzura said obligingly. "Hey, wake up."

Jaime's eyelids twitched slightly. "I'm awake."

"Well, answer your mother."

"So I'm answering. What's she want?"

"I don't know."

"Ask her."

Dulzura leaned over the front seat. "He wants to know what do you want?"

"Tell him not to let that Chinaman breathe in his face."

"She says don't let the Chinaman breathe in your face."

"He's not breathing in my face."

"Well, if he tries, don't let him."

Jaime closed his eyes again. The old lady was getting kookier every day. Personally, he hoped he'd be lucky like Mr. Osborne and die before he got senile.

ON THE COURTHOUSE STEPS pigeons preened in the sun and walked up and down, looking important like uniformed guards. Beside one of the colonnades Devon saw her lawyer, Franklin Ford, surrounded by half a dozen men. He caught her eye, gave her a quick warning glance and turned away again. As she went past she heard him speaking in his soft slow voice, enunciating each syllable very distinctly as though he were addressing a group of foreigners or idiots:

". . . bear in mind that this is a non-adversary proceeding. It is not being opposed by an insurance company, for instance, with a large policy to pay out on Robert Osborne's life, or by a relative who's not satisfied with the disposition of Mr. Osborne's estate. The amount of Mr. Osborne's insurance is negligible, consisting of a small policy taken out by his parents when he was a child. The terms of his will are clearly stated and have not been challenged; and of his survivors, his wife petitioned the court for this hearing and his mother concurred. So our purpose in today's hearing is to establish the fact of Robert Osborne's death and to prove as conclusively as possible how and why and when and where it occurred. Nobody has been accused, nobody is on trial."

As Devon went into the building she wondered which came closer to the truth, Ford's "Nobody is on trial," or Agnes Osborne's "Of course we are on trial, all of us."

The door of courtroom number five was open and the spectators' benches were nearly full. On the right side near the windows Agnes Osborne sat by herself. She wore a blue hat that perched like a jay on her careful blonde curls, and a ribbon knit dress the same dark grey as her eyes. If she felt that she was on trial, she gave no sign of it. Her face was expressionless except for one corner of her mouth fixed in a half-smile, as though she was mildly, even a little contemptuously, amused by the situation and the company she found herself in. It was her public face. Her private one was uncertain, disordered, often blotched with tears and mottled with rage.

She watched Devon walk toward her down the aisle, thinking how incongruous she looked in this place of violence and death. Devon should still be wandering around the halls of some college with other nice mousy girls and earnest pimply boys. *I must be kinder to her, I must try harder to like her. It's my fault she's here.*

Mrs. Osborne had thought that if she sent Robert away from the ranch for a couple of months, the scandal about Ruth Bishop's death would blow over. It was a double error. His absence merely intensified the gossip, and when he returned he brought Devon with him as his wife. Agnes was shocked and hurt. She wanted her son to get married eventually, of course, but not at twenty-three, not to this odd little creature from another part of the world. *"Robert, why? Why did you do it?" "Why not? The girl loves me, she thinks I'm great. How about that!"*

Devon leaned over and the two women touched cheeks briefly. There was an air of finality about the cool embrace, as if both of them knew it would be one of the last.

AT THE BACK OF THE COURTROOM, sitting between his father and Dulzura, Jaime was like a patient coming out of an anesthetic and discovering that his moving parts could still move. He did a couple of secret isometric exercises, cleared his throat, hummed a few bars of a TV commercial—"Shut up," Estivar said—stuck another piece of gum in his mouth, pulled up his socks, cracked his knuckles—"Stop that!"—scratched his ear, rubbed one side of his jaw, pushed the greasy stump of a comb through his hair—"For God's sake, sit still, will you?"

Jaime crossed his arms over his chest and sat still except for the swinging of a foot against the bench in front and the practically inaudible grinding of his teeth. The scene was different from what he'd expected. He'd thought there would be a lot of fuzz hanging around. But in the whole courtroom only one cop was in sight, an old guy of thirty-five having a drink at the water cooler.

The judge's bench and the jury box were both empty. Between them a large drawing had been set up on an easel. Even by narrowing his eyes to slits and using all his powers of concentration, Jaime couldn't make out the contents of the drawing. Maybe it was left over from yesterday or last week and had nothing to do with Mr. Osborne. In spite of the cool act Jaime put on for his friends and the somnolent pose he assumed within the family circle, he still had the lively curiosity of a child.

He whispered to Dulzura, "Hey, move over so I can get out."

"Where you going?"

"Out, is all."

"You can get past."

"I can't. You're too fat."

"You're one fresh little big-mouth kid," Dulzura said and heaved herself up and into the aisle.

Casually, hands in pockets, Jaime walked to the front of the courtroom and sat down in the first row of benches. The cop had turned away from the water cooler and was watching him as though he suspected Jaime might pull a caper. Jaime tried to look like the kind of guy who could pull a caper if he wanted to but didn't feel like it at the moment.

The drawing on the easel was a map. What had appeared from the back of the room to be a road was the riverbed which marked the east and southeast boundaries of the ranch. The little triangles were trees, indicating the lemon orchard on the west, on the northeast the avocado grove, and on the north the rows of date palms with grapefruit growing in the shade between. The circle showed the location of the reservoir; and the rectangles, each of them lettered, were buildings: the ranch house itself, the mess hall, the bunkhouse and storage sheds, the garage for all the mechanized equipment and, on the other side of the garage, the house where Jaime lived with his family.

"Are you looking for something, fellow?" the cop said.

"No. I mean, no, sir. I was just studying the map. It shows where I live. The square marked C, that's my house."

"No kidding."

"I'm a witness in the case."

"Is that a fact."

"I was driving the tractor when suddenly I looked down on the ground and there was this knife lying there."

"Well, well, well. You'd better go back to your seat. The judge is coming in and he likes things tidy."

"Don't you want to know what kind of knife it was?"

"I can wait. I have to sit through the whole thing anyway, I'm the bailiff."

The clerk of the court, a young man wearing horn-rimmed glasses and a blue serge suit, got up and made the first of his four daily announcements: "Superior Court of the State of California in and for the County of San Diego is now in session, Judge Porter Gallagher presiding. Please be seated."

The clerk took his place at the table he shared with the bailiff. The hearing of probate petitions was usually the dullest of all judicial procedures, but this one promised to be different. Before putting it aside to file, he read part of the petition again.

> In the Matter of the Estate of Robert Kirkpatrick Osborne, Deceased, the petition of Devon Suellen Osborne respectfully shows:
>
> That she is the surviving wife of Robert Osborne.
>
> That Petitioner is informed and believes and upon such information and belief alleges that Robert Osborne is dead. The precise time of his death is not known, but Petitioner believes and therefore alleges that Robert Osborne died on the thirteenth day of October, 1967. The facts upon which the death of Robert Osborne is presumed are as follows:
>
> The Petitioner and her husband, Robert Osborne, lived together as husband and wife for approximately half a year. On the night of October 13, Robert Osborne, after dining with his wife, left the ranch house to look for his dog, which had wandered off in the course of the evening. When Robert Osborne failed to return by half past nine, Mrs. Robert Osborne roused the foreman of the ranch and a search was organized. It was the first of many searches covering a period of many months and an area of hundreds of square miles. Evidence has been collected which proves beyond a reasonable doubt that between 8:30 and 9:30 o'clock on the night of October 13, 1967, Robert Osborne met his death at the hands of two or more persons . . .

3

JUDGE GALLAGHER tugged impatiently at the collar of his black judicial robe. Even after fifteen years on the bench he still dreaded this moment when he walked into the courtroom and people stared up at him as if they expected the robe to endow him with magic qualities like Batman's cape. Occasionally, when he caught a particularly anxious eye, he wanted to take time out to explain that the robe was merely a piece of cloth covering a business suit, a drip-dry shirt and an ordinary man who couldn't perform miracles no matter how badly they were needed.

Gallagher looked around the room, noting with surprise that the only empty seats were those in the jury box. To his knowledge there'd been no publicity about the hearing except the legal notices in the newspapers. Perhaps the legal notices had a larger public than he imagined. More likely, though, some of the people were drop-ins who had no real interest in the case: the lady shopper resting her feet between sales; the young marine who seemed to be suffering from a hangover; a small group of high school students with notebooks and clipboards; a teen-aged girl, thin as a reed, carrying a sleeping baby and wearing a blonde wig and sunglasses as big as saucers.

Some of the spectators were courtroom regulars who came for the excitement and because they had nowhere else to go. A middle-aged German woman knitted with speed and equanimity through embezzlement trials, divorces, armed robberies and rapes. A pair of elderly pensioners, one man on crutches, the other carrying a white cane, appeared even in the worst weather to sit through the dullest cases. They carried sandwiches in their pockets and at noon they would eat outside on the steps, feeding the crusts to the pigeons. To Gallagher, looking down on them from the windows of his chambers, it seemed a very good way to spend the noon hour.

Even without years of practice it would have been easy for Gallagher to pick out the people closely connected with the case: Osborne's wife and mother pretending to be cool in the heat of the morning; some leather-faced ranchers looking out of place and uneasy in their city clothes; the ex-policeman, Valenzuela, almost unrecognizable in a natty striped suit and orange tie; and sitting at the counsels' table, Mrs. Osborne's lawyer, Ford, a soft-spoken, gentle-mannered man with a ferocious temper that had cost him hundreds of dollars in contempt fines.

"Are you ready, Mr. Ford?"

"Yes, your Honor."

"Then go ahead."

"This is a proceeding to establish the death of Robert Kirkpatrick Osborne. In support of the allegations contained in the petition of Devon Suellen Osborne, I intend to submit a considerable amount of evidence. I beg the indulgence of the court in the manner of submitting this evidence.

"Your Honor, the body of Robert Osborne has not been found. Under California law, death is a rebuttable presumption after an absence of seven years. The presumption of death before this seven-year period has passed requires circumstantial evidence to show first, the fact of death, i.e., there must be enough evidence from which a reasonable conclusion can be reached that death has occurred; and second, that absence from any cause other than death is inconsistent with the nature of the person absent.

"The following quote is from the People versus L. Ewing Scott: Any evidence, facts or circumstances concerning the alleged deceased, relating to the character, long absence without communicating with friends or relatives, habits, condition, affections, attachments, prosperity and objects in life which usually control the conduct of a person and are the motive of such person's actions, and the absence of any evidence to show the motive or cause for the abandonment of home, family or friends or wealth by the alleged deceased, are competent evidence from which may be inferred the death of one absent or unheard from, whatever has been the duration or shortness of such absence. Unquote.

"We intend to show, your Honor, that Robert Osborne was a young man of twenty-four, mentally and physically well-endowed, happily married and the owner of a prospering ranch; that his relationship with his family, friends and neighbors was pleasant, that he was enjoying life and looking forward to the future.

"If we could follow any man around on any particular day of his life, we would find out a great deal about him, his character, the state of his health, his mind, his finances, his interests, hobbies, plans, ambitions. I can think of no better way of presenting a true picture of Robert Osborne than to reconstruct, as completely as I am able, his final day. Bear with me, your Honor, if I elicit from witnesses details that are seemingly irrelevant, and opinions, suppositions and conclusions that would not be admissible evidence in an adversary proceeding.

"The final day was October thirteen, 1967. It started on the Yerba Buena ranch, where Robert Osborne was born and where he lived most of his life. The weather was very warm, as it had been since early spring, and the river was dry. A late crop of tomatoes was being harvested and crated for shipping, and the picking of dates was scheduled to begin. The ranch was a busy place and Robert Osborne a busy young man.

"On October thirteen he awoke before dawn as usual and began his preparations for the day. While he was in the shower his wife, Devon, also awoke but she didn't get up. She was in the early stage of a difficult pregnancy and under doctor's orders to stay as quiet as possible . . . I would like to call as my first witness Devon Suellen Osborne."

The courtroom stirred, rustled, whispered, shifted its weight. Then everything was suddenly quiet again as Devon walked toward the stand. *"Do you swear . . . ?"* She swore, her raised right hand steady, her voice flat. Ford could scarcely remember the wild weeping girl of a year ago.

"Would you state your name for the record, please?"

"Devon Suellen Osborne."

"And where do you live?"

"Rancho Yerba Buena, Rural Route number two."

"Displayed on the easel is a map. Have you seen it before?"

"Yes, in your office."

"And you had a chance to study it?"

"Yes."

"Is it a true representation of a portion of the property known as Rancho Yerba Buena?"

"To my knowledge it is."

"Do you own any portion of Rancho Yerba Buena, Mrs. Osborne?"

"No. The deed has been in my husband's name since he was twenty-one."

"During the early part of Mr. Osborne's absence, how was the ranch business carried on?"

"It wasn't. Bills piled up, checks came in which couldn't be cashed, purchases were at a standstill. That's when I went to you for help."

Ford turned to Judge Gallagher. "Your Honor, I advised Mrs. Osborne to wait until ninety days had elapsed from the time her husband had last been seen and then appeal to the court to appoint her as trustee of the missing man's estate. The appointment was granted, Mrs. Osborne was bonded, as required, and through my office made periodic accountings to the court of receipts and disbursements and the like."

"And that is your present position, Mrs. Osborne," Gallagher said, "trustee of the estate?"

"Yes, your Honor."

"Continue, Mr. Ford."

Ford went over to the map and pointed to the small rectangle bearing the letter O. "Is this the ranch house, Mrs. Osborne?"

"Yes."

"And it was here that you saw your husband before sunrise on October thirteen last year?"

"Yes."

"Did any conversation take place at that time?"

"Nothing important."

"In the reconstruction of a man's final day it is difficult to say what's important and what isn't. Tell us the things you remember, Mrs. Osborne."

"It was still dark. I woke up when Robert came out of the shower and turned on the bureau lamp. He asked me how I felt and I said fine. While he was getting dressed we talked about various matters."

440

"Was there anything unusual about the way he dressed that morning?"

"He put on slacks and a sports jacket instead of his working clothes because he was driving into the city."

"This city, San Diego?"

"Yes."

"Would you describe the slacks and jacket, Mrs. Osborne?"

"The slacks were lightweight grey gabardine and the jacket was grey and black dacron in a small plaid pattern."

"Why was he driving into San Diego?"

"A number of reasons. In the morning he had a dental appointment, and after that he was going to drop in and see his mother and then pick up a tennis racket he'd ordered, one of the new kind made of steel. I reminded him too that it was Dulzura's birthday—she is our cook—and that he should buy her a present."

"Did he, in fact, do all of these things?"

"Except the present, he forgot that."

"Wasn't there a luncheon meeting at noon which he was expected to attend?"

"Yes."

"Do you know what the meeting was about?"

"It concerned problems of migrant labor in California agriculture."

"Did he go to the meeting?"

"Yes. Robert had the idea that the problem must be solved at the source, the crops themselves. If crops could be regulated chemically, such as by hormones, perhaps harvesting could become a twelve-month-a-year business which would give steady employment to agricultural workers and do away entirely with migrant labor."

"Now, Mrs. Osborne, that morning after your husband finished dressing, what did he do?"

"He kissed me goodbye and told me he'd be home for dinner about seven-thirty. He also asked me to keep a sharp lookout for his spaniel, Maxie, who'd taken off the night before. I thought Maxie had caught the scent of a bitch in heat and gone to find her, but Robert suspected something more sinister might be involved."

"Such as?"

"He didn't say. But Maxie was never allowed near the bunkhouse or the mess hall, and at night he was kept inside the house."

"Was this for the dog's protection or yours?"

"Both. At certain times of the year there were quite a few strangers around the ranch. Maxie was our watchdog and we were—well, I guess you could call us his watchpeople."

At the unusual word a little hum of laughter vibrated through the courtroom and bounced gently off the walls.

"The dog, then," Ford continued, "was not friendly toward any of the workers on the ranch?"

"No."

"In the event of an attack on your husband, do you think the dog would have gone to his defense?"

"I know he would."

Ford sat down at the counsels' table and spread his hands in front of him, palms up, as if he intended to read in their lines the past as well as the future. "When and where were you and Robert Osborne married?"

"April twenty-fourth, 1967, in Manhattan."

"How old was Mr. Osborne at that time?"

"Twenty-three."

"Had you known him long?"

"Two weeks."

"Since you were willing to marry him after so brief an acquaintance, I must assume he made a considerable impression on you."

"Yes."

A considerable impression.

They had met at a Saturday afternoon concert at the Philharmonic. Devon arrived during the opening number and slipped quietly and apologetically into her seat. As her eyes gradually adjusted to the darkness she became aware that the seat on her left was occupied by a large young man with fair hair and horn-rimmed glasses. Every minute or two he turned to stare at her and at intermission he followed her into the lobby. She wasn't used to such uninvited attention and it made her a little uneasy and more than a little curious. The young man gave the impression of having walked into the concert hall either by mistake or because someone had given him a ticket and he didn't want to waste it.

She was the first to speak. "Why are you staring at me?"

"Was I staring?"

"You still are."

"Sorry." His smile was shy, almost melancholy. "I guess I can't help it. You remind me of someone back home."

"Someone nice, I hope."

"She used to be."

"Isn't she nice anymore?"

"No."

"Why not?"

"She's dead." After a moment's hesitation he added, "A lot of people think I killed her. I didn't, but when people want to believe something, it's hard to stop them."

Now it was Devon who stared, and a pulse began to beat rapidly in the back of her head like a warning signal. "You shouldn't go around saying things like that to strangers."

"I never did before. I wish you'd—"

But she had already started to walk away.

"Please wait," he said. "Did I frighten you? I'm sorry. It was a dumb thing to do. It's just that I haven't talked to anyone since I came to town and you looked nice and gentle like Ruth."

Her name was Ruth, Devon thought. *She looked nice and gentle and a lot of people think this young man killed her and maybe he did.*

"I'm sorry I frightened you," he said. "Wait just a minute, will you?"

She turned to face him. "Appearances are deceiving. I'm not very nice and not at all gentle, so you'd better forget whatever you had in mind."

"But—"

"And I suggest that for the balance of the concert you go and sit somewhere else."

"All right."

For the next hour the seat beside her remained empty. She wanted to look around to see if he was sitting anywhere nearby but she forced herself to keep her eyes on the stage and to concentrate on the music, applauding when other people applauded.

After the concert he was waiting for her in the lobby. "Miss? Would you let me talk to you for a minute? I've been thinking over what a stupid thing I did. It's no wonder you were scared."

"I wasn't scared. I was annoyed."

"I'm sorry. My only excuse is that I felt I should be honest with you right from the start."

"There hasn't been a start," she said. "Nothing has started. Now if you'll—"

"My name is Robert Osborne, Robert Kirkpatrick Osborne. What's yours?"

"Devon Suellen Smith."

"I like that. It's pretty."

While she explained that her parents wanted something different to make up for the "Smith," she became aware that she'd been wrong and the young man right: there was a start.

It continued through coffee and éclairs at Schrafft's, and the next morning they met for a walk in Central Park. It was the first warm Sunday of the year. There must have been people everywhere in the park, but the only one Devon could remember seeing was Robert as he strode across the grass toward her, his pockets bulging with peanuts he'd bought to feed the squirrels. He told her about his ranch in California, which was really a farm, and about the squirrels on it that lived in holes in the ground instead of trees. He talked about Maxie, the spaniel; about his father, who had died years ago in a fall off a tractor; about the land, which was irrigated desert, and the crazy river that was either flooding or bone-dry. By the end of the day Devon knew that her life had changed abruptly and would never be the same again.

". . . please respond to the question, Mrs. Osborne?"

"I'm sorry, I didn't hear it."

"Was your husband a big man?"

"Six feet one and about a hundred and seventy pounds."

"He was in good health?"

"Yes."

"Active and strong?"

"Yes."

"Did he have any physical disabilities? For instance, did he wear glasses?"

"Yes."

"What kind?"

"To correct his short-sightedness—I think myopia is the right word."

"Did he have more than one pair?"

"Yes. Besides his ordinary horn-rimmed glasses he had prescription sunglasses which he used especially while driving. During the early part of the summer he'd been fitted with contact lenses, and he wore them for tennis and swimming and other times when his ordinary glasses would have been a nuisance."

"These contact lenses were prescribed and fitted by an ophthalmologist?"

"Yes."

"Do you happen to recall his name?"

"Dr. Jarrett."

"Where is his office?"

"Here in San Diego."

Ford consulted some notes on the table in front of him. "Now, Mrs. Osborne, you stated that one of your husband's reasons for driving to the city was to pick up a new tennis racket he'd ordered. Did he actually try the racket out during the afternoon?"

"Yes. He played several sets on one of the courts in Balboa Park."

"Did he wear his contact lenses?"

"Yes."

"Are you certain of this?"

"I'm certain that he was wearing them when he got home."

"Did he continue to wear them through dinner?"

"Yes."

"And after dinner when he went out looking for the dog, Maxie, was he still wearing the contact lenses?"

"Yes."

"Who has these lenses at the present time, Mrs. Osborne?"

"The police."

"What about his prescription sunglasses—where are they now?"

"In the glove compartment of his car."

"Where he left them?"

"Yes."

"What about his ordinary horn-rimmed glasses? Where are they now?"

"I don't know."

"You mean they were lost or misplaced?"

"Neither."

"When was the last time you saw them, Mrs. Osborne?"

"Three weeks ago. If you want the exact time it was the day you phoned to tell me this hearing had been scheduled. My husband's glasses were among other things of his which I packed in cartons. I intended to store the cartons in the attic. Then I realized that this would be merely postponing the inevitable, so I decided to give the stuff to the Salvation Army in the hope that some use could be made of it. I know Robert would have approved."

"Did you deliver it to the Salvation Army yourself?"

"No. Mrs. Osborne, Robert's mother, offered to do it."

"When you were packing those cartons, were you pretty sure what the outcome of today's hearing would be?"

"I was sure my husband was dead. I'd been sure for a long time."

"Why?"

"Nothing would keep Robert from getting in touch with me if he were alive."

"You were happily married?"

"Yes."

"And expecting a child?"

"Yes."

"Did you carry the child to term, Mrs. Osborne?"

"No."

SHE REMEMBERED THE TRIP to the hospital in the back of Estivar's station wagon, with Dulzura beside her, strangely silent and dignified, and a police car clearing the way, its siren screaming. It took a long time to come home from the hospital. Autumn was nearly over, the migrants were gone, the crops harvested.

The return trip was quieter. There was no police escort. She rode in a taxicab instead of the station wagon, with Agnes Osborne beside her instead of Dulzura. Mrs. Osborne talked to her in a flat, low-pitched voice which gave no indication that the loss of the child was a more severe blow to her than it was to Devon. For Devon there would be other chances, for Mrs. Osborne it was the end of the line. She told Devon what to do, sounding as though she were reading off a list she'd written down in a corner of her mind: get lots of sleep and fresh air, avoid worry, be brave, exercise, replace Dulzura with a more responsible person, take up a hobby, eat plenty of protein . . .

". . . attention to me, Devon?"

"Yes."

"We'd probably be wise to ignore Christmas this year, it's such an emotional occasion anyway. Perhaps you'd enjoy going off on a little holiday by yourself. Don't you have an aunt in Buffalo?"

"Please stop bothering about me."

"I hate the thought of you staying alone at the ranch. It's not safe. Dulzura is unreliable, you should be aware of that by now."

"I know she drinks a little bit now and then."

"She drinks a whole lot and whenever she can get her hands on the stuff. As for Estivar, how can we really tell whose side he'd be on in an emergency? He's learned English and the ranching business and a few manners in the last twenty-five years, but he's just as Mexican now as when he crossed the border—What happened to your aunt in Buffalo?"

"She died."

"Everyone's dying. Oh God, I can't stand it. Everyone's dying . . ."

FORD GOT UP, walked slowly around the end of the counsels' table and stood leaning against the railing of the empty jury box. The move was deliberate, to give Devon a chance to compose herself.

"Mrs. Osborne, you stated previously that before your husband left the house on the morning of October thirteen he told you he'd be back for dinner at seven-thirty. Did he come back by seven-thirty?"

"Yes."

"And you had dinner together."

"Yes."

"Was it a pleasant meal?"

"Yes."

"And when it was over, Mr. Osborne went outside to try and find the dog, Maxie."

"Yes."

"What time was that?"

"Eight-thirty, approximately."

"After he left the house, what did you do?"

"A new record album had arrived in the mail that day and I played it."

"How big an album?"

"Three records, six sides."

"What kind of music was it?"

"Symphonic."

"In most symphonies there are soft passages which require the volume to be turned up quite high if they are to be heard properly. Was the volume turned up high, Mrs. Osborne?"

"Yes."

"This would make the louder passages very loud, would it not?"

"Yes."

"Where in the ranch house was the stereo equipment installed?"

"The main living room."

"And that's where you sat and listened to the album?"

"Yes, but I didn't just sit. I walked around, did some dusting and straightening up, glanced at the evening paper."

"Were the windows closed or open?"

"Closed. It was a hot night and the house stayed cooler when it was shut up."

"What about the drapes?"

"I opened them after the sun went down."

"What direction do the windows in the living room face?"

"East and south."

"What do you see from the windows facing east?"

"In the daytime I can see the riverbed and, on the other side of it, the ranch belonging to Leo Bishop."

"And at night?"

"Nothing."

"Is there a view from the windows facing south?"

"You can see Tijuana in the distance both night and day."

"What about the blacktop road leading into the ranch, is this visible from the main living room?"

"No. It's west of the ranch house. You can see it from the study and the kitchen and a couple of the bedrooms upstairs."

"But not from the living room where you were sitting listening to music."

"Not from there, no."

Ford went back to the counsels' table and sat down. "As time passed and your husband remained absent, did you begin to worry, Mrs. Osborne?"

"I tried to tell myself there was nothing to worry about, that Robert had been born on the ranch and knew every inch of it. But around nine forty-five I decided to check the garage to see if maybe Robert had taken the car to search for Maxie instead of going on foot as he usually did. I turned on the outside floodlights from the kitchen. Dulzura was in her room adjoining the kitchen, I could hear the radio playing."

"Did you find the garage door unlocked?"

"Yes."

"Was Mr. Osborne's car in the garage?"

"Yes."

"What did you do then, Mrs. Osborne?"

"I went back in the house and telephoned Mr. Estivar."

"The foreman?"

"Yes. His cottage is on the other side of the reservoir."

"Did he answer immediately?"

"No. He goes to bed around nine and it was almost ten by this time. But I let the phone keep ringing until he woke up and answered. I told him Robert was missing, and he said I was to stay in the house with all the doors and windows locked while he and Cruz made a search with the jeep."

"Cruz?"

"Estivar's oldest son. He had a jeep with a searchlight on it."

"Did you do as Mr. Estivar suggested?"

"Yes. I waited in the kitchen by the window. I could see the lights of the jeep as it went up and down the little dirt roads that crisscross the ranch."

"Did you notice any other signs of activity, any vehicles in motion, any people, any lights?"

"No."

"Is it possible to see the mess hall and the bunkhouse from any of the windows of the ranch house?"

"No. A row of tamarisk trees shields the main house from the men's quarters."

"How long did you wait in the kitchen, Mrs. Osborne?"

"Until a quarter to eleven, about forty-five minutes."

"Then what happened?"

"Mr. Estivar came to the door."

"Was he alone?"

"Yes."

"What did he say to you?"

"He said we'd better notify the police."

"And did you?"

"Mr. Estivar called the sheriff's office in Boca de Rio."

"The sheriff's men arrived when, Mrs. Osborne?"

"Shortly after eleven o'clock. The man in charge was Mr. Valenzuela. The other man was younger, I don't recall his name, but he was the one who found all the—the blood in the mess hall."

"Were you informed of his discovery?"

"Not directly. Mr. Valenzuela came back to the ranch house about eleven-thirty and asked if he could use the phone to call the sheriff's office in San Diego. I overheard him say that a great deal of blood had been found and it looked like the result of a homicide."

"What did you do then, Mrs. Osborne?"

"Dulzura was up by that time. She made a pot of coffee and I think I drank some. Pretty soon I heard a siren. I'd never heard a siren on the ranch before, it's always so quiet late at night. I looked out the kitchen window and saw several cars moving along the road and red lights flashing."

IN ADDITION TO THE SIREN there was the sound of Dulzura praying in Spanish, very loudly, as though she had a bad connection. Then suddenly the cuckoo clock above the stove began striking midnight, a mocking reminder that Robert had been gone for three and a half hours and it might be too late for prayers or policemen.

Devon went into the study, closing the door behind her to shut out some of the noise. For the first time she became physically aware of the child in her womb. It felt heavy and inert as a marble cherub.

She dialed the number of Agnes Osborne's house in San Diego. Mrs. Osborne answered on the third ring, sounding a little annoyed, as though she'd been watching a late show on TV and didn't like being interrupted by a wrong number.

"Mother?"

"Is that you, Devon? Why aren't you in bed at this hour? The doctor told you—"

"I think something's happened to Robert."

"—get plenty of sleep. What did you say?"

"The police are here now searching for him. He went out to look for Maxie and he hasn't come back and there's blood in the mess hall, a lot of blood."

There was a long silence, then Mrs. Osborne's voice again, stubbornly cheerful. "It's not the first time blood's been found in the mess hall. Why, I can remember a dozen brawls in there, three or four of them quite serious. The men frequently quarrel among themselves, and of course they all carry knives. Are you listening to me, Devon?"

"Yes."

"What probably happened is this: while Robert was out looking for the dog he heard a fight going on in the mess hall and went in to investigate. Perhaps one of the men was badly injured and Robert had to drive him into Boca de Rio to a doctor."

"No."

"What do you mean, *no?*"

"He didn't drive anywhere. His car's here."

There was another long pause. Then, "I'll come right out. For the baby's sake, don't get overexcited. I'm sure there's a perfectly logical explanation and Robert will be quite amused when he learns that the police were looking for him. Do you have any tranquilizers to take?"

"No."

"I'll bring some with me."

"I don't want any." There was no need to tranquilize the stone mother of a marble cherub . . ."

". . . ANY MORE QUESTIONS at this time," Ford was saying. "You are excused for now, Mrs. Osborne."

He watched with interest as she stepped down from the witness stand and went back to her place in the spectators' benches. Long experience in probate work had taught Ford to be suspicious of meek little women. They had a tendency to inherit if not the earth, at least some large chunks of worldly goods.

"Call Mr. Secundo Estivar."

4

FORD SAID, "Please state your full name for the record."

"Secundo Alvino Juan Estivar."

"And your address?"

"Rancho Yerba Buena."

"That is the area depicted on the map to your left?"

"Yes, sir."

"You're employed there?"

"Yes."

"In what capacity?"

"Foreman."

"You're responsible for the operation of the ranch?"

"The court appointed young Mrs. Osborne boss during Mr. Osborne's absence. I take orders from her. If there are no such orders, I do the best I can without them." A suffusion of scarlet spread across Estivar's cheeks and into the whites of his eyes. "When the ranch makes money, I don't claim any credit; when there's a robbery and a murder, I'm not about to take the blame."

"No one is putting the blame on you."

"Not in words. But I can smell it a mile away, so I think I'd better clear something up right now. I hire people in good faith. If it turns out their names and addresses are phony and their papers forged, that's not my fault. I'm not a cop. How can I tell whether papers are forged or not?"

"Kindly simmer down, Mr. Estivar."

"I'm in the hot seat, it's not so easy to simmer down."

"Suppose you try," Ford said. "A couple of weeks ago, when you and I discussed your appearance here as a witness, I told you this proceeding is to establish the fact that a death has occurred, not to hold anyone responsible for the death."

"You told me that. But—"

"Then please bear it in mind, will you?"

"Yes."

"When did you first arrive at the Osborne ranch, Mr. Estivar?"

"In 1943."

"From where?"

"A little village near Empalme."

"And where is Empalme?"

"In Sonora, Mexico."

"Were you carrying border-crossing papers?"

"No."

"Did you have any trouble finding employment without such papers?"

"No. There was a war on. Growers needed help, they couldn't afford to bother about little things like immigration laws. Hundreds of Mexicans like me walked across that border every week and found jobs."

"A lot of them are still doing it, are they not?"

"Yes."

"In fact, there's a profitable underground business in Mexico which consists of supplying such men with forged papers and transportation."

"So I've heard."

"We'll go into this subject more thoroughly a little later in the hearing," Ford said. "Who hired you to work on the Osborne ranch in 1943?"

"Robert Osborne's father, John."

"Have you worked there steadily since then?"

"Yes, sir."

"So your relationship with Robert Osborne goes back a long time."

"To the day he was born."

"Was it a close relationship?"

"From the time he could walk he followed me around like a pup. I saw more of him than I did my own kids. He called me Tío—uncle."

"Did this relationship continue throughout his life?"

"No. The summer he was fifteen his father was killed in an accident, and things changed after that. For all of us, I guess, but especially for the boy. In the fall he was sent off to a prep school in Arizona. His mother thought he needed the influence of men—she meant white men." Estivar glanced briefly at Agnes Osborne as though he expected her to issue a public denial. But she had turned her head away and was looking out the window at a patch of sky. "He stayed at the school two years. When he returned he wasn't a kid anymore tagging along behind me asking questions or coming over to my house for meals. He was the boss and I was the hired man. And that's the way it stayed until the day he died."

"Was there any ill-will between Mr. Osborne and yourself?"

"We disagreed once in a while, about business, nothing personal. We had nothing personal between us anymore, just the ranch. We both wanted to operate the ranch as profitably as we could, which meant that sometimes I had to take orders I didn't like and Mr. Osborne had to accept advice he didn't want."

"Would you say there was mutual respect between you?"

"No, sir. Mutual interest. Mr. Osborne had no respect for me or any other members of my race. It was that school she sent—he was sent to. That's what changed him. It taught him prejudice. I was used to prejudice, I'd learned to live with it. But how could I explain to my sons that their friend Robbie didn't exist anymore? I didn't know the reason. I thought many times of asking her—his mother— but I never did. After he died it bothered me that I didn't try harder to find out why he'd changed, maybe talked it over with him like in the old days. Deep down I kind of expected that eventually he'd tell me all about it on his own and I shouldn't try to hurry it because there was lots of time. But there wasn't."

Estivar stopped to wipe the beads of sweat off his forehead. A hush had fallen over the courtroom, as if each person in it were straining to hear the sound of time running out, the slow drag of the minutes, the quick tick of years. Ford said, "On the morning of October thirteen,1967, did you see Robert Osborne?"

"Yes, sir."

"What were the circumstances?"

"Very early, while it was still dark, I heard him whistling for his dog, Maxie. About half an hour later my wife and I were eating our breakfast when Mr. Osborne came to the back door and asked me to step outside. He sounded upset and mad, so I got out there fast as I could. The dog was lying on the ground with froth all around its mouth and its eyes kind of dazed-looking, like it might have been hit on the head or something."

"You stated that Mr. Osborne was 'upset and mad.'"

"Yes, sir. He said, 'Some filthy so-and-so around here poisoned my dog.' Only he didn't say 'so-and-so,' he used a very insulting term meaning the lowest kind of Mexican. For myself, I don't care about names. But my family heard it, my wife and my younger children who were still at the breakfast table. I ordered Mr. Osborne to go away and to stay away until he had his temper under control."

"Did he do so?"

"Yes, sir. He picked the dog up in his arms and left."

"Did you see Mr. Osborne again later?"

Estivar rubbed the back of his hand across his mouth. "No."

"Will you please speak louder?"

"That was the last time I saw him, heading for the ranch house with the dog in his arms. The last words we spoke to each other were in anger. It weighs heavy on me, that goodbye."

"I'm sure it does. Still, it was not your fault."

"Some of it was. I knew how much the little dog meant to him. It had been a present years ago from someone who—from a friend."

Ford began pacing up and down in front of the empty jury box, partly from habit, partly from impatience. "Now, Mr. Estivar, it is not my intention during this hearing to explore the complicated subject of migrant labor in California agriculture. We must, however, establish certain facts which affect the case, bearing in mind that you, as foreman, are caught in the middle of the problem. On the one hand you represent the growers whose business it is to market the crops for a profit. On the other hand you are aware that the present system—or lack of system—encourages the breaking of laws on the part of Mexican nationals, and the exploitation of these nationals on the part of the growers. Is that a fair statement of your situation, Mr. Estivar?"

"Fair enough, I guess."

"All right, we'll proceed. In the late summer and early fall of 1967, who was employed at the Osborne ranch besides yourself?"

"In August my three oldest sons were there, Cruz, Rufo and Felipe. My cousin, Dulzura Gonzales, acted as the Osbornes' housekeeper, and my youngest boy, Jaime, worked several hours a day. We employed half a dozen border-crossers, Mexican citizens with permits that allowed them to cross the border every day and work on ranches within commuting distance. We also had a part-time mechanic who came out from Boca de Rio to service the machinery."

"That was in August, you said."

"Yes, sir."

"Were you using any migrant labor at the time?"

"No. We couldn't get any. The grape strike was going on up in Delano and Mexican nationals were being used as strikebreakers. A lot of them were lured away from this area by the promise of higher wages in the vineyards up north; the rest were taken by the larger growers. The Osborne ranch is a comparatively small family operation."

"What happened in September with regard to this operation?"

"Plenty, all of it bad. My second son, Rufo, got married and went to live in Salinas so his wife could be near her family. My third son, Felipe, left to try and find employment in another line. I lost even Jaime, because school started and he could only help on Saturdays. The border-crossers had their minibus stolen off a street in Tijuana and couldn't come to work without transportation. By the end of the month only Cruz, my oldest son, was still with me working full-time. We were putting in sixteen-hour days until that old G.M. truck arrived with the men in it."

"You're referring to the men you subsequently hired to harvest tomatoes and dates."

"'Subsequently' makes it sound like I sat around thinking about it first. I didn't. I hired them as soon as they could pile out of the truck. Then I phoned Lum Wing at his daughter's place in Boca de Rio and told him he had a job cooking for a new crew."

"How many men were in this crew, Mr. Estivar?"

"Ten."

"Were they strangers to you?"

"Yes."

"They were not, as far as you knew, wetbacks or *alambres*."

"No. They were *viseros*, Mexican nationals registered as farm hands with visas that allowed them to work in this country. Anglos usually called them green-carders because the visas are in the form of green cards."

"Did the crew present their visas, or green cards, to you?"

"Yes."

"What did you do then?"

"I told the men they were hired and entered their names and addresses in my books. My son, Cruz, showed them where they were to eat and sleep and store their gear."

"Did they have much gear?"

"Migrants travel light," Estivar said. "They live light."

"Did you examine the visas carefully when they were presented to you?"

"I looked at them. Like I mentioned before, I'm not a cop, there's no way for me to tell by looking at a visa whether it's genuine or not. If I hadn't hired those men they'd have just gone over to Mr. Bishop's place across the river or to the Polks' ranch east of that. All the small growers were desperate for help because of the *huelga*, the grape strike, and because it was the height of the harvesting season."

"Did the crew have a leader?"

"I'm not sure you could call him a leader exactly, but the man who drove the truck did most of the talking."

"You said it was an old G.M. truck."

"Yes."

"How old?"

"Very. It was burning so much oil it looked like a smokestack."

"Who owned the truck?"

"I don't know."

"Didn't you check the vehicle registration?"

"No."

"Why not?"

"I never thought of it. Why should I? If you drove up to the ranch and asked for a job picking tomatoes, I wouldn't check your car registration."

Ford raised a quizzical eyebrow. "Would you give me a job, Mr. Estivar?"

"I might. But you wouldn't last." There was a burst of laughter from the spectators. Estivar did not join in. Color had spread across his face again except for a thin white line around his mouth. "You're too tall. Tall men have a rough time doing stoop labor."

"What day was it when the crew arrived at the ranch in the old G.M. truck?"

"September twenty-eighth, a Thursday."

"So that by the time Robert Osborne disappeared, October thirteen, the men had been working at the ranch for two weeks."

"Yes, sir."

"Did you get to know any of them personally?"

"I don't run a social club."

"Still, it's possible that one or two of the men might have told you about their wives and families back home, things like that."

"It may be possible but it didn't happen. The men were paid by the lug. They didn't want to talk any more than I wanted to listen."

"How often were they paid, Mr. Estivar?"

"Once a week, same as all the other crews."

"On what day?"

"Friday. Mr. Osborne wrote the checks on Thursday night and I handed them out in the mess hall while the men were having breakfast."

"What did they do after work on payday?"

"I don't know for sure."

"Well, what do crews usually do?"

"They go into Boca de Rio and cash their checks. The bank is closed on Saturday, so on Friday nights it stays open until six. The men settle accounts with each other and some of them buy money orders to send back home. They go to the laundromat, the grocery store, the movies, a bar. There's usually a crap game in somebody's back room or garage. A few get drunk and start fights, but they're generally pretty quiet about it because they don't want to attract the attention of the Border Patrol."

"What kind of fights?"

"With knives, mostly."

"Do they all carry knives?"

"Knives are often used in their work. They're tools, not just weapons."

"All right, Mr. Estivar, did the crew that was working for you on October thirteen, 1967, leave the ranch right after work?"

"Yes, sir."

"In the truck?"

"Yes."

"Did they return that night?"

"I was just going to bed when I heard the truck drive in shortly after nine and park outside the bunkhouse."

"How do you know it was the old G.M.?"

"The brakes had a peculiar squeak. Besides, no other vehicle was likely to park in that particular spot."

"Nine o'clock is pretty early for a big night on the town to conclude, isn't it?"

"They were scheduled to work the next day, which meant they had to be in the fields before seven. You don't keep bankers' hours on a ranch."

"And were the men in the fields the next morning before seven, Mr. Estivar?"

"No."

"Why not?"

"I didn't get a chance to ask," Estivar said. "I never saw any of them again."

5

AT ELEVEN O'CLOCK Judge Gallagher called for the morning recess. His bailiff opened the massive wooden doors and people began moving out into the corridor, the elderly men on cane and crutches, the students hugging their notebooks across their chests like shields, the lady shopper, the trio of ranchers, the German woman with her bag of knitting, the ex-cop, Valenzuela, the teen-aged girl holding her baby now half-awake and fussing quietly.

Estivar, self-conscious and perspiring, rejoined his family in the last row of seats. Ysobel spoke to her husband in staccato Spanish, telling him he was a fool to admit more than he had to and answer questions that hadn't even been asked.

"I think Estivar did real good," Dulzura said. "Talking up so clear, not even nervous."

"You keep out of this," Ysobel said. "Don't interfere."

"I'm obliged to interfere. I'm his first cousin."

"Second. *Second* cousin."

"*My* mother was *his* mother's—"

"Mr. Estivar, kindly tell your second cousin, Dulzura Gonzales, not to express her opinions until they're asked for."

"I think he did real good," Dulzura repeated stubbornly. "Don't you think so, Jaime?"

Jaime looked blank, pretending not to hear, not even to be a part of this loud peculiar foreign family.

On the opposite side of the room Agnes Osborne and Devon sat silent and bewildered, like two strangers who were being tried together for a mysterious crime not described in an indictment or mentioned by a judge. No jury had been summoned to decide guilt. Guilt was assumed. It hung heavy over both the women, keeping them motionless in their seats.

Devon was thirsty, she wanted to go into the corridor for a drink of water, but she had the feeling that the bailiff would follow her and that the unnamed crime she was accused of committing had canceled even so basic a right as quenching her thirst.

Mrs. Osborne was the first to speak. "I told you Estivar couldn't be trusted when the chips were down. You see what he's trying to do, don't you?"

"Not exactly."

"He's blackening our name. He's making it appear that Robert deserved whatever fate he met. All the business about prejudice, it wasn't true. Mr. Ford shouldn't have allowed him to speak lies."

"Let's go outside and take a walk in the fresh air."

"No. I must stay here and talk to Mr. Ford. He's got to straighten things out."

"What Estivar said is a matter of record. Mr. Ford or anyone else can't change it now."

"He can do *something*."

"All right, I'll stay with you if you want me to."

"No, go take your walk."

To reach the main door Devon had to pass near the row of seats where Estivar still sat with his family. They seemed uncertain about what a recess was and how they were expected to act during it. As Devon approached, all of them, even Dulzura, looked up as though they'd forgotten about her and were surprised to see her in such a place. Then Estivar rose, and after a nudge from his father, so did Jaime.

Devon stared at the boy, thinking how much he'd grown in just the short time since she'd seen him last. Jaime must be fourteen now. When Robert was fourteen he used to follow Estivar around everywhere, he called him Tío and pestered him with questions and ate at his table. Or did he? Why had it never been mentioned to her by anyone, Robert himself, or Estivar or Agnes Osborne or Dulzura? Perhaps the man, Tío, and the boy, Robbie, and their relationship had never existed except in Estivar's mind.

She said, "Hello, Jaime."

"Hello, ma'am."

"You've been growing so fast I hardly knew you."

"Yes, ma'am."

"I haven't seen you since school started. Are you liking it better this year?"

"Yes, ma'am."

It was a polite lie, just as every answer she'd get from him would be a polite lie. The ten years' difference in their ages could have been a hundred, though it seemed only yesterday that people were telling her how much she'd grown and asking her how she liked school.

In the corridor men and women were standing in small clusters at each window, like prisoners seeking a view of the world outside. Here and there cigarette smoke rose toward the ceiling. The teenager in the blonde wig came out of the ladies' room. The baby was fully awake now, kicking and squirming and pulling at the girl's wig until it slipped down over her forehead and knocked off her sunglasses. Before the baby's hand was slapped away and the sunglasses and wig were put back in place, Devon had a glimpse of black hair, clipped very short, and of dark troubled eyes squinting even in the subdued light of the corridor.

"Hello, Mrs. Osborne."

"Hello."

"I guess you don't remember me, huh?"

"No."

"It's my weight, I lost fifteen pounds. Also the wig and sunglasses. Oh yeah, and the kid." She glanced down at the baby with a kind of detached interest as though she still wasn't quite sure where he'd come from. "I'm Carla, I helped Mrs. Estivar with the twins summer before last."

"Carla," Devon said. "Carla Lopez."

"Yeah, that's me. I got married for a while but it was a drag—you know? So we split and I took my real name back again. Why should I be stuck for the rest of my life with the name of a guy I hate?"

Carla Lopez, you've grown so much I hardly know you. Devon remembered a plump smiling schoolgirl hardly older than Jaime, walking down the road to meet the mailman, her thigh-high skirt emphasizing the shortness of her legs. *"Buenos días, Carla." "Good morning, Mrs. Osborne . . ."*

Carla ironing the kinks out of her long black hair in the ranch-house kitchen, with Dulzura helping her—half admiring because she'd heard this was the latest style, half reluctant because she knew Devon would eventually come to investigate the smell of scorched hair that was pervading the house. *"What on earth are you doing, you two?"* Dulzura explaining that curls and waves were no longer fashionable, while the girl knelt with her hair spread across the ironing board like a bolt of black silk . . .

Carla sitting at dusk under a tamarisk tree beside the reservoir.

"Why are you out here by yourself, Carla?"

"It's so noisy in the Estivars' house, everyone talking at once and the TV on. Last summer when I worked for the Bishops, everything was real quiet. Mr. Bishop used to read a lot and Mrs. Bishop took long walks for her headaches. She had very bad headaches."

"You'd better go inside before the mosquitoes start biting. Buenas noches."

"Good night, Mrs. Osborne."

Devon said, "Why are you here today, Carla?"

"I think it was Valenzuela's idea, he's got it in for me."

"You mean you were subpoenaed."

"Yes, I was."

"For what reason?"

"I told you, Valenzuela's got it in for me, for my whole family."

"Valenzuela has no control over subpoenas," Devon said. "He's not even a policeman anymore."

"Some of the muscle stayed with him. Ask anyone in Boca de Rio—he still swaggers around like he's wearing a cop suit." She switched the baby from her right arm to her left, patting him between the shoulder blades to soothe him. "The Estivars don't like me either. Well, it's mutual, one hundred percent mutual . . . I hear Rufo got married and Cruz is in the army."

"Yes."

"It was the other one I had a crush on—Felipe. I don't suppose anyone ever hears from him."

"I wouldn't know." Devon remembered the three oldest Estivar boys only as a trio. When she used to meet them individually she was never certain whether she was seeing Cruz or Rufo or Felipe. They were uniformly quiet and polite, as though their father had spelled out to them exactly how to behave in her presence. There were rumors, passed along to her mainly by Dulzura, that away from the ranch the Estivar brothers were a great deal livelier.

Beneath the girl's platinum wig a narrow strip of brown forehead glistened with sweat. "My old lady was supposed to meet me here, she promised to look after the kid when I go on the stand. Maybe she got lost. That's the story of my life—people I count on get lost."

"I'd be glad to help if I can."

"She'll turn up sooner or later. She probably wandered into some church and started praying. She's a great prayer but it never does much good, least of all for me."

"Why not for you?"

"I got a jinx."

"Nobody believes in jinxes anymore."

"No. But I got one just the same." Carla glanced down at the baby, frowning. "I hope the kid don't catch it from me. He's gonna have enough trouble without people dying all around him, disappearing, drowning, being stabbed like Mr. Osborne."

"Mr. Osborne didn't die because of your jinx."

"Well, I feel like if it wasn't for me he'd still be alive. And her, too."

"Yes?"

"Mrs. Bishop. She drowned."

Mrs. Bishop had had headaches and took long walks and drowned.

THE TABLE RESERVED for the press when court was in session had been vacated for recess. Across its polished mahogany surface Ford and Mrs. Osborne faced each other. Mrs. Osborne still wore her public face and her jaunty blue hat, but Ford was beginning to look irritable and his soft voice had developed a rasp.

"I repeat, Mrs. Osborne, Estivar talked more freely than I anticipated. No harm was done, however."

"Not to you, nothing touches you. But what about me? All that talk about prejudice and ill-feeling, it was embarrassing."

"Murder is an embarrassing business. There's no law stating the mother of the victim will be spared."

"I refuse to believe that a murder occurred."

"Okay, okay, you have a right to your opinion. But as far as this hearing today is concerned, your son is dead."

"All the more reason why you shouldn't have allowed Estivar to blacken his name."

"I let him talk," Ford said, "just as I intend to let the rest of the witnesses talk. This Judge Gallagher is no dope. He'd be highly suspicious if I tried to present Robert as a perfect young man without an enemy in the world. Perfect young men don't get murdered, they don't even get born. In presenting the background of a murder, the victim's faults are more pertinent than his virtues, his enemies are more important than his friends. If Robert wasn't getting along well with Estivar, if he had trouble with the migrant workers or with his neighbors—"

"The only neighbors he ever had the slightest trouble with were the Bishops. You surely wouldn't dredge that up again—Ruth's been dead for nearly two years."

"And Robert had no part in her death?"

"Of course not." She shook her head, and the hat jumped forward as though it meant to peck at a tormentor. "Robert tried to help her. She was a very unhappy woman."

"Why?"

"Because he was kind."

"No. I meant, why was she unhappy?"

"Perhaps because Leo—Mr. Bishop—was more interested in his crops than he was in his wife. She was lonely. She used to come over and talk to Robert. That's all there was between them, talk. She was old enough to be his mother. He felt sorry for her, she was such a pathetic little thing."

"Is that what he told you?"

"He didn't have to tell me. It was obvious. Day after day she dragged her trouble over to our house like a sick animal she couldn't cure, couldn't kill."

"How did she get to your house?"

"Walked. She liked to pretend that she did it for the exercise, but of course no one was fooled, not even Leo." She paused, running a gloved hand across the surface of the table as though testing it for dirt. "I suppose you know how she died."

"Yes. I looked it up in the newspaper files. She was attempting to cross the river during a winter rain, got caught by a flash flood and drowned. A coroner's jury returned a verdict of accidental death. There were indications that she suffered from despondency, but suicide was ruled out by the finding of her suitcase a mile or so downstream, waterlogged but still intact. It was packed for a journey. She was going some place."

"Perhaps."

"Why just 'perhaps,' Mrs. Osborne?"

"There was no evidence to prove Ruth and the suitcase entered the water at the same time. It's easy enough to pack a woman's suitcase and toss it in a river, especially for someone with access to her belongings."

"Like a husband?"

"Like a husband."

"Why would a husband do that?"

"To make people think his wife was on her way to meet another man and run away with him. The easiest method of avoiding blame is to cast it on someone else. That suitcase turned Leo into a poor grieving widower and Robert into an irresponsible seducer."

"What was in it?"

"You mean exactly?"

"Yes."

"I don't know. What difference does it make?"

"A woman preparing for a rendezvous with her lover wouldn't pack quite the same things as a man would pack for her, even a husband. I presume the contents of the suitcase were exhibited at the coroner's inquest."

"I didn't attend the inquest. By that time I'd stopped going anywhere because of the gossip. Oh, nothing was ever said in front of Robert or me, but it was there on everyone's face, even the people who worked for us. If she hadn't died it would have been laughable, the idea of Robert running off with a woman twice his age, a pale skinny little thing who looked like an elderly child."

"What do you think happened to Ruth Bishop, Mrs. Osborne?"

"I know what didn't happen. She did not pack a suitcase and start across that river in order to keep a rendezvous with my son. It was raining before she left the house, and she was well aware of the danger of a flash flood."

"You believe that she walked into the river deliberately?"

"Perhaps."

"And that Leo Bishop packed a suitcase and put it into the water so it would be found later downstream."

"Again, perhaps."

"Why?"

"A wife's suicide puts her husband in a bad light, starts people asking questions and prying under surfaces. As it was, all the bad light was on us. I sent Robert on a trip East to give the scandal a chance to blow over. That's where he met Devon and married her two weeks later. Funny how things repeat themselves, isn't it? The first thing that struck me about Devon was how much she looked like Ruth Bishop."

People had begun returning to the courtroom: the high school students; Leo Bishop and the ranchers; the Estivars, with Lum Wing shuffling along behind like a family pet that was currently out of favor; Carla Lopez, freshly groomed and without her baby, as though she'd suddenly decided she was too young to be burdened with a child and had left it somewhere in the corridor or the ladies' room.

Ford's only reaction to the people coming back in was a slight lowering of his voice.

"You also sent Robert away after his father's death, is that right?"

"Yes."

"How did his father die, Mrs. Osborne?"

"I've already told you."

"Tell me again."

"He fell off a tractor and fractured his skull. He was in a coma for days."

"And after his death Robert was enrolled in a school in Arizona."

"I was depressed and poor company for a growing boy. Robert needed men to guide him."

"Estivar claims that the guidance was the wrong kind."

"He exaggerates. Most Mexicans do."

"Do you agree with Estivar that Robert had changed when he returned home?"

"Of course he'd changed. They're years of change, between fifteen and seventeen. Robert went away a boy and came back a man who had to take over the management of a ranch. I repeat, Estivar exaggerates. The relationship between him and Robert was never as close as he likes to remember it. Why should it have been? Robert had a perfectly good father of his own."

"And they were on friendly terms?"

"Of course."

"How did Mr. Osborne fall off the tractor, Mrs. Osborne?"

"I wasn't there when it happened. And my husband didn't tell me because he never regained consciousness. Just what are you trying to prove anyway? First, you bring up Ruth Bishop's death and now my husband's. They were totally unconnected and half a dozen years apart."

"I didn't bring up the subject of Ruth Bishop," Ford said. "You did."

"You led me into it."

"By the way, it's not exactly easy to fall off a tractor."

"I wouldn't know. I've never tried."

"The rumor is that your husband was drunk."

"So I heard."

"Was he?"

"An autopsy was performed. There was nothing in the report about alcohol."

"You said a minute ago that Mr. Osborne lay in a coma for days. All traces of alcohol would have disappeared from the bloodstream during that time."

"I'm not a doctor. How would I know?"

"I think you know a great deal, Mrs. Osborne. The problem is getting you to admit it."

"That was an ungentlemanly remark."

"I come from a long line of ungentlemen," Ford said. "You'd better go back to your place. The recess is over."

Judge Gallagher was striding back into the courtroom, his black robe flapping around him like the broken wings of a raven.

"Remain seated and come to order," the clerk said. "Superior Court is now in session."

6

THE NAME OF JOHN LOOMIS was called, and one of the men in ranchers' clothes came to the witness box and was sworn in: John Sylvester Loomis, 514 Paloverde Street, Boca de Rio; occupation, doctor of veterinary medicine. Dr. Loomis testified that on the morning of October 13, 1967, he was asleep in the apartment above his place of business when he was awakened by someone pounding on the office door. He went downstairs and found Robert Osborne with his dog, Maxie, on a leash.

"I gave him hell, if you'll pardon the expression, for waking me up so early, since I'd been at a foaling until three o'clock. But he seemed to think it was urgent, that someone had poisoned his dog."

"What was your opinion?"

"I saw no evidence of poison. The dog was lively, his eyes were clear and bright, nose cold, no offensive breath odor. Mr. Osborne said he'd found Maxie in a field before dawn, that the dog's legs were twitching violently, it was frothing at the mouth and had lost control of its bowels. I persuaded Mr. Osborne to leave the dog with me for a few hours, and he said he'd pick it up on his way home from San Diego in the late afternoon or early evening."

"And did he?"

"Yes. About seven o'clock that night."

"Meanwhile you'd had a chance to examine the dog."

"Yes."

"And what did you find out?"

"Nothing absolutely positive. But I was pretty sure it had suffered an epileptic seizure. Such seizures are not uncommon in dogs as they get older, and spaniels like Maxie are particularly susceptible. Once a seizure is over, the dog makes an immediate and complete recovery. It's the speed of the recovery, in fact, which helps with the diagnosis."

"Did you explain this to Mr. Osborne, Dr. Loomis?"

"I made an attempt. But he had this thing in his mind about poison, that the dog had been poisoned."

"Was there any basis for his belief?"

"None that I could see," Loomis said. "I didn't argue with him, though. It seemed a touchy subject."

"Why?"

"People often identify with their pets. I got the impression that Mr. Osborne thought someone was trying to poison *him*."

"Thank you, Dr. Loomis. You may step down now."

Leo Bishop was called as the next witness. His reluctance to take the stand was evidenced by the slowness of his movements and the look of apology he gave Devon as he passed her. When he responded to Ford's questions about his name and address, his voice was so low that even the court reporter, who was sitting directly below the witness box, had to ask him to speak up.

Ford said, "Would you please repeat that, Mr. Bishop?"

"Leo James Bishop."

"And the address?"

"Rancho Obispo."

"You are the owner as well as the operator of the ranch?"

"Yes."

"What's the location of your ranch in relation to the Osborne ranch?"

"It's just to the east and southeast, with the river as the boundary line."

"In fact, you and the Osbornes are next-door neighbors."

"You might put it like that, though it's a long way between doors." *A long way and a river.*

"You knew Robert Osborne, of course."

"Yes."

"Had known him for many years."

"Yes."

"Will you tell the court when and where you last saw him, Mr. Bishop?"

"On the morning of October thirteen, 1967, in town."

"The town of Boca de Rio."

"Yes."

"Would you explain the circumstances of that meeting?"

"One of my green-carders showed up for work suffering from stomach cramps. I was afraid his symptoms might be the result of an insecticide we'd used the previous day, so I drove him into Boca to a doctor. On the way I saw Robert's car parked on Main Street outside a café. He was standing on the curb talking to a young woman."

"Did you honk your horn or wave at him, anything like that?"

"No. He seemed busy, I didn't want to interrupt. Besides, I had a sick man in the car."

"Still, it would have been the natural thing to do, taking a second or two to greet a close friend."

"He wasn't a close friend," Leo said quietly. "There was a generation between us. And some old trouble."

"Would this 'old trouble' have any bearing on the present case?"

"I don't think so."

Ford pretended to consult the pages of yellow foolscap on the table in front of him, giving himself time to decide whether to pursue the subject further or whether it would be wiser to stick to the main theme he'd chosen to present. Overkill might be a mistake in view of Judge Gallagher's skeptical mind. He said, "Mr. Bishop, you've been present in the courtroom all morning, have you not?"

"Yes."

"So you heard Mr. Estivar testify that he hired a crew of Mexicans to work on the Osborne ranch at the end of September, and that these men disappeared on the night of October thirteen . . . As a grower you're familiar with the pirating of work crews, are you not, Mr. Bishop?"

"Yes."

"In fact, in the summer of 1965 you had occasion to report that a crew which you'd hired to pick melons had disappeared during the night following a payday."

"That's correct."

"Now, on the surface, what happened to your crew and what happened to Mr. Estivar's crew appeared to be similar. There was, however, an important difference, was there not?"

"Yes. My men were located by noon the next day. A grower near Chula Vista had simply convinced them they could do better at his place, so they left. But the men from the Osborne ranch were never found. Chances are they crossed the border before the police even knew a crime had been committed."

"When did you learn that a crime had been committed, Mr. Bishop?"

"I was awakened about one-thirty in the morning by a deputy from the sheriff's department. He said Robert Osborne was missing and the surrounding ranches were being searched for traces of him."

"What did you do then?"

"I got dressed and joined the search. At least I tried to. The deputy in charge sent me back in the house."

"What was his name?"

"Valenzuela."

"Why did he refuse your offer of assistance?"

"He said a lot of searches had been messed up by amateurs and this wasn't going to be one of them if he could help it."

"All right, thank you, Mr. Bishop. You are excused."

Ford waited until Leo returned to his place in the spectators' section, then asked the clerk to call Carla Lopez to the stand.

Carla rose and walked slowly to the front of the room. In the hot dry air her pink and yellow nylon shift clung to her moist body like a magnet. If she was embarrassed or nervous she managed to conceal the fact. Her voice was bored when she took the oath, and the huge round sunglasses gave her an Orphan Annie look of complete blankness.

"State your name, please," Ford said.

"Carla Dolores Lopez."

"Miss or Mrs.?"

"Miss. I'm getting a divorce, so I took back my maiden name."

"Where do you live, Miss Lopez?"

"431 Catalpa Street, San Diego, Apartment Nine."

"Are you employed?"

"I quit my job last week. I'm looking for something better."

"Did you know Robert Osborne, Miss Lopez?"

"Yes."

"A few minutes ago Mr. Bishop testified that he saw Mr. Osborne on the morning of October thirteen talking to a young woman outside a café in Boca de Rio. Were you that young woman?"

"Yes."

"Who initiated the conversation?"

"What do you mean by that?"

"Who started talking first?"

"He did. I was just walking along the street by myself when he pulled up to the curb beside me and asked if he could speak to me for a minute. I had nothing better to do, so I said yes."

"What did Mr. Osborne talk to you about, Miss Lopez?"

"My brothers," Carla said. "They used to work for him, my two older brothers, and Mr. Osborne wanted to know if they might want to come and work for him again."

"Did he give any reason?"

"He said the last crew Estivar had hired was no good, they had no experience, and he needed someone like my brothers to show them how things were done. I told him my brothers wouldn't be caught dead doing that kind of labor no more. They didn't have to squat and stoop like monkeys, they had respectable stand-up jobs in a gas station."

"Did Mr. Osborne make any further remarks about the crew he had working for him?"

"No."

"He gave no indication, for instance, that he suspected they might have entered the country without papers?"

"No."

"Did he use the terms wetback, *mojado* or *alambre*?"

"Not that I remember. The rest of the talk was personal—you know, like between he and I."

The girl's long silver-painted fingernails scratched at her throat as if they were trying to ease an itch deep inside and out of reach. It was her first sign of nervousness.

"Was there anything in the conversation," Ford said, "which might have bearing on the present hearing?"

"I don't think so. He asked me about my baby—I wasn't showing yet but the whole town knew about it, it being that kind of town—and he said his wife was having a baby, too. He seemed kind of jumpy about it. Could be he was scared it would turn out like him."

"What do you mean by that?"

"Well, there was a lot of gossip about him when Mrs. Bishop drowned. Maybe some of it was true. Or maybe he just had a jinx like me. I'm an expert on jinxes. I've had one ever since I was born."

"Indeed."

"For instance, if I did a rain dance there'd probably be a year's drought or even a snowstorm."

"The court must deal in facts, Miss Lopez, not jinxes and rain dances."

"You have your facts," the girl said. "I have mine."

7

THE EXODUS from the courtroom for lunch was faster and more complete than it had been for the morning recess. Devon waited until only the bailiff remained.

He glanced at her curiously. "This room is locked up during the noon hour, ma'am."

"Oh. Thank you."

"If you're not feeling well, there's a ladies' lounge in the basement where you can get coffee and things like that."

"I'm all right."

Agnes Osborne had driven back to her apartment to rest, suffering more from weariness than from hunger. With her out of the way Devon thought Leo might be waiting for her in the corridor and they would have lunch together. But there was no sign of him. The corridor was deserted except for a pair of tourists taking pictures out of one of the barred windows and, in an alcove beyond a row of telephone booths, the ex-policeman, Valenzuela, talking to a short stout Mexican woman who was holding a baby on her left arm. The child was sucking on a pacifier and regarding Valenzuela with mild interest.

Valenzuela, so dapper earlier in the day, had begun to show the effects of the increasing heat and tension. He'd taken off his coat and tie and under each arm of his striped shirt there was a dark semicircle like a stain of secret guilt. When Devon approached he looked at her with disapproval, as though she were someone from a remote corner of his past and had no right to be popping up in the present without warning or permission.

As she walked by she nodded but didn't speak. Everything had been said between them: *"I've done what I could, Mrs. Osborne. Searched the fields, dragged the reservoir, walked up and down the riverbed. But there are a hundred more fields, a dozen more reservoirs, miles and miles of riverbed."* *"You must try again, try harder."* *"It's no use. I think they took him into Mexico."* The following spring Valenzuela phoned Devon and told her he'd quit his job in the sheriff's office and was now selling insurance. He asked her if she wanted to buy any and she said no, very politely . . .

A few blocks from the courthouse she found a small hamburger stand. She sat at a table hardly bigger than a handkerchief and ordered a burger with French fries. The odor of stale grease, the ketchup bottle with its darkening dribble, the thin round patty of meat identical to ones she'd eaten in Philadelphia, New Haven, Boston—they were all so normal and familiar, they made her feel like an ordinary girl who ate lunch at hamburger stands and had no business with bailiffs or judges. She ate slowly, prolonging her stay in the little place, her role of ordinary girl.

After lunch she began her reluctant return to the courthouse, pausing now and then to stare out at the sea. *"I think they took him into Mexico,"* Valenzuela had said. *"Or maybe dumped him in the sea and a high tide will bring him in."* A hundred high tides came and went before Devon stopped hoping; Mrs. Osborne had never stopped. Devon knew she still carried a tide table in her purse, still walked for miles along the beaches every week, her eye on specks in the water that turned out to be buoys or harbor seals, pelagic birds or pieces of floating lumber. *"In salt water this cold it would take a week or two for gases to form in the tissues and bring a body to the surface."* The first week passed, and the second, and fifty more. *"Not everything that goes into the sea comes out again, Mrs. Osborne."* With each tide things floated into shore and were stranded on the beach—driftwood, jellyfish, shark eggs, oil-soaked grebes and cormorants and scoters, lobster traps, plastic bottles, odd shoes and other pieces of clothing. Every scrap of the clothing was collected and taken to a room in the basement of the sheriff's department to be dried out and examined. None of it belonged to Robert.

Devon turned away from the sea and quickened her pace. It was then that she spotted Estivar. He was sitting alone on a bus-stop bench under a silver dollar tree. At the slightest stirring of air the silver discs of leaves twitched and jumped, eager to be spent. Their quick gay movements altered the lights and shadows, so that Estivar's face from a distance appeared very lively. As she drew closer she saw that it was no livelier than the concrete bench. He rose slowly at her approach, as though he was sorry to see her.

She said, "Aren't you having lunch, Estivar?"

"Later. The others wanted a picnic at the zoo, they left me a sandwich and an avocado. Will you sit down, Mrs. Osborne?"

"Yes, thanks." As she sat down she wondered if the bench had been made of concrete because it was a durable material or because its cold roughness would discourage people from remaining too long. "Don't you like the park?"

"Live things shouldn't be put in cages. I prefer to watch the sea. All that water, think what we could do at the ranch with all that water . . . Where is Mrs. Osborne?"

"She went home to rest for a while."

"I know she resented some of the things I said on the stand this morning. But I couldn't help it, they were true, I was under oath. What did she expect from me? Probably some of those nice lies she believes herself."

"You mustn't be too hard on her, Estivar."

"Why not? She's too hard on me. I heard her at recess this morning talking to the lawyer. I heard her clear across the room speaking my name like a dirty word. What's she got against me? I kept that place going for her when her son was too young to be any help and her husband was too—" He drew in his breath sharply, as though someone had given him a warning poke in the stomach.

"Too what?"

"He's dead, it doesn't matter anymore."

"It does to me."

"I thought you'd have found out on your own by this time."

"I only know he died by accident."

"That was the verdict."

"Didn't you agree with it?"

"If you go around looking for accidents, asking for them, they can't be called accidents anymore. Mr. Osborne's 'accident' happened before ten o'clock in the morning, and he'd already drunk enough bourbon to paralyze an ordinary man." Estivar spread his hands in a little gesture of despair. "It wasn't a case of bad luck killing him when he was just forty-three years old, it was a case of good luck keeping him alive that long."

"When did he become an alcoholic?"

"I'm not sure. Between the two of them they managed to keep it secret for years. But eventually it reached a point where a new crew would take one look at him and label him a *borrachín*."

"Is that why Robert spent so much time with you as he was growing up?"

"Yes. He'd come over to my house when things got too rough. I didn't say any of this on the witness stand, naturally, but I told Mr. Ford last week. He was asking me a lot of questions about the Osbornes. I had to tell him the truth. I knew she wouldn't, she never told anyone. She had this game she played. If Mr. Osborne was too drunk to come out and work, she said he had a touch of flu or a migraine or a toothache or a sprained back. Once he had to be carried in from the fields, out cold and reeking of whiskey, but she claimed he must have suffered a heat stroke, though it was a winter day with a pale cool little sun. She couldn't bring herself to admit the truth even while she was hiring my boy, Rufo, to haul away the bottles every week." He raised his head, frowning up at the round silver leaves as though they represented the dollars and half-dollars Rufo had been paid to dispose of the bottles. "It was silly, the whole cover-up business, but you couldn't help admire how hard she worked at it and what guts it took, especially when he got quarrelsome."

"How did she handle him then?"

"Oh, she tried lots of things, same as any woman married to a drunk. But eventually she developed a routine. She'd maneuver him into the living room one way or another, close the doors and windows and pull the drapes. Then the arguing would start. If things got too loud she'd sit down at that piano of hers and start playing to cover them up, a piece with good firm chords like 'March of the Toreadors.' She couldn't admit that they quarreled any more than she could admit that he drank. Everybody caught on, of course. Even the men working around the place, when they heard that piano, they'd look at each other and grin."

"What about Robert?"

"Lots of the arguing was about him and how he should be brought up, disciplined, educated, trained. But they would have argued even if the boy had never been born. He was just a peg to hang things on. When he got older, ten or eleven, I tried to explain this to him. I told him he hadn't caused the trouble and he couldn't stop it, so he might as well learn to live with it."

"How could a ten-year-old understand such a thing?"

"I think he did. Anyway, he used to show up at my place when he sensed trouble on the way. Sometimes he didn't make it in time and he'd be caught between the two of them. One day I heard the piano music start in real loud and I waited and waited for Robbie to show up. Finally I went over to the ranch house to find out what was happening. She had forgotten to pull the drapes across a side window and I could see the three of them inside the room. She was at the piano, with Robbie sitting on the bench beside her looking sick and scared. Mr. Osborne was propped up against the mantel, the veins in his neck sticking out like ropes. His mouth was moving, so was hers. But all I could hear was the bang bang bang of that piano, loud enough to wake the dead. 'Onward, Christian Soldiers.'"

"What do you mean?"

"That's what she was playing, over and over, 'Onward, Christian Soldiers.' It seems funny now, her using a hymn. But it wasn't funny then. That fight was the same as all the others, long and mean and deadly, the kind nobody can win, so everybody loses, especially the innocent. I wanted to get Robbie out of that room and away from that house until things quieted down. I went inside and started pounding on the living-room door as hard as I could. A minute or so later the piano stopped and Mrs. Osborne opened the door. 'Oh, Estivar,' she said, 'we were just having a little concert.' I asked her if Robbie could come over and help my son, Cruz, with his homework. She said, 'Certainly. I don't think Robbie cares much for music anyway . . .' Sometimes when I wake up in the night I swear I can hear the sound of that piano, though it isn't even there anymore, I helped the movers take it out of the house myself."

"Why are you telling me all this?"

"No one else will, and it's time you knew."

"I didn't want to know."

"You wanted to know more than I wanted to tell you, Mrs. Osborne, especially today. But who can be sure? I may not get another chance to talk to you like this."

"You sound as if something is going to happen."

"Something always does."

"The ranch will remain the same," she said. "And you'll continue on as foreman. I don't plan on changing anything."

"Life is something that happens to you while you're making other plans. I read that somewhere, and it's like the piano music, it keeps running through my mind. Robbie's life was planned—high school, college, a profession. Then his father fell off a tractor and things changed before they had a chance to begin."

A silence fell between them, emphasized by the noise all around: the roar of freeway traffic and planes landing and taking off from Lindbergh Field and from the Naval Air Station across the bay. At the top of a palm tree nearby a mockingbird had begun to sing. It was October, the wrong time to be singing, but the bird sang anyway, with loud delight, and Estivar's face softened at the sound.

"*Sinsonte*," he said. "Listen."

"A mockingbird?"

"Yes."

"Why is he singing now?"

"He wants to—that's reason enough for a bird."

"Maybe he thinks it's spring."

"Maybe."

"Lucky bird."

A carillon began chiming the first quarter of an hour. Estivar rose quickly. "It's time I went and picked up my family."

"You didn't eat your sandwich."

"I'll have a chance in the car."

She rose, too. Her eyes felt hot and dry and tired, as though they'd seen too much too quickly and needed a rest in some quiet sunless place.

"I'm sorry I had to tell you things you didn't want to know," he said.

"You were right, of course. I need all the information I can get in order to make sensible plans."

"Yes, Mrs. Osborne." *Life, Mrs. Osborne, is what happens to you while you are making sensible plans.*

She began walking slowly back to the courthouse as if by delaying her return she could delay the proceeding and the verdict. There was no doubt in her mind what the verdict would be. Robert, who had died a dozen times to the strains of "Onward, Christian Soldiers" and "March of the Toreadors," would die this time to the tuneless hum of strangers and the occasional beat of a gavel.

8

COURT RECONVENED ten minutes late because Judge Gallagher was caught in a traffic jam on the way back from his club. Even with this extra time allowance Agnes Osborne, scheduled to be the first witness of the afternoon, was still absent at one forty-five. A conference was held at the bench and it was decided not to delay the proceeding further by waiting for Mrs. Osborne but to call the next witness.

"Dulzura Gonzales."

Dulzura heard her name but she didn't respond until Jaime jabbed her in the side with his elbow. "Hey, that's you."

"I know it's me."

"Well, hurry up."

Already breathless from fear Dulzura had trouble getting to her feet and out into the aisle; and once she was in motion she walked too rapidly, so that her giant dress swirled around her like a tent fighting a storm.

"Do you swear that the testimony you are about to give in the matter now pending before this court shall be the truth, the whole truth, and nothing but the truth?"

She swore. Her hand left moist prints on the wooden railing around the witness box.

"State your full name, please," Ford said.

"Dulzura Ynez Maria Amata Gonzales."

"Miss or Mrs.?"

"Miss." Her nervous giggle swept through the room, raising little gusts of laughter and a flurry of doubt.

"Where do you live, Miss Gonzales?"

"The same place as the others—you know, the Osborne ranch."

"What do you do there?"

"Well, lots of things."

"I meant, what are you paid to do, Miss Gonzales?"

"Cook and laundry, mostly. A little cleaning now and then."

"How long have you worked for the Osbornes?"

"Seven years."

"Who hired you?"

"Mrs. Osborne, Senior. There wasn't anybody but her around. Mr. Osborne was dead and the boy away at school. My first cousin, Estivar, gave me a nice recommend on a piece of paper."

"Miss Gonzales, I want you to try and recall the evening of October the thirteenth last year."

"I don't have to try. I recall it already."

"There were special circumstances that fixed the day in your memory?"

"Yes, sir. It was my birthday. Usually I get time off to celebrate, maybe go into Boca with a couple of the boys after work. But that day I couldn't, it was Friday the thirteenth. I'm not allowed to leave the house on Friday the thirteenth."

"Not allowed?"

"A *quiromántico* told me never to because of strange lines in my hands. So I just stayed home like it was no special day and cooked dinner and served it."

"At what time?"

"About seven-thirty, later than usual on account of Mr. Osborne had been to the city."

"Did you see Mr. Osborne after dinner?"

"Yes, sir. He came out to the kitchen while I was cleaning up. He said he forgot to buy my birthday present, like Mrs. Osborne asked him to, and would I accept money, and I said I sure would."

"Was Mr. Osborne wearing his spectacles when he came out to the kitchen?"

"No, sir. But he could see okay, so I guess he was wearing those little pieces of glass over his eyeballs."

"Contact lenses."

"Yes."

"What did he give you for your birthday, Miss Gonzales?"

"A twenty-dollar bill."

"Did he take the bill from his wallet in your presence?"

"Yes, sir."

"Did you notice anything of interest about the wallet?"

"It was full of money. I never saw Mr. Osborne's wallet before and I was surprised and kind of worried, too. The boys don't get much pay."

"Boys?"

"The workers that come and go."

"The migrants?"

"Yes. It would of been a real temptation to them if they found out how much money Mr. Osborne was carrying."

"Thank you, Miss Gonzales. You may—"

"I'm not saying any of them did it, killed him for the money. I'm just saying that a lot of money is a big temptation to a poor man."

"We understand that, Miss Gonzales. Thank you . . . Will Mr. Lum Wing take the stand, please?"

Lum Wing, encouraged by his sunny hour in the park, gave his name in a high clear voice with a trace of southern accent.

"Where do you live, Mr. Wing?"

"Sometimes here, sometimes there. Where the work is."

"You have a permanent address, don't you?"

"When there's nothing better to do I stay at my daughter's house in Boca de Rio. She's got six kids, I share a room with two of my grandsons. I keep away from there as much as possible."

"What is your profession, Mr. Wing?"

"I used to be cook with a circus. What my daughter tells the neighbors, I retired. What happened, the circus went bust."

"You come out of retirement and take a job now and then?"

"Yes, sir, to get out of the house."

"Your work has brought you to the Osborne ranch at various times?"

"Yes."

"You're working there now, in fact?"

"Yes, sir."

"And you were there a year ago, on October thirteen?"

"Yes."

"Where do you stay when you're working at the ranch?"

Lum Wing described his living arrangements in the curtained-off corner of the former barn that served as a mess hall. In the late afternoon of October 13 he had cooked supper as usual. After the men departed for their payday fling in Boca de Rio he'd drawn his curtain, set up a chess game and opened a bottle of wine. The wine made him sleepy, so he lay down on his cot. He must have dozed off, because the next thing he remembered was the sound of voices speaking loud and fast in Spanish on the other side of the curtain. On occasion other basic needs besides eating were satisfied at the mess-hall tables and Lum Wing made it a habit to ignore what went on. Moving quietly in the darkness he checked his case of knives, his pocket watch and chess set, the rest of the bottle of wine, and finally the money belt he wore even when sleeping. Finding everything intact he returned to his cot. The voices continued.

"Did you recognize any of them?" Ford asked.

After a moment's hesitation Lum Wing shook his head.

"Did you hear what they were saying?"

"They talked too fast. Also I didn't listen."

"Do you understand Spanish, Mr. Wing?"

"Four, five words."

"I gather that you didn't overhear any of those four or five words spoken on that occasion?"

"I'm an old man. I mind my own business. I don't listen, I don't hear, I don't get in trouble."

"There was a great deal of trouble that night, Mr. Wing. You must have heard some of it whether you listened or not. You appear to have normal hearing for a man your age."

"I fix it so it's not so normal." He showed the court how he made earplugs out of little pieces of paper. "Beside the plugs, there was the wine. It made me sleepy. Also I was tired. I work hard, up before five every morning, doing this, doing that."

"All right, Mr. Wing, I believe you . . . You've been employed at the Osborne ranch quite a few times, haven't you?"

"Six, seven."

"Did Robert Osborne speak Spanish?"

"Not to me." Lum Wing stared blandly up at the ceiling.

"Well, did you ever hear him speak to the men in Spanish?"

"Maybe two, three times."

"And maybe oftener? A lot oftener?"

"Maybe."

"It would, in fact, have been quite possible for you to recognize Mr. Osborne's voice even if he was talking in a foreign language?"

"I wouldn't like to say that. I don't want to make trouble."

"The trouble is made, Mr. Wing."

"It could be worse."

"Not for Robert Osborne."

"There were others," the old man said, blinking. "Other people. Mr. Osborne wasn't talking to himself. Why would he talk to himself in Spanish?"

"Then you did recognize Mr. Osborne's voice that night?"

"Maybe. I'm not swearing to it."

"Mr. Wing, we have reason to believe that a fight which ended in a murder took place in the same room in which you claim to have been sleeping. Do you realize that?"

"I didn't commit a murder, I didn't commit a fight. I was sleeping innocent as a baby with my earplugs in until Mr. Estivar woke me up by shaking my arm and shining a flashlight in my face. I said what happened? And he said what happened, Mr. Osborne is missing and there's blood all over the floor and the cops are on their way."

"What did you do then, Mr. Wing?"

"Put on my pants."

"You got dressed."

"Same thing."

"I take it that your earplugs had been removed by this time."

"Yes, sir."

"And you could hear perfectly well?"

"Yes, sir."

"What did you hear, Mr. Wing?"

"Nothing. I thought funny thing how quiet, where is everybody, and I look out my window. I see lights on all over the ranch, the main house, Estivar's place, the garage where they keep the heavy machinery, the bunkhouse, even in some of the tamarisk trees around the reservoir. I think again what's the matter, all those lights and no noise. Then I see the big truck is gone, the one the men came in, and the bunkhouse is empty."

"What time was that, Mr. Wing?"

"I don't know."

"You mentioned previously that you had a pocket watch."

"I never thought to look at it. I was scared, I wanted to get out of that place."

"And did you?"

"I opened my door—there are two doors to the building, the front one the men use and the back one that's mine. I stepped outside. Estivar's oldest son, Cruz, was standing between me and the bunkhouse with a rifle over his shoulder."

"Did you speak to him?"

"He spoke to me. He told me to go back inside and stay there, because the police were on their way and when they asked me if I touched anything I better be able to say no. So I sat on the edge of my cot, then in five, ten minutes the police arrived."

There was a sudden audible stirring throughout the courtroom, as if the arrival of the police marked the end of a period of tension and gave people freedom to move. They coughed, changed position, whispered to their neighbors, sighed, stretched, yawned.

Ford waited for the sounds to subside. Without actually turning to face the audience he could see that the place where Agnes Osborne had sat during the morning was still empty. His uneasiness over her absence was tinged with guilt. He had probably talked to her too harshly. Women like Mrs. Osborne, who were blunt themselves and seemed to invite bluntness from others, were often the least able to tolerate it.

Ford said, "What happened after the police arrived, Mr. Wing?"

"Plenty, plenty of noise, cars moving around, doors banging, people talking and shouting. Pretty soon one of the deputies came to me and started asking questions like what you asked, did I see anything, did I hear anything. But mostly he wanted to know about my knives."

"Knives, Mr. Wing?"

"I carry my own knives to cook with—cleaver, choppers, parers, slicers, carver. I keep them clean and sharp, locked up in a case and the key in my money belt. I opened the case and showed him they were all there, nothing stolen."

"Did you ever hear of a butterfly knife?"

Lum Wing's impassive face looked as surprised as possible. "A knife to cut *butterflies*?"

"No. It's one that resembles a butterfly when the blade is open."

"I leave such silly things to the Mexicans. Around here they all carry knives, the fancier the better, like jewelry."

"When the deputy questioned you that night, you were not able to give him any more information than you have given the court this afternoon?"

"No, no more."

"Thank you, Mr. Wing. You may return to your seat . . . Will Jaime Estivar come to the stand, please?"

As they met in the aisle the old man and the young one exchanged glances of puzzlement and resignation: it was a middle-aged world, which Lum Wing had passed and Jaime hadn't yet reached and neither of them cared about or understood.

9

"FOR THE RECORD," Ford said, "would you state your name, please?"

"My church name or my school name?"

"Is there a difference?"

"Yes, sir. I was christened with five names, but at school I just use Jaime Estivar because otherwise I'd take up too much room on report cards and attendance sheets, things like that." He had sworn to tell the truth, but the very first thing he uttered was a lie. What's more, it tripped off his tongue without a moment's hesitation. The boys he admired at school were called Chris, Pete, Tim, or sometimes Smith, McGregor, Foster, Jones; he couldn't afford to have them find out he was really Jaime Ricardo Salvador Luis Hermano Estivar.

"Your school name will be sufficient," Ford said.

"Jaime Estivar."

"How old are you, Jaime?"

"Fourteen."

"And you live with your family at the Osborne ranch?"

"Yes, sir."

"Tell us about your family, Jaime."

"Well, uh, I don't know what's to tell." He glanced down at his parents and Dulzura and Lum Wing, seeking inspiration. He found none. "I mean, they're just a family, no big deal or anything."

"Do you have brothers and sisters?"

"Yes, sir. Three of each."

"Are they living at home?"

"Only me and my two younger sisters, they're twins. My oldest brother, Cruz, is with the army in Korea. Rufo is married and lives in Salinas. Felipe's got a good job in an aircraft plant in Seattle. He sent me ten dollars for Christmas and fifteen for my birthday."

"When your brothers were at home, they all had chores to do around the ranch, did they?"

"Yes, sir."

"What about you?"

"I help after school and on weekends."

"Do you get paid?"

"Yes, sir."

"How?"

"My pop just hands me the money and says go buy yourself a Cadillac."

"What I meant was, do you get paid by the hour or by the job?"

"The job usually. Also for the last three years I've been in business for myself part of the time. Pumpkins."

"You're pretty young to be in business for yourself."

"Well, I don't make much money," Jaime said earnestly.

Ford smiled. "How do you go about getting in the pumpkin business, Jaime?"

"I just took over from Felipe, the way he did from Rufo and Rufo from Cruz. It all started with old Mr. Osborne lending Cruz a field for a crop that would bring him money to put away for his education. Cruz and Rufo grew a lot of different things. It was Felipe who thought of pumpkins. They grow fast and don't take much work and you harvest them all at once at the beginning of October."

"And is this what you did at the beginning of October 1967?"

"Yes, sir."

"After the pumpkins were picked and sold, you plowed the vines under?"

"I did when my dad said I'd better get to it or else."

"What date was that?"

"Saturday morning, November four, three weeks after Mr. Osborne disappeared. The vines were drying up by that time and a lot of them were broken and, you know, trampled down by people looking for clues and stuff like that."

"Did anyone find any 'clues and stuff like that'?"

"I don't think so, not in the pumpkin field."

"Did you?"

"I found the knife," Jaime said. "The butterfly knife."

"Where was it in the field?"

"The southwest corner."

"The corner nearest the road leading out of the ranch?"

"Yes, sir."

"Was it buried in the ground?"

"No, sir. It looked like maybe somebody flung it out of a car window to get rid of it and it sort of stuck in the ground underneath one of the vines."

"I'm going to show you a knife and ask you if it is the one you found." Ford held up the knife, now labeled with an identification tag. "Is this it, Jaime?"

"I'm not sure."

"Here, take it in your hands and examine it."

"I don't want—well, okay."

"Is it the knife you found?"

"I think so. Except it looks cleaner now."

"Some of the bloodstains were scraped off for analysis in the police lab. Allowing for that difference, would you say this is the knife you picked up in the pumpkin field?"

"Yes, sir."

"Was it open with the blade operable the way it is now?"

"Yes, sir, open."

"Had you ever seen a knife like it before that time?"

"A couple of the boys at school carry butterfly knives."

"For show? For fun?"

"No, sir, for real."

The knife was offered in evidence, numbered, then replaced on the court clerk's table. Two of the high school students in the audience stood up to get a better view of the knife but the bailiff promptly ordered them to sit down.

"Now, Jaime," Ford said, "I want you to go over to the map on the board, and using one of the colored marking pencils, indicate the location of the pumpkin field."

"How?"

"Draw a rectangle and print the words pumpkin field beside it."

Jaime did as he was told. His hand shook and the boundaries of the pumpkin field were uneven, as though old Mr. Osborne had laid them out himself on one of his drunk days and no one had bothered to straighten them. The area where the knife was found, Jaime indicated by a circle with the letter K inside it. Then he returned to the witness box and Ford went on with the questioning.

"Jaime, I understand the pumpkin business occupied your time only for a couple of months out of the year."

"Yes, sir. Late summer and early fall."

"The rest of the year you were engaged in other projects around the ranch, is that right?"

"Yes, sir."

"Did these other jobs bring you in contact with the various crews of migrant laborers?"

"Not much. I did my work mostly after school and on weekends and holidays. Also my dad gave me orders to stay away from the mess hall and the bunkhouse."

"So you didn't become acquainted with any of the men personally?"

"No, sir. At least not very often."

"Referring now to the crew which was employed on the ranch during the first half of October 1967, I'll ask you if any of the men were known to you by name."

"No, sir."

"Do you recall anything in particular about the crew?"

"Just the old truck they came in. It was painted dark red. I noticed that specially because it was the same color red as the pickup Felipe used to teach me to drive. It's not there anymore, so I guess Mr. Osborne sold it on account of its gears being stripped too often." He added, half in contempt, half in envy, "The kids in driver education at school learn in cars with automatic shifts."

"I have no more questions, Jaime. Thank you."

Jaime went back to his place very quickly, as though he were afraid the lawyer might change his mind. But Ford's attention was already directed elsewhere, to the empty seat beside Devon.

"My witness is still missing," he told Judge Gallagher. "Robert Osborne's mother."

"Where is she?"

"I don't know."

"Well, find out."

"I'll try. I need a short recess."

"Ten minutes?"

"Half an hour would be better."

"Mr. Ford, somewhere in the county of San Diego right now, at least one irate taxpayer is figuring out exactly how much a minute this case is costing him. Do you realize that?"

"I do now, your Honor."

"Court is recessed for a period of ten minutes."

As the room began to empty, Ford walked over to where Devon was sitting. He would have liked to sit down beside her. His legs were tired and the lower part of his body felt as if the vertebrae had softened and the connecting discs had been unfastened. "Where is Mrs. Osborne?"

"She went home to rest during the noon hour but she intended to be back by one-thirty."

"I told her I was going to put her on the stand right after the lunch break. Perhaps it slipped her mind."

"I hardly think so. Mrs. Osborne is very meticulous about such things, and very punctual."

"Then perhaps one of us had better find out why she's suddenly not meticulous and punctual anymore."

"Mrs. Osborne hates to be checked up on. It makes her feel old."

"It's time she got used to it," Ford said briskly. "There are pay phones at the end of the corridor."

"She might take it better if you called her."

"That's unlikely. I'm the big bad man who asks her embarrassing questions, you're her loving daughter-in-law."

"Am I?"

"Until the conclusion of this proceeding you are."

Of the half-dozen pay phones at the end of the corridor five were being used. The booths looked like upended coffins whose occupants weren't actually dead but had been put into a state of suspended animation to await a better world. The sixth booth had its door open, inviting Devon to step inside and wait, too. She closed the glass door behind her, and as she'd done fifty or a hundred times in the past year, started to dial the number of Agnes Osborne's house. But her hand seemed to freeze on the dial. She couldn't remember more than the first two digits and had to look up the number in the directory as she would any stranger's. "*You're her loving daughter-in-law . . . Until the conclusion of this proceeding you are.*"

The ringing of the phone was loud and sharp. She held the receiver away from her ear, so that the sound seemed a little more remote, more impersonal. Six rings, eight, ten. Agnes Osborne's house was small and she could get to the phone from any room in it, or from the patio or back yard, in less than ten rings, less than five if she hurried. And during the past year, when any call might be about Robert, she always hurried.

The booth was hot and smelled of stale tobacco and food and people. Devon opened the door a few inches, and with the little gust of new air came the sound of people talking in the alcove adjoining the row of phone booths. One of the voices was a man's, hoarse and low-pitched:

"I swear to you I didn't know a thing about it until a few minutes ago."

"Liar. You knew it all the time and wouldn't tell me. So did they. The whole bunch of you are liars."

"Listen, Carla, I'm warning you, for your own good stay away from the ranch."

"I'm not scared of the Estivars. Or the Osbornes either. My brothers see to it nobody pushes me around."

"This isn't kid stuff anymore. Stay out of it."

"Look who's giving orders again like he's wearing his old cop suit and tin badge."

"Trouble, you've been nothing but trouble to me ever since I laid eyes on you."

"You laid more than eyes on me, *chicano.*"

Devon waited for another half minute, six rings, but there was no answer from Mrs. Osborne's house and no more talk from the alcove. She opened the door and stepped out into the hall.

The girl had gone. Valenzuela stood alone at the barred window of the alcove, his eyes somber and red-rimmed. When he saw Devon his mouth moved slightly as though it were shaping words he wasn't ready to speak. When he did speak, it was in a voice quite unlike the one he'd used on Carla, soft and sad, with no hint of authority in it.

"I'm sorry, Mrs. Osborne."

"What about?"

"Everything, how it's all turned out."

"Thank you."

"I wanted you to know I hoped things would be different, and the case would be solved by now. That first night when I was called out to the ranch to look for Mr. Osborne, I was sure he'd show up. Every step I took, every door I opened, every corner I went around, I expected to find him—maybe beat up a little or sick or even up to some mischief. I'm sorry things turned out this way."

"It's not your fault, Mr. Valenzuela. I'm sure you did the best you could." She wasn't sure, she'd never be sure, but it was too late now to say anything else.

"I could maybe have done better if they'd given me more money. Not more salary. Bribe money."

"*Bribe* money?"

"Don't be shocked, Mrs. Osborne. In a poor country everything's for sale, including the truth. I believe someone saw that old red truck at the border or on the road going south to Ensenada or east to Tecate; someone noticed the men in it, maybe recognized a couple of them; someone may have watched them bury the body in the desert or dump it into the sea."

"Mrs. Osborne offered a substantial reward."

"Rewards are too official, too many people are involved, too much red tape. A bribe is a nice simple family type of thing."

"Why didn't you explain the situation to me a year ago?"

"A cop can't ask a private citizen for bribe money. It wouldn't look pretty in the newspapers, it might even cause an international scandal. After all, no country likes to admit that a lot of its police, its judges, its politicians are corrupt . . . Anyway, it's over. All I'm saying now is I'm sorry, Mrs. Osborne."

"Yes. So am I."

She turned and walked toward the courtroom, holding herself rigid to counteract the feeling she had inside that vital parts had come loose and were bleeding. Someone saw the truck—noticed the men—watched them bury the body or dump it in the sea. She thought of the dozens of times she'd watched the men stooping in the fields, but they were always in the distance, always anonymous. She had wanted to get to know them a little, to be able to tell them apart, to call them by name and ask them about their homes and families, but Estivar wouldn't allow it. He said it wasn't safe, the men would misinterpret any friendliness on her part. The men, too, had obviously been given orders. When she drove past a field being harvested, they would bend low over their work, their faces hidden by the big straw hats they wore from dawn to dusk.

The light had been switched on in the sign above the door: *Quiet Please, Court Is in Session.* By the time Devon entered, the room was nearly full, the way it had been before the recess, but now the Lopez girl, as well as Mrs. Osborne, was missing.

In the aisle beside the seat Devon had occupied since the hearing began, Ford stood talking to Leo Bishop. Both men looked impatiently at Devon, as though they'd been waiting for her and had expected her to come back sooner.

Ford said, "Well?"

"There was no answer."

"Did you let it ring several minutes, in case she might be outside or in the shower or something?"

"Yes."

"Then I guess you'd better go over to the house and check up on her. Mr. Bishop here has offered to drive you or let you use his car, whichever you prefer."

"Exactly what am I supposed to do?"

"Find out if she's all right and when she intends showing up to testify."

"Why are you forcing her to testify?"

"I'm not forcing her. When I brought the subject up she seemed perfectly willing to be a witness."

"That was just a front," Devon said. "You mustn't be taken in by it."

"Okay, so I don't know her front from her back. I'm a simple man. When people tell me something I believe it, I don't immediately conclude that they mean the opposite."

"She—isn't ready to admit Robert is dead."

"She's had a whole year to get used to it. Maybe she's not trying hard enough."

"That seems a very cynical attitude."

"You'd better watch it," Ford said with a wry little smile. "You're beginning to sound like an honest-to-God loving daughter-in-law."

The door to the judge's chambers had opened and the clerk was intoning: "Remain seated and come to order. Superior Court is again in session."

"Call Ernest Valenzuela."

"Ernest Valenzuela, take the stand, please."

10

WHEN THEY REACHED LEO'S CAR in the parking lot, he unlocked the right front door and Devon stepped inside without protest. She didn't like being dependent on Leo but she liked even less the idea of driving a car she wasn't used to in a city that was still strange to her.

Leo got in behind the wheel and turned on the ignition and the air conditioning. "I've kept away from you all day because you asked me to."

"It was Mrs. Osborne's idea," Devon said. "She thought people would talk if they saw us together."

"I'd like to think they had something to talk about . . . Do they?"

"No."

"No period, or no not yet?"

Her only response was a slight shake of her head that could have meant anything.

She had taken off the white wrist-length gloves which she'd worn almost continuously since early morning. They lay now in her lap, the false passive immaculate hands she'd exhibited to the spectators in court and strangers in the hall and on the street. Her real hands, sunburned and rough, with calloused palms and bitten nails, she showed only to friends like Leo who wouldn't care, or to people she saw every day like the Estivars and Dulzura who wouldn't notice.

"I worry about you," Leo said.

"Well, stop. I don't want you to worry about me."

"I don't want to, either, but that's the way it is. Did you have a decent lunch?"

"A hamburger."

"That's not enough. You're too thin."

"You shouldn't fuss over me, Leo."

"Why not?"

"It makes me nervous, self-conscious. I like to feel at ease with you."

"All right, no fussing. That's a promise." The humming of the air conditioner muffled the rasp in his voice.

He turned north on the freeway. Traffic had been slowed down to boulevard speed by its own volume. People passing were without names or faces or any identification except their cars: a red Mustang with Florida plates, a blue Chevelle, a VW camper decorated with daisies, a silver Continental with matching silver smoke coming from its exhaust, a yellow Dart with a black vinyl roof, a white Monaco station wagon trailing a boat. It was as if human beings existed merely to keep the vehicles in motion, and the real significance had shifted from the Smiths and the Joneses to Cougars and Corvairs, Toronados and Toyotas.

"Turn west on University," Devon said. "She lives at 3117 Ocotillo; that's three or four blocks north."

"I know where it is."

"Did Mr. Ford tell you?"

"She told me. She called me one day and asked me to come and see her."

"I thought you were barely on speaking terms."

"We barely were," Leo said. "In fact, we barely are. But I went."

"When was that?"

"About three weeks ago, as soon as she found out the hearing was scheduled for today. Well, after a lot of chitchat she finally got to the point—she wanted to make sure my wife's death wasn't brought up during the hearing. She said it was irrelevant. I agreed. She offered me a drink, which I refused, and I drove back to the ranch. That's all. At least as far as I was concerned it was all. I can't be sure what was in her mind, perhaps something quite different from what was actually said."

"Why do you suggest that?"

"If what she really wanted was to keep Ruth's name out of the proceedings, she would have called Mr. Ford, not me. I'm only a witness, he's running the show."

"Maybe she called him, too."

"Maybe." He ran his left hand around the scalloped rim of the steering wheel as though it were a bumpy road he'd never explored before. "I think she was trying to make sure I didn't say anything against her son. She had to believe—and to make other people believe—that Robert was perfect."

"What could you have said against him, Leo?"

"He wasn't perfect."

"You were referring to something specific."

"Nothing that should make any difference to you now. It was over before you even knew the Osbornes existed." He added, after a time, "It wasn't even Robert's fault. He just happened to be the boy next door. And Ruth—well, she happened to be the girl next door, only she was pushing forty and afraid of growing old."

"So the gossip about them was true."

"Yes."

"Why didn't you tell me before?"

"I started to, many times, only I never went through with it. It seemed cruel. Now—well, now I know it's necessary, cruel or not. I can't afford to let you believe Mrs. Osborne's version of Robert. He wasn't perfect. He had faults, he made mistakes. Ruth turned out to be one of the bigger mistakes but he couldn't have foreseen that. She was pretty appealing in her role of defenseless little woman, and Robert was a setup for her. He didn't even have a girlfriend to stand in the way, thanks to Mrs. Osborne. She'd managed to get rid of all the girls who weren't good enough for him, and that meant all the girls. So he ended up with a married woman nearly twice his age."

Devon sat in silence, trying to imagine the two of them together, Ruth seeing in Robert another chance at youth, Robert seeing in her a chance at manhood. How often did they meet, and where? Beside the reservoir or in the grove of date palms? In the mess hall or bunkhouse when there were no migrants working on the ranch? In the ranch house itself when Mrs. Osborne went to the city? No matter where they met, people must have seen them and been shocked or amused or sympathetic—the Estivars, Dulzura, the ranch hands, perhaps even Mrs. Osborne before she shut her eyes tight and finally. Mrs. Osborne's references to Ruth had all been similar and in the same tone: "Robert was kind to the poor woman . . ." "He went out of his way to be neighborly . . ." "It was pitiful the spectacle she made of herself, but Robert was always patient and understanding."

Robert—kind, patient, understanding and neighborly. Very, very neighborly.

Devon said, "How long had it been going on?"

"I'm not sure, but I think a long time."

"Years?"

"Yes. Probably ever since he came back from school in Arizona."

"But he was just seventeen then, a boy."

"Seventeen-year-olds aren't boys. Don't waste sympathy on him. It's possible that Ruth did him a favor by distracting him from his mother."

"How can you say such a terrible thing so calmly?"

"Maybe it's not so terrible. Maybe I'm not so calm." But he sounded calm, even remote. "When Estivar was on the witness stand this morning he blamed the school for teaching Robert prejudice and keeping him away from the Estivar family. I don't believe it was prejudice. Robert simply had something new in his life, something he couldn't afford to share with the Estivars."

"If you knew about the affair, why didn't you try to stop it?"

"I did. At first Ruth denied everything. Later we had periodic fights, long and loud and no holds barred. After the last one she packed a suitcase and set out on foot for the Osbornes'. She never got there."

"Then nothing was planned about her running away with Robert?"

"No. I think it would have been a real shock to him to look out and see her heading for his house with a suitcase. But he didn't see her. It had started to rain heavily and he was in the study catching up on his accounts. Mrs. Osborne was in her bedroom upstairs. Both rooms faced west, away from the river, so nobody was watching it, nobody knew the exact time of the flash flood, nobody saw Ruth try to get across. She was small and delicate like you, it wouldn't have taken much to knock her off her feet."

Small and delicate . . . *You remind me of someone back home,*" Robert had told her at their first meeting. "*Someone nice—or she used to be. She's dead now. A lot of people think I killed her.*"

"Leo."

"Yes."

"Her death was an accident?"

"According to the coroner."

"And according to you?"

"To me," Leo said slowly, "it seemed a crazy way to die, drowning in the middle of a desert."

THE HOUSE AT 3117 OCOTILLO STREET was built in the California mission style, with tiled roof and thick adobe walls and an archway leading into a courtyard. The archway was decorated with ceramic tiles and from the top of it hung a miniature merry-go-round of brass horses that twitched and pranced and chimed against each other when the wind blew.

The inner court was paved with imitation flagstones and lined with shrubs and small trees growing in Mexican clay pots. The orange of the persimmon leaves, the pink of the hibiscus blossoms, the purple of the princess flowers, the crimson of the firethorn berries, all seemed lusterless and pale compared to the gaudy high-gloss paint on their containers. The word WELCOME printed on the mat outside the front door looked as though nobody had ever stepped on it. Devon's sandals sank into the thick deep velvety pile until only their tops were visible, crossed straps like two X's marking the spot: *Devon Osborne stood here.*

She pressed the door chime. Her arm felt heavy and stiff like a lead pipe attached to her shoulder.

"I don't know what to believe," she said. "I wish you hadn't told me any of it."

"Sometimes it's easy to make a hero out of a dead man, especially with the help of his mother. Well, I can't compete with heroes. If I have to cut the opposition down to size in order to win, I'll do it."

"You mustn't talk like that."

"Why not?"

"She might hear you."

"She only hears what she wants to. Anything I say isn't likely to be included."

A gust of wind blew across the courtyard. The horses on the tiny merry-go-round danced to their own music. Royal petals escaped from the princess flowers, and bamboo clawed and scratched at the living-room window.

The drapes were open and most of the room and its contents were visible. Side by side along one wall were the special possessions Mrs. Osborne had taken with her from the ranch house—the mahogany piano and the antique cherrywood desk. Both were open, as if Mrs. Osborne had played a tune and written a letter and disappeared. The rest of the furniture had come with the house, and Mrs. Osborne hadn't bothered to change any of it—a pair of flowery wing chairs facing each other across a backgammon table, a glass-fronted bookcase, and on the walls oil paintings of someone's childhood, remembered rivers, clear and sweet, emerald meadows, golden forests of maple.

Leo had walked around to the side of the house to check the garage. He returned looking irritable and worried, as though he suspected fate was about to pull another trick on him, that wheels were in motion he couldn't stop and booby traps set in places he didn't know.

"Her car's here," he said. "You'd better try the door."

"Even if it's unlocked we can't just walk in."

"Why not?"

"She wouldn't like it."

"She may not be in a position to like or dislike it."

"What does that mean?"

He didn't answer.

"Leo, are you suggesting she might have—"

"I'm suggesting we make an attempt to find out."

The knob turned easily and the door swung inward, slowed by its own weight and Devon's reluctance. As the door opened, a draught of air blew several of the papers off the desk. Leaning over to pick one up, Devon saw that it was covered with printing done with a thick-tipped black marking pen. There were sentences and half-sentences, single words, phrases, some in English, some in Spanish.

> Reward Premio (Remuneracion? Ask Ford)
> The sum of $10,000 will be paid to anyone furnishing information
> (No, no. Keep it simple.)
> On October 13, 1967
> Robert K. Osborne, age 24, blond hair, blue eyes, height 6'1" weight 170
> (More money? Ask Ford)
> Have you seen this man? (Use 3 pictures, front, side, 3/4)
> ¿
> !Atencion!
> Please help me find my son

Devon stood with the paper in her hand, listening to the sound of Leo moving around the dining room and the kitchen. She wondered how she could tell him that this wasn't to be the last day after all. Mrs. Osborne intended to offer another reward and the whole thing was going to start over again. There would be still another round of phone calls and letters, most of them patently ridiculous, but some reasonable enough to raise faint new hopes. The lady who claimed to have watched Robert land in a flying saucer in a field near Omaha needn't be taken seriously, yet some consideration had to be given to reports that he'd been seen working as a deckhand on a yacht anchored off Ensenada, picking up a suitcase at the TWA baggage-claim department at Los Angeles International Airport, drinking rum and Coke at a swish bar in San Francisco, running an elevator in a hotel in Denver. All reports within reason had been checked out. But Valenzuela said, "He's not working or drinking or traveling or anything else. He lost too much blood, ma'am."

Please help me find my son.

Devon put the sheet of paper back on the desk very carefully as if it were contaminated material. Then she followed Leo into the kitchen. The room had been used recently. There was a pot of coffee on the stove, the heat turned low under it, and on the work counter of the sink half a head of lettuce, two slices of bread curling a little at the edges, and an opened jar of peanut butter with a knife stuck in it. It was an ordinary table knife, blunt-tipped and dull-edged, but it may have reminded Mrs. Osborne, as it did Devon, of another more deadly knife, and she had fled the memory.

"It looks as though she started to make a sandwich," Leo said, "and something interrupted her—the doorbell maybe, or the telephone."

"She told us she was too tired to eat, that she wanted just to rest."

"Then we'd better check the bedrooms. Which is hers?"

"I don't know. She keeps changing."

The front bedroom had a window on the courtyard protected by iron grillwork and framed with bougainvillea blossoms that fluttered in the slightest breeze like bits of scarlet tissue paper. It was fully furnished, but it had an air of abandonment about it as though the people who really belonged there had long since left the premises. The closet door was partly open and inside were half a dozen large neatly stacked cartons with Salvation Army printed in red marking pencil on each one. Devon recognized the printing as her own and the cartons as those she'd packed with Robert's stuff and given to Mrs. Osborne to deliver to the Salvation Army.

The other bedroom was occupied. Its sleeper lay face down across the bed, her body wrapped in a faded blue silk housecoat. Her arms were bent at the elbows and both hands were pressed against her head as if they were trying to protect the places where the hair was thinning. On the bureau was a Styrofoam wig stand holding the orderly curls Mrs. Osborne showed to the public. The blue hat she'd worn in court had fallen or been thrown on the carpet and her ribbon knit dress hung limply across a chair like an abandoned skin.

Both windows were shut tight. Suspended in the still air was the faint sour odor of regret, of little sins and failures mildewing in closets and damp forgotten corners.

"Mrs. Osborne," Devon said, but it sounded wrong, as if this silent helpless woman was a stranger with no right to the name.

"Mrs. Osborne, answer me. It's Devon. Are you all right?"

The stranger stirred, disclaiming the identity, protesting the invasion of her privacy when Devon leaned over and touched her temple and felt the pulse in her thin white wrist. The pulse was slow but as steady as the ticking of a clock. On the night table beside the bed there was a half-empty bottle of yellow capsules. The label identified them as Nembutal, three-quarter grain, and the prescriber as the Osbornes' family doctor in Boca de Rio.

"Do you hear me, Mrs. Osborne?"

"Go—way."

"Did you take any pills?"

"Pills."

"How many pills did you take?"

"How—? Two."

"Is that all? Just two pills?"

"Two."

"When did you take them?"

"Tired. Go away."

"Did you take them when you came home at noon?"

"Noon."

"You took two pills at noon, is that right?"

"Yes. *Yes.*"

Leo opened the windows, and the incoming air smelled of a forgotten harvest, overripe oranges whose thickened pockmarked skins covered pulp that had gone dry and fibrous. Mrs. Osborne turned over on her side, knees bent and hands over her head like a fetus trying to ward off the pain of birth.

"If she's leveling with me, she took only a hundred milligrams," Devon said. "The stuff should be wearing off pretty soon. I'll stay with her until it does."

"I'll stay, too, if it will help."

"It won't. She'd be upset if she woke up and found you here. You'd better go back to the courthouse and tell Mr. Ford what happened."

"I don't know what happened."

"Well, tell him as much as you do know—that she's all right but she won't be able to testify, at least not this afternoon."

11

FORD addressed the bench.

"Your Honor, the testimony of this witness, Ernest Valenzuela, has presented a number of problems. Since he is no longer employed by the sheriff's department, the files on the case are not available to him. However, I obtained permission for Mr. Valenzuela to refresh his memory by going over the files in the presence of a deputy and making notes for his appearance here today. I also arranged for a deputy to bring into the courtroom certain reports and pieces of evidence which I consider vital to this hearing."

"These reports and pieces of evidence," Gallagher said, "are they now in your possession?"

"Yes, your Honor."

"All right, proceed."

Valenzuela took the oath: the testimony he was about to give in the matter now pending before the court would be the truth and the whole truth and nothing but the truth.

Ford said, "State your name, please."

"Ernest Valenzuela."

"Where do you live, Mr. Valenzuela?"

"209 Third Street, Boca de Rio."

"Are you currently employed?"

"Yes, sir."

"Where and in what capacity?"

"I'm a salesman with the America West Insurance Company."

"How long have you held your present position?"

"Six months."

"Before that, what was the nature of your employment?"

"I was a deputy in the Boca de Rio division of the sheriff's department of San Diego County."

"For how long?"

"Since 1955 when I got out of the army, a little more than twelve years."

"Describe briefly the situation in the sheriff's department in Boca de Rio on Friday, October thirteen, 1967."

"The boss, Lieutenant Scotler, was on sick leave and I was in charge."

"What happened that Friday night, Mr. Valenzuela?"

"A call came in from the Osborne ranch at a quarter to eleven asking for assistance in searching for Mr. Osborne. He'd gone out earlier in the evening to look for his dog and failed to return. I picked up my partner, Larry Bismarck, at his house and we drove out to the ranch. By this time the search for Mr. Osborne had been going on for about an hour, led by Mr. Estivar, the foreman, and his son, Cruz. Mr. Osborne hadn't been located but there was considerable blood on the floor of the mess hall. I immediately phoned headquarters in San Diego and asked for reinforcements. Meanwhile my partner had found small fragments of glass on the floor of the mess hall and part of a shirt sleeve caught on a yucca spike just outside the main door. The shirt sleeve also had blood on it."

"Did you take any samples of blood?"

"No, sir. I left that to the experts."

"What did the experts do with the samples of blood they collected?"

"Sent them up to the police lab in Sacramento for analysis."

"This is the usual procedure?"

"Yes, sir."

"And at a later date you received a report of that analysis?"

"Yes, sir."

Ford turned to the bench. "Your Honor, I hereby submit a copy of the full report for you to read at your convenience. It is, naturally, detailed and technical, and in the interests of saving time—not to mention the taxpayers' money—I suggest Mr. Valenzuela be allowed to give in his own words the facts essential to this hearing."

"Granted."

"I will give Mr. Valenzuela a copy of the report also, in case his memory needs further refreshing."

Ford took two manila envelopes out of his briefcase and handed one to Valenzuela. Valenzuela accepted his reluctantly, as though he didn't need or didn't want his memory refreshed.

"The report from the police lab," Ford said, "deals with blood samples taken from four main areas—the floor of the mess hall, the piece of shirt sleeve caught on the yucca spike, the butterfly knife found by Jaime in the pumpkin field, the mouth of the dead dog. Is that correct, Mr. Valenzuela?"

"Yes, sir."

"Let's take them in the order mentioned. First, the blood on the floor of the mess hall."

"Two types were found in considerable quantity, type B positive and type AB negative. Both are uncommon types, AB negative, for example, being found in only five percent of the population."

"What about the blood found on the piece of shirt sleeve?"

"Again there were two types. The smaller amount matched some of the blood on the floor, type B, and the rest was type O. This is the commonest type, found in approximately forty-five percent of the population."

"What blood type was found on the knife?"

"AB negative."

"And in the dog's mouth?"

"Type B positive."

"Did the amount of blood found and the fact that it was of three different types lead you to any conclusions?"

"Yes, sir."

"Such as?"

"Three persons were involved in a fight. Two of them were injured seriously, the third injured to a lesser extent."

"The type O blood found on the shirt sleeve belonged to this third man?"

"Yes, sir."

From his briefcase Ford took a clear plastic bag containing a piece of blue and green plaid material. "This is the sleeve referred to?"

"Yes, sir."

"I offer it in evidence."

A few of the spectators leaned forward in their seats to get a better look, but they soon sat back. Last year's blood appeared no more interesting than last year's coffee stains.

"Now, Mr. Valenzuela, tell us what facts were established by the contents of the plastic bag."

"The sleeve belongs to one of thousands of similar shirts sold by Sears Roebuck through their catalog and retail stores. The shirt is a hundred percent cotton and comes in four color combinations and in sizes small, medium, large. Price in the catalog is $3.95. The style number and lot number are contained in the report of my investigation."

"In your estimation, Mr. Valenzuela, how many shirts of that style, color and size were sold by Sears Roebuck last year and the year before?"

"Thousands."

"Did you try to pinpoint the sale of that particular shirt to one particular person?"

"Yes, sir. We couldn't do it, though."

"But you were able to ascertain some facts about the man who wore the shirt, were you not?"

"Yes, sir. He was small for one thing, probably less than five foot six, a hundred thirty-five pounds. A number of hairs adhering to the inside of the sleeve cuff indicate that he was from one of the darker but not Negroid races."

"In view of the proximity of the Mexican border and the fact that a large percentage of the population in the area is Mexican or of Mexican descent, there is considerable likelihood that the owner of the shirt was Mexican?"

"Yes, sir."

"You didn't examine the sleeve cuff yourself, did you, Mr. Valenzuela?"

"Just superficially. The real examination was done at the police lab in Sacramento."

"Was anything significant discovered in addition to the hairs?"

"Quite a bit of dirt and oil."

"What kind of dirt?"

"Particles of sandy alkaline soil of the type found in irrigated-desert sections of the state like ours. There was a high nitrogen content in the soil, indicating the recent addition of a commercial fertilizer which is used on most ranches in the area."

"And the oil mixed with the dirt?"

"It was sebum, the secretion of human sebaceous glands. This secretion is usually abundant in younger and more active people and decreases with age."

"So a picture begins to take shape of the man who wore the shirt," Ford said. "He was small and dark, probably Mexican. He worked on one of the ranches in the area. He was young. The blood on his shirt was type O. And he got into a fight in which at least two other people were involved. Would it be possible to reconstruct this man's part in the fight?"

"I think so. The evidence seems to indicate that in the first stage of the fight he was hurt enough to bleed and that the left sleeve of his shirt was torn. He decided to escape before things got any rougher. As he ran out the door the torn sleeve caught on one of the spikes of the yucca plant and ripped completely off."

"And the other two men?"

"They finished the fight," Valenzuela said dryly.

"What can you tell us about these two men?"

"As I indicated earlier, they had different blood types, B and AB. Both of them bled considerably, especially AB."

"On the floor of the mess hall?"

"Yes, sir."

"Were samples of blood scraped off the floor and transported to the police lab in Sacramento?"

"No, sir. A section of the floor itself was removed and sent up there. This method allows a more precise analysis."

"To simplify matters I will refer to each of the three men by their blood types. Is that agreeable to you, Mr. Valenzuela?"

"Yes, sir."

"Then O would be the dark young man who wore the green and blue plaid shirt and left the fight early after sustaining a superficial wound."

"Yes."

"Now let's turn our attention to B. What do we know about him?"

"Traces of type B blood were found in the dog's mouth."

"Robert Osborne's dog, Maxie?"

"Yes."

"Since it's highly unlikely, if not impossible, that Robert Osborne would have been attacked by his own dog, we know first of all that B was not Robert Osborne."

"There is other evidence to that effect."

"Such as?"

"Bits of human tissue, skin and hair found in the dog's mouth indicate that B was dark-skinned and dark-haired. Mr. Osborne was neither. In addition, a small shred of cloth was caught between two of the dog's teeth. The cloth was heavy-duty navy-blue cotton twill of the kind used to make men's Levis. When Mr. Osborne left the house he was wearing grey gabardine slacks. In fact, he didn't own any Levis. He wore lighter-weight, lighter-colored work clothes because of the heat in the valley."

"Getting back to the dog for a moment, when and where was it found?"

"It was found the following Monday morning, October sixteen, near the corner where the Osborne ranch road joins the road leading to the main highway. The exact spot is out of range of the map on the display board."

"What were the circumstances?"

"Several children from the Polk ranch, which adjoins Mr. Bishop's, were on their way to meet the school bus when they spotted the dog's body under a creosote bush. They told the bus driver and he called us."

"Was an autopsy performed on the dog?"

"Yes, sir."

"Tell us briefly the pertinent facts."

"Multiple fractures of the skull and vertebrae indicated that the dog was struck and fatally injured by a moving vehicle such as a car."

"Or a truck."

"Or a truck."

Ford consulted his notes again. "So we had definite knowledge that the man we have called B was dark-skinned and dark-haired, that he wore Levis, that he was bitten by the dog. What else?"

"He owned, or at least used, the butterfly knife."

"How can you be sure of that?"

"The blood on the knife belonged to the other man, AB."

"Do you know who that other man was?"

"Yes, sir. Robert Osborne."

Though there was no one in the room who hadn't anticipated the answer, reaction to the spoken name seemed to be one of group surprise, simultaneous intakes of breath, sudden stirrings and rustlings and whispers.

"Mr. Valenzuela, tell the court why you're so sure the third man was Robert Osborne."

"The pieces of glass found on the mess-hall floor were identified by Dr. Paul Jarrett, an ophthalmologist, as fragments of contact lenses he had prescribed for Robert Osborne during the last week of May 1967."

"Dr. Jarrett's report is on file as part of the record?"

"Yes, sir."

"Without going into technicalities, can you tell the court to what degree contact lenses are distinctive?"

"They're not absolutely unique the way fingerprints are, for example. But each lens has to be fitted to each eye with such precision that it's highly unlikely a mistake in identification could be made."

"Since you've brought up the subject of fingerprints, Mr. Valenzuela, let's pursue it. In reading your report of the case I was struck by the small amount of attention given to fingerprints. Will you explain this?"

"A large number of prints were lifted off the doors, walls, tables, benches, and so on. That was the trouble. Everybody and his little brother had been in and out of that mess hall." Valenzuela paused, looking guilty, as though he'd committed a punishable offense by using language not condoned by the official rule book. "There were too many fingerprints in and around the building to allow for proper classification and comparison."

"Now, Mr. Valenzuela, on November eight, nearly four weeks after Robert Osborne's disappearance, a man named John W. Pomeroy was arrested in an Imperial Beach bar. Is that correct?"

"Yes, sir."

"What was the charge?"

"Drunk and disorderly."

"Was anything pertinent to this case found among Mr. Pomeroy's effects when he was booked?"

"Yes, sir."

"What was it?"

"A credit card issued by the Pacific United Bank to Robert Osborne."

"How did it come into Mr. Pomeroy's possession?"

"He said he found it, and his story checked out. At the beginning of that week the valley had its first rain of the season. The river flooded—or, more accurately, it appeared—and a lot of debris washed down that had been accumulating for months. Pomeroy was a lifelong vagrant; searching through piles of debris was second nature to him. He picked up the credit card about a quarter of a mile downstream from the Osborne ranch."

"Is Mr. Pomeroy available for questioning in this proceeding?"

"No, sir. He died in the County Hospital of pneumonia the following spring."

"Except for the credit card found in his possession, was there anything linking him to Robert Osborne's disappearance on October thirteen?"

"No, sir. Pomeroy was in jail in Oakland on October thirteen."

"We offer in evidence exhibit number five, the credit card issued to Robert Osborne by the Pacific Union Bank . . . There is one more point I'd like to bring up at this time, Mr. Valenzuela. You stated a while ago that the blood on the butterfly knife was AB negative, an uncommon type found in approximately five percent of the population. Was Robert Osborne one of this five percent?"

"Yes, sir."

"Can you offer proof of that?"

"In the summer of 1964 Mr. Osborne underwent an appendectomy. Preoperative blood tests were routinely conducted and the hospital records indicate that Robert Osborne's was AB negative."

Judge Gallagher had slumped further and further into his chair, his arms crossed over his chest giving his black robe the appearance of a strait jacket. For the most part he kept his eyes closed. The lighting in the courtroom had been cunningly engineered by experts to be too bright to look at and too dim to read by.

He said, without opening his eyes, "There is no precise law on this point, Mr. Ford, but in trying to establish the death of an absent person, it has become general practice to include an averment of diligent search."

"I was coming to that, your Honor," Ford said.

"Very well. Proceed."

"Mr. Valenzuela, did you conduct a diligent search for Robert Osborne?"

"Yes, sir."

"Indicate the time covered."

"From eleven P.M. on October thirteen, 1967, to the morning of April twenty, 1968, when I submitted my resignation from the department."

"And the area covered?"

"By me personally, or by everyone connected with the case?"

"The whole area covered during the investigation."

"The full details are in my report. But I can summarize by saying that the search for Mr. Osborne and the search for the missing workers ultimately became the same thing. It spread out from the Osborne ranch to all the large agricultural centers of California where migrant labor is used—the Sacramento and San Joaquin and Imperial valleys, certain sections of various counties like San Luis Obispo, Santa Barbara, Ventura. Out-of-state areas included places that had served as reception centers during the bracero program, Nogales, Arizona, and El Paso, Hidalgo and Eagle Pass, Texas."

"Was there a particular part of the investigation for which you were personally responsible?"

"I checked out the names and addresses given to Mr. Estivar by the men who'd arrived at the Osborne ranch during the last week of September."

"Do you have a list of those names and addresses with you this afternoon?"

"Yes, sir."

"Would you read them aloud to the court, please?"

"Valerio Pinedo, Guaymas. Oswaldo Rojas, Saltillo. Salvador Mayo, Camargo. Victor Ontiveras, Chihuahua. Silvio Placencia, Hermosillo. Hilario Robles, Tepic. Jesus Rivera, Ciudad Juárez. Ysidro Nolina, Fresnillo. Emilio Olivas, Guadalajara. Raul Guttierez, Navojoa."

There was a brief delay while the court reporter checked with Valenzuela on the spelling of certain names. Then Ford continued: "Did anything about this list strike you as peculiar right from the beginning?"

"Yes, sir."

"Tell the court what it was."

"Well, Mexicans are very much family-oriented. It struck me as odd that no two of the men had the same name or even the same hometown. They were traveling as a unit in a single truck, yet they came from places as far apart as Ciudad Juárez and Guadalajara, nearly eighteen hundred miles. I wondered how such a mixed group had gotten together in the first place and how the truck they were driving managed to cover the distances involved. From Ciudad Juárez to the Osborne ranch, for instance, is another seven hundred fifty miles. The truck was described to me by various people as an ancient G.M., and on the stand this morning Mr. Estivar said it was burning so much oil it looked like a smokestack."

"Did you, on seeing the list, immediately sense that something was wrong?"

"Yes, sir. Normally a group of ten men like that would come from just two or three families, all living in the same area and probably not far from the border."

"So when you started into Mexico to try and find the missing men, you already suspected that the names and addresses they'd given Mr. Estivar were fictitious and their papers forged?"

"Yes, sir."

"Did you, in spite of this, conduct a diligent search of all the areas?"

"I did."

"And you found no trace of Robert Osborne or of the men who'd been employed at the Osborne ranch?"

"None."

"During this time other police departments in the Southwest joined the search and bulletins were circulated throughout the country?"

"Yes, sir."

"At the end of November, Robert Osborne's mother offered a ten thousand dollar reward for information about her son, dead or alive."

"You know more about that than I do, Mr. Ford."

Ford made a quarter-turn to face the bench. "Your Honor, this reward was handled through my office at Mrs. Osborne's request. Notices of it were posted in public buildings, and ads were placed, in two languages, in newspapers both in this country and Mexico. There was also considerable news coverage on radio and TV, mainly in the Tijuana-San Diego area. I rented a P.O. box to receive mail and a special phone was installed in my office for calls. The reward generated plenty of interest—ten thousand dollars usually does. We had a lot of crank calls and letters, a couple of false confessions, anonymous tips, astrological readings, suggestions on how the money might better be spent and a few assorted threats. One woman even appeared at my office carrying a crystal ball in a bowling bag. No useful information was received from the crystal ball or any other source, so on my advice Mrs. Osborne withdrew the offer and all ads and notices were canceled."

The judge opened his eyes and gave Valenzuela a brief penetrating glance. "As I understand it, Mr. Valenzuela, from October thirteen, when Robert Osborne disappeared, until April twenty, when you resigned from the sheriff's office, your full time was spent in trying to locate Robert Osborne and/or the men allegedly responsible for his disappearance."

"Yes, your Honor."

"That would seem to constitute a diligent search on your part."

"Many others were involved. Some still are. A case like this is never officially closed even though the deputies are assigned to other jobs."

"I believe it's legitimate for me to ask whether your resignation from the sheriff's department was due in part to your failure to locate Mr. Osborne and the missing men."

"It wasn't, your Honor. I had personal reasons." Valenzuela rubbed one side of his jaw as though it had begun to hurt. "Nobody likes to fail, naturally. If I'd found what I was looking for, I would have hesitated before going into another line of work."

"Thank you, Mr. Valenzuela." Judge Gallagher leaned back in his chair and recrossed his arms on his chest. "You may continue, Mr. Ford."

"Has diligent search been proved to your Honor's satisfaction?"

"Of course, of course."

"Now, Mr. Valenzuela, during the six months you worked on the case you must have reached some conclusions about what happened to the ten missing men."

"There is no doubt in my mind that they crossed the border, probably before they were even missed at the ranch and before the police knew a crime had been committed. The men had a truck and they had papers. Once they were back in their own country they were safe."

"How safe?"

"Let's put it in terms of figures," Valenzuela said. "At that time Tijuana had a population exceeding two hundred thousand and a police force with only eighteen squad cars."

"All vehicles are stopped at the border, aren't they?"

"The Tijuana-San Diego border is said to be the busiest in the world, twenty million people a year. This averages out to fifty-four thousand a day, but in actual fact weekday traffic is much lighter and weekend traffic much heavier. Between a Friday afternoon and a Sunday night three hundred thousand people or more travel between the two countries. Numbers alone present a very serious problem to law enforcement agencies. There are also other factors. Mexican laws differ from U.S. laws, enforcement in many areas is inconsistent, bribery of officials is a general practice, policemen are few and usually poorly trained."

"How much chance did you figure you had of locating the missing men once they'd crossed the border into their own country?"

"When I started out I thought there was some chance. As time went on, it became obvious there wasn't any. The reasons have been mentioned—generalized corruption, overcrowding and understaffing at the border, lack of training, discipline and morale among Mexican police officers. Such statements aren't going to make me very popular among certain people, but facts must be faced. I'm not inventing anything in order to justify my own failure in this case."

"Your candor is appreciated, Mr. Valenzuela."

"Not by everybody."

Valenzuela's smile appeared and disappeared so fast that Ford wasn't quite sure he'd seen it and not at all sure it had been a smile. Perhaps it was merely a grimace indicating a twinge of pain in the head or stomach or conscience.

"One more item of interest, Mr. Valenzuela. There's been considerable talk about the blood found on the floor of the mess hall. Between the mess hall and the bunkhouse there's an area of blacktop. Was any blood found on it?"

"No, sir."

"Near it?"

"No, sir."

"What about the bunkhouse?"

"It was a mess, as the photographs in the file clearly indicate, but there were no bloodstains."

"Was it possible to determine if anything had been taken from the bunkhouse?"

"Not that night. The following day a careful examination was made with Mr. Estivar present and it was discovered that three blankets were missing from one of the bunks, a striped flannelette, more like a double sheet, and two brown wool, army surplus."

"Did you connect the fact that no bloodstains were found outside the mess hall with the fact that three blankets were missing from the bunkhouse?"

"Yes, sir. It seemed reasonable to assume that Mr. Osborne's body had been wrapped in the blankets before it was removed from the mess hall."

"Why three blankets? Why not two? Or one?"

"One or two probably wouldn't have been adequate," Valenzuela said. "A young man of Mr. Osborne's height and weight carries between six and a half and seven quarts of blood in his system. Even if as much as two quarts were found on the floor of the mess hall, there would have been enough left to cause a lot of trouble for the other men."

"You mean the other two men who were involved in the fight?"

"Yes, sir—O, who left the fight early, and B, who lost a considerable amount of blood."

"Your previous evidence indicated that both of these men were small."

"Yes, sir."

"Did you know Robert Osborne personally, Mr. Valenzuela?"

"Yes, sir."

"How would you describe his physique?"

"He was tall, not heavy but well-muscled and strong."

"Could two small men, both wounded, one of them quite badly, have been able to wrap Mr. Osborne's body in blankets and carry it out to a vehicle?"

"I can't give you a definite answer to that. Under special circumstances people can sometimes do things which ordinarily would be impossible for them."

"Since you can't give a definite answer, perhaps you will tell the court your opinion."

"My opinion is that O, the man who was wounded slightly, went to get help from his friends."

"And got it?"

"And got it."

"Mr. Valenzuela, in California jurisprudence it is held that where absence from any cause other than death is inconsistent with the nature of the person absent, and the facts point to the reasonable conclusion that death has occurred, the court is justified in finding death as a fact. However, if the person at the time he was last seen was a fugitive from justice or was a bankrupt, or if from other causes it would be improbable that he would be heard from even if alive, then no inference of death will be drawn. That's perfectly clear, is it not?"

"Yes, sir."

"Now as Mr. Osborne's lawyer I can testify he was not a bankrupt. Was he a fugitive from justice, Mr. Valenzuela?"

"No, sir."

"Was there, to your knowledge, any other cause, or causes, which would prevent Mr. Osborne from getting in touch with his relatives and friends?"

"Not to my knowledge, no."

"Can you think of any reason at all why an inference of death should not be drawn?"

"No, sir."

"Thank you, Mr. Valenzuela. I have no more questions."

As Valenzuela left the stand the court clerk rose to announce the usual afternoon recess of fifteen minutes. Ford asked that it be extended by half an hour to let him prepare his summary, and after some discussion the extra time was granted.

The bailiff once again opened the doors. He was getting bored and weary. Dead people took up a great deal of his time.

12

LIKE AN ANIMAL that had sensed danger in its sleep, Mrs. Osborne awakened abruptly and completely. Her opening eyes were alert, ready to spot an enemy, her voice distinct, ready to challenge one: "What are you doing here?"

"You didn't answer your phone," Devon said, turning from the window. "I came out to see why. The front door was unlocked, so I walked in."

"To check up on me."

"Yes."

"As if I were some doddering old fool."

"No. Mr. Ford suggested I find out why you didn't return to court this afternoon. He thought he'd made it clear that you were expected to testify."

"He made it quite clear." Mrs. Osborne sat up on the bed, running her fingers along her chin and cheeks and forehead like a blind woman reacquainting herself with her own face. "I don't always do what's expected of me, especially when I think it's wrong. I couldn't stop the hearing but at least I could keep from playing a part in it."

"And you feel that's a victory?"

"It was the best I could do at the moment."

"At the moment," Devon repeated. "Then you have something else in mind?"

"Yes."

"Such as a new reward?"

"So you saw the paper on my desk. Well, I was going to tell you anyway." She stood up, holding the collar of the blue robe tight against her throat as if to protect a vulnerable place. "Naturally you disapprove. But it's too late. I've already arranged for the first ad in the paper."

"It seems like a useless gesture."

"Ten thousand dollars is more than a gesture. It's a good solid chunk of reality."

"Only if it buys something," Devon said. "And there's nothing to buy. The other reward didn't bring in a single usable piece of information."

"This second one will be different. For instance, I'm going to arrange for a much wider distribution of reward posters. And the posters themselves will be redesigned. This time we'll use at least two pictures of Robert, full face and profile—you can help me choose—and the wording will be kept very simple and direct so that the meaning will get across even in the smaller Mexican villages where hardly anyone is literate." She let out a sudden little laugh, almost like a schoolgirl's giggle. "Why, I feel better already just talking about it. It always cheers me up to take positive action on my own instead of waiting for other people to make the decisions. I'll put on a fresh pot of coffee to celebrate. You'll have some, won't you, dear?"

She left the room without waiting for an answer, and after a brief hesitation Devon followed her out into the kitchen. Mrs. Osborne poured water into the percolator and measured the coffee with a plastic scoop, humming to herself in a loud nervous monotone intended to cover up awkward silences, discourage awkward questions. It was like the piano playing Estivar had told Devon about during the noon recess: "*She'd start playing to cover up, a piece with good firm chords like 'March of the Toreadors' . . . 'Onward, Christian Soldiers' . . . Bang bang bang . . . Sometimes I swear I can hear the sound of that piano, though it isn't even there anymore, I helped the movers take it out of the house myself.*"

Suddenly the humming stopped and Mrs. Osborne turned, frowning, from the window. "I don't see your car in the driveway. How did you get here?"

"Leo brought me."

"Oh."

"He had no trouble finding the place," Devon said in a careful voice. "Apparently he'd been here before."

"I sent for him two or three weeks ago to discuss a personal matter."

"Ruth."

"He told you, then."

"Yes."

Mrs. Osborne sat down at the table across from Devon, one corner of her mouth hooked in an iron smile. "He probably repeated that ugly story about Ruth and Robert."

"Yes."

"Of course you didn't believe it. Why, Robert could have had dozens of girls, young, pretty, rich. It's unthinkable that he'd have bothered with a woman like Ruth who had nothing. It simply doesn't make sense, does it?"

Devon said, "No," because it was expected of her. She no longer knew what to believe, what made sense and what didn't. Each new piece of information cast a shadow instead of a light; Robert was gradually disappearing into darkness, and the months they had spent together were losing their outlines, changing shape like clouds on a stormy day.

The coffee had begun to percolate and for a time its cheerful bubbling was the only sound in the room.

Then Mrs. Osborne spoke again: "After she died, the gossips had a field day, of course. The funny thing was, they didn't blame Leo for neglecting his wife, or Ruth for seeking the company of another man. They blamed Robert."

"Why?"

"Because he was young and vulnerable."

"That's not reason enough."

"His very existence was reason enough for some people. Wherever Robert and I went, we stepped into the midst of whispers. The phone would ring and there'd be no one on the line, just the sound of breathing. Letters arrived, unsigned. I finally called the Sheriff's office and they sent Valenzuela out to the ranch to discuss the situation. Well, we talked but there was no communication. He was carrying around in his mind a picture of Robert as the neighborhood seducer and destroyer of women, and I couldn't shake it loose. He's been prejudiced against Robert right from the beginning, that's why he never really tried to find him. He didn't want to. Oh, he put on a good show, taking all those trips to the labor camps and into Mexico. It fooled his superiors for a while but they caught on eventually and fired him."

"I heard that he quit because he got married again and his new wife didn't like him being in police work."

"Nonsense. He'd never have given up the power of such a job, let alone his seniority and his pension, for the sake of some little tramp."

"How do you know she was a little tramp? She might—"

"Word gets around. Valenzuela was fired. I heard it on the valley grapevine as well as the Mexicans' *parra grande*."

"I talked to him this afternoon," Devon said. "He apologized for the way things have turned out. He seemed very sincere. I can't believe he didn't do his best to find Robert."

"Can't you . . . ? How do you take your coffee?"

"Black, please."

"I'm afraid it's rather weak."

"That's all right."

Mrs. Osborne poured the coffee, her hand steady. "What else did he have to say? Surely he didn't just walk up to you and tell you he was sorry."

"He said the case is over."

"As far as he's concerned it's been over for a long time."

"No. He meant that I—you and I—shouldn't go on hoping."

"Well, his advice was wasted on both of us, wasn't it? You never really started hoping, and I don't intend to stop."

"I know that," Devon said. "I saw the cartons."

"Cartons?"

"In the bedroom closet. The ones you told me you were going to take to the Salvation Army."

"I made no promise. I agreed to take them because I didn't want to argue with you. You were so anxious to get them out of the house. It seemed the natural move to make, bringing them here instead of giving them away to strangers. Some of the things in the cartons were very personal. His glasses." Her voice tripped over the word, fell, rose again. "How could you do that, Devon—give away his *glasses*?"

"They might help someone to see. Robert would have approved."

"It saddened me terribly to think of a stranger wearing Robert's glasses, perhaps using them to see ugliness Robert would never have seen because he was such a good boy. No, I couldn't bear it. I put his glasses away for safekeeping."

"What are you going to do with the rest of his stuff?"

"I thought I'd fix up the front bedroom, just the way his room was at the ranch, with the kind of things boys like— college pennants on the walls, and surfing posters and, of course, the maps. Did Robert ever show you his old maps?"

"No."

"My sister sent them to him for his birthday one year. They were framed copies of early medieval maps showing the world as it was presumed to be then, flat and surrounded by water. At the edge of one map there was a notice saying that further areas were unknown and uninhabitable because of the sun's heat. Another said simply, 'Beyond this point are monsters.' The phrase appealed to Robert. He printed a sign and taped it outside his door: BEYOND THIS POINT ARE MONSTERS. Dulzura hated the sign and wouldn't go past it because she believed in monsters, probably still does. She refused to clean Robert's room unless I stood in the doorway to protect her, just in case. Dulzura's lucky. The rest of us have monsters too, but we must call them by other names, or pretend they don't exist . . . The world of Robert's maps was nice and flat and simple. It had areas for people and areas for monsters. What a shock it is to discover the world is round and the areas merge and nothing separates the monsters and ourselves; that we are all whirling around in space together and there isn't even a graceful way of falling off. Knowledge can be a dreadful thing."

Devon sipped the coffee. It was like hot water, slightly colored, barely scented. "How old was Robert when he was given the maps?"

"I'm not sure."

"Jaime's age?"

"A little more than that, I think."

"Fifteen, then."

"Yes, I remember now, it was the year he grew. He'd been rather small until then, not much taller than the Estivar boys, and he suddenly started to grow."

He was fifteen, Devon thought. *It was the year of his father's death and she sent him away to school. He never really came back. She's still waiting for his return to a room decorated with school pennants and surfing posters and a warning sign on the door.*

13

FOR THE LAST TIME that day the bailiff announced that court was in session, and Ford addressed the bench:

"Your Honor, I would like at this time to summarize the events which led to the filing of the petition by Devon Suellen Osborne alleging that her husband, Robert Kirkpatrick Osborne, met his death on the night of October thirteen, 1967, and asking the court to declare him officially dead and to appoint her as administrator of his estate. Nine witnesses have been heard. Their testimony has given us a fairly complete picture of Robert Osborne.

"Robert Osborne was a young man of twenty-four, happily married, in good health and spirits, and planning for the future, both the very near future—he was driving into San Diego that morning to pick up a new tennis racket, attend a growers' luncheon, visit his mother, and so on—and the distant future—his wife was expecting a child. He was the sole owner of a ranch. It would never have made him a millionaire but it was operating in the black and he had only himself and his wife to support, his mother having inherited money from her sister. The troubles in his life were minor, mainly concerned with the management of the ranch, the difficulty of getting adequate help at harvest time, and so on.

"On the morning of October thirteen, 1967, Robert Osborne rose, as usual, before dawn, showered and dressed. He wore grey lightweight gabardine slacks and a dacron jacket in a grey and black plaid pattern. He kissed his wife goodbye, asked her to be on the lookout for his dog, Maxie, who'd been gone all night, and told her he'd be home for dinner about seven-thirty that evening. Acting on doctor's orders, Mrs. Osborne remained in bed. Before she went back to sleep she heard her husband outside calling the dog.

"Mr. Secundo Estivar, the next witness, testified that Robert Osborne appeared at his door while the family was having breakfast. He had the dog with him and acted very upset because he thought it had been poisoned. There was an exchange of angry words between the two men, then Robert Osborne departed, carrying the dog in his arms. It was still early when he appeared at the veterinary hospital run by Dr. John Loomis. He left the dog at the hospital for diagnosis and continued on his way to San Diego. As he drove toward the highway he saw Carla Lopez walking along the street and stopped to ask her about the possibility of her two older brothers coming back to work for him. He told Miss Lopez his present crew was no good and had no experience.

"The crew he referred to was composed of ten *viseros*, Mexican nationals with visas which allowed them to do agricultural work in the United States. Mr. Estivar made a record of the names and addresses of the men but he didn't examine their visas carefully nor did he check the registration of the truck they arrived in. Such things seemed unimportant at the time. The tomato crop was ready to be picked and crated and the need for pickers was aggravated by other factors. During the preceding month one of Mr. Estivar's sons, Rufo, had married and moved to Northern California; another, Felipe, had left to look for a non-agricultural job, and the border-crossers who'd been working the fields had their minibus stolen in Tijuana and were without transportation. It was a critical period at the ranch, with Mr. Estivar and his oldest son, Cruz, putting in sixteen-hour days to keep things going. When the ten *viseros* showed up, they were hired on the spot, no questions asked.

"They remained for two weeks. During those two weeks they kept, and were kept, to themselves. As Mr. Estivar remarked from the witness box, he was not running a social club. The bunkhouse where the *viseros* slept, the mess hall where they ate their meals were out of bounds for Mrs. Estivar and Jaime and his younger sisters, for Mrs. Osborne, for the cook, Dulzura Gonzales, and even the Osborne dog. This isolation made the job of the sheriff's department not only difficult but, as it turned out, impossible. The men Mr. Valenzuela spent six months searching for were hardly more than shadows. They left no tracks and no pictures in anyone's memory, no gaps in anyone's life. Their main identity was an old red G.M. truck.

"The truck departed from the ranch late in the afternoon of October thirteen. Around nine o'clock that night, as Mr. Estivar was preparing for bed, he heard the truck return. He recognized it by the peculiar squeak of its brakes and the fact that it parked outside the bunkhouse. The Estivar family kept ranchers' hours. Shortly after nine they were asleep, Mr. and Mrs. Estivar, the two sons who were still living at home, Cruz, the oldest, and Jaime, the youngest, and the nine-year-old twin girls. We have reason to believe they all slept through a murder.

"The victim, Robert Osborne, had arrived home about seven-thirty from his trip to the city. He had his dog with him, completely recovered and eager to run after being cooped up at the vet's all day. He let it out and proceeded into the house, where he had dinner with his wife. According to her it was a pleasant meal lasting an hour or so. At approximately eight-thirty Robert Osborne went into the kitchen to give Dulzura Gonzales some money for her birthday, since he'd forgotten to buy her a present in San Diego. He took a twenty-dollar bill out of his wallet. Miss Gonzales noticed that the wallet contained a lot of money. We don't know the actual amount, but it hardly matters—murders have been committed for twenty-five cents. What matters is that when Robert Osborne left the house he had in his possession enough money to constitute what Miss Gonzales called 'a real temptation to a poor man.'

"While Robert Osborne was outside looking for the dog, his wife, Devon, went into the main living room to play an album of symphonic music which had recently arrived by mail. It was a warm night after a hot day and the windows were still closed. The drapes had been opened after sunset, but the windows faced east and south toward the riverbed, the Bishop ranch and the city of Tijuana. Only the city was visible. Devon Osborne did some straightening up around the room while she listened to the music and waited for her husband's return. Time passed, too much time. She began to worry in spite of the fact that Robert Osborne had been born on the ranch and knew every inch of it. Finally she went out to the garage, thinking that her husband might have driven to one of the neighboring ranches. His car was still there. She then telephoned Mr. Estivar.

"It was almost ten o'clock and the Estivar family was asleep, but Mrs. Osborne let the phone ring until Mr. Estivar answered. When he learned of the situation he asked Mrs. Osborne to stay inside the house with the doors and windows locked while he and his son, Cruz, searched for Robert Osborne with a jeep. Following instructions Mrs. Osborne waited in the kitchen. At a quarter to eleven Mr. Estivar came back to the ranch house to call the sheriff's office in Boca de Rio. Mr. Valenzuela, with his partner, Mr. Bismarck, arrived at the ranch within half an hour. They discovered a great deal of blood on the floor of the mess hall and called the main office in San Diego for reinforcements.

"More blood was found later that night on a piece of cloth caught on a yucca spike outside the mess-hall door. The cloth was part of a sleeve from a man's shirt, small in size. On the following Monday children waiting for a school bus came across the body of Robert Osborne's dog, which an autopsy later showed had been struck by a car or truck. About three weeks later, on November four, Jaime Estivar spotted the butterfly knife among the pumpkin vines. The floor of the mess hall, the sleeve, the dog's mouth and the butterfly knife—these were the main areas where blood was found and from which samples were sent to the police lab in Sacramento for analysis. Three types of blood were classified, B, AB and O. Type O was confined to the sleeve; both B and AB were in considerable quantity on the floor; B was in the dog's mouth and AB on the butterfly knife.

"Additional clues turned up in the lab. Tiny fragments of glass from the mess-hall floor were identified as the contact lenses Robert Osborne was wearing when he left the house. The torn sleeve contained particles of sandy alkaline soil with a high nitrogen content indicating recent use of a commercial fertilizer. Such soil is typical of the Valley area. Mixed with the sample taken from the sleeve was sebum, the secretion of human oil glands which flows more copiously in young people, and a number of straight black hairs belonging to someone from one of the dark but not Negroid races. Similar hairs and bits of human tissue were found in the dog's mouth, as well as a shred of cloth, heavy-duty blue cotton twill of the kind used to make men's work pants.

"From a police lab five hundred miles away, a picture began to emerge of the events which took place on the Osborne ranch that night and of the men who participated in them. There were three. The only one whose name we know was Robert Osborne. Let us refer to the other two, as we did previously, by their blood types. Type O was a dark-haired, dark-skinned young man, small in stature, probably Mexican, who worked on a ranch in the area. He wore a blue and green plaid cotton shirt of the kind sold by the thousands through Sears Roebuck. He was slightly wounded near the beginning of the fight and left early, catching his sleeve on a yucca spike as he ran out the door. Perhaps O was merely trying to escape further trouble, but it seems more likely that he went to get help for his friend, seeing that things were going badly. The friend, B, was also dark-skinned, dark-haired and probably Mexican. He wore Levis and carried a butterfly knife. Lum Wing referred to such a knife as 'jewelry,' but it was lethal jewelry. A butterfly knife in the right hands can be almost as quick and deadly as a switchblade. We know that B was bitten by the dog and also that he was fairly seriously injured in the fight.

"I will not attempt to reconstruct the crime itself, how and why it started, whether it was actually planned as a robbery or a murder, or whether it was a chance encounter that turned into a homicide. We simply don't know. The lab that tells us a man's age, race, stature, blood type, clothing can't reveal what's going on inside his head. Our only clue concerning events prior to the crime was provided by Lum Wing, the cook, whose quarters were in a partitioned-off area at one end of the mess hall. Mr. Wing testified that he dozed off on his cot after drinking some wine. He was awakened by the sound of loud angry voices talking in Spanish. He didn't recognize the voices or understand what they were saying, since he doesn't speak the language. Nor did he attempt to interfere in the argument. He made earplugs out of small pieces of paper, put them in his ears and went back to sleep.

"While the circumstances leading up to the crime itself are and will probably remain obscure, what happened afterward is somewhat clearer. First, there is the evidence of the blankets missing from the bunkhouse—a double flannelette sheet-type blanket and two brown wool army surplus—plus the fact that no bloodstains were found outside the mess hall. Mr. Valenzuela has testified that the body of a young man Robert Osborne's size contains between six and a half and seven quarts of blood. It's a reasonable assumption that the body was wrapped in the three blankets and carried out to the old red G.M. truck. Ten men had arrived in that truck. Eleven left in it.

"As the vehicle moved toward the main road three things occurred: the murder weapon was tossed out into the pumpkin field; the dog was struck and killed as it chased the truck in pursuit of its master; and some of the contents of Robert Osborne's wallet, if not the wallet itself, were thrown into the riverbed. One item, a credit card, was subsequently found downstream in a pile of debris after the season's first heavy rain. Unlike other cards Robert Osborne carried in his wallet, the credit card was made of a heavy plastic, indestructible in water. If the men had been ordinary robbers they'd probably have kept the card and tried to use it. But the chances are that the *viseros* didn't even know what it was, let alone that it could be useful to them.

"In hearings like this one, as your Honor pointed out, an averment of diligent search should be included. The search was diligent, indeed. It began the night Robert Osborne disappeared and has continued until the present time, a period of one year and four days. It covered an area from Northern California to Eastern Texas, from Tijuana to Guadalajara. It included the posting, by the victim's mother, of a ten-thousand-dollar reward, none of which was ever paid out because no legitimate claim was filed.

"When a man drops out of sight, leaving behind evidence of foul play but no body, questions inevitably arise in people's minds. Was the disappearance voluntary and the evidence faked? Would a presumption of death benefit the man or his survivors? Was he in trouble with the law, with his family, his friends? Was he depressed? Ill? Broke? In the case of Robert Osborne such questions are easily answered. He was a young man with everything to live for. He had a loving wife, a devoted mother, a child on the way, a successful ranch, good health, good friends.

"I will let Devon Osborne's own words conclude this summary. She said in her testimony this morning: 'I was sure my husband was dead. I'd been sure for a long time. Nothing would keep Robert from getting in touch with me if he were alive!'"

14

ON THE WAY HOME LUM WING, exhausted by his mental battles with the law and his unexpected victory, fell asleep in the back of the station wagon.

The day had had the opposite effect on Jaime. He felt excited and restless. Splashes of bright red crossed his face, disappeared and came back again like warning lights turning on and off. Around his family and friends he was used to playing it cool, limiting his reactions to blank stares, noncommittal shrugs or barely perceptible movements of the head. Now suddenly he wanted to talk, talk a great deal, to anyone. Only Dulzura was available, massive and quiet in the seat beside him. All the talking was being done in the front seat. It wasn't loud, it didn't sound like quarreling, and yet Jaime knew it was and listened to find out why.

"... Judge Gallagher, not Galloper."

"Very well. Gallagher. How did he get to be a judge if he can't make up his mind?"

"He can," Estivar said. "He probably already has."

"Then why didn't he announce it?"

"That's not the way it's done. He's supposed to go over all the testimony and study the reports from the police lab before he reaches a decision."

When Ysobel was angry her speech became very precise. "It seems to me the lawyer was attempting to prove the *viseros* killed Mr. Osborne. Accusing men who are not present to defend themselves is not American justice."

"They weren't present because they couldn't be found. If they'd been found they would have had a fair trial."

"Men do not just disappear into the air like smoke."

"Some do. Some did."

"Still, it doesn't seem rightful to read names out loud and in court the way they did. Supposing one of the names had been yours and you weren't given a chance to say, 'That's me, Secundo Estivar, that's my name, don't you go accusing—'"

"The names read in court were not real, can't you understand that?"

"Even so."

"All right. If you don't like the way Mr. Ford handled the case, call him up and tell him as soon as we get home. But don't drag me in."

"You are in," Ysobel said. "You gave him the names."

"I had to, I was ordered to."

"Even so."

It was a dangerous subject, this business of the migrants, and Estivar knew his wife wouldn't give it up until she was offered another to take its place. He said, "You'd have handled the case much better than Ford did, of course."

"In some ways maybe I could."

"Well, keep a list and send it to him. Don't waste time telling me. I'm no—"

"I don't think he should have brought the girl into it, Carla Lopez." Ysobel rubbed her eyes as though she were erasing an image. "It was a shock to me seeing her again. I thought she'd left town, and good riddance. Then suddenly up she pops, in court of all places, and no longer a girl. A woman, a woman with a baby. I suppose you saw the baby when she had it with her this morning."

"Yes."

"Do you think it looked like—"

"It looked like a baby," Estivar said stonily. "Any baby."

"What fools we were to hire her that summer."

"I didn't hire her. You did."

"It was your idea to get someone who'd be good with the kids."

"Well, she was good with the kids, all right, only it was the big kids, not the little ones."

"How was I to foresee that? She looked so innocent," Ysobel said. "So pure. I never dreamed she'd dangle herself in front of my sons like a—like a—"

"Lower your voice."

Jaime leaned toward Dulzura and spoke in a whisper: "What's that mean, dangled herself?"

Dulzura wasn't certain but she had no intention of admitting it to a fourteen-year-old boy. "You're too young to know such things."

"Bull."

"You get fresh with me and I'll tell your father. He'll knock the bejeez out of you."

"Oh, come on. What's it mean, she dangled herself?"

"It means," Dulzura said carefully, "that she paraded around with her chest stuck out."

"Like a drum majorette?"

"Yes. Only no music or drums. No costume or baton, either."

"Then what's left?"

"The chest."

"What's so great about that?"

"I told you, you're too young."

Jaime studied the row of warts along the knuckles of his left hand. "Her and Felipe used to meet in the packing shed."

"Well, don't you tell nobody. It's none of their business."

"There are cracks between the boards where I could watch them through."

"You oughta be ashamed."

"She didn't dangle herself," Jaime said. "She just took off her clothes."

THE FIVE O'CLOCK RACE to the suburbs had begun and cars were spilling wildly onto the freeway from every ramp. With the windows open, the way Leo liked to drive, conversation was impossible. Above the din of traffic, only very loud noises could have been audible, shouts of anger, excitement, fear. Devon felt only a kind of grey and quiet grief. The tears that stung her eyes dried in the wind and left a dusting of salt across her lashes. She made no attempt to wipe it away.

Leo took the off-ramp to Boca de Rio and it was then that the first words of the journey were exchanged.

"Would you like to stop for a cup of coffee, Devon?"

"If you would."

"It's up to you. You're a free agent now, remember? You have to start making decisions."

"All right. I'd like some coffee."

"See how easy it is?"

"I guess so." She didn't tell him that her decision had nothing to do with coffee or with him. She only wanted to make sure she wouldn't be returning to an empty house, that Dulzura would have plenty of time to get home before she did.

They stopped at a small roadside *cantina* on the outskirts of Boca de Rio. The proprietor, after a voluble exchange of greetings with Leo in Spanish, led the way to a table beside the window. It was a picture window without much of a picture, a stunted paloverde tree and a patch of weeds half-dead of drought.

She said, as though there'd been no lapse of time since midafternoon and the ride to Mrs. Osborne's house, "Robert must have had some girlfriends."

"Temporary ones. None of them hung around after a few bouts with Mrs. Osborne."

"Robert wasn't a weak or timid man. Why didn't he stand up to her?"

"She was pretty subtle about it, I guess. Maybe he didn't realize what was going on. Or maybe he didn't care."

"You mean he had no need of anyone besides Ruth." She stared out at the patch of weeds dying hard like hope. "Leo, listen. There's no—no reasonable doubt that he and Ruth—"

"No reasonable doubt."

"All those years, ever since he was a boy?"

"I repeat, seventeen-year-olds aren't boys. Some fifteen-year-olds aren't either."

"What are you hinting at?"

"He was fifteen when she sent him away to school."

"But that was because his father died."

"Was it? The usual pattern in such cases is for the mother to lean more heavily on the son, not send him away."

The proprietor brought mugs of coffee and a dish containing slivers of dark sweet Mexican chocolate to sprinkle on top. The chocolate melted as soon as it touched the hot liquid, leaving tiny fragrant pools of oil which caught the sun and shone iridescent like little round rainbows.

Leo broke up the rainbows with the tip of a spoon. "I've been thinking a lot lately about those two years he was gone, remembering things, some trivial, some important. Ruth was depressed—I remember that well enough. It colored our lives. She told me that every hour was like a big blob of grey she couldn't see through or over or underneath."

"What about Mrs. Osborne?"

"She kept pretty much to herself—normal enough for a woman who'd just lost her husband. The Osbornes had very little social life because of Osborne's drinking, so Mrs. Osborne's seclusion wasn't particularly noticeable. We'd never seen much of her anyway, now we saw less." The miniature rainbows in his cup had re-formed and he broke them up again. "I recall one occasion when I asked Ruth to go over and visit Mrs. Osborne, thinking it might do them both some good. Ruth surprised me by agreeing right away. In fact, she even baked a cake to take with her. She started out on foot toward the Osborne ranch—she couldn't drive a car and she turned down my offer of a ride. She stayed away for hours. She was still gone when I finished work for the day, so I went to look for her. I found her sitting on the edge of the dry riverbed. There was a flock of blackbirds beside her and she was feeding the cake to them piece by piece. She looked quite happy. I hadn't seen her look that happy for a long time. Without saying a word she got in the car and we drove home. She never told me what happened, I never asked. That was nine years ago, yet it's one of the most vivid pictures I have left of Ruth, her sitting quietly on the riverbank feeding cake to a bunch of blackbirds."

"She liked to feed things?"

"Yes. Dogs, cats, birds, anything that came along."

"So did Robert." She looked out at the falling sun. "Perhaps they were just good friends, just very good friends."

"Perhaps."

"I'd like to go home now, Leo."

"All right."

THE PUNGENT SMELL of oregano drifting out of the kitchen windows welcomed her home.

Dulzura was at the work counter shredding cheese for enchiladas. She said, without turning, "Are you okay?"

"Yes. Thank you."

"I thought, an early dinner with a little wine—How about that?"

"Fine."

"Did I do right in court? I was nervous, maybe people couldn't hear me."

"They heard you."

"What kind of wine would you like?"

Devon was on the point of saying "Any kind," when she remembered Leo's insisting that she start making decisions on her own. "Port."

"All we got is sherry. The only reason I asked is because you always say you don't care what kind."

So much for decisions, Devon thought, and went upstairs to take a shower.

After dinner Devon walked by herself in the warm still night. The sound of her footsteps, inaudible to a human being, was picked up by a barn owl. He hissed a warning to his mate, who was hunting for rats outside the packing shed and underneath the bleachers where the men ate their lunch. Devon sat on the bottom step of the bleachers. Both owls flew silently over her head and vanished into the tamarisk trees that ringed the reservoir. She had often heard the owls between twilight and dawn, but this was the first time she had more than a glimpse of their faces, and it was a shock to her to discover that they didn't look like birds at all but like monkeys or ugly children, accidentally winged.

The water, which in the daytime appeared murky and hardly fit even for irrigating, shone in the moonlight as if it were clean enough to drink. She remembered a giant scoop probing the muddy depths for Robert, and bringing up old tires and wine bottles and beer cans, pieces of lumber and rusting machinery, and finally, the baby bones which Valenzuela had carried away in a shoe box. Months later she'd asked Valenzuela about the bones. He said the baby had probably been born to one of the girls who followed the migrants. Staring down at the water Devon thought of the dead child and the long-gone mother, and of Valenzuela simultaneously crossing himself and cursing as he packed the bones into the little shoe-box coffin.

Suddenly a match flared on the opposite side of the reservoir and moments later the smell of cigarette smoke floated across the water. She knew that members of the Estivar household were forbidden to smoke—"The air," Estivar said, "is already dry and hot and dirty enough"—and she was a little uneasy and more than a little curious. She rose and began moving quietly along the dusty path. She had a flashlight in her hand but there was no need to turn it on.

"Jaime?"

"Yes, ma'am."

In the moonlight Jaime's face was as ghostly white as the barn owl's. But he was neither winged nor wild and he made no attempt to escape. Instead, he took another deep drag of the cigarette, letting the smoke curl up out of his mouth and around his head like ectoplasm. Nothing materialized except a voice: "Smoke is supposed to keep the mosquitoes away."

"And does it?"

"I've only been bit twice so far." He scratched his left ankle with the toe of his right shoe. The wooden crate he was sitting on creaked rheumatically at the joints. "You going to tell my folks on me?"

"No, but they'll find out some time."

"Not tonight, anyhow. She went to bed with a headache and he's gone."

"Where?"

"He didn't say. He had a phone call and left the house, looking like he was glad of an excuse to get away."

"Why would that be, Jaime?"

"Him and Mom were fighting, they'd been at it ever since court."

"I didn't know your parents ever fought."

"Yes, ma'am." He took another drag on the cigarette and blew smoke, slowly and scientifically, at a mosquito that was buzzing at his forearm. "He gets mean, she gets nervous. Sometimes vice versa."

"Money," she said. "That's what most couples fight about, I suppose."

"Not them."

"No?"

"They fight about people. Us kids mostly, only like tonight it was about other people."

She realized that she shouldn't be standing in the dark prying information out of a fourteen-year-old boy but she made no move to leave or to alter the course of the conversation. It was the first time she'd ever really heard Jaime talk. He sounded cool and rational, like an elderly man assessing the problems of a pair of youngsters.

She said, "What other people?"

"Everybody whose name came up."

"Did my name come up?"

"A little bit."

"How little?"

"It was just about you and Mr. Bishop. Him and my dad don't groove, and my dad's afraid Mr. Bishop might get to be boss of the ranch some day. I mean, if he married you—"

"Yes, I see."

"But my mom says you'd never marry him on account of his *mal ojo,* evil eye."

"Do you believe in things like that?"

"I guess not. He's got funny eyes, though. Sometimes it's better not to take a chance."

"Thank you for the advice, Jaime."

"That's okay."

The owls appeared again, flying low and in utter silence over the reservoir. One of them had a rat in its claws. The rat's tail, bright with blood, swung gently in the moonlight.

"People with *mal ojo,*" Devon said, "what do they do?"

"They just look at you."

"Then what?"

"Then you got a jinx."

"Like Carla Lopez."

"Yeah, like Carla Lopez." Jaime hesitated. "She was one of the people my mom and dad were quarreling about tonight. There was a big argument over which of them hired

"Do you remember the name of it?"

"I never been out of state."

"Would you remember if you heard it again?"

"Maybe so."

"Seattle," Devon said.

"Seattle." The young woman passed her fingers across her mouth as though she were trying to feel the shape of the word. "Seattle, is that way, way up north?"

"About as far as you can get without leaving the country."

"That sounds like the place."

"Did you see Carla leave?"

"Couldn't help it. I was standing right where I am this minute."

"Was the man with her?"

"He waited down on the street beside the car." Her eyes fired up for a moment like pieces of coal. "Maybe the car was stolen, eh?"

"Had you ever seen the man before?"

"No. But I kind of suspicioned from the way the two of them acted that he was a relative, not a boyfriend. Her uncle, maybe."

"Then he wasn't a young man?"

"No. He moved heavy."

"Uncles don't ordinarily go on vacations with nieces."

"Oh, he didn't want to go, I could tell that. He kept leaning against the car, hungover maybe, or maybe just blue. Anyhow, it was a funny scene, her flying around like a bird and him dead on his feet."

A girl flying happy like a bird, Devon thought, *and a hungover uncle dead on his feet.*

She said, "Thank you, Mrs.—"

"Harvey. Leandra Harvey."

"Thanks very much, Mrs. Harvey."

"Sure. Any time."

The two women stared at each other for a moment as if they both knew there wouldn't be another time.

DEVON STOPPED AT A GAS STATION and put in a call to Ford's office. She had to wait several minutes before Ford's voice came on the line, soft and precise: "Yes, Mrs. Osborne?"

"I'm sorry to bother you."

"No bother."

"It's about the girl who testified at the hearing yesterday morning, Carla Lopez. She has no phone and I wanted to ask her some questions, so I drove into the city to see her."

"And did you?"

"No. That's why I'm calling. The woman who lives next door told me Carla left this morning on a vacation with a man."

"Nothing illegal about that."

"I think I know who the man was and I'm pretty sure I know where they're going. There's something peculiar about it. I'm worried."

"All right, come on over to the office. I was going to get in touch with you anyway—I've had a couple of queries from Judge Gallagher. You may be able to answer them. Where are you?"

"On Bewick Avenue about three blocks from Catalpa."

"Keep heading south and you'll hit the freeway. It should take you fifteen minutes."

It took twenty. She wasn't used to California freeways, and on the other occasions when she'd gone to consult Ford someone else had driven her and she hadn't paid much attention to the route.

Everything in Ford's office had been designed to shut out the city, as if its noise might shatter a thought and its polluted air suffocate an idea. The picture window with its view of the harbor was double-plate glass, the ceiling was cork, the walls and floors were covered with thick wool. The chairs and the top of the massive desk were made of leather and even the ashtrays were of a non-resonant material, myrtle wood. The only metal in the room was the gold wedding band Ford wore to protect himself against overeager clients. He wasn't married.

"Good morning, Devon," he said. "Please sit down."

"Thanks." She sat down, a little puzzled. It was the first time he'd called her Devon. She knew it hadn't been done on impulse, that years in the practice of law had left Ford with a minimum of spontaneity. What he said and did, even the gestures he made, seemed planned for hidden judges and secluded juries.

"So Carla Lopez has gone on a vacation," he said. "Why should that bother you?"

"I'm pretty sure she went to Seattle."

"Seattle, Peoria, Walla Walla—what difference does it make?" He stopped suddenly, frowning. "Wait a minute. Someone referred to Seattle during the hearing. The Estivar boy."

"Jaime."

"As I recall, it was simply a casual remark to the effect that one of his brothers worked in Seattle and had sent him money for Christmas."

"The brother's name is Felipe and Carla had a crush on him. She still has."

"Who told you?"

"Carla herself. So did Jaime when I met him last night at the reservoir. He said that during the summer Carla worked for his family she made a play for all the brothers. The two older ones didn't pay much attention but Felipe really twitched."

"*Twitched?*" His shock was genuine. "Where did you get—"

"That's the expression Jaime used."

"I see."

"Felipe left the ranch, and the area in general, more than a year ago."

"Before or after the girl got pregnant?"

"Oh, I think after. She's apparently been trying for a long time to get in touch with Felipe and no one would give her any information about him."

"Did Jaime tell you that, too?" Ford asked.

"No. I overheard a conversation in the hall yesterday afternoon when I went to phone Mrs. Osborne. The phone booth was stuffy and I kept the door open a little. There were two people talking just outside. One of them was Carla, the other was the policeman, Valenzuela."

"Ex-policeman."

"Ex-policeman. He said something like 'not knowing a thing about it until a few minutes ago.' But she claimed he was lying to her the way the Estivars had. He warned her to stay away from the ranch and she told him she wasn't afraid of the Estivars or the Osbornes or anyone else because she had her brothers to protect her."

"What made you jump to the conclusion that they were referring to Felipe?"

"It wasn't a very long jump. Carla had a crush on Felipe and the chances are he's the father of her child. She'd naturally be angry if someone knew where he was and refused to tell her."

"So she found out where he was and now she's going there?"

"Yes."

"With another man? That seems a bit tactless."

"Necessary, though. She doesn't have money for a trip like that. She had to talk somebody into taking her."

"And you're pretty sure of that somebody's identity?"

"Yes. It was Valenzuela."

He leaned forward in his chair and the leather made a soft patient sighing sound. "Would you like to see my file on the girl?"

"Of course."

He pressed the intercom. "Mrs. Rafael, please bring in the Carla Lopez file."

It was brief: *Carla Dolores Lopez, 431 Catalpa St., Apt. 9. Age 18. Waitress, currently unemployed. Uses her maiden name though not yet divorced. Married Ernest Valenzuela Nov. 2/67 in Boca de Rio. Gave birth, March 30/68, to male child registered as Gary Edward Valenzuela. Separated from husband July 13/68 and moved to present address in San Diego. Juvenile record for shoplifting, habitual truancy.*

"The baby," Ford said, "may or may not be Valenzuela's. Under the law any child born to a married woman is presumed to have been fathered by her husband unless proven otherwise. Nobody's tried to prove otherwise. Maybe there isn't an otherwise." He turned the file face down on his desk. "If the girl left town this morning with Valenzuela, it might simply indicate a reconciliation."

"But they're heading for Seattle, where Felipe is. She couldn't very well ask her estranged husband to help her track down her former lover."

"My dear Devon, many bargains are struck in this life that you wouldn't understand or condone. The girl wanted to go to Seattle and one way or another was willing to pay for the trip."

"So you think everything is just dandy."

"I think practically nothing is just dandy. But—"

"I'm worried about Carla. She's very young and emotional."

"She's also a married woman with a child, not a runaway kid who can be picked up and held in juvenile hall for her own protection. Besides, I have no reason to believe Valenzuela poses any threat to her, or to anyone else. As far as I know, his record with the sheriff's department over the years was good."

"Mrs. Osborne told me he was incompetent."

"Mrs. Osborne thinks most people are incompetent," Ford said dryly. "Including me."

"She also told me that he didn't resign, he was fired."

"When he left the department various stories were heard around the courthouse. The official one was that he resigned to take a job with an insurance company—true as far as it went. Privately it was rumored that he'd begun to slip because of heavy drinking. His marriage didn't improve the situation. The Lopez family is large and trouble-prone and Valenzuela's connection with it was bound to cause friction in the department." He frowned up at the ceiling like an astrologer looking for stars to read. "How he got involved with the girl in the first place I wouldn't know. Affairs of the heart are not in my sphere of competence. Or interest."

"Really? You asked me enough personal questions about my life with Robert."

"Only because it was my business to present to Judge Gallagher the picture of Robert as a happily married young man."

"You sound as if you doubt that he was."

"My doubts, if any, are irrelevant. I think I've proved to the court's satisfaction that Robert is dead. Of course I won't be absolutely sure until Judge Gallagher announces his decision on the hearing."

"And when will that be?"

"I don't know yet. When he called me earlier this morning I expected him to set a time for the announcement. Instead, he asked me some questions."

"What about?"

"First, the truck."

"The old G.M. belonging to the migrant workers?"

"No. It was the pickup Jaime referred to at the end of his testimony yesterday afternoon. I didn't pay much attention, since Jaime seemed to be merely making a passing remark. But Judge Gallagher's a stickler for details. He read that section of the transcript to me over the phone. I'll repeat it for you: Q. Jaime, do you recall anything in particular about the crew? A. Just the old truck they came in. It was painted dark red, I noticed that specially because it was the same color red as the pickup Felipe used to teach me to drive. It's not there any more, so I guess Mr. Osborne sold it on account of its gears being stripped too often."

Devon nodded. "I remember, but why is it important?"

"Judge Gallagher wants to know what happened to the truck and where it is now."

"I can't answer that."

"Who can?"

"Estivar is responsible for all the vehicles used on the ranch. I'll ask him about it when I get home. I'm sure there's a perfectly logical explanation and that the truck had nothing to do with Robert's death."

"You'll take Estivar's word for it?"

"Of course."

He watched her carefully for any signs of doubt. There were none, and after a moment or two he continued. "Judge Gallagher is also curious about the weapon, the butterfly knife. So am I. A great deal of effort went into the disposing of the body. The knife could have been disposed of at the same time and in the same place. Instead, it was tossed into a pumpkin field. The pumpkins had been gathered for market at the beginning of October and the field was due to be cleared and plowed. Any agricultural worker would have known this."

"So the knife was meant to be found," Devon said. "Or else whoever threw it into the field was not an agricultural worker. I'm inclined to believe the first theory."

"Why?"

"Everyone in our area is connected with agriculture. Even the strangers passing through are ranch hands or migrant laborers."

"Gallagher made a further point: no poor Mexican field worker would have discarded a knife like that. He would have washed it off and kept it, no matter what it had been used for."

A sonic boom shook the building like an explosion. Ford got up and hurried over to the windows as though he hoped to catch a glimpse of the offending plane. Seeing none, he returned to his desk and made a note on his memo pad: REPORT S. BOOM, 11:32. His report would be one of many, followed by an equal number of protestations of innocence from every air base within a thousand miles.

Ford said, "The real question is why the knife, if it was meant to be found, did not implicate anyone. Ownership was never proved, which would indicate either that something went wrong or that somebody did a cover-up."

"Who?"

"Valenzuela was in charge of the case. Suppose he knew who owned or had access to the knife but kept quiet about it."

"Why would he do that?"

"Let's ask him when he gets back from vacation."

"That might not be for weeks," Devon said. "Will we have to wait that long for Judge Gallagher to make his decision?"

"No. It's already been made, unofficially—he's convinced of Robert's death, and the points he raised over the telephone aren't going to affect that. But, as I told you previously, he's a stickler for details. He's also presided at a lot of murder trials, and if yesterday's hearing had been a trial, any questions about the knife and the pickup truck would have had to be considered very carefully."

"Were those the only points he brought up?"

"The only physical ones," Ford said. "The other was psychological, having to do with Estivar's testimony. You may recall that I asked Estivar how long he'd known Robert. He stated that he'd known him since birth, that as a boy Robert used to follow him around; that Robert spent a great deal of time at the Estivar house and this close relationship

"Yes. What did he want?"

"He left two messages. I wrote them down."

The messages, printed in large careful letters, were on a sheet of paper beside the telephone: *Meet Ford in court 1:30 for judge's decision. See morning paper page 4A and 7B.*

Above the story on page 4 there was a picture of a car smashed beyond recognition, and another of Valenzuela in uniform, looking young and confident and amused. The account of the accident was brief:

A former deputy in the sheriff's department, Ernest Valenzuela, 41, and his estranged wife, Carla, 18, were killed in a one-car accident late yesterday afternoon a few miles north of Santa Maria. The car was traveling well in excess of a hundred miles an hour according to Highway Patrolman Jason Elgers, who was in pursuit. Elgers had been alerted by an attendant at a gas station in Santa Maria where Valenzuela had stopped for refueling. The attendant said he heard the couple quarreling loudly and saw a half-empty bottle of bourbon on the front seat. The ex-deputy was killed instantly when his car smashed through a guard rail and struck a concrete abutment. Mrs. Valenzuela died en route to the hospital. They leave a six-month-old son.

The other newspaper item was a box ad on page 7. It offered $10,000 reward for information on the whereabouts of Robert K. Osborne, last seen near San Diego, October 13, 1967. All replies would be kept confidential and no charges of any kind would be pressed. The numbers of a P.O. box and of Mrs. Osborne's telephone were given.

She put the paper down and said to Dulzura, "Valenzuela is dead."

"I heard it on the radio," Dulzura said, and that was Valenzuela's epitaph as far as she was concerned.

DURING THE MORNING Devon called Leo's house half a dozen times before getting an answer at eleven o'clock when he came in from the fields for lunch. He sounded tired. Yes, he'd heard the news about Valenzuela and Carla—one of his men had told him—but he didn't know about Mrs. Osborne's advertisement or about the time set for Judge Gallagher's decision.

"One-thirty this afternoon," he said. "Do you have to be there?"

"No, but I'm going to be."

"All right, I'll pick you up—"

"No, no. I don't want you to—"

"—about twelve-fifteen. Which doesn't leave much time for arguing, does it?"

She was waiting when he drove up to the front door. Before she stepped into the car she glanced up and saw the vulture still circling in the air above the house. He was riding so high now that he looked like a black butterfly skimming a blue field.

He noticed her watching the bird and said, "Vultures are good luck."

"Why?"

"They clean up some of the mess we leave behind."

"All they mean to me is death."

Once inside the car she couldn't see the bird anymore, but she had a feeling that when she returned it would be there waiting for her, like a family pet.

Leo said, "I haven't heard any details about Valenzuela's death, or Carla's."

"The newspaper called it an accident and that's how it will go down in the record books. But it won't be right. He was drinking heavily, they were quarreling, the car was going more than a hundred miles an hour—how can all that add up to an accident?"

"It can't. They just don't know what else to call it."

"It was a murder and a suicide."

"There's no proof of that," Leo said. "And no one wants proof. It's more comfortable for everyone—the law, the church, the survivors—to believe it was an act of God."

511

Devon thought of Carla telling the judge earnestly about her jinx—*"Like if I did a rain dance there'd be a year's drought or maybe a snowstorm"*—and of the last time she'd seen Valenzuela outside the courtroom. He was standing alone at the barred window of the alcove, somber and red-eyed. When he spoke his voice was muffled:

"I'm sorry, Mrs. Osborne."

"What about?"

"Everything, how it's all turned out."

"Thank you."

"I wanted you to know I hoped things would be different . . ."

She realized now that he'd been talking about himself and his own life, not just about hers or Robert's.

"Devon." Leo spoke her name sharply, as though he'd said it before and she'd failed to hear it.

"Yes."

"Whenever I see you these days we're in a car or some place where I can't really look at you. And we talk about other people, not about us."

"We'd better keep it that way."

"No. I've been waiting for a long time to tell you something, but the right moment never came around and maybe it never will. So I'll tell you now."

"Please don't, Leo."

"Why not?"

"There's something I should tell you first. I won't be staying here."

"What do you mean by 'here'?"

"In this part of the country. I'm putting the ranch up for sale as soon as I can. I'm beginning to feel the way Carla did, that I have a jinx and I must get away."

"You'll come back."

"I don't think so."

"Where will you go?"

"Home." Home was where the rivers ran all year and rain was what spoiled a picnic and birds were seagulls and hummingbirds and swallows, not *gaviotas* or *chupamirtos* or *golondrinas*.

"If you change your mind," he said quietly, "you know where to find me."

HER BRIEF REAPPEARANCE in court was, as Ford had told her it would be, merely a formality, and the moment she'd been dreading for weeks came and went so fast that she hardly understood the Judge's words:

"In the matter of the petition of Devon Suellen Osborne for probate of the will of Robert Kirkpatrick Osborne, said petition is hereby granted and Devon Suellen Osborne is appointed executrix of the estate."

As she walked back out into the corridor tears welled in her eyes, not for Robert—those tears had long since been shed—but for Valenzuela and the girl with the jinx and the orphaned child.

Ford touched her briefly on the shoulder. "That's all for now, Devon. There'll be papers to sign. My secretary will send them on to you when they're ready."

"Thank you. Thank you for everything, Mr. Ford."

"By the way, you'd better call Mrs. Osborne and tell her the court's decision."

"She won't want to be told."

"She must be, though. That ad has put her in a very vulnerable position. If she knows Robert has been officially declared dead, she's not so likely to pay some con artist ten thousand dollars for phony information."

"Mrs. Osborne has always been quite practical about money. When she buys something, she gets what she pays for."

"That's what I'm afraid of."

Devon telephoned from the same booth she'd used two days previously. This time Mrs. Osborne answered on the first ring, a sharp impatient, "Hello?"

"This is Devon. I thought I'd better tell you—"

"I'm sure you mean well, Devon, but the fact is you're tying up my line and someone might be trying to reach me."

"I only wanted to—"

"I'm going to say goodbye now because I'm expecting a very important call."

"Please listen."

"*Goodbye,* Devon."

Mrs. Osborne hung up, hardly even conscious that she'd told a lie. She wasn't expecting the call, she'd already received it and made the necessary arrangements.

19

THE NEXT STEP was to get the house ready for his arrival. He wouldn't come before dark. He was afraid to move around the city in daylight even though she'd told him no one was looking for him, no one wanted to find him. He was safe: the case was over and Valenzuela was dead. It was sheer luck that she'd chosen to buy this particular house. The California mission style suited her purpose—adobe walls as much as two feet thick, heavy tiled roof, enclosed court, and more important than anything else, iron grillwork across the windows to keep people out. Or in.

She returned to the front bedroom and her interrupted task of fixing it up. The cartons, marked Salvation Army in Devon's small square printing, were nearly all unpacked. The old map had been taped to the door: BEYOND THIS POINT ARE MONSTERS. Robert's clothes hung in the closet, his surfing posters and college pennants decorated the walls, his glasses were on the top of the bureau, the lenses carefully polished, and his boots were beside the bed as if he'd just stepped out of them. Robert had never seen this room, but it belonged to him.

When she finished unpacking the cartons she dragged them to the rear of the house and piled them on the service porch. Then she brewed some coffee and took it into the living room to wait until the sun set. She'd forgotten about lunch and when dinner time came she felt light-headed and a little dizzy, but she still wasn't hungry. She made another pot of coffee and sat for a long time listening to the little brass horses dancing in the wind and the bamboo clawing at the iron grills across the windows. At dusk she switched on all the lights in the house so that if he was outside watching he could see she was alone.

It was nearly nine o'clock when she heard the tapping at the front door. She went to open it and he was standing there as he'd been standing a hundred times in her mind throughout the day. He was thinner than she remembered, almost emaciated, as if some greedy parasite had taken up residence in his body and was intercepting his food.

She said, "I thought you might have changed your mind."

"I need the money."

"Come in."

"We can talk out here."

"It's too cold. Come in," she said again, and this time he obeyed.

He looked too tired to argue. There were dark blue semicircles under his eyes, almost the color of the work clothes he wore, and he kept sniffling and wiping his nose with his sleeve like a child with a cold. She suspected that he'd picked up a drug habit along the way, perhaps in some Mexican prison, perhaps in one of the local *barrios.* She wouldn't ask him where he'd spent the long year and what he'd done to survive. Her only questions would be important ones.

"Where is he, Felipe?"

He turned and stared at the door closing behind him as if he had a sudden impulse to pull it open and run back into the darkness.

"Don't be nervous," she said. "I promised you on the phone that I wouldn't press charges, wouldn't even tell anyone I'd seen you. All I want is the truth, the truth in exchange for the money. That's a fair bargain, isn't it?"

"I guess."

"Where is he?"

"The sea, I put him in the sea."

"Robert was a very strong swimmer. He might have—"

"No. He was dead, wrapped in blankets."

Her hands reached up and touched her face as though she could feel pieces of it loosening. "You killed him, Felipe."

"It wasn't my fault. He attacked me, he was going to murder me like he did the—"

"Then you wrapped him in blankets."

"Yes."

"Robert was a big man, you couldn't have done that by yourself." Her voice was cool and calm. "You must come and sit down quietly and tell me about it."

"We can talk here."

"I'm paying a great deal of money for this conversation. I might as well be comfortable during the course of it. Come along."

After a moment's hesitation he followed her into the living room. She'd forgotten how short he was, hardly bigger than Robert had been at fifteen, the year he suddenly started to grow. Felipe was twenty now, it was too late for him to start growing. He would always look like a boy, a sad strange sick little boy with a ravenous appetite and poor digestion.

"Sit down, Felipe."

"No."

"Very well."

He stood in front of the fireplace, pale and tense. On the backgammon table between the two wing chairs the game was still in progress but no one had made a move for a long time. Dust covered the board, the thrown dice, the plastic players.

She saw him staring at the board. "Do you play backgammon?"

"No."

"I taught Robert the game when he was fifteen."

Backgammon wasn't the only game Robert had learned at fifteen. The others weren't so innocent, the players were real and each throw of the dice was irrevocable. During the past year she had spent whole days thinking of how differently she would handle things if she had another chance; she would protect him, keep him away from corrupters like Ruth, even if she had to lock him in his room.

She said, "Where have you been living?"

"Tijuana."

"And you saw my reward offer in the paper?"

"Yes."

"Weren't you afraid of walking into a trap by coming here tonight?"

"Some. But I figured you didn't want the police around any more than I did."

"Are you on drugs, Felipe?"

He didn't answer.

"Amphetamines?"

His eyes had begun to water and he seemed to be looking at her through little crystal balls. There was no future in any of them. "It's none of your business. All I want is to earn the money and get out of here."

"Please don't shout. I hate angry sounds. I've had to cover up so many of them. Yes, yes, I still play the piano," she said, as if he'd asked, as if he cared. "I make quite a few mistakes, but it doesn't matter because nobody hears me, and the walls are too thick . . . Why did you kill him, Felipe?"

"It wasn't my fault, none of it was my fault. I wasn't even living at the ranch when it happened. I only went back that night to try and get some money from my father. I was a little roughed up from fighting—I ran into Luis Lopez in a bar in Boca—and that put my father in a bad mood. He wouldn't give me a nickel, so I decided to go over to the mess hall and touch Lum Wing for a loan. If my father had given me some money, like he should have, I'd never have been anywhere near that mess hall, I'd never—"

"I don't want to hear your excuses. Just report what happened."

"Rob—Mr. Osborne saw the light in the mess hall and came in to investigate. He asked me what I was doing there and I told him. He said Lum Wing was asleep and I wasn't to bother him. And I said why not, money's no use to an old man like that, all he does is carry it around. Anyway, we started arguing back and forth."

"Did you ask Robert for money?"

"No more than what he owed me."

"Robert had borrowed money from you?"

"No, but he owed it to me for my loyalty. I never said a word to anybody about seeing him come in from the field right after his father's accident. He was carrying a two-by-four and it had blood on it. I had climbed up one of the date palms looking for a rat's nest and I watched him throw the two-by-four into the reservoir. I was just a kid, ten years old, but I was smart enough to keep my mouth shut." He blinked, remembering. "I was always climbing up crazy places where no one would think of looking. That's how I found out about him and Mrs. Bishop, I used to see them meet. It went on for years, until he got sick of her and she walked into the river. It was no accident, like the police claimed . . . Well, I never said a word about those things to anybody. I figured he owed me something for my loyalty."

"In other words, you tried to blackmail him."

"I asked him to pay me a debt."

"And he refused."

"He came at me, he hurt me bad. He'd have killed me if it hadn't been for the knife I took from Luis Lopez. I hardly remember the fight, except he suddenly fell on the floor and there was blood all over. I could tell he was dead. I didn't know what to do except get away from there fast. I started to run but I caught my sleeve on a yucca spike outside the door. I was trying to get loose when I looked around and saw my father. He was staring at the knife in my hand. He said, 'What have you done?' and I said I got mixed up in a fight between Mr. Osborne and one of the migrants."

"Did he believe you?"

"Yes. But he said no one else would. I had a bad reputation for fighting and Mr. Osborne was an Anglo and things would go hard for me."

"So he helped you."

"Yes. He thought we should make it look like a robbery, so he gave me Mr. Osborne's wallet and told me to throw it away like I was to throw away the knife. He brought some blankets from the bunkhouse and we wrapped Mr. Osborne in them and put him in the back of the old red pickup. My father said no one would miss it. That was when the dog suddenly appeared. I kicked at him to make him go away and he bit me, he bit me on the leg, and when I drove off he chased the truck. I don't remember the truck hitting him."

"Did you leave the ranch before the migrants returned from Boca de Rio?"

"Yes."

"And of course it was quite simple for Estivar to handle them. He had hired them, he paid them, he gave them their orders; he spoke their language and was a member of their race."

All he had to do was tell them the boss had been murdered and they'd better get out of there fast if they wanted to avoid trouble. Their papers were forged, they couldn't afford to argue, so they left."

"Yes."

"And you, Felipe, what did you do?"

"I dropped the body off the end of a pier, then I drove across the border. It was the beginning of a weekend, there were hundreds of other people waiting to cross. No one was looking for me and no one at the ranch noticed the pickup was missing. If they had, my father would have covered for me."

"I'm sure he would. Yes, Estivar is very sentimental about his sons. You can hear it in his voice when he says *my sons. My sons,* as if he were the only one who had ever had a son—" Her voice had begun to tremble and she paused for a minute to regain control. "And that's the whole story, Felipe?"

"Yes."

"It hardly seems worth all the money I offered, especially since there were two quite serious mistakes in it."

"I told you the truth. I want my money."

"Both mistakes concerned Robert. He didn't get sick of Ruth Bishop. On the contrary, they were planning to go away together. I naturally couldn't allow that. Why, she was old enough to be his mother. I ran her off the place like a stray bitch . . . The other mistake was about the two-by-four you saw Robert throw into the reservoir. It had blood on it, his father's blood, but Robert hadn't put it there. He was protecting me. We must keep the record straight."

"I want my money," he said again. "I earned it."

"And you'll get it."

"When?"

"Right now. The safe is in the front bedroom. You can open it yourself."

He shook his head. "I don't know how. I never—"

"You just turn the dial according to my instructions. Come along."

The safe was built into the floor of the bedroom closet and concealed by a rectangle of carpeting. She removed the carpeting, then stood aside while Felipe knelt in front of the safe.

"Left to three," she said. "Right to five. Left to—"

"I can't make out the numbers."

"Are you short-sighted?"

"No. It's too dark in here. I need a flashlight."

"I think you're short-sighted." She picked up Robert's horn-rimmed glasses from the bureau. "Here, you'll be able to see better with these."

"No. I don't need—"

"Try them on. You may be surprised at the difference."

"I have good eyes, I've always had good eyes."

But even while he was protesting she was putting the glasses in position on his face. They slid down past the bridge of his nose and she pushed them back in place. "There. Isn't that an improvement? Now we'll start over. Left to three. Right to five. Left to eight. Right to two."

The safe didn't open.

"Gracious, I hope I haven't forgotten the combination. Perhaps it's left to five to begin with. Try again. Don't hurry it. I can't let you rush off immediately anyway." She reached out and touched the top of his head very gently. "We haven't seen each other for a long time, son."

DURING THE NIGHT one of the neighbors woke to the sound of a piano and went to sleep again.

COLLECTED MILLAR

The Complete Writings of Margaret Millar in Seven-Volumes

Collect all seven to complete the illustration on the spine!

THE FIRST DETECTIVES
ISBN: 978-1-68199-031-6
$17.99

The Paul Prye Mysteries
The Invisible Worm (1941)
The Weak-Eyed Bat (1942)
The Devil Loves Me (1942)

Inspector Sands Mysteries
Wall of Eyes (1943)
The Iron Gates [*Taste of Fears*] (1945)

DAWN OF DOMESTIC SUSPENSE
978-1-68199-030-9
$17.99
Fire Will Freeze (1944)
Experiment in Springtime (1947)
The Cannibal Heart (1949)
Do Evil in Return (1950)
Rose's Last Summer (1952)

THE MASTER AT HER ZENITH
978-1-68199-027-9
$17.99
Vanish in an Instant (1952)
Wives and Lovers (1954)
Beast in View (1955)
An Air That Kills (1957)
The Listening Walls (1959)

LEGENDARY NOVELS OF SUSPENSE
978-1-68199-028-6
$17.99
A Stranger in My Grave (1960)
How Like an Angel (1962)
The Fiend (1964)
Beyond This Point Are Monsters (1970)

THE TOM ARAGON NOVELS
978-1-68199-029-3
$17.99
Ask for Me Tomorrow (1976)
The Murder of Miranda (1979)
Mermaid (1982)

FIRST THINGS, LAST THINGS
978-1-68199-032-3
$17.99
Banshee (1983)
Spider Webs (1986)
Collected Short Fiction (2016)
It's All in the Family (1948) (semi-autobiographical children's book)

MEMOIR
978-1-68199-033-0
$16.99
The Birds and the Beasts Were There (1968)

THE COMPLETE WRITINGS OF
MARGARET
MILLAR
AVAILABLE AS EBOOKS FOR THE FIRST TIME

PAUL PRYE NOVELS
The Invisible Worm
ISBN: 978-1-68199-000-2

The Weak-Eyed Bat
ISBN: 978-1-68199-001-9

The Devil Loves Me
ISBN: 978-1-68199-002-6

INSPECTOR SANDS NOVELS
Wall of Eyes
ISBN: 978-1-68199-003-3

The Iron Gates
ISBN: 978-1-68199-004-0

TOM ARAGON NOVELS
Ask for Me Tomorrow
ISBN: 978-1-68199-005-7

The Murder of Miranda
ISBN: 978-1-68199-006-4

Mermaid
ISBN: 978-1-68199-007-1

NOVELS OF SUSPENSE
Fire Will Freeze
ISBN: 978-1-68199-008-8

Do Evil in Return
ISBN: 978-1-68199-009-5

Rose's Last Summer
ISBN: 978-1-68199-010-1

Vanish in an Instant
ISBN: 978-1-68199-011-8

Beast in View
ISBN: 978-1-68199-012-5

www.syndicatebooks.com